THE DEADLY DECISIONS

THE
Deadly Decisions

Decision At Delphi
The Venetian Affair

BY

HELEN MacINNES

HARCOURT, BRACE & WORLD, INC.
NEW YORK

DECISION
AT
DELPHI

The lines from Constantine Cavafy's poem "Waiting for the
Barbarians," which Cecilia quotes on pages 175–176, can be found
in *The Poems of C. P. Cavafy*, translated by John Mavrogordato,
and published in 1952 by Grove Press, Inc., New York.

Printed in the United States of America

To G., as ever

AUTHOR'S NOTE

The plot and the fictional characters of this novel are wholly imaginary. Any resemblance to real names and living persons is purely coincidental.

On the other hand, the historical background, and the historical characters who are part of it, are perfectly true and real. Such are the Greek guerrilla leaders—Ares, Psarros, Zervas—who were active during World War II; and such are the political events of 1940 to 1958 which are the basis of this novel. These things did happen, and are now part of the tragic history of Greece.

DECISION AT DELPHI

ONE

Now there's a pretty girl, Kenneth Strang thought, as he relaxed his efforts to open the porthole of his cabin and glanced down at the cluster of upturned faces planted along the pier's edge. For a moment, he wondered who was the lucky fellow on the deck above who had won that smile and wave. Then, quickly, he renewed his attack. The porthole swung open with a surprised shriek, letting the cold March air pour into the overcrowded cabin.

"Oh, Ken! Must you?" his sister Jennifer called, pointing his penknife, which she had borrowed to spread caviar, at the open window. "This is still New York, you know. You aren't in the Mediterranean yet!" Josephine, his other sister, had her own comment. "You are breaking all the rules and regulations, Kenneth," she warned him, exchanged her usual isn't-that-just-like-him glance with husband Carl Underwood, and went on listening in her peculiarly intent way to Mason Farmer. Farmer must have been astounded twice in a row, which was quite a record for a publisher, when Josephine again interrupted her understanding nods and extreme concentration on his smooth prose to say, "To whom were you waving, Kenneth?" But that was Josephine, correct to the last dative.

"A pretty girl," Strang told her. No one believed him, of course.

Except Lee Preston, who had left his own pretty girl—a beauty, this one, an astounding smooth-haired brunette, and why had he brought her to this party?—in the austere care of Jennifer's husband, Philip Beecham, and was making his way determinedly through the packed cabin toward Strang. He glanced at the heavy window and shook his head. "Forceful, aren't you? I thought you were about to lose your right hand there. If it isn't valuable to you, it's valuable to me," he reminded Strang with a smile. Lee Preston was a small man with an energetic body and a restless head, a

3

generous mouth, sharp eyes under black eyebrows. His hair was, appropriately, iron-gray. "Perhaps we ought to have insured it with Lloyd's," Preston was saying, still smiling easily, but there was a brief uneasy flicker in his watchful eyes: perhaps, in all his carefully arranged plans for Kenneth Strang's assignment, he had forgotten something.

"There are only two ways to deal with an inanimate object," Strang told him. "Either you sneak up on it when it isn't looking or you double the charge of explosive and use a hammer." He studied Preston unobtrusively, wondering what had brought him down to the ship. Lee Preston had a reputation, certainly, for carrying all his projects through, from his first bright idea for a three-part series right up to the supervision of layout and color reproduction. He was more than editor of *Perspective,* a monthly magazine dealing with architecture and its decorative arts: his proper title, Strang had often thought, should be inspirer-in-chief. But to pay a last-minute visit to a man he had commissioned to travel to southern Italy and Greece was a refinement of efficiency.

Strang's briefing was long since complete: suggestions and discussions had been exhausted in those last four months of hectic preparation; his research was finished, all carefully compressed into a thick sheaf of notes, now lying between the absolutely necessary reference books in his heavy brief case. He had carried the brief case and his specially constructed portfolio on board ship himself, trusting only his suitcase to someone else. His job for the next five months was to visit the ruins of ancient Greece and its western empire, to reconstruct in his drawings—based on the facts that were known, bolstered by his own close guesswork—the temples and theaters as they had once stood. These drawings were to be published in three major installments in *Perspective,* along with photographs of the temples and theaters as they appeared today, in all their stark ruin.

Stefanos Kladas was to be the photographer. He was flying next week to Italy, to start his part of the job. Unlike most Greeks, he was a bad sailor. Besides, he had become so accustomed in those last few years of success to fly to Peru, or Alaska, or Bali, complete with all his elaborate gear, that the idea of taking a ship would have astonished him as much as traveling by covered wagon to reach Chicago. In any case, as a photographer, Steve Kladas had no need of the specialized knowledge that Strang had had to accumulate to make his reconstructions of the past. He didn't need the peace of ten nicely anonymous days at sea to review his homework and get his notes into order. Perhaps I ought to have become a photographer, Strang thought, instead of an architect who has never been freed from his ambition to paint, and is now trapped by archaeology. Steve's career seemed so pleasantly simple and assured.

4

Lee Preston glanced again out of the porthole at the increasing bedlam of good will on the dock, then at his watch. "Ken," he said urgently, "just one final point—"

Strang had been watching the dark-haired girl who had come to this party with Preston. She was still standing near the door of the cabin. Shy? Poised for flight, if only the corridor behind her were not so jammed with laughing people and worried stewards? Or simply trapped? She was listening, anyway, to Philip Beecham. (Who would have thought the old boy had so much talk in him?) "And what's that?" he asked Preston now. He was amused. Had Preston come here to give him one of those little afterthoughts that plague the perfectionist?

"About Kladas—" Preston began, and then stopped, watching Jennifer Beecham in dismay. "There's your sister bringing us some of that stuff she's been spreading."

"What about Steve Kladas?" Strang asked quickly.

"He left yesterday for Italy."

"Did he? I thought he was flying next Friday."

"So did I."

Well, what of it? Strang thought. Steve had probably wanted to dodge any send-off parties like this one. "Hello, Jenny," he said to his sister's round flushed face. "Keep your mink out of the caviar, will you?"

"Thank you, no," Preston said.

"He doesn't like small black eggs tasting of fish oil," Strang explained. "I'll tell you what, Lee, I'll trade. You don't eat caviar. I don't like champagne. Have my glass, untouched, with beaded bubbles winking at the brim. It was standing just behind me here—" He turned to search for the ledge where he had set his glass before his assault on the window.

"It gave one wink too many," the practical Jennifer said.

"Be an angel and bring Lee another glass."

"And if you find some way of steering Miss Hillard over here," Lee Preston added to that, seeing a chance to have at least two minutes more alone with Kenneth Strang "—oh, not immediately, but in a little while. After all, she came to meet Ken."

"Did she?" Strang was startled for a moment. Then he smiled. Preston's excuses always had the ring of truth. He had almost believed that one.

"You know what?" Jennifer asked. "I don't think you want me around. And I had a poem of farewell all ready to deliver. I learned it especially."

"I'll hear *The Isles of Greece* later."

"Oh, Ken—how could you guess? You won't have time later," she said gloomily. "The first warning has gone; didn't you hear it? The second is due any minute. Where's the rest of your luggage?"

5

"There's only a suitcase still to come."

"Heavens, don't tell me that's all you're taking for five months. Ken, I warned you! Just wait until you find yourself in one of those bathrooms with no shower-curtain rod—then where will you hang any drip to dry?"

"I'll hammer a nail into the wall."

"I believe you would."

"What about that drink for Lee?"

"I'm getting it, don't you see?"

"I see."

"Beaded bubbles. Coming up, sir," she called back over her shoulder. (But the beautiful brunette might be more difficult to deliver on time. Behind Philip, those two mad friends of Ken were already lining up, in position to pounce once Philip stopped talking about his fishing trips.)

Lee Preston said thoughtfully, "I never had any sisters." He looked grateful for a moment. Then he was back to business. "Kladas—I like him. Don't misunderstand me, Ken. Steve Kladas is first-rate. I know that. Does splendid work. Those studies he brought back from Yucatan, two years ago, when you made the drawings of the Mayan sites—excellent, yes, excellent. He works well with you, Ken. That's why I agreed to get him for the Greek assignment when we started talking about this trip. If you remember—" He paused delicately.

"Yes, I remember. You suggested Johnnie Kupheimer or C. L. Hillard for the job. But Kladas and I have worked together. I know his ways, he knows mine. We like a certain amount of freedom, of independence, not always breathing down the back of each other's neck." Strang could pause delicately, too.

Preston said, with a touch of stiffness, "I have little interest in a man who is not independent. But—" his worry humanized him into a quick rush of words—"it's just that we must have dependable men, too. Are we going to have the photographs we want by this summer? The end of July is the absolute deadline. We must have his first prints by then. And your first sketches. It's a matter of planning layouts and space. You can finish the sketches we choose, later. But we've got to see the general shape of this series by the end of July."

"You'll see it. But if it would help you stop worrying, I'll remind Steve about July when I meet him in Taormina."

"Taormina? Aren't you seeing him before that?"

"I doubt it. We thought we'd each work on our own in Sicily, following our joint plan, of course. Then, before we leave Sicily, we'll meet at Taormina and compare notes on what we've done. Steve has the name of a first-rate photographer in Taormina who will rent him his dark room, so

6

he can make some test prints and—well, make sure they are just what he wants." He gave Preston's shoulder a reassuring pat. "Steve won't slouch on the job. You'll have his prints and my sketches by July."

Then, as Preston still frowned at the floor, Strang said sharply, "What *is* worrying you, Lee?"

"Kladas has other things on his mind besides our assignment."

"You think he's doing work for other publications on the side?" There was no written law against that. Some might consider an all-expenses-paid trip, and a rousing fee, as a natural restraint on any other work until *Perspective* had got all the material it wanted; others, however, did not see things in that light. Provided he did the job for *Perspective* and did it well, Steve might feel free to tackle a few other projects on the side.

"Perhaps. Greeks are keen businessmen. I was prepared for that," Preston said.

"Then what weren't you prepared for?"

"A young woman who came to the office this morning, saying that she had something urgent to tell me about Steve Kladas, that she had only a few minutes . . . Miss Taylor believed her, and got me out from an editorial meeting. The girl was terribly upset. No doubt about it. And frightened. But her words were quick and clear, as if she had been rehearsing what she had to tell me, as if she did indeed have only a few minutes. She said she couldn't telephone Kladas. But he had to be warned. He must cancel his visit to Greece. Or postpone it. For two months, at least. And then, as I stared at her, she looked at the clock on my desk, said, 'Oh!' and ran out. Ran! Miss Taylor, in the office outside, followed her. She didn't wait for the elevator—she kept on running down the stairs."

"What was she like?"

"Small, slender, expensively dressed. But no coat, no hat or gloves. A chiffon scarf over her head. Miss Taylor said her hair was in pins under the scarf."

"In pins?" Strang restrained an impulse to laugh.

"The kind of torture females endure in a beauty parlor."

"Oh!" Strang thought over the strange array of little facts. No coat in early March, pin curls. "Is there a hairdressing place in your building?"

"Two floors below."

"Oh!" Strang said again.

"Miss Taylor agrees with you. She went downstairs, made some excuse to get into the beauty salon, or whatever fancy name the damn thing is called. No luck, though. About twenty cubicles, some with curtains drawn across them. But she did notice there was a back entrance to the place be-

7

side the washroom. The staircase is just outside the back entrance. You follow me?"

Strang nodded.

"What do you make of it?"

Strang thought for a moment. "You've got a very efficient secretary."

"That's all we'll ever know about this whole thing," Preston agreed gloomily. "I had Miss Taylor send off a letter to Kladas, telling him someone seemed very much against his trip. If there was any real reason for the girl coming to worry us like that, I thought Kladas could fill in the details for himself."

"But you took the girl seriously enough to write Kladas. Where?"

"At the first address on his itinerary. Naples. But you know Kladas," Preston added fatalistically. "He probably won't even go there. Probably, he'll decide to stay at Sorrento, or someplace. . . ."

"Perhaps you'd have done better to hire Johnnie Kupheimer or C. L. Hillard, after all," Strang said dryly. The truth was that Kladas and Preston had respect for each other's talent but little liking for each other's personality. It was a case of complete emotional incompatibility, and Strang began to wish he had never even tried to act as the hinge between a door and a wall that were off-angled.

"He is the best man for the job," Preston said generously.

"And he speaks Greek," Strang said with a grin. "That's no small accomplishment, let me tell you. After my struggles with the language this winter, I begin to think that all Greek two-year-olds are geniuses."

"How is your own Greek coming along?"

"A little more bite in the consonants and rasp in the vowels, and I'll make the eighth grade." So, Strang thought, as he watched Preston's tight lips relax, we end our little talk with smiles all around. That was much better. "And there is sister Jennifer with the last bottle of champagne," he added. Jennifer was really a very good girl in many ways. She had, for instance, timed the end of their conversation quite neatly. Now, she was detaching the dark-haired girl from Wallis and O'Brien, no mean accomplishment. Strang said to Preston, "Your Miss Hillard is attractive. Any relation to C. L. Hillard?"

"She *is* C. L. Hillard." Unashamedly, he enjoyed the jaw-dropped look on Strang's face. "And she is not mine, I am sorry to say. We were lunching together—discussing an assignment for her in Mexico, this April—and I thought it might be amusing to bring her along to the ship."

"Amusing for whom?" Strang asked wryly. His idea of C. L. Hillard had been—and why did men jump to conclusions about successful women they had never seen?—one of those tremendously capable battle-axes who

8

chopped their way to success. From the tantalizing distance of fifteen feet or so, partially blocked by other people's heads and annoyingly screened by other people's voices, Miss Hillard had looked young, serenely beautiful, quietly elegant. Within handshaking distance, she still was young, serenely beautiful, quietly elegant. But now were added the sudden warmth of her wide-set dark-blue eyes, the smile on her lips. Weeks later, he still couldn't remember what he said to her as they shook hands.

"I wanted to tell you—" she began, almost shyly, but her voice was blotted out. There was a wild beating of gongs, a procession of stewards calling their warnings in high Italian fortissimo, raised voices, more gongs echoing down the corridor, a rush, a bustle, a surge of people outside the cabin door, the frenzied excitement of expected departure. The girl laughed and looked at Strang helplessly. The crushing weight of noise lifted. She was about to speak.

"Second warning bell has gone," Josephine interrupted. "Kenneth, I didn't get a minute to talk to you!" She began making up for lost time. Behind her, husband Carl was saying decided good-bys to everyone. He was a hale, explosive type, with prematurely white hair, who had done very well on Madison Avenue with his capacity to make up other people's minds for them. Now he had decided it was time to get off this ship, and everyone here was going to get off this ship, too; he'd see to that. He thumped Strang's shoulder. "What a racket you're in!" he told everyone. "Five months' vacation, while all the rest of us are chained to the desk! Tell me"—he turned to Lee Preston—"is there really any demand for the kind of stuff Ken does?" He gave a genial nod of dismissal and passed on to say good-by to Mason Farmer, signaling Josephine to follow.

Josephine finished her advice about brucellosis, gave a cheek to kiss, a jangle of bracelets as a farewell salute, and then said, "Oh, I nearly forgot —the rest of your luggage came. Carl had it put under your bed, out of the way. He took care of the two stewards."

Strang, now shaking Mason Farmer's hand, looked startled. "Two?"

"They came separately." And as he stared at her, she added a little sharply, "Yes—your two cases. The large one and the little one. They're under your bed. You'll remember that?"

Strang looked at his sister's retreating back, then at Farmer in amazement. But the publisher had his own immediate problem. In his quiet, diffident way, he was saying, "You won't forget that we'd like very much to see your work when it's completed? I think you'll have a book there."

"I shan't forget," Strang promised, a little dazed by the hint of Farmer's real interest. Normally, such a moment would have rocketed him through the ceiling, but now he was still half thinking about some fellow passenger's small suitcase stowed neatly under his bed. Carl's brisk efficiency was often self-defeating: why hadn't he looked at the labels to make sure?

"*After* our three installments are published," Preston was reminding Farmer with professional friendliness.

"Of course, of course. By the way, Strang, why not take in Asia Minor? There's a good deal of Greek remains at Pergamum and—"

"Not this trip," Preston said firmly. "Ken has enough on his plate as it is. We're leaving the Greek eastern empire for another year. You'll just have to plan a two-volume job, Mason." He enjoyed the worry on his friend's brow. "Cheer up. If you charge fifteen dollars a volume, you'll clear all expenses. Time you had a prestige book."

"My, my, and is this how it's done?" Jennifer asked, lining up in turn for her good-by hug. "You do know how to parlay your talents, brother." She looked a little triumphantly at her husband, Philip. Of all the family, Jennifer had been the only one not to take a dim view of Kenneth Strang's change in career. Philip, even with the evidence all around him that his brother-in-law was not exactly destitute, still had regret in his eyes for Maclehose, Mitchem and Moore, the firm of architects where Kenneth's career would have been so nicely assured. Still, they'd always take Kenneth on again, if he decided to return to architecture once he got these mad ideas out of his system. Too bad Kenneth had not married the Bradley girl; there was nothing like a wife and a first mortgage for keeping a man's feet firm on his own piece of ground. Then Philip put these thoughts aside and shook hands warmly. He liked his young brother-in-law despite the fact he never quite knew what to talk to him about. He wished him well.

Then came the others—Jerry Garfield, from *Perspective*; Judith Robbins, from Maclehose, Mitchem and Moore; Tom Wallis and Matt O'Brien, old friends from Strang's Navy days.

O'Brien was saying, "Wouldn't mind seeing Athens again myself. At least you won't be dodging machine-gun bullets this time, Ken."

"What's that?" Preston asked quickly. "Machine-gun bullets?"

"After the Germans cleared out," Wallis explained, making everything still more bewildering.

"December, 1944," added O'Brien. "Boy, what a Christmas that was! Everyone starving and shooting each other." He shook his head, remembering his introduction to power politics in action. "And the British caught in the middle—trying to chase the Communists back into the mountains without blowing Athens or the Athenians to pieces."

"Wonder if that Greek is still alive?" Wallis speculated. He ignored the worried steward who had suddenly appeared at the cabin door. "The one who smuggled us through the street-fighting back to the ship. What was his name again? Chris— Chris something—"

"Christophorou," Strang said. "Alexander Christophorou."

"All visitors must leave, all visitors ashore!" the steward announced loudly. "All—"

"That's it! Christophorou," said Wallis. "Quite a guy. As crazy as they come. Took Ken right up to the Acropolis walls to let him get a close look at the Parthenon by moonlight. We could have wrung both their necks."

"Not so much by moonlight," Strang said, giving the steward a reassuring signal. "It was more by the rocket's red glare. Just coming, steward."

But the man was crossing, much perturbed, to close the opened porthole. He kept saying, "It is not permitted. *Vietato—*"

"I know, I know," Strang said in Italian, "but this lady fainted, and so . . ." He shrugged helplessly. The steward eyed Miss Hillard doubtfully, and she restrained the beginning of a laugh. Did she understand Italian? Strang wondered, and was caught off balance. He turned quickly back to the steward. "There is a small case under the bed. It isn't mine. Take it to the right cabin, will you?" And then he was finishing the last good-bys. "I'll walk to the gangplank with you," he told Lee Preston and Miss Hillard. I'll have that one small chance to talk with her, he thought, to watch those incredible eyes.

But, as they all left the cabin, the steward called to him urgently. "Signore Strang! Signore Strang!" The man was bending over the small case he had pulled out from under the bed. "This is your case, signore."

Strang halted at the door. "Can't be. I know what I packed," he told Miss Hillard. Then, as the steward pointed at the label, he came back into the cabin. The label, in heavy block letters, all too clear, said KENNETH C. STRANG. It was the regulation label for the Italian Line, first class, main deck, with the correct cabin number most definitely marked. "All right, all right," he said, completely defeated. "I'll straighten this out later. Thanks." He turned back to the door. The others had gone.

Preston was waiting outside in the corridor. Miss Hillard was far away, escorted by Wallis and O'Brien. Too late now, Strang thought; Wallis and O'Brien would not give her up so easily. There's a general conspiracy, he told himself, to keep me from talking to that girl.

"Don't forget, Ken, to tell Kladas about my strange visitor," Preston was saying as they reached the promenade deck, where the covered gangplank was secured. "And when you see the temple at Segesta, give it a salute from me, will you? It's a beauty, almost intact in spite of the Carthaginians. Been standing there for twenty-five hundred years and still—" He stopped shaking Strang's hand, looked past him. "By God," he said in a startled voice, "she's sailing!"

"Who?"

From above their heads, the siren's blast seared every eardrum, even set the deck tingling under their feet.

Preston waited, frowning, impatient. "The profile," he could say at last. "The girl who was frightened. The girl in my office. Don't look now, you damn fool, she's got her duenna right at her elbow."

"Did she recognize you?"

"Sure. She froze. No pin curls now, but plenty of mink. Platinum, at that! Yes, yes, officer, I'm just leaving." He waved and ran, barely reaching the pier before the gangway was being swung off. His exit, thought Strang, was scarcely what Preston had planned. The final bon mot about Segesta was forever silenced. The siren gave a last and triumphant blast, overwhelming the babel of voices on the pier, the shouts, the laughter. He couldn't see Preston, any more. Where were the others? His eyes searched the mass of faces and waving handkerchiefs. Was he expected to stay and wave? Possibly. Before beginning that duty, he turned to light a cigarette. Now he could look at the girl in the platinum mink coat. Yes, that profile would be hard to forget. Standing beside her, a small squat woman, in somber black, was speaking in a torrent of sharp syllables.

"This is all that is to be seen," the woman was saying in Greek. "You will catch cold, and your aunt will blame me. Come!" She stumped away in her sensible, black leather shoes. "Katherini!" she called over her shoulder. And the girl, who had been looking at the laughing crowd below her with an expression of—yes, it had been sadness—turned obediently and followed. She passed two feet away from Strang. She glanced at him for a brief moment. Her eyes flickered as if she had identified him, known who he was. Suddenly, they were blank again. Her face had become a cold, impersonal mask. She was very young, he saw, probably no more than twenty; much too young to need any mask on that pale, dark-eyed face.

So she is Greek, he thought, as he took his position at the rail. Lee Preston had not guessed that; her English accent must be good. Well educated, traveled, mink, pearls, expensive gloves holding a large crocodile handbag, a vague perfume of roses. The very best roses. Her father must own three shipping lines, at least.

Strang couldn't find any face he could recognize on the pier below him. Hundreds were pressing forward from under the roof of the shed, to see and be seen; but there was no one he knew. Then, just as, unexpectedly, he felt a chill of loneliness among all the warmth of emotion sweeping around him, he saw O'Brien's red hair and Wallis's semaphoric arm. And, between them, he saw the Hillard girl. He gave a shout and waved wildly. Suddenly, she was waving, too. It was very pleasant, after all, to have someone to whom you could wave.

The bustling tugs hauled and pushed and prodded the towering ship, until its prow pointed down the Hudson toward the ocean. Then, with chests proudly out and heads held high, they gave a piercing hoot of farewell before they sped, skirts gathered up and around them, back to the long row of piers on the Manhattan shore. From Jersey, the late-afternoon sun turned the high windows of the tall buildings into flaming gold. Strang stood, collar turned up against the cold Hudson wind, watching the midtown skyscrapers, shadow behind shadow, wheel and recede into a world that was both a dream and a reality.

He went back to his cabin for his overcoat. The steward had worked a miracle—the place had been cleared of glasses and bottles and cigarette stubs. The telegrams were stacked neatly on his dressing table beside the penknife Jennifer had used. It smelled of caviar, the one witness left to the noise and confusion of an hour ago. Oh, yes, there was that damned suitcase, too. He stood looking at it, the intruding stranger sitting so calmly on his floor with his name tied round its neck. He'd see about that. He rang for the steward.

The man came, bringing three more telegrams and a special-delivery letter with a receipt to sign for the purser's office. The letter was addressed to him in Steve Kladas's handwriting. It felt as if something solid were enclosed. He slit the envelope with his knife. Yes, there was a key inside, a very small key which would fit the lock of a small suitcase. And a sheet of cheap yellow paper filled with Steve's large letters. "Knew you were traveling light," Steve had scrawled. "I'm weighed down with more excess baggage than usual. Can you help me out? The extra film is necessary, or I wouldn't bother you. Be seeing you. Stefanos."

"Everything all right, signore?" the steward asked anxiously.

Strang nodded, and began opening the last telegrams. The steward hesitated. The small suitcase no longer seemed to trouble the American. Signore Strang must have made a mistake; it was understandable—all that champagne, and scarcely a half-bottle left.

But when the man had gone, Strang dropped the telegrams, took the key, and opened Steve's small case. It was packed with rolls of color film, each in its sealed yellow box. They were the type he could use in his own Stereorealist camera. For that he was thankful. Otherwise, how was he going to explain them through customs? So he locked the small case—it was the size of an overnight bag, easy to handle, and for that he was thank-

13

ful, too—pushed it back under the bed with his foot, attached its key to his own ring, tore up the letter, found his coat, remembered to remove his camera from its pocket, and went upstairs again. He'd get some exercise and air until the three-mile limit was passed. This might be an interesting sea voyage, after all. It shouldn't be too difficult on this ship to find an excuse to talk to Miss Katherine (how would a Greek say that?—oh, yes. *Despoinis Katherini*) and find out why she was so frightened. After all, duennas did not dance.

TWO

Duennas did not dance. But neither did Katherini. Nor did she sit and read in any of the deck chairs around the pool. Nor play shuffleboard, nor write letters, nor take the air, nor go to the movies, nor visit the library. Nor did she eat: not once did she, or the duenna, or the aunt, appear in the dining room for meals. And not even the romantic moment of sailing among the islands of the Azores in a strange effect of cloudburst and sunset—where one huge mountaintop, rising blackly from dark waters, was almost blotted out by rain while the island opposite, across a short stretch of sea, lay golden and placid under flame-tinged skies, with whitewashed houses scattered on green hillsides—brought any of the three women into view.

Apart from an entry in the passenger list that might possibly refer to the invisible travelers ("Signora Euphrosyne Duval, of Athens; and niece, Signorina Katherini Roilos, of Athens"), and a second glimpse of the girl herself one evening, when everyone was crowding into the cocktail bars or dressing for dinner, the women might have been only something he had dreamed up to break the monotony of the interminable, gray Atlantic.

Strang had worked dutifully that afternoon, and at six o'clock had come up to the emptying decks for a brisk walk. Eight times around the ship, or some such nonsense, made a mile, it was said. But that gave him a feeling of imitating a phonograph needle, and so he preferred to climb stairs as he came on them and twist his way vertically through the layers of decks. He had reached the topmost stretch of scrubbed white wood, where the suites of rooms had doors that opened out onto the deck itself, as private a veranda as one could have on a public carrier. He might not have noticed the girl, so still was she standing at the rail's edge in the shelter of a lifeboat, had the blue chiffon scarf round her head not streamed wildly out in

15

the wind. It escaped her hands and blew toward him. She turned quickly —this time she was wearing a voluminous dark fur coat, no doubt one of the little old minks she kept for horizon-gazing—and saw him.

The scarf had whipped round the line on the davit of the lifeboat near him. By standing on the lower bar of the open rail, holding on to the lacings of the tarpaulin covering the lifeboat, Strang could just reach the fluttering tip of the scarf. He played it free slowly, bracing his thighs against the upper bar of the rail, telling himself he'd look a damn fool bobbing around in the white froth of cut waves far below him. He stepped back onto the solid deck with admitted relief. The girl had vanished. A round small man in a long dark overcoat, hands in pockets, was standing at the side of the lifeboat with a look of sardonic amusement on his sallow-skinned face. Now where had this particular little goblin, with the sharp black eyes, well-oiled black hair, and thin black mustache, been hiding? Strang wondered. Probably something that crawled out from under the tarpaulin.

The man took one small hand from his pocket and held it out for the scarf. The smile under the thin mustache grew more irritating. Strang stretched out his arm politely, and just as the man was about to grasp the scarf, he let it go. The wind was a perfect ally: it caught the transparent piece of silk and blew it high and around and over and higher and away. It ended its flight on a taut rope, high on the rigging above the swimming pool. "Too bad," Strang said. "Now it's your turn, I think." He resumed his steady pace along the empty deck.

"Private. Private," the man said, pattering after Strang on quick, small feet. His pointed shoes were as light and thin as his high-pitched voice.

"Who says so?"

"Private, private," the little man repeated. He spoke the word with excessive care, in an accent Strang couldn't place.

"This is getting monotonous," Strang told him, as the magic word was repeated twice again. "Is that all the English you know? Never mind, you've learned it well. I'll give you a big E for effort. Now go away. Stop dancing at my heels. Where's your hair net?" For emotion, or the wind, was raising long strands of oiled-together hair. Strang kept his voice easy, his pace steady. He had passed three doorways to private suites of rooms, a series of real windows heavily curtained. The pattering footsteps stopped, as if reassured. Strang kept walking until he reached the short flight of stairs that led to the radio room. Now this is really private private, he told himself, but the little gate saying *Vietato l'ingresso* could easily be stepped over.

Before he entered the narrow doorway leading to the radio room, Strang gave his first glance back at the little man, still watching. He looked uncertain, baffled, drooping. Either his unsuccessful struggle with the English language or his overlong coat weighed heavily on his shoulders. Strang gave him a cheerful wave and stepped out of the wind.

The radio operator was having a cosy little chat with a Portuguese freighter. He looked more annoyed at the interruption than startled by such an abrupt entrance. "I want to send a cablegram," the American told him. "This way?" He was already walking into the passage toward the cable room before the radio operator could answer. "Sorry," he told his Portuguese friend, "just another passenger lost at sea." But later, he wondered about the American with the broad smile—what had entertained him so much? He even looked out of his door, checked the locked gate, and noted that the rich woman's chauffeur was still standing his watch on the wind-swept deck. So there was nothing to report. There could have been, he thought with some disappointment; for why did anyone travel with so much security unless she expected trouble?

Strang actually did send a cable. To Lee Preston. FORTRESS IMPREGNABLE. DRAWBRIDGE UP, PORTCULLIS DOWN. ADVISE WE CONCENTRATE ON GREEK TEMPLES. There's a limit to curiosity and wasted time, he thought as he paid for the cable and went down to the bar. Like all men who value their own personal independence, he disliked meddling in the private affairs of other people. In the last five minutes, he had decided that the girl and Steve Kladas could work out the difficulties between them. There would be plenty. The very rich knew how to protect their investments, and a marriageable daughter was a big one.

The little tables in the bar were crowded. (Cocktail Lounge, it was called, but euphemisms had a tendency to curdle Strang's blood.) The blue-haired ladies were in full regalia, earrings and fur scarves and beaded bags and dependable lace. The few younger women were already welcoming the Mediterranean in brightly flowered, low-cut dresses; it was amazing how pretty shoulders could keep a girl warm even in the cold Atlantic drafts. The men were mostly retired, if not retiring, coaxed into that little trip which they had been promising their wives for the last ten years. Some of them, sitting carefully in new dinner jackets, feeling their empty hands, watchful, wary, were going back, along with their completely silenced wives, to their native villages for the triumphal visit. It was just a pity that their friends could not see them traveling, right in the Bella Vista Cocktail Lounge.

Captain's dinner tonight, Strang remembered: tomorrow, the ship would be reaching Gibraltar. He chose a seat at the small bar itself, keeping company with a Hollywood actor who seemed to spend most of his waking time in self-imposed silence on that same high stool, and ordered a Scotch. He studied the decorative panel behind the rows of bottles—the Italians were good at that kind of graceful abstract design—and, in order to keep the actor from realizing he had been recognized, got lost in his own thoughts again.

It was his guess that Miss Katherini, in her startling visit to Lee Preston's office, had been terrified by her aunt's warning: stop that man from following you to Europe, or else your father and your brothers and your sisters and your aunts will find a way to discourage him permanently. And Strang, remembering the Greeks he had seen in action back in Athens on that grim Christmas of 1944, did not underestimate their capacity to even the score. The avenging Furies were a Greek invention. Surely Steve Kladas hadn't become so Americanized in the last ten years that he had forgotten that.

Hardly, Strang decided, and ordered another drink. The Hollywood star was watching him covertly. Don't worry, friend, I shan't ask for your autograph or describe all the finer points in your last picture; I shan't even exchange a glance with you. Doesn't that make you happy? What's your problem? Can't be money, can't be women; you have plenty of both. But one thing is certain: if people don't have problems, they do their best to invent them. You're in good company, chum. I invent mine hard. All I have to do is to persuade myself that Steve Kladas can take care of his own troubles, and I begin to think and think, just little driblets of thought, nothing to worry Erasmus or Einstein that a new star is swimming up in the heavens to outshine them. Odd, isn't it? Here we are sitting, with a background of satisfied customers all congratulating themselves that the seasick days are over and that, tonight, they even can risk all the free champagne, caviar, and pressed duck. And there will be balloons, and cute paper hats, and miles of streamers, and isn't that all such merry, merry fun? And there you are, profile, worrying in case people don't recognize you, hating them if they do. And I am just worrying, period.

I wish to heaven I knew why. Perhaps I've been thinking too much about Athens as I last saw it. Perhaps, too, if I'd stop trying not to think about it, and just let the pictures take hold of my mind, I'd work this whole damned thing out of my system. Not very happy pictures, actually. It is never a happy sight to watch brave people crucifying themselves. . . .

You know what? I've just talked myself out of the captain's dinner. (Who am I, anyway, the man who never can find room in his suitcase for a dinner jacket, to lower the tone of an *haut monde* evening with my simple little tweed?) I'll settle for a ham sandwich and a pot of coffee in my cabin.

18

Because Gibraltar is going to swing into view tomorrow, and I have a letter to write. Sure, it's an important letter. I ought to have written it before this. Why didn't I? Now that's a question without an answer. But I'll write it tonight. To a man called Alexander. Alexander Christophorou. It's possible he won't remember a very young seaman from a United States destroyer. On the other hand, he is the kind of man who might just remember.

Wallis, back in New York, was wondering if Alexander were still alive. I hope so. I'd like to look at the Acropolis with him again. This time, we wouldn't be pressing our bellies into the cold hard ground on a little rock-covered hill, shivering in the bitter night wind from the north, listening to random blunt-nosed bullets striking the southern colonnade of the Parthenon instead of the British paratroopers who were garrisoned up there. Yes, the Brits and the Parthenon, with sandbags piled high around them both. I kept hoping the sandbags were high enough. And I'd give a silent cheer when a mortar bomb hit the rock face itself instead of the temple above. I guess there were some good Athenians among the artillerymen: they aimed low, at least. And above us all rose the white marble pillars turned to red in the glare of burning buildings in the city below.

Remember that, will you, if you ever visit the Parthenon? Sure, it's true. December, 1944. A Christmas of siege and civil war and savagery. You can't believe it? No; nor could the Athenians. The ones who spoke English would stop me on the street when they saw my American uniform. "It isn't Greeks who are doing this," they told me. They'd catch me by the arm to make me listen, as if some—oh, sure, laugh at me, but that's what I saw in their eyes—as if some agony inside them drove them to talk to the stranger who was seeing their city in a way no city should ever be seen. A place of hate and hurt and vengeance. "It's the Bulgarians," they said. "Bulgarians and Albanians and German deserters. It can't be Greeks." Then they'd leave me. And there was something in their haunted faces that even an embarrassed kid of nineteen couldn't shake himself free from. These were proud people, and proudest of their civilization. They had just discovered that barbarians lived among them.

Perhaps there was guilt mixed with shame, too. Some of them, you see, had welcomed the barbarians only four weeks before, thinking of them as heroes of the resistance, men of force and action who would straighten out the eternal quarrels and talk talk talk around the Athenian café tables. So the quarrels were straightened out, and corpses lay in the streets. I remember what a Greek reporter said, I can't forget it: "It is not only bodies lying in the gutters. It is not only people who have been mutilated with axes or torn to pieces by human hands. It is also our beliefs and our pride. A Greek does not enjoy the taste of shame in his mouth." The Greek didn't enjoy saying that, either. But it is only the civilized who can feel the taste of shame. A barbarian wouldn't even know what it was. . . .

I'm getting too serious? You know, I just can't raise a smile over barbarians. And what is a barbarian, you ask? A man dressed in skins? Not in this century, friend. He's the type who likes to destroy. That's all. He wants to be boss-man, whether it's with a hatchet or a gun or a bomb, or with nice cold-eyed justifications such as "You can't make an omelette without breaking eggs." As if we were only something laid by a clucking hen for breakfast.

Strang's lips tightened. He stared at the last inch of Scotch and melted ice. He caught the actor's side glance, and raised his glass. "Down with all barbarians!" he said crisply, and finished his drink. As he left, the actor was looking—for the first time—directly at him.

Well, I broke through his boredom for at least a minute, Strang thought as he went down to his cabin. And don't thank me, pal; I thank you—for letting me talk my head off to myself. A man needs that, every now and again. But it would be better if I could talk out loud to someone who'd listen; and then she could talk her head off, and I'd listen; and then we'd go to bed and make love, and fall deep asleep and wake up happy. That's my recipe for a good marriage. When I meet a girl who can listen, and talk, and make love, all equally well, then I'll get married so damned quick that sisters Jennifer and Josephine won't even have time to raise a penciled eyebrow.

The steward Gino, like most Italians, was desolated at the idea of anyone missing a party. So he brought an elegant tray with cold turkey and fruit and sweet cakes and a half-bottle of champagne smuggled out of the dining room. When someone was taking so much delight in providing champagne, it was totally impossible—for Strang, at least—to ask for a Scotch and soda. Or a bottle of beer. And he listened while Gino talked about his native Genoa and the little farm outside the city which his wife worked while he sailed the Atlantic. It was a hard life, but Italy was a poor country. Yes, Strang was thinking as the flood of English helped out by Italian poured over him, we are now sailing into a world of poor countries —the Mediterranean, where most people have to scrabble for a very bare living. Yet ask anyone in America or England or the northern countries of Europe what the Mediterranean conjured up for them, and you'd be given sweet dreaming for an answer: sunshine and beaches and yachts in the harbors, music and flowers, long meals and lazy siestas.

Gino left, and Strang could eat some supper, and begin his letter to Christophorou.

He kept it as brief as possible. First, a piece of self-identification; next, the purpose of his visit to Sicily and Greece, mentioning *Perspective* and Stefanos Kladas. Then, the dates in April when he expected to be in Athens. He would be staying at the Grande Bretagne. It would give him the greatest pleasure if Christophorou were able to dine with him. He was, most sincerely . . .

He reread the page he had written, grateful that Christophorou's excellent command of English saved him from floundering into beginner's Greek. His letter was brief, all right, and clear enough. Then he wondered if Christophorou were still living in Athens. Had he gone back to teaching law at Athens University? It would be pretty silly if Strang found he had missed Christophorou by twenty miles or so, on his visit to the Peloponnese or one of the islands, simply because neither had known the other was there. So, as a safeguard, he added a postscript: "If you will not be in Athens around the middle of April, I hope you'll drop me a note and let me know where I might possibly see you somewhere along my itinerary. Any letter reaching the San Domenico Hotel, Taormina, Sicily, will find me there until April 6. After that, the Spyridon Makres Travel Agency in Athens (Churchill Street) will forward all my mail to me. Yours, K.C.S."

He hoped the postscript was clear enough, too. He would have been astounded to hear that it was the most important part of the whole letter.

Then it was only a matter of finding the small notebook he had carried around with him during the war—it contained sketches, innocuous enough to avoid a censor's disapproving eye, of people and places which had caught his imagination; and a scattering of addresses, of names now mostly half-forgotten. Christophorou's address was jotted on the corner of his sketch of the distant Acropolis as he had watched it when he sailed away from the Piraeus, Athens' port. Its white columns gleamed on top of its high hill in a sudden shaft of sunlight piercing the cold winter sky, serene and beautiful, aloof from the occasional belches of artillery fire on the other hills of Athens or from the black pillar of smoke sent up by a burning building in Piraeus itself.

As he copied the address carefully, he had another pessimistic moment wondering if perhaps Alexander Christophorou's family had moved. But this whole attempt to get in touch with Christophorou was a gamble; what had he to lose? So he sealed the envelope, picked up his coat for a late stroll on deck, and made his way to the purser's office.

One of the assistant pursers was still on duty, filling up another batch of forms, looking doggedly martyred as he worked to the muffled throb of music from the ballroom. "Gibraltar," he explained, pointing to the small pile of passports and landing cards on his desk, and he sighed. "Let us hope it will be calm, and the passengers for Spain will leave us gracefully. A little ferryboat comes out to take them away. But perhaps you have seen it?"

"No, I've never seen it."

"You have never seen Gibraltar?"

"Yes, I've seen Gibraltar."

The assistant purser was puzzled, and then blamed it on the difficulties of the English language. "This time, you must go on deck and watch. It can be very amusing."

"I'm sure it is. Sorry to trouble you about this airmail stamp. Are you sure it is sufficient?"

"You would like to pay more?" The young man reweighed the letter. "I am sorry. I must disappoint you."

"*Molte grazie.*"

"Prego. And do not miss Gibraltar tomorrow!" Then he looked concerned as he noticed Strang's overcoat. "You are not going to dance?"

Strang shook his head, smiled reassuringly to show he had no criticism of the band or the floor or his hosts' indefatigable hospitality, and bade the assistant purser good night.

On deck, there was a freshening western wind which seemed to blow the ship through the darkness toward the narrow gap between Europe and Africa. This was a journey he had made, on convoy duty, at least half a dozen times during the last year of the war. Oil tankers, ships with food and clothing and medical supplies, had moved like a straggling herd of arthritic sheep poked and prodded by their darting escorts through the narrow passage into the Mediterranean. As he looked over the black rolling water of the Atlantic, wave swallowing wave, he admitted why he had chosen to come by ship. Not for any of the reasons he had given his friends so easily that he had almost come to believe them himself; only for one, hopelessly sentimental reason. He was no longer nineteen years old, on board a small destroyer trying to outwit a pack of German submarines. But looking at the cold, impersonal sea covering this giant stretch of burial ground, he tried to ignore the lighted deck, the rise and fall of distant music. Gradually, the dark horizon lined up before his eyes; and, watching the constant surge of water beat against the wall of black sky, he could almost recapture the emotions of fifteen years ago. Almost. Emotions could be remembered only vaguely, at best. All the variables, the textures, the proportions of feeling that made them so overwhelming once became blurred with time. Too much happened to most of us: the clouds of glory and the vision splendid died away.

He turned on his heel and went below. It was always a mistake to try to breathe life into the past; the man of thirty-four was not a youth of nineteen. He wished now that he had never mailed that letter to Alexander Christophorou. He actually did go back to the purser's office, but it was closed. The letter was beyond recall.

He overslept next morning, and arrived on deck almost at the end of the Gibraltar halt. The liner was anchored in the wide circle of bay, with the Rock rising bluntly at one end of the horseshoe of land, while the flat Spanish coast line curved back and around. Overhead, small soft white clouds chased like tumbleweed across the blue sky. The strong breeze chopped the water, but had not discouraged the little bumboats, bobbing around the ship with their tourist cargoes of garish scarves, tawdry ornaments, and dubious sherry. The clear cool air was filled with raucous cries and harsh Spanish curses as the rowers kept their boats in place until their baskets of souvenirs, pulled up to the ship's open decks by highflung ropes, could be lowered back to them with the dollar bills they had bargained for so strenuously.

Strang, watching the pantomime of the bumboats as the rowers astutely jockeyed a competitor aside or tried to edge in closer to the ship only to be turned back by a watchful police launch, had paid little attention to the disembarkation from a lower deck, where a small steamer dipped and swayed as it hugged the liner's side and waited to carry the passengers to Algeciras across the bay. But, suddenly, a white cabin cruiser with red leather cushions, brass that glittered, windows that gleamed, two white-uniformed sailors at stiff attention beside a pile of trunks on its afterdeck, swept away from the liner's side, made a wide curve, elegant and disdainful, between the clusters of bumboats, and headed for the Algeciras side of the bay. As Strang's eyes were following it, admiring its compact lines and powerful drive, the assistant purser came to stand beside him at the rail.

"I told you it would be amusing." The assistant purser indicated the heaving deck of the ferryboat below them. Then he noticed the direction of Strang's eyes. "That is the way to travel! You see the yacht, over there?" He pointed across the bay. "They say she has two of them, so that one is always ready while the other is being overhauled. She travels much. I wonder when she can enjoy her five houses?"

"She?" Strang asked sharply.

"Signora Duval. They say that if she would only tell how much she

23

owns, she could call herself the richest woman—well, in the Levant at least, perhaps in the whole Mediterranean. I do not think that even in America you have such a fortune."

"In America, we pay our income taxes," Strang reminded him dryly. So the dragon aunt and her frightened niece had left, servants and baggage complete. They had faded out of his life as quickly as they had stepped into it. His cable to Preston had shown some sense, after all.

He watched the cabin cruiser become a little white arrow darting across the water. By comparison, the yacht must be of quite a respectable tonnage. "A very cautious woman," he remarked, "if she wouldn't trust that yacht to the Atlantic."

"Very cautious. She never travels by air, either."

"Is that what makes so much money—caution?"

"Women don't make money," the assistant purser said with a touch of bitterness. "They spend it. It was Étienne Duval who made the fortune. A Frenchman who lived in Syria. He took Syrian nationality to protect his investments. But you must have heard about him. His suicide, two years ago, was in every newspaper. You did not read about it?"

"I guess I had other things on my mind, two years ago." Yucatan, for instance, and Mayan tombs.

"A pity. It was a very strange end to a romantic life. He had a palace in Syria, a villa on Rhodes, a *palazzo* in Venice, a castle in Spain, a fortress in Casablanca."

"Adequate. No château in France, I suppose."

"None." The assistant purser caught the joke and explained it. "But of course not. To protect his investments." He enjoyed it, too. "Ah, well," he said at last, "I, for one, am glad to see Signora Duval leave." His lips tightened, his eyes narrowed broodingly.

"Was there trouble?" Strang asked sympathetically. He could guess the kind of difficulties that someone like Madame Duval could stir up.

The Italian was silent, but he must have remembered something that had stung his pride, for he looked at the distant yacht and his brown eyes, normally pleasant and gentle, hardened with anger. He said bitterly, "Trouble?" And then, to cover the momentary indiscretion, "Nothing important for anyone—except me."

"What on earth did you do?" Strang asked in surprise. Had the handsome young purser slipped past Mr. Private Private, and managed to meet Miss Katherini? If so, it was good to hear the girl had at least a few minutes of pleasure before the prison walls had closed in on her again. "Don't tell me they caught you kissing the niece's hand."

The assistant purser was horrified. And now he must end such a story before it started. "No, no," he said urgently. "Nothing such as that, but nothing. It was only the little matter of their names on the passenger list."

"You got them wrong, did you?"

"No. They were correct."

"Then why—"

"Signora Duval did not want them on the list at all."

"And she complained about that? Well, some people—"

"Complained?" The assistant purser gave a short and mirthless laugh. "You should have heard her! You should have seen her face! She is not a woman. She is a tornado."

"She actually sent for you?" Strang was incredulous.

"She sent for the captain. The purser was told to go. He sent me." The young man sighed deeply.

Strang said with a smile, "They owe you a medal for facing the old tornado."

"She is not old." The assistant purser had both a literal mind and some professional discretion, for the lady's age and any other interesting details that her passport must have entrusted to him were held secret. His face even cleared, as if he were a little cheered by the idea that someone thought him worthy of a medal. He said, less mournfully, "But the niece was grateful. She stood behind her aunt, and her eyes thanked me."

"For what?"

"Because I kept silent. What else could a man do? It was the niece, you understand, who had filled out the details for the passenger list and sent them to our office by a steward. Fortunately, I questioned him before I went to see Signora Duval. He had promised the young lady not to betray her. And when I saw her, standing so still, so very frightened, I kept silent. What else could a man do?"

Strang looked at him. "Good for you," he said quietly.

The assistant purser was almost restored to his natural good humor. "Oh, well, there are always strange situations on board ship. One never knows what to expect." He glanced at his watch, then at his immaculately white uniform; he flicked an impertinent speck of soot from his white shoes. "We are due to sail. You will excuse me? Perhaps you will be at the dance tonight? Then we can talk about more pleasant things. *Arrivederci!*"

Strang stayed at the rail, now watching the bargaining boats in their last frenzy of raucous effort to make another dollar, now studying the neat rigging of three British naval vessels, austere gray ladies withdrawn behind the long breakwater that sheltered the Gibraltar dockyards from the various hazards of the open bay. Once or twice, in spite of himself, he found his eyes drawn to the large white yacht, with its clean lines, its excellent proportions. Beauty was always worth a long moment of homage.

With a rattle of chains, a tremble of engines, a blast of siren, the liner swept round in a half-circle to point into the Straits once more. This maneuver brought them closer to the yacht. Strang could see her flag quite clearly. He stared at it in amazement. It was not the blue-and-white flag of Greece.

"What's that flag? Do you know?" a woman's voice asked beside him. She was a nice, motherly creature with a pleasant face.

"Yes." He remembered the flag of the freighters he had sometimes seen from a destroyer's deck, miserable hulks, rust-streaked, as if they carried deckloads of dysentery patients like the hospital ships he had read about in that long-ago campaign of Gallipoli. "That's a Liberian flag."

"So it's a Liberian boat? My, isn't it pretty!"

"Very few ships flying the Liberian flag are Liberian." And as the round, pink-cheeked face looked at him blankly, he added, "The flag only means the yacht is registered there." And a damned mean trick that was, too, to escape Greek taxes.

"*Medea,*" the woman read carefully just before the liner's course carried them out of eye range of the yacht's prow. "Now that's a pretty name. *Medea.* What does it mean? Do you know?"

"She was a woman who killed her two children."

The round cheeks blanched under their pink rouge. "Whatever for?"

"Revenge on their father."

She obviously didn't believe him. Such things didn't happen in Larchmont. She gave a nervous smile, and edged away.

Strang noted the changing color of the water. The soft white clouds had increased and become shadowed with gray; darker clouds were blowing from the rain sky to the east. We are running into the Mediterranean and a sizable squall, he thought. He wondered if he should advise the pink-cheeked lady to eat only dry crackers and an apple for lunch, but he decided against it. She had received enough shocks for one morning: he couldn't destroy her beliefs in the blue Mediterranean, too.

So he went below, settled himself on his bed, and picked up his notes on the history of Paestum. There was nothing like a dose of solid work to keep one's mind off the Mediterranean's sudden treacheries. Besides, time limits were fixed on this assignment; he had to read and think himself into the picture before he arrived at each chosen place. Paestum, south of Naples, was his first stop. Next, over to Sicily for the four "musts": Segesta, Agrigentum, Syracuse, Selinunte—although what he could do with that jumble of broken pillars and smashed pediments was something that

26

terrified him even from this distance. Taormina, although it did possess a Greek theater adulterated with Roman additions, had been chosen rather as a delightful place to finish his Sicilian sketches. When your travels were defined for you, you might as well make them as comfortable as possible. He thought of the next five months, a neatly planned stretch of his life which lay before him most invitingly. Odd, in a way, that he would be living almost entirely in a world created by men between two and three thousand years ago; odd, and—considering the state of the present-day world—not unattractive.

THREE

The arrival in Naples was not, in any way, according to plan. Kenneth Strang, if only he had been clairvoyant, would have seen it as symbolic and taken it as an omen for the rest of his trip. But he only felt annoyance when a force-eight wind, for almost two hours, kept the liner circling the water-lashed bay—Capri hidden behind a black curtain of rain, Vesuvius lost in the low dark sky—before the pilot boat could risk coming out to take her safely into harbor.

When they docked at last, Strang's annoyance sharpened. According to plan, he could have walked off the ship, carrying his suitcase, brief case, and portfolio. But there was also the small case Steve Kladas had sent him. The total load was impossible in the high wind that raked the long, exposed pier. So he had to depend on a porter to help him, after all. It was the usual slow and tedious business, waiting in the giant customs shed for his suitcase to arrive. Portfolio and brief case he had carried, and Steve's small case. He spent this patch of interminable dreariness watching his fellow passengers freezing (now that the excitement of the little adventure in the Bay of Naples was over) in their thin suits and light coats. Spring, and the Mediterranean—what dreams had it roused, aided and abetted by the enchanting travel advertisements? The addition of an advisory "but" was needed after the ecstatic eulogy.

Eulogies were fine, very fine, full of upbeat and uplift. *But* let's keep a balance, boys. Let's advertise: "Come to Jolly Old England, *but* not when April's there unless you bring wool underwear and a coat to wear indoors." Or: "Come to Romantic Brittany, *but* bring a sweater for suntanning on the beach." Or: "Come to Subtropical Heaven, fanned by summer breezes, *but* these three-inch things with wings to fly when they get tired running over the floor or crawling into your bureau drawers are only roaches. Ladies, short skirts for dancing on the terrace are preferable, so that land crabs won't cling and climb. Gentlemen, your job is to empty out all shoes each morning." Or: "Come to the Sunny Riviera, *but* hire a pneumatic mattress for lazing on the pebbles." Or—no, this game could go on forever, and the suitcase was now being trundled past him under a pile of many people's luggage.

He had a brief battle of wills with the porter, who wanted to trundle to some distant section of the shed, but he won it by yanking his possession clear. "All ready," he told one of the waiting men behind the low wooden counter marked "S." He lined up his luggage not without a sense of achievement, produced passport and camera, took out his keys and began unlocking. Customs officers who had had their siestas interrupted for a ship's afternoon arrival, and then had to stand in a cold shed for nearly three hours, might be less patient than usual.

"Nothing open until all here," one hard-eyed man said, and kept his hands in his overcoat pockets. He was both angry and bored with tourists' stupidities.

"It is all here," Strang said.

The expression did not change, but the examination was thorough though brief. Strangely, it was the portfolio that caused the customs officer most doubt. He was so interested in it that he accepted the small case of camera film without a second glance. He went over to confer with the colleague who had taken Strang's passport and was now studying it with great intensity. That's right, Strang thought as the passport man looked down at the little green book and then up at the American and then down again, then up: this is Kenneth Clark Strang. Height: 5 ft. 11 in. Hair: brown. Eyes: gray. No visible marks. Born: Princeton, New Jersey, on February 7, 1925. Occupation: architect. Address: 124a East 54th Street, New York City. Yes, indeed, that is I, as my more refined friends would say.

"You are *arquitetto?*" the officer asked suspiciously.

Strang nodded. "An architect," he assured the man.

"But this is for a *pittore*—a paint—" He looked most dubiously at the opened portfolio, lifted a tube of color as if the Hope diamond had decided to cross the Atlantic in gamboge.

"I am an architect who draws buildings." That didn't appear to be helpful. Desperately, he said, "Paestum. I go to draw the temples at Paestum."

"There are only ruins at Paestum."

"I shall draw ruins."

The two men looked at each other. At this moment, they reminded him of his two brothers-in-law.

"Ah," said one, dawn breaking at the end of a cloudy night, "it is a little thing to amuse oneself?"

Strang grappled with that. "A hobby?" My God, perhaps they *are* my brothers-in-law in disguise. But he nodded gravely: it was the easiest way out. And all was well. With many understanding nods, the opened cases were commanded to be closed and carried away. That was more difficult to do than giving a commanding wave. The crowd along the counter had reached the desperate stage of elbowing and pressing. He locked the cases with a struggle, could find no porter who wasn't already trundling (there must have been a law against carrying, in Naples), and chose to battle his way to the exit barrier with a precarious but painful hold on his luggage. Listing slightly to starboard as the heavy brief case in his right hand and the portfolio slipping from under his right arm outmatched the two cases on his left side, he headed grimly for a door that might lead to the street. A voice said, "Hi, Ken! You look like a man who could use a third hand." It was Steve Kladas.

Strang said slowly, "What the hell are you doing here?"

Steve grinned happily. His blunt-featured, rugged face, olive-complexioned, looked as if a ravine of white rock had suddenly split the furrowed surface of light-brown earth. His thick black hair, usually carefully combed, was ruffled by the wind. His raincoat glistened. But his fine dark eyes, almost as black as his hair, sparkled with delight. Surprises were his specialty. "That's a nice way to welcome a friend." His voice and manner were completely American, which was not surprising, since he had been born in Philadelphia and had lived there for the first twelve years of his life, until his family had decided to return to Greece. "Hand over!" he said, and took a firm hold of his own case, and—almost as an afterthought—the brief case. "What's in here?" he asked. "Rocks?" He pretended to stagger and then brushed aside a porter, who, no longer needed, had suddenly appeared, with a short flow of ungrammatical but understandable Italian. He told Strang, "It's only a few steps down to the street." He wasn't tall, a full head shorter than Strang, but he used his shoulders —he had become fairly thickset in the last few years—to push his way through the groups of small, thin men loitering around the door. "No," he snapped at one whispering character with the usual furtive hand holding out three fountain pens, "we don't want anything. Go away!" The effect of that last simple phrase was magic. "At first I tried a few Italian curses. That just made these guys all the more eager. Then a waiter told me to say 'Go away!' That's all. And boy, do they go away! It's the final insult. Can you figure that out?" He gave his short, deep-chested laugh, and then went on talking in his usual torrent of words. "Got your nose sun-stripped, I see. Don't tell me you found any warm weather on that damned Atlantic."

"It could have been worse. In fact, there were a couple of days when we could even go swimming." But Steve wasn't really listening. They had come out onto a street that was almost dark—perhaps dusk came early to Naples at this time of year, or maybe the black clouds were swallowing up the city—with the shimmers of scattered street lights reflected on the soaked pavement. Gusts of wind ripped off hats while tourists and short-order porters searched for taxis.

"There's one thing I *won't* do," Strang said firmly, remembering Steve's sometimes irritating sense of economy. "I am not going to walk to the hotel."

"Now, now," said Steve, "I've got a cab waiting, just across the street. Cost me two good American dollars." He led the way at a half-run. "If he's gone, I'll spend tomorrow morning searching for the son of a bitch."

And he would, Strang had little doubt. "Why not tomorrow afternoon, too?" he asked with a grin as he followed Steve over the hard surface of stone blocks, slippery with rain.

"Because I leave for Taormina then," Steve said crisply. "There he is!" His cabdriver was yelling at them to run, while he struggled to keep his taxi door closed against the strong pull of a porter's right arm. "Sorry, lady, the cab is taken. This gentleman has urgent business at the American Consulate," Steve said to a tourist who had been standing hopefully behind the porter, and settled the question of who was going to open the door by dropping the brief case smartly down on the porter's arm. "In!" he told Strang.

Strang had recognized the dismayed round face of the pink-cheeked lady, now retreating. "Just a minute, Steve—"

"In!" Steve gave a shove with his shoulders, and Strang was in. Steve followed, slammed the door, just missing the porter's fingers. "Do you know how long it took me to find a cab that would wait? Listen, Ken—for a man who fancies himself as a hard-boiled bachelor, you're as easy to cut into as a poached egg on toast." His annoyance wore off. "I've often wondered how you ever did stay free. You're just the type to be caught by a sweet-faced widow, with five children, and two of them crippled. Now don't get sore! All I'm saying is that you're a romantic. And I'm a realist. It's a good thing you've got me around, this trip." He settled himself in the seat of the high-walled taxi, smoothed his hair back from his brow, and gave one of his broad grins. "If that had been a man, back there," he said, "you'd have told him to get the hell out. But what's the difference? Women got the vote, didn't they? They're equal, aren't they? That's what they wanted. So they've got it, and we're all happy. Or aren't we?" He broke into Italian. "Not that way! Take the direct route. To your right! By God," he said to Strang, "you would think I was a newly arrived tourist, too."

In the large, carefully appointed hotel overlooking the sea front, Strang was given a room with a small balcony and a large-scale view of the bay. That pleased him. And the room itself would be a good place to finish his sketches of Paestum—plenty of light from the wall of window, plenty of air from the glass door that led to the balcony, gray tiled floor, white walls, simple furniture, a desk that was steady to the touch, an adequate lamp.

Steve Kladas prodded the bed, tried the two armchairs, ran the shower, flushed the toilet, and pronounced everything—much to his surprise—to be all right. He ordered Scotch and soda and ice, hung up his raincoat in the little entry hall, switched on all the lights, and chose the more comfortable chair. "Haven't you had enough of sea breezes?" he wanted to know, for Strang had pulled aside the panel of pleated gray silk curtain and opened the glass door that was part of the window wall. He was now watching the high spring tide sending its surging waves across a causeway that led to the little island not much more than fifty yards offshore. Lights were on, down there, blazing cheerfully in the empty restaurants grouped around the island's small harbor; behind them rose the dark massive shadow of the old castle whose rugged walls plunged into the sea. Usually, the little restaurants were filled with people and noise and music, making the castle only a backdrop for *Il Trovatore*. But tonight it had reasserted itself. It was the Castel dell' Ovo, guarding the tiny pleasure harbor of Santa Lucia from the storm as stoutly as it had once fought against Saracen invaders from the sea.

"Shut that door, Ken! You're blowing the curtains off their hooks."

Strang came back into the room and made everything fast against the night. "I like it this way," he said. "It smells better."

"Better than what?"

"Better than Naples in August."

"And when were you here in August?"

"At the end of the war."

"Oh—that!" Steve Kladas lost interest.

Strang said jokingly, "You know, there was a war—in fact, five or six wars—outside of Greece."

Steve looked at him sharply, and then laughed. "Well, I like Naples at any time of year."

"Sure. It was founded by the Greeks."

32

Steve said, "When Preston started enthusing over the Greek western empire, I thought he was nuts. Nuttier than usual, that is. But now, sure I admit it, I'm beginning to catch some of that excitement he kept talking about."

"Did you never feel it before? When you lived in Greece, did you never look at the ruins and—"

Steve cut in, with a laugh. "Ken, my good friend, if you lived in a village like a thousand other villages where people spent all their days working in the fields and half their nights worrying about the food they couldn't produce from a rocky hillside, you wouldn't have much time to admire the beauty of a line of pillars. It was the foreigners, with books in their hands and stars in their eyes, who had time to admire. Archaeologists did not have to plow a hillside before they could eat." Steve shook his head. "Now I hear the tourists are following the archaeologists. The ruined temples have become big business. So—" he shrugged and smiled—"perhaps the peasants can start catching this general excitement. There's nothing like money to stimulate cultural interest. But we won't tell Lee Preston all that." Steve shook his head again. "How is our bright idea-boy?"

"He came down to see me off."

"Doesn't trust anyone to blow his own nose, does he?"

"He's worried about you."

Steve didn't give the guffaw that Strang had expected. "About me?" he asked quietly, blandly innocent.

"Didn't you get his letter?"

"Not yet."

"It's waiting for you downstairs."

"I'm not staying here," Steve admitted, and glanced at Strang. "Look, if I'm arranging my expense account to suit me, that doesn't mean I'm cheating Preston. I'm cheating myself." He looked round the comfortable room. "And I won't charge him a penny more than it would have cost me to stay here."

"If you needed money," began Strang in embarrassment, "Lee Preston would have—"

"I don't borrow," Steve said quickly. "And I don't need the money for myself. I just need it for—well, for someone else. And I need it pretty damn quick." He looked at the door irritably. "Where's that boy with the drinks? What's he doing?"

"Distilling the Scotch," Strang suggested.

But Steve had laid aside his comic mask for a tragic one. Morosely, he asked, "You've got a sister, haven't you, Ken?"

33

"Two, bless their funny hats."

"And married—"

"Thank God."

Steve nodded agreement to that. "But they didn't need a dowry," he said slowly. Then, back to the brisk, don't-give-a-damn-for-anyone Steve, "What's worrying old Preston? Is he thinking I'm going to take photographs for *Life*, *Look*, and *Holiday*, too? Well, he can drop that idea. I've got plenty ahead of me, as it is—plenty."

"That's what's troubling Preston. He thinks you may have your mind on too many things."

"It's none of his damned business. I'll do his job, and do it as well as I can. I suppose he began fussing when I left New York before his final pep talk could be delivered? It was just as well I came here early: I got the Paestum pictures before the weather broke. I spent all of these last two days developing them."

"How are they?"

"Beautiful," Steve said with his usual frankness. Modesty was something he considered strictly for hypocrites. "But you should have seen me prowling around Paestum, trying to keep the telephone wires and bungalows out of my backgrounds."

"Then no retakes are necessary?" Strang asked in relief. "When can I see the prints?"

"I'll leave the copies at your hotel in Taormina."

"*Leave* them? Look, Steve—you're going to *be* there when I'm there. In the first week of April. That was the arrangement, remember?"

Steve Kladas looked at him in surprise.

"I need a week at Taormina to get my sketches into shape. Don't try to talk me out of that, just because you are going to Taormina out of schedule. What's the rush to get there tomorrow?"

"What does it matter where we begin or end the Sicilian tour? We could just as well have the final get-together in Palermo."

"And be kept awake by motor scooters until three o'clock each morning? And up again at four, when the peasants yell their news to each other as they drive their donkey carts to market? No, thank you. I'll work at Taormina." On a terrace filled with flowers, high over steep hillsides falling down to a blue sea; and Etna, snowcapped, rising slowly into the sky, with a thin spiral of smoke drifting over the volcano.

"Say, you got around in that war," Steve said appeasingly. "All right, all right. I'll see you at Taormina. My, oh my," he added softly, with a touch of admiration, "when you dig your heels in, you dig them in."

"What's the rush to get to Taormina tomorrow?" Strang asked again.

"That the drinks?" Steve was on his feet, halfway to the door even before the waiter knocked on its panel. "Let me handle this, Ken." And he did, in Italian that was far from accurate but remarkably effective.

"You know," Strang said when the boy had left, "that waiter can talk perfectly good English."

"I like giving orders in Italian. I took plenty of them during the occupation. Funny—we fought the Italians and beat them. Then came the Germans. And what did we get for occupation troops over most of the countryside? Italians. The Germans, of course, kept the big jobs for themselves—like Athens and Salonika." He paused. "And reprisals," he added grimly.

"You've never told me about your war," Strang said, curiously.

Steve measured the drinks with more than usual care. "It is something to forget."

"Is?" Strang echoed the present tense.

"Some things don't stay buried." Steve handed Strang his drink. "Here's to us, anyway!" He added, almost awkwardly, "I mean that. You are just about the only person left I can trust."

It was always difficult to handle a compliment gracefully. Strang, as usual, retreated into a topic as far away from himself as possible. "How long," he asked, "have you known the Roilos girl?"

Steve, who had begun walking around the room in a fit of restlessness, halted and stared. "Roilos," he said very slowly. "What do you know about Roilos?"

"If you'd only collect your mail—"

"You mean Preston wrote me about Roilos?" Steve was tense, grim, and amazed.

"Yes. Katherini Roilos came to his office, just before she left New York. She wanted to—"

"Katherini Roilos?" A look of immense relief spread over Steve's face. "Never heard of her."

"No?" asked Strang with a smile.

Steve sat down, searched for a cigarette, and ended by borrowing one of Strang's. "What does she look like?"

Strang described her.

"And what did she want?"

Strang told him.

Steve's eyes were worried again, but he still kept shaking his head. "Never met any Katherini Roilos in my life," he said most finally.

"But," Strang reminded him frankly, "you recognized the name when I first mentioned it."

"Why shouldn't I? There were twenty people called Roilos in our village —twenty in the next one—it's a common name in some parts of the Peloponnese."

And feuds were common, too, in the Peloponnese, that large southern stretch of Greece now joined to the mainland only by a bridge over the Corinth Canal; the man-made island of scattered towns where Homer's heroes had been kings, of lonely farming and fishing villages, of wild mountains and cruel coasts, of hardy people and long memories.

"I've heard there are two things that can start a blood feud in some parts of Greece," Strang said lightly, but he was watching Steve closely. "Kill a man, even in fair fight, and his relatives will kill you."

"I killed Germans, Italians, collaborators. But it didn't start any blood feud." Steve was amused. "So that's one thing you can stop worrying about. What's the other?"

"Women."

"Sure. Greeks take a pretty serious view of their women's honor. So do I, my friend. I'm still Greek enough for that." He laughed. "Boy, for an American, you know a lot about Greeks. You'll stay alive." He put down his glass, rose, and crossed over to the neatly stacked luggage. He lifted his own case onto the dressing table. "By the way, did I thank you for bringing this little object across the Atlantic?"

"Repeatedly. So much so, I became embarrassed."

"Okay, okay. . . . Thank you." Steve turned and gave an elaborate bow. Then, in earnest, "Thank you, Ken."

"There's one thing I kept wondering about. How did you have it sent on board ship in New York?"

"By a friend." He didn't elaborate on that. "Did it give you any trouble?" He was searching for a key to open the case.

"When?" Strang could tantalize, too.

"Back at the customs shed."

"Just about paralyzed my right arm."

"That all?" Steve had got the case open. He looked inside, searching with his hands, nodded approvingly and closed it.

"Not quite." Strang's jesting was over. His tone of voice made Steve turn to look at him. "I wasn't helping to run any contraband, was I?" he asked quietly.

"No. Nothing like that." Steve was equally grave. The cynicism, and its half-joking half-serious manner, was gone. "I wouldn't let you in for that kind of business, Ken," he said reproachfully.

"I'm glad to hear that."

Steve said angrily, his pride wounded, "Don't you trust me?"

"Sure. More than you trust me, pal." But Strang's broad grin took the edge from his words. "Glad you found everything intact."

"Hell, I didn't check the case because of you. Just making sure that no steward had decided to sneak some of the film." Strang looked startled. "You're a trusting guy, Ken. Maybe that's why no one ever steals from you."

"No challenge in that?" Strang shook his head. "And there I was, imagining that nothing got stolen from me—so far, that is—because I kept things locked up. Which reminds me—" He began to unhook from his own collection the key that Steve had sent him.

"Would you do me a favor, Ken? Another one?"

Strang waited, half expecting the bad news.

"You haven't much luggage, and you should see the stuff I'm groaning under. The load will get easier, though. By Athens—" He could look very pleading.

"You want me to cart that damn case around until Athens? What if some sneak thief thinks a trusting guy is a challenge, after all?"

"It will be safer with you than with me." Steve paused. Then, in desperation, "Come over here, come on!"

Kenneth Strang rose, the key in his hand. "Here it is," he said, polite but definite.

Steve Kladas didn't take it. "Look for yourself." He opened the case again. "No heroin, nylons, furs, or diamonds. Only film, honest-to-goodness film, and this envelope." He drew it out from under the first row of films, and opened it. "It just holds a couple of private letters. From my sister. But they are important."

"And these neat little yellow boxes—there are no crisp twenty-dollar bills folded and wrapped round the spools instead of film?" Strang was joking, but Steve did not react with any of his usual quips.

He shook his head slowly. "No, Ken. On my honor, no!"

Strang believed him. When Steve brought honor into his conversation, you could trust him.

Impulsively, Steve said, "All the film is fresh, waiting to be used. Except these three boxes." He searched for them. "See, I made a small ink blot on each of them. They contain negatives of pictures I took in Greece. Years ago. But they are important."

"Like the letters?"

"Look, Ken, they are only personal documents. I swear. On my honor." Strang rehooked the key to his ring. "What about dinner?" he asked. He watched Steve lock his case carefully and drop it beside the rest of the luggage.

"It's a family matter," Steve explained with a last glance at his small suitcase, "just a family matter." He fell completely silent.

Steve was still silent as they left the elevator and came into the red-carpeted lobby. In summer, this hotel would be as busy as a hill of ants at a picnic. Tonight, one could even notice the white-and-gold-paneled walls, the silk lamp shades, majolica vases, mirrors, showcases of coral jewelry and cameos and Sorrento lace flowers, the gray-uniformed bellboys standing as idly as the potted plants just inside the huge glass entrance door. The few guests were either in the restaurant or watching television in the darkened ballroom, hypnotized by a ghostly voice explaining the grace, the delight, the beauty of a vacuum cleaner's spare parts. People paid the hard way for their amusements nowadays.

"We could eat here," Strang said as they walked the half-mile of carpet toward the door, "but I'd like to try one of those little fish restaurants on the island just across the causeway." Steve said nothing. "That is," Strang went on, "if you don't object to wave-dodging. Or have you any better ideas?"

Steve halted abruptly, his eyes on the entrance. The bellboys started into life as the glass doors opened to let a wild gust of wind blow two guests into the hall. They were a middle-aged man, handsome in a thin-faced way, and a young and attractive woman, well dressed, but bedraggled like all new arrivals on such a night, cold, probably hungry, and certainly a little dazed by the sudden blaze of warmth that threw its welcoming arms around them. He was helping her remove her coat, and she looked up at him and laughed at something he had said in a grave way.

Nice picture, Strang thought approvingly, a nicer picture than that of two lonely men going out to find a place to eat. "Come on, Steve," he said sharply. "The rain seems to have stopped. Only your sea breezes left to battle."

But Steve had turned his back on the door. He was walking to the porter's desk. "Better collect my mail while I'm here," he said.

Waiting for Steve, Strang found he was watching the newcomers. The man had checked the luggage, but he refused to give up his brief case to any helpful hands. He was walking with large strides, a little noticeable in a man of less than medium height, toward the reception desk. He had taken off his narrow-brimmed felt hat; his gray hair was closely brushed to his neatly shaped head. Everything about him was neat and restrained, from the well-built dark suit and striped tie to the narrow shoes so carefully and firmly set down on the bright-red rug. English, thought Strang, and was amused at himself for starting to play the old guessing game so early on his travels. But it was a game, once started, that was difficult to stop. Probably ex-army, Strang made his next guess. Or present army in mufti, trying to look like a diplomat? The wife was obviously English—pink-and-white complexion, soft golden hair, and, no doubt, violet eyes. She had set the bellboys' rows of polished buttons bristling.

He wondered what could be keeping Steve. There appeared to be some kind of argument at the porter's desk. Steve was looking round—he was angry, Strang could see by the way his brows came down in that thunderous straight line—and signaled for help.

Strang went forward. It was only a matter of identification. "Yes, this is Mr. Stefanos Kladas. His plans were unavoidably altered and he had to cancel his reservations, much to his regret. I believe there is a letter waiting for him. Would you be good enough to look again? Yes, I think that's it. From *Perspective* magazine? . . . Thank you." He led his simmering friend away. "Why the hell don't you carry your passport around?"

"Do you?" Steve tore open the envelope roughly. "Thanks for all the four-syllable words. When I get mad, all I remember are the four-letter ones. That damned Italian!"

"He's probably Swiss. Come on, you Greek. You can read that over a plate of red mullet. Say, do you know that Englishman? He has looked over in your direction twice. And that's once too often for that type." The man had left the registration desk and veered toward them.

"No," Steve said gruffly, thrusting the letter in his pocket, not looking at anyone, suddenly in a hurry to reach the door and that plate of red mullet.

"Yannis!—It is Yannis, isn't it?" The man was English, all right. His thin face softened with the moment of recognition. He put out his hand. Delightedly, he said, "Yannis—my dear fellow!"

"Sorry." Steve's voice and face were quite expressionless. "You are mistaken." He walked on; stiffly, Strang noted, as he caught up with Steve. Steve's walk, Steve's voice were both a very simple-minded attempt not to be Steve. They went into the blustering night.

"The rain has ended," Strang said, giving Steve time to recover.

In the darkness, Steve's face grimaced with pain. "Some things won't stay buried," he said thickly, and cursed.

"Over here." Strang led the way across the wide, deserted, gust-torn street that edged the bay. As they reached the beginning of the causeway which would take them onto the little island, he added, "The dinner and drinks are on me. We'll have a bachelor's evening—all hiccup and happiness."

39

The phrase caught Steve's fancy and fetched him half out of his black mood. "All hiccup and happiness," he repeated.

"Not mine. Credit Byron. But all good things have been said before. It's like women—the pretty ones are already married." Strang remembered C. L. Hillard, the girl with the misleading name; not married, seemingly, but most certainly engaged ten times over. He concentrated on the problem of the wave-swept causeway. "Now the idea is this: we'll time the waves. And calculate. And make a bet on it. And run like hell."

Steve's wide grin came back. Leaning forward, against the force of the wind, they waited, watching the waves smash against the rocks on their right and hurl their broken crests at the narrow causeway. On its lee side, to their left, was the little Santa Lucia harbor, surging and restless as its swollen waters rose and dipped almost on a level with the restaurants' front doors. Steve said, "I hope you calculate right. One second out, and we'll end up there." He looked at the harbor's straining tide. As he watched, he could see the water spill over the narrow sidewalk toward the restaurants' steps.

"Then we'll have to swim for our supper." Strang counted three more seconds. "Now!" he yelled.

They raced across the dripping causeway, staggering once against a sharp buffet of wind, carried along by Steve's war cry, which began as a shout and ended in a sustained, piercing scream. They reached the shelter of the fort's huge gateway, and collapsed, fighting for breath, against its wet rugged stones. When the breath came back into their lungs, they began to laugh and kept on laughing, collapsing now against each other, now against the enormous wall.

Then sanity, and appetite, prodding them, they took the back road around to the service side of a restaurant. The cook and his enormous collection of family looked up in surprise, as the two strangers, hair and coats soaked with spray, came into the kitchen.

"I hope you don't mind us using the back door tonight," Strang said. "We don't like getting our feet wet." No joke is a poor one in Italy. This one, as usual, paid off handsomely. Surprise gave way to laughter, a burst of welcome, a dozen hands helping them out of their wet coats. They had five waiters, three musicians, the full lights turned on in the empty dining room to do them honor, and the most carefully cooked dinner in all of Naples.

After that, they talked until three in the morning, mostly about Greece. Casually, impersonally, as if he were speaking about a stranger, Steve Kladas lifted the curtain he had dropped around his life in Greece. The curtain was lifted just here and there, a quick glance in that direction, a brief look in this: no complete unveiling, just a broken sequence of memories which he described quietly, without emotion, making them still more painful to hear.

Tomorrow, thought Strang, I'll take a quiet hour and try to piece these anecdotes together, and make them into the pattern that Steve thinks he's giving me. It is all clear and logical to Steve. He thinks he is telling me something. And yet, if I were to interrupt him and say I wasn't quite following—would he explain this or that more clearly?—he would probably stop altogether, and I'd hear no more. That's the way he is: take what he gives but don't try to force out anything more than that. Tomorrow, I'll piece this jigsaw puzzle together. No, tomorrow would be spent at Paestum, and tomorrow and tomorrow. Then, someday, Strang promised himself, someday, when I've a quiet hour. But now, it was enough to let Steve talk some of the memories out of his mind.

"So you see," Steve ended, "why I must go back to Greece. It's now a great necessity. I'm the head of the family. There is no one else to take charge, to kill this threat, to see that no more dishonor comes to our name." He had sounded more and more Greek as he talked, as if he were making a translation into English.

"Threat?" Strang picked up the word, in spite of his self-warnings. "What threat?" There had been no talk of the future. All Steve's words had been of the past. Threats dealt with the future.

Steve looked at his watch. "Good God, it's almost three. Let's get moving."

The storm had spent itself, the tide was ebbing. They could walk out of the restaurant's front door and along the sidewalk edging the harbor to the causeway. They crossed it in silence. The bay was still sullen, but no longer raging.

"One thing I meant to ask you, Steve—" Strang stopped, noticing Steve's guarded look. He smiled and went on, "Do you know anything about C. L. Hillard?"

Steve Kladas relaxed. "A damned good photographer." He grinned widely. "Almost as good as I am."

"She's prettier than you."

"So you've met Hillard! When?"

The use of the second name jarred Strang unexpectedly. "Very briefly. Didn't even have the chance to ask her what the initials stand for."

"She isn't married, if you're wondering about that, too."

"Oh?" Strang responded most casually. "That seems strange."

"She was engaged, once. The guy got killed. Korea."

"Korea is a long time ago."

"Well, that's the way she sees it, I guess. Some, of course, say it's all part of her line. But I like her, so the hell with them." They had reached Strang's hotel. Kladas stopped and put out his hand. "See you in Taormina, Ken." He added, with a laugh, "And I'll make sure you meet little Hillard when we get back to New York. She is just offbeat enough to please you." He left. The sharp echo of his brisk footsteps faded into nothing.

FOUR

It was Strang who arrived two days late in Taormina. Steve Kladas had already been there, spending almost a week developing negatives and making prints, and then had left for a retake job of the theater at Syracuse. He explained it all in a sprawling note left at Strang's hotel with a parcel of his photographs. "Got trapped, this time, by telephone wires. Thank God, Greece doesn't have those modern improvements near *her* ruins. Hope you like the rest of the prints. Will be back to receive congratulations. This Syracuse trip will take no more than three days. Stefanos."

Strang read the letter, standing in the porter's lodge of his hotel. "When was this delivered?" he asked one of the battery of black-suited men, serious-faced, keen-eyed, who stood behind the desk. This morning, he was told. So Steve would be back by Friday. And three days would give Strang a lot of working time on his own sketches. Too bad, though, that he had missed Steve: other retakes, in spite of Steve's enthusiasm, might be necessary. It was a pity Steve hadn't waited to make sure. Unless, of course, he liked jaunting around Sicily. That could be true, too. Steve was usually adept enough at discovering telephone wires long before his finger pressed down on his camera's release. However, three days of peace were welcome; doubly welcome in a place like this after all the varied hotels he had stayed at. Even the flies looked as if they would be thoroughly tame here.

He followed the boy carrying his luggage around the long stretch of sixteenth-century cloisters (the pillars were now glass-enclosed, the flagstones carpeted) to the front wing of the old monastery. The Dominicans in Taormina had given themselves plenty of room between the thick walls. The passages were broad. The cells, each with a monk's name still painted above its carved door, now made comfortable bedrooms with whitewashed walls, dark massive furniture and—once he had opened the tall shutters—a view. He stood at a window which was framed by the shocking puce of bougainvillaea climbing over the front of the hotel. Below was a broad terrace, a long terrace, laid out with flowers and shrubs, benches and tables. There was enough room there, too, to please him. He might find a working corner, hidden behind that row of orange trees.

He went out to investigate. The key to his room measured a foot. "The keys are left in the locks," a quiet voice said behind him. "I am always on duty." He looked at the maid who had stepped out from the shadows of the broad corridor, her feet silent on the heavy carpet. "All right," he said, and hoped it was all right. "I need another lamp, more light, more light for working at night. Another lamp. You understand?" She nodded. But he left, wondering.

He found his way onto the terrace with only two mistaken turns. (This whole place was one vast stretch of museum pieces and unexpected doorways; a guest might be lost for days until a search party found him babbling by a seventeenth-century chest or a sixteenth-century wood carving.) The hill slope, on which the hotel was perched, dropped steeply to the sea far below. To his left, the little town spread along a ledge cut into the hills. To his right, more falling hills; and Etna, towering.

"It's too much," he told himself regretfully. There were palm trees and almond trees, and orange trees bearing both fruit and blossom, just to please everyone. And the flowers—spring and summer bloomed at the same time, it seemed. Roses and hyacinths, violets, and geraniums and freesia. Too much, far too much. Back to your cell, Brother Kenneth, he told himself gloomily. He left the terrace, with a glance of pure envy at the guests who had nothing to do but enjoy it.

There was no one in his corridor when he did find it again. Always on duty, was she? His door was ajar; the maid was inside, studying the labels on his suitcases. She looked more astounded by his quick return than by his silent entry.

"The lights are good. I tested them," she told him. She pointed to the bulb set into a wrought-iron decoration on the ceiling, and to the bed lamp.

"Yes, they are good." All twenty-five watts of them. "I need another light here. And here." He pointed to the writing and dressing tables. "Okay?" She left, nodding. He still wondered.

He turned the writing table away from the window so that he wouldn't be distracted by the view. He pulled the dressing table nearer to his chair, and propped several of his sketches against its looking glass. Now, slave, back to your galley! But before he began work, he gave himself ten minutes with Steve's photographs. (He would be going over them, in detail, with Kladas himself.) They were excellent. He looked across at his sketches, then back at the photographs. We'll manage this job, he thought, we'll manage it. With a feeling of purest pleasure, he began to work.

But there was a discreet knock at the door, and a housekeeper entered with the maid. The housekeeper spoke English. "Your maid says you cannot make the lights work." She switched them on and off. "See, it is very simple. This one is for the ceiling. That one is for the bed."

"I want one here, and here." He pointed. "For this work."

"In daylight?" She frowned at the opened shutters which let the flies come into the room, and then noticed his sketches.

"I work at night, too."

"Ah—you are a painter?"

He had given up arguing about that. He nodded.

"I shall send the lamps to you."

"Thank you."

She pushed the maid out of the door and followed. She stopped to say, "It would be pleasanter to work on the terrace."

He looked hard at the door she had closed, and repeated to himself, "I do like women, I do like women," until his temper cooled, and he could resume his thin-line architectural drawing of a Doric temple.

The rest of the day was peaceful, except that, when he returned from an early dinner rather more quickly than might be expected and entered the long corridor that led to his room, he saw the solemn-faced maid locking a door some distance away. It could be his door. He was still too far away to be sure. The girl saw him, stopped, and—to his surprise—hurried toward him. But the boot boy, in white shirt sleeves, black waistcoat, and green apron, had entered the corridor just behind Strang, and the maid halted abruptly. She said, "The two lamps are in your room. *Buona notte, signore.*"

"Thank you. Good night."

She turned and walked quickly away to the other end of the corridor. Very obliging, Strang thought, to come out of her way to tell me what will be obvious as soon as I open the door. He reached it and began the usual battle of the strange lock. The boot boy passed him quickly, giving him a polite good night, and hurried to overtake the maid. "You are late going off duty," Strang heard him say. "You are late coming on," she replied. Their voices faded as Strang entered his room and closed the door.

The two lamps had been installed, all right. But he shook his head at their size: long on charm, short on strength. Travel had its delights, but at this moment he would have given a lot for a simple hundred-watt bulb, and a screen for the window.

Then he saw that someone had been looking at the work he had left on the desk. The top drawing, in a set of three, had been shifted askew. He swore, and studied the heavy sheet of paper for any ruinous thumb-marks. But the drawing and those beneath it were as clean as he had left them. He relaxed. Yet, instinctively, he went over to his luggage and examined each case. All were locked. He took the trouble, though, to open them and check. Nothing was out of order.

He became half annoyed, half amused by his suspicions. Everyone loved to look at pictures: the maid had just the same curiosity as all the rest of us. He remembered the small boys who had materialized out of nowhere on a lonely hillside, did not even try to cadge a cigarette for at least five minutes while they grouped round his elbow and chattered in Sicilian dialect; the black-haired, black-mustached laborers who had stopped heaving a pickax to become equally energetic art critics; the peasants who pulled their long-suffering donkeys to a halt while they sat silently watching a fellow artist from their bright, hand-painted carts.

Suddenly, he saw that Steve's bundle of photographs had been moved from the dressing table. For a moment, he really panicked. Then he caught sight of them, neatly arranged, of all places, on his chair behind the desk. Neatly arranged, yes. But the first one was missing. His lips closed in a grim line as he hoped someone's love of pictures hadn't tempted her to take a pretty pin-up for her room. He began checking the photographs, and relaxed when he found the missing one in third place. On top of it was a sealed, unaddressed envelope.

He counted the photographs to make sure they were all there, placed them back on the dresser, and then, baffled and bewildered, ripped the envelope open. The page of narrow pointed writing was signed, simply, "Aleco." Aleco. What Aleco? The letter began quite abruptly. "My thanks for your invitation to dinner in Athens, which I accept with pleasure." (Alexander Christophorou, he thought, astounded. Here, in Taormina?) "Perhaps we may even meet for dinner when my business is completed in Taormina. On Sunday? Meanwhile, if you could help me in a most urgent matter? I must see S. K. but discover he has left Taormina for a few days. Where can I find him? If you would let me know his address early tomorrow morning, I would be in your debt. Please leave the message where you found this note. I am sorry this matter needs so much urgency and discretion. Aleco."

There was a very small postscript. "How are your two friends? Wallace and the Irishman with red hair?" And that, Strang decided, was a most tactful piece of identification. He hadn't mentioned either Wallis or O'Brien by name in his letter to Christophorou. So Aleco was Alexander, in short, and no fake.

Why should he have even thought of a fake? Only because the surprise of discovering Christophorou in Taormina was almost too big to swallow at one gulp. Or because Christophorou wanted to see Steve Kladas? Why not? Lawyers could turn publishers or editors of magazines. Kladas was a photographer in demand. What more in keeping with good Greek business sense than to combine a holiday at Taormina with signing up Kladas for some photographs before any competitor could make contact with him in Athens? Except that most Greeks with vacations headed straight for their own islands; and most people didn't send their letters by a chambermaid with elaborate instructions (and a tip to match) for such fantastic secrecy.

Yes, he was puzzled. He reread the letter thoughtfully. Aleco was the diminutive, familiar, and affectionate for Alexander. He wasn't quite on Aleco terms with Christophorou. And yet the letter's phrases were too precise, too calculated, to slip into Aleco at the end without a purpose. It was as if Christophorou were telling him, "I am your friend." And friends trusted each other—all right, all right—and had dinner with each other. But not until Sunday. He had to smile. He caught sight of himself in the looking glass. And a damn fool he looked, grinning by himself in an empty room. This was one hell of a way to get his work done.

So he wrote a brief note. It said, "S. K. is in Syracuse until Friday. Don't know his address. Sunday will be fine. Ken." He added a very small postscript as his own piece of identification: "Hope the sandbags on the Acropolis did their job." He was smiling again as he slipped the note (in a sealed, unaddressed envelope) into the neat pile of Steve's photographs. He didn't bother to disarrange them. The maid knew where to look for his note when she came tomorrow morning. His smile broadened in spite of himself, and he ended in a fit of laughter. It was difficult, sometimes, even with all the good will in the world and lavish applications of international understanding, not to find foreigners comic. And how they must find him, sitting in here, when everyone else was dancing or drinking or walking a pretty girl on the terrace, was something he didn't even want to imagine. They'll think I fancy myself as the reincarnation of the old monk who once lived in this cell, he decided. And settled to work.

FIVE

Late on Friday afternoon, the siege was lifted. All-or-nothing Strang, he reflected, looking around the battlefield. The bedroom was in complete chaos, not one horizontal surface uncovered, not one vertical that wasn't a prop. But he had won, only six hours later than the deadline he had set himself, which wasn't too bad. Neither were the drawings. He looked at them again, anxiously, critically; then felt the stirring of excitement. They were all right, they were very much all right. All right, so they're all right, he told himself sharply, all right! Keep your hat on and your overcoat buttoned, Strang. But it gave him sweet pleasure to file the finished job carefully away in the waiting compartment in his portfolio.

He looked as much a mess as the room. He had been needing a haircut for a week. Now, too, he needed some exercise and sun. But most of all he needed some empty hours, doing what he damned well wanted to do, and no more must's, don't forget's, or have to's. For two days he'd have a holiday.

He shaved and showered quickly, chose a crisp blue shirt (bless the Sicilian laundress who made a traveler's life worth living) and a dark red tie to lend a festive touch to his gray suit. He was going to walk out, quite aimlessly, not even a sketchbook to bulge the pocket of his newly pressed coat, and look at the town and the people. For the first time in weeks, he felt free. This was the evening he had been looking forward to.

He stopped at the porter's lodge to see if there was any message from Kladas. There was none. So Steve had not yet returned from Syracuse. That was not surprising; Steve's sense of timing was a little haphazard. If you asked him to come round and have a drink at six, he would arrive at half past seven and think he was early.

Strang passed through the gate at the lodge into a small courtyard

48

sloping up toward a broad street, almost a square, of quiet houses and walled gardens and a long row of empty tourist buses from practically every country in Western Europe. He closed his eyes, and turned away to open them at a more pleasing prospect: the rising tiers of old buildings and Norman towers laced together by flights of worn stone steps. He began to climb, up into a compact little world of many centuries, and reached the next ledge on the hillside—a narrow, main street, broadening into a piazza: three sides for cafés and teashops, the fourth for a magnificent view toward the sea, if one could see the view for the hillocks of sun-pink shoulders and the forest of reddened thighs. It was a pity that people thought they had to start undressing when they went traveling; few were built for it.

Nothing, thought Strang as he sat down at a table and ordered a beer, would have pleased him more than to see a lot of beautiful girls with bare shoulders and pretty legs; but the beautiful girls were few and wore masses of skirt. There was a cruel twist, apparently, to the simpler enjoyments of life. He had another beer, listened to the snatches of six or seven languages drifting into one unintelligible human voice, and then decided to continue along the main street and find a barbershop.

The Corso was narrow, crowded, lined with small shops. Everything from embroidered blouses to cheese and wine, but he must have missed the barber's. A car drove slowly past, and the pedestrians either flattened out against windows and walls or dodged into doorways. Strang was doing just that—fortunately, it was a bookshop with a good display of foreign periodicals and newspapers on the racks by the door—when a woman's voice said, "Excuse me." She had been coming out of the shop, with a selection of magazines under her arm, and he, trying to decide between *Harper's* and *The Atlantic Monthly*, had blocked her way.

"Sorry," he said, stepping aside. She was young, no more than twenty-four or -five, dressed in cool green linen. She didn't walk past him. She stood, her large eyes widening (almost green they were in color, and not violet, after all) as she recognized him. She was the Englishwoman with golden hair and a perfect skin, now lightly tanned into what Italians called, not peaches and cream, but carnations, who had stood in the lobby of a Naples hotel and watched Steve Kladas cut her husband dead.

Some of the embarrassment that Strang had felt now came flooding back over his face. She noticed it. She said, "How do you do? We were nearly introduced once. Or don't you remember?"

"Naples," he said, recovering himself, "on a cold and empty night."

"In a hot and glittering lobby."

They laughed. And then there was a small silence. "I suppose," she

49

said, "we should finish the introduction which your friend didn't want. I am Caroline Ottway."

"And my name's Strang, Kenneth Strang."

She transferred her pile of magazines (they were mostly American, he noted) to her left arm, and they shook hands formally. She was studying him. Then she seemed to come to a decision, for she nodded and said, "Yes."

"Yes, what?"

"Yes, I am going to talk with you."

"You are?"

"Yes. After you buy your magazines."

"They can wait."

"They won't. This lot will vanish in the next hour. You had better make your choice while there is still one to make." She patted her own collection proudly.

Quickly, he selected four American magazines, *Encounter, Réalités.* "I was reduced to reading the travel folders," he remarked. "Very forceful prose, too. Did you know that Taormina offers 'revigoration of the health'? It also 'represents an oasis of peace in an over-anxious world.' Isn't that reassuring?"

She watched him, thinking: Kenneth Strang, Kenneth Strang, I've heard or seen that name; I'm almost sure I've seen it someplace. For a moment, she wondered if George would be cross about all this; he never had become accustomed to her way of reacting so instinctively to people. And she could never quite change herself, however much she tried. And she had tried, she really had tried in those last five years. Perhaps everything would ease out, just a little, now that George had this new post in Athens and felt he was useful again and could be among his beloved Greeks.

She stopped worrying about her husband, and decided, as Kenneth Strang paid for his magazines and made a couple of pleasant remarks to the nice man who ran this shop, that she was right—this time, at least —in her instinctive reactions. It wasn't just that Kenneth Strang had the kind of face she liked. He was not so handsome as George, she thought loyally, but he was good looking, certainly: strong, even features, thoughtful gray eyes, and a smile not too frequent but quite original; in this day of polite masks and guarded emotions, it was refreshing to see a smile that seemed real, not just a forced grin or a deprecating smirk. But most of all she liked the way he had looked, back in Naples, when George had put out his hand to that dreadful Yannis who said he wasn't Yannis, and had been met by a brick wall. Mr. Strang had looked as if he himself had felt the blow. Yes, she decided, I think he would listen to me, and help.

"Now," Strang said as he rejoined her, "where is your favorite café, or shall we talk here and block up the doorway?"

She laughed and began walking along the Corso. "There's a café at the end of this street, not so fashionable as those back on the piazza, but you can look at the Norman gateway and admire an Arab tower when my conversation runs low. Besides," she added wistfully, "sometimes you do see a real native there, and one of those beguiling little donkeys."

"I was wrong about you."

She looked perplexed.

"You aren't English." She has tried hard, he thought: voice, clothes, looks, all seemed English. But she wasn't. "What part of America do you come from?"

She looked as if he had given her a jolt. She said, stiltedly, "I was educated in England, I married an Englishman, I live in England, most of my friends are now English. But, technically, you're correct. I'm an American."

"And it keeps breaking in. Beguiling."

"What else can you say about a Sicilian donkey? Sweet, darling, amusing, enchanting? No. It's beguiling."

"More beguiling than most of the other donkeys wandering around," he said, as he stepped aside for the fifth time in two minutes.

"You are like my husband. Tourist shy. But, you know, we are tourists, too."

"Yes. That's what worries me."

She laughed. "I can't get George to admit that. He has retreated into our room and says he has work to do. George is my husband," she added, unnecessarily.

I should hope so, he thought, or you aren't the girl I took you for.

"We've been here three weeks."

"Three weeks?"

"Don't look so appalled. It sounded divine when we planned it in a January London fog." They had come to the end of the Corso, into a small square sloping down to the old town wall and its main gateway. She led the way to a little café, where icy stares greeted them from some permanent foreigners who had adopted Taormina, their refuge against materialism, as long as the checks from home arrived on time.

"We are two more of those damned tourists," Strang observed cheerfully. "The real natives are kinder." The group of workmen who had gathered round a metal-topped table for small cups of bitter, black coffee were watching them, certainly, as far as Caroline Ottway was concerned, with far from disapproving eyes. "What will you have?" he asked her as the waiter approached. He smiled. "Tea?"

"I'll have American coffee just to disappoint you."

"They'll bring you a can of that make-it-yourself-with-a-spoon stuff," he warned her. "We'd better play safe and order Cinzano. Okay?"

She nodded. She was frowning at the table, not so much at the over-friendly flies enjoying the last customer's beer rings, as at some problem shaping up in her mind.

"You know," he said, watching her, "I think it has been so long since you had a good cup of coffee that you've forgotten its taste."

"Possibly," she admitted. But she was thinking of something other than coffee, or café table, or people passing by.

He tried again. "When did you leave America?"

"I only lived there during the war." And there was one of her beguiling little donkeys, but she did not even see it.

"So it has its uses," he suggested.

She looked at him indignantly, stung into attention. "I was a child then. My father was Peter Drew Martinson." Silence again, with a frown from the beautiful dark brows to underline it.

"Oh?" he asked politely. I'm ready to give up, he thought; this isn't exactly the pleasant talk it promised to be. You've got another wrong number, Strang.

"He was a news correspondent in Europe. Mother and I trekked around with him. Until the war. After that—Mother had died—I joined him again. I was brought up all over the place. England for school, Paris and Geneva for the hols." A little smile came back into her face. "Sorry. For vacations."

"Keep that smile," he said.

She blushed a little. "I didn't become uprooted through choice," she said. "It just happened."

Peter Martinson, he remembered. "Oh, yes," he said, remembering, too, Martinson's death in a car crash outside of London five or six years ago. "I saw your father once. At the bar in the Grande Bretagne, in Athens." She looked puzzled. "Christmas, 1944," he explained. "He was arguing with a crowd of other reporters who were all preparing to shoot poisoned darts into Churchill. The old boy had just arrived to see for himself what was going on. Your father was trying to get them to ask a few questions and listen to a few answers before they started aiming for Churchill's heart."

"Aiming for his back, you mean," she said bitterly. "Did you ever see so much one-sided reporting as was done then? How could it happen? How?"

"Those were the days before the pattern of political take-over became clear," he reminded her.

"So you excuse people who had to have a blood bath in Hungary before they could see the pattern?"

"I'm not excusing. Just explaining," he said patiently. "We've all learned a little since then."

"My father didn't need the example of Hungary."

"No," he agreed quietly. "I expect he didn't."

She dropped the edge in her voice. "Sorry. But if you knew how my father was cold-shouldered for years! Oh, well—" For a moment, she was silent. "And what on earth took you to Athens, just then?"

"Sulfa drugs and powdered milk. A sort of special express job from the Piraeus docks."

"Were you Red Cross, or what?"

"Strictly Navy. We unloaded the stuff from one of the supply ships we had convoyed to the Piraeus—there was an emergency call for it, you see. And then we couldn't get anyone to run the stuff up to Athens, either, so we borrowed a bus and did that job, too."

"Was that when you met Yannis?" she asked. She was completely and intensely interested.

He looked at her for a long moment. He began to laugh.

"Now why?" she wanted to know.

"Just a little joke against myself." And the second one today, he thought. First, Alexander Christophorou. Now you. What secret charms has Steve Kladas got that I haven't? He glanced at his watch, and counted out enough lire to take care of the drinks and the tip. Then, as she stared at him in astonishment, he said, "I'd suggest another Cinzano, but your husband is probably beginning to think you've been kidnaped on a beguiling donkey to the upper slopes of Etna."

"So you did meet Yannis in Athens," she said slowly.

"I never met any Yannis," he said shortly. "My friend in Naples is an American. I met him in New York. His name is not Yannis. It's Steve—" He stopped there. He would leave it to Steve himself to broadcast Kladas.

"Please—" she said, gathering up her magazines, letting them slip, "Oh, thank you, I'm so sorry to be such a nuisance. Please—" She looked up at him in utter confusion. She was close to tears. "It's all so very important to me," she finished lamely, her voice dragging.

"All right," he said more gently. "We'll find another café and begin all over again."

"Perhaps I ought to go back to the hotel," she said doubtfully. "It's later than I thought."

Women, he thought, women. . . . If they were all ugly and dull and stupid, they would be easier to bear.

"All right," he said again.

"And walk with me," she said almost pleadingly. "I must explain a little."

That, he decided, was much needed.

"Because you really have been so very nice," she added.

"And may I carry your schoolbooks, ma'am?" He took the load of magazines under his arm. "Which way?"

"This street, just here. Our hotel is almost at the end of it." They began walking up the long, gradual hill. "It's rather a sweet little place. We stayed there five years ago, just after we were married. George was terribly ill in London last winter. Pleurisy. I thought it would be a marvelous idea to spend a holiday here, before we went on to Athens." She sounded as if she had doubts now about that idea. Perhaps a honeymoon was not easily recaptured.

"Athens? I am headed that way, too."

"Are you? George has been given a post at the embassy there. That is, he is sort of attached to the embassy. He is an expert on Greek affairs, you know. He has spent so much of his life, or rather the most important part of his life, with the Greeks."

Strang hid his astonishment. If I had a wife who looked like this, he thought, the most important part of my life would damned sure not be spent with other people.

"You see," she was saying, "George knows so many Greeks. He spent two years with them in the mountains during the war. A number of British officers were smuggled in, you know, to join the bigger resistance groups as liaison between them and headquarters in Cairo."

"I've heard about that." And he was remembering an empty restaurant in Naples, and Steve Kladas talking.

(Steve was saying, "Oh, yes, there were Englishmen in the mountains with us, types who learned classical Greek at school and came to visit the ruins and sail among the islands in peacetime—just the same kind of romantic idiots as you, Ken, who thought we were all Homeric heroes. They grew beards like us; slept on cold mountainsides, hid in peasants' houses with us; starved like us; marched with us; fought with us against

54

the Germans. . . . God, did they have a rough awakening! But no rougher than I had, and thousands like me.")

She had been talking about George's experiences with the guerrilla forces. Blowing up bridges became his specialty. That wasn't so easy in the last year of the Nazi occupation, because the leaders of George's group became more evasive about taking orders from Cairo or London.

"What group was that?" Strang asked quickly.

"The biggest of all. To begin with, there were many groups of resistance fighters, but George's group had good organizers. So it grew. In the end, it was an army."

(And Steve was saying, "Our group was getting bigger and bigger, and some of these ways of getting bigger were not so pretty. We would surround a resistance group who did not share our leaders' politics: either they joined us or they were wiped out. Very simple. Same rule with villages and the peasants: give no help to any other guerrilla bands, or watch your men be killed. And I'm not talking about collaborators; I shed no tears for them. I am talking about how to deal with the opposition, how to wipe it out before peace comes, and the elections. Sometimes the killing was not so pretty, either. Have you seen a man flayed? Have you seen a man crucified? There was one of our leaders, Ares, he called himself, the god of war. He used to boast he had killed two thousand men with his own hands. He was always a braggart, but cut that estimate in half and you still could not overestimate him. He had a special band of followers, a punitive force, about fifty of them; they liked to wear astrakhan hats and beards—by God, I never want to see their like again come upon any poor pitiful village. What's the matter, Ken? Isn't this your idea of underground resistance? You look just like the Englishmen, unable to believe or understand. Later, they did believe the truth, but I doubt if they ever understood it. Sure, they were good men, most of them, but they kept stumbling over their schoolboy learning. What did they think the ancient Greeks were, anyway? Only a set of handsome profiles on a high frieze?")

She said, "But you aren't listening—"

"I'm listening," he said grimly.

"It really *was* a well-organized group," she insisted, watching his face worriedly.

Strang nodded. "Except in following orders from H.Q. in Cairo?"

"It's no joking matter," she said sharply, widening her green eyes at such sarcasm. "The war was still going on, in Africa, Italy. . . . But George had one man in his unit, a sergeant, who'd carry out any orders that came through. When George found the leaders evasive about blowing up a bridge or ambushing a German patrol—goodness knows why they

55

were so wary about spending dynamite or bullets; the British were sending in quantities of ammunition and gold—then he would go quietly to this sergeant, and together they'd get enough men and do the job. The sergeant was called Yannis." She halted. "Now do you see that George couldn't have been mistaken in Naples? He and Yannis were always together in the last few months before Yannis disappeared."

(Steve's voice was saying, "Maybe some of us were fighting the Germans too hard, or perhaps we just didn't keep our mouths shut or the black look out of our eyes when we saw Ares and his men at work. Anyway, accidents happened to us. Or we were caught by German patrols. Strange how even the most careful were caught! The trap was set for me, too. But I didn't walk in.")

She said, "You just can't forget a man like Yannis. He was the closest friend George ever had."

"What was his full name?"

"No one knew. Most of the guerrillas took a false name. It protected their families if the Germans ever caught them."

"But look—didn't Yannis, like all the others, have a beard? How could your husband recognize him so quickly in Naples, when he was clean-shaven?"

"Once, George took him on a special mission into Athens. They shaved off their beards before they entered the city so that they'd look more normal. They nearly ran into disaster, all the same. You see, Yannis was fascinated by cameras. He had found one among the pile of loot taken from an Italian division at the time of the Italian surrender. Others were taking boots and overcoats and arms, but he only wanted that camera. Then, in Athens, he saw the German cameras. He liberated one, and so much film that he bulged. George thought they'd never get back to the mountains." She shook her head.

(Steve Kladas was saying, "What does a man do when everything turns sour? Oh, it was sweet for Ares, sweet for his political friends. They had, gradually, taken over the real power. In the end, our military leaders were helpless. So were the English. So were the rest of us. We had been outmaneuvered from the start, when Ares arranged everything to be run by Committees of Three. Everything to be decided by democratic vote; and each Committee of Three had two Communists. We had joined a National Army of Liberation to fight the invaders, and we had been turned into an army waging civil war. A man can go crazy when he sees that. He keeps hoping it isn't true, he keeps thinking he must be mistaken, he keeps quiet, and then—. But I found a way to keep sane. I began taking photographs. If I shot pictures, I might not have to shoot Greeks. I was only a good soldier when there was a real enemy in my sights, not just someone Ares called an enemy. So I liberated a camera and some film, and became a kind of war photographer. We smuggled these photographs into Athens, pictures of villages after Nazi reprisals, that kind of thing. At first, Ares liked the idea; he was chief of Propaganda and Enlightenment, as well as leader of his own little band of terrorists. Then, suddenly, he didn't like it. Maybe I was becoming too handy with a camera. I could use it hidden under a torn sheepskin cape. I could work pretty close to my subject, too. . . . One night, I was given orders to leave for a village that had been destroyed by the Nazis the week before. Routine stuff for me: a long walk over wild country, a long climb over a mountain. Except that I kept wondering why I had been sent out of camp so secretly, without a chance to say good-by to my friends. So when I came to the village, I didn't enter it. I lay on a hillside and watched it, a burned village with blackened walls, deserted. And that was strange, too. Survivors usually came back to search for something they could save. When you are so poor that you cannot buy a bowl, then even a broken one is valuable. I waited for a day, a night, and part of another day. At last, men came out of a half-ruined house. German soldiers, they were. They must have thought they had been given the wrong information, or that something had happened to me on the way. Anyway, they left. That night, so did I. I began the long walk to Athens. Ares did not go raiding there, not at that time. I found shelter with friends. I shaved my beard, hid my camera, borrowed clothes, invented a name and a story to go with it. None of Ares's informers ever found me. So I stayed alive. That seems important when you are twenty-one.")

Caroline Ottway looked at Strang sharply. Was he really listening to all she had been saying about George, and the way he valued old friends, and how much he needed their good will in his new job? "What is wrong?" she asked. "Have I said something you didn't like?"

He shook his head.

"And here is the hotel!" she said in dismay. "I haven't even told you what I wanted to say most of all." She glanced up at a corner window which overlooked the street. Oh, well, she thought, George has probably seen us by this time. If I'm to be read a lecture again, I might as well earn it. "Let's walk on," she said.

There were only two or three houses more, all standing within walled gardens, before the long street ended its slow climb in a high promontory of rock where ruined columns and broken arches were raised into the sky.

"There's the Greek theater!" Strang said, halting in sudden surprise.

I wish, she thought angrily, that he would listen to me as intently as he looks at that pile of old bricks and marble. "Mr. Strang, I haven't much time. I am late as it is. And what I have to ask is so important."

"Sorry." And he was. "All right. Go ahead and ask me for Steve's address so that you can write him."

She opened her large eyes wide. "However did you guess?" He must have been listening, after all. She said, "I just want to clear up everything. I want Yannis—or Steve—to know that George has always believed in him. When he was denounced as a deserter and traitor, it was George who defended him."

"He was denounced as a traitor?"

"Yes, at an emergency meeting in the camp just after he had disappeared. They said he had gone over to the Germans, and that enemy patrols were now moving against the camp, so everyone had to scatter and regroup. It must have all been a lie, of course. But George couldn't prove it, because he wasn't allowed to go back to the camp site to see if German patrols had moved up. He wasn't allowed any freedom of movement at all; he was almost a prisoner after he had defended Yannis. His mission became a total failure. So—" she drew a deep breath—"do you think it was fair of Yannis to wound George so deeply when they met in Naples? Why, George was the only one who defended him."

"What were his other friends doing?" Strang asked bitterly.

"But it was his brother who denounced him. Who could argue with a brother? Besides, who would argue? See what happened to George! And he had the protection of being a British officer."

"I see" was all Strang said. But he was thinking, Steve never told me anything about a brother. He looked at her, wondering if she had got the story wrong. "His brother?"

She nodded. "George can tell you all about it."

Strang said nothing. George, he was fairly sure, would never again even mention the name of Yannis. To a man, a snub was a snub. It was women, poor darlings, who thought that if only they explained enough, then everything would be made all right.

"One thing puzzles me," she said slowly.

Only one thing? he wondered. "Shall we climb up to the theater," he asked, "and talk about it there?" They could hardly stand rooted beside a garden wall for another five minutes.

"I—I don't know if I have time." She glanced back at the high, corner window of her hotel. Then she looked at the gateway to the Greek theater. "It will soon be closed for the night," she said, watching a girl and an elderly woman coming slowly through the gates. She noticed that Mr. Strang had seen them, too. "They always go up there, each evening, and leave just before the gates are closed. I think she's lonely. Every morning down on the shore, every evening up on that hill. And always with that old woman trailing along. They bicker, constantly. It's a very peculiar household—George and I are fascinated—just the girl, always exquisitely dressed; the old woman, always complaining; and a rather strange man-servant. At least, he wears a uniform when he drives their car, and yet he lounges about the garden as if he owned it. He was sunbathing yesterday, without a stitch on."

Strang looked away from Miss Katherini Roilos and her duenna arguing sharply on the other side of the road, but the girl hadn't even glanced in his direction.

"That's their house, just across from our hotel," Caroline Ottway told him, "the one with that heavenly almond tree inside its high wall. They only arrived a week ago. If I had a divine house like that, I'd have been here since early spring, wouldn't you?"

He pretended to lose interest in the house. "You were puzzled by one thing," he reminded her, and started to edge her slowly back to her hotel.

"Oh, yes—about Yannis. Was it Cyprus, do you think?" As he looked blankly at her, she explained, "Cyprus caused so much bitterness. It's all settled now, of course. But so many Greeks turned against the English. That could be why Yannis was so—so—well, you saw how he behaved. And that's so unfair, too. Because George was pro-Greek, right through the Cyprus trouble. It was a miserable time for him during these last four years. He was stuck in London. In fact, it was only recently that he was given a real job to do again—working with the Greeks—that's something which really interests him." She fell silent. Almost sadly, she added, "Do you understand what I'm trying to say? But why should you? I don't even know why I am talking to you like this. You listen so well—perhaps that's the reason."

"Or perhaps because I'm American?" he asked. Or perhaps because she was as lonely as Miss Katherini, he was thinking. He glanced up at the high, corner window as they reached the hotel, and frowned for a moment.

"You haven't given me your friend's address," she reminded him.

"There's no need. He's probably in Taormina right now. He's going on to Athens, too. So your husband can see him there."

"No, not that way!" she said. "Let me see him first, talk to him. That will make things easier."

"You should be the diplomat in your family. Where can Steve meet you?"

"But George isn't a career diplomat," she said quickly. "He isn't Foreign Office, one bit. Why don't you tell your friend that I'm always at the

English Café on the main piazza every afternoon at four o'clock? George has been so busy this last week that he has scarcely left the hotel. Reports and things . . ." she added vaguely. "Well, good-by, Mr. Strang. You know, your name sounds so familiar." She gave a dazzling smile and a firm handclasp. She looked past him, toward the doorway of the hotel, and her smile became shy, embarrassed.

"Don't you want your magazines?" He began dividing them from the pile under his numb left arm.

"Tell me," she said urgently, in a low voice, "what do you do? Why are you going to Greece? On holiday?"

"Not exactly. I visit ruins and try to draw reconstructions of them." He noticed her amazement. He grinned. "What was your guess?" If she had any time for guessing about me, he thought, with all her worries about George. Even her interest in Steve was only because of dear George.

"George!" she said delightedly, holding out her hand. Her husband walked past Strang to stand beside her, his back turned to the street and the houses opposite. "I am so glad you came down to meet Mr. Strang. Kenneth Clark Strang. Don't you remember, darling? That book about the Mayan temples?" Her eyes were laughing. "I gave it to my husband for his birthday," she told Strang. "You are one of his favorite authors."

It was a masterly introduction. George Ottway's face, not particularly genial at this moment, unfroze just enough so that his eyes couldn't revert to the cold stare he had been preparing for the last two minutes within the shadows of the hotel doorway. Kenneth Strang's amusement turned to appropriate embarrassment. He glanced at Caroline Ottway, but she was too clever a little piece to show she had disarmed them both. "We've had such a wonderful talk," she told her husband, cuing Strang at the same time, "all about the Greek theater"—she waved her magazines toward the rising crags at the end of the street—"and—and things. . . ."

It was a lame ending. But Caroline was no liar, Strang decided; she was just a sweet little finagler with a tendency to be the defending tigress. George didn't look as if he needed much defense, though. Strang looked at the fine-boned face, the well-shaped head with its neatly brushed gray hair, the controlled lips, the quietly appraising eyes. "Good-by, again," he told Caroline Ottway. "Good-by, sir."

"Perhaps we'll meet in Athens," she said. "I hope you're going to have the same photographer with you. His pictures of Yucatan were so good. He had a Greek name, hadn't he?" Her eyes were laughing again. "Stefanos or Steve something-or-other, wasn't it?" George Ottway took his wife's arm. "Caroline, I'm afraid we are keeping Mr. Strang from his evening's engagements." And to Strang, "It was kind of you to help my wife home with her load of magazines. Good-by to you."

Strang walked down the long street, even forgetting to look at the house with the almond tree inside its high wall until he was far beyond it, while he brooded over Caroline Ottway's last words. So, she had identified Yannis: she would find Steve's full name in that damned book. Not that it mattered. When she met Steve tomorrow, she would melt him into telling her not only his name but his life story.

He was back at the little square by the town's gate. The main street was more crowded than ever. He plunged into it, wondering if he would have the good luck to run into Steve. Or perhaps even meet Alexander Christophorou. Or see Miss Katherini and her strange household. Everyone else in Taormina seemed to be here, walking as slowly as possible, looking at the little shops, looking at other people.

Strang searched for half an hour and then entered a barbershop. He called his hotel, first, but there was no message waiting for him. Blast Steve, he thought irritably, why can't he be on time, just for once? He had his hair cut, in a thoroughly bad temper.

For he was beginning to worry. There were just too many Greeks gathered together in Taormina. Coincidence? He would like to believe that, and enjoy the pleasant, relaxed night he had planned for himself. Instead, after dinner, he walked around the narrow dark streets, climbed innumerable steps, sat at café tables, looked into restaurants and a couple of night clubs, made three telephone calls to his hotel. There was no sign of Steve.

Exhausted, worried, and depressed, he returned to his hotel around midnight—and that wasn't what he had planned, either—to find the unexpected. "Signore Strang," the porter called to him, "that message you have been expecting—it came only ten minutes ago. By telephone."

He took the slip of paper and unfolded it. The message was simple: "Weather disappointing. Delayed. Kladas."

Yes, that's Steve, he thought wearily: one cloud missing and he can't get the composition he wanted for the sky. "Thanks," he said to the porter, and made his way through the dimly lit cloisters. From the distant hotel bar came the strange effect of a samba tune played by a sweet mass of Strauss violins. But tonight, completely wasted, didn't put him in any humor even for the incongruous. He wasn't worried and depressed any longer; he just felt foolish and a little baffled.

He decided to have a drink in his room, and read a magazine article on "Night Life in Paris." And so to bed.

61

SIX

Bright sunshine and blue sky, for a late breakfast on a terrace high above a sparkling sea, were a good remedy for last night's gloom. As Strang drank his third cup of coffee and looked at a small orange tree displaying its golden fruit against the distant background of Etna's snow-covered peak, he decided he would mix a little business with a good deal of pleasure. He would spend the morning at the beach.

He took his swimming trunks, a magazine, and a taxi, for the constant twists and turns of the snakelike road around gardens and villas trebled the journey down to the blue sea. Straight distances, here, would be measured not as the crow flew but as the stone dropped.

The beach was a small crescent of sand, guarded by immense black rocks jutting out of the clear waters. Today, most people were of the bob-and-splash school, so it was easy to count not only heads, but torsos and hips. There was no one of the size and shape of Miss Katherini. "Every morning down on the shore," Caroline Ottway had said. But there was no one of the size and shape of Caroline, either.

He swam out to the rocks and found no sea nymphs there, only two small, thin, brown boys in a small, thin, brown boat, who shouted to him hoarsely. He hoped it was encouragement and not a warning against octopus.

By one o'clock, he admitted defeat, dressed, lunched at the small restaurant beside the bay, and caught a bus back to Taormina. The streets were empty now, bleached white by the early-afternoon sun. It was the time for the Mediterranean sleep behind cool shutters. He went back to his hotel, found no message from Steve, exchanged swim trunks for his sketchbook, and wandered out again. By this time, his irritation with Steve was returning. He wouldn't get another two-day break like this for a long time, and instead of being able to enjoy it, he was restless, unsettled. All he wanted was one small note from Steve giving time of arrival; better still, one small message saying: "Here I am. Where are you? See you in the piazza."

He went along there, anyway. He was early for the appointment with Caroline Ottway. (If she meant to keep it, that was. Perhaps she had decided not to take tea today, just as she had decided not to go swimming. Steve's full name might be all she had wanted. Or needed.) He chose a seat under a wide awning of a café, well to the back of the broad sidewalk, where he could have a clear view across the rows of little tables to its neighbor. That was where she had said he could find her. At four o'clock. Ten minutes to go. The tables were still mostly empty. The piazza looked stripped. He would wait here and see if she did come. Time enough, then, to go forward. Today, he had some questions of his own to ask.

It was almost as if a faucet had been gently turned on, and people, instead of water, came slowly streaming out. Now the piazza was flowing with them. They were seeping into their favorite cafés. The tables were no longer bare blobs surrounded by empty chairs. The quiet lazy silence was wrenched from its sleep by footsteps and voices and laughter. It was almost four o'clock.

He pretended to read a travel folder which had been bequeathed to his table. (Taormina, he was delighted to hear, had "a wonderful air saturated with energy-restoring oxygen.") But he kept a watchful eye on the street by which she would arrive. Two minutes to go. And, walking briskly into the piazza, never slackening his pace as he approached the English Café, making his way to the back row of tables with a quick but no doubt comprehensive look around him, came George Ottway. He chose a table as far from anyone as possible, consulted his watch, and opened a newspaper. Dressed as he was, in a dark-blue shirt, no jacket, no tie, he became just another tourist who liked to wear sunglasses.

For a moment, Strang was startled enough. Then, in quick succession, curious and amused. Caroline Ottway wasn't so adept at keeping secrets from her husband, after all. Perhaps that was the reason she so enjoyed surprising other people's secrets out of them: we all needed our little triumphs to balance our defeats. The best thing to do, Strang decided, was to produce a little surprise of his own. He left money beside the check on his saucer, and walked over to the neighboring café, approaching it from the side so that George Ottway, his eyes watching the front rows of tables from behind his newspaper, didn't even notice him until he said, "Sorry to have kept you waiting." He was delighted to see that Ottway looked startled enough for a moment, too. We begin even, he thought.

63

"Four o'clock exactly," Ottway said, recovering himself quickly. "Do sit down, Strang." As he spoke, he rose and offered his chair, taking another which would let him sit with his back turned to the other tables and to the piazza. "I believe you like Cinzano," he said, and called a waiter.

So he got everything out of her, Strang thought. He said, "I'll have a beer, thanks, today." I've been promoted, too: Strang, not Mr. Strang. And I've been honored: he has dropped the work that has kept him glued to his room for a week in order to come out here and meet me. Why?

"My wife had a headache," Ottway explained, removing his sunglasses.

"That's too bad." Strang was quite aware that he was being carefully studied. I suppose if I had a pretty young wife, he thought, I'd be sizing up any man she had produced out of nowhere. Except that Caroline hadn't even tried to hide that; she could have walked with Strang in twenty different directions instead of right under her husband's window. But it was none of his business, thank God, to delve into Caroline's motives. That was a job for her husband. And if Ottway had dragged himself away from the reports on his desk just to have a closer look at Strang and freeze him off— No, he discarded that idea. There was something more to this meeting than that. For Ottway was waiting, and watching Strang as he waited, as if he were deciding something. The drinks came. The waiter left.

"Now," Ottway said, his waiting over, "I think we needn't argue that I did know your friend as Yannis?"

Strang nodded. There wasn't any doubt left in his mind about that.

"And is he working with you on your new book?"

"On a series of articles, first. Eventually a book, we hope."

"Then it is true that he is here and will be going on to Greece?"

"That's the idea."

"Would he cancel it?"

"No."

"Why not? If I were to ask you to persuade him that he is running into serious danger, wouldn't he listen to you?"

Strang stared at the quiet face opposite him. In spite of the controlled voice, Ottway could not hide the anxiety that had invaded his normally calm, pale-blue eyes. "I've already passed on one warning to him," Strang said. "It made no impression."

"Then he knows?"

"Frankly, I couldn't say." Knows what? Strang wondered.

"If he knows," Ottway said thoughtfully, "he will be on his guard. And if he is on his guard, he probably can take care of himself. He always could." Ottway's anxiety had lessened. He lit a cigarette. "Yannis—" he went on, and then broke off. "Let's bury the name of Yannis, for his safety, shall we? You call him Steve, I believe."

"Your wife will be able to tell you his full name when she unpacks your art books in Athens," Strang reminded him.

Ottway didn't find that funny. He frowned. "Yes. Caroline would do better not to meddle. None of us should." He looked very directly at Strang. "It was made quite clear to me in Naples that your friend wanted the name of Yannis, and everything that was connected with Yannis, to be completely forgotten." He paused. With bitterness he did not even disguise, he added, "I find it rather difficult to make my wife understand this."

"I suppose any wife is curious about any mysteries in her husband's past," Strang suggested. He had meant that as a simple generalization, but Ottway's eyes focused, tight and hard, on his face. There was an awkward pause. Strang said, "I am grateful to your wife, actually. She filled in a lot of gaps for me yesterday."

"Such as?" The words were quick and sharp.

"The brother, for one. What was his name?"

"I only knew him as Sideros."

"That means—?"

"Steel. Appropriate? Only in his affection for the use of cold steel."

"What was he like?"

"Didn't Steve tell you?" Ottway was still tense.

"He never mentioned him," Strang said. "Nor did he ever mention you. In fact, he mentioned no one at all, except Ares. Where is that peculiar monster, by the way?"

Ottway relaxed. His voice became as easy as Strang had kept his. "He caught it, thank God. He was killed by Greek regular army troops who had chased him back to the mountains. That was a few months after his attack in Athens failed. A long time ago, now—1945, to be exact."

"Are you sure he is dead?"

"They cut off his head and displayed it in the marketplace of Trikkala. The peasants came in from miles around, just to make sure."

"My God!" Strang recovered himself. "Well, that's final enough," he admitted. "Steve can forget about that one. I must admit that Ares had me worried. He and Steve had a real grudge feud; more than just politics, I felt."

Ottway nodded. "Steve almost persuaded his brother to leave Ares's special band of followers. Ares never forgot that."

"What?" Strang was really upset. "Steve's brother was one of that crowd?"

65

"He became one of Ares's favorite young men," the calm English voice said. "He was scarcely twenty."

"You use the past tense. He is dead?"

Ottway looked down at his fine hands. "I am not certain," he said at last. He thought for a long moment. When he spoke, it was to change the subject back to Steve. "As I was saying—your friend Steve wants Yannis forgotten. I know of only three people who could definitely identify Steve with his past experiences: you, my wife, myself."

"No others? If the brother is alive—"

"If," Ottway emphasized. He paused. "Ares's friends were killed with him, except for two or three who escaped to Bulgaria. I imagine they would be safer to stay there; their records are too well-remembered. Unless, of course, they have changed. A man can change. . . ."

It was Strang's turn to study the table in front of him. Was Ottway only judging from his personal experience? So many did. Because they could regret mistakes made in their past, they thought all men could. But some would never admit a mistake; and nothing admitted meant nothing regretted. "No others?" Strang repeated.

Ottway said, "Steve and I were very close friends. Yet he never told me his real name, never talked about his family or village, or town or wherever he came from. He spoke English with an American accent, but he could have learned that from a Greek-American teacher. I have known Indians who speak English with a Welsh accent, and Poles who have a Scots accent: it all depends on who taught them English. Steve gave nothing away to anyone. Perhaps he didn't want Sideros, his brother, identified with his real name. Greek pride runs deep."

"All right. There is just you and your wife and myself who could harm Steve by identifying him as Yannis, the man who was supposed to have deserted. As far as I'm concerned, Yannis is only a name in a story that someone once told me about the war. And as for you—"

"Steve is an American photographer whose work I much admire."

"And I think you can persuade your wife to concentrate on that, too," Strang said with a smile.

"She must," Ottway said grimly. "None of us talk, none of us even think about Yannis. And if ever I do meet your friend Steve in Athens, it will be as a complete stranger. Tell him I understand that, won't you?"

"I'll tell him."

"But never that my wife discussed him, at all, with you?"

"Of course not." What was troubling Ottway so much? "Isn't it clear to Yannis's old comrades that he wasn't a deserter or a traitor?"

66

Ottway said slowly, "I think most people know now who the real traitors were."

"Then it is just the two or three survivors of the Ares band that are worrying you?" There was no answer from Ottway. "Particularly Sideros— Steve's brother—if he is one of them?"

Ottway picked up the check and studied the price of two drinks. "Naturally," he said. "If he is alive, and out from the safety of the Iron Curtain, he would not want himself identified. I imagine—if he has not changed— that he would not particularly enjoy having any attention drawn to the name of Sideros."

"Could Sideros recognize you?"

"Possibly." There was a slight flicker of an eyelid. "I never went in for heavy disguises. When my beard itched, I shaved it off. Several times." And then, before Strang could ask one more question, he dropped some lire beside his half-finished drink, and rose, saying, "Keep an eye on Steve, won't you?"

"I'll do my best." Strang rose, too. "Look, I'm going to the Greek theater. We can walk together as far as your hotel."

"No," Ottway said sharply. "I would rather we were not seen together." Then he looked puzzled. "Aren't you rejoining Steve? Didn't he come here with you?"

"No. He is still in Syracuse."

"Oh—I thought, perhaps, that he had seen me here and refused to come over with you. Well, that makes it all the better; he doesn't have to know we had this little talk. He never did like interference. Good-by, Strang. Don't follow me too closely. That makes me nervous." He nodded, put on his dark glasses, picked up his newspaper, and left.

Strang lit a cigarette and sauntered slowly across the crowded piazza to its open side, where he could pretend to look down at the view of steep falling hillside. When he decided that he had given Ottway time enough, he set out himself, at his usual walking pace. But Ottway must have really hurried. He was, in the far distance, already entering his hotel by the time that Strang was starting up the long straight street that led to the theater.

Taormina is a town of views. Strang thought he had become accustomed to them, but the one from the Greek theater seized him by the throat. For a long moment, he couldn't breathe or think. He stood on the grass-covered stone of the topmost tier of broad steps, which once had been seats, and looked far down over their wide half-circle to the open stage. The shape and graceful proportions of the stage were still visible, marked by slender marble pillars, some broken, some fallen, some standing with a delicate arch miraculously preserved. And beyond all this lay nature's incomparable backdrop: Etna sloping down to a rippling sea shimmering like beaten gold under the late-afternoon sun. Sharp precipices to his right rose behind the town itself. To his left was more dark-blue sea; behind him, sea again with the Calabrian mountains of Italy shadowy in the white mist of the far horizon. Above him was a vast stretch of bright clear sky; around him, the sweet smell of wild flowers and herbs warmed by the sun, the gentle constant hum of bees.

He sat down on the stone seat and opened his sketchbook. Back in New York, his archaeologist friends had warned him that there was little worth recording here: the Romans had ruined the Greek theater with all their additions and afterthoughts. But although the purists could be right about the Roman brickwork—now pathetically exposed, its marble facing ripped away through the centuries by Christians and Arabs, either to decorate their own villas or just in a frenzy of general religious destruction—there was something that delighted an architect's eye: the Greeks had known not only how to build, but where to build. Neither Romans with their eternal brickwork, nor thieves nor barbarians with their jealous hands, could destroy this site. He forgot everything else—even his chief reason for coming here, at this hour—and began to draw.

At half past six, he took a break, lit a cigarette, decided to stretch his legs and rest his eyes, and walked along the back of the top tier. The shadows were deepening. He glanced down at the other visitors to the theater, perhaps forty or fifty in number, but so scattered over the giant steps and stairs formed by the rows of stone seats that he had scarcely noticed them. Most of them were sitting quite still, completely subdued, as he had been. He remembered to look for Miss Katherini and her elderly watchdog. They weren't here. Perhaps he had missed them, after all; or perhaps they were late this evening. His eyes searched the amphitheater again, its lower seats now lying in cold shadows. But they were not there. He did see someone he knew, though, and she had seen him, too. Caroline Ottway waved, and began the long steep climb toward him. Resigned, he closed his sketchbook and put away his pencils. Work was obviously over for this evening.

He was looking out toward the sea when she arrived, flushed and breathless, but prettier than ever. She was wearing white today, which set off the carnations in her cheeks; and the beads twisted around her throat were green, of course. Her eyes were bright and glancing.

"You've been here a long long time," she said, quite frankly admitting that she had seen him enter the theater. "Have you been working?"

"I made a start."

"May I see?" She touched his sketchbook.

"No," he said firmly.

"You never show anyone your work in progress?"

"No."

"Don't you want compliments?"

He laughed. It was no use trying to resist Caroline. "How's your headache?"

She glanced at him, and then smiled for an answer. She looked toward the sea. "There are some fishing boats! And a tramp steamer!" She pointed delightedly at a small coastal freighter. "Where is it coming from?"

He judged its course. "From Messina, probably."

"Just around the corner from here? And where do you think it's going?"

"It's hugging the coast line. Possibly it's heading for Syracuse." He wasn't watching the freighter, any more. Farther to the east, there was another ship, a white yacht.

"Let's say North Africa," Caroline suggested. "That's much more romantic."

"Not in that little tub."

She noticed the yacht. "*There's* a ship to sail anywhere!"

He nodded. The yacht was too distant for its flag to be identified. But there was no doubt about her beautiful, simple lines. He had seen that yacht, or her twin sister, across the bay at Gibraltar.

"She must be coming from Messina, too," Caroline said, adopting a good sea eye. "Oh, she's leaving us," she added in disappointment. The yacht certainly wasn't going to hug the coast to Syracuse. She was already drawing away from Sicily to the southeast, to the toe of the Italian boot. "For the Adriatic? Or Egypt? Or Greece?" Caroline was asking.

He looked at her quickly, but she had not been expecting any answer. She was simply speaking the guesses that drifted in and out of that pretty little head with alarming rapidity. Her last guess produced another jump in thought. "We are leaving for Greece tomorrow."

"I didn't know you were leaving so soon."

"Nor I. But George is so eager to reach Athens. We shall have to pack in a hurry."

"Then it's time you were getting back to your hotel." He had a vision of Ottway, finishing his reports at his desk, outwardly businesslike, inwardly fuming about his wandering wife. Strang took her arm to help her down over the rows of seats.

"Oh, George isn't there. He went back into town to send off a cable. I came up here to say good-by." She looked around her, memorizing the view. She laughed. "I came to say good-by to you, too. And to tell you I'm sorry if

I bothered you. And to let you know that I *can* be discreet. See, I haven't even mentioned you-know-whom. I can keep my promises, can't I?"

"For the first hour or so, certainly."

"Oh—now! I'll prove it to you. When we meet in Athens—"

"Shall we?"

"Of course! Everyone meets each other in the Grande Bretagne bar. By the way, I told George you had met my father. But you did, you know."

"I only saw him."

"You don't have to go into details, do you?"

"Not if it upsets your story."

"I don't tell stories," she said indignantly. "It is just that sometimes, occasionally, I—I have to find minimum explanations. You do understand, don't you?"

"Vaguely. I've never been married."

She glanced at him with one of her quick, now-what-do-you-really-mean-by-that looks. "You ought to be married," she said. "You'd be a great comfort to some girl."

"Is that all I'd be?"

She began to smile. "No," she answered. "I imagine—" She didn't go on.

"What?"

"Oh! We'll have to hurry." Her eyes were laughing, her cheeks flushed. "It's closing time, don't you see?"

"But how could you know? Your usual time signal isn't here today."

She frowned for a brief moment. "Oh, you mean the girl in the Dior dress? She left. This afternoon. Just about the time you were having a drink with George. They all left—the girl and the old woman and the chauffeur and five suitcases."

"Did they, indeed?" Then the yacht that he had seen sailing away from Messina could very well have been the *Medea*. "What is the chauffeur like, by the way? A small round type with well-oiled black hair? Sort of patters as he walks, dances around when he is excited?"

"Nothing like that. Dark hair, yes; but he is almost as tall as you are. Not fat, either. An athletic-looking bloke, as George said when he first saw him."

"In the garden, having his sun bath."

She concentrated on the last steep steps, leading them round the ruined stage.

"Well," said Strang, almost to himself, "he can't be Greek." When she looked at him sharply, he added, "The modern Greek doesn't strip down easily."

"I know. They are quite the opposite of the ancient Greeks in that kind of thing. And yet—George thought he could be Greek."

"How on earth could he tell?"

"The man reminded him, I think, of someone he once knew."

"Pretty good eyes, your husband has." Pretty good field glasses, too, perhaps.

"Yes," she said slowly, looking straight ahead. "He has seen me." They were now on the sloping path that led down to the entrance gate. George Ottway had stopped there, by the ticket booth, and was studying the post cards for sale.

"You would have told him everything," Strang reminded her. "This will save you finding that minimum explanation. By the way, does your husband know the Greeks have left?"

"Of course." She smiled. "Didn't you just say I told him everything?"

Ottway looked up to face them, at the exactly right moment. "Hello, there!" he said cheerfully. "Had a pleasant climb?"

SEVEN

Strang went back to his hotel in a thoughtful mood. Ottway had even asked him to join his wife and himself for a drink, but he had begged off. He gave an excuse which, to his amusement, Ottway had accepted with a long look: he had some work to finish before dinner. "Perhaps we'll see you later," Caroline had said, glancing at her husband. "We are going dancing at the San Domenico tonight." So, thought Strang, the Greeks have left and Ottway can step out again like a free man; no more subterfuges such as dark glasses, or standing with his back carefully turned to the Greeks' house, as he did when we met yesterday. "That would be pleasant," Strang had said, "but I may have to keep pretty close to my room tonight. Steve will be turning up any time now."

And when he met Steve, Strang was thinking as he reached the hotel, there was going to be quite a lot of talk. Steve was going to have to listen to some frank advice. Because, Strang decided, I'm on the side of Lee Preston, this time certainly; alarms and excursions are no way to run a business, and we have a serious job to do. It is all very well to be erratic, offbeat, independent, but this job is a good job, worth doing, and let's keep our minds on that, shall we, pal?

At the porter's lodge, there was still no message from Steve.

After an early and lonely dinner, Strang settled in his room to wait. And, of course, just as he had arranged the desk and the light and spread out his sketches and picked up a pencil, there was a knock on the door. It was the sad-eyed maid, returning his laundry. That was a little surprising; it had been promised for the next day. More surprising was her low voice, saying, "Your friend is on the terrace." Then, in her normal tones, she added, "I hope the gentleman is pleased with the shirts?"

"Yes, thank you. Just lay them on the bed. Good night."

She hesitated at the door, glancing into the corridor. "Is the gentleman leaving tomorrow? I wish him a good journey and a quick return."

It was a tactful hint. "Is it your day off, tomorrow?" he asked, and rose and found his wallet. "I probably won't leave until early Monday, but in case I don't see you again—thank you for your most efficient services."

To an Italian, the phrase of thanks spoken earnestly was almost as important as the tip. Her tired face came to life for a delighted moment. She wished him a good journey, for the second time. As Strang closed the door on her thanks, he heard the *facchino* outside say, with a laugh, "You made sure of that one, eh?"

"Why not?" the maid asked sharply. Their voices blurred in half-joking argument and faded into silence.

For a moment, as he pulled on his jacket and tightened the knot of his tie, Strang felt ridiculous. Play acting was something to be kept strictly for a stage. Yet human beings were odd: he had picked up his cue so easily from the maid, had backed her excuse for her visit to his room at this hour, as if he actually accepted this play acting as something quite natural. His feeling of foolishness passed into one of worry. If Steve had to send messages like this—or was it Steve?

He left his desk with his work spread out over it. He opened the shutters wide to let in the air, switched off all lights to keep the night moths out. In the corridor, the half-joking argument was still in progress. It was silenced abruptly as he appeared, and then, as he left the corridor, he could hear it begin again. He found himself a little envious. For at this moment, somehow, traveling was a lonely business.

He halted at the top of the steps leading down to the terrace, and lit a cigarette. There were bright lights spaced overhead, but there were enough patches of deep shadow among trees and flower beds to please the romantics. The terrace appeared empty; people were still at dinner in the restaurant on the other side of the hotel. More mysteries, he thought with rising annoyance, and he walked slowly down to the front balustrade. Then, to his right, almost at the side of the terrace that looked toward Etna, he saw a man. The man had seen him, too. He was standing still, waiting, not under full lamplight, yet not in deep shadow. But he wasn't Steve. He was thinner, much thinner. For a moment, Strang hesitated. All right, he thought, all right. . . . He threw away his cigarette and began walking slowly toward the stranger. It was Alexander Christophorou.

Strang halted. Christophorou stepped back into the shadow of some trees, and Strang followed him. In the darkness, they gripped hands. "I would have known you," Christophorou was saying delightedly. "Even if I had not been expecting you, I would have known you." The warmth in his voice, speaking English fluently, was unmistakable.

Strang relaxed. With undisguised relief, he said, "It's good to see you again. It has been a long time."

"Over here," Christophorou directed, still keeping his voice low, as he led the way between flower beds and fruit trees, "we shall find a pleasant place to sit and talk." They passed under a light, and each glanced at the other automatically. Christophorou smiled and said, "Yes, let's have a close look." Then they entered another patch of deep shadow. "Careful! There are little chairs here. And a table."

"Last time we met, you were saying, 'Careful! There is a deep hole here, a rock there.' And we kept to the shadows then, too." But why here? Strang wondered.

"Here, we can sit," Christophorou said. "And this time, too, we still have something beautiful to watch while we talk." He gestured to the dark outline of Etna against the ink-blue sky. "Your face has changed a little, Kenneth. Have you? I hope not."

"Fifteen years older," Strang reminded him.

"And I am fifty years older. But you noticed that."

Strang thought of the face he had seen under the lamplight for a brief moment. Alexander Christophorou was still a handsome man, but he had aged rapidly. His dark hair was now receding, his face had become thinner, so that the aquiline nose and high forehead were more accentuated. His deep-set brown eyes were still remarkable under the thin black eyebrows, but they had sunk further into their large sockets, just as his cheeks were now gaunt. The lips, once full and sensuous, were now almost severe. His smile was quick, fleeting. Fifteen years ago, he had probably been no older than twenty-seven or -eight. Now, he looked like a man in his late fifties. What, Strang wondered, has he been through?

"I'm sorry we must sit in this darkness," Christophorou said.

Strang recovered from his shock at Christophorou's appearance. "Is it really necessary?" he asked lightly.

Christophorou laughed softly. (And that, Strang was glad to note, had not changed.) "I am afraid so. Some people have become very interested in my visit to Sicily. I should like to keep them puzzled as much as possible. In fact—I am sorry, but I think it would be safer if we did not have dinner together tomorrow night. We shall postpone that until Athens."

"I'm glad to hear that Athens is safer." Strang's disappointment added a slight edge to his voice.

Christophorou said quickly, "For you, certainly. Because in Athens, I meet so many people. But here, I have met no one except on—certain business."

The implication was clear enough. "Your business has to do with Steve Kladas?"

"Yes. I would rather you were not connected with it, in any way. And so, let us postpone our little dinner."

"It seems to me I'm pretty well connected with Steve already."

"But only in your own work. Let us keep it that way, Kenneth."

Strang said nothing. Was a postponed dinner the only reason for this meeting? Perhaps Christophorou had thought that the voice explained more kindly than a brief note.

"No other questions?" Christophorou asked.

"Plenty," Strang said. "But they would put me at a disadvantage."

"I know. Questions make a man sound inquisitive or naïve. You were never either of these things."

"They can also embarrass one's friends," Strang reminded him, letting the compliment fall to the ground. Whether it was truth or flattery no longer interested him: he had become older, too, evidently. "Frankly, what questions may I ask you?"

"Have I become so much a mystery?"

"You always were, you know," Strang said with a laugh.

"I was?" Christophorou was serious, a little hurt. He hadn't taken the remark as a small joke. "How?"

"Just the way we met, remember?"

"In the Grande Bretagne bar. But what was mysterious about that? It was crowded with soldiers, a general headquarters for the government forces—"

"But you were the only man there who didn't laugh when I said over a drink that before I left Athens all I wanted to see was the Parthenon. I remember you standing quite quietly at one side of the bar. You looked over at me and said, 'Why not?' And you did get me close up to the Acropolis, street-fighting or no street-fighting."

"A mad impulse," Christophorou remarked, "but hardly mysterious."

"I used the wrong word, I guess. I ought to have said 'romantic' or something like that." Strang was embarrassed a little. "And how is Athens?"

"Quiet."

"Are you still teaching law at the University?"

75

"No. But I haven't given up the practice of law, entirely." Christophorou was speaking carefully. Strang had the feeling that he was choosing his words. "Shall we say that I have moved into a field where my training can be very useful?"

Intelligence work, obviously, thought Strang; something confidential, at least.

"I'm a journalist."

Strang wondered if he had guessed wrong. He said, "I thought that perhaps you were here on some kind of police business, or intelligence work, or something like that."

"Not police business," Christophorou said definitely. "I am here as a journalist interested in a story."

"I'm sure you are a very good journalist and the story is a very good story, too." If Christophorou had become an intelligence agent, he could scarcely admit it, but the inflection in his voice and his new passion for secrecy might be a calculated warning to a friend: I am here on official business, he seemed to be saying, but I can't tell you that in actual words.

"The story belongs to Stefanos Kladas," Christophorou said. "My job is to ask him to tell it. I think it will be a very important story."

"For Kladas, or for you?" Strang asked bluntly.

"For many, many people," the quiet voice said. Then Christophorou laughed that small touch of grimness away. He reached out and grasped Strang's shoulder for a moment. "Don't worry, Kenneth. You will not have to divide your loyalties between Stefanos Kladas and me."

I hope to God I won't, Strang thought. Steve's story, he was beginning to feel, was much more than the family matter Steve had talked about. "What do you intend to do with this story when you get it?"

"That will be decided on the highest level. This is a very grave security matter. I can't explain more."

Strang thought of Steve's small case lying so peacefully in his room. He moved restlessly. "Well," he said, "when you get to Athens, call me at the Grande Bretagne and we can arrange—"

Christophorou stopped him as he rose. "There are some things I can explain, though. It is absolutely imperative that we find Stefanos Kladas."

"Why?"

"Because he has certain knowledge, certain information about certain people, which is vital to us. His story, as I call it, could be disastrous if it were to get into the wrong hands. I *must* see Stefanos Kladas. You understand?"

Strang nodded politely. The matter was urgent; that he did understand. He said, "So my letter to you turned out to be very useful."

"Incidentally, yes. When your letter reached me in Athens, we already had a man in Taormina waiting to interview Stefanos Kladas when he arrived from Naples."

So that explained Steve's hurry to get to Taormina. "Didn't he see your man?"

"Yes. But the meeting was not altogether satisfactory. Stefanos Kladas wanted to deal with his story in his own way, on his own terms. Perhaps he wanted time to think about our proposals. He arranged for another meeting here, in Taormina, this week. And that is where your letter was not only a pleasant surprise, but something useful. For I decided to come and interview him myself. If he still had doubts about us, then I thought you could at least vouch for me. Or was I wrong?"

"Steve makes up his own mind."

"But aren't you close friends?"

"Yes, but still I don't know any of his secrets. That's the way he is." Strang tried to see Christophorou's expression, but the shadows defeated him. Would Christophorou have ever bothered to meet me at all, he wondered wryly, if I couldn't have introduced him to Steve? "I thought you said you wanted me kept out of all this business."

"I do, since coming to Taormina. Back in Athens, the interview seemed a much simpler matter. But here, in Sicily, our competitors have learned that Stefanos Kladas is around."

Strang half smiled. "Are they working for a rival newspaper?"

"You could express it that way." Christophorou's voice was grim.

"And you are both after the same information?"

"Yes. But their methods—" Christophorou's shrug could be felt through the darkness.

"How will they try to get it?"

"By threats, or bribery, or even blackmail."

"Steve isn't the kind to be easily threatened." Or bribed, or blackmailed.

"Perhaps not. But—in any case—our problem has widened. It is not only a matter of persuading Stefanos Kladas to give us that information. It is a matter of protecting him."

"He won't like that."

"He won't know."

"He will. Any intelligent man would know at once if he were being followed around."

There was a slight pause. "Did you know that you have been followed for almost two days?"

"What?" There was a longer pause. "Why?"

"You might have been interesting."

"And was I?"

"Until last night."

"And what did I do last night to make them lose interest?" Strang's sense of the ludicrous became swamped in anger. "And who the hell are—"

Christophorou's hand was on his arm. "Quietly," he advised. "Last night, you searched this town. Obviously, you were looking for Stefanos Kladas. Obviously, you did not even know his hotel."

"And obviously, if he didn't trust me with his address, he never trusted me very much about anything." Strang was still angry.

"Or did he?"

Strang hesitated for a moment. "He told me about his sister. She's alone now, in some small village in Sparta. There was some problem about a dowry. But that isn't the story you want from Steve, is it? I don't know any other."

Christophorou was silent for a few moments. "You haven't seen him since you came here?"

"No."

"No letter? No message?"

"There was a telephone call, last night."

"You spoke with him?"

Strang, sensing the change in Christophorou's face, cursed the deep shadows once more. It was only when you talked in the dark that you realized how much you listened, not only with your ears, but with your eyes.

"No. The message came just ten minutes before I got back to the hotel. He was delayed in Syracuse." Strang shook his head and added, "But after what you've told me, I wouldn't be surprised if Steve didn't send that message. Perhaps the men who followed me around last night thought they'd send me a note and get me to stop searching."

"Stefanos Kladas did not send that message."

Strang, who hadn't really believed his own suggestion, looked startled.

Christophorou rose to his feet. "I went to Syracuse. I found where Stefanos Kladas had been staying. But he had already left Syracuse, yesterday morning."

"Then where is he?" Strang was on his feet, too. If Steve had left Syracuse yesterday morning, he could have reached Taormina by noon. Unless, of course, he had stopped off to photograph Etna, or Catania.

"Don't start worrying! Stefanos Kladas is bound to return to Taormina. He left some of his luggage at his hotel. Two cameras and a suitcase."

"He wouldn't leave Sicily without collecting all his cameras," Strang agreed. "I think I'll get in touch with the local police, though."

"That's unnecessary. I've already been in touch with them."

Strang stared through the darkness.

Christophorou said, "That isn't as bad as I made it sound. Just a precaution. That is all. Really, Kenneth, I did not mean to worry you like this. You seemed to be taking everything so calmly—" Christophorou himself sounded worried. But not so much by Kladas, for he asked, "When do you plan to leave here?"

"I was supposed to leave for Rome by the early plane from Catania on Monday." Supposed to . . . but what now?

"Then straight on to Athens? Keep that plan."

"But if Steve—"

"Keep it!" Christophorou's hand gripped Strang's. "I want to see you in Athens. So keep it. Tomorrow—what were you going to do tomorrow?"

"Spend the morning at the Greek theater, the afternoon working in my room."

"Keep that plan, too. Good-by, Kenneth."

"Good-by—" Strang paused in embarrassment. He couldn't say "Christophorou." That might sound like a rebuff. Alexander? Aleco? Too familiar. "But I don't think I'll concentrate much on my work," he said quickly. "Where is Steve's hotel?"

"I would rather you did not visit it. That would only complicate my life still more. I don't want you in the picture at all, Kenneth. It is quite enough to have to worry about Stefanos Kladas."

"Are you sure you are not overworrying?" Strang asked slowly.

"Quite sure." Christophorou sounded most definite. "Good-by, Kenneth."

"Good-by," Strang said again.

Christophorou smiled as he moved out into the half-shadows. "Aleco would be quite suitable," he said gently. "After all, one doesn't measure friendship by length of time only; depth of time is just as valuable. And danger gives the greatest depths of all."

Now they could see each other's faces again.

"You aren't quite sure of me, Kenneth, are you?" The smile on Christophorou's face faded. "Yet I haven't changed. I am still fighting, in my own way."

"I had hoped the fight was over." Then Strang added, "But I suppose the barbarians never leave us."

"Barbarians?" Christophorou looked puzzled. At last, he remembered. "Ah, yes," he said. "How can they leave? They are part of us all, perhaps." He turned, stepped into the pool of lamplight, and made his way to the steps. The trees hid him.

Strang walked by another path toward the balustrade. Now he could light a cigarette. He smoked it slowly, without any pleasure. "You aren't quite sure of me, Kenneth, are you?" Aleco had asked, mistaking Strang's worry and indecision for distrust. Come to think of it, Aleco had not been quite sure of Strang, either. That was a most unsatisfactory meeting in every way, Strang thought: I don't know much more than I did, except that there is a feeling of disaster all around Steve. Disaster—he could feel it as deep and black as the night around him. Suddenly, he was chilled. The late breeze had a sharp edge. So had this feeling of inadequacy; this sense of having disappointed, this admission of having been disappointed. The truth was that he couldn't tell Aleco about Steve's case and its documents; they were Steve's business, not his. And Aleco couldn't have told Strang more about his problems; he felt, probably, that he had reached the farthest point of indiscretion, stretching it as far as he could because of—what? Friendship? Or necessity?

I'd like to think it was both, Strang decided. He looked down for a moment longer at the vast stretch of sea so far below him. Three torches moved slowly across the dark water, just off shore. They were night fishing, down there. Now that's what I'd like to be doing, he thought; right now, I'd like to be in one of those small boats, drifting along, nothing to think about except the curious fish swimming nearer and nearer the flickering torches, nothing to worry about except making the oars dip silently, keeping our voices low, nothing to watch except the scattered lights on the hillsides under this huge canopy of star-sprinkled sky.

He dropped his cigarette, ground it out with his heel, and started the long walk back to his room. If Steve didn't turn up by tomorrow morning, he was going to the police.

Among the antiques in the shadowed corridor, the *facchino* was dozing in a high-backed chair. But the sound of Strang's light footstep, deadened as it was by the heavy rug, was enough to rouse him. He called over, "There is a message in your room, signore. It came ten minutes ago." He acknowledged Strang's thanks with a polite, *"Buona notte!"* and lapsed into his private brooding again. The hotel, thought Strang, had become message-conscious after last night's constant inquiries. Also, his room was guarded well. Nothing, he verified as he glanced around it, had been disturbed. As always, his luggage and Steve's small case lay neatly together. He looked at Steve's case for an extra moment, and turned to pick up the large envelope propped against his traveling clock on the dressing table. Another fake, he thought bitterly, and then saw that the address was in Steve's handwriting.

The envelope was, strangely, unsealed. Did Steve not care if anyone read his business? It contained two photographs of the Greek theater at Syracuse, and a lined page torn roughly from a cheap notebook. In Steve's hand, and it *was* Steve's large sprawl, read the bleak message: "Sorry I haven't been able to see you, but must leave immediately for Greece. I have mailed all photographs and negatives to Papa Preston. Here are copies of the final Syracuse effort. Hope you approve. Stefanos."

Strang's first reaction was one of enormous relief: Steve had collected the rest of his luggage and left; Christophorou worried too much. Then he reread the note, and—unbelievingly—read it a third time. He sat down on the edge of his bed. What was that about mailing photographs and negatives to Lee Preston? Steve was running out on the job. No, he couldn't be. Steve had too much good sense to end his career with a whimper. Strang looked at the enclosed photographs. They were magnificent. Fine composition, dramatic use of shadows, good texture of stone, silk-smooth sky, and a perfect balance of gentle cloud.

But the note—he looked back at it again. Not so good. Too casual. Not one mention of a meeting in Athens, or of that blasted case he had been carrying around for Steve. In a way, Steve's off-hand attitude was completely comic when you balanced it with all the worry and fuss he had been stirring up in Taormina. Either you had to laugh at yourself or you had to lose your temper with Steve. He decided to laugh. And then he wondered if the unsealed envelope and the casual note were not connected: anyone reading it would see that he had not met Steve in Taormina, would have no suspicion that Steve's case was among his luggage.

He rose, threw the note and photographs on the dressing table. Lee Preston had been right, all along. Steve hadn't his mind fixed on his job, not on this trip. He wondered gloomily if he should sit right down and compose a letter to Preston now; it might be wise to prepare him for the idea that another photographer might be needed for Greece. But he was depressed enough, as it was. He decided he had had quite enough of duty for one day; tonight, he was going out on the town. There had been a little place, when he had been making the rounds last night in search of Steve (and where had Steve been then—in a cosy little room with one of those cheerful Swedish blondes who had invaded Taormina by the bus load?) which looked a very promising spot to begin an evening.

He was changing his shirt, struggling with a stiff cuff link, when the telephone rang.

"Yes?" he asked curtly.

"Kenneth?" It was Christophorou. "I have good news for you."

"Let me guess. Could it be that our friend has arrived and left?"

"Yes. How did you—"

"I got a note."

"Telephone?"

"Not this time. Handwritten. The genuine article."

There was a little pause. "Could I see you?"

"Well—I was just going out."

"Just a brief visit." Aleco sounded anxious. "I am leaving early tomorrow morning."

Ah, well, thought Strang resignedly, wasn't this always the way? "How long will it take you to get here?"

"Forty seconds," Aleco said with a laugh, and put down the receiver.

Aleco's sense of humor was returning, Strang thought. Or was he staying at this hotel? On this corridor? That could explain the sad-eyed maid who played courier for a nice fat tip. He began buttoning his shirt with all speed, and crossed over to the door to unlock it and leave it open one small inch. He was reaching for a tie when Christophorou stepped in, closed the door quietly, and locked it again.

"Aren't you taking a chance," Strang asked with a grin as he knotted his tie, "walking all that distance of three doors away to my room?"

"Four doors away." Christophorou was smiling, too; but he was still security-conscious to some extent, for, as he walked over to the desk, ostensibly to look at the sketches, he closed the shutters.

"We'll be parboiled in here."

"Better that than broadcasting our voices all over the terrace," Christophorou said a little sharply. "Even if you did get a note that reassured you, you must still be careful. Please remember that, Kenneth!"

Strang turned away from fixing his tie in the looking glass and picked up Steve's note. "I suppose you'd like to see it," he said. "It came with these photographs in that envelope."

"Thank you," Christophorou said gravely. He began to read. Strang could study his face properly. Perhaps the cold glare from the terrace lights had been too cruel. Certainly Alexander Christophorou was much older, and thinner; but now, his face seemed less taut, less bleakly sculptured. It was a quiet, thoughtful face, restrained, as all his movements were restrained. Even his clothes—a dark-blue suit, a white shirt, a narrow dark-blue tie tightly knotted—were neat understatement. Here, Strang felt, was a capable man, a clever man, with few illusions left. The optimism and confident hope that had marked him so strongly, fifteen years ago, might still be there; but now they were under strong discipline, strong control. "So Stefanos Kladas has left," he was saying now. He handed the note back to Strang. "You accept this? It is definitely in his handwriting?"

"Most definitely."

"I wonder," Christophorou said slowly, "when this note arrived. And how."

"That's easy enough to find out," Strang said, and moved quickly to the telephone. His call to the night porter did not take long. "The envelope was delivered at ten o'clock, by a taxicab driver."

Christophorou was watching him thoughtfully.

"What's wrong with that?" Strang asked quickly.

"Nothing," Christophorou said reassuringly. "I suppose Stefanos Kladas hired a cab to get to the station, and gave the driver the envelope to deliver to you."

"To get to the Catania airport," Strang corrected him. "Steve always travels by air. Hates the sea."

Christophorou looked surprised. "But with all his equipment, surely—"

"Always by air. His expense account takes care of any excess baggage. No, you wouldn't catch Steve taking any train to get on to the Messina ferry for the mainland. Besides, he seems to be in a hurry to get to Greece."

Christophorou was frowning down at the desk by which he still stood.

"You are worried," Strang said. He began to worry, too. "You don't like Steve's letter being delivered so late? Should we check on that cabdriver?"

Christophorou roused himself. "The cabdriver?" He considered that question. "No. He was probably only following definite instructions. By ten o'clock, Stefanos Kladas would be well away from Taormina, and you would not feel tempted to call the airport to try to get in touch with him."

"I might call the airport, at that, and find out exactly when Steve did leave."

"That's hardly necessary. I'll have to make inquiries at the airport, so why should you? Let Stefanos Kladas have his way. He obviously wanted to slip out of Taormina."

"I wish everything else was as obvious," Strang said sharply. "It seems to me that if everyone would just stop being so damned enigmatic—"

"Including you, Kenneth?"

Strang looked at Christophorou in surprise.

"We all have our reasons. Mine are, simply, that I want to localize this danger, keep it from spreading. I think that is Stefanos Kladas's idea, too. Certainly he has been avoiding all contact with you. Otherwise, you would have found your life becoming extremely—complicated."

"What do you call it now?" Strang wanted to know. "All right, all right —I'm lucky. I'm the one who has nothing to worry about." He restrained himself from looking over at Steve's case. "So Steve has gone into hiding. Is that what you are telling me? But from whom?"

"You have no idea?"

"None."

"The difficulty with a man like Stefanos Kladas is that he thinks he can fight trouble by himself."

"Would it be tactless if I were to draw your attention to my poor little question left hanging in the air? It's turning black in the face."

Christophorou smiled. "Have you ever heard a Greek admit he did not know the answer to a question?"

"Only a Greek could say that. I wouldn't dare."

"Perhaps," said Christophorou, "I can answer your question when we meet in Athens."

"You need to consult the files, is that it?" Strang asked half jokingly. And certainly not newspaper files. "You really have become security-minded."

But Christophorou's joking mood had passed. "You think I am too cautious, that I worry too much? Twice in my life, I worried not enough. And twice, I paid for that." His voice was harsh, stilted, as if bitter memories had him by the throat.

"Aleco—" Strang began impulsively, and stopped.

Christophorou's voice became gentle. "Perhaps you feel that I trust nobody. Is that what really upsets you?"

"Perhaps your job doesn't allow much trust in anybody," Strang said. "And I'm not upset." Or am I? A ridiculous word, in any case.

"Yet what is this talk we are having, except a demonstration of trust? Yes, I still trust my friends. The only change in me, Kenneth, is that I no longer trust the enemy, not even when he smiles, not even when he offers gifts. He is always dangerous; most dangerous when he seems most innocent."

"But if your enemy has a change of heart?"

"The more he changes, the more he is the same."

"You've become a thorough pessimist, Aleco," Strang said, but his voice was sympathetic. "You have had reason enough," he added, remembering Greece in 1944.

Christophorou's eyes were just a little amused.

"But don't be too harsh on the Westerners," Strang said quickly. "If we seem a little slow in understanding Greece, well—there's always a big difference between those who were actually in a fight for existence and those who watched. All the sympathy in the world doesn't quite bridge that gulf. Take that terrible story of mass kidnaping, for instance."

Christophorou looked at him. In surprise?

84

"We aren't totally ignorant in America," Strang said. "How many children in Greece were kidnaped by the communists, after the Nazi war was over? Fifty thousand?" The number defeated any civilized mind. Thousands of children, thousands, had been seized in raids on the villages, had been taken north over the borders by the Communist bands operating out of Albania, Yugoslavia, Bulgaria. "And how many ever got back?" Strang asked. "Oh, yes, eleven thousand were returned from Yugoslavia when Tito quarreled with Stalin. But the others?"

Christophorou said nothing. His face was hard, a suffering mask of stone.

I shouldn't have talked so much, Strang thought. I'm a man from a country that has never known that kind of ruthless, political blackmail, has never had its children kidnaped by the thousands and taken into hostile countries. I should have kept my mouth shut. He turned away. "I'm sorry," he said quietly, and picked up Steve's photographs.

"That is your job," Christophorou said, pointing to them. "Stay with it." Then he added, surprised, "I had no idea you felt so strongly—"

"Who wouldn't?" Strang asked sharply. "My God—" He stared at Christophorou. He tried to lighten his voice. "You really must have a pretty low opinion of Westerners."

"No, no! It is just that your own interests are so far removed from present-day politics."

"This isn't an escape into the past," Strang said, holding up the photographs. "Every time I look at its ruins, I remember the barbarians who made them. I also remember the men who built. What is left of their work has still got enough vision to silence most of us. And give us some much-needed hope, frankly. If man can build, he isn't altogether lost. If he has done it once, he can do it again." His own seriousness embarrassed him. He could never talk about this adequately, somehow. "The past and the present aren't so far removed," he added, still on the defensive, but smiling. "They are just separate rooms in the same house, and if you unlock the doors they all connect."

"I wonder," said Christophorou. He was preparing to leave. He seemed abstracted. "You are an incurable optimist, Kenneth. But have you ever given serious thought to your—opposition? The barbarians, you've always called them. They are formidable people, a powerful enemy. They just can't be dismissed in a contemptuous phrase, you know." He reached the door and hesitated. "Do you know anything about nihilists?"

Strang, half annoyed, was yet surprised. He thought of *The Possessed*. "Only what I read in Dostoevski," he admitted. He waited.

But Christophorou merely nodded. He unlocked the door. "Stefanos

Kladas ought to be in Athens by this time. Stop worrying about him, Kenneth."

"Will you?"

"That is my job. Or perhaps I am an incurable pessimist." He smiled, then. His voice was confident, reassuring. *"Kalé nichta!"*

"Good night, Aleco. *Kalé nichta sas!"*

The door closed gently behind Christophorou. Strang opened the shutters. There were several people on the terrace. Soft voices, laughter, the click of high heels, the fragrance of flowers in the cool air; the night was inviting him to enjoy it. And so he would. But first things first. "Stop worrying," Christophorou had urged. The way to stop worrying was to break up the problem; to rearrange that case of Steve's, for instance. This was a well-run hotel, yet tonight was Saturday, with a good deal of movement, of extra visitors around. And ahead of him, there was a lot of travel, with several changes, porters, intervals when his luggage might be out of his sight. He might as well attend to Steve's case, right now, and then be able to go out and concentrate on the general fun and games.

He closed the shutters and lifted Steve's case onto his bed. One of the locks seemed to have rusted a little on his travels. He had to use his penknife to force it open. There was a slight smell of fish oil in the room: caviar, he remembered. How many weeks ago had that farewell party been? It felt like years. New York was not only in another continent, it was in another world. What would Lee Preston or his brothers-in-law think if they were to see him now, emptying out the contents of this case, searching for the three yellow boxes that were marked by Steve's small, careful ink blot, checking the letters in the envelope and—he saw, as he counted them quickly—a closely typed sheet of paper? He read nothing; as far as he was concerned, this was Steve's most private property. A family matter.

In his own suitcase, he had some extra film for his own use, not much, only half a dozen boxes jammed into the odd corners. (He believed in practical, rather than elegant, packing.) He added Steve's three boxes, mixing them with his. The envelope he took over to his brief case, inserted it among his own envelopes and folders. Then he rearranged the boxes of film in Steve's case and locked it. Only one lock would answer to the key; the knife, or the caviar, hadn't agreed with the other. It didn't matter now, anyway.

He replaced his luggage exactly as it had been. Quickly, he washed his hands, brushed his hair, checked the money in his wallet. He left, thinking only about the remains of the night ahead of him. Life had become almost normal again.

EIGHT

Athens welcomed Strang with a frown and a smile. Rain clouds had blown in from the bay just as he was arriving at Phaleron airport, turning the stretch of small dancing waves from a sheet of rippling gold into a matted blanket of sullen gray. The rain moved northward and covered the city and all its vast sprawl of light-colored houses. The Acropolis, with its marble temples, became a shadow island, raised high into a dark-tempered sky. The bare, yellow hills behind the city were blotted out. And then—as he was being driven up the long stretch of highway, past the new houses and apartment buildings thrown up by the city's spreading tide—the rain ended, the clouds thinned and scattered, the sun threw a quilt of clear light and sharp shadow over the hills and slopes of Athens.

People jammed the sidewalks. The shops (now open after the three- or four-hour lunch period) were filled with women. The coffeehouses were filled with men. The streets themselves were a torrent of traffic. And new buildings were going up everywhere. The sound of drill and hammer reminded Strang of New York: noise and noise, every variety of man-made noise. He looked at a placid woman clothed peasant-style, long black dress, long black head scarf, standing beside her daughter in silk frock and high-heeled shoes: what did she make of it all?

The change in Athens since he had last seen it was fantastic. But it was pleasant to be startled in this way. For this is how a city should be, he thought. Not with shattered walls and windows, bullet holes and barricades. Not with people huddled in unheated houses, shivering in their last remnants of worn clothes, starving; not with shops bare and boarded up; not with desolate streets given over to armored cars and patrols, to armed bands and snipers. My God, he thought as his taxi drew up at the front of his hotel in a line of other two-tone latest models from Detroit, what a bloody mess it all had been.

The contrast followed him into the busy lobby of the Grande Bretagne. For a moment, he stood quite still under its bright chandeliers, remembering how it had once been. He shook himself free from the old memories. But he wondered how a Greek like Alexander Christophorou must feel every time he entered here.

He took his place in line at the reception desk. In front of him were a French businessman and his smart wife, behind him a German professor talking to two archaeologists about Olympia. Two Egyptians watched. An American dramatist was making conversation with a Greek-American couple, returned to show their three restless sons the old country. Two very tall men were speaking Dutch. A Texas oilman was finding his plane schedules inaccurate. Three Vassar girls were worrying about bus reservations for Delphi. Greek women in flowered hats and elderly men in gray suits walked slowly through the lobby, talking their way toward some reception. A black-skirted priest, his long black hair knotted and pinned in place under his high black hat, stalked in silence, followed by his black-clothed wife at the proper, respectful distance. Americans, Greeks, Indians, French, Israelis, English, Swedes—Strang made his guesses by their clothes and voices. If all queues offered this kind of entertainment, he would have little objection to waiting. The hotel lobby seemed to be a general meeting room. At least half of the people here were not even hotel guests: they were simply casual visitors come to meet their friends, or old Athenian hands walking through the lobby to the bar as confidently as if they were in their own private club.

As Strang waited for his reservation to be confirmed, a small man in a shabby but neatly pressed gray suit came hurrying toward him. Like so many Greeks, he was dark of hair, mustache, and eye. Breathlessly, either from hurry or nervousness or both, he identified himself as Yorghis, a representative of the Spyridon Makres Travel Agency. Strang restrained himself from asking bluntly where the hell Yorghis had been at the airport, when some fluent Greek would have eased the way through the usual exhaustions of arrival; instead, he made a short reply to Yorghis's perceptive comments on the weather. Then Yorghis, relieved that no excuses were necessary—after all, his charge (marked *Highest attention* on the files) had arrived safely with luggage intact, so what was over was over—turned on the reception clerk with an authoritative voice and sharp words. The clerk, an elegant figure, distinguished of face, quiet in manner (more elegant and distinguished and quiet than most of the people in the lobby), raised a cold eyebrow and replied with unexpected vehemence. Another three minutes of this, Strang thought, and I'll end up in an attic bedroom.

"Yorghis—" Strang said, putting out his hand with a couple of dollar bills hidden in the palm, "everything is under control now. Thank you. Good-by."

Yorghis looked at him, made sure there was no criticism in Strang's face, shook hands politely, and then nodded delightedly.

The clerk's sardonic eye watched the small, hurrying figure of Yorghis leave. Then he looked at Strang quite impassively. "A bedroom and bathroom, and a sitting room attached. One of our nicer suites. With a balcony. Would that be suitable?"

"Very suitable." A sitting room would give him plenty of space to work.

"Did you hire a taxi to come here?" the clerk asked as he completed the register. "Then be sure to deduct, from your account with the Spyridon Makres Agency, the cost of the Cadillac that they supplied." He gave almost a smile in the direction of the door, as if administering his own particular last word to Yorghis.

The sitting room was small, with a charm of faded pink brocade and rose velvet which Strang could have done without. It was lit—it had no windows—by delicate silk tulips spaced on paneled walls. The bedroom was larger, with a massive double bed draped in pink again. All he needed was a wife to complete the décor. The French windows in the bedroom opened on to a balcony over the main street. From there, he had an oblique view of Constitution Square and the Old Palace. Evzones, in their stiffly pleated white skirts and long white stockings, stood at attention in front of two sentry boxes. He retreated from the motor horns and screeching brakes, and walked back into the sitting room.

"I'll need a large table, two good lamps, and a solid chair," he told the young woman who had conducted him with polite conversation and a light rustle of silk to his suite. She was a little distressed as she looked round the room's small elegance and visualized its ruin. "For my work," Strang explained, opening his brief case and piling its heavy books on the little Louis XXII coffee table. He opened his portfolio, too.

She said, dismayed, "This room is so pretty, just as it is. You don't like it? Another room might be difficult to find."

"Oh, this is splendid." Very splendid, he thought, Louis XXIII chairs and all. And he could always sleep sideways on the bed: that would give him a whole new perspective on his dreams. "I just need a desk, lights, and a chair that I can tilt myself back in." He showed her what he meant. "See?"

She saw at once. "I shall speak to the reception clerk," she said, leaving hurriedly. "I am sure there will be another room. . . ."

There was always, Strang thought, an S.O.P. for every situation. Find that Standard Operating Procedure, and life was simple. He settled himself carefully in the delicate-legged chair and began to open the mail which had been gathering for his arrival. A letter from Jennifer, another from Josephine, an invitation to buy Greek scarves in the hotel gift shop, a cleaner's bill for four dollars and thirty-five cents from New York, and a small note in hotel script telling him that Mr. Lee Preston of New York had tried to reach him twice today; would he call the New York operator as soon as he arrived? Her number was given most clearly, making everything sound so simple.

It was after six. Not yet lunchtime in New York. He thought of the bar downstairs where all sensible folk were gathering, and picked up the receiver.

Eventually, he reached New York. But not before complications were compounded: the polite and pleasing person with the rustling petticoat (taffeta?) came to lead him to his new room through several stretches of carpeted corridor. The new room was worth the walk. It was large, white-walled, light. There was a tweed-covered couch which became a bed, big armchairs, solid tables, movable floor lamps, a desk that didn't shake, a full wall of windows with a door onto a balcony; plenty of space, too, and less noise from the street below. "This is fine," he told her. It was, indeed.

"The chair at the desk tilts very nicely," she said, with a suspicion of a smile. "So I shall have the rest of your luggage sent here?"

"As soon as possible," he said urgently, suddenly remembering the cases, still standing downstairs among the incoming quantity of luggage in the lobby. He mastered the short spasm of worry. "I'll have to change before I go downstairs to the bar," he added more calmly. "And I'm very thirsty."

She nodded sympathetically and left. The sympathy was real. Within a few minutes by Greek time, his luggage was all intact in his room. He was unlocking his suitcase to check it when his call to New York summoned him to the telephone.

Preston's voice came through with a sudden boom and sizzle. "Ken, is that you?"

"Hooray for us! We made it. Only forty minutes down the drain."

"Ken, is that you?" Telephones always made Preston sound querulous. "What's all this about Kladas?"

I wish I knew, Strang thought wearily. "What?" he asked cautiously.

"He is not going on with the job. Got a letter from Syracuse, this morning. He's quitting. Just like that."

"Did he give any reason?"

"But don't you know? Didn't he talk with you in Taormina?"

"I didn't see him there."

There was a silence that throbbed with anger.

"Don't get too upset, Lee," Strang said. "He isn't enjoying this any more than we are."

"Then why did he—"

"Your little friend with the profile could answer that, possibly."

There was a shorter silence, completely blank this time.

"At least," Strang went on, "he did finish the Sicilian pictures. He sent you the prints and negatives."

"By sea mail" was the glum reply. "I'll know in two or three weeks whether they are any good."

Strang shook his head over Steve's thrift. "You don't have to worry about them. They'll knock your eye out. He sent some copies to my hotel at Taormina. They are the best thing he has ever done."

"They are?" Then Lee Preston's delight changed to gloom. "And what good will that do us? We shall have to find another photographer for the whole job."

"You could find a photographer for Greece, and keep Steve's pictures of Sicily."

"Not so easy."

"Why not? *Perspective* carries a lot of weight. Kudos. Cash. Offer the new man top billing, if he starts turning prima donna."

"Whom would you like, Ken?"

"Well—there's Johnnie Kupheimer; there's Bradley Summers; there's Sean O'Malley."

"What about C. L. Hillard?"

"No."

"No?"

"No."

"What's your prejudice against women?"

"I'm all for them," Strang said with a laugh.

"She's every bit as good as Kladas."

"I know that. But pleasure doesn't mix with business."

"When she's on a job, she doesn't let pleasure interfere with work, Ken."

"That's what I'm afraid of." He had won a real laugh from Preston, at least. "Try Kupheimer, et cetera," he said, "and let me concentrate on my drawings."

"How is your own work coming along?"

"It's coming," he admitted.

"It is?" Preston sounded relieved, delighted. "That's fine, that's just fine. I'll try to get a photographer over there at once. I'll keep you posted."

"Do that. Good-by, Lee."

"Take care of yourself. Good-by, Ken."

Strang put down the receiver and went over to check his suitcase, but he was still thinking about C. L. Hillard. He hadn't altogether been joking to Preston: she was much too disturbing. When I meet a girl like that, he thought, I don't want any work, or worry about Steve, to keep me from concentrating. It would be worth concentrating hard on that girl.

His suitcase was in good order: Steve's three small boxes of film were still safely tucked away among shoes and socks. He looked at them thoughtfully, remembering that short, but unpleasant, spasm of worry. Then he knew how to deal with this little problem: a sealed envelope in the safe downstairs in the manager's office would be the simplest solution. He could leave the envelope there during his field trip out of Athens, even forget about it until Steve came asking for his possessions.

When Strang reached the bar, twenty minutes later, he had the receipt for his sealed envelope hiding, most comfortably, behind his driver's license. The cure for worry was simply to feel you had done all you could have done; and then forget it.

The bar had its usual quota of journalists, attachés, and businessmen. The rest of the room (large and square and high-ceilinged, with mirrored walls, long white curtains billowing over dark windows, solid little tables and chairs set on thick carpeting, brightly lighted) was given over to a mixture of Athenians and foreigners, both men and women, who all shared one thing in common—a polite and carefully concealed interest in all newcomers. For the place was more than a bar: it was an institution with its own various ways of after-six-o'clock life. In one remote corner, around a table of polite tea cups and sweet cakes, were grouped the Athenian ladies with their flowered hats, formal dresses, and heavy *maquillage* over aging faces. Near them, at another swollen table, were their husbands and friends in gray elegance, drinking little, discussing much. The visiting scholars and businessmen and pilgrims of all conditions, from plain tourist to guest musician, were gathered around the rest of the tables. Their women, hatless, more casual in dress, sat with them and tried to make their cocktails last. It was almost half past seven now, but no dining room would open for another hour, and no proper Athenian would think of sitting down to dinner before ten o'clock.

It was, Strang reflected as he stood at the wide doorway and looked around the room, very hard on Westerners trying not to appear gauche or uncivilized: stomachs did not appreciate fashions in dining. Not his, at least. He had traveled far today, and he was hungry. He hoped there would be an adequate supply of potato chips at the bar. He left the doorway to try his luck.

He ordered a Scotch over the top of a group of heads. In one of the odd angles of a mirrored view, he had a glimpse of Alexander Christophorou standing quite near him with some friends, watching him quietly. Christophorou's eyes met his and traveled on to someone else. So that's how we play it, Strang thought, and concentrated on his Scotch and soda.

"Hello, Strang! Remember me?" asked a pleasant voice at his elbow.

Strang looked at the stranger blankly. Gradually, the thin tanned face lost ten years: it rounded out, the lines under the eyes disappeared, the bristle of close-cut gray hair became a shaggy thatch of solid brown. "Beaumont. Henry Beaumont," Strang said slowly.

"Recognized you at once. But I had the advantage. I knew you were coming to Athens. What about bringing your drink over to our table?" Beaumont led the way to a corner where three men were arguing amicably.

"How did you know I was coming?" Strang asked. He hadn't seen Beaumont since they were at college together.

"You were in all the Greek papers." Beaumont grinned and quoted, "Famous American architect to study our temples."

"Good God—no!" Strang was remembering more about Beaumont: a classicist turned archaeologist. No wonder he was amused by the newspaper publicity.

"Good God—yes!" said Beaumont. "Welcome to our ruins, Strang. If you discover anything new, you'll let me in on it?"

"Go and—"

"Later. Meanwhile, meet my friends."

Three faces looked up at Strang. Beaumont sprinted over the names, so well known to him, and left Strang with a clear impression only of their occupations: an Australian historian; an American who was some kind of attaché at the embassy; an elderly Englishman, schoolmaster retired. Then their argument continued. It dealt with the Long Walls which Athens had built some two thousand five hundred years ago to keep the Spartans out.

Strang listened (all four men were on their own particular hobby horses, rocking off in every direction) and was grateful for a chair at the table. He could see, from here, that the doorway was no place to linger unless one wanted a marked entrance. Even the Long Walls discussion ebbed a little as each newcomer filtered into the room and stood a little uncertainly as his eyes searched for a place to sit.

"There's the new English attaché," the Australian said. "Not a bad sort, I hear."

"Pretty wife," the American attaché observed, quickly finishing his drink, looking at his watch. "Which reminds me—" He called the waiter to pay the bill before he left.

The elderly Englishman said, "I heard he married Peter Martinson's daughter." He put on his glasses, making his round jovial face still rounder, to have a sharper view. "Charming," he decided as he looked at Caroline Ottway. "Used to know her husband. He was a captain, then. Army man. Met him here, in the war, odd as that may seem." He turned to Strang. "This hotel was almost the only part of Athens that was not taken over in the first surprise attack by the Communists in 1944. Actually, this bar was the headquarters of the resistance to them. In fact, you might say the resistance began here— What, are you all leaving?"

The American—a tall, light-haired man with pleasant gray eyes, pleasant features, pleasant smile, probably about thirty years old, quietly dressed —said diplomatically, "My wife has been waiting—"

The Australian said, "Beaumont and I were due at the American School ten minutes ago."

Beaumont said, "Call me at the School, Strang, whenever you have a free moment. No, no, you stay here and Tommy will put you in the picture about everyone and everything. He taught school in Athens for forty years. All these English accents you hear around you can be blamed on him."

The old schoolmaster's face beamed. "There is a touch of Paul Bunyan in most Americans," he said as he watched Beaumont and his two friends leave. His blue eyes rested on George Ottway. "Strange. I thought he had seen me." He was more than a little disappointed as the Ottways found seats at a table some distance away. His amiable, red face frowned.

"What are you drinking? Scotch?" Strang asked tactfully, and caught a waiter's quick eye.

"Thank you." The Englishman was still looking perturbed. "I hope Ottway didn't *choose* to sit at that table over there. Do you see that elderly female who has begun talking to him?"

94

"I had the impression she sent a waiter to ask them to join her. Perhaps they couldn't refuse."

"Most unfortunate, most unfortunate."

Strang looked surprised. The elderly lady was Greek, dressed like all the other elderly ladies. Her only difference was that she had sat alone, rather proudly, almost defiantly.

"She is quite the most objectionable person in all Athens," the Englishman said with marked distaste. "Really, one would think our attachés would be adequately briefed." He pursed his lips. "Ah, well, where were we? Oh, yes . . . In this bar, December, 1944."

And Strang sat and listened to a description of the hotel, and its bar, exactly as he had seen it for himself in 1944. He ought to have said, right at the beginning, "I know. I was here." But having let the chance slip, he was stuck with his Ancient Mariner. The old man, gentle-voiced, courtly in his manners, was not to be interrupted. At last, he ended. "You don't believe me," he said, quite equably, as if he had met disbelief too often to become indignant any more.

Strang stopped watching Caroline Ottway being extremely polite to the most objectionable person in all Athens. (George Ottway had refused a drink and was obviously waiting for the first possible moment of disengagement.) "But I do," Strang answered.

Surprise and pleasure swept over the retired schoolmaster's face. "What's your name again?"

"Strang."

"You probably did not catch mine, either. Thomson. How long are you staying here?"

"A few months in Greece. Some weeks in Athens."

Thomson nodded in approval. "People nowadays have such an odd idea of travel, never settle in one place, take countries as if they were vitamin pills—one with breakfast each morning." He studied Strang for a moment. "You must come and see me. I have a little flat, just across the street and up the hill."

"I'd like to," said Strang. He was watching Alexander Christophorou as he circulated among the tables and talked briefly to friends. (But he passed the Ottways' table without one glance, very marked this was, at their companion. So he shared Thomson's dislike.)

"I have lived there for years," Thomson went on. "Except, of course, during the war, when I had to go into hiding from the Nazis. My friends risked a great deal to keep me safe." He was looking at Alexander Christophorou. "There's the son of one of them. I stayed with his family for almost four months, at one time." He shook his head. "Strange," he said slowly, "strange to think that they all escaped imprisonment and death throughout the war. Then, at the end, when all the Nazis had gone—" Thomson's placid face clouded over. "An appalling story, really. But when one makes friends here, one finds that all have a story to tell. If one could make them talk about it, which I rather doubt." He fell silent for a moment. "Now, where was I?"

"You were talking about the family who hid you from the Nazis."

"Oh, yes. The name is Christophorou. They were a large family. The parents, three unmarried sisters; two other sisters, widowed by the war, and their five children. And Aleco, of course, who spent most of the war in the mountains. That's another grim story—he was with the guerrillas under Colonel Psarros. They were practically all killed in a surprise attack by other guerrillas under the command of a terrorist called Ares. Ares . . ." Thomson shook his head.

"I've heard of him," Strang said grimly.

"Aleco was one of the few survivors of that slaughter. Their escape was pure luck. They had been away from camp on some mission. They came back to find their comrades murdered. On a slope of Mount Parnassos itself." The place chosen for the massacre seemed to horrify the old schoolmaster almost as much as the treachery involved.

"What about his family's story?" Strang asked.

"Ares was to blame for that, too. You see, when the Communist attack on Athens failed, the terrorists took hostages along with them on their retreat. Some fifteen thousand civilians, stripped of coats and shoes. They were herded toward the mountains. Aleco's family was seized, all of them. It was a January of bitter weather, sleet and rain; many froze to death. The weaker ones—the old and the very young and the wounded—were shot if they couldn't keep up with the retreating partisans."

The crowded room, with its warmth and lights and amused voices, was suddenly suffocating. Strang said, "How many of that family survived?"

"The father. Two unmarried girls. One of the married daughters—although she has died since."

"And the children?"

"Two were found frozen in a ditch with their mother. The other three—no one knows what happened to them."

And all that, thought Strang, was in January, 1945, a few weeks after I first met Christophorou. No wonder he blanched when I talked in Taormina of the mass kidnaping three years later. Good God, what made me do such a thing? Strang stared at the old schoolmaster.

Thomson, who had been sipping his Scotch decorously, took a large gulp. "I spent forty years of my life trying to teach character as well as

English prose style. A man must be honorable or he is not a man. Gentleness makes strength bearable. Politeness is thoughtfulness. Truth is wisdom. . . ." He shook his head, sadly. "Perhaps I ought to have taught my pupils how to use a machine gun, how to expect treachery and practice hate. Some of them might have been better prepared." He lapsed into his own dark shadows.

Strang said nothing at all. He finished his drink. He saw that Aleco Christophorou had stopped to talk at the next table. "I have to leave, I'm afraid." He signaled to the waiter and rose. And at that moment Christophorou's elbow caught the small of his back. "Sorry," Strang said, glancing round.

"I beg your pardon," Christophorou said with exact politeness. "Hello, Tommy!"

"Aleco!" Thomson said, rousing himself. "If you would stop bumping into this agreeable American, I should like him to meet one of my old pupils."

"Very, very old," Christophorou added, abandoned his friends at the other table completely, and bowed to Strang. "How do you do?"

"Strang is leaving, but do sit down, Aleco. What have you been up to recently? Traveling again?" And then, to Strang as he started a firm good-by, "If ever you need a guide to the Acropolis, Aleco is your man. He used to know a great deal about the excavations. Long, long ago. Before he became a journalist. But I don't suppose he has much time left for ruins —or old friends—nowadays."

"Now, Tommy!" Christophorou shook hands in a formal good-by with Strang, bowed once more, and sat down. And Strang, as he left, hoped Thomson wasn't hurt because he hadn't shaken hands with him, too. But he couldn't; in his right palm was the small slip of paper which Christophorou had left there.

Out from the crowded bar into the crowded lobby, nonchalantly, not too eagerly, the note still concealed in his hand, Strang stopped to look at a concert advertisement, light a cigarette, and read Christophorou's message. "Meet you in ten minutes. Your room."

Strang turned toward the group of people waiting at the elevators. One of them, a thin-faced man, seemed to decide that walking might be quicker, and made a dash for the staircase that encircled the elevators. An original type, Strang thought idly; the lobby might be busy, but no one hurried. He forgot the man, until he had reached his own floor and set out for his room. He had made one false turn, retraced his steps back to a junction of corridors, started down the right direction at last, when there—coming to meet him—was the original type, still hurrying.

The man had company. His friend was small, nattily dressed in silver gray, light on his quick-stepping feet, his gray-gloved hand carrying a neat attaché case. As soon as they saw Strang, the two men began to talk suddenly—much too suddenly—in a fast flow of Greek. The little man's voice was thin and high and sibilant. The other spoke Greek as if he really belonged to the language. Their look of bland innocence was strangly mixed with wariness.

Strang had his own mask in place—a careful pretense that he had not even noticed them. For the small, globular man, sallow-faced, with thin black mustache and glove-button eyes, well-oiled hair in perfect place and no longer blown into thick strands by an Atlantic wind, was the same little Kewpie doll who had pattered after Strang on a liner's top deck. It took more than a little restraint not to say, "Private, private!" as the neat feet passed him and hurried around the corner.

Now Strang's corridor was deserted. And quiet. From a distant pantry came a subdued murmur of maids' voices. That was all. Deserted and quiet enough to suit any intruders. Strang entered his room, a little worried.

But the room was in good order. One of the maids had drawn the shades, transformed the couch into a bed. Everything else was exactly as he had left it, except that his soiled shirt had been hung up neatly on the bathroom door.

Strang stood in the middle of his room, considering. It could be that the impatient man whom he had noticed downstairs had come hurrying here to warn his light-footed friend that Strang had left the bar. Or perhaps I just dislike that little man, Strang thought, and don't believe he ever did a day of honest work. He recognized me, certainly. But more important, he hoped I did not recognize him. All right; foolish or not, I'd better make sure.

He had made it easy for any thief, though. Tonight he had been in a hurry. His portfolio and brief case were unlocked, his suitcase open. He examined their contents carefully. I'm being foolish, he decided as he found nothing apparently disturbed. The wave of suspicion ebbed, but methodically he finished his check. He inserted Steve's key in the good lock of the small case and heard it click obediently. He pressed with his thumb on the other latch, reminding himself for the tenth time that he had better get an expert to attend to it, so that it could be locked with a key again. To his amazement, it wouldn't unlatch.

He tried again, pressing harder with his thumb. It was stuck fast. Hell, he thought, that penknife really wrecked it. Yet it had opened easily enough at the customs shed. He stared at it, not quite believing his new thought: was it locked? He tried the key. It could turn. It could, and did, unlock.

His astonishment gave way to a vision of the little round man with his neat small hands hastily working on the broken lock, cursing at his bad luck in having damaged it, congratulating himself on his skill when he managed to fix it, smiling in triumph as he locked it, thinking now that nobody would ever guess.

The vision was too much for Strang. He began to laugh. He hadn't laughed as much as this in weeks.

Then Alexander Christophorou slipped quietly into the room, looked at his helpless friend, and stood, astounded and worried.

"I'm all right," Strang assured him. "Come in, Aleco. Let me tell you a funny story."

NINE

The story was told, but Christophorou was more horrified than entertained. He looked at Strang incredulously; at the case, now safely locked, thanks to the expert; at Strang again. "Never," he said at last, "shall I understand American humor."

Strang began, with a trace of disappointment in Christophorou's own sense of humor, to tell the story another way. But Christophorou cut him short. "I grasped its significance, Kenneth," he said quietly. "But do you? They thought your luggage was worth searching."

"I got that message, too," Strang said abruptly. Had he appeared as stupid as that? "I have been put back on their doubtful list, whoever they are." He looked at Christophorou, but there was evidently no explanation forthcoming about the people called "they."

"In spite of all my efforts to keep everything as secret, as innocent as possible—" Christophorou was worried.

"I still think it's comic, the expert who came prepared to botch a job."

"I shall laugh later, I think." Christophorou glanced at the case again. "At least you could not have had anything valuable in it, if you are so amused."

Strang thought of the envelope now sitting in the manager's safe. "That's right," he said cheerfully. "It wasn't my case, anyway."

"What?"

"It was Steve's."

Christophorou stared at him. "What?" he asked again. "When did he give it to you?"

"In New York."

"And you have not met him since?"

"Yes. Briefly in Naples."

"Were you seen together?"

"Obviously. Or why am I now back on that doubtful list?" Strang looked at Steve's case and frowned. "George Ottway and his wife met us, by accident, in Naples. But I'm pretty sure Ottway is not going around talking about that."

"No," agreed Christophorou.

"Do you know Ottway?"

"By reputation. He is discreet." Christophorou smiled. "He was with British Intelligence at one time."

Strang was startled, not so much by the information as by the casual way it had been dropped. But it was always easy to be indiscreet with other people's secrets. Or perhaps Christophorou was really saying, "See, I am being frank with you. Be frank with me." What is so damned painful, Strang thought, is that I like Aleco Christophorou, I like him and I trust him. But when I'm talking to him, I'm not talking for myself alone. If I were, it would be easy. I have no problems such as Steve must have, no emotional involvements in past politics, no secret fears for any brother whose war record in killing went far beyond military duty. So I hedge, and wait, and play safe for Steve. I wish to God he'd appear and do his own answering. He has weighed me down with more than that damned case. Strang looked over at it again, with annoyance and dislike.

Christophorou noted the quick glance. He sat down, and searched for his cigarettes. He had decided to stay a while, evidently. He looked at the case, too. "Nothing in it except unused film?" he asked, with a smile.

Strang smiled back. "That's a pretty good guess."

"Nothing else?"

"What else would you expect?"

Christophorou studied him thoughtfully. He appeared to be making a difficult decision. He said very quietly, "Documents. Photographs and letters, which Stefanos Kladas was bringing to Greece. So he told the agent who met him in Taormina when he first arrived there. They concern his brother, Nikos Kladas." There was a definite pause. Another difficult decision was made. Then, grimly, Christophorou added, "I am interested in Nikos Kladas."

"So he has got himself involved again, has he? What is it now?"

At first, Christophorou said nothing. He was studying Strang again. Then, slowly, he answered, "Conspiracy. Conspiracy against the state."

Strang took a deep breath.

"I can only add," Christophorou went on, "that it is a serious conspiracy. Well-planned, well-organized, dangerous. Not only for Greece."

"Steve didn't know anything about a conspiracy. I'm sure of that."

"He only knew that his brother Nikos had joined a group of people who seemed to him to be—undesirable. He could guess that there might be serious trouble, but he had no idea of the extent of his brother's involvement. Or he would never have wasted any time on the idea of arguing with his brother. Yes, that is what he wanted to do: persuade his brother to leave his friends, get away to America, start a new life. And if persuasion failed, Stefanos Kladas was going to use these documents— whatever they are—to expose his brother's friends." There was a small smile hovering around Christophorou's lips. "He blamed everything on those friends."

"Steve was going to use these documents, you say. How?"

"He said he would hand them over to the American Embassy in Athens, with instructions that they should be transferred to the proper Greek authorities for action to be taken."

"He would not give them to you?"

"I did not meet him," Christophorou reminded Strang. "Besides, I am a journalist."

"Yes. So I heard. Well—Steve is certainly being cautious. Or perhaps he didn't trust your colleague. It's a pity you didn't see him yourself."

"Stefanos Kladas probably wanted to make quite sure of my colleague's credentials. After all, he has been away from Greece for ten years or more. He is out of touch. Trust is always a very delicate business when big stakes are involved."

Trust, thought Strang, is more than a delicate business when involved politics are at stake. Steve did not trust Christophorou's man at all. That is the unpleasant truth. Christophorou is trying to excuse his subordinate, but the man blundered. "So Steve wants to talk with his brother before he takes any action on those documents. How much success will he have in persuading Nikos to leave his friends?"

"None whatsoever."

Strang looked at Christophorou. "You sound pretty definite."

"Nikos Kladas is one of the top men in this conspiracy. So the police found out. They have proof. And now, various branches of Intelligence are—" Christophorou broke off, as if he had said too much. "You see, Kenneth, this conspiracy does exist."

"I don't doubt that."

"And it is about to explode. You realize that?"

Strang said nothing. Steve's documents are not mine to hand over, he told himself again. Yet there was an urgency, a desperation in Christophorou's voice that was completely real. What do I do? Strang wondered.

"I haven't had a proper night's sleep for seven weeks," Christophorou said. He passed a hand over his eyes, and then reached up to switch off the lamp beside his chair. He sat, staring at nothing, his face taut with worry.

"What about a drink? Shall I ring—?"

"Better not." Christophorou lit another cigarette. Again he was deciding something. He watched the match flare down to his fingers. He blew it out. "Seven weeks," he said bitterly. "Ever since two men were found by the police, on a lonely stretch of the Megara road. That is west of Athens, down by the sea. It was night; their bodies were lying on the roadway as if they had been struck down by a truck. Two local policemen—by pure luck—were cycling back to their village and saw the rear lights of the truck, standing, then backing toward them. As they approached, the truck stopped again and started away very quickly. They found the bodies almost at once." He paused, stubbed out his cigarette.

"One, however, was not quite dead. He kept asking for the other man. When he heard the man had been killed, he began to rage. His talk was incoherent, wild. But he kept repeating the same wild ravings. Over and over again, the dying man repeated his story. The policemen listened. One of them, when they got back to their village, made out a report and sent it to Athens. There, the police studied it. And called in Military Intelligence." Christophorou lit another cigarette.

"Who were the men?"

"A father and son. Originally from a small village in Sparta. They left Greece in 1945, and took refuge in Albania. But, of course, they had kept in touch with their friends. Last July, they had been ordered to work in Yugoslavia. There they had made all the contacts, all the preparations necessary for the assassination of—" He hesitated. He said, "Of a major political figure. They were experts in that line of business." Christophorou shook his head sadly. "And the man who had chosen them for this assignment? A man who had once lived in the same village in Sparta—a comrade called Nikos Kladas."

"Why were they killed? Had they failed in their mission?"

"No. When it was completed, they made their way back into Greece to report to Nikos Kladas. Once that was done, their work was finished. So were their lives. The son died, too; but he had lived, by sheer will power, long enough to implicate Nikos Kladas most thoroughly."

"Belated patriotism."

Christophorou shook his head. "Vengeance," he said softly. "So there's the story, Kenneth. By purest luck, three small pieces of information came to light. First, a conspiracy did exist, its plans completed, ready to go into action. Second, a man called Nikos Kladas, originally from the village of Thalos, in Sparta, who had been considered dead for the last fourteen years, was one of the important men in that conspiracy. Third, the members of the conspiracy were of the extremest of the extreme left —frustrated Communists, possibly, who had turned impatiently from Karl Marx to follow the teachings of Nechayev."

"Nechayev—the nihilist? But he was a raving lunatic!"

"Was he?" Christophorou almost smiled. "Lenin did not think so. Or else he would not have based his teachings partly on Marx, partly on Nechayev. One needs both of them, perhaps, if one wants complete power: the theorists and the terrorists—yes, they each serve their turn, depending on whether one wants skillful dialectic or violence. The only danger is that sometimes the terrorists cannot be kept under control. They swing loose and away—as they did in the bloody twenties in Russia."

Strang looked at him in surprise.

"You never thought of that period, in that way? I suppose not. Most people think of it as a struggle between Czarists and Bolsheviks. But a struggle for power is not just one opposite against another."

Strang now looked at him curiously. What is he trying to tell me? he wondered. Or was this simply an overflow from one of Christophorou's particular interests—the study of anarchy, the history of violence?

"There are undercurrents, Kenneth, that can become very powerful."

"An undercurrent isn't a tide."

"No? Given proper direction, it can become a tidal wave."

"If you're talking about nihilism, I don't agree."

"Not if all its forces were organized, and channeled?"

"Look—I don't know much about this—"

"That's another of its hidden strengths: people ignore it."

"But it's completely negative. What does it preach?"

"Complete freedom."

"Yes, freedom from civilization. Burn the books, destroy the records, abandon law, down with religion, down with all government, kill those who disagree or stand in your way, end the cities, return to the fields, wipe the slate clean, start all over again at the animal level."

"That's going very far back," Christophorou said. "I think most nihilists would be content if they could recapture the neolithic age, or at least a simplicity of life where corruption and decadence and oppression are ended. True, they would have to destroy much to get what they wanted. In the civilized world, evil and good are so often entwined round each other that the quickest way to end evil is to cut back both. Ruthless? Yes. So was the man who cut out his offending eye and cast it away." Christophorou gave a short laugh. "Don't Americans glorify the noble Indian? What could be more neolithic? Even mesolithic?"

"Look," said Strang jokingly, "you aren't trying to convert me, are you?"

"It's a fascinating subject, you'll agree."

"No, I don't."

"Have you studied it?"

"Not studied. I did pick up a book on the history of nihilism yesterday. In Taormina." Strang grinned as Christophorou looked surprised. "I went to the bookshop for a copy of *The Possessed*. I saw this history, and bought it. All I can say is that I'm damned glad there are not many nihilists around."

"There do not need to be many. They have no armies, but what if they think they can use other people's armies?"

"By a well-timed assassination?"

"By several well-timed assassinations."

"You're crazy!"

"Well-timed, well-placed. Enough to set the Balkans and Asia Minor on fire. There is enough tinder lying around, you'll agree. And as for Eastern Europe—suppose you were a Hungarian, or a Pole. You had a taste of Fascists and hated them. Nazis—you hated them. Communists—you hated them. And what do the democracies do? They send kind words, sympathy; food, which only helps your masters to sit more firmly on your back. But you are the one who suffers and is left to go on suffering. What would you believe in then? Nothing. What would you feel? A burning sense of injustice. Revulsion. Hatred. And there are the forces of nihilism."

"Not all men, even in misery, turn negative. Some, yes. But not everyone."

"How many people," Christophorou asked gravely, "all through this world, see nothing ahead for them? Life is meaningless, a cruel joke where injustice is made into law, and religion only talks about the next world. But what about this world, where a man still has twenty, thirty, forty years to live? In conditions he never made or chose or wanted? Where he sees no hope of ever struggling free? Why must he live like this? The fools never ask that question; they are animals, willingly caged. But the men who do ask it find only one answer. They may hide it deep within them. But the answer is there, waiting. Destroy everything that has trapped us, caged us, made life meaningless. All gods have died, all reason disappeared from this world, leaving only one sovereign force—the Absurd. Destroy, and build anew."

"And that's their fallacy. They are already trapped in their own cage."

Christophorou looked at him sharply.

Strang said, "A nihilist believes in nothing. A man who believes in nothing cannot build anything. Therefore, a nihilist can reduce everything to chaos, but he can only keep living in chaos."

"I think that you must do a little more reading on the subject of nihilism."

"Perhaps," Strang said equably, but he hadn't expected that kind of remark from Christophorou. That was always one way of dealing with a point that wasn't too easy to answer. It was the kind of reply you'd be given at a dinner party where a self-appointed expert was brushing aside some unexpected opposition. "How interesting, Mr. Strang, but I think if you were to read more on this . . ." He smiled and shook his head.

Christophorou said, "You find nihilism amusing?"

"No." Strang was deadly serious now.

"Some people find conspiracy a comic subject," Christophorou observed with a touch of acid.

"Yes, until they are destroyed by it."

"So you don't laugh at me when I talk about men such as Nikos Kladas?"

"No, I don't laugh at you," Strang said quickly. He thought for a moment. "I think you might be in less trouble, though, if you had told Steve Kladas about the conspiracy and his brother's connection with it. Steve wouldn't have laughed at you, either."

"I didn't get the chance to see him," Christophorou reminded him again. "Your colleague did."

"His assignment was simply to find out if Nikos Kladas was alive. Besides, he had not the authority to disclose—"

"You didn't even know that Nikos Kladas was alive?"

"All that was known was a name."

"There's a sister still living in Sparta. She could have told you—"

"Nothing," cut in Christophorou. "I went to see Myrrha Kladas just over six weeks ago."

"Nothing?" Strang asked unbelievingly.

"That's what she said."

"She is a Communist?"

"I don't think so."

"Then why—"

"She was too unhappy—uncertain—I think, afraid. When people have held extreme opinions, they always seem a little nervous about trusting."

"Or perhaps one should never send an Athenian to argue with a Spartan."

Christophorou looked at him. "No one," he said a little stiffly, "would have had much success with Myrrha Kladas. In fact, I regard it as a triumph that she did give us one small piece of help. At the end of our talk, or rather my talk, for she kept mostly silent, she suddenly said, 'My brother Stefanos in New York is coming to Greece. Speak with him.' And the interview was over."

"A nice sisterly touch, that, shifting the responsibility onto Steve."

"I was grateful for it. Without it, we could never have arranged that meeting in Taormina, never have learned that Nikos Kladas is known to be alive."

"Could the villagers in Thalos not tell you anything about Nikos?"

"Very little. They distrusted the Kladas family who came back from America. He was only remembered as a boy of sixteen or seventeen who went off with his older brother to fight the Italians. Nothing had ever been heard of him since. They all thought he was dead, like so many others."

"Well," said Strang slowly, "your one hope seems to be Steve. Only, this time, tell him everything."

"I've told *you*, Kenneth. I've told you much too much."

"I've been wondering about that," Strang said. But he had been worrying about that, too.

"In desperate situations, one has to use one's own judgment; one has to talk, even to the point of being indiscreet."

"I understand. The word got through. What do you want from me, Aleco?"

"Anything you can tell me about Stefanos Kladas and his visit to Greece —his friends, his problems. Anything."

"But he said practically nothing—"

"What is 'practically nothing' to you might mean a great deal to us. You see—all trace of Stefanos Kladas has been lost. He has disappeared. Completely, this time."

That had been a swift jolt, in spite of Christophorou's quiet bedside manner. Strang's mind and face went blank for a moment. Then, remembering Steve's past performance, he said wryly, "He is getting to be pretty good at that, isn't he?"

"But this time he may not have arranged his disappearance."

"*What?*"

"The Sicilian police are working on his disappearance now. The Italian police have been alerted. So have our police. So has your embassy."

"Good God!"

"Stefanos Kladas took the morning train to Messina on Saturday. And that is all that is known."

"He was traveling by train?" Strang couldn't believe it. That train, after a halt at Messina, crossed on the ferry to Italy. It was a slow way to reach Greece.

"Yes. Taormina station was the last place he was seen."

"He never reached Calabria? What's the name of that place over on the mainland—Reggio?"

"The Italian police searched. They report no sign of him."

"When did they start looking?"

"Sunday morning. We wasted no time. When I left you on Saturday night, I got the local police to make inquiries at the Catania airport. That drew a blank. So then they checked at the Taormina station. By Sunday morning, the search had spread across to Calabria."

"Then Steve must have got off the train at Messina before it went onto the ferry for Italy."

"Why should he get off at Messina?"

"He might have taken passage on a freighter to Greece." But even as he spoke, Strang felt his doubts increase.

"All sailings from Messina on Saturday have been checked. No freighter picked up any passenger."

Strang rose to his feet. With his doubts came fears. He was remembering a yacht, possibly the *Medea*, possibly sailing from Messina, possibly bound for Greece. How did that sound? Too many possibles . . . And yet, he was remembering, too, the strange household on the street that led up to the Greek theater in Taormina. They were more than strange, since Mr. Private Private had shown a capacity for searching other people's luggage. Where had they gone when they had left at four o'clock on a Saturday afternoon? To Messina, where the *Medea* was waiting for them? "How far is it, by car, from Taormina to Messina?" Strang asked suddenly. "Thirty miles?"

Christophorou was startled; then interested. "About thirty miles," he agreed. "Why do you ask?"

It could have been the *Medea*, Strang thought. Now, that was more than a possibility. "What would these people do with Steve? Kidnap, question him? Would they even kill him?"

Christophorou's grave dark eyes only looked at him somberly. "I over-worry. So you told me in Taormina."

"I was a damn fool in Taormina," Strang said angrily. The interested spectator, the man who talked down worry, the reasonable-explanation guy. "We went to two very different schools, you and I," he told Christophorou, "and I don't mean the kind where you learned to speak English from old Tommy, either." He went over to his case for his emergency flask of brandy. "How much time have you got?"

"Time? It's running out fast."

"No, no, I mean how much time have you got right now? Can you spare me another half hour?" He handed Christophorou a water glass with a couple of inches of brandy. "Not just for a drink," Strang said, noticing Christophorou's slight impatience, "or for some general chitchat. I am going to tell you a very odd story. It's more like a theme running through a piece of music, all dependent on two people. One is Steve Kladas; the other, a woman I have never even seen, Euphrosyne Duval, whose husband, Étienne Duval, left her an outsize fortune. And there's a sort of counterpoint to this theme which I heard from Caroline Ottway in Taormina. It deals with Steve and his brother during the occupation, when they fought in the mountains. Nikos Kladas called himself Sideros then."

"Sideros!"

"You recognize that name, I see."

"Many people have good reason to remember Sideros." Christophorou was still staring at Strang. "But Sideros is dead. He is officially listed as dead."

"If Nikos Kladas is alive, as you told me, then Sideros is alive."

"Are you sure they can be identified as the same man?"

"Steve has only one brother."

"Well—" said Christophorou, and drew a deep breath. "There is a very full record on Sideros," he added softly.

"Then tell your colleagues to start digging into the files and it might be surprising how easy the search for a man called Sideros would be. They'll find his description, habits, friends—right?"

"Most possible."

"And then the conspiracy might start unraveling just enough. Isn't that why you are all trying to find Nikos Kladas? He is the loose thread."

"He is the only loose thread." Then Christophorou shook his head in wonder. "But how did you ever learn the name of Sideros?" He set down his brandy glass untouched, and put out his cigarette.

"I'll begin with the first thing I learned—the visit of a very frightened young woman, called Katherini Roilos, to *Perspective*'s office." And Strang began his story, omitting nothing—not even the documents in Steve's small case—giving only the facts, wasting no time on his own inferences or deductions.

When he ended, there was a long silence. Strang was still trying to remember if he had forgotten anything. "No," he said at last, drawing the final line. "That just about covers everything."

Christophorou was watching him with a completely new expression on his usually guarded face. He was interested, astounded, but also amused.

"Just about everything," he agreed, a hint of a smile lingering around his lips.

"Except, of course, where Steve's documents are now hidden," Strang said quite frankly.

"I hope you have hidden them well."

Strang couldn't restrain his own smile. "Sorry, Aleco. They don't belong to me. I hand them over to Steve. They are still his property. Right?"

Christophorou looked aghast. "Good heavens, do you think I want them?"

"Yes." Strang's smile broadened into a grin.

Christophorou was deadly serious. "I wouldn't *touch* them," he said emphatically. "Can you imagine how the authenticity of these documents could be torn to shreds, by any defense counsel in a court of law, if you were to give them to me without witnesses? Fabrications, invented evidence, collusion between two friends. My dear Kenneth, the only thing for you to do, meanwhile, is to keep these documents. Either Stefanos Kladas will collect them or—you can hand them over to me in the presence of one of your own State Department officials. There is an aide at your embassy, Pringle is his name, who is watching developments closely. After all, Nikos Kladas is technically an American."

"How long can we afford to wait for Steve?"

"This is Monday—" Christophorou frowned. "Let's say until Friday. No later than that."

"Can we hold off as long as that?" Strang was doubtful.

"If you feel you can't, just let me know," Christophorou suggested. "I was only trying to follow your own inclinations, Kenneth." He waited. And then, as Strang kept silent, he said crisply, "Let us review your story. This girl, Katherini Roilos—I think she could tell us a great deal. She must be desperate if she could think of no other way to let you know she would be in Athens than that pitiful little attempt to reach you through a passenger list."

"It seemed to me," Strang said, "that her aunt's name on that list was the important one, all the more so when the Duval woman wanted her visit to Athens to be kept so secret. Why?"

Christophorou shrugged his shoulders.

"Is Madame Duval a political exile? I mean—shouldn't she be in Athens?"

"I know of no reason why she shouldn't be. She's just one of those obnoxious rich women, too much money, too little sense. She lives in the kind of way that would almost turn me Communist. Senseless display."

Christophorou spoke with marked aversion. "Completely self-centered. Irresponsible."

"The yacht *Medea* worries me, frankly. Its timing was—"

"I'll pass on your information about that."

"And the little light-footed lock-fixer—"

"I'll see to him, too. In fact," Christophorou frowned, "I'll pass on all your information. You can forget about it, Kenneth."

"Good," Strang said, glad to be rid of it all.

"You think Ottway would really tell what he knows?"

"Why not? He's pro-Greek."

"Yes. But—his private life is his own."

Strang shot a quick glance at him.

"I am talking about the past, Kenneth, and a very personal past it was —nothing to do with politics." Christophorou paused. "Frankly, I was surprised to hear he had married."

Strang said nothing.

"His wife seems charming."

"Yes."

It was Christophorou's turn to glance sharply at Strang. "Why did she talk so much to you? Could it be possible that she was feeding you all that information?"

"No. She was only trying to find out more. That's all."

"Oh?"

"About the past," Strang said abruptly. He didn't like this turn in the conversation.

"She is jealous of it? With reason, I might say." Christophorou thought for a moment. "And Ottway is jealous of you. They must be in love, after all."

"Jealous? No, Aleco. Wrong tree."

"Why did he risk coming out of his hotel room to keep that appointment with you? You told me he had been lying low for a week. If Ottway did that, he had a good reason. He is no fool. Yet you pulled him out—"

"You flatter me. He isn't the kind who gets jealous."

"Then he was worried about his friend Stefanos Kladas?"

"Like all of us," Strang said, trying to ignore the implication in Christophorou's voice.

"Like all of us," Christophorou agreed, and rose. He looked at Strang as he shook hands. Again that odd expression—interest, astonishment, amusement—came over his face. This time, amusement won. "And I thought, in Taormina, that I was keeping you out of all this trouble." He regained his seriousness with an effort. "Now, *there* is a truly comic situation. Isn't it?"

It was ironic, Strang thought, that Americans who could take perfectly good care of themselves at home seemed to have earned a general reputation of needing protection abroad. But it was fine to see Aleco Christophorou with a real smile again.

"So," Christophorou was saying with some of his old lightness, "a Greek *can* see a joke against himself." With evident relief, he added, "And I also see that you can keep information to yourself. That is a very pleasant reassurance for me. My lapse of discretion tonight won't give me any bad hours tomorrow."

There certainly had been no lapse of tact, thought Strang. What could have been a more gentle reminder that Aleco's story must be considered as dead and buried as the two terrorists who had started it all? "You don't have to waste any worry on me. I'll—"

The telephone rang.

"Strang?" an American voice said.

"Speaking." He nodded good-by across the room to Christophorou, who was just about to leave. "Pringle?" he echoed, giving all his attention to the voice on the telephone.

"We met today. Your friend Beaumont introduced us. At Tommy's table."

"Of course—a long conversation about Long Walls."

"That's right." Pringle seemed relieved. "Could I see you?"

"That's a good idea. Tomorrow for lunch?"

"Tonight?"

"Something wrong?" Strang asked quickly. He looked over at Christophorou, waiting at the doorway, alert, worried.

"You could say that. Have you had dinner?"

"Not yet." Strang glanced at his watch. It was now almost ten o'clock. "I could see you around eleven fifteen or eleven thirty." Christophorou had crossed quickly over to him. Strang covered the mouthpiece. "There's some trouble," he said.

Pringle was saying, "Why don't you drop over to my apartment? It is just across the street and up the hill. Take Voucourestiou Street—that's also called Jan Smuts. My apartment is—"

"Just a moment. Voucourestiou?" Strang turned to Christophorou, who had touched his arm. Christophorou held out a slip of paper. "Find out what trouble," Strang read. "Right," he told Pringle, "I've got all that. But tell me—what's the trouble?"

"Time enough after you've eaten."

"My dinner is ruined, in any case. Can you tell me what's wrong? Is it something about Steve?"

"Yes. He has been found."

"Where?"

"I am afraid it's very bad news," Pringle said heavily.

Strang looked at Christophorou. "Steve is dead," he said. Half prepared as he had been, the finality of his own words, three small words, caught him in shocked surprise. Christophorou took the phone from him.

Christophorou was saying to Pringle, "Bob? Aleco, here. Sorry you couldn't find me. There was a slight alteration in my engagements. But here I am now. I'm listening."

Christophorou listened for four full minutes. "The documents are here," he said at last. "Yes, Strang has them. No, I haven't seen them. It would be better if we three got together right away. You can be our witness of transfer. Just a moment—" He looked across at Strang, sitting very still on the arm of a chair. "Anything you want to add, Kenneth? Pringle says eleven fifteen at his place would be all right."

Strang said, "Why not follow Steve's idea? Tell Pringle I'll meet him at the American Embassy. We'll do it the way Steve wanted."

Christophorou hesitated. He shrugged, and talked to Pringle again. "Yes, yes," he insisted. "I'll get in touch with the right department at once. They'll send two of their experts over to the embassy tonight. That's what Strang wants. Let's say half past eleven?"

Strang stared down at Steve's small case. They didn't silence Steve, he thought. He turned away, opened the door onto his dark terrace and stepped out into the cool, crisp night. High above the quietening street, looking over the broken succession of flat roof tops opposite him, the neon signs, the scattering of lighted rooms, the glow from the main avenues, he forgot the city. He was remembering another dark night, the gale-swept causeway at Naples, the mounting wave and Steve yelling as they ran, defiant and triumphant.

Strange that, of all the memories of Steve, the one that would always stay with him would be that moment.

At his elbow, Christophorou said quietly, "Here is my telephone number. Memorize it. Don't keep it." He handed over a slip of paper. "Two Intelligence officers will take charge of the Kladas documents tonight. You can rely on them to take appropriate action. Don't be surprised if you see me around, somewhere in the background. And don't be surprised, either, if you see a man dressed in a dark suit and striped tie staying close to you at dinner—he is a friend."

Strang shook his head. Nothing would surprise him very much any more. "There's no need for that," he said.

"Pringle is responsible for that idea. He's a pleasant fellow, but he is inclined to double-lock the stable door once the horse is stolen. If only he had listened to me when I told him Stefanos Kladas was in grave danger!" Christophorou touched Strang's arm for a moment. "I am sorry," he said, and was gone.

Strang came back into the room. He finished the brandy, memorized Christophorou's telephone number, and burned the scrap of paper. Now, he thought as he looked at his watch, I'm supposed to get some food inside me. The idea was nauseating, but when had he last eaten? Nine, ten hours ago. Better make the effort. There was a long night ahead of him.

The large dining room was aglitter with light, well filled with sedate guests, astir with polite murmurs. He found a small table, impressed on a horrified captain the fact that he really wanted something light, something quick, swallowed some soup and choked down mouthfuls of omelette. He would long remember his first dinner in Athens. At a table near the door, a small dark man in a dark-blue suit and striped tie seemed to be adept at making one very small cup of coffee last, in the Athenian way. Was all this really necessary? Strang wondered with irritation.

Yet, as he signed at the reception desk for the envelope containing Steve's strange legacy, it was—oddly enough—most comforting to see the small dark man in his neat dark suit waiting in the lobby with an expertly detached and aimless air. Strang looked inside the envelope to make sure, and was sure: that worry could at least be crossed off his little list. The last problem was only to get to the embassy. Suddenly, he felt no longer annoyed by the grave-faced, dark-suited man so close on his heels, but only grateful. He took back his hard feelings about Pringle's misplaced efficiency.

This will all end in an anticlimax of complete ignorance, he told himself as he waited for the doorman to signal a taxi. I shall be conveyed carefully to the embassy, I'll make my little explanation to Pringle, I'll hand over this envelope; a couple of Greeks in dark-blue suits will bow gravely, take charge of it, and vanish; I'll probably have to sit in a small office and talk some more to Pringle about Steve, Aleco may come in, and they'll tell me how Steve died, or they may not; and that will be all I shall ever know, except what I read in the newspapers. That's the way it will be. Anticlimax. Thank you, Strang; now good-by, good-by. . . .

And it was very much like that. Except that one of the Greeks wore khaki with four rows of close-packed ribbons on his solid chest.

When he left Pringle, the first threat of dawn was streaking the placid sky gray-green. The white and yellow houses were softly luminous ghosts behind still trees. "Put this all behind you," Pringle had said sympathetically. "You have your own job to do, you know." That was the voice of good sense and quiet reason. But when had emotions listened to logic?

The bar at the Grande Bretagne was open, but the large room was empty, the lights reduced to one faint chandelier, the long counter without anyone at all. That certainly solved one problem: there was no place to go but bed, with bitter thoughts for company.

TEN

Next morning, apart from sleeping until the lazy hour of ten, Strang found everything almost back to routine. He shaved, showered, and dressed briskly, had breakfast in his room after a bleak attempt to sit on the terrace in the thin, wind-cooled sunlight of early spring, read the English-language papers which had arrived along with bacon and eggs, and made a determined if gloom-filled effort to follow Pringle's advice.

He became increasingly restless. He looked at his portfolio, and closed it again. He picked up his notes on the Acropolis, and put them down. A pleasant little waiter, brisk and friendly, came to wheel away the breakfast table. The elderly, sensible-looking maid peered in, and retreated, but not too far from his room. He was glad to take her cue. He needed fresh air, some exercise, anything to end this restlessness. He laid aside the book he was trying to read, didn't even look for his sketch pad or pencils, and left. He passed quickly through the crowded lobby, out into the noisy street. It was half past eleven. Athenians were already homeward bound toward their midday meal.

He began walking along Venizelou, a broad and busy thoroughfare with a mixture of shops and cafés on one side and public buildings, more or less, on the other. Smaller side streets fed it so that it bulged with traffic of all kinds—speed seemed to be the only common denominator—and resounded with all varieties of honks and screeches, as if wild geese and night owls were competing overhead. Overfilled trolley buses, bristling with dark mustaches (high fashion, evidently, for the gray-suited young men) and the hatless heads of serious-eyed women, asserted their lawful rights among the quick flowing traffic. A certain independence of spirit was very evident, adding to the gaiety of the battle against the pedestrian whose wits had to be as quick as his feet. Strang, at least, achieved one purpose of this excursion: he wasn't given much time to think about anything else than having his tail lopped off by a speeding taxi or being sideswiped by an impatient bus.

He had explored what might be called the main-street section of Athens —for Athens, he had decided, was a collection of towns, from city towns to country towns, self-contained and yet interwoven like the patches on a New England quilt—and now he was back on the smarter end of Venizelos Street, only two or three blocks from his hotel. Here the sidewalk was broad and paved and the bigger cafés had rows of tables and chairs under their awnings for the usual collection of hop-skip-and-jump tourists (four-day visit, with Delphi and Sunium thrown in); Greek dowagers in flowered hats and smooth gloves; stay-and-see visitors (two weeks' residence, at least); and some young men, with short haircuts, rebelling against the coffeehouse ritual of their elders by enjoying ice-cream sodas. And just as Strang was debating whether he would cut down the next side street to a coffeehouse where he could sit indoors in a large bare room with a dusty floor and close-packed tables jammed tight with men sitting over a thimbleful of fine ground coffee, or whether he'd flop here and enjoy a beer and have some more deep breaths of exhilarating carbon monoxide, he saw Caroline Ottway. She had seen him, too. She gave a wave of her hand beckoning him toward the table where she sat. With her other hand, she said good-by to a man in gray, small, dark-haired, black-mustached, who bowed over it with great politeness. He turned to bow to Strang, too, before he left, saying in his sibilant English, "I hope Mr. Strang is enjoying himself? Such a fine spring day!"

"Who's that?" Strang asked, watching the man's retreating shoulders.

"Oh, yes, he's the fellow who didn't meet me at the airport."

"Yorghis," said Caroline Ottway.

"That's the character." Strang shook her hand and sat down.

"He is teaching me Greek."

"Good heavens—does the Spyridon Makres Agency run classes, too?"

"Oh, this is only some extra work that Yorghis does on the side. I got his name through a friend of a friend. *You* know. . . . He's really very good, I think. And not expensive."

"He has original ideas in classrooms."

"But where else, meanwhile? We are still searching for a flat—I think we've got one, actually—and I couldn't have Yorghis in our hotel bedroom, and I certainly couldn't go to his room, and we tried the hotel lobby, and so we came here." She pushed over a notebook for Strang to admire. "See what I learned in one hour—all about streets and traffic and people. It's really a very practical way of doing things."

"You don't waste time, do you?" He signaled to a waiter.

"Well, I haven't much time to waste. I have to know how to manage a household in Greek, you know."

"Unless you got an English-speaking cook."

She shook her head. "George likes to speak Greek. We are going to get a maid from one of the islands."

"That's much more authentic," he agreed. "I hope she comes from an island strong on decorative costume."

She looked at him, and then decided to smile. "And how are you?"

"All right." He signaled again for the waiter. "Don't they want people to order?" he asked.

"Now," she said gently, "you know that time doesn't matter here."

"Oh, so that's the explanation for all that slow traffic. I wondered."

"Now," she said again, a little anxiously, "you don't sound like yourself at all. Are you feeling all right?"

"Fine, just fine."

"How is your work?"

He was amused in spite of himself. Whenever George's work was going badly, his temper must obviously shorten. "I've just had too little sleep. And I'm thirsty," he said. "And how have you found Athens?" There was no need to ask how she felt. She was glowing. Today, she was wearing black, but nothing could dull down her skin and eyes.

"I've never met so many people so quickly and all at once. They're terribly hospitable, aren't they? I didn't quite expect all this—Cyprus, you know. However, lots of people seem to remember George. And that's nice."

"So you've been partying like mad." He looked once more for the waiter.

"George is too busy. I have to go and make excuses for him, so no one feels we aren't grateful. Two on Sunday, three yesterday. . . . Imagine!"

"You love every moment of it, so don't expect sympathy," he told her. "But didn't you just arrive on Sunday?"

"Yes," she said delightedly, "and there were the invitations, all waiting for us. George, of course, was hauled away to a meeting, scarcely had time to wash his hands, one of those all-evening-into-night sessions." She lowered her voice. "Cyprus. It's all settled, but it isn't settled, if you know what I mean. Terribly worrying. I've scarcely seen George in those last two days. —There's a waiter now!" she said quickly.

"Impossible! It must be a mirage." But he could order, at least. Now all he had to do was to wait for the beer to be brewed.

The theme of parties seemed to fascinate her, for she went on about them. Or perhaps, with that small frown knitting her eyebrows, she had some doubts which she hoped to talk out and away. That is the trouble about having a hard-worked husband, Strang thought gloomily: she has to find a sympathetic uncle with a bendable ear, and I'm it.

She was saying, at the end of a description of her first party, "Wasn't that just my luck? George says I was an idiot to go to that one. But how was I to know? I wouldn't have gone, really, if Evgenia Vasilika had not telephoned and said she had known my father, and I was just to come without George, and she even sent her car to collect me and bring me back in time for a dinner with some of the other embassy wives. I was all alone at the hotel, and it seemed such a good way to put in the next three hours. But I did have to pay for it all, next day." She sighed. "You saw her inviting us to her table in the bar, didn't you? I couldn't snub her. And George couldn't snub me. So I had to go and sit with her, and George had to follow. Oh, dear!" she ended, probably remembering an after-scene with an angry husband. "But it was really such a pure party—just tea and cakes, and people sitting around talking about art and literature. Lots of people, too, mostly foreigners: Americans and English and French. Even some diplomats from the smaller legations. If they all like Evgenia Vasilika, why don't the Greeks?"

"Perhaps she is a social-climber using a checkbook and a sharp elbow."

"Oh, no! Her family was terribly distinguished—all generals and patriots and heroes in the long-ago wars. George says she is a dabbler, trying to prove she is better than they were."

"What does she dabble in? Politics?"

"She used to. That was the trouble, perhaps. But now it's all art and literature. She seems to know everything and everyone." Caroline Ottway hesitated. "She talked about you. I shouldn't be surprised if she asks you and your friend Mr. Kladas to her next *salon.*"

Strang recovered from his own surprise. "Thanks for the warning."

Caroline was delighted. "How nice and quick you are! Of course, you might have wanted to go, but George says she is really pure arsenic to him. Men often agree on women, don't they?"

Strang looked at her in amazement. So all this conversation had been leading up to just that: a friendly little warning about an invitation that might descend on him unexpectedly.

"I think George is too cruel about her," she said, registering her own small opinion. "I must leave. I have a luncheon at one o'clock." She began putting her notebook away.

"Not so fast," he said. "I'm a bit stupid this morning. Who talked about Steve and me? Miss Vasilika or you?"

She looked a little flustered. "It was just part of a conversation. You know. . . ."

"But I don't know."

"I mean, your name came up and I said how nice you were. But if you make me late for my luncheon, I'll take it all back, Kenneth Strang!"

"So my name came up, did it?"

"Well, she was interested in your work for *Perspective*. That came up first. She knows quite a lot about ruins."

"And she wondered however such a job could be done, and did Kladas and I work closely together, so very difficult with two such different media as photography and drawing?"

Caroline Ottway's radiance had gone. "Not exactly." She looked at him wanly. "But I did say you were working alone when I met you in Taormina."

"And that Steve and I had probably planned our work ahead, when we were together in Naples?"

"Not exactly," she repeated. "But shouldn't I have mentioned Naples?"

He looked at her. Evgenia Vasilika had questioned her on Sunday. Monday, he had arrived, and within a few hours his luggage had been searched. "It doesn't matter now," he said at last.

"I never even breathed the name of—" she lowered her voice—"of Yannis."

"Of course you didn't."

"And I brushed all mention of Stefanos Kladas aside, I really did. I said I had never actually met him, just seen him with you in Naples. What was wrong with that? I mean—you weren't there in secret, were you?"

"No, no. It's just that I don't like people sticking their long, sharp noses into something that is none of their blasted business."

"You sound like George. Only your choice of adjectives is different." She shook her head, still contrite, but recovering visibly. "Honestly, I didn't start that conversation. It just—"

"I know," he agreed. "It just happened." He rose. "You'll be late for your luncheon."

"So will everyone else; only women are going to be there." She tried to laugh. It was a little nervous, but her natural good humor was returning. "I am sorry, Kenneth." The use of his first name was a nice little bit of appeasement. "You must come to dinner as soon as we are settled in our flat," she called over her shoulder. "And do bring your friend Mr. Kladas, too, won't you?" She waved a prettily gloved little hand, and passed the rows of admiring tables. God in His Heaven, all well with the world.

Pringle had said, "Put this all behind you. . . ." But that wasn't so easy, not with Miss Caroline around. The question had been raised, and it would not lie down: what had the descendant of generals, patriots, and heroes to do with all this? Six weeks ago, in New York, he would have raised an eyebrow, murmured something about mere coincidence. But in the last few days he had learned one small truth: coincidences were not always meaningless pieces of chance—they only seemed that way to the unsuspecting. What a blissful state ignorance had been!

The porter's desk had a cable for him. "It came just after you went out, Mr. Strang," the porter said, tactfully disclosing his efficient interest in all his guests. It was a very long cable from Lee Preston. Strang went into the bar to study it in comfort. There were fewer flowered hats and more men at this time of day. He chose a table in the farthest corner from the door and ordered a Scotch. He needed some stronger support than beer. Long cables didn't carry birthday wishes.

Translated from its peculiar jargon into good republican English, the cable was quite clear. The search for an immediate replacement in photographers had been intense. Johnnie Kupheimer was in Alaska. Bradley Summers had shingles. Sean O'Malley had three weeks to go in Reno. Only possible solution: C. L. Hillard, arriving immediately.

I knew it, Strang told himself, I *knew* it! Preston wanted her, in the first place.

Then he calmed down, admitting that if he had accepted C. L. Hillard, in the first place, there wouldn't be any present difficulties for *Perspective*. He read on. Preston's next words hinted as much. NO PROBLEMS NOW. HILLARD FULLY BRIEFED. KNOWLEDGEABLE ABOUT ANCIENT GREECE, BUT NERVOUS. PLEASE TREAT KINDLY, YOU LUMMOX.

As if, Strang thought angrily, I didn't know how to handle women. Then the comic side of the message struck him; only, today, he wasn't feeling very comic. This morning, he had made a good attempt to hold back thoughts about Steve. Now, the wall had been breached, the flood of questions kept pouring through. How had Steve walked into the trap that had cost him his life? Steve had dodged traps before; he knew what the words "treachery" and "ruthlessness" really meant. How had he been caught this time? And who had set the trap, who had closed it?

This isn't doing any good at all, he admitted with his third Scotch. I am just circling around, not even pointing at any solution. Leave it to Aleco and Pringle and those impressive four rows of medals. That combination ought to be able to pounce on the answer. Which reminds me, I ought to get in touch with Aleco and tell him of this woman Vasilika and her most opportune questions about Naples. And I ought to phone Preston and tell him to delay C. L. Hillard for one week, perhaps two, for safety, until this mess is all cleared up; there's no need to drag her into the contamination area. How quick is "immediately"? She'll need passport and shots and vaccination. . . . I'd better start that call to Preston right away. And I'll have to break the news about Steve, too.

He postponed that, by calling Aleco first. A man's voice said that Mr. Christophorou wasn't at his desk; any message? Strang left his name and said he could be found at his hotel.

Then he started a call to Preston's home number—it would be just about shower-and-shaving time in New York—and had a sandwich and coffee while he waited for contact. His meals, he thought, were symbolic of the way his life was going these days: haphazard. He had better warn Preston that he would be doing no real work for a week or so. How could anyone concentrate on prostyle or peripteral, on the balance of a cornice over an architrave or the composition of the frieze between? That only sounded like double talk to him at this moment. Who could keep his mind on his work if he knew that tomorrow might see another Sarajevo that began with the assassination of one man and ended in the deaths of millions?

His call never did reach Preston, who had already left to catch a plane to Washington. So Strang went out to one of the little kiosks at a nearby corner, bought every variety of newspaper, from extreme left through liberal and moderate to extreme right, and went back into the bar to wait for Aleco. The papers would keep him usefully occupied, giving him some idea (allowing for his by-guess-and-by-God method of translation) of present-day politics in Greece, and some much-needed practice in the language itself. But nowhere could he find any mention of Steve's death.

There probably was a reason for that. Yet it was odd to feel himself so thoroughly shut away from all news of developments: for almost a week —yes, it had been a week ago since he had arrived in Taormina—he had known something was going on, even if he had only seen part of the story. Now, nothing. He was on the outside, completely, and couldn't even glimpse in.

Gradually, the bar began to fill. What a hell of a way to spend a good afternoon, he thought angrily, noticing his mound of cigarette stubs, pushing the papers aside, ordering another drink to keep his elbow hold on this table. A flotilla of flowered hats had eyed it as an excellent vantage point for tea, and then had sailed on regretfully when he showed no signs of gallantry or surrender.

Bob Pringle came in with two other Americans, left them to speak to some Greek friends, circulated a little, stopped to speak again, and then —apparently—caught his first glimpse of Strang and came over for a quick handshake. "Can't stay but a minute," he said. He glanced down at the newspapers. "I see you're doing what I've been doing."

Strang said in surprise, "I thought you never needed to read newspapers."

"It's always interesting to see how stories are treated."

"I'm too impatient, I guess." Strang dropped his voice. "But it would have been nice to read that a bunch of crooks had been rounded up. Just so that we could all go back to our own jobs again." Pringle's pleasant, even-featured face, whose chief distinction was its total lack of expression, gave him no clue. So he risked a direct question. "Were the documents of any use at all?"

Pringle looked at him for a thoughtful moment. "I can't say. Because I don't know." He sat down, with his back to the room, and said, "Do you know what they were about?"

"No."

Pringle looked actually baffled. "I hope they are handling it properly," he said, almost to himself.

"Greeks aren't stupid."

"Not even their enemies can call them that," Pringle conceded, but his face hadn't recovered its usual benign diplomatic calm. "Those two men last night—when I saw them, I almost flipped. Too late, then, of course, to say anything."

"Didn't you know them?" Strang was alarmed.

"Oh, they are authentic, all right. But—" He paused, shrugged with a good Greek accent. "The Colonel had a fine war record. All those medals are for real. In the last ten years, though, he has just been collecting dust, ever since they put him in an office and called it Intelligence. The other guy you met last night is temporarily attached to Intelligence as a political expert. But his politics keep interfering with his intelligence. Also, he's nursing a bad ulcer." Pringle paused again. "Oh, blast all political ambitions," he said angrily.

"Perhaps the two of them work well together."

"That is what worries me most. On the surface, all politeness. Underneath, they hate each other's guts. The civilian is quite sure the Colonel's medals are eatable, chocolate wrapped in gold foil. That's the only kind he ever had himself."

"Then why," asked Strang, "did Aleco contact them?"

"They were the only ones available last night at such short notice. Everything was arranged pretty quickly, you'll agree."

"It might have been wiser to have postponed my visit to you till today."

"Well, we didn't," Pringle said dryly, sharing the blame with Aleco.

"Too much haste—that old toe-stubber." He thought for a moment. "If I hear nothing but the thunders of silence, I'll make inquiries in a few places to see that these two aren't wasting valuable hours jockeying for position. They will each want full credit for solving this problem. That may be the trouble, I'm afraid. I don't know much about Zafiris—that's the Colonel—but four rows of medals aren't going to give way to any ulcerated civilian. What do you think?"

"Aleco will keep an eye on them, I'm pretty sure. They are his choice, after all."

"Both eyes, I hope. By the way—I came over to tell you about Steve Kladas. The Italian police think his death was either accident or suicide."

"How?"

"He fell from the ferry, between Sicily and Italy."

"You told me his body had been found on the southwestern tip of Italy."

"The currents in the Strait of Messina play peculiar tricks. His luggage, certainly, came across in the ferry. The police found it in Reggio yesterday. Some of the cameras had disappeared, which is only to be expected."

"Yesterday? But they looked in Reggio on Sunday and found nothing." That was what Christophorou had said.

It was Pringle's turn to look surprised. "No," he said, "the police only entered the picture after the body was found. That was at dawn, Monday. Yesterday. Kladas, I'm afraid, wasn't very recognizable, but tracing him was easy because of his clothes and passport and money. Nothing had been stolen from him. So the police started checking his movements. Not much success there, but they did find that his luggage had gone over to Reggio on the ferry from Messina. It had been lying there since Saturday." His voice was sympathetic. It was a very ugly business, altogether. "We'll never know the real story," he said. Then he rose, and his voice became brisk once more. "About that other matter—I'll keep prodding quietly. But it's a tricky business, you know, making inquiries without giving the appearance of interfering in Greek affairs. That's taboo, definitely. Goodby, Strang. My wife will call you toward the end of the week and ask you to dinner." Pringle had a most engaging smile when he was not worried. "I hope you'll come," he added warmly.

"I'd like to. Thanks. And I hope—"

"There's Aleco!" Pringle cut in quickly. He lowered his voice. "No need to tell him I am a little depressed by his choice."

"No need at all."

"Have you considered Henry Beaumont, by the way?" Pringle's voice was normal again. "He is just the man to write the text for your drawings.

He's a missionary, really. Wants to convert everyone to the beauty of the classics. Hello, Aleco! No, I can't sit down. Just leaving."

"Hello!" Strang said. Then to Pringle, "But are you sure Beaumont can write English?"

"He is one of the chosen few."

"Thanks for the tip. I'll pass it on to *Perspective*."

"Delighted to give it. Good-by, both! See you. . . ."

"You know," Strang said to Christophorou, "if Beaumont can really write, then that is a big headache solved for Lee Preston."

"Is it so difficult to find a scholar who knows how to express himself?" Christophorou was bland. And yet there was a certain curiosity in the way he was watching the retreating Pringle.

"That's something we inherited from the German universities—the more difficult, and therefore unreadable, we make our writing, the greater our scholarship must seem."

"Only seem?" Christophorou was relaxing.

"Appearance and reality," Strang said, "sometimes have little connection." He looked at Christophorou and forced a smile. "Take me for instance—"

Christophorou looked worried. He glanced at the littered table, and at Strang's drink in particular.

"Yes," said Strang, "that's just it. Everyone who looks at me thinks I've been having a whale of a time all afternoon. Actually, this has been just as miserable a day as I can remember."

"Kenneth—"

"I'm all right. Just a little delayed shock, I guess. Also—it's sort of lonely. No one following me around, no one breaking and entering. Even you didn't go to any trouble. You just came right over and sat down here."

"Only for a moment," Christophorou said equably. "What have you to tell me?"

"Nothing," Strang said.

"But you telephoned—"

"Nothing to report; something to ask."

"Yes?" Christophorou's eyes were puzzled.

"I am calling Lee Preston in New York. What do I tell him about Steve? Can I break the news of the murder?"

"Of course."

Strang pointed to the newspapers. "I thought it might still be classified material."

"No, no. But you'll have to call it suicide. That is the way it will appear in the later editions."

"*What?*"

"You and I don't believe it was suicide, but who is going to believe you and me? And it's a clever trick to play on the murderers. They will read of suicide and assume they are safe. You see?"

"I also see that unless some others, besides you and me, don't believe it, then the murderers will probably be quite right in their assumption."

"You are much too depressed, Kenneth." He glanced at Strang's drink, once more. "I know how you must feel. But that is not the way." He was honestly perturbed.

How do I feel? Strang wondered grimly. I need time to think this out. At the moment, I can't quite believe he lied to me deliberately: Sunday was the day, he said. Sunday, quite definitely. The police were searching everywhere all Sunday, were they? Or had that been a slip of the tongue, a mistake in memory? Hardly. He was too insistent on the exact facts. Everything he told me was carefully selected, urgent, important. We weren't discussing the weather, a new play, his vacation plans. We were talking about Steve's disappearance, perhaps his death. A lie about a serious matter can be a dangerous lie. Or was he so eager to make me blurt out any information I had on Steve's documents? And how many other equivocations, or lies, did I swallow? But why? Why did he have to bother to lie? . . . Strang said, keeping his voice lighter than his thoughts, "Oh, I haven't been sitting here all day. I tried walking around the city. Saw some sights. Including the beautiful Ottway."

"Beautiful? No. Pretty—yes. But not beautiful. Her looks will disappear by the time she is fifty."

Strang looked at Christophorou in surprise. "You sound like a connoisseur. I didn't think you left yourself much time for that."

Christophorou looked bland. "Did you talk to the pretty Mrs. Ottway?"

"We talked. Or rather, she talked. About apartments and maids and parties."

"Parties? She seems to have made a quick start on her career."

"And she's taking Greek lessons, right on Venizelou, over a café table! The real joke is that it makes good sense."

Christophorou's interest died away as quickly as "parties" had aroused it. What had he expected to hear? Then Strang felt a little ashamed that he could even have thought of that interpretation. Christophorou was glancing at his watch. "The art of circulating is part of my job as a journalist. I must leave." He smiled as he repeated, "Journalist. You won't forget that, will you, Kenneth?"

"What makes you think I'd forget that little detail?"

"I hope you won't. A lot depends on your silence and tact, you know. A misplaced word—"

"I shan't misplace any words," Strang said sharply.

"Thank you again, Kenneth."

"That sounds a very final good-by. Is it?"

"I hope not. But I may be prevented from seeing you for some time. You understand?"

"Of course."

Christophorou began to rise, hesitated, sat down again. "Why are you so troubled, Kenneth?"

Strang said, very softly, "Were they worth it all?"

Christophorou looked at him quickly.

"Steve's death, all your efforts, all this upset in so many lives—were the documents worth all that? Are they of any use?" Anxiously, he waited for the answer, praying it would come right.

"You are being indiscreet." There was a pause. "What made you doubt their usefulness?"

"Not doubt. Just the usual human impatience to know how our side is doing." Strang tried to smile.

Christophorou seemed to relax. "It would be doing very much better," he said quietly, "if Stefanos Kladas were alive to interpret his photographs. That's all I can tell you."

"That's all we needed," Strang said bitterly. All that haste—and now, blank inaction. "But surely your experts—"

"Oh, it's only a short delay in solving the problem. Just a matter of much work, co-ordination, and a little time." Christophorou got up and held out his hand. "Good-by, Kenneth."

But, Strang wondered, have we got even a little time? Christophorou's complete calm annoyed him. "Good-by," he said shortly, and his eyes drifted away from Christophorou to sweep around the room. He hoped he had hidden his feelings. He was looking with bogus interest at the doorway. Suddenly his interest was real. "Good God!" he said.

"What?"

"She's here! She has arrived!"

"Who?"

"Steve's replacement. The new photographer Preston was sending out."

"A woman?" Christophorou was openly startled. He turned to look. He was astounded now. "And, even from this distance, a beauty."

Strang gave him a grin, which—thank heavens—was completely natural. He started toward the doorway.

"I think your luck is holding," Christophorou called softly after him.

ELEVEN

It was a slow journey from Strang's corner to the entrance of the bar. Luck, he was thinking, as he made his way through the crowded tables past blocking chairs and burdened waiters, luck . . . What kind of luck? Good for me or good for Alexander Christophorou? Someone to help me get my mind back into my own world or someone who will stop me worrying about what progress Christophorou and his two chosen experts are making? "Blast all political ambitions," Pringle had said. Could that be Christophorou's own private weakness, too? After all, the Greeks had invented politics. And yet, he still couldn't see Christophorou maneuvering for personal glory and the power that went with it. A political finagler might have had important papers turned over to a couple of prestige-boys who, he knew, couldn't really cope with them; and then what easier than to step in, retrieve defeat, become the hero? But Christophorou wasn't like that: he was too brilliant to play astute little games, too much the dedicated man to gamble with his country's safety. The truth probably is, Strang told himself sharply, that your vanity is hurt because a friend told you a lie; and Pringle is hurt because he was given a very sudden brush-off; and between you and Pringle, you're chin-deep in a bog of damn-foolish doubts. Come out of it, Strang, come out of it! And with that sharp injunction, he reached the doorway.

She wasn't there, of course. She probably wasn't the kind of girl who stood waiting for any man. She was in the lobby, though, studying the list of concerts with great concentration.

"Miss Hillard!"

She turned, smiled, held out her hand.

Yes, she looked exactly as he remembered her, with those deep-blue eyes shadowed by dark lashes. The eyes and the smile—that was what he had noticed first, and always: a warm smile, gentle and generous, making the pretty lips prettier. There were such other details as flawless skin, alive and glowing, smooth over finely proportioned bones, crowned by a shining cap of dark silken hair. Quickly he looked away, released her hand, brought himself back onto solid ground once again. "Well—it seems as if we are really going to be allowed to talk to each other, this time." Not a brilliant opening, he admitted, but it was all he could think of, at this moment.

"I was beginning to wonder," she said, her smile breaking into a little laugh. "Every time I looked into the bar, you were much too busy. Did I interrupt something? I'm sorry."

"Not at all. Why didn't you come in?"

"I am not brave enough." It was truth covered by a joke.

"Come along now—if I've still got that table. You can drop in here any time by yourself without breaking any taboo. This place is a home away from home. You can get tea and bun, coffee and cakes, mothers' meetings, breakfast at noon. But how they still keep it looking like a men's club is something beyond me." He steered her toward his corner, quite aware that Miss Hillard was having all the attention, covert or otherwise, that she merited. And then he thought, she must be accustomed to this kind of thing, accustomed to idiots like me gawking into those big beautiful eyes, and he felt less happy, somehow. His euphoria totally vanished when he saw that his table was still waiting for them simply because Alexander Christophorou was sitting guard. Christophorou rose as they reached him.

"I fought everyone off," he told Strang, but he was looking at Miss Hillard.

"Thank you, friend," said Strang, and rushed the introduction.

"Also," Christophorou said, "I wanted to see if my eyes were as good as I hope they are." He smiled for Miss Hillard. "I am happy to say they were."

"He told me you were beautiful," Strang said brusquely. "Now, Aleco, don't let us detain you." For Christophorou had pulled out a chair most gallantly. Christophorou glanced at him and turned to Miss Hillard.

She thanked him as she took the chair he offered, but she avoided his eyes, looked only at Strang.

Christophorou took her cue quickly. "Good-by, Miss Hillard. You are staying at this hotel? Then we shall meet again, I hope."

She bowed and looked down at the table, breaking all contact.

"We've said good-by," Strang told Christophorou. "It's bad luck to repeat it."

"But in a way, you have," Christophorou said gently, and left.

Strang watched him for a moment. He felt tense and miserable. Then he sat down and looked at the blue eyes. "Thank you," he said quietly.

"He didn't like that very much," she said reflectively, watching Alexander Christophorou walk over to the bar.

"I expect he didn't. But—oh well—" He fell silent.

She glanced at him, and then looked around the room with interest. "Goodness, what a mixture! American Express gray flannel, Thomas Cook tweeds, faces straight out of Byzantine paintings, and even"—she noticed the dowagers at tea—"a get-together for the Daughters of the Greek Revolution. And who are the men ten-deep at the bar?"

"Journalists, junior diplomats, professors, tentative businessmen, ex-playboys, writers."

"And not a secret agent among them? You disappoint me."

He looked at her in surprise.

"You can tell I've been on a plane trip," she explained. "I've had a steady diet of magazines. There was one article, all very serious and fact-finding. Athens, it seems, is now one of the great espionage centers, like Rome and Berne. I don't think the author could have been here at teatime, though."

"What will you have?" he asked her, as the waiter came over to them. "And how was the trip?"

"The same as you, if it's Scotch," she said, glancing at his unfinished drink. "And the trip was bewildering. My last three meals have all been breakfasts."

"I didn't know you were arriving so soon. You vaccinate very quickly."

"I was practically yanked off a plane to Mexico City, so I was all complete for travel. I only hope clothes for Mexico will be right for Greece, that's all. But didn't Lee Preston tell you I was coming?"

"Only vaguely. Or else I'd have met you at the airport."

"Oh, that was all right. The travel agency had a man to steer me in the right direction. But how like Lee!" She shook her head. "He left the breaking of the bad news to me."

"What bad news?" he asked.

"Me."

"Now—" he began awkwardly.

"But," she said quickly, "you didn't really want me here, did you? I know that. But don't worry, it won't be so difficult to work with me. I do try to keep tantrums to a minimum. I hardly ever stamp my foot." She was watching his face. "And I promise not to breathe down the back of your neck."

He recognized himself. "Where did you get that phrase?"

"Lee. That's why you liked working with Steve, wasn't it? How is he, by the way?"

He was grateful to the waiter for arriving at that moment. "Lee seems to have briefed you very fully about me. What else?"

"You don't like mixing business and pleasure. But I don't, either."

"He got that slightly wrong. I don't like business interfering with pleasure."

"Oh!" She showed the first sign of embarrassment, and the nervousness which she had been hiding so gaily forced itself to the surface. "I can be *very* businesslike," she said. "I can be so impersonal that you'll call me Hillard quite naturally."

"Heaven forbid!" he said with such dismay that she broke into a real smile. "We'll manage this job," he told her, "we'll manage it very nicely."

"If my work is good enough—" she began, worriedly.

"It is," he said. "Everyone knows that, except you, seemingly. But that's all right, too. There's only one direction for people who know they're damned good, and that is backward. You're hired, Miss Hillard. Will you take the job?"

"Yes."

"And what about me—am I hired?"

"Yes."

"See," he said, "how simple it all was!"

"Not what I expected," she admitted, and glanced at the doorway. "When I stood there, I was beginning to wonder when the next plane back to Rome would leave."

"Not what I expected, either," he admitted, frankly, in turn. And if anyone had told him an hour ago that he would even now be planning an evening with actual enjoyment—"Incredible," he said.

"What is?"

"I am."

"How?"

He smiled and shook his head.

She was wise enough not to trespass, and changed the subject. "I'd love to see your sketches of Sicily and Paestum. And Lee told me you had a set of Steve's first prints. He said you liked them."

He nodded. When do I tell her about Steve? he wondered. Now? No, don't spoil her first day in Athens. "We could look at them before we go on to dinner," he said. "But that will be some time away. Ten o'clock is about the usual hour."

"Ten?" She was horrified. "Don't restaurants open before that?"

"About half past eight, I'm told."

"And I am starving," she said.

"So am I. My last proper meal was in Taormina."

She gave that small quick glance which he was beginning to recognize. It will be difficult to keep all the truth about Steve from this girl, he thought, partly because she has a bright little intelligence burning behind those deceptively gentle eyes, partly because I don't want to mislead her. She's someone I want to keep liking me, somehow. No lies. They're the deadliest sin between two people. No lies . . . But how? I can't tell her much, that's certain. What shall I tell her, and how?

"When my father had a problem," she said, "he used to take a long walk. Why don't we do just that? I'd like to have my first look at the Acropolis." Watching his face, she added, "But perhaps you've been spending all day wandering over it?"

"No, I haven't seen it yet. Not this trip."

She did more than glance at him this time, but she only said, walking lightly over the unknown ground, "Last time, you saw it by night, didn't you?"

"Who told you about that?"

"Tom Wallis and Matt O'Brien. They make a very good story out of it."

"Don't believe all they tell you," he warned her.

"No?" She looked at him thoughtfully. "But I just loved the bit about why you were chosen to go along with them and the J.G. on that mission."

"They have three versions of that story." He sounded alarmed.

"Then I was given the one about the lieutenant thinking you could speak Greek because you had a copy of Homer in your locker."

He could laugh over that memory. Then he frowned.

"All right, I shan't believe everything Matt and Tom told me. Is that better?"

"Yes. Memories are always exaggerated." His voice had hardened unexpectedly. "Either they leave you in a rosy glow or they cover you with blue murk. There's no balance in them."

She said nothing at all to that. She had memories of her own, perhaps, which she did not want attacked. Her eyes looked away to the billowing curtains over the dark windows.

"One thing is certain," he said, easing his voice. "You know more about me, however romanticized, than I know about you. Let's even things up, shall we? What's your name?"

She looked back at him, blankly. "Oh, that C. L. Hillard business? It's protective coloring. If you want yourself accepted as a serious photographer, you have got to have something serious in the way of a name."

"C is for—?"

"Cholmondeley, spelled C h u m l e y."

"Come on, now," he said with a grin. "Give me a name. I need it."

"Cecilia. Cecilia Loveday Hillard. How is that for a professional name competing with Kupheimer, Kladas, and Sean O'Malley?"

"It's a very pretty mouthful." He thought over it. "I see what you mean. It really belongs to a young girl who writes poetry and wouldn't venture to publish it."

"Or photographs old girls who write poetry and insist on publishing."

"Or takes studies of moonlight through mist."

"Or of bright-eyed twins hugging a flop-eared puppy which belongs to the dear old doctor next door."

"How would you fit the horse and buggy into that? An interesting problem in composition."

"The horse could be looking over the white picket fence."

"Oh, there's a garden?"

Suddenly, she wasn't joking any more. She nodded. "With masses of roses and phlox and Sweet William. And somewhere, up at the left-hand corner of the picture, an apple tree." Her face was serious. She could talk herself into sad thoughts, too, it seemed.

"You know," he said, "you made that sound rather attractive?"

"Did I?" She had recovered.

"I've an idea," he said. "We can bribe someone to cook something early. And after dinner, we'll go exploring around the Acropolis."

"But first of all, your drawings. And Steve's photographs," she reminded him.

"First before first of all, you'd better tell me what to call you. It's very disturbing to walk around with a nameless girl. Cecilia? It's good enough for an ode to be written about it."

"That's where it came from," she said gloomily. "But please don't quote it against me. It has been done too often."

"And Loveday?"

"It's one of those family things."

And a very nice tradition, too, he thought as he signed the waiter's check and added a tip in real money. "My name is no problem. People hack it down to handling size. But I wouldn't like to tamper with Dryden. So Cecilia it is. And I'm glad I don't stutter."

She began to laugh. Then she tried to be serious to make a correct exit from the room. But the laugh kept breaking out; and, even when it was controlled at last, still shimmered in her voice. "Why don't you just call me Jane?" she asked.

"Who calls you that?" he asked quickly.

"No one. I just thought of it. I've an essentially simple mind."

Jane and roses and phlox and an apple tree. "Thank heaven for that," he said, most seriously. "But I'll stay with Cecilia."

Christophorou was leaving just ahead of them. She had noticed him, too. She said, "What does he do?"

"He's a journalist."

"Newspaper or free lance?"

"A little of either, I'd imagine."

She had detected something in Strang's voice. "Don't you like him?"

"I have liked him a lot," he said carefully. "What was your first impression of him?"

"He would photograph well." She hesitated. "Is he the same Christophorou whom you and Matt and Tom—"

"The same."

"The Homeric hero—" she said delightedly.

"Yes. You must photograph him as that." But whether as Achilles or the wily Odysseus might be more difficult to decide. Strang avoided the quick glance that swept his way from under dark eyelashes. "There's Thomson," he said, glad to find a diversion. "Nice old guy." Tommy was talking to another scholarly type, forming a solid blot right in the middle of the exit from the room. "He's lived so long here, he's caught the Athenian habits. What's a better place to talk than bang in the middle of a doorway, unless it's in the center of a crowded sidewalk?"

As they squeezed past, Tommy said, "But how pleasant to see you, Strang! I was just leaving, too." He broke away from his friend and came into the lobby with them. "Hillard," he repeated thoughtfully, after the introduction. "I knew some Hillards once. They came from Wessex."

"We are completely Wyoming," Cecilia said.

"Ah! Horses!" said Tommy, quite enchanted. "Then you will enjoy the Parthenon frieze. I once wrote a paper on the affinity of the fifth-century Greek with your West American cowboys. They would have got on very well together, these young men. And are you staying long, Miss Hillard?"

"Miss Hillard is a photographer," Strang began explaining, but only partly, for Tommy was running as mettlesome as any Parthenon horse. His own affinity was with dark-blue eyes which really listened.

"Indeed? How interesting. I used to take a great number of snapshots. You must come and see them. Perhaps tea, tomorrow? Half past four? Strang knows where I live."

"I don't," said Strang.

"Dimocritos Street." Tommy searched abstractedly in his pockets. "It's easy to remember."

"Street of the Laughing Philosopher," Strang said.

Tommy found his card case at last. "Now," he said, as he presented Strang with a neat little piece of embossed cardboard, "you will have no excuse to forget. The printed word is always so impressive. Tomorrow, then? Splendid, splendid." And on that upbeat note, he left, his gray tweed jacket flapping open, his fine white hair raised in a startled aura around his amiable red face.

"Tea and snapshots," Strang said with some misgiving, looking at Cecilia.

"I'd like it," she said, and pleased him. "Any man who sees a likeness between Greek horsemen and cowboys is worth visiting."

"Good." And I'll have a little talk with Tommy, he thought. Perhaps Tommy can put me in touch with George Ottway. Ottway could help the experts with Steve's photographs, possibly. After all, Ottway had fought in the mountains along with Steve. It was an idea certainly worth exploring.

"Tell me about Mr. Thomson," Cecilia said. "I'm the stranger here."

Aren't we all? he thought. But he told her what he knew. It didn't take long; it was quicker, in fact, than either of the elevators. She smiled to someone, as they waited, and he turned to see who it was. But it was only Yorghis, the travel-agency man, bowing now to them both, between reassuring phrases to a bewildered tourist and his nervous wife. "So he met you at the plane," Strang said, as they were loaded into a crowded car. "That is more than he managed to do for me."

"He was terribly upset about that," she said soothingly. "Seemingly, he—" But a broadly built gentleman, breathing heavily (either a claustrophobic, or too tightly corseted, or a passionate lover en route—Strang couldn't decide which) inserted his well-braced bulk between them. She raised her eyebrows and fell silent with a helpless shrug.

"Evkharisto," Strang said to the attendant as they left the elevator. The man bowed, answered, "Parakalo," with a sudden gleam of teeth in a somber face.

"He's my friend," Strang explained as they walked down the long stretch of corridor. "He is the only one who lets me practice Greek. Everyone else is too busy practicing his English on me."

"Evkharisto—that's 'thank you.' And he said?"

"'Please.' In our language, 'you're welcome.' Or, as Tommy would say, 'not at all.'"

"Evkharisto," she said carefully.

"Parakalo."

She laughed. "You make it seem so easy. Which it isn't. I'm still trying

135

to memorize the alphabet. It's lucky for me that *Perspective* is so rich. Lee has hired a car and an English-speaking guide to take me around the Peloponnese. That's my first project."

"Oh?"

"Yes. I begin there, the day after tomorrow," she said, looking him straight in the eye. "You are planning to concentrate here first, aren't you?"

"I was. But I probably shan't start any real work for another week or so. In fact, I was preparing myself to telephone Preston about that."

She hesitated. "What's wrong?" she asked. Then, "Sorry." She was annoyed with herself.

He opened the door to his room. It was neat enough, thank heaven. "About this Peloponnese trip—I hope you've got a reliable guide. It isn't Yorghis, by any chance?"

"It might be. He is really quite a nice little man. Businesslike. I wouldn't have any trouble with him."

"I'm sure you could deal with him. But businesslike? I doubt that. Unless you mean he has a knack of making extra money." He didn't like the idea of Yorghis, somehow. "You'd do better to travel alone, provided you have a first-rate driver. You'll find the Greeks polite and helpful; they are a good people, on the whole. Do you know, there were hundreds and hundreds of stray British soldiers left stranded here after the German invasion, and not one of them was betrayed? The Greeks fed and hid them, and neither was easy."

"Then why worry about Yorghis?"

"He is not always reliable."

"It wasn't altogether his fault that he didn't meet you at the plane. He had to go to Nauplion yesterday: some people from a yacht wanted to go sight seeing. Now that really would be a cosy way to travel around."

"To Nauplion and back here, in one day, in time to pick me up at the airport? He has plenty of confidence." He began opening his brief case for Steve's photographs of Paestum and Sicily.

"He must certainly know his way around the Peloponnese. You know, I think I'll stay at Nauplion myself. It's easy to reach Mycenae and Epidaurus from there. And it's right on the bay where Agamemnon sailed away to Troy. You can see the mountains of Sparta just across the water, and the plains of Argos. . . ."

"You're getting yourself into the mood, I see." She would do good work, he thought. "But I am still against Yorghis." For if he had clients at Nauplion yesterday, then the Spyridon Makres Agency hadn't known about them; or else they would have sent someone else to meet Strang at the air-

136

port, that was certain. Yorghis couldn't resist the job-on-the-side, evidently. "Oh, come," she said, laughing, "you won his heart. Don't break it! He called you a 'very nice gentleman' several times. He really was sorry. He wouldn't admit he had been wrong, of course; just apologized sideways by impressing on me how rich and important his client at Nauplion was. That excused everything, apparently. He wanted me to tell you that it was all unavoidable. His client was a 'very great lady,' and he couldn't hurry her sight seeing. As a very nice gentleman, you see that, don't you?"

"He only called me that because I didn't report him to the agency," Strang said, unimpressed.

"You wouldn't have done that, would you?" She looked at him, uncertainly, almost anxiously.

"No," he agreed, "you can't report a man whose shirt collar is fraying."

She looked at him thoughtfully. She said, holding out her hand, "Are these the photographs?"

She spent a long time with them, examining each of them critically, while Strang watched her. She was intent, unnoticing, absorbed in Steve's work. The impersonal C. L. Hillard, he thought, in her simple, elegant gray suit: smooth-haired, calm-faced, intelligent, competent, charming; and in complete control of any situation. But, relieved in one way as his mind was, he was glad he had met Cecilia first. Without Cecilia, C. L. Hillard would be a little overwhelming. And yet, without C. L. Hillard, Cecilia would be just a very pretty girl, enchanting for three months. But for thirty years?

She looked up at him. "Oh, Lord!" Cecilia said. "I'll have my work cut out to come anywhere near this. He's so good, he's so very good!" She gathered the photographs together. "He ought to have finished the job," she said regretfully. "Why didn't he, Ken?"

Strang opened his portfolio and drew out some of his drawings.

"All of them," C. L. Hillard said, coming over to the desk, "I want to see all of them, if I may." She switched on the lights.

He didn't watch her, this time. He went out onto the terrace and watched, instead, the soft dusk gathering its violet-gray cloak around the city.

She didn't come out in five minutes, not even in ten. When she looked at drawings, she looked at drawings, he thought. Politeness? No. C. L. Hillard was too honest for that. Or perhaps she hadn't liked them, had found them lacking, and Cecilia was standing now in an agony of indecision, not wanting to hurt him. He lit a third cigarette, and switched his thoughts to Nauplion, with its broad bay where a yacht could anchor. There must be many yachts coming there through the sight-seeing season, enough, at least, to establish acceptance among the shore dwellers. Nauplion with its view of the mountains of Sparta . . .

He heard the light sound of her thin high heels on the terrace behind him. He turned around quickly. "You're better than Steve," she said slowly. She gave a deep sigh. "Or perhaps photography is not enough. Perhaps I ought to try to learn to draw."

"You think they are all right?" He watched her carefully.

"All right?" She was honestly scandalized. "They are better than your Mayan pictures, and that's quite something." She stood looking at him, remembering his drawings with such delight and absolute pleasure that he could have stood there looking at her with both delight and pleasure for the next half hour. "You really love those ancient Greeks, don't you?" she asked softly.

He nodded. So that had come through, had it? "They soared," he said, "while other men were crawling in the mud." He broke his mood with a grin. "Come on," he said, taking her arm, "let's find out where we'll have dinner. And you'd better take a coat—it gets cool here at night." He noticed the amazed look in her eyes. "Something wrong?"

"No," she said, conscious of the touch of his arm. "Nothing's wrong." She hid her own surprise. It is so wonderfully easy to be with him, she was thinking; so simple, so natural. But why should you feel so happy, Cecilia Hillard? This won't do at all, she told herself. She said, very crisply, "See you in the lobby. In ten minutes?"

The problem of dinner was solved by the avuncular eye of the night porter. He had looked at the two Americans, tried to gauge them with an accuracy sharpened by years of observation, wasn't quite sure, refused all defeat by playing safe, and recommended a restaurant that had food not too difficult for Western digestion, wine that would not be resinated, music, soft lights, and general atmosphere. "It is a tourist place, of course," he had added, guarding his own reputation as a gourmet; but, then, who knew better than he that foreigners' stomachs were not always as strong as their ambitions? And as the expected shadow fell over the foreigners' brows, he brushed it away by saying, "But, of course, the tourists don't arrive until ten o'clock."

"Oh, let's risk it," Cecilia said while they waited for a cab, as if she sensed something of Strang's annoyance and hesitation.

"I'd like to have known a special kind of place for your first dinner in Athens, but I honestly just don't know," he admitted unhappily. He felt inadequate.

"We'll keep the special kind of place for a night when I don't have to eat at half past eight." Besides, she thought, I expect I'd find any place, even a hamburger stand, exciting with him. Doesn't he know that? And that was something else she liked about him.

"Thank you for taking the blame." Any place would be wonderful for him if he could just sit opposite this extraordinary girl. "The truth is I haven't yet found my way around Athens."

"I suppose, last time you were here—" she began, but the cab arrived and carried them down and around Constitution Square. "It was different," he said, and he looked out at the huge square, now hiding its bitter memories under spring-green trees. By way of a brightly lit thoroughfare with smart shops, they entered the older part of the city, the Plaka. Here, low houses, capped with gently sloping tiles, pressed in on twisting streets; the heavy balconies overhung the narrow sidewalks of worn and half-sunken flagstones; the lights were mellowed into a soft yellow glow. Many of the houses needed plaster to cover their cracks, paint to cover their plaster, but decay was strangely mated with vitality. The numerous food shops meant numerous kitchens cooking for numerous families gathered in the numerous small dark rooms.

"Crowded and cosy," Strang said, keeping his eyes well open for street names. He had a small map in his pocket, a fairly good memory for places, an adequate sense of direction, and a hearty dislike for feeling lost.

"Romantic," decided Cecilia. "This is the kind of place I'd like to stay. One could convert a house like that—" She looked with interest at one with a small secretive garden, only betrayed by the thick branches of a tree behind a high wall.

"Takes a little money, though," said the practical architect.

"Then some money and offbeat taste has been moving in around here. There is a house already converted."

"Quite a good job. Windows widened to chase out tuberculosis, all the rats fumigated, plumbing added."

She laughed. "I didn't really like it. Bright-pink plaster and a picture window. That's too much conversion for me."

"There's a better job across the street, all shuttered up, probably closed; but that's nice detail over the doorway—" Strang looked back quickly at the man who had come out of the house. It had not been so closed, after all. But the man—the man was Alexander Christophorou. "Slow, slow down!" he told the driver, who obliged with a shriek of brakes as the cab skidded around a corner and then jolted to a halt. "Sorry," he said, catching Cecilia round the shoulders to steady her. "I didn't mean him to be so damned literal about it." He tried to see the street name, but his view was blocked from this angle. "Just a moment," he said, getting out of the cab. He walked quickly back to the corner to make sure. Kriton Street, it was called. He glanced along at the shuttered house, standing so quietly by itself, protected from its less-affluent but more cheerful neighbors by its high-walled garden. Alexander Christophorou had walked a little distance to a waiting car. He got in, quickly, and the car drove off.

Strang went back to the cab, wondering what impulse had made him behave in this way. "Sorry," he said to Cecilia again, and was grateful for her silence. "That was Kriton Street. But don't ask me why I got out to look. I honestly don't know." He hoped he didn't seem as foolish as he felt. "Did you notice the man who came out of that house?"

"Your friend Mr. Christophorou, wasn't it?"

He nodded. So I wasn't mistaken, he thought.

"I like his house. But you should tell him to have those wooden storm windows taken off. It's strange how dead a house looks with its shutters all closed, as if pennies were lying on its eyes." She stopped and considered. "That's a gruesome thought to take us to dinner."

"Cheer up," he said, "we are going to have a gypsy orchestra all to ourselves."

"I thought you were looking a little worried," she said cheerfully. "Don't you like violins breathing down the back of your neck, either?" Good, she thought, I got a real smile out of him. But he *is* worried. What is wrong? When I first saw him this evening he was unhappy about something. Watching him from the doorway of the bar, I thought I was the cause of it all. It wasn't a joke, really, when I told him I had thought of catching the first plane back to Rome: I was scared that Lee Preston had talked me into a job where I wasn't wanted. But, when we met, I didn't feel that way any more. I thought, then, that he must have had a quarrel with Steve Kladas in Sicily, and Steve had resigned in his own impetuous way. But I don't feel that is true, either, now. And yet, there is something troubling him. What is it? Why doesn't he mention Steve?

The cab was drawing up in front of the restaurant with as much flourish as if the driver had been reining in four mettlesome horses. "This looks charming," she said.

"You're the most tactful girl I've ever met," he told her. But he was relieved, and generously calculated the tip in cents and translated it into drachmas.

"What does it say?" she asked, looking at the restaurant's name.

"The Five Gypsies."

"Poached rabbit for dinner? How exotic."

He laughed. "Probably Maryland chicken or London grill. Time, yet, to wander on and look for something more authentic."

"People who are hungry can't afford to be snobs. Besides," she said, as they entered, "Steve did warn me not to rush too quickly into the authentic places."

"Steve?" The name was jolted out of him. When shall I tell her? he wondered for the tenth time. Not now, not yet . . . He looked down at her enchanting face and was startled to see something like very real sympathy in her eyes. His hand, quite unconsciously, tightened its grip on her arm. He led her through the subdued lights of the little entrance hall into the large and completely empty dining room. "Well," he said, looking at the huge, well-polished barrels lining one wall, "we at least have wine casks for company. Where shall we sit? Under that cluster of grapes or over by the draped mimosa?"

He helped her off with her light cashmere coat. She had used every one of those ten minutes, back at the hotel, to put on a dress of blue that made her eyes devastating. Or perhaps it was the way she smiled as she looked up at him. He sat down opposite her, pretending to study the handsome menu. For a long minute he stared at it, seeing nothing, hearing nothing, his body numb, his mind paralyzed. Then the revelation hit him, and he looked at her.

This is the girl I'm going to marry, he told himself.

TWELVE

"Tell me," she said, as dinner was ending, "about Athens when you were last here."

"In 1944?" He didn't hide his surprise.

"Yes. We've talked so much about me—" she paused, laughed—"there isn't really much of my life story left, is there?"

Only the most important part, he thought: only about the man to whom she had been engaged, the man who had been killed in Korea. She must have been about nineteen or twenty then. "I didn't learn so much."

"What? An only child, brought up in Philadelphia, father an English teacher, mother a pianist, summers in Wyoming with my grandparents; then after my parents died, New York, living in one large room euphemistically called a studio, when I'm not being sent to photograph the Grand Canyon or Mesa Verde or Rio apartment houses or Loire châteaux—"

"Why," he interrupted, "did you choose photography? And why do you always photograph stone?"

"Stone?" She was startled. "Well—yes—that has become sort of my particular thing, somehow. Now let's talk about you."

"How old are you, Cecilia?"

"Twenty-seven. Twenty-eight next month, to tell you the cruel truth."

"You've come a long way, for twenty-seven years."

"Oh—I didn't have many distractions."

"You mean you didn't allow yourself many," he said gently.

She looked at him. "It wasn't so difficult," she said. "You wait, and you work, and you wait. It becomes a habit. Two years slip away, three—"

"How many now—seven?"

She looked down at her hands, bare of rings, slender and graceful to match her slender, graceful body. "Did Steve tell you about Jim?" she asked quietly.

"He told me that you had been engaged once."

She hesitated. Why should I want to tell him all this? she wondered. I don't go around telling people. . . . She said quietly, simply, "Jim was listed as missing in Korea."

Ah, that was it! Missing . . . Killed in action, died of wounds—these were grimly definite. But missing . . . And so, he thought, she waited. And she worked. And she waited. Success came and added new meaning to work, a new pattern of life. "And when do the years stop slipping away?" he asked. He regretted the question as soon as it had been uttered; that was always the danger with thinking aloud. But when he glanced at her face, he surprised a smile in her eyes.

"Is twenty-seven such an advanced age?" The smile spread to her lips. Then she opened a little escape doorway for them both. "Tell me about Athens when you last saw it."

"If you really want to hear about that—" He looked at her doubtfully, but she nodded. "Then we'll walk to the Acropolis and I can tell you on the way. But first, what about some cognac, with our coffee? Or would you risk some ouzo? It's an *apéritif*, actually, but it's definitely authentic."

"Ouzo," she said reflectively. "I know a good place to go and drink ouzo. Just a moment!" She searched in her handbag and drew out a small notebook. "Travel addresses," she told him. "Everything from darkrooms and camera shops to hairdressers." She searched through the little book impatiently. "It was here," she reassured herself. She turned the notebook upside down and shook it. A piece of paper fell out. "There it is! See— Steve wrote two addresses on it for me. Places where we can have Greek music and ouzo."

"When did Steve give you this?"

"Last summer, when I was planning a month's vacation in Greece. But then I got the Loire châteaux job, and I had to cancel everything else. Can you make out Steve's writing? He jotted down all this at a party, so it's a little high-flown."

It was. There was a Kilroy mark, two large round eyes over a wall, opposite one of the addresses on a street called Erinna, and a scrawled warning: "Positively no *kokoretzi!*" There were two other afterthoughts in the margin: "Under Acropolis wall, big tree"; and "Petros," with a brief Greek sentence scratched after the name. The other address was somewhere down in the Piraeus, but it lacked any similar enthusiasm.

"Petros is a very old friend," Cecilia was explaining. "I was to ask for him, especially."

Strang looked at the Kilroy sign. "Steve went there a lot, did he?"

"He lived there for eighteen months. Fantastic, isn't it? Restaurants where you can stay. Or is it an inn of some kind?"

"He lived there?"

(Steve's voice was saying, "None of Ares's informers even guessed where I was. So I stayed alive.")

"When was that?" Strang asked.

"Oh, years and years ago. But Steve said there was an enormous family who runs the place, so some of them were bound to be still around. Why don't we visit them for a drink and Greek music?" She frowned at the gypsy band, a sedate group of dark-suited men, who had been stealing expertly from Brahms and Enesco, and now—as the guests started to arrive in numbers—were breaking into a song from *My Fair Lady*. "Poor darlings," she said, shaking her head. "Do they think we came five thousand miles to hear that?"

Carefully, Strang replaced Steve's memorandum in her notebook, and handed it back to her. "All right. Let's try Erinna." He glanced at his watch. "It's almost ten o'clock, though. We may not have much time left for the Acropolis tonight."

"Of course we shall. The Acropolis at dawn—what could be more romantic?"

"You've been doing a lot of traveling—"

"You think I must be tired? On my first night in Athens? I'm far too excited to sleep."

"All right," he said, watching her radiant face. She was hard to refuse. "Just let me study this map for a moment. The lighting in the streets in this part of town isn't too good." He drew his map out of his pocket. "Besides, the Greeks are very polite; even if they don't know the way to a place, they will give you directions." He searched carefully, and at last found a small street, very short indeed, leading right up to the wall of the Acropolis and stopping blankly there.

"We are near the Acropolis now, aren't we? But where?"

"Roughly, to its north." He showed her on the map.

"And Erinna Street?"

"Northwest by north."

"Nautical, aren't we? But of course—" she added. "And the front view of the Acropolis is from the west, more or less? So Erinna Street is on our way to the Acropolis. It's just a kind of side shoot from this main stem of street." She pointed to a street on the map that ran parallel with the wall. "Let's try it. Shall we?"

"Could you walk there? I'd like to talk." He paused. "About Athens in

1944, and the time Steve was hunted." She was watching him, her eyes wide, her face expectant but no longer excited, as if she sensed there was something unpleasant underlying his quiet words. "It isn't a pretty story," he said. But, he thought, it will lead quite naturally into the telling of Steve's death.

They walked slowly, taking almost an hour to cover a distance that could have been traveled in a quarter of that time. The streets were twisting, narrow, dimly lit and quiet, with only an occasional car jolting past or small groups of young men strolling arm in arm. Strang chose careful detours so that they would not be altogether lost: they returned to their route, broke away from it again, returned, retraced steps, continued once more in the right direction, while Strang talked and kept on talking. Once he had started, there seemed no end to what she could draw out of him, simply by letting her eyes question him. He had taken her arm to steady her high heels over the broken sidewalks, and he could feel the shock that sometimes hit her body or sense the sympathy even before it welled into her face. There was no disbelief, no scorn for his worry, no—and that would have been worse—politely correct remarks to conceal wandering attention. His story, in all its bits and pieces, held her as firmly as his hand on her arm. And in the end, he had told her—except for the conspiracy, which wasn't his story to tell—just about everything: Athens and civil war, the resistance in the mountains and Steve's escape; Naples, Taormina, Steve's death.

I've lost all my senses, he thought in sudden alarm as he realized how much he had talked. No, I haven't, he decided, and knew that was the truth. How else could she ever understand my doubts about Steve's death, or the way I'm going to keep on and on until I see the murderers caught?

She stopped, and turned to face him. "Steve—" She shook her head as if she couldn't really believe he was dead. Then she said, "His sister—I wish she could be told all this. Otherwise, she will believe it's suicide. And it wasn't, was it?"

"I don't think so."

"After what you've told me—" she gestured helplessly—"I don't think so, either. But surely when the police get your report—your friend Mr. Christophorou will have sent it to them, won't he?"

"Yes, I suppose so." He was a little surprised by her question, for the simple reason he hadn't thought of it.

"Then they *will* take a different view, won't they?"

"It will have to be decided, first, what country is responsible for the investigation," he reminded her. "There's Italy; there's Sicily, which has its own state rights, I think; there's Greece, and there's America. It may take a little time—" Too much time, he thought bitterly. "Don't worry about the sister. I'm going to visit her, see what can be done—" He paused awkwardly, thinking of that damnable dowry which had brought Steve back to Greece. "I'll tell her what I've told you, if you think that's of any use."

"It will be. Truly, it will be. When will you go?"

"This week. Soon." He stopped to verify a street sign. He pulled, gently, at her arm. "Only one short lap to go. There's Erinna Street, over there."

She went with him, slowly, then still more slowly. As they entered the mouth of the narrow street, she halted. "I don't know," she said, "if I want to go now." She turned her head quickly away from him.

He looked up the dim, unpaved, dusty street, no more than fifty yards long. It mounted between high uneven walls hiding more than gardens (there was the smell of farmyard around here, the sound of a light bell around a goat's neck, the bark of a dog, the rustle of chickens alarmed out of sleep), and ended in a cluster of small houses. From the farthest of these—and the largest, for it boasted two stories—a pool of white light was cast, from a naked lamp attached under the rippling edge of its tiled roof, on the hard-packed earth in front of its door where a solitary tree, large and strong, grew out of the dusty road. Above the wide spread of green leaves, vivid, almost unreal in the sharp light, soared a backdrop of dark rocks, which formed the base of the Acropolis walls, so high overhead, so deeply shadowed that they became part of the clouded mystery of the sky itself.

I'll come back here alone, he thought. I'll see Petros then. "All right," he told her gently. "That's all right." There was the light sound of the bell's sweet note, one small last bark from the dog. A breeze rustled the leaves with a caressing hand, and left. Stillness and peace, darkness and sleep: night had come to this little village within a city.

Just at that moment, on the point of turning away, he heard footsteps behind him. He swung around to face a man who had come out of a shadowed recess in the uneven wall. He was well dressed, of good height, dark-haired, clean-shaven. He smiled pleasantly. "You have lost your way," he said in English. "May I help you?"

Cecilia had drawn close to Strang, but the man stopped a little distance away from them. Strang could feel her relax even as his own tension mounted. He was thinking, there is another man behind him, another man keeping hidden. He said, "We were looking for a small *taverna* on Erinna Street."

"This is Erinna. But there is nothing here."

"I hear music," Cecilia said to Strang. From the farthest house, there came the faint sound of a song, sad and plaintive. "Greek music."

"A very rough place," the man said quickly, contemptuously. "It is not a place that the lady would enjoy. There is a good night club only three blocks from here."

"We were not looking for a night club," Cecilia said coldly. "We wanted a *taverna* with Greek music."

Strang, who had been letting his eyes grow accustomed to the shadows against the wall, could see the other man now—a small round shape in a light-colored suit. He said to Cecilia, "Look—we can come here another night. You must be tired. Let's call it a—"

"Listen!" Cecilia said. The last notes of the song were dying away, leaving a sudden emptiness in the night. "I'd like to hear the beginning of that song."

And I'd like to see Petros, he thought. But the man hidden in the shadows worried him.

"Oh, let's try it," said Cecilia, and walked past the unhelpful stranger without a glance. Strang hurried after her. "I bet," Cecilia said, "his cousin runs that night club only three blocks from here."

"Sound carries," he warned her, keeping his own voice very low.

"Didn't you want to come here?" she asked in dismay.

"If I were alone, yes," he told her frankly. "But at this moment—" He searched quickly for a cigarette.

"That's what I guessed," she said, relieved.

Sounds did carry on this calm night. He could hear the footsteps of the two men as they walked back to the main street. The small man's voice was thin and light, as light as his footsteps, pattering like a woman's, beside his companion's firm tread.

"Damn, I've dropped my lighter," Strang said. He turned as he bent down to pick it up. He had a moment's clear view of the two men. They had halted at the corner and were looking back up the hill, interested yet uncertain. Strang lit his cigarette. "Let's put on a little show for them," he said quietly. He slipped an arm around her waist as they began to walk, slowly, toward the lighted house.

At first, her body had tautened. Then she relaxed with a little laugh. She slipped her arm lightly around his back. "Is this what you mean?" She laughed again, and leaned her head against him.

"You're good," he told her. "You're very good."

"I can be obedient," she admitted, "and not even too inquisitive about the other man in the shadows."

147

He laughed, this time, as he looked down at her by his side. In a moment, he forgot the need for any pretense, even the pretense itself. His step slowed, halted. Then he remembered the watching men. He'd be damned if he'd make any show out of real emotions for them. He pulled himself away from his impulse, slackened the pressure of his arm, glanced at her to see if she had noticed that sudden moment. He hoped not. He said, "Remember the little man who played watchdog on the liner? That was the one in the shadows, back there."

"The man who searched your room?" Her voice was excessively low, too. "I thought Mr. Christophorou would have had him locked up by this time. Who was the other man?"

"A stranger to me." But was I a stranger to him? I doubt that, thought Strang. That had been an unpleasant encounter, somehow. And then, just ahead of them at the open door of the house, a man and a boy appeared. "Here's the welcoming committee," Strang said lightly. Cecilia dropped her arm and moved a few inches away from him. She glanced quickly back over her shoulder.

"They've gone," she reported with relief.

"Good." But he had his doubts about that, too. They hadn't been watching Erinna Street in order to check where Miss Cecilia Loveday Hillard spent an evening with Mr. Kenneth Clark Strang. He had given them as much of a surprise as they had given him. "Kalé spera sas!" he said to the man and the boy.

"Good evening," the boy answered in careful English. He was young —only thirteen or fourteen years old—small, thin, with bright black eyes and an engaging smile on his white, anxious face. He wore a once-white cotton jacket, too loose on his narrow shoulders, with a folded napkin carefully placed over his left forearm, which he held stiffly across his concave waistline. He bowed gravely. At a sharp nudge from the man standing beside him, he said, "Closed. Closed tonight."

"Kleisto!" the man said, making "closed" sound most complete.

Strang looked at the man. His face had a marked resemblance to the boy's, with the addition of a fine Greek mustache, long and dark, a scar at the side of his broad brow, and some ten or fifteen years onto his age. There was always difficulty in guessing a Greek's age if he was anywhere between twenty and thirty-five. There was this fashion of the long mustache, which made the young seem older; and the smooth, unlined skin, tight-drawn over thin faces, kept the lean appearance of youth. The man's black eyes were as bright as the boy's. But, although he might have been interested in the two Americans, his face was totally impassive. Polite, yes, in the gestures of his hands; not menacing. A neat, compact individual, Strang decided, with neat, compact conversation. For the man again said, "*Kleisto!*" firmly, impersonally.

"Please—" Cecilia said very softly, "we have come to see Petros."

The man spoke quickly in Greek to the boy. "Why?" the boy asked.

"Steve Kladas told me Petros was his friend."

"Stefanos Kladas," Strang amended very quietly.

There was a flicker in the man's eyes. He might not want to speak in English, but he could understand it. He stood aside, and pointed to the open door. The boy darted ahead to stand at the threshold and bow Cecilia into the room. Strang followed, bending his head to pass under the low doorway. Any man over five feet six, he reflected, must enter humbly. He cast a quick glance around the room, and relaxed. There were three customers at dinner, two women and a man, pleasant, ordinary people who looked most comfortingly reassuring. The boy was escorting Cecilia to a corner table. We've made one friend, at least, Strang thought, as he chose a seat with a view of the room.

It was square-shaped, small, low-ceilinged, with one window high in the wall just over his head. There were exactly eight tables, three of them now occupied, and one of those, nearest the kitchen door, where four men sat together, was more for family than for customers. Strang studied the four men carefully, and wondered which was Petros. Two were fairly young, with the usual dark mustache. The third was definitely middle aged, with a thickening body and a heavy face. The fourth was old but with powerful shoulders, white-haired, his strong-featured face tanned and wrinkled, a noble head. His dark eyes had been studying Strang quite openly from under white eyebrows, as thick and untamed as his heavy white mustache. There was a fifth chair waiting at that table for the man who had stopped Cecilia and Strang at the doorway. He joined the little group now, and all the men began talking in low voices. But none of them even looked across the room at the two strangers.

"We'll have to order something," Strang told Cecilia. The young waiter had been standing expectantly at their elbows, and he now began a brief recital: lamb, lamb, and lamb.

Cecilia broke off her own quiet inspection of the room: lower walls newly painted in a blue glossy enamel ending, at her waist level, in not too exact a line under the upper stretch of white. Either someone had run out of blue enamel or had considered the painting of the upper wall as a sheer waste of money. The small tables were covered with white oilcloth, the chairs were of cane, the stone floor clean. There was one vase of wild flowers, which the boy had whipped off a neighboring table to place before her. And the only other decoration, a matched pair of fading enlargements of the King and Queen in full regalia, was carefully hung above the old man's chair. Overhead, the unshaded light from a central bulb, its wire snaking openly across the ceiling, shone impartially on the five men crowded around the far table, on the three neighboring customers finishing the last mouthfuls of their supper, on Ken trying to look completely unconcerned but watching her anxiously. She wondered which would be less impolite: to order food, as was expected, and leave it uneaten, or merely to order an after-dinner drink with some coffee. She said, uncertainly, "Brandy?"

Strang saw the slight shake of the boy's head. Cecilia must have noticed it, too, for she glanced over at the old man, maintainer of all the unwritten laws. "All right," she said, "coffee. And may I be allowed a glass of wine?"

The boy's face brightened, and he nodded.

"It will be *resinato,*" Strang warned her.

"But I love turpentine," she told him, and admired the way he could smother a smile. I like a man, she thought, who can notice a small attempt at a joke even when he is tense with worry. She slipped her arms free of her coat sleeves as the boy hurried away with their order. "I like it here," she told Strang. "And I'm glad you told me so much tonight. Does that cross off two of your lesser problems?" And, as he looked at her, she said, "Truthfully, how could I even begin to understand the Greeks I meet, if I don't know something of what they've been through? Although at the moment," and she glanced at the ceiling, through which disturbing noises were drifting down into the little room, "I can't pretend to understand what's going on up there." For there were restless footsteps on the wooden floor of the room overhead, women's voices in muffled argument, then silence, then the bitter voices again, then silence.

"Someone seems to have been nursing her wrath to keep it warm," Strang said, as the older woman's voice, harsh and declamatory, broke out again. The other voice was young, pleading and indignant in turn. "A family discussion. Daughter wants to go out, mother wants her to stay home. Something like that." Actually, though, the argument sounded the other way around: mother wanted the girl to go out, the girl wanted to stay. My Greek, decided Strang gloomily, must be in a worse condition than I thought. The words overhead were not altogether distinct, but the occasional phrase came clear as anger mounted and then merged into a low mumble as the volume of sound was abruptly lowered.

"Well," Cecilia said, "if everyone else pretends they don't exist, why shouldn't we?" The five men were talking together, grouped into their own private world. The three customers had their own world, too: the man was counting out payment for their small check with complete absorption in his arithmetic, while the women waited in anxious silence. They're just like me, Cecilia thought, worrying in case they have cost too much. See, poor dears, how relieved they look now as they are leaving and their husband and brother isn't bankrupt after all. Her feelings for them seemed to attract their attention: at the door, as their escort exchanged a friendly word with the men, the women turned to give a quick, shy bow to Cecilia and a gentle good night. Then they were gone, and four cats came out from under their table, all fallen crumbs having been devoured, to prowl around Cecilia and Strang until the boy arrived with a tray. They were lean cats, striped, and still hungry.

"Pavlov's cats," Cecilia said. "You clatter a tray and the saliva starts." She looked in dismay at the bottle of wine, brandy, minuscule coffee cups and two small tumblers of water, which the boy was now setting carefully before Strang and herself. "And not a crumb possible. Will they start on my ankles, do you think?" They were already under the table, waiting.

"I'll get them out—" Strang began. "Don't you like cats?"

"Yes, except when I start wondering what would happen to us all if they were the size of horses. Oh, let them be. Who says I can't be as Spartan as any Athenian?"

The boy had poured her a glass of amber-colored wine, and waited. The voices upstairs had begun again.

"Petros—" Cecilia said, no longer disguising her worry. The bitterness in the recriminations upstairs was upsetting her. Involuntarily, she glanced up at the ceiling. "Is he really here, do you think?"

Strang said, "We've told them why we came here. That's all we can do. The next move is theirs. They've been discussing us forward and backward."

"Wouldn't it be easier just to come over and ask us questions?"

"Perhaps we have to be dominated, first of all," Strang said with a grin. "Your young friend is waiting to see you enjoy the wine he has poured."

Cecilia took a sip.

"Good," the boy told her. "Good?" He looked anxious.

"A very interesting little wine," she observed, "with a personality all of its own."

"The lady speaks very good English," the boy said.

"Thank you," Cecilia said. "Where did you learn to speak it so well?"

"At school."

"And you work here, at night?"

"I live here. That is my father." He looked at the old man proudly. "He is from Crete."

"And are those men your brothers?"

"One is my uncle. The others are my—" He wrinkled his brow.

"Cousins?"

"No. No. Almost they are my brothers."

"Half-brothers? And your mother is upstairs?"

He nodded. "Is the gentleman your husband? How many children do you have?"

Strang said, watching her retreat with amusement, "I was wondering how long you'd get away with all your questions. Better have another sip of wine. The eyes of the room are upon us."

It was true. The discussion at the men's table was over. Five pairs of eyes were watching, calmly, objectively.

"You will explain," she told him, "that ladies, where I come from, are not supposed to have more than two sips of wine." She took the second sip without flinching. "My quota," she warned him, and drank her coffee quickly.

"It's an acquired taste," he told her sympathetically.

"I know. But the trouble about an acquired taste is the acquiring of it." And, she thought, as the cats under the table lost some of their patience and began to prowl restlessly, brushing their thin bodies lightly over her insteps, against her legs, at this moment I'm thoroughly dominated and I don't care who knows it. She gave a start as the women's voices above her head burst out anew. Someone had thrown herself down on a bed, for the springs had clanged. Someone was being pulled off the bed. Even the men gave a brief glance at the ceiling. The old man suddenly crashed his fist on the table and shouted. There was silence overhead, immediate, complete.

"This may be a tactical error," Strang said, "but we have waited long enough." He rose to his feet, and went toward the men's table. The man with the scar rose, too, and came forward. But it wasn't a case of being met halfway: it was a neat maneuver to block, politely, any approach to the table. Strang said, in the Greek sentences he had been rehearsing, silently and painfully, for those last ten minutes, "I came to see Petros. Is he here? I want to talk with him about Stefanos Kladas, who was his friend and mine. This is serious, important business."

The men looked at each other. The man with the scar spoke.

Strang said to Cecilia, "He is asking why I brought a woman here if I wanted to talk to Petros about serious things." He shook his head. "Apparently, they've decided we are doubtful characters."

Indeed, thought Cecilia, and studied the old brigand chief across the room. What was going on here that made them so distrustful? Greeks were hospitable people. "Do you think some credentials would help?" she asked. She searched in her handbag for Steve's page in her small notebook, and handed it over to Strang.

Strang said to the man with the scar, "This is Miss Hillard. My name is Strang. We both knew Stefanos Kladas. He told her to come here, to ask for Petros. See—here is his writing." He handed over the page, which was then carefully studied and passed around among the men. It had some effect. The old man's white eyebrows, which had bristled into a straight line of doubt, looked less awesome. We're half a league onward, anyway, thought Strang with relief, watching the man with the scar. Either he had had more time to get accustomed to Cecilia and Strang or he was more sympathetic. Strang said, "I need help." He paused and added grimly, "I want to find Nikos Kladas and his friends."

The faces, watching him, went rigid.

"Why?" asked the man with the scar very softly.

"Because Stefanos Kladas is dead."

"Dead?" The echo went around the room. "Dead?"

"When was this?" the man with the scar demanded. "When?"

"Three days ago. Perhaps four. It will be published in the newspapers tomorrow. The Italian police found his body. They say it was suicide. Or perhaps an accident."

"Suicide!" The word was contemptuously spat out.

"I agree," Strang said. "And if it was an accident, then it was a very clever accident."

The quick mind behind the quick brown eyes caught his meaning. "You think he was killed?"

"Yes."

"That is why you search for Nikos," the man said, through tight lips.

"I see you know Nikos," Strang said slowly.

"He killed Stefanos?"

"We shall know that when Nikos is caught. And his friends."

The old man, watching Strang through half-closed eyes, silenced the surge of angry voices at the table with a gesture, and said, "Nikos Kladas is a man to whom all evil is possible. But first—let us hear this story. Tell it!"

He was a hard man to convince, Strang thought. "First," he said, equally firmly, "where is Petros?"

There was a deep silence.

"All right," Strang said. "We leave. I shall come back tomorrow when

Petros is here. Or the next day. Or the day after that. But I must talk to Petros. He is the only one who can help."

The man with the scar said, "How can Petros help?"

"When Stefanos hid here, for many months, he must have told Petros many things. For Petros was his friend."

The man nodded.

"Did he tell Petros about his life as an *andarte*, about the battles in the mountains, about the leader called Ares?"

The old man's eyes opened wide in anger, his lips drew back to spit out the name of Ares with a mouthful of curses.

Strang waited. The man with the scar nodded again. "Did Stefanos tell about the photographs he took? Were they of Ares"—there was a rumble of thunder from the old man—"and of Nikos, and of their special friends?"

"He took many photographs." The man's interest was drifting: photographs were pieces of paper, not battles and courage and treachery and death.

"Did he leave any photographs here?"

"He took them to America," the man said impatiently. These questions were unimportant.

"Did Petros know the people in those photographs? Could he identify any of them?"

"Perhaps. Perhaps not. Petros did not fight under Ares against the Germans. He fought under Zervas, in the west."

"*Zito* Zervas!" one of the younger men said. There was more qualified approval from the old man, who was obviously a royalist. Zervas had been a republican, a guerrilla leader who had been a bitter enemy of Ares, but one with enough distrust and cunning. At least, Strang thought, Zervas and his army had not been massacred wholesale like so many other guerrilla bands. They had been able, most of them, to retreat from the trap Ares had set for them.

"How," he asked, puzzled, "could Petros be a friend of Stefanos?"

The man with the scar looked at him, distrust returning to his eyes. "You ask many questions."

"I need many answers," Strang said quite simply. "Without answers, how can we find those who killed Stefanos?"

"Stefanos came from Thalos. So did Petros," the man said grudgingly. "They were good friends there. Politics was something they left to others." His voice had softened. He stood for a moment, silent. Then he said, "Stop talking about such foolishness as photographs. Why was Stefanos killed? Where? How?"

"The friends of Nikos did not want Stefanos to come to Greece and talk about them. They were afraid of him, afraid of the photographs he took years ago."

"Ah!" said the man, and began to understand. "And what is Nikos planning now? Politics and death? Always politics, always death."

"It will not matter what is planned if we can find those who do the planning. They are nameless. But Petros might help to give them a name."

"You have the photographs? Where did you get them?"

"That is part of my story. But first—will Petros help?"

The man hesitated.

"It may be dangerous," Strang told him.

"I will do it," the man flashed back at him. "I am Petros."

The old man burst into a laugh. "I will do it, I will do it," he parroted. "The American speaks of Stefanos, and help, and danger, and you promise your life before you know all the truth. Why was there so much trouble here in Greece? Because men did not know all the truth. In Crete, we did not have trouble with Communists like Ares. And how? We did not let them make trouble. We kept them in one corner of the island, and let them tell their lies to each other. And we made a line which we guarded, over which none crossed, or—" He drew a finger across his throat and smiled benignly. "So we had no trouble. We drove out the Germans. We did not waste time and blood on killing our neighbors. And how? Because we had thought out the truth about the Communists. For whom were they so suddenly brave? Such patriots overnight? For what? For what they wanted." His voice quietened. "That is what you must find out first. The truth about a man." He looked at Strang. "What is the truth about you? Who sent you here?"

"No one."

"And the girl—you did not follow her here?"

Strang stared at the watchful faces. "What girl?" he asked. He glanced over at Cecilia, wondering if his Greek had gone completely haywire.

"Not that one," the old man said sharply. But the shrewd dark eyes, deeply set in his strong-boned face, were less belligerent. He pointed to a chair opposite him. "Sit," he said. "Let us hear this story about Stefanos Kladas."

"I shall speak in English, and the boy can translate. That would be quicker."

"Quicker, quicker. Americans want everything quicker. Speak in Greek. We have plenty of time."

"You are mistaken. We have very little time. This I know. And you do not."

Petros said in English, "I will translate."

Strang gave him a look of thanks. He was too exhausted by his struggles with a strange and difficult language to feel much astonishment at this belated revelation. All he felt now, as he sat down opposite the Cretan's angry frown, was relief: at last, he could gather his thoughts in English and set them out, neatly, clearly; even the pauses for translation would give him a better chance to make everything exact, for the problem was not in telling the story but in the selection of what could be told as simply as possible. But most of all, there was comfort in the feeling that Petros had somehow shifted over to his side. Perhaps Petros had heard about Crete too often. Strang took a deep, steadying breath and began. The old man watched his face as if he could read truth or lie by the flicker of an eyelid or the tightening of a lip.

Ordeal by listening, Cecilia thought as she watched Kenneth Strang. He never gave up, did he? Ten minutes ago, it had seemed as if there was nothing left to do but retreat back into Erinna Street, and walk away defeated. But now the grave faces around Kenneth Strang were no longer distrustful. They listened to him, as if they could understand every word of English, and then listened just as intently to the translation. Carefully, she moved her cramped legs. At least she had solved her own small problem with the cats. They were asleep now, still near her feet, but no longer rubbing their long thin backs against her legs or brushing their bodies unexpectedly over her instep.

Kenneth Strang was ending his story. There were new details, which he had spared her earlier this evening. Steve's body had been identified by his clothes, papers, travelers' checks, passport. Nothing had been stolen. His face had been smashed by the rocks where the body had been found by a fisherman at dawn on Monday. Suicide or an accident: that was what the police believed. That was what everyone would believe.

Petros finished his translation. There was a long moment of silence. Then the old man asserted his authority again. "You say that Stefanos Kladas is dead."

"Yes." What else have I been saying? Strang thought, with a quick surge of annoyance. Or perhaps he had misheard the Cretan's words.

"Then," the old man said softly, with great enjoyment, "who is lying?"

Petros said quickly, "The girl was lying to get our help."

"The American also wants our help."

"Not for himself. For the sake of Stefanos."

That scored a point. The old man weighed it, and nodded.

Petros said, "She came here bargaining for help. 'Hide me,' she said, 'and I will give you news about Stefanos Kladas.' News? Now, we see she was lying."

"But"—the clever old eyes were watching Strang's bewilderment—"she was bargaining. One does not tell everything when one bargains."

"You were the first to disbelieve her. You said she had lived with lies for years; she had forgotten truth."

"If I had disbelieved her altogether, I would not have kept her here. I would not have hidden her from our guests. The girl is afraid. That is real. Not a lie."

"She did not tell us Stefanos Kladas was dead."

"No," agreed the old man. "But why should she come here in the first place? Her family is no friend of ours."

"Friend?" Petros gave a bitter laugh.

"There is much to think about here," the Cretan said happily. He half closed his eyes.

Strang rose, completely baffled. "Then you must think about it," he said abruptly. "I'll wait until you have talked together." He crossed the room to his own table and Cecilia. "It's an all-night session," he told her. "My God, how did I ever get into all this?" He slumped down in his chair. His foot hit something soft and roused a muted protest. "What the—" He lifted the long flap of oilcloth and looked under the table at four placid bodies. "They're *still* there?"

"They are just sleeping it off. Let's keep them that way. It's much more peaceful." She poured him a drink. He noticed that the two coffee cups were saucerless and the wine bottle half empty. "Sh!" she said quickly, "don't spoil your advantage. You were wonderful, so serious and earnest. I'd hire you as my defense lawyer, any day."

"Not against the old man." He shook his head admiringly, both for the Cretan and for Cecilia. He looked at the cats again. "It's one hell of an evening for you." Then he wished his language didn't slip unconsciously out of his control when he was worried sick. "Sorry," he said awkwardly, apologizing for everything.

"I shan't forget this evening. What's happening, do you think?"

"We've run into some kind of a snag. It's beyond me. All I wanted was to get Petros to help."

"How?"

"Steve spent how long here—eighteen months? How many nights of secret talk and reminiscence in eighteen months?"

"Quite a number, I'd think." She looked reflectively at the men's table.

"Petros was shown the photographs. Perhaps he will remember what

Steve told him about them. It's a chance, I know; and a small one. But—" He shrugged his shoulders.

"If you got that Englishman to look at the photographs—" she began. "He would do that, wouldn't he?"

"Ottway? Yes, I think he would."

"Then with Ottway and Petros, you have a slightly better chance."

He did feel better, too. Less exhausted, less depressed. "You are a strange mixture," he told her. "Whatever it is, it's good for me."

She looked away, at the men across the room. "I think the curtain is about to go up again." For the old man had raised his eyes, and now his voice, to the ceiling. Overhead, footsteps hurried. There was a clatter on a flimsy staircase, which must, by the sound of it, lead down into the kitchen next door. "I can see," Cecilia observed, "how the Greeks invented the five-act drama."

The woman entered first, elderly, small, thickset. Not so old, Strang reconsidered quickly, not much more than fifty, but with a face whose premature wrinkles and furrows were marked cruelly under the bright glare of light from the naked bulb overhead. Her long black hair, streaked with gray, was drawn back without mercy into a knot at the nape of her neck. Her lips and cheeks were colorless. A plain woman and no nonsense, even to her ankle-length black skirt, her long-sleeved, high-collared blouse. There was a long black scarf over her shoulders, falling almost to her knees. Her dark eyes flashed briefly over Cecilia and Strang. "Who are they?" she asked the old man.

"They are friends of Stefanos Kladas."

The woman's face softened. "Then they are welcome," she said with simple dignity.

Strang thought, We have been named friends: that is something at least.

"What more had the girl to say?" the old man asked.

"Nothing. What did you expect?" The woman's voice was harsh with irritation.

"We heard a lot of talk."

"The same old thing. Ask her, and waste your breath. She will tell us nothing more until we help her. Help *her*? What has she ever done for us? Never in twenty years has she even looked at my shadow. She didn't even know I was alive! And now—" She plunged into a full account of all that had been said upstairs, her hands at her waist, elbows stiffly out, feet planted solidly on the ground, and ended with a declaration addressed to the ceiling. "So she is in danger, she says. She helped Stefanos Kladas because her father and brother were murdered, she says. And she comes running here, saying that they were of my blood, asking if that means

158

nothing to me." She threw up her hands to her head. "It meant death to my husband in the war, it meant I was a refugee in Athens with my children, it meant we left everything and lost everything. And I have to weep tears for her father, the man who controlled our village for three years of nightmare? I have to weep for the death of that man and his son? Killed by their own friends. The only honest work *they* ever did! And I must weep?" She whirled around toward the doorway, where the girl stood hesitating, her head bent, her dark hair disheveled, half falling over her face. "They made me weep all my tears, years ago. I have none left, for them, for you. My village—" She burst into deep sobs, ripped her hair loose, pulled at the throat of her blouse. The two younger men and the boy ran to her, began talking quietly, tried to pull her hands down to her sides. The sobs deepened.

Cecilia flinched. "I can't bear this," she said almost to herself, and half rose, and then sank back in her chair again.

Very quietly, he said to her, "You were the one who reminded me of Greek tragedy." He put his hand over hers.

"It isn't real?" She belied her own question, for her eyes filled with tears, and she bit her lip.

"Very real," he said gently. If calling up emotion from great depths was not real, then what was? Grief was not complaint or self-pitying tears. Grief was mourning for all of us, he thought.

The woman was being led to a chair. She sat down, covering her head with the long black scarf, drawing it over her mouth. She didn't even look up as the old Cretan turned his head sharply toward the kitchen doorway. "Well?" he asked the girl.

Strang had almost forgotten her. He looked now, with interest, but with no recognition. Not at first. Then, as she looked around the room, at the old man and his sons, at the two Americans, at the woman sitting with her head covered and bowed, something quickened in Strang's memory. The white, drawn face, the pale lips, the fall of unkempt hair, the shapeless black coat, too large for her thin body, all belonged to a stranger. But the profile was unmistakable. It was Katherini Roilos. His grip tightened on Cecilia's hand. "The girl who tried to help Steve," he said quickly. He rose. And then he hesitated.

The girl was saying, "I did not know these things. I was four years old when the village was burned. I—" She looked at the woman's bowed head. "I shall leave." And then, defiantly, "I would never have come here if Stefanos Kladas did not need help."

"How does a dead man need help?" Petros asked. "Charon has taken him beyond all help."

"Dead?" She looked at them in horror. "When? Where?"

The old Cretan gestured to Strang.

Strang said, "The Italian police found his body. They believe it was suicide."

The girl stared at him, but the look of terrified dismay left her face. She said slowly, "That is what everyone is supposed to believe. But it was not suicide. It was murder." She took a deep breath. "Murder of another man, Mr. Strang. Your friend Stefanos Kladas is alive."

THIRTEEN

In the small square room, there was a silence so intense that Cecilia could hear the purring sleep of a cat near her feet. Then there was a growl of triumph from the old Cretan, an exclamation of disbelief from Petros, a quick exchange of glances among the men, a lifting of the black-shawled woman's head, a look of mixed emotions on Strang's face—amazement, uncertainty, relief, doubt, hope. He gripped Katherini's shoulder. "Steve is alive?" he asked in English.

"Yes." She looked at the old man, and began speaking in Greek. "He was alive, yesterday, on the yacht *Medea,* when it arrived in the Bay of Argos." She broke into English again for Strang's benefit. "He was a prisoner. They took him away in the darkness, in a small boat. They were rowing toward the coast of Sparta." She looked again at the old man, who was frowning with impatience.

"Speak in Greek," Strang said quietly. "If I don't understand, I'll signal."

Katherini said, "They took him ashore when darkness fell. I watched them, praying that the moon would rise so that someone in Nauplion, on the other side of the bay, might see what was happening. But they had planned everything carefully. Even I, standing on the yacht, could not see the little boat after the first few minutes."

"Was he injured?" Strang asked.

"Drugged."

"Why did they keep him alive?"

"Yes," said Petros, grimly, "that is a good question."

"Because of the photographs he took during the war. They will keep him alive until they can find out where he has sent them. They are afraid of these photographs, I think. Very afraid."

Petros glanced at Strang. "Do you believe her?" he asked bluntly.

"She tried to help him in New York," Strang said slowly. "And if that is known, then she is in danger." He thought for a moment. "How did she recognize me? How did she find out my name?"

"They have their own photographs, too," she said with a bitter smile. "I saw one of you, taken when you were walking on Madison Avenue. Nikos said you were the man who was coming to Greece with Stefanos. Oh, they knew all about you, about the magazine—"

"All about me?" Strang asked, unbelieving.

"Enough, at least," she answered, "to decide whether you were only a business friend of Stefanos or a very close friend—like Petros—who might know much of his life. But they decided you were harmless. So no accident happened to you."

He looked around at the listening faces. None seemed to find her last remark ridiculous. "And where," he asked, "would that accident have happened?"

"In the middle of the Atlantic," she said calmly.

"You seem to know a lot about them," he said, watching her.

"For years, I paid no attention. But since I found out that my father and brother were killed by Nikos Kladas I—I have paid attention. I listened. I watched. And I began to learn. And I did not know what to do with what I learned. I did try to warn Stefanos Kladas. I did try to tell you that we were coming to Athens. But that was all I could do. So little. It is horrible to know something and not be able to do anything."

"You could have gone to the police."

"Police?" She was shocked. "But they would have said my aunt was guilty. And she is not. She is being used. That is all."

"She doesn't know what is going on, even on board her own yacht?" Strang asked sharply.

"But they explain it to her in such a way that she believes they are right," the girl said. She wasn't altogether happy about her own explanation, Strang thought.

"I owe her everything I had," the girl went on, with sudden passion. "She took me out of a miserable village; she educated me and fed me and clothed me—"

"Half a dozen fur coats put your aunt beyond suspicion?" Strang asked. "Is that it?"

"Why doesn't your aunt help you now?" asked Petros. "Why do you need help from us?" His distrust was still evident.

Katherini Roilos looked at him contemptuously. "I don't ask your help, any more. All I do now is to give you the message from Stefanos. After that, I leave."

"They let you talk to Stefanos?" Petros asked. "This is a fine story, a very fine story."

"They did not let me talk," she said with annoyance over his stupidity. "But I talked with him. Yesterday, at dawn, my aunt went ashore. Later, the others went, too, to sight-see. It was an excuse, to make the officials in Nauplion think that everything was normal. Many yachts come to Nauplion with people who want to visit Mycenae, Epidaurus. So they went, but I said I was ill and I stayed on board. I talked with Stefanos for five or six minutes. He had been drugged, but he was beginning to be conscious. I gave him a knife. I warned him that his food would be drugged again, that he would be taken off the ship that night. He promised he would not eat anything, or drink. That he would pretend. And go with them. And once he reached the shore, he would try to escape. If he managed, he said he would hide. I was to get this news to Petros, who lived on Erinna Street. That is how I knew to come here."

"Where would Stefanos hide?"

"He said he would try to reach the old place."

"Where is that?" asked the Cretan.

"He did not tell me. Just—the old place." She looked anxiously at the watching faces.

Was this, wondered Strang, another devious trick, one to trap Petros this time? He, too, knew something about those damn photographs. The same idea had entered the old Cretan's eyes. He said nothing, only tossed his head back twice, abruptly, which was the Greek way of making a silent but emphatic "no!"

Strangely enough, it was Petros and the woman, sitting so still at the side of the room, who believed the girl now. They looked at each other. Petros said, "He may be there."

"If he escaped," said the girl. She pulled the loose coat around her and began walking to the door.

"One minute," Strang said in English. "How did you come here?"

The girl looked puzzled. "I walked," she said.

"Alone?"

"But of course." She paused. "I thought I was running away. Leaving my half-dozen fur coats—" she flashed a sharp glance at him—"beginning all over again." She shrugged her shoulders.

"Who gave you this coat?" He touched the loose sleeve.

"My maid, Maria."

"She knew you were coming here?"

"She is devoted to me."

"Did she know you were coming here?"

"Someone had to find out where Erinna Street was. I'm a stranger in Athens. Maria went out this afternoon, and found it. Tonight, when they were all downstairs talking, she unlocked my bedroom door. I slipped down the back stairs and came here." Katherini Roilos looked at him anxiously. "I *can* trust Maria. She helped me escape."

The Cretan was muttering with annoyance at the use of English, his curiosity overreaching his polite patience. Petros began translating roughly.

Strang said, "Why were you locked in your room?"

"I was not told why. When I arrived this afternoon in Athens, my aunt locked me into my room. She had learned about my visit to *Perspective*, about my putting our names on the passenger list on the liner." Katherini shivered. She forced herself to go on. "Tonight, there was a meeting of them all. They were discussing me. Maria brought me the news. She guarded me while I went down the back staircase."

"Two men followed you here."

"No one followed me. I made sure."

"Then two men came, afterward. They were waiting when we arrived here."

The girl's thin, white face turned toward Cecilia.

"Yes, that's true," Cecilia said, and rose a little stiffly. She came over to the girl, and took the slender white hands, so cold and trembling. "It's all right, we'll take care of you." But how on earth, she wondered dismally, do we do that? She exchanged glances with Strang.

The Cretan had risen. "What is this? What is this?"

Petros said, "I've just told you. Two men are waiting."

"What men?" The white eyebrows and mustache bristled.

In slow Greek, Strang described them. The girl's cold hands tightened, fear spread across her face. "Boris. He is the little man. A Bulgarian."

"A Bulgarian!" the old man repeated, with contempt and hatred. He spat on the floor, and rubbed the mark out with his foot.

"And the tall man?" Strang asked her.

"Nikos." She stared at him helplessly.

"Nikos Kladas!" Petros was tight-lipped.

My God, thought Strang, we spoke to him. We actually spoke to him. Here, in Erinna Street . . . He recovered himself. Quickly, he asked the girl, "Did you tell your maid what house you were looking for in Erinna Street?"

She shook her head.

"Did you tell her you were searching for Petros?"

She shook her head.

"You must have given *some* excuse," he said in exasperation.

"Only that a cousin of my father lived in Erinna Street."

"But no mention of Petros?" he insisted. Thank God for that, he thought, as she shook her head again. He glanced at his watch. "How long will they stay out there?"

"All night, if necessary," Petros said. He exchanged glances with his brothers. They moved toward the door.

"What?" the old man stopped them sharply. "We sit here for an hour of nothing, the door closed. And then you open the door and rush out to look? No, no. We must think of a better way. We must trick them a little." The prospect pleased him. Yes, thought Strang, that's wise: we had better think of what we are going to do before we start doing it. And as the men started thinking in close argument, he turned to Cecilia. "She can't stay. She can't leave. We are in one hell of a fix."

"Well, at least she can sit," Cecilia said, and led the girl to a chair. "She's freezing cold."

In this room, Strang wondered, with its closed high window and heavy door and thick walls? The temperature, with all the excitement, must have reached a communal ninety degrees. "I'll get her a drink," he said, a little abstractedly, for he had his own thinking to do. He walked slowly across the room to pick up the wine bottle and a glass. The boy followed him, ready to help, smoothing his badge of office, the undisturbed napkin which he never seemed to unfold, into its correct place over his arm. He looked a little astounded as the cats, one by one, began to emerge from under the table, pausing, stretching, picking their way slowly into the light. A dark, heavily striped tiger reached up, not too steadily, to try out its claws on Cecilia's coat, lying over the back of a chair. "Damn and blast you," said Strang, making a grab for the coat. The boy, ever helpful, landed a kick. "They need some air," Strang said as the boy—he must have seen the saucerless coffee cups—frowned and then looked under the table. He picked up the saucers, smelling them, and broke into a wide smile. He called over his shoulder to the men, and began to laugh as he talked.

A laugh was a strange sound in that room, but it was a good sound. The men stopped their argument, looked surprised, annoyed, and—as they understood—relaxed a little. Strang said, "There's your excuse to open the door and send someone outside." He pointed to the cats. Then he concentrated on pouring wine for Katherini.

The old Cretan was quick to see the chance and elaborate on it. "Take the cats out. Leave the door wide open. They will hear voices and music. Play!" he told one of the young men. "And you—" he said to the girl—"go into the kitchen. Keep out of sight. Not you!" he told Cecilia. "Sit there and listen to the music. If anyone is near this house and looks inside, he will see what should be seen, hear what should be heard."

"Unless he has climbed up to look in the window," Strang told Petros.

Petros shook his head. "First, he would have to climb into our yard. The wall has spikes. And then there is also a dog."

"Stop talking in that foolish tongue," the old man said, "and tell your girl she's to stay here." For Cecilia was trying to follow Katherini into the kitchen, and the old man was holding her back by her wrist. "If she has so much strength, this one, why didn't she kick the cats out of her way? Wasting good wine . . . Tell her that, too."

"Oh!" Cecilia said, and sat down again, as Strang explained.

"I thought she was a woman without nerves," the old man went on, as he signaled to Petros. The door was opened wide, and the cold sharp air streamed in. The cats ran out. The boy followed, shouting. The old man stood, looking down at Cecilia. "All evening, she sat. Very still. The cats at her feet. I said to myself, There's a woman with great calm. But I now see she's just a woman, with all the little tricks." He was enjoying himself immensely.

"He is talking about me, isn't he?" Cecilia was even forgetting she sat in full view of the open door.

Strang told her, amused by the expression on her face.

"You mean he actually noticed me this evening?"

"Probably counted every cigarette you smoked, and pitied Americans who have chimneys instead of women." And so now the three of them were amused, quite naturally. Anyone looking in from the street through the door would find this harmless scene a little difficult to fit into any suspicions. One of the young men had picked up a strange-looking instrument with a single string, and was plucking a slow, lamenting accompaniment to his song. The others listened, eyes half closed. The woman had let her head scarf fall back over her shoulders. It was, thought Strang, a picture he would never shake out of his memory.

The boy stood at the threshold. "About time, too," the old man said crossly. "It is cold. Shut that door!"

Indeed it was. Cecilia had gathered her coat round her shoulders. The door closed. And they all looked at the boy.

"Well?" asked his father.

"There was one man outside."

"Which one?"

"He was my height."

"Where?"

"Just across from this door. He hid behind the big tree."

Petros said, "And you stared at him?"

"No, I didn't." The boy was hurt.

"He did well, Petros," the old man said. "You could have done no better."

"But where has Nikos gone?" Petros wanted to know.

"That is not our problem at this moment." The old man looked at Strang and Cecilia. "You must leave together. You must be seen, walking away just as you walked in."

"And the girl?"

"She can stay here—" The old man glanced at his wife, but there was neither approval nor objection from her. "They can wait and watch, outside, but it will do them no good. She can stay here for months, as Stefanos once did."

"But no one knew Stefanos was here. These men know she came to the street. There will be danger."

The old man looked at his son, his stepsons, his brother-in-law. "We are enough," he said.

"The girl has information she ought to tell."

"She has told us all that is needed."

"But there is more than Stefanos to think of," Strang said desperately.

"What is more than Stefanos?" the old man asked abruptly. He looked around, sharply, as the girl came quietly to the kitchen doorway. "You stay here," he told her. "No one will get near you."

She looked past him at Strang. "I know what you mean," she told him. "But I will not go to the police with my story. There would be scandal, newspapers. My aunt does not deserve that."

"Not to the police," he said. "There are others—"

"Counterintelligence? Military intelligence? My aunt would be branded as a traitor. Our family is too much hated already. Would you never have our name free of that?"

"You could free it."

"By being a traitor to my aunt? No. All I have done is to try to save the life of Stefanos Kladas. That is all I will do."

"And you do not care if other people lose their lives?"

"Who?" She was angry, defiant.

"You know quite well," he told her sharply. In English, he added, "You know what a political conspiracy means to ordinary people, the people you saw in the street today when you came to Athens, the people in your village. You were only four, you said, when your village was burned. By whom? Did the people rejoice? Or was it only a few men, like your father, who were glad? Surely, even someone four years old could remember flames and screams of terror and, afterward—yes, afterward, what did you hear? Or were the survivors scattered in the hills so you couldn't hear them weep?"

My God, he thought, taking a deep breath, where did that all come from?

She stared at the ground and said nothing. But, at least, the anger and defiance had gone.

He said, very quietly, "Money is like all weapons: it can be used for good or for evil. I could think of a hundred ways in which your aunt's fortune could be spent to bring good to Greece. Instead, she spends it in the one way that is bound to bring suffering. Does she hate Greece so much?"

The girl looked up at him. Her eyes dilated.

"No one is forcing her to spend her money this way. She made her own choice, didn't she?"

"She has suffered—you don't know what she has suffered. You hear *their* side of the story," she gestured to the others. "She has her story, too, just as terrible as theirs."

"I know," he said. "Every side in politics has its own reasons. But we are not arguing about rights and wrongs in politics. We are talking of something more honest than that. We are talking of suffering."

"Suffering changes people. It makes them different," she said haltingly. "My aunt has suffered much."

"It doesn't change. It strips them down to what they really are. It only shows them naked. It shows what lay hidden inside them." He paused. "For God's sake, can't you see that?"

The Cretan and his family were standing quite still, listening intently, although only Petros and perhaps the boy could have understood anything that had been said. The old man hadn't even blustered for an immediate translation, as if the emotion in the two voices demanded the respect of silence.

Strang made his last appeal to the girl. "These people here have no reason to like you, yet they've offered you shelter. Your aunt loves you, yet what does she offer you now? There's a difference in the kind of people they are and the kind of woman your aunt is. If you think she is as human as they are, why don't you walk out of that door and put your little hand right into the Bulgarian's? Ask him to take you back to all those dear sweet people who are only twisted by what they've suffered?"

The girl flinched, then became angry with herself for the instinctive gesture, and, in turn, translated the anger on to him. "What do Americans know about suffering?" she demanded, facing him.

Strang's lips closed tightly, stopped his quick comment that her time might have been better spent in reading some American history than on choosing the minks for her coats, if only to keep herself from being as stupid as she sounded. He said, very quietly, making his sarcasm twice as bitter, "That's right: we fought our civil war with rose petals."

She turned away from him. She turned away from the others, too, as if she didn't want to be reminded that people could suffer and still remain human beings. She looked at Cecilia.

Cecilia's voice was gentle. "Who killed your father and brother, Katherini?"

Katherini stared at her. "It was not my aunt. She was angry when she heard."

"But she knew their murderer."

"Yes."

"Did she have him arrested?"

"No." For a moment, the girl seemed almost scornful at the American's naïveté about police. As if *they* could solve anything like this!

"She never saw him again—she cut him out of her life—she said how evil he was—" Cecilia ran out of suggestions. But she had given enough, it seemed.

"No," the girl said slowly.

"So, if she was angry, it wasn't with him."

"But—" the girl began, and fell silent.

"Perhaps she was angry because the murders were badly planned. Perhaps they did not look like suicide or an accident?"

The girl stared at her.

"After all," Cecilia said, getting up from the table, "who pays the murderer? I mean—what does he live on? How does he earn his money for food and clothes? Someone employs him. Or has he been discharged? Is he out of favor?"

The girl's eyes widened still more.

Cecilia took her arm. "Then what are we arguing about?"

Katherini Roilos didn't pull her arm away. Instead, her hand suddenly gripped Cecilia's. It was still ice-cold. "If only," Cecilia said to Strang, "we could get a good hot meal inside her, put her in a comfortable bed, let her sleep, with friends sitting near."

Strang nodded. But where could they find all that? Not only food and a bed, but complete safety, too. Where? And then he knew. He said to the girl, "Will you come with us?"

"You want me to tell—everything?" Katherini Roilos asked.

"I think you ought to. But it's your choice."

"Perhaps," she said slowly, "perhaps it is the only choice." She looked at Cecilia. "Yes," she said softly. "I'll go with you. But how?" She looked at the door to the street. "How?"

"Petros," Strang called over to the group of talking men, "we need your help."

FOURTEEN

"Good night," the boy said solemnly, smoothing the folded napkin over his arm, ducking his small round head in a little bow. Overhead, the naked bulb shone down from the edge of the rippled roof and cast a net of light over the boy and the two men beside him.

"Good night," said the Cretan. He was a massive and imposing figure, standing erect before the doorway of his house, his feet planted securely on the earth road, his wide breeches tucked into his long heavy boots, his waistcoat now buttoned and a handkerchief twisted around his head, low on his brow, against the night air.

"Good night," said one of the stepsons, and flashed a smile.

"Good night," said Cecilia and Strang, and turned from the little group to walk down Erinna Street. Halfway, Cecilia turned to wave back to them: three still figures under the roof's hard light; to one side of them, the tree with its spread of shadows; behind them, the steep face of rough rock.

"At least," she said lightly, "I did get one view of the Acropolis tonight." She was more tired than she would allow, though. Her weight was beginning to rest on Strang's arm.

"We won't have much chance of finding a taxi at this hour. Not here," he said worriedly, as they reached the corner and found the street deserted. "Can you walk three or four blocks?"

I'll have to, she thought. "Of course." She dropped her voice. "Did you see the Bulgarian anywhere?"

"He was under the tree as I opened the door. He drew behind its trunk."

"What's the plan?" she asked. "You were all talking Greek so busily that no one had time to translate anything."

"Petros will smuggle Katherini out by the yard, and through some other yards that stretch along under the Acropolis wall. He is borrowing a light truck he almost shares with one of his neighbors—I couldn't get that part quite straight; it was all very digressive. Seemingly, he drives a truck in winter, a bus in the summer. In any case, he can get hold of some kind of transportation. He will bring the girl to the corner of Dimocritos Street, and that's only a block from Pringle's doorstep."

"Pringle?"

"An attaché at the embassy. Married. Katherini will be safe there. In the morning, she can see some people. And if she will only tell them what she knows—" He shook his head, remembering his defeat. "Without you, she would have told nothing. Or as little as possible. Or much too late to do any good."

"I hate to admit it, but logic and sweet reason are often lost on a woman. We're more personal and practical in our arguments. You'd have won, though; it would just have taken longer."

"I doubt it."

"But she had already made her choice when she came to Erinna Street. And that's another strange thing about women: we decide somewhere deep inside us, and then we want to be persuaded that what we have decided is right. We can argue ourselves back into a corner where we can't do what we decided to do, in the first place, before we started being persuaded that what we had wanted to do was the only thing possible. See what I mean?"

"No."

"But it's quite simple. Women are really very simple."

"Yes. I've noticed that."

How many women has he known? she wondered suddenly, inexplicably. What were they like? No—what *are* they like?

"Cheer up," he said, "we've only one block to go. The restaurant should be just around the corner."

"We're going back to the gypsies?" They were, she thought, the most-dressed gypsies she ever had seen.

"There are bound to be some taxis around there. Besides, I'd like to telephone Pringle."

"Ask his wife to have some soup heated for Katherini. That's about all she can digest, right now, poor dear. Funny thing, you know . . ." She lapsed into silence.

"What's so funny?"

"Everything you said—about suffering and its effects—was being proved by her, right there; and she never knew it. I mean, she's been through her own private little agony for weeks, and what came to the surface? An attempt to save a life."

He looked at her thoughtfully. "No," he said, "I just don't understand women."

"You aren't supposed to." She was equally serious.

He looked at her in surprise. Perhaps that has always been my trouble, he thought. He said, "Here's the restaurant."

The headwaiter remembered them with one glance. "Certainly," he told Strang, pointed to a telephone in the small lobby, and found a chair for Cecilia.

"It won't take long," Strang reassured her, searching through the telephone directory, privately cursing the deeply shaded light. He found the number, got through, and then—as he waited for someone to pick up the receiver—wondered if Pringle was out, if Pringle was asleep, if Pringle was in the arms of his loving wife, if Pringle was allergic to phone calls at ten minutes after one in the morning and never answered on principle. But Pringle was neither out nor asleep nor et cetera. His voice was hearty, if a little surprised. In the background, there were other voices, distant laughter.

"I hear you're in the middle of a party. I'm sorry—" Strang said. He was more than sorry.

"Oh, they're just about to leave. But why don't you come along and I'll get them to stay? It's only the Ottways, and a couple of fellows who wanted to talk about Cyprus, and Alexander Christophorou. He dropped in to see me and stayed for a drink." The good humor left Pringle's voice. "He's a little depressed. So am I, frankly. Come along, and we can have a quiet five minutes together."

"Not tonight. Miss Hillard is with me."

"Bring her along. Why not?"

"With Aleco around?"

Pringle laughed and spoke to someone beside him. "He is out on the town with la Hillard, but won't bring her around. Seems to think you would make heavy competition." Then Pringle spoke into the telephone again. "Aleco says you overestimate him." There was a short pause. "Anything else?" It was a reminder that telephone calls usually meant something.

"I called you," Strang said slowly, thinking quickly, "to ask for Beaumont's address."

That obviously surprised Pringle. "You'll always find Beaumont through the School."

"I know that. But where can Lee Preston be sure of reaching him, definitely?"

"Oh, *Perspective*," Pringle said. "Just a moment. I have his phone number and address somewhere here." He gave them, carefully. He still sounded a little puzzled.

"Sorry to bother you at this hour. Miss Hillard and I thought we'd call Preston in New York. It's a good time to reach him. He will just be mixing his first batch of Martinis."

"Lucky fellow," Pringle said with a laugh and a touch of nostalgia. "They never taste the same anywhere else."

"It's the ice," Strang said. "See you later," he added very softly.

"See you—" Pringle repeated automatically, and then stopped. "Soon," he ended. He sounded thoughtful.

"Slight change in plans," Strang told Cecilia, as he helped her rise. He tried to look unconcerned. He pulled her coat properly onto her shoulders, and began buttoning it for her. "You are one tired girl," he said, worriedly.

"I've another hour in me. Provided no one puts me into a comfortable chair again. What's wrong?"

"Pringle's place is filled with people."

"Oh? Then what?"

"We'll think of something. In the taxi."

"We'll think. . . ." That was a sweet inclusion. "*You* will," she murmured. All she could think of, at this moment, was something simple and practical, like taking Katherini Roilos back to the hotel with her. What was there against that?

"Hi!" an American voice said, and a hand gripped Strang's arm. "Shipmate ahoy! And how are the barbarians?"

Strang stared at the handsome face.

"We came over on the same boat," its owner was explaining to Cecilia, without waiting for the introduction. "Come on, let's have a drink together. I'm with a bunch of stuffed shirts. Very lovely people, but definitely overweight. We'll ditch them and go on our merry way." He managed to get his eyes off Cecilia. "You know, old boy, that was a very neat toast you pulled out of your cuff. Damned good exit line. *Down with all barbarians!* I've been using it, I don't mind telling you. Say, this place is quite something." His eyes were back to Cecilia again, and looked as if they'd stay there permanently. "There's nothing like seeing the real people, is there? Interesting types."

Straight from Wichita, Kensington, and Heidelberg, Strang thought, took firm hold of Cecilia's arm and began steering her to the door. "Sorry. Have to go. Another time. Old boy."

He came after them. "I didn't say good-by to the lady." He caught Cecilia's hand and held it with exaggerated grace. "Parting is such sweet sorrow," he said sadly.

"Another time," Strang repeated firmly, and pulled Cecilia into the cab. "We're stayed for, Bassanio." As the cab started away, he looked at her. "And what was so funny about all that? Damned nuisance—" He looked at his watch and scowled. "The Church of St. Dionysios," he told the driver, who nodded with pleasure, seeing a long, clear run through the almost empty streets, and the cab leaped forward.

"Hold tight," Strang warned her.

"Don't you like him?"

"Used to be one of my favorite film stars."

"Now what did he do, except quote Shakespeare?"

"Murdered him. That's Juliet's speech, not Romeo's."

"Purist! You murdered Shakespeare a little yourself."

"Just giving him another variation in exit lines."

"Oh, yes—what was that about barbarians?"

For a moment, he said nothing. "It just proves you should never think aloud. Or some idiot is going to seize what you say and turn it into another of his stock clichés. My God, how many bars have heard that one!"

So that's what really angered him, she thought.

"If he understood what he was talking about," Strang went on, "he wouldn't go around repeating it, not with that smile on his face."

"Perhaps you ought to send him the poem that Cavafy wrote about the barbarians. That would take the smile off anyone's face."

He looked at her quickly. "You know modern Greek poetry?"

She shook her head. "Only that poem," she admitted honestly. "'Waiting for the Barbarians.' Steve sent me a translation."

He asked the question that had troubled him a little before, "How well did you know Steve?"

"I only met him twice. Once, he talked about Cavafy. Once, he told me about—" she glanced at the driver's neat, well-brushed head—"about authentic Greek music." She paused. "How does it go again—the poem?" Slowly, hesitantly, she began it, almost speaking it to herself.

> "What are we waiting for, all crowded in the forum?
> The Barbarians are to arrive today.
> Within the Senate house why is there such inaction?

The Senators, making no laws, what are they sitting
        there for?
Because the Barbarians arrive today.
What laws now should the Senators be making?
When the Barbarians come they'll make the laws."

She paused again. He was silent, watching the empty streets with a frown, as if he were puzzling out a long and difficult problem. So she fell silent, too.

"Go on," he said. He was still watching the streets.

"Why did our Emperor get up so early in the morning?
And at the greatest city gate why is he sitting
        there now,
Upon his throne, officially, why is he wearing
        his crown?
Because the Barbarians arrive today.
The Emperor is waiting to receive
Their Leader. And in fact he has prepared
To give him an address. On it he has
Written him down all sorts of names and titles."

And then she forgot the exact lines—something about the chief men in the city going out in all their richest clothes, with bracelets and amethysts and splendid flashing emeralds, because the Barbarians would arrive today; things of this sort dazzled the Barbarians.

And none of the orators would be speaking, all would stay silent, because the Barbarians would be here today; and they were bored with eloquence and speechmaking. Yes, she thought sadly, remembering the last bitter lines, everything is ready to welcome and appease the Barbarians, and then when the Barbarians don't arrive—

"Why are all the streets and squares emptying so
        quickly . . .
Because night has fallen and the Barbarians have not
        come. . . .
And now what will become of us without Barbarians?—
Those people were some sort of a solution."

She shivered. "Its end always depresses me," she confessed. "I just don't want to believe that people can become so decadent that nothing is worth fighting for."

He came out of his own thoughts. "That's the poem's value," he said.

"If it makes a man say 'I'll be damned if I'll do!' then that's something. It's a spine-stiffener."

"If one has a spine left. That's the horrible thought."

"There are plenty of good stiff spines still around," he said. "Just ordinary people like Steve and Petros. And do you see the old Cretan's spine bending?"

"No," she agreed. She looked at him. She thought, I don't see yours bending, either. "All right," she told him, "I'm on their side." She shook her head. "Imagine an American saying she is on the royalist side, though!"

"Petros must be a republican, if he is as proud as he is of having fought under Zervas. Steve is a socialist." He looked at her with a smile. "Our side is a mixed bunch, thank God! When we've all got the same labels around our neck, then we are halfway to defeat. The group mind makes things very easy for Barbarians to take over."

"Dissension can be dangerous, too, if I remember anything of my Greek history."

"Not as long as you don't develop curvature of the spine." He noticed her worried face. "Don't forget that the poem could have ended on a worse note. It could have said that Barbarians were the only solution. When a civilized man begins to believe that—well, he has had it."

"But no intelligent civilized man would ever believe that."

"Wouldn't he?"

"But do you really know *anyone* like that?" she challenged him, unconvinced.

He didn't answer, at first. "I hope not," he said at last. He wished to God he didn't keep thinking of Christophorou.

The taxi sped away, leaving them on a broad street lonely with night, standing in front of a row of steps and the yawning entrance of a twin-towered church.

"This way," Strang said, and they began retracing their direction.

Ten minutes ago, Cecilia was thinking, I was walking along narrow streets of old houses, low and clustered; now I'm somewhere high on the side of a hill of straight streets crisscrossing, with public buildings and apartment houses. She was a stranger, deaf and blind; she could neither understand the spoken language—these two men, passing now, what were they talking about?—nor recognize the street names. She stared up at the corner sign, quite hopelessly: Δημοκρίτου.

"Dimocritou," Strang told her, "or, as we say, the street of Dimocritus. See, it slopes down toward the main drag. Got your bearings now?"

How shall I ever manage, traveling around by myself? she wondered desolately. "Dimocritou," she repeated, and looked down the long hill. So this is where we go to tea tomorrow with Mr. Thomson, she thought. If ever, she added, I wake up in time. She looked at the street sign again. "I thought I knew the alphabet, at least. And some phrases. You know what, the taxi driver didn't pronounce one word like any records I ever learned from!" She sighed, thinking of the Peloponnese this week. "Lee told me not to worry. Famous last words. Everyone speaks English, he said; and if they don't, use your French. French in the Peloponnese?"

"You'll get on famously," he told her. "You don't need words to help you along. This is the hour of depression, that's all." He had tried to sound more cheerful than he felt.

But she glanced at him. "Let's talk of someone with real worries. Katherini. What are we to do with her?"

"Get her off the street as quickly as possible. Keep her safe until we know that Pringle's place is clear, I suppose. Then—" he almost sighed himself—"take her there, make sure she feels safe, let Pringle contact the right people." After that, he thought, I can start worrying about Steve.

"What's wrong with our hotel? She could stay in my room until the morning."

He shook his head. "I don't want you mixed up with all this." He looked sharply across the street at two young men: students, perhaps? He relaxed.

"Aren't I?"

"Not so far. Not openly, at least. I hope. And if we had the time now, I'd take you back to the hotel. But—" There was a light truck driving slowly toward them. He grasped her arm. But it drove past them. "Wrong guess," he admitted. A car passed quickly, and three men talking busily. He didn't know whether to be relieved or worried that this district had a scattering of life in it, even at this hour. "Now, it's all right," he reassured her. "This is the street. Petros gave me careful directions. Or else I'd be as lost as you are."

The truck is late, she thought nervously, as she saw him look at his watch again.

"We can't loiter here." They had reached the corner of Jan Smuts Street. They began to retrace their steps toward Dimocritou again. "We can't risk walking too far away, either, from the meeting place."

"Where is it?"

"Just here. Anywhere about here." His eyes searched for a shop doorway, or the entrance to a block of apartments which could shelter them. "There are some houses over there being turned into apartments," he said.

Canvas sheets were spread all over the working front, and scaffolding partly covered the sidewalk. But even if it looked bleak, the work-in-progress offered some shadows and protection from the open street. "Let's cross over," he suggested. "We can wait there."

"What about a night watchman?" She followed him quickly.

"It doesn't seem as if one is needed around here." Mounds of lime were all that greeted them. It was as desolate as it had looked from across the street. "Yes, I know," he told her. "I'm wondering for the tenth time to-night how we ever got into all this."

"But we are, and that's that," she said. "You said something to Katherini, down at the *taverna*, about political conspiracy." She glanced at him. "Sorry. But I'm just so lost, in every way. You think Katherini's aunt is behind it all?"

"She has the money. There must be two or three others on the top level."

"No more than that?"

"A secret isn't as well kept as this one if you start spreading it around several people."

"So then you think that if the top men were caught—"

"Cut off the head, what use is the body?" That had been too abrupt, too sharp, he thought. He turned his eyes away from the street, so irritatingly empty now, and looked at her. He took her arm and gripped her hand. "Sorry," he said. "I'm getting on edge." He looked at his watch again, and then back at the street.

"Could three or four people plan so much trouble?" she asked, if only to keep him from staring silently at the street.

"The trouble exists. It may be dormant, but they know how to waken it. That's their way of working. They have money, brains, and a ruthless philosophy. They must have organized well; all orders radiating out from the top committee, no one knowing who else is in the conspiracy except the leaders. I heard of two men who could identify one of the leaders—Nikos Kladas—and they were murdered."

She looked at him in horror. "What kind of people are these?"

"Extremists. And for once, I use the word correctly. They've traveled so far to the left that the next step is straight into a padded cell. That's my personal opinion. A Khrushchev Communist would call them leftist deviationists, I expect. But the jargon boys make things too blurred, too complicated. It is simply that there are people in this world who want to build, and there are others who want to destroy. And all the nastiest human failings belong to that group: spite, revenge, jealousy, false pride, greed, ambition, and just plain hate. Oh, they doll up their politics with fine phrases and slogans; they find excuses for their anger. But it all ends in anarchy and destruction."

He could sense her disbelief. Or perhaps, more kindly, her unwillingness to accept any such philosophy as nihilism.

"Look," he said, "if I could have told your father in 1932 that within ten years Hitler was going to get men not only to build gas chambers but to run them, destroy other human beings by the million, what would your father have said?"

"I see now," she said slowly, "I see what you mean." And then, angrily, "They are mad, all of them! Crazy mad."

"Ask Katherini," he said quietly, "if her aunt and her friends are mad. Crazy mad."

"You mean, she'd think I was crazy for suggesting it?" There was more than a hint of a sharp edge to her voice.

He didn't give an inch. "Yes," he said. "She'd think just that. They are a collection of ruthless power-politicians who are making sure they are going to win, this time."

"But if they believe in complete destruction, then they'll be destroyed, too."

"They'll take that chance. After all, who is more likely to survive—a pack of wolves or a flock of sheep?"

"But—" she began, and stopped. Together, they looked along the street as they heard the heavy sound of an engine pulling up a hill.

It was a light truck, they could see now, as it turned sharply around the corner and came toward them. It slowed down a little; not much, though. Strang stepped out to the edge of the sidewalk, so that he could be more clearly recognized. Cecilia followed him, and stood beside him. Surely Petros will notice us, she thought. If it was Petros. Alarm and dismay swept over her, for the truck was not stopping. It slowed down only enough to let a small, thin figure jump out, her head wrapped in a black scarf, her loose coat flapping. Katherini almost fell, recovered herself, and then ran with amazing speed toward their outstretched hands. She grasped them and pulled toward the shadows. "Hide!" she said. "Hide!" She covered her mouth, and knelt down. Strang crouched and pulled Cecilia with him. They heard the sound of another engine coming up the hill. Strang looked at Katherini. She nodded. So they *had* been followed.

The waiting only lasted a minute, but to the three still figures, motionless behind the barricade of lime heaps and wooden props, each second stretched out interminably. Strang listened tensely. The truck had traveled some distance before the car—its tires hissing as the corner was taken too sharply—turned into this street and gathered speed on the level stretch of roadway. It was passing them, a sleek, tail-finned body of green and white and chromium. It was gone.

Strang kept them all within the shadows until he saw that the slant-eyed taillights had disappeared. "Now!" he said, taking each girl by an arm and hurrying them along the sidewalk and across the street.

"Where?" asked Cecilia.

"Tommy's," he said, and increased their pace. The streets were empty at this moment; he might as well make the most of that.

"You know him well enough to trust him?"

"Fifteen years ago, he was being hunted and hidden." I'll trust that memory, he thought, any day.

They had turned the corner and started down Dimocritos Street. "It's on the other side," he said, his eyes on the numbers at the doorways. "Cecilia, you cross over, walk down to this address"—he gave her Tommy's card—"and keep inside the doorway. We'll walk down this side of the street. See you there!"

She nodded and left them, walking lightly, her coat collar turned up and held at her throat against the sharp night air. Their hiding place had been dank and cold. Another five minutes and she would have been chilled to the bone. She was too alert—all right, let's name it truthfully, she told herself—too afraid, to feel tired or sleepy. Strange what effect one car chasing a light truck had had on her. No more arguments. No more doubts that Kenneth Strang might be taking excessive precautions. In fact, as scared as she was at this moment, eying every doorway, every shadow, she wondered if Ken were taking enough precautions. But, like the green-and-white monster chasing Petros, you cut corners for the sake of speed. She ascended two steps into Tommy's doorway. I'm here, she thought, now where are they? And where is Petros? She shivered, and drew her collar more tightly around her neck.

"What happened?" Strang asked Katherini as Cecilia left them. He slackened his pace.

"Petros led me out through the back, and then into a lane. The truck was there, all loaded and ready for tomorrow morning—Petros had deliveries to make in Corinth and—"

"Yes, yes," he said. "What happened?"

"We started very quietly, very slowly. And at the end of the lane, just as it curved round to join a street—we saw Nikos Kladas. He was walking toward us, with a man called Andreas. They had left their car down on the street. They must have been searching the lane."

Petros had been a little too optimistic, Strang thought, when he had insisted that no one would calculate where the back entrance of the *taverna* could lead. Or Nikos Kladas had a good detailed map and a cold analytical eye. "And then?"

"Petros put on full speed. He ran them down. They had to jump. Nikos was struck. A little. He fell, at least." She sounded pleased. Perhaps in all the years she had known Nikos Kladas, she had never seen him being forced to jump. "Then we were driving down the street, and twisting and turning, onto a big road, and then up a long hill and around. I saw the Acropolis. We drove halfway to the Piraeus, and turned back on a side road, and up and around, and twisted and turned."

"And they followed?"

"I looked back at their car as we left the street where it was standing. I saw Andreas helping Nikos into it. I think his leg was hurt. They started after us as quickly as they could."

Petros could drive, Strang admitted to himself: that was one thing he had not overestimated. "Petros—"

"Oh, he will be all right!" The new confidence in Katherini's voice was startling. "He would have shaken off that car completely if he hadn't had to come to this district. He will take them down into the market. He has friends there, he said. He would leave the truck with them, well hidden. They'll take it back to the lane tomorrow, and explain to his partner—"

"Where is Petros going after that?"

"To the Peloponnese."

"Alone?"

"He has friends there, and all along the way. He drives a bus in summer to Sparta."

"I told him to wait until tomorrow, when I could go with him," Strang said angrily. So Petros had won their last-minute argument, after all, in his own fashion.

"Stefanos needs help *now*," she reminded him softly.

"I know, I know." He was angered by his own helplessness. He looked across the street. A couple of minutes had elapsed since Cecilia had vanished into that doorway, over there. Time enough to let any inquisitive observer think she had little connection with Katherini and him. "Come," he said, and they crossed quickly.

"Petros says," Katherini was explaining patiently, as if Strang were a five-year-old and not too bright for his years, "that what we need is one scout, not a pack of soldiers and policemen. So that is what he is going to be—a scout. To find out what he can. Alone. And then when he sees what has to be done, he will get his friends to help him. They are much more clever than soldiers or policemen. You see?"

"Sh!" he warned her, as they entered the small, stone-floored hall where Cecilia waited, close to the door.

Katherini's face softened as she pulled back the head scarf from her hair. "My father's cousin at Erinna Street gave me this," she whispered to Cecilia, smoothing its folds with her thin hands. "And I know what you'll say," she jibed at Strang. "It cost her more than it cost my aunt for six fur coats. I know that!"

"Sh!" he warned again, and pointed to the small self-service elevator. Cecilia nodded, took Katherini's arm, and drew her toward it. Strang studied the small notice board, its roster of names displayed by visiting cards inserted into narrow brass frames. There were four tenants in this house: J. J. Thomson; Louizis Michalopoulos; Demetrius Drakon; A. Christophorou. His hand, reaching for the receiver on the house telephone beside the board, paused. A. Christophorou? The girls had already reached the elevator. In sudden alarm, he started after them, worried, trying to think, instinctively wanting to get them out of this building. And then, in the street outside, a car drew up abruptly, footsteps hurried across the sidewalk.

He didn't wait for the front door to open. He was already inside the elevator, closing its solid door, his finger on the top-floor button, pressing hard. For a moment, nothing moved. Through the small square of glass inserted in the door's upper panel, he could, by bending his head, see the newcomer. It was a woman. Flat heels—they had deceived him into thinking it was a man's step—tweed coat thrown over her shoulders, reddish hair severely upswept, a sculptured face, now too haggard for beauty, but with definite remnants of what once must have made an astonishing picture. The elevator groaned, roused itself from sleep, and started up with surprising swiftness. His last glimpse was of the red-gold head turning quickly away. There's someone who doesn't want to be recognized, either, he thought, with a touch of amusement.

He shook his head warningly, put a finger to his lips. There was little need for his caution. Katherini's weight sagged against his arm, her eyes still looking in horror at the small square of glass. Cecilia was holding her, startled, frightened. He slipped his arm around Katherini's waist, and held her, too. Over her head, his eyes met the deep blue of Cecilia's in an interchange of silent questions. Neither had any answers. Except that, for a few moments, lost in that deep deep blue, he could almost forget everything else.

The fourth floor was reached; they stood in a small hallway listening to the elevator start its descent. In front of them was a dark-brown door, a well-polished brass bell. Strang, holding Katherini, again gestured for silence. If he rang the doorbell now, would the woman in the hall hear Tommy's surprised voice? He glanced at Katherini, wondering a great deal. All her new-found confidence had left her. She was in a state of collapse, her body trembling inside the curve of his arm. He remembered a spaniel he had picked up once after it had been lolloping around a field near his father's house outside Princeton and had flushed a ground hog instead of the usual rabbit from a tangle of bushes. He was now feeling against his side the same pathetic, spasmodic shudders of fear. The sooner we clear out of here, the better, he thought as he listened to the elevator. The woman had entered it. He could hear it droning its way up again.

Katherini said, "She is coming here!"

"Who?"

"My aunt. She's coming. . . ." The whisper died away, hopeless, and left Strang and Cecilia staring at each other.

"No. Not here," he said, as he heard the elevator stop. It had not traveled far, only to the second floor. Demetrius Drakon, he remembered, and took a deep breath of relief as the elevator was sent down once more. I'll call it back up here, he thought, as soon as it reaches the hall. We'll get the hell out. He looked at Thomson's solid door; he liked old Tommy, but he didn't care much for the house he lived in.

But, at that moment, the door opened. Tommy stood there, wrapped in a heavy dressing gown, his white hair ruffled into a startled fuzz around his head, his red face frowning, his light-blue eyes wary, his hand gripped round a heavy walking stick.

"Wondered who was whispering on my door mat," he began, relaxing.

Strang made an instinctive gesture for silence and, although the surprised Tommy could hardly be expected to understand, pointed downward to the second floor. But Tommy at least understood the urgency of the pointed hand.

He looked at Strang, then he looked at Cecilia, then at the white face of the girl. He stepped back, opening his door wide. "Come in, come in," he said irritably. "Can't have her fainting out there!"

FIFTEEN

Tommy hadn't been asleep. He hadn't even been in bed. His comfortably dented armchair, with a footstool in front, a reading lamp at its side, and a table at elbow level on which a pot of tea, a large cup, an opened book face down, reading glasses, pipe, and massive ash tray were lying, showed he was a long-established bachelor with his own agreeable answer for insomnia. Everything in the room was dark and crowded, worn and comfortable: a woman's nightmare, and a man's delight.

It was a solid little place, secure, permanent, with its walls covered with memories of old friends in framed photos and bookcases. Nothing changed much here, unless another book was jammed into a packed shelf, another magazine added to the piles that covered solid, dark tables, another enlarged snapshot inserted among the mosaic of frames on the wall. Armchairs and sofa looked as if they had been enjoyed for years, their plush covering worn threadbare. The blue velvet curtaining the windows had faded into streaks of slate gray, and one of its long panels was pulled back, with more practicality than grace, to jam a glass door half open, so that a cool wedge of night air could swirl the pipe smoke out of the room. Hence the heavy dressing gown, Cecilia thought, and decided to keep her coat on. For a moment, she let her eye follow Kenneth Strang as he went forward to the opened door among the windows. Then she heard Katherini's sharp choke on the smidgen of brandy that Tommy was letting trickle between the girl's lips, and she turned back to the sofa with her questions still unasked.

Strang glanced outside and saw a narrow terrace, a balustrade, and then the yawn of street. He stepped quietly through the opened door and looked cautiously down into the street. The car had gone. It looked as if Madame Étienne Duval planned to stay some time.

Opposite him, the houses were dark and asleep. Their owners hadn't Tommy's reading habits. Strang stepped back into the room, closing the door enough to let the curtain fall over it more adequately. Katherini was now sitting up on the sofa, Cecilia beside her, Tommy standing over them with an empty glass in his hand and a look of complete astonishment, which he was trying very hard, and most politely, to control. Cecilia was saying, "She's in danger. She's a—a refugee."

"Oh?" Tommy waited.

"We've been trying to help her. And we came here because you—well, we don't know many people, and you're the only one we felt we could trust."

"Indeed," said Tommy, but he softened a little.

I'll keep out of this, Strang decided, and glanced into the little hall where they had entered the apartment. I'll leave it all to those beautiful eyes; they have a truth in them that words can't compete with.

"Because," Cecilia was saying, "Ken said you know what it is to be hunted. And Katherini is being hunted. Could we hide her here, just for half an hour? It's a dreadful imposition, I know. But please . . . We're so sorry. We had to find shelter. . . ."

"Hm!" Tommy said, and then whirled around on Strang as he re-entered the room. "Have you quite finished your tour of inspection?"

"I'm sorry," Strang said. He decided to be completely frank. "I was just making sure that we couldn't be overlooked or overheard." This apartment was certainly compact. Out in the hall, he had found a small bathroom next to a minuscule kitchen, and a door which he had guessed would lead to the bedroom. "There's a high window in the kitchen. Is that for ventilation or a view?"

"Ventilation."

"And the door in the kitchen—that's the service entrance?"

"Naturally," Tommy said a little acidly.

"Is there a back staircase, or is it a service elevator?"

Tommy's most perceptive eyes were studying Strang's face. He answered, at last, "A staircase. Which leads down to the caretaker's flat in the basement of the house, a very respectable woman with two children, all fast asleep, I am sure. You needn't worry so much. The front door is locked, the back door is bolted and barred, as you no doubt saw. And the high window in the kitchen is closed. You are perfectly safe here."

"Thank you." It looked as if Tommy wouldn't turn them away. But there was still one small worry. "Could anyone getting out of the elevator at the second floor have heard you speak to us?" He waited anxiously.

Tommy's eyes and voice softened. "Dear me, you are in trouble, aren't you? No. The lift doesn't conduct any noises. It makes quite enough by itself when it's in action." He pointed to one end wall of the sitting room. "It's just through there, blast it. But it does warn me to expect visitors. Except, of course, they usually telephone from the hall downstairs first." He looked a little severely at Strang for a moment.

"We hadn't time. A car arrived just as I was about to call you. There was a woman—"

Katherini's hands went to her lips. She turned her head away, for a moment. Tommy's eyes flickered back again to Strang.

Strang said, "We heard her take the elevator to the second floor. By that time, we were huddled outside your door, afraid even to ring the bell in case she heard it."

"The second floor?" Tommy was surprised. "To Michalopoulos? But how extraordinary—I mean, at this hour!" He glanced, in sudden confusion, at the two girls.

"Michalopoulos is on the second floor?" Strang asked.

"Of course. And a more respectable, retired wool merchant would be hard to find." Tommy grinned over his own thoughts. Strang wasn't sharing them. He was watching Katherini now. The name of Michalopoulos had had no effect on her.

He said to her, "You never heard of anyone called Michalopoulos?"

She shook her head.

Tommy said, "I know what you need—a nice cup of tea."

Cecilia said, "Or soup? If you have any, that is. I don't think Katherini has had much to eat today."

"Soup!" Tommy looked doubtful and a little upset. "I'm rather afraid— or would Bovril do? And lots of bread and butter? I do have that."

"Wonderful!" Cecilia rose. "I'll put water on to boil," she said, and went into the hall toward the kitchen. Katherini struggled to her feet to follow.

"No, no," Strang said gently. "You rest here. This is Mr. Thomson. He is English, but he has lived here most of his life. He is a very good friend of Greece." The girl looked at them both. Then she sat down obediently, her head drooping. She began to cry, silently.

Strang looked at her, aghast. "I'd better get Cecilia—"

"Leave her," Tommy said quickly, drawing Strang toward his armchair. "She'd much rather we didn't even notice," he whispered. "Pull in that chair, won't you? Now, tell me—what's all this commotion?" He settled himself in his chair, picked up his pipe to prod its ashes with his finger, while he watched Strang carefully.

Strang looked at the telephone, hesitated, and decided to talk to Tommy first. This invasion deserved a little explanation. He said quickly, "The girl is running away from her aunt. The aunt is involved in a political intrigue, a very nasty mess, and the girl wants no more of it." There, he thought with relief, is the truth and no secrets divulged, either.

"That doesn't sound too desperate," Tommy said, knocking the ashes out of his pipe and then relighting the remaining wad of tobacco. "Politics usually end in a mess of some kind, I find."

"These particular politics start off where most other political troubles end."

"Indeed? What are they?" Tommy's interest had sharpened. "Fascist or Communist?"

"As far as I can make out, her aunt belongs to a group that is a terrorist faction of Communists. That is, they are definitely leftist, not rightist. But they are so far to the left that they've written off Tito as a bourgeois reactionary and they think Khrushchev—except for his action in Hungary —may be going the same way. When they talk of revolution, they mean revolution."

"Ah—one of those extremist groups," Tommy said, with the equanimity of someone who had spent too many years in the Balkans to be astounded by political intensity. "They always are so set on remaking the world in their own unpleasant image. I can't think why." His pipe was drawing, nicely, at last. He glanced over thoughtfully at the girl. She was crouching forward on the edge of the sofa, her elbows on her knees, her hands covering her face. "And just what *kind* of political intrigue were we talking about?"

Strang looked embarrassed. He tried to search for a few careful phrases.

"All right, all right," Tommy said testily, letting him off that hook. He drew at his pipe, frowning, his curiosity increased. But he would ask no more questions.

Strang glanced at his watch. "May I use your phone? I've been trying to get in touch with one of the attachés at our embassy here. Last time I telephoned, he had several people at his apartment. I've been waiting until they have all left. I don't want to take Katherini to his place until I'm sure of that." He crossed quickly over to the telephone, aware that Katherini was watching him. Then he put down the receiver, cursing silently as the only answer to his call was a busy-signal.

Tommy's shrewd eyes were studying his face again. "You seem to be taking this very seriously."

"It is serious. In the last few days, one man has been murdered, another has been kidnaped and—unless he has escaped—will be murdered, too.

This girl was hunted all over Athens tonight. If she is caught—she will be silenced. Yes, I think we can take this all quite seriously."

Tommy's equanimity was gone. "Good heavens!" he said. He added, angrily, "And what on earth are you doing dragging Miss Hillard into all this?"

Strang said sharply, "Don't start thinking that Cecilia isn't one of my chief worries." He picked up the receiver again. And, again, there was that damned go-away, drop-dead signal. He said angrily to Tommy, "Sure I'm to blame, but all this is none of my choosing. Everything is breaking so fast. . . ." He calmed down, added wearily, "I think we've struck the climax of a conspiracy. It has been organizing itself for months, if not years—careful recruiting, planning, preparation, complete secrecy. And in a few days, I walked bang slap right into the middle of it."

He took a deep breath, searched for his cigarettes, found one left in a crumpled pack, straightened it, and lit it. "Tonight, believe it or not, Miss Hillard and I just went out to dinner. That's all. To dinner. Afterward, we went to a little place where we could hear some Greek music. Instead—" he halted, as he looked over at Katherini Roilos. She was watching them, listening. "Well, that's the way the tide runs," he said to Tommy.

Tommy rose. "You look like a man who needs something stronger than Bovril." He went over to a cupboard in a bookcase, and took out his one bottle of Scotch. "And I think I'll join you. This is, after all, a rather unusual night." He looked around vaguely. "Glasses . . . water . . . just one moment." He left for the kitchen.

Katherini said, her large eyes two dark hollows in her white face, "I am trouble. Trouble for everyone."

"Nonsense," he said awkwardly.

"Why do you help me?"

He stared at her in surprise. "You didn't expect us to leave you wandering around Athens by yourself, did you?"

"Because you need me? Is what I know so valuable that you put yourself and your girl and the old Englishman in danger?"

"Look—" he began patiently, and glanced over his shoulder for help. What had kept Cecilia so long? From the kitchen came the cheerful rumble of Tommy's voice and Cecilia's laugh.

"But you aren't Greek. Why do you help me?"

"You're someone very much in need of help. That's enough. Isn't it?"

She stared at him. "So is Maria in need of help," she said.

"Maria?"

"You don't even remember who she is!" she said angrily.

He remembered now. "Of course I do. Your maid. But look, Katherini,

189

one person at a time! First you, then Maria. And there's Steve, too. Remember him? There is a lot of help needed tonight."

She said slowly, "Is Maria still alive? She may still be in that house." The worry in her voice was mounting. "She may be hurt. Alone."

"Now, Katherini," he said, "you calm down, and let me put this call through. That's the quickest way to get help for both you and Maria." He had his hand on the telephone. "Where is that house?"

"You will tell your friends where to go and find her?"

"That's why I'm asking for the address," he said, concentrating on patience.

"It's in the Plaka."

That was the last place he had expected to hear. He said, unable to conceal his surprise, "Your aunt has a house down in the Plaka?"

"It isn't her house. That's what she always does. In New York, in Mexico City."

"Always does what?"

"She gets a friend to lease a house. Then she borrows it. This one, in Athens, is in Kriton Street. It is all—all made like new. I don't know the number. But it is big, and it is painted in the color of rich cream. And the shutters are of chocolate brown. There is a garden at the side, and a high white wall."

"And a door with steps in front and carved decorations overhead?" he asked quickly.

"You know it?" Her eyes widened. "Then you can find Maria and—"

"Who was the man who left there, tonight, around eight o'clock?" His excitement had died away, leaving only the chill of unpleasant realization.

She wouldn't admit she didn't know. "Boris?" she asked.

"No. It wasn't the little Bulgarian. It wasn't Nikos, either. And it wasn't the man who drove with Nikos in the green car—what's his name?"

"Andreas. It wasn't Andreas?"

"No. Who?" He waited for her to say the name and wished he were five thousand miles away, back in New York.

"Then it was Metsos. He is dark, thin, quite tall. Very serious. Very important."

And so were a thousand men. "Have you ever heard the name of Christophorou?"

"And who is he?" she asked. "If it were not Nikos, not Boris, not Andreas, then it was Metsos—Metsos Drakon. He used to visit my aunt in Syria. Long long ago, during the war, she knew him well. Then, his code name was Odysseus, my aunt was Elektra, and Nikos was Sideros. They use these names still, among themselves."

"Then they are all old friends?"

"They have always worked together. My aunt was a courier in the war —she carried messages from Athens into the mountains. That was before she was married." Katherini paused. Then she said proudly, "Do you know how dangerous it was to be a courier? My aunt was a very great heroine, a patriot, during the war against the Nazis."

Strang looked at the girl. "I'm sure she was," he said slowly. But had she fought so well before June, 1941, and the invasion of Russia? That was the date no one should forget when they talked of heroes and heroines and staunch allies. Before June, 1941, it had been an imperialist war. After that, a holy crusade. So how did one measure such a patriot? The kind of patriot who needed clearance orders from a foreign power before he decided he could fight for his country?

"I do not like the way you said that," she said angrily. "Women can be as brave as men. Braver. The world would have died long ago if men had to produce the children."

"No doubt about it," he told her with a grin. "Now let's get back to Kriton Street. In whose name was the house rented for your aunt?"

Cecilia and Tommy were coming back into the room with a loaded tray.

"Evgenia Vasilika." Katherini's indignation had subsided. She added, almost listlessly, "She came to Nauplion to meet my aunt."

"*That* woman!" Tommy burst out. He put the heavy tray down, to let him concentrate on Evgenia Vasilika. "That woman is a friend of your aunt's?" A raw nerve end had been touched: now, he was quite prepared to believe the worst about such an aunt. He looked at Katherini with evident sympathy.

Strang said to Cecilia, "Would you get Katherini to calm down and eat something? She won't listen to me." He walked back to the telephone.

Katherini was watching him. "You tell them about Maria?" she asked sharply.

Strang looked at her. "Yes," he said, and picked up the receiver.

"I see what you mean," Cecilia murmured, and lifted two cups of steaming brown liquid. At that moment, the sound of a car came gently humming into the room from the quiet street. The engine was easing to a careful halt. Too careful. Strang moved swiftly. He jammed the receiver back on the telephone, switched off the light, pulled aside the heavy folds of velvet, stepped onto the terrace.

"Oh!" Cecilia said softly, left standing in the dark in a strange room with two scalding cups in her hands. "Ken does choose his moments, doesn't he?"

"Keep very still," Tommy's anxious voice warned her unnecessarily. "And what's all this hullabaloo over a car stopping below my window?"

No one answered him. He fell silent, too, staying close to the lamp, his hand ready to switch on the light as soon as the mad American stopped playing little games. But, "Sh!" he found himself saying as the first drag of the elevator's cables sounded through the end wall of the room. Can I really be taking this seriously? Tommy wondered. Certainly he found he was listening carefully. "Someone for Drakon, this time," he announced cheerfully, and then stared at the sofa in sudden amazement as he heard a terrifying, small, half-strangled cry of fear.

SIXTEEN

"Now what did I do?" Tommy was demanding, switching on the light quickly as Strang stepped back into the room, closed the door, and pulled the curtains together. "I only said that was someone for Drakon, this time." He looked in amazement at the frightened Katherini. "At least, I'm pretty sure the lift traveled no farther than the first floor. Really, Strang, you are making me behave as oddly as you. Counting lift stops!" He humphed with pretended indignation and handed a glass of Scotch and water to Strang. "Have your drink and calm down, my dear fellow. Let us all calm down." He looked at Katherini, and nodded approvingly as Cecilia took charge of that situation.

Katherini said accusingly to Strang, "Drakon lives here? And you didn't tell me!"

"Let's eat and drink first," Cecilia coaxed her.

"That's best," Strang said. "Eat first, and then we'll talk." He took a large gulp of Scotch. He needed it. He said to Tommy in a low voice, "Tell me—isn't the name Metsos an abbreviation for Demetrius?"

Tommy nodded. "Why do you ask?"

"I was just making quite sure." He looked over at Katherini, who, at last, had begun to eat and drink. She would need every ounce of that encouragement. He looked at the telephone, decided to postpone his call to Pringle until he had broken the latest piece of news to Katherini, or otherwise there would be incoherent interruptions to his talk with Pringle. And when he did make a call, interruptions were the last thing he would need. He would have to be quick, calm, concise, and very sure of the facts. They were building up unpleasantly.

"I'm sorry," he said to Tommy. "I thought that all I had to do was to put in a telephone call, prepare Pringle to receive boarders, and then leave you with many many thanks. But the fact is, we're sort of beleaguered here. And I don't know quite how to handle it." He finished his drink, and frowned down at a large stain on the rug. Someone had spilled a bottle of ink there, one time. He pulled his thoughts back into disciplined ranks again. "I recognized the man in that car," he went on, "the one you say went to Metsos Drakon's flat." Then he stopped, looking sharply at Tommy. "The first floor?" Lord, he thought, my brain is turning to cheese: you don't need an elevator to reach the first floor.

"The first floor," Tommy insisted.

"I think—" Cecilia called across the room, and then stopped apologetically. It was difficult to contradict such a patient host. "I'd have called it the second floor," she ended tactfully.

"Oh, you Americans!" Tommy said delightedly, as the truth dawned. "Why don't you call things by their right names? There's the ground floor, then the first floor, then the second, then the third, where you now are. Naturally! I suppose you'd call this the fourth?"

Strang smiled politely. "That's right. Now let's straighten me out. No one has gone to Christophorou's apartment, which is on the first floor, American style. Both visitors have gone to Drakon's, on the second. Right?"

"American style? Right!" Tommy said, still diverted. "And so we return Michalopoulos to his usual state of virtue. I must admit I was rather surprised."

Strang glanced at his watch. "Feeling better?" he asked Katherini. "All right, here's the latest news: I saw Nikos Kladas get out of the car—yes, the same green car that chased you and Petros all over Athens—and come into this house. He is in Drakon's apartment, right now, along with your aunt."

Katherini surprised him. She said, with an interest that chased her fears away, "And the green car?"

"It left. Andreas was driving. I don't think there was anyone else in the car, for Andreas got out to help Nikos Kladas into the hall. That leg must have been badly hurt."

Katherini laughed. "Then Petros escaped. He escaped! They didn't find him. I knew it!" She looked at Strang triumphantly.

"You were right and I was wrong," he said, thinking, as he watched her, that there was nothing like two thick slabs of butter-coated bread to soothe raw nerves. But he wished he didn't always get a feeling of some underbattle of the sexes between that girl and him. All right, all right: so men were stupid oafs, bumbling braggarts. Who had taught her to dislike men so much? Men? Or her aunt? "And now—if you'll go on eating?" He picked up the telephone. Cecilia had laughed, and perhaps that cheered him up. Or perhaps it was the knowledge that Petros had managed to evade the great Nikos. One thing was quite certain: Nikos wouldn't be here if Petros had been caught. Katherini was right about that. He waited impatiently for Pringle to answer at his end.

"See—you *are* safe here," Cecilia was reassuring Katherini. "They think you are with Petros. And now they'll be scared—they'll think you and Petros are both in some police station, talking a hundred and twenty words to the minute."

I wish that were so, Strang thought; that would have solved a lot of problems, but we had Miss Katherini's tangled loyalties to treat lightly. Still, we've managed one thing: somehow, in our stumbling, improvising way, we have sent Madame Duval into temporary hiding; the house on Kriton Street is no longer so safe. That's why she came here. And now Nikos, too. They are off balance. They've got to decide what to do next, if Petros and Katherini can't be found. They don't know how catastrophic, or how negligible, Katherini's escape may be for them. And in spite of the nagging anxiety of this long wait by the telephone, Strang's spirits began to lift. Good for old Petros, he thought with sudden and intense gratitude.

At last, Pringle's receiver was lifted, and Pringle's voice came through, brusque, impatient. "Later—" Pringle cut him short. "I'm busy right now. Got someone here. See you tomorrow."

"Is that Christophorou with you?"

"No. He left ten minutes ago. He's probably—"

"Good! Now listen—"

"I can't. Not right now." Pringle dropped his voice. "The Colonel is here."

"The rows of medals I met last night? Is he still dragging his feet?"

"Far from it. I underestimated that situation, I'm glad to say."

"So did someone else, I think."

"What are you getting at?"

"I have urgent news for the Colonel. Better listen and pass it on."

"About what?"

"The conspiracy."

There was a silence more explicit than words. Then Pringle's voice said sharply, "Shut up, you damn fool! How do you know about that?"

"Through the old confidence game. He tells me all; I trust him completely; I hand over the documents. What's more, how could this damn fool get you to listen, unless he mentioned the unmentionable? We are at Tommy's apartment, beleaguered. Yes, Tommy's. Miss Hillard is with me. And a girl who can tell you a lot about the people involved in the unmentionable you-know-what. We're trying to keep her hidden, and alive, until we can bring her around to your place."

"Not here!"

"But—"

"Not here! There's trouble starting up—rumors that I've been interfering in Greek affairs."

"That's nonsense!"

"But dynamite. Christophorou was worried enough by it to come around this evening and tip me off."

"He would."

"What do you mean?" Pringle's voice was very quiet. "That's the third crack you have made this—"

"It's a scare job."

"The Colonel agrees with you. But the embassy won't take it quite so calmly. There is a pretty unpleasant paragraph in a newspaper, tomorrow, that—"

"Who planted it? And why? It's a scare job, I tell you. You have every right to work on Steve's case. He's an American."

"You seem to forget he is dead."

"He isn't. At least, he was alive last night. Katherini Roilos can tell you all about him. Also about Madame Duval and Nikos Kladas, who are in an apartment, right this moment, second floor, this building. Tenant's name is Demetrius Drakon. Also, there is a house on Kriton Street, newly renovated, cream color, brown shutters, white-walled garden. Rented by Evgenia Vasilika for Duval as her headquarters in Athens. Inside that house, you'll find . . ."

"Good God!" Pringle said. "Stay there! Do nothing! I'll call you right back." The line went completely blank.

"Damn," Strang said to the receiver, and replaced it. He looked over at the others ruefully. The girls were talking, close-cosseted. Tommy had picked up a magazine and was concentrating on it with studied politeness. Strang thought, I'll give Pringle exactly three minutes to tell the Colonel all that, and then I'll call back. And, this time, I'll finish what I have to say. What did people do in emergencies before the telephone was invented? Bless Mr. Alexander Graham Bell for solving people's problems so quickly. And then he wondered what problems were being solved downstairs in the Drakon apartment, right now, by the speed of telephone? Whatever we can do, they can do, he reminded himself. Then he resisted this gloomy idea and forced himself to remember that, whatever was happening in that apartment downstairs, they were still off balance.

Katherini had interrupted a long flow of words to Cecilia. She rose, looked at Strang. "Did you tell them about Maria?"

"Not yet. I was cut off. They will call me back." And then, as a look of distress passed over her pale face, he said, "Don't worry, Katherini, I shan't forget. And the other news is good. There is a colonel in Greek Intelligence right now with my friend Pringle. I think we'll see some quick action." He picked up the telephone again, but there was only that old depressing sound of a line already engaged. He replaced the receiver and tried to look cheerful, for Katherini was still watching him. "The Colonel is working on that, right now," he told her. "This waiting will soon be over."

She said slowly, "And after they listen to me? What then?" She didn't wait for his answer. She turned back to Cecilia, sat down beside her.

Cecilia said gently, "Don't worry, Katherini. We'll see that . . ."

"Don't worry?" It was the first time that Katherini had snapped at Cecilia. "Everyone keeps saying *don't worry, don't worry!*" She bit her lip, regained control. "Let me talk some more. Then I forget to worry."

Cecilia said, "Are you sure you want to—"

"Yes." Katherini sat down, and began talking, almost in a whisper.

Tommy came forward, the magazine open in his hands. "So we're locked out, are we?" he asked, with a humorous glint in his eyes as he glanced briefly at the two girls on the sofa. "All right, let's adjourn to the smoking room." He drew Strang over toward his armchair. "Pull in a chair and make yourself comfortable. If Pringle is ringing you here, it would be wiser simply to wait; his telephone may be needed, at this moment. You've probably stirred up quite a little hornet's nest with that call of yours. Oh, yes, indeed, I was listening. But it's always important to appear not to listen. A conspiracy, you said. How interesting—"

Strang stopped looking at the telephone, and took a chair opposite Tommy.

"Now this is very Greek," Tommy said genially. "Men here; women there." He waited. The word "conspiracy" was still in his eyes.

"I'll have to disappoint you, at the moment," Strang said. "But I'll promise one thing: as soon as I can, and when I can—" he paused.

"You'll tell me the whole story?" Tommy was not quite believing.

"As much as I know of it. That's possibly very little."

Tommy glanced at him in surprise, his disbelief now evident.

"Look—" Strang said, "I'm only an architect who is interested in Greek temples."

Tommy looked. His sharp eyes studied the American. Then he smiled. "I've seen stranger incidents than this. During the German occupation, and in the Communist troubles afterward—" He broke off, remembering. "Yes, most of us have strange stories to tell, many of them incomplete, fantastic, with at least five explanations. I sometimes think that normal, everyday life is only a delusion. We walk on a thin crust of earth which we call peace; and every now and again we can hear a rumble below our feet; and sometimes the crust splits and we see that, underneath, there is a glowing inferno ready to erupt. Sometimes it does, sometimes it doesn't, but it is always there." He glanced over at Katherini, who was still talking intently to Cecilia. His tone changed. "At least she *is* calmer now. It's a very difficult thing, you know, to be a refugee. At first, all you want to do is to escape. Once you have escaped, you start to think about the friends who didn't escape. And you're torn between staying and returning, and you don't know what to do. There's a very bad hour, indeed, when you ask yourself the question she asked tonight. You noticed it?"

Strang nodded. *What then?* "And I couldn't answer it."

"Just as well. No one can answer it for any refugee. It is a cruel question. You ask it when you realize that escape is not enough. You have exchanged one set of problems for another, that is all. Are you brave enough to start all over again? That's the real question. And a refugee has to answer that for himself." He shook his head, sadly.

"I think," Strang said, groping tactfully for the right words, "that it would be best for everyone if you didn't mention the fact that we brought Katherini here tonight. Not even to a very close friend, like Aleco Christophorou."

"I shouldn't dream of discussing this with anyone," Tommy said stiltedly. He was hurt at the unnecessary suggestion.

"I didn't mean a discussion," Strang said hastily. "What I had in mind was more of a—well, a neighborly little chat in the front hall, one morning."

"I hardly ever see Aleco."

"I thought he was a friend."

A shadow drifted over Tommy's brow. "He was one of the brightest pupils I ever had."

"How long did he hold his professorship?"

"Professorship?"

"Professor of Law at Athens University, wasn't he?"

"Where on earth did you pick up that idea?" Tommy had recovered his equanimity as Strang looked completely dumfounded. "No, he never was given any appointment at the University, although I think he would have liked one. It was a bit of a disappointment, I gather. But he *would* spread his talents around as if they were butter. I warned him repeatedly when he was a boy. He never would listen to anyone, though." Tommy sighed. "First, he was going to be an archaeologist. Then he went to Oxford and read history. Then to the Sorbonne. Then to Geneva and political science. Then back to Athens—for law. We all thought he was settled in a career, at last. But he had that disappointment, and then he went off to fight in the war. He did very well in it, I hear. He's extraordinarily brave, you know."

"And after that?"

"Politics. He made some excellent speeches, stood for election to parliament, and lost. I rather think the voters couldn't take an existentialist quite seriously. Oh, yes, that had become his postwar enthusiasm." Tommy shook his head. "Life to most Greeks may be either tragic or comic or a mixture of both; but one thing it never is—and that is, meaningless. They would never have survived if they had believed that."

"And since then?"

"I've rather lost track of him. Traveled a good deal, I heard. Now, he is a free-lance journalist, writes very superior articles on international politics. If he doesn't watch out, he will end as a pundit." Tommy laughed. "Careers are extraordinary things. So much wasted—then so much retrieved, unexpectedly."

So much wasted? Strang wondered about that. Or had everything contributed its share to the complete education of Aleco Christophorou? "What about his family?" Strang asked. "How do they feel about all this?"

Tommy said, "Now there's one situation that *is* completely meaningless." He pushed himself out of his comfortable chair. "Let me give you another drink, Strang." Then he looked at the magazine still lying open on his table. "Dear me! I meant to show you where I first heard about you." He pointed to a column of print, took Strang's glass, and walked across to his cupboard.

The opened page seemed to deal with notes on art and music, each given a separate paragraph under its own headline. But at this hour of the morning, it was indeed all Greek to Strang.

"Can you understand it, or shall I translate?" Tommy called over his shoulder.

"Which paragraph is it?"

"The one beginning 'Famous Greek photographer commissioned by *Perspective*, renowned American magazine.' Clumsy, but appropriately exuberant. You are mentioned, too, in the last line. But you aren't a Greek."

"Neither is Steve Kladas, technically," Strang said, trying to cover his sudden alarm. "*Perspective's* publicity department seems to have been supplying us with a lot of advance billing. When was this published?"

"January, I think."

January it was.

"You look thoughtful," Tommy said, handing him his drink.

"I am," Strang said grimly. So Steve's arrival in Greece had been announced before he left New York. Christophorou could have heard about it even before he went visiting Steve's sister in Sparta. Even before Christophorou got my letter, Strang thought, he probably knew all about the *Perspective* job. "Is this magazine read much?"

"A great deal."

"And talked about?"

"That's why it is read! What would one do for conversation if one couldn't repeat what one reads? I borrow it steadily from Christophorou—Aleco's father, that is. I visit the family every week, you know. The father hasn't been at all well for some years now; confined to his room, most depressing."

Strang put down the magazine. "Don't you ever meet Aleco there?"

Tommy's face changed. A blank mask stared back at Strang. "Not since the war." He sat down in his chair again. "He never visits his family. They never talk of him."

"They forward letters to him."

"You would scarcely expect them to burn them."

Strang looked startled.

"I told you it was a strange situation. I never can discuss Aleco with his father, of course. But one of his sisters did try to explain things to me. Seemingly, at the start of the civil war in Athens, Aleco warned his father that hostages would be taken into the mountains if the Communists had to retreat. His father wouldn't believe him. The family stayed in Athens. Then, at the end, they were seized as hostages and marched toward the mountains. But I told you about that, didn't I?"

How, wondered Strang, could such a warning be given? "Surely, he can't blame his father for staying in Athens. After all, that forced march was a surprise move."

"It was also an idiotic, cruel, and completely bankrupt piece of blackmail," Tommy said angrily, too absorbed in his own thoughts to catch Strang's reasoning. "Anyhow, there's the situation in the Christophorou family. Aleco does blame his father, for he has never seen his father since."

"And his father?"

"Quite silent."

Because he never could solve the problem of how his son had been able to give such a warning? Or had the old man solved it and, out of pride, kept silent? No, no, Strang told himself quickly, you are reading too much into that incident. All it proves is that Christophorou always did keep a close ear to the ground, a very close ear.

"I seem to have depressed you," Tommy said, wondering.

Strang stared at the drink in his hand and finished it quickly. "What the hell is keeping Pringle?" he asked angrily, and went over to the telephone again.

This time, the line was not engaged. There was a short wait, though. Then a woman's voice answered. It was American, polite but impersonal, and smothered with sleep.

"Mrs. Pringle? Is your husband there? This is Kenneth Strang." But he could sense the answer before he heard it.

"I'm sorry. He left. With Colonel Zafiris."

"Where can they be reached, do you know?"

"Haven't the faintest. Sorry."

"So am I. Sorry for waking you, too. Good night." He put down the receiver quickly. "No luck," he said to Tommy. "You are still stuck with us, I'm afraid. All we can do is wait." He glanced over at the sofa. Katherini had finished her slow, quiet monologue. She looked at him. "It won't take long now," he reassured her, and felt relieved when she nodded calmly. He noticed Cecilia had been writing something down in that notebook she carried in her bag. What's going on? he wondered, took a step toward her, and then was halted by Tommy's voice.

"Pringle has left his apartment?"

"Yes."

"Well, he will telephone you whenever he reaches wherever he is going. It must have been urgent."

"Yes." Urgent enough to push Pringle farther into the Greek political maze. Poor old Pringle, trying to keep a balance between helping and interfering. It was a slender line to walk.

"Waiting is always so difficult," Tommy tried tactfully. "Let us comfort ourselves that we also serve. Please don't be alarmed if I fall asleep around three o'clock. I always do."

"We'll be out of here long before then," Strang said determinedly. Still thinking of Pringle and his problems, he asked, "You know George Ottway, don't you? Would you pass on a warning to him?" He looked around sharply, as Katherini rose and walked into the little hall. The bathroom door opened and closed. Cecilia was studying the book on her lap. "Anything wrong?" he asked. She looked up and shook her head reassuringly.

"A warning for Ottway?" Tommy was startled enough to drop all comfortable drowsiness. He sat bolt upright, his amiable face contorted between a banished yawn and growing surprise.

"He could be facing some very nasty trouble. I've got a feeling that anyone who seems dangerous to this conspiracy is being eliminated. Neutralized, as it were. There's an attempt to get Pringle moved out of Greece, for instance. The same thing could happen to Ottway."

"Why?"

"Because he could identify a man called Nikos Kladas, whom he knew as Sideros during the war."

"Ottway's a fairly hard-bitten type, quite capable of taking care of himself."

"But he's vulnerable." Strang thought of Caroline Ottway.

"How?"

"He had a fairly close friendship with Nikos, back in the mountains."

"Back in the mountains," Tommy said a little stiffly, "close friendships were common. There is such a thing as comradeship—"

"I know, I know. Nikos was nineteen, perhaps less. A hero-worshiper, probably. The closer-than-glue type. Difficult to shake off. Until he transferred his admiration to Ares, and became one of his select little group. You have heard of Ares?"

Tommy had. He recovered himself. "But Ottway avoided Ares and his group of sadists like the plague. He admires soldiers, but he has nothing but contempt for killers. I have heard him on the subject of Ares. He certainly wouldn't even exchange two sentences with this Nikos, once he became attached to Ares."

"I'm sure that's all true, too. But his past friendship could be twisted."

"How?" Tommy was short, both in manner and voice. But his eyes showed he clearly understood.

"I heard the first innuendoes, yesterday."

"Preposterous!"

"Will you warn Ottway?"

"You've been talking to the wrong kind of people, Strang."

"That's very possible," Strang agreed wryly.

"Who invented such a piece of nonsense?" Tommy demanded indignantly.

It took something of an effort to refrain from saying that Christophorou had at least passed on that particular piece of nonsense, even if he hadn't invented it. "The rumor may be spread, that's our worry," Strang said patiently. "If Ottway has to leave Athens because of rumors he can't pretend to ignore—"

"Sh!" said Tommy, glancing nervously at Cecilia, who had risen and was coming over toward them.

"Will you warn Ottway?" Strang insisted. "Put him on his guard, at least? For instance, his wife seems to trust a man called Yorghis, who has been giving her Greek lessons pretty openly. Yorghis will soon be visiting the Ottways' new apartment."

"Really—what have you against Yorghis?"

"I don't trust him."

"That is hardly sufficient reason—" Tommy began, but this time Cecilia did contradict him.

"Ken is right, you know," she said gently. "I've just been hearing all about Yorghis. Evgenia Vasilika hired him to drive to Nauplion yesterday morning. Somewhere near there, he picked up Madame Duval and drove her back to Athens. How did she get off her yacht without being noticed? Quite simple. The yacht arrived before dawn; Madame Duval was taken ashore in the darkness to a lonely inlet."

"Good heavens!" Tommy said.

Cecilia's quiet voice changed. "How can people live like that?" she asked angrily. "Lies, deceit, treason, treachery—how can they bear it?"

Strang said, "Katherini told you everything?"

"Just about."

"She's crazy!" But why, he wondered worriedly, why did she talk?

"No, she isn't. She's incredibly realistic. Even spelled out the names for me." Cecilia handed over her notebook to Strang. "And it *is* safer to share such information."

"Safer for whom?" Strang asked angrily. "Five hours ago you knew nothing at all, and now—"

"It's incredible, the ignorance we can live in," Cecilia admitted.

"You're crazier than she is," he told her. He examined the list of names and places and dates. The style was cryptic, but decipherable. The information, in six well-filled pages, was considerable. Why did Katherini do this? he wondered again. "See if she is all right," he told Cecilia, quickly. And quickly, too, he ripped out the six pages.

"Don't destroy—"

"No. I'm keeping them." Not you, my sweet, crazy darling. "Do I go into that bathroom, or do you?" he threw the notebook down on Tommy's table, and jammed the dangerous papers into his pocket. Cecilia was already in the hall.

"Do you think the girl—?" Tommy was too alarmed to finish his sudden thought. He was on his feet, following Strang into the hall, his face white at the notion of suicide.

But there was no one in the bathroom. In the kitchen, they found the back door unbolted and unchained.

"Kriton Street!" Cecilia said. "Can she have gone to help Maria?"

"That's just the kind of wild idea she'd have," Strang said. He opened the door and listened. No sound of footsteps, of movement. He closed the door so that he could talk. "I'm going down to have a look. What's the geography, Tommy?"

"There's a short corridor in the basement. At one end, there's a flight up to the front hall. At the other, a door to a small back patch of ground, surrounded by walls."

"Any door or gate there?"

"An old iron gate, high. Never used. Padlocked and chained. I remember it well: I had to climb over it when the Germans were coming in by the front entrance."

"What's outside the gate?"

"A rabbit warren of concrete and wood. But she'll never climb over that gate. It's ten feet high or more. I had a rope, hidden for such an emergency. Otherwise, I could never have managed it. As it was, I nearly broke my leg on the other side of the gate."

"And how did you get out of the rabbit warren?"

"By guess and by God," Tommy said. "There were several exits then. But that was seventeen years ago. They may be closed now—all this rebuilding, since the war, you know."

"Chain this door," Strang told him. "I'll knock three times when I get back." He nodded reassuringly to Cecilia and stepped outside, pulling the door closed behind him to end any argument.

Quietly, he ran down the staircase, a monotonous repetition, between bare yellow walls, of flight and landing, flight and landing; a thing of little beauty but a temporary joy, for the solid stone stairs had no creak to them. The third floor, he noted, had a high ventilation window in its kitchen, just like Tommy's, except that Mr. Louizis Michalopoulos, dreaming of past triumphs in the wool market, had left his window open on its hinge. It would be too much to expect that Mr. Demetrius Drakon would be as generous.

He was not. When Strang reached the second floor, he found the same type of window, but this one was covered by iron bars. The light in Drakon's kitchen was on. But there was no sound from the apartment. The door, he noticed as he passed quickly, was the same as Tommy's: no outside keyhole to be picklocked, everything held fast by interior bolts and chains.

Quickly, too, he passed the back of Christophorou's apartment on the first floor. It was blacked out, blankly silent. And then there was only a short flight of steps to the basement corridor and the door leading out into the yard. At the other end of the corridor was another flight of stairs, leading up into the main hall. From the caretaker's door, a zone of sleeping respectability, came a softly muted mezzosoprano snore, steadily rhythmical.

The door into the yard was unlocked. He opened it carefully, but there was no creak in its hinges. A well-oiled door, he decided, his surprise deepening. In the cold darkness, broken by clouded moonlight, he saw a little stretch of bare earth, bounded by a high wall and a forest of buildings. The gate stood opposite him. He picked his way past a coil of rusted chicken wire, battered crates, a small hen coop. The iron gate's padlock was open, its rusty chain hung loose. He pushed the gate; it swung open a couple of inches, quite soundlessly. Someone had been busy with his little oilcan around here.

He pulled the gate back into position, retreated back inside the house. Katherini had had the most fantastic luck, he thought, as he closed the door carefully behind him. That was, he added, if she had used the back exit. But she might have been in too much of a hurry to waste time in exploring an unknown yard; she might have come running down the service staircase and headed straight for the front hall, a territory she at least knew. In which case, he would have quite a sprint ahead of him, trying to catch up. Or, perhaps, he wouldn't; perhaps he would be too thankful to see that she had managed to escape out of this house alive. For that, he admitted as he walked quietly past the caretaker's door and then started up the short flight of stairs that led to the front hall, had been the fear that had sent him rushing down from Tommy's apartment, the fear that one of Madame Duval's thugs had been guarding the service stairs and that Katherini had been caught. But Drakon's apartment had been peaceful: no sound of questioning, of forced answers, of violence. Peace and unsuspicion everywhere, thank God.

And then, just as he reached the main hall, two men stepped out from the wall on either side of him and seized his wrists in an iron grip.

SEVENTEEN

Strang's first instinct was to struggle, free himself, hit out, run. But as he looked at the grave faces of the two compact men and saw the dark mistrust in their quick, observant eyes, he hesitated. They were neither Boris nor Andreas. And if they had been guarding Madame Duval, they wouldn't be holding him by the wrists. By this time, he ought to have been cracked over his skull with that handy-looking revolver which the smaller of the men had produced in a businesslike way. "And who are you?" the small man asked now. The tone was inimical, but the man was curious, at least.

That decided Strang. Thugs did not ask questions. These men might not be dressed in police uniform, but they had the confidence of those who acted on the side of the law. He identified himself quickly. "Do you speak English?" he added urgently. He had a feeling that his Greek might not be adequate enough for this kind of situation.

The small man nodded. He glanced at the front door, where two other men were entering, and nodded again, this time approvingly. "Search him," he said to his companion.

"Did a girl come this way in the last ten or fifteen minutes?" Strang asked, ignoring the adept hands that slapped his pockets and found them flat enough.

"A girl?" The man's sharp eyes were wary but not astonished. He was a neat little man with neat expressions; dark of hair, eyes, mustache, and suit; as sparing of movement as he was with words.

"I sent a message—" Strang paused. He glanced across the hall at Christophorou's door, and wondered for a split second if Christophorou had returned home and could hear them. He dropped his voice almost to a whisper. "Then she must have gone out through the back gate." The searching hands were at his waist, at his ribs. He resisted the impulse to tell their owner that he never did believe in shoulder holsters. The searcher found his wallet and was studying his driver's license. He seemed satisfied, for he slipped the wallet back in place.

"The gate?" the small man asked, too carefully.

"There is a gate from the yard at the back of the house." And I don't carry a knife strapped to my leg, either, he refrained from telling the man with the practiced hand, who was insisting on completing his search. The man—even if he didn't speak English could certainly understand it, for his hand froze on Strang's ankle—looked up quickly.

The other man let go of Strang's wrist. He gestured down the staircase to the corridor. "Show me this gate," he said. "You first!"

Strang started down the stairs, trying to rub some of the paralysis out of his wrist. There was no use losing his temper; he was at this moment, quite frankly, a nuisance of an amateur who was complicating a professional man's difficult job. He said, "The girl ran away. I came down from the top floor to see if I could find any—"

"Sh!" the man silenced him abruptly. They both halted. There was the sound of a light footstep. From the door at the end of the corridor, there came a decided click, as if a heavy key had been turned too quickly in its lock. The Greek shoved Strang aside and leaped down into the corridor and raced toward the back door. It was locked.

Strang tried the handle for himself. He looked at the Greek, and the Greek looked at him. Outside, in the small courtyard, there was only the silence of stealth. They heard the brief rattle of an iron chain, abruptly stilled. "That," said Strang, "was someone locking the gate." Now, there was no sound at all except the sudden crackle of a child's night cough.

The Greek moved quickly to the caretaker's door and thumped hard on it. Then he raced back along the corridor, called sharply up to the hall, set a flurry of footsteps in motion and a quick fluster of low voices in canon-like echo. He came running back to the caretaker's door and crashed his fist impatiently on its panel again. "Open, open!" he kept repeating. Over his shoulder, he asked, "That gate outside—where does it lead?"

"I don't know. Perhaps to the next street."

"I have sent two men to look there." He was still worried, and angry. "All that time wasted—with you!" he said bitterly, as the caretaker's door opened, and a woman stood, frightened, wary, uncertain, her eyes still puffed with sleep. She screamed. The whimpering child in the room behind her burst into a terrified yell. The woman screamed again.

That's all we needed, thought Strang. He looked up the service staircase, listening for any sound of a door being opened. But he could hear nothing. The little man had quieted the woman and got the back-door key. Strang said, "There was only one pair of footsteps, wasn't there?" But the Greek was already in the yard, examining the gate. Strang waited anxiously, watching the staircase, wondering who would come down first —Duval or Nikos Kladas, feeling naked with only his two bare hands to cope with that problem, wishing that he had borrowed Tommy's stick at least, willing the Greek to come back from the gate with that revolver, which had become a most comforting object. But when the man did return, the look of deepened suspicion on his hard-set face was far from comforting.

"Look—" began Strang, and stopped. Explanations might only confuse everything still more. He asked, "Why haven't they come down? They must have heard the woman's scream."

"We shall wait here," the man told him. He looked at his revolver, then at the staircase.

I suppose that makes sense, Strang thought. Two men had been sent to the other street; one man left to guard the front hall, one man here alone with an unarmed nuisance of a foreigner: that wasn't much of a boarding party to force its way into a barricaded apartment. But wait for how long, wait for what?

Behind him, he heard the Greek question the woman. And her answers were exactly as one might expect: she had the only key for the door to the yard, she kept it in her kitchen, it was always there unless she was using the yard; the gate was always locked; she had a key for that, too, but no one else had these keys; why should they?

Why should they, indeed? Strang thought wryly. This whole setup was perfect for anyone leading a double life, for a conspirator who needed an unobtrusive exit in that emergency for which all conspirators must plan.

"Your child is crying," the Greek told the woman severely. "Why do you stay here? Go inside. Lock the door. Let no one enter. Keep out of the way!"

Strang said, "I'm going upstairs. You'll find me in the Englishman's apartment on the top—"

"You will wait here," the man told him, and he meant it. And then, as he heard the sound of cars from the front of the house and quick footsteps entering the hall above him, he relaxed a little. "Now," he said, "you can lead the way. I shall follow."

Strang heard him stop at Christophorou's door. He was studying it curiously. "No lock?" he said softly, almost to himself. He reached out and turned the handle gently. But the door was bolted from within. He seemed puzzled. This man is no fool, Strang thought; whoever came down the staircase and slipped into the yard must have left an open door behind him. It was so obvious the minute the Greek made his quiet check, but it was the kind of thing I'd have remembered to do by the time I reached Tommy's doorway. And then he thought, Was that a routine check or was there any particular interest in Christophorou?

The Greek signaled to him to wait. Behind them, four men were ascending the staircase quickly. For a moment, Strang stared in amazement at Colonel Zafiris, no less, who was leading the way. Is this usual? he wondered in surprise, and then found his answer in the look of stupefaction that showed on his companion's face for a moment, to be quickly covered by a slightly nervous smile. He began explaining the series of small disasters in a quick, low voice. (He didn't blame himself. But he didn't blame Strang, either. Strang was impressed.)

"Enough, Elias, enough!" The Colonel waved him into silence, and pointed up the stairs toward the next floor. He wasted no time, either, on greeting Strang. A brief nod, a quick sharp look, and his eyes were turned to Christophorou's door as he passed it. He took a decided grip on its handle and tested it for himself. And that, Strang decided as he noted the Colonel's pursed lips and drawn brow, had not been a merely routine test. Then the Colonel was ascending the staircase. Strang had to stretch his legs to keep up with him. It was surprising that a man so solidly built and compact in shape could move so quickly, so lightly.

Nothing seemed to have changed at Drakon's apartment. The light still shone through the barred kitchen window. The silence was complete.

The Colonel gestured to the window, and one of his men was given a hoist up to its level. But he must have seen and heard nothing, for the expression on his face as he looked around at the Colonel was blank. They have gone, the woman Duval and Nikos have gone, Strang thought worriedly; they slipped through that confounded gate while I sat upstairs and waited for a telephone call. And then Drakon went out, after them, carefully locking door and gate behind him. They've gone, that's certain; there is no one in there. Strang looked at the Colonel and wondered how this volcano would erupt when he heard the witness had vanished as well. He watched the men fan out on either side of the door, while one of them tried its handle gently. The door was not bolted. It moved a cautious inch. The gap widened to six inches. The door wasn't chained, either. The men looked at the Colonel. And at that moment the silence was cracked by the sharp clack of loose slippers overhead.

Strang looked upward. An elderly man, sparse hair fuzzed into a gray mat above a long and doleful yellowed face, his hands clutching his dressing gown around him, peered down. "Did a woman scream?" he asked Strang. His eyes traveled to the group of men around the door. His toothless gums gaped. He turned and scuttered back to his own apartment. "Police!" he was screaming in a piercing falsetto. "Police! Get the police!" His door rattled shut. Silence returned.

Well, thought Strang, we can now all break into a song and dance. Anyone inside, if there is anyone there, has certainly been fully briefed on this situation by now. "Civilians are always so helpful," he said very quietly. The Colonel heaved a deep sigh, walked briskly over to the door as he unbuttoned the flap of his gun holster, kicked the six-inch gap into a wide open sweep and drew sharply aside for a few moments. Strang counted silently, in the photographer's formula: one bloody second, two bloody seconds, three bloody seconds, four—and the Colonel was in the kitchen. Impatient fellow, Strang thought, or very brave. Or a man with all his hunches in good working order. For the Colonel had been right: there was no resistance. And Strang had been wrong: the apartment was not empty.

Nikos Kladas was lying in the hall, spread-eagled and stiff, face twisted sideways, mouth open in a last protest, a neat hole between his eyes. Madame Duval, in the sitting room, was resting permanently in a high-backed chair. One side of her face was unrecognizable. There was a small revolver at her feet, dropped—it could have been—from the hand that hung limply by her side.

Strang turned away.

"Can you name them?" the Colonel asked.

"Madame Étienne Duval. Nikos Kladas. So Duval's niece said, at least."

"And what is her name?"

"Katherini Roilos."

The Colonel was surprised enough to say "Ah!" Then his eyes became expressionless again. "Is she the witness you have upstairs?"

"She was. She left."

"You let her go?" There was the hint of real anger in the careful voice.

"She slipped out by the back door. That is why your men found me downstairs. I thought she might still be in the building, or in the street outside."

The Colonel took a deep breath. "So you let her escape," he said. He sounded sad now, and fatalistic, as if so many disappointments had come his way that one more was not too hard to bear.

"She wasn't a prisoner. She could have walked out any time. She didn't have to leave like that." Strang's own anger was showing. He muzzled it. "At least, they didn't get her." He looked at Nikos Kladas. "Katherini said he was also known as Sideros. And Duval used the name of Elektra. The man Drakon was known as Odysseus. They all worked with Ares, during the war."

The Colonel was quite impassive. It would be impossible for him not to recognize the name of Ares, Strang thought; everyone, even people like Tommy, knew that name. So it was also possible that he recognized the other aliases, too. Strang searched in his pocket and drew out the sheets of paper from Cecilia's notebook. "You'll find all that, and more, written down here."

The Colonel took the sheets of paper. "Your handwriting?"

And Strang, who hoped he had managed very neatly to keep Cecilia's name out of all this, looked at him and said, "No."

"Whose writing?"

"Miss Hillard's."

"Ah!" The Colonel seemed to know about Cecilia. He frowned at her notes. "Don't worry," he said, "we shall arrange for someone to guard her, of course."

Strang looked at him. "Thank you," he said very quietly. "Is it necessary to ask her any questions?" He glanced at his watch. "I'd like to get Miss Hillard back to the Grande Bretagne. She is dropping with exhaustion. If you need me, I'll come back and fill you in on any of these details." He pointed to the notes in the Colonel's hand, tried to conceal his own fatigue.

The Colonel studied the American's face. "I have enough to work on, tonight, both here and at my office." He gave his first smile. "Do not be so depressed, Mr. Strang. We may know more than you think we do." His brown eyes were bland, friendly, sympathetic. "Who told you about the conspiracy?" he asked.

"Christoph—" Strang began. He took a deep breath. "He was explaining the urgency of the situation to me. That's how I heard. No details. Or very few. Just enough to let me know that—" he paused again—"everything was very urgent," he ended lamely.

The Colonel's eyes showed a brief gleam of sardonic humor. "Indeed it is," he murmured.

Strang glanced at the men, hands carefully gloved, who were quickly searching the room with complete absorption. They had opened every drawer and closet, examined every book shelf, picture frame, chair. Not that there was so much to search; the apartment was a stilted place, barely furnished, characterless. The only thing that didn't attract any attention, now that pockets had been examined, was the two bodies.

The Colonel said, as if he had been following Strang's thoughts, "They are police business, now."

"Double murder," Strang risked guessing.

A heavy dark eyebrow was raised. "Execution," the grave voice corrected him.

Strang hid his surprise. "Drakon must be pretty desperate if he'd kill them right here, in his own special hideaway."

"It might be the only place where he could get them together without any suspicion of danger. They obviously expected nothing." He glanced down at the wrist of Nikos Kladas's outstretched arm. "He didn't even have time to throw that knife." It was true; the hilt of a knife had been slipped out of Nikos's cuff, but not quickly enough. "This is all very far removed from your world, is it not, Mr. Strang?" the Colonel asked, watching the American's amazement. "I think you should return to it. Your friends will be anxious. By this time, Mr. Pringle will have joined them." He paused, and then said, "Do not worry so much about these two. They would never have worried about you. We have been spared much trouble. If they had come to trial, there would have been organized protests; and they would have been described as great patriots during the Nazi war. Their guilt would have been covered in a cloud of doubt, so that those who had proof of their treason would have been made to look tyrants. It is strange, is it not, that the real patriots of the war, who were killed by these two and their friends, should so seldom be remembered? I had a friend. Colonel Psarros. He was murdered by them. On Mount Parnassos." The Colonel looked down at Nikos Kladas. "There we have complete justice: the traitor betrayed, the murderer murdered." He seemed to have forgotten Strang.

A car drew up outside the house.

"That is the police coming to take charge," the Colonel said, steering Strang decisively toward the kitchen door. "Come and see me tomorrow at ten o'clock. Elias will bring you. He will meet you in your hotel lobby, fifteen minutes before." The neat little man who was superintending the search of the apartment, with as much grave concern as he had watched Strang in the basement corridor, looked up briefly, nodded, and concentrated on his job again.

"Ten o'clock," Strang said, and made some quick calculations; with luck, he might get five hours of sleep. Then he remembered the Colonel's work "here and at my office." He halted at the door. "Tell me one thing, Colonel. When do you sleep?"

He left a startled look behind him, and an unexpected smile. Even colonels liked sympathy.

Strang found Tommy's kitchen door wide open, with Cecilia and Tommy at its threshold and Bob Pringle, determinedly nonchalant by contrast, sitting on a corner of the small table. Strang closed the door and bolted it.

"Thank heavens!" Tommy said.

"And about time, too!" said Pringle. "Don't you ever look at your watch, Strang?"

Cecilia said nothing at all. Her face was pale, tense. He took her hand and held it. He asked Tommy, "How long have you had that door open?"

"We thought we heard a woman scream. It wasn't the girl?"

"No."

"Then I arrived," Pringle said, "or they would both have been down there, complicating the Colonel's life still further. What happened?"

"We found the Duval woman and Nikos Kladas in Drakon's place. Both dead."

Pringle's nonchalance vanished. "Murdered?"

"Here—in this house?" Tommy asked, equally aghast. Neither of them could quite believe it. "And the murderer?"

"Slipped out by your back gate."

"This is appalling," Tommy said, "appalling."

"I told you these boys play rough," Strang reminded him gently.

"But who could have done this? Drakon? But the man is never here. The caretaker tells me he travels constantly. He seems to keep that apartment simply to put up friends when they visit Athens."

"Let's move toward a chair," Pringle said, leading the way to the room. "Now, what happened?"

Strang said, "I'll tell you later. I must get Cecilia back to the hotel. Colonel's orders."

"But," Tommy protested, "am I only to hear a little bit of the middle of a story; no beginning and now no end?"

"We'll come back some afternoon and have that cup of tea you promised us."

"How's the Colonel taking all this?" Pringle wanted to know.

"I guess he has been defeated before and come up winning."

Pringle nodded. "And just when everything was going so well," he said thoughtfully. "He had one terrific success tonight. Well, you can't win all the time, I suppose."

"What success?" Strang had found Cecilia's coat, where she had dropped it by the sofa. He began finding the right armholes for her.

"Oh, that's what kept me from calling you back at once. The Colonel got a telephone message just after you spoke to me. It seems there was a burglary over in his office while he was visiting me, a very neat little job. Those photographs were lifted—"

"Steve's?" Strang asked, unbelieving, horrified. "*Steve's?*"

"Now, now—" Pringle said soothingly, "no need for tremors." He looked so unperturbed that Strang's horror changed to amazement. Pringle didn't give him any chance for questions, though. "Good night, Tommy," he said. "I'd better see these two safely back to the Grande Bretagne and justify my existence. Thanks for taking care of them."

It was such a well-mannered good-by under decided control that Tommy could only say, "There's no rush, really. I don't usually go to bed until three o'clock."

"It's nearer four now," Pringle said, took Cecilia's arm, and led her toward the front door.

"Good-by," she called back to Tommy. "We'll come and see you—" She gave him, tired as she was, one of her warmest smiles.

"Don't forget," Tommy said. He seemed a little crestfallen, after all, at the sudden end of this extraordinary visit. "Well—" he said to Strang.

"We shan't forget," Strang promised.

"And"—Tommy's voice dropped to a conspiratorial whisper—"I'll get in touch with Ottway. First thing tomorrow morning. Indeed, yes."

Strang paused at the front door. "You know, if Ottway liked to get in touch with Colonel Zafiris, he could do a lot of good."

"How?"

"He could identify these two bodies, for one thing. Clear up all doubts about them. He knew them, I think, in the old days."

"That doesn't seem too much to ask him."

"It might be asking him to lay his head on the block."

Tommy pursed his lips. "Did you tell Colonel Zafiris to expect him?"

"No. Didn't mention his name."

Tommy nodded approvingly. "No good putting people into difficult situations. Much better to let them decide for themselves."

Pringle was standing by the elevator door, listening to its approaching drone. "Nearly here," he warned Strang. "What are you two whispering about?"

"We're starting a conspiracy of our own," Strang told him. Pringle looked shocked. Tommy laughed delightedly. A good host, thought Strang, should always be presented with something to cheer up his suddenly empty living room. He stepped into the elevator quickly, took Cecilia's arm away from Pringle's charge, and said as they started down, "We'll find police in the hall, no doubt. I'll leave it all to you, Talleyrand."

The distance to the hotel was short, so Pringle drove his ancient Buick around several streets. His mood, away from Tommy, had changed. He was serious, worried. "And so the girl disappeared—" he began, frowning at the sleeping city.

"Now, now—" Strang reminded him, "no need for tremors."

"How?"

"She left a sort of testament behind her."

"You gave it to the Colonel?"

"I have a few brains, if scattered."

"But why did she leave? My God, she may get herself killed."

"Several reasons, probably. There usually are."

Cecilia said softly, "They mount up. They usually do. If only I had had the sense to stop her!"

"How?" asked Strang. "By force? I don't see any of us holding a struggling girl. When a woman makes up her mind, boy—it's made up. But" —he still felt a little aggrieved, not so much as before, but still a little—"she didn't have to sneak out like that. She could have walked out, any time."

"Except her world didn't let people walk out when they felt like it. That was why her brother, and father, too, died on the Megara road."

Pringle looked at Cecilia quickly.

"Keep your eyes straight ahead," Strang advised him. "And her name is Roilos, if that means anything to you, too."

It did. Pringle recovered his poise. "How things come out, and start fitting together! And Steve Kladas—where is he?"

"He's either still a prisoner, in which case he's a dead man; or he's free, and in hiding."

"They'd kill him, *now?*"

"Because of the fact that I handed over an envelope, last night. Until then, they needed Steve alive to find out from him where it was. Now, they know. And they've got the envelope, too." Strang's voice was bitter.

"Hold it, hold it—" Pringle said. "The theft went according to plan."

"It was a trap? They caught the thief?"

Pringle glanced at Cecilia.

"I'm asleep," she told them, her eyes closed.

Pringle said, "It was a trap. The thief is being followed. Also, there was a concealed camera registering every step of his little operation in the Colonel's room."

"But the envelope?"

"Listen, will you? The Colonel had been expecting some general skulduggery. I told you we underestimated him. He had copies made of everything in that envelope—the old negatives carefully printed, blown up. The technicians have been working on that steadily since this morning."

"But why 'since this morning'?"

"That was when his colleagues decided that a lot of 1943 photographs taken of life in a guerrilla camp were of little use in 1959 if Steve Kladas wasn't around to say who the people were and why he had taken their photographs. So, this morning, the Colonel took charge of Steve's envelope. His way of looking at these old photographs was this: they had to be important, simply because at least one man had been murdered because of them. The Colonel takes murder as a more serious omen than most civilians, it appears. Then he got some of the best men from Military Intelligence to start working on the photographs. They've got something, I hear. And the thieves have got a false sense of success. Neat tactics."

"Just a minute," Strang said. "Is the Colonel in Military Intelligence?"

"He was at one time. Some months ago, he was lent to a civilian counter-intelligence unit to work with them on illegal border crossings. There's been a good deal of that recently, you know. Communists returning secretly after spending the last ten years or so in special training schools and camps in Bulgaria and Albania."

"Any link between them and the conspiracy?"

Pringle would give neither a yes nor a no to that question. "All the Greeks can do is to make sure that doesn't happen. If they can eliminate the conspiracy, it obviously won't happen. That's the dangerous thing about those extremist groups: they join forces, not because they love each other, but simply because they are willing to use any help to get power. And they always think that their group can control the others, and come out on top. They gamble on that, the criminal fools. All they do is create so much violence and bloodshed that the extreme right can step in to seize control. Then bang goes an elected government, predominantly left of center but moderate, at least, and what happens? Dictatorship."

"What are the Colonel's politics?"

"He was one of the old Venizelist army group: liberals, strongly republican, antiroyalist, but what the English call 'loyal opposition.' That's the reason Zafiris and his fellow officers spent several years in exile before the war, when the old rightist Metaxas dictatorship was in power. No opposition, loyal or otherwise, was allowed then."

"That's a strange inversion: army officers who were republicans."

"This is Greece, and politics are strange. For instance, who were indirectly responsible for putting a king back on the throne after the war? The Communists. They shocked people into being royalist. And if they are planning any more terrorist trouble, this time they may well put back a rightist dictatorship in power."

"I can see how the Colonel and his republican friends are very loyal opposition. If that trouble started, they might have to go into exile again."

"If he were lucky. There's no love lost between the liberals and the extreme right or the extreme left." Pringle took a deep breath and shook his head slowly. "Don't get me wrong. I love the Greeks. But, sometimes, they can break your heart." He drew the car up beside an arcade of shuttered shops. "Your hotel is just around the corner to your right. It would look better if you arrived on your own two feet. What are your plans for tomorrow?"

"I'm being taken to see the Colonel at ten o'clock."

"And after that?"

"I'm waiting to hear news of Steve."

"Let me know when you do hear."

"Sure." Strang glanced quickly at Pringle's set face. "But don't cut me out then. I'm still in the game, Bob."

Pringle said, "You've done your stint. Retire gracefully. It's my job to make sure Stefanos Kladas is all right. See?"

"No, I don't see," Strang said equably. He rubbed Cecilia's cheek gently. "Come on," he told her, wakening her fully—she had drowsed almost into sleep.

"You're a stubborn man," Pringle told him. "You'll add to all my headaches, blast you."

"I hope not. And I'm not stubborn, either. Just someone who doesn't like being played for a sucker," Strang said with a grin.

"Look—" Pringle began worriedly.

"Good night, my friend." Strang helped Cecilia out of the car. Then, thinking that he owed Pringle more of a warning than that, he ducked his head inside the car again to say, "And don't believe everything that Alexander Christophorou tells you."

"Oh?" The question was sharply pointed.

"No answer to that—as yet."

"You and Zafiris make a strange pair," Pringle said slowly. "That's why he came to my apartment, you know: to warn me sideways." His normally pleasant and amiable face was hardened by an ugly frown. "I don't believe either of you," he said flatly, "but I'll listen."

And that is something, Strang thought. "Thanks, anyway, for rallying round," he said. He slipped his arm through Cecilia's and headed toward the hotel.

The hotel porter handed Strang both bulky keys. "I hope you had a pleasant evening," he said politely.

Strang was equally polite. "Very pleasant," he assured the porter cheerfully, and led Cecilia across the half-lit lobby to the darkened elevator.

For a brief moment, the porter's eyes followed them with tired approval; it looked as if they had had a *very* pleasant evening. He was now quite accustomed to that look of bland triumph combined with disarming innocence: people were always so convinced that no sharp eye could guess. He shook his head over the dissimulations of lovers—if only men would put as much energy into their business as they did into disguising their adventures, there would be a surfeit of millionaires—switched off some more light in the lobby, and went back to adding up his stamp receipts.

"There's no need," Cecilia protested, but not too hard, as Strang got out at the second floor with her. "Only twenty yards to go. I'll manage that."

"I'll just make sure you do."

He unlocked her door and recognized the little room. "So they gave you the Petit Trianon? Well, you'll have pretty pink dreams. Do you mind if I look around?"

She sat down in the nearest velvet chair, slipped off her shoes, and sighed with pleasure. Next time I go exploring in the Plaka, she thought, I shan't wear three-inch spikes for heels. Strang didn't take long with his tour of inspection.

"You're sure there's no one under the bed?" she teased him. "Ken—you really have to stop worrying about me."

"That's my pleasure, ma'am."

"Besides, there's a balcony, right over the main street, outside my bedroom. If anyone scares me, I just run out there and scream."

"You'd be quite a sensation," he said with a broad grin. Particularly in that gossamer nightdress which had been so artistically draped by an enchanted maid over the turned-back sheet of her bed. Then, brusquely, partly to shake off the memory, "Two things before I go, Cecilia. You said something, tonight, about the reason why Katherini's father and brother were killed. What was it, exactly?"

Oh dear, she thought, we're back there again. She said, "Her brother had a girl in Athens. When he returned from Yugoslavia with his father, they were told to stay out of sight in a house near Delphi. But he came secretly into Athens. The father followed his son, tried to get him back to

Delphi instead of reporting him right away. So they were liquidated. I've got the place where the bodies were found written down in the notes. And the dates of their mission into Yugoslavia. Katherini didn't know much more about it than that, though."

So, Strang thought, the Roilos son had risked breaking security, the Roilos father had lost control of his son, both had become liabilities, and they were dead. "That's strong discipline," he said. But was that how their organization had remained so secret? Where, then, did Madame Étienne Duval stand when she lost control of her niece? Where did Nikos Kladas, whose name had been placed on the police files ever since the Megara road murders, and who could be identified as Sideros by Ottway and Steve? Yet, neither Duval nor Nikos Kladas had been expecting death tonight. Or perhaps terrorist leaders had one set of rules for their followers, another for themselves. They could always persuade themselves that they were too important, too necessary for the ultimate success of their plans. But someone tonight had thought they were more of a liability than they were indispensable.

"And the second thing?" she reminded him gently. And then, she thought, I can get to bed and sleep and sleep and sleep. . . . The word was too soothing, with all those sibilants and soft sounds. She smothered a yawn and concentrated on sharper consonants: keep awake, keep awake!

"In your notes about Drakon, I saw some place names."

"Syria, where he visited her aunt, twice, for long periods. They also met in Alexandria, in Paris, and—about a week ago—in Taormina."

"In the house where Katherini was staying with Maria and a chauffeur? Who was the chauffeur, did she say?"

"Nikos Kladas."

"The house with the almond tree in its garden," he said softly. No wonder Ottway had been so interested in it. But even Ottway had to sleep. "I suppose the meeting there was by night?"

"Yes. Madame Duval drove in from Messina, where she was staying on board her yacht. Drakon was staying somewhere in Taormina."

"Somewhere?"

"Katherini didn't know exactly."

He sat, staring at the pink-velvet chair in front of him, remembering a monk's converted cell in Taormina.

"I wonder where she is," Cecilia said.

He kept wondering about that, too. He forced himself to sound confident. "Any girl who can slip away as expertly as she did has a pretty good chance of survival. She has quick brains and a lot of courage."

"But you *were* worried about her—or you wouldn't have gone down that staircase after her."

"She got away safely. That was the main thing."

"You really thought she might have been caught?" There was an unexpected note of alarm in Cecilia's voice.

"If there had been a guard at Drakon's back door—yes, she'd have had it."

"And what good would you have been, Kenneth Strang, without a weapon or anything?" She was almost angry. "Oh, you men!" she said. "You all think you are indestructible!" He looked at her in amazement. "You know," she said, trying to sound very matter of fact, "we have a job of our own to finish." But C. L. Hillard wasn't able to take over. Cecilia tried to smile. "Or do we?" She didn't sound too sure about that.

"Yes," he said. "We'll finish it." He gave an encouraging grin, and rose. "I've an appointment at ten tomorrow morning. What about lunch together?"

"If I'm awake by that time," she said doubtfully as she followed him to the door. "Tell you what, I'll meet you for lunch at five o'clock."

"Getting into proper Mediterranean habits, aren't you?" That's better, he thought, watching her face. "Keep this door locked," he said. "I don't want you walking in your sleep." Good, he thought again, as she nodded seriously and then began to smile. For a moment, his hand on the door, he looked down at her. Without her shoes, she didn't even reach his shoulders. "You have very pretty feet," he told her, and bent down and kissed her cheeks. She had a very pretty mouth, too, but this was hardly the night to start anything he couldn't stop. "That's what the French do when they pin a medal on you. I'm pinning a very big one, right now." He stepped quickly through the narrowly opened door, and drew it quietly closed behind him. For almost a minute, he waited, listening. There wasn't a sound from the other side of the door. Had she forgotten to lock it, after all? Then he heard the safety catch click sharply, and she moved away. He started along the corridor to the staircase.

As he passed the half-closed pantry door, not far from Cecilia's room, the mild clatter of plates halted him. He looked inside the pantry, where a waiter was arranging breakfast trays. "Are you on duty all night? I wonder if you'd keep an eye—" he began, and noticed the quietly dressed man sitting in the corner behind the pantry door. With its dark grave eyes, thick black hair, thin black mustache, it was a face he had seen a thousand times in Athens; but with its slight hint of polite amusement around the lips and its small warning of recognition in the quick twitch of an eyebrow, it was the face that had studied his wallet in the hall of Tommy's house. "That's all right," he told the waiter, added "Good night!" and left. Perhaps, he was thinking as he slowly climbed the staircase through the silent hotel, I'll be able to spend the next four and a half hours in some real sleep. It was a blissful prospect.

EIGHTEEN

Colonel Zafiris seemingly, and rather surprisingly, had his office within walking distance of the Grande Bretagne. It was a sparkling, clear morning with a benign spring sun touching lightly on the bare heads in the crowded street. Strang, only half awakened by his shower and shave and quick breakfast, found that twenty deep breaths of the cool, golden air had lifted his headache, opened both his eyes, and put him into an almost amiable mood, something that had seemed totally impossible three quarters of an hour ago. Elias, keeping thirty paces or so ahead, cut his way quickly through the streams of people. Strang just managed to stay within seeing distance of the neat, dark bobbing head. Suddenly, the head vanished, swept away in the current, through a colonnaded entrance into an arcade of shops.

Strang entered the arcade. I've lost him, he was thinking worriedly. But Elias was standing in front of a tobacconist's highly polished window. As Strang appeared, he went into the shop. All right, thought Strang, I buy some cigarettes, too. He followed Elias. "You first," Elias said politely to Strang, and nodded to a door at the back of the shop. The owner of the shop didn't even seem to be aware that Strang existed, busy as he was with arranging the flat boxes of Greek cigarettes into neat stacks. Strang obeyed Elias, and went quickly through the door. After that, there was only one direction to follow: up. A circular iron staircase was all that was contained behind the door.

Up he went, curiosity and humor beginning to reassert themselves. At the top of the round-and-round, come-and-be-found staircase there was a bleak corridor. And this, decided Strang, is where I stop. He leaned against an unprepossessing buff-colored wall, studied the long empty passage lit by a window at its far end, decided that the window looked out onto an interior courtyard judging by the dimness of its light, listened, could hear not even the distant clack of a typewriter, gave up trying to guess. Four minutes later, he heard light footsteps running up the stairs toward him. It was Elias, all right, with a nod of approval for the patient American. It was fortunate, at that moment, that Elias, with all his innumerable gifts, hadn't the knack of mind reading.

After another corridor and one more flight of stairs, Elias seemed to be quite content with an unpretentious brown door marked AMFISSA OLIVES EXPORT COMPANY. Inside, there was a small room, windowless, green-shaded light bulbs over two men at large typewriters, two telephones on their desks, a wall of filing cabinets, two wooden chairs, and another brown door leading into an inner room. "Sit!" said Elias, and disappeared through the plain brown door. It was exactly one minute before ten o'clock. Elias was not only careful; he delivered on time.

The two typists inspected Strang politely (or memorized?) and went back to their work. Elias appeared at the brown door and led him through the inner office (three walls of filing cabinets, several telephones, one man writing at a desk) into a third room. In the middle of the bare wooden floor was a large table covered at one end with paper folders which a clerk seemed to be arranging for a game of solitaire. Three wooden chairs stood at attention beside it. Around the cracked plaster walls, once cream-colored, stood a shoulder-high safe, a small filing cabinet, another door (which looked much more important than the one Strang had used), a collection of large-scale maps of Greece and adjacent countries, a blackboard, and—tucked into a corner—a low army cot with a neatly folded, gray blanket on its thin mattress. There was a window in this room, but the outside shutters were propped at an angle that would discourage any curious eyes from across the courtyard. The rest of the floor space was occupied with people—the clerk at the table; another man bringing in a tray of coffee cups; Colonel Zafiris, looking remarkably wide awake, carefully shaven, crisp in a fresh khaki shirt; Elias, unexpectedly nervous; and the slightly embarrassed Strang. For it was a strange feeling, like standing in the center of one of the rooms at the Benaki Museum, to have four pairs of Byzantine eyes all focused on him at once. Then the clerk and Elias left, and there were only two pairs of eyes.

The Colonel's morose and heavy face was lightened by a fleeting smile. He edged around the loaded table and shook hands with polite formality. "Our interpreter," he said, waving a hand to the man who was grouping the three chairs beside the coffee cups. Strang nodded, noted that the interpreter was offering him the chair nearest to an outsize wooden cigarette box, smiled, and said, "Hardly necessary. Your command of English is excellent."

"Thank you. It was one of the few compensations for six years of exile. Now, are we all ready?"

Indeed we are, thought Strang as he took the offered chair and glanced away from the wooden box almost at his elbow. What if I ask for a cigarette and reach out to lift that lid? But the Colonel took care of that by pulling out a neat white cardboard box of Papastratos cigarettes from the table drawer and pushing it over to Strang along with an ash tray advertising a Dutch airline. "Now," he said again, enjoying a delicate sip from his small cup of coffee, lighting a Papastratos, looking down at a page of typescript in front of him, taking quiet but complete charge.

They had gone crisply over Katherini's information, point by point. Strang enlarged where he could, keeping his own additions as brief as possible, while the interpreter listened intently and the Colonel scribbled occasional notes of his own on the broad margin of the typed page in front of him. At the end, he handed the page to the interpreter. "Have copies sent to the others, at once," he said in Greek. The interpreter rose and left. "And bring more coffee," the Colonel called after him. Then he looked at Strang, relaxed, and stretched his arms to fold his hands behind his head. "That wasn't so bad, was it?" he asked. "Nor so long, either," he added, and Strang, who had been stealing a quick glance at his watch, gave a broad grin.

The Colonel took one arm down from the back of his head, and reached casually for one of the paper folders. As he opened it and selected a couple of sheets from the top of its file, he was saying, "Can we believe Katherini Roilos? What was her reason, or her motive, for breaking with her aunt?"

Strang told him.

"And how did you come to meet her, in the first place?"

Strang told him that, too.

The Colonel said, in the same quiet voice, his body still relaxed, his face placid, "Why don't you take off your jacket, Mr. Strang, and make yourself comfortable? It's a very good American habit. And now, tell me—I am sometimes slow to understand so many involved details—all the little things that happened and brought you, one by one, to my office here this morning."

Strang looked at him quickly. "Just what do you want to know?"

"Everything to do with Stefanos Kladas, or the yacht *Medea*, or Taormina. . . ." His voice drifted away. "You must forgive me, Mr. Strang. There are many questions I must ask out of sheer curiosity. Perhaps the easiest and quickest way to answer them would be simply to tell me your story." His hand, upturned, weighed that suggestion. "After all, Mr. Strang, I did meet you in rather strange circumstances last night. Do you blame me for being curious?"

"No," Strang admitted frankly. "But I'll have to go a long way back—to New York harbor, in fact. Just after I had heard about the girl who came to *Perspective*'s office—"

"Our stories always start a long way back. Longer," the Colonel said sadly, "than most of us realize." He frowned as the door opened, but relaxed into approval.

The interpreter had returned, bringing a large discolored copper coffee-pot. The Colonel poured carefully, settled himself at another angle in his hard wooden chair. "Now," he said once more.

The telling was fairly simple, partly because he had already told this story—or most of it—to Cecilia, partly because he had been eating, drinking, breathing it for the last forty-eight hours.

The Colonel listened without comment. There was no change of expression on his face. But, halfway through, his eyes left Strang's face and fell, quite casually, on the two sheets of paper lying before him. Strang had almost forgotten them. Now, quietly, unobtrusively, the Colonel was reading their contents as Strang talked. Yet, he was listening. Strang was disconcerted enough to stop and light another Papastratos. The two things are connected, he decided as he snapped his lighter closed: what he is reading, what I am talking about. Strang continued, recounting Christophorou's visit to his room at the Grande Bretagne and the disclosure of the conspiracy, the news of Steve's death and the surrender of Steve's documents. But when he described the following evening with Cecilia, the Colonel was no longer reading. Now, he seemed to be listening with doubled intensity; perhaps his comparison between what he had read and what he had heard had made him twice as interested.

"And so we arrived at Tommy's doorstep," Strang ended. "He took us inside. I telephoned Pringle. You know the rest."

There was a pause. The Colonel frowned at his desk, then looked at the interpreter. "We need more coffee, Yorghis, and more cigarettes."

Yorghis, a tall, thin man with a highly intelligent nose and a receding hairline which turned his high brow into a formidable precipice, took the coffeepot and said, "I shall fill the cigarette box, too." He left, with extreme speed, carrying the box carefully. So, thought Strang, the recording session has been completed.

"My right-hand man," the Colonel said, watching the door close. "Not at all like the Yorghis you mentioned." He laughed. "Did you see his face when you talked about your Yorghis?" Then his amusement was over. He picked up the two sheets of paper.

"I noticed you gave me only the facts. No opinions. No judgments. Why?"

"I don't know enough of the facts to start making comments."

"But you must have formed some opinions. A man must ask the reasons why. Is that not so?"

"Yes."

"What is your opinion of Alexander Christophorou?"

Strang lit another cigarette very carefully.

The Colonel said, "You must have asked why you saw him yesterday evening leaving a house on Kriton Street which Katherini Roilos identified as the one rented for her aunt by Evgenia Vasilika. Miss Hillard saw him, too? There is no doubt that it was he?"

"None."

"Then why? You asked yourself that question, I am sure. What was your answer?"

"I keep thinking Christophorou must be a double agent." He looked up quickly and surprised a look of astonishment.

"That could have been a good answer, if Christophorou had been working for us."

"But isn't he attached to—to some intelligence unit?"

The Colonel asked sharply, "Did he tell you he was?"

"No," Strang said slowly.

"Did he give you that impression?"

Strang hesitated. "Perhaps I was too quick in picking it up. He told me, actually, that he was a journalist."

"And that is what he is, neither more nor less."

"But why was he in Sicily? Where did he get all his information?"

"Very interesting questions." The Colonel didn't answer them, though.

"Why," tried Strang again, "did you listen to him when he told you I had documents to deliver? Why did you even—"

"He is a good journalist. And good journalists are detectives, too. They have informants, they check the stories they hear, they can discover vital facts. And when they come across something of great importance that deals with state business, they make contact with official sources. Their discoveries, in other words, can be too dangerous to be treated as ordinary news. Supposing you were a journalist, Mr. Strang, and discovered a serious plot to assassinate your president. What do you do? Burst into headlines and become famous? Or do you give that information to your Secret

Service and F.B.I.? And let them find out the whole plot, and arrest the plotters, and end the danger to your country, before you publish what you know? It is a matter of ethics. Personal gain or public service? That is the question. So, two nights ago, when Christophorou made contact with me and my colleague, we were interested, curious. But not astounded. Any reliable journalist would have followed the same course. You understand?"

"Yes. But what puzzles me is the fact that the documents *were* handed over to you. It would have been easier just to take them—" He halted, remembering that there had been one attempt to steal them.

"Easier in some ways. But more dangerous, too. The sudden death of another American would have caused serious complications. You did not give up those documents easily. You were very tenacious." The Colonel paused. "Why? You were not in a trusting mood, last Monday. I think you had some doubts about Alexander Christophorou, even then. Am I right? Please do not look so embarrassed, so very unhappy. After all, in your work with ancient ruins you are something of a detective, too. Perhaps you like to make reconstructions of people as well as of temples? Tell me frankly, off the record as you say in America: do you think Drakon is only another name for Christophorou?"

The Colonel, thought Strang, had his own technique for the raw wound: first, the lanolin; then, the sudden jab of iodine. He said, "Does it matter what I think? My ideas won't interest any court of law. I've no proof."

"Thinking is the beginning of the search for proof," the Colonel said coldly. "If we do not think, we do not find reasons for doubt. If we do not doubt, we do not start the search for proof. Oh, we'll find the proof of either innocence or guilt, if we work hard enough and have enough time. But without thinking, doubting, we would not know even where to begin our work. You understand?"

"Katherini Roilos could give you the proof. Let her meet Christophorou. She can tell you whether he is Drakon or not."

The Colonel looked at him searchingly. Then he sighed, and stretched out his arm to a bell on his table. He frowned, as he jabbed its button. He said sadly, "It is a little more complicated than that, Mr. Strang." Yorghis opened the door at once. He had the copper coffeepot in his hand. "Is it cold?" the Colonel wanted to know. "No? Good. Set up the screen. Get the photographs." The orders were almost conversational.

Strang drank the hot, sweet coffee cautiously. You had to be careful to leave almost an inch of liquid at the bottom of the little cup if you didn't want a last mouthful of delta mud. He watched the Colonel with equal care. Those two sheets of paper were still in his hand.

Casually, the Colonel held them up. "This is the report made to us, yesterday, by Alexander Christophorou. It is a statement of how he became interested in Stefanos Kladas, and discovered that certain documents, which might be of some importance to us, were in your hands." The Colonel studied the two sheets of paper for a long moment. "Not one word of your story, Mr. Strang, coincides with his."

The coffee silt touched Strang's teeth. He put down the cup hastily, and found his handkerchief to clean his lips.

"You must not drink our coffee so trustingly, Mr. Strang."

"Not one word?" Strang echoed.

"Oh, perhaps a few words—where he says he was visiting Taormina and renewed an old friendship. But after that—" The Colonel consulted the top sheet again. "You were extremely worried about the nonappearance of Stefanos Kladas. You asked Christophorou's advice, and in return, over several drinks, you told him everything that Stefanos Kladas had confided in you. Including—" the Colonel raised his eyes, opened them wide, and smiled—"all that Stefanos Kladas knew about a conspiracy in which his brother, Nikos, was implicated."

Strang said softly, "And that is how Christophorou came to know about the conspiracy?"

The Colonel nodded and sipped his coffee.

Strang could only stare at Christophorou's report. My word against his, he thought grimly.

"Only," the Colonel said, slapping the two sheets down on the table, "how could Stefanos Kladas, in New York, have known such vivid details about the murder of the Roilos father and son on the Megara road? He was not in contact with his brother, Nikos. That is obvious from the two letters from the sister, Myrrha Kladas, to Stefanos Kladas in New York that were among the documents he gave you. The first letter was written last November, after she had received a secret visit from Nikos. She was worried about Nikos then. In a letter written last February, she seemed to have become frightened about Nikos. She hoped Stefanos could persuade him to stay clear of his old friends, who always led him into trouble."

"Yes," Strang said bitterly, "he always was a good boy."

The Colonel, who probably had little time to read New York newspaper reports on juvenile delinquents and their doting mamas, looked momentarily perplexed. Then, "Yorghis, please get Elias to come in here. I want him to see this, too." And when Elias stood within the door, the Colonel said, "Now, Yorghis—are we ready?"

Yorghis was ready. The screen was in place over the blackboard. The projector was pointing at it. He closed the window's shutters completely.

The small room was dark and warm, smelling of aromatic coffee, delicate cigarettes, starched shirts, and hair oil. "But first," said the Colonel, now that the shutters were closed, "perhaps you should see the actual photographs, before our experts went to work on them." He switched on the table lamp, scattered some small snapshots from an envelope into the little pool of light. Strang rose and examined them: the usual aging snapshots, not too defined, not much variety in light and shade, not too clear. But, even then, Steve's sense of composition had been good.

"Do they make any sense to you?" the Colonel asked.

"None." Just people under trees, a group beside a burned-out house. "What's this fellow doing? Cleaning a rifle?"

"You'll see." The Colonel was delighted. He switched off the table light; they sat down; Yorghis took command.

On the screen was flashed a series of photographs, blown up to enormous proportion, coarsened in texture, but with outlines and shadows skillfully sharpened. Faces had become real, actions understandable. Yorghis, in the dispassionate voice of a research scholar, first analyzed the backgrounds to suggest the possible localities (Steve had been clever at using the shape of a mountain, a ruined church, a high-perched village above a precipice, even eagles circling over cliffs, to identify the scenes), and then explained the groups of men in the foregrounds. The photographs seemed to deal with one small district of Greece: the slopes of Mount Parnassos and the area surrounding them. The men were *andartes*, the guerrilla fighters, bundled into bulky shapes by strange mixtures of clothing—captured uniforms, tattered civilian jackets, sheepskin tunics as wild as their hair and beards, wool caps, twists of knitted scarves, anything to keep out the savage cold of the mountains. Sometimes they were returning from a raid, sometimes jubilant around a few captured weapons. They were usually in small bands, five or six lonely men, straggling as they climbed a rough mountainside, or resting as they lay under a sheltering tree.

"These photographs were included," Yorghis was saying, "presumably to identify the area of operations against the Nazis. Here is one, dealing with a less-heroic operation in this same area. The season is different, you will note from the trees and the hillside. There are other differences. The commander of this band of guerrillas is Ares. There he is, with his men. The bodies which are lying scattered on the sloping meadow are Greeks, too. Their commanding officer, Colonel Psarros, lies with them. The few survivors stand with hands held up in surrender."

The photograph flashed on the screen. The dead were scattered; the survivors, in a pathetic small group; the victors, in considerable force. To get this scene, Steve had taken a distance shot. Only the gestures of the men were discernible. In clothes, they were the same. Faces couldn't be distinguished.

"Here is one detail," Yorghis said. And now four of the survivors were on view: three ghostlike, bewildered faces; the fourth head, with a battered old cap pulled down rakishly over his brow, was bent slightly as the man lit a cigarette. He wore, so it looked, an officer's long coat.

"And now," said Yorghis as he flashed another photograph onto the screen, "the survivors who refused to join Ares are executed. One changes his mind just before he is shot, and breaks away to join the victors. They find it amusing." The man did not. He was weeping. He was a big man, powerful. His face was contorted with anguish and tears. "A shepherd in ordinary life, perhaps," Yorghis's calm voice went on. "So we have been told. Name unknown as yet, but identified by his light hair, height, and that sheepskin tunic which he always wore. And now, in the next picture, those who are willing to join Ares are marched away."

"March" was scarcely the word. The new photograph showed a straggle of men, melting away from the meadow with its abandoned dead. It had focused on that rakishly tilted, battered old cap again. (Steve must have taken a dislike to its owner.) And again the head had avoided a clear picture. "Until we saw these photographs," Yorghis said, "we had thought no officer had surrendered. But this one did. Notice that the shepherd is following him faithfully. Notice, too, that one of Ares's men has come over to talk to that officer. They walk together. Look carefully: the friendly man is Sideros."

Indeed it was. Sideros had not had much success with a beard. The face of Nikos Kladas, turning toward the camera in surprise, was not too difficult to recognize.

"And last of all, a picture taken at a rest camp some months later, judging by the clothes. Locality undiscovered. But this is not a usual camp. The men seen here are known to have been closely associated with Ares. Most of them died with him, in 1945."

The men had left off their bulky clothing, except for the shepherd, who still wore his sheepskin tunic. Most of them were smiling as they sat around a glade, except for the shepherd again, a desolate crag of a man, who stood in the background. One had even stripped, and was lying asleep, face down in full sunlight. "Sideros, the sun-worshiper," Yorghis said bitingly. "Notice that mark below his right shoulder blade. Definitely identified by a British liaison officer who knew Sideros before he joined Ares's special unit."

Strang looked sharply at Colonel Zafiris beside him. The Colonel, who had grunted his approval of the earlier guerrilla photographs, had lapsed into complete silence since the massacre of Colonel Psarros and his men. Now, he only gestured back to the screen, as Yorghis said, "Notice this small group sitting apart from the others." Strang took the Colonel's hint, stopped mentally congratulating George Ottway on his amazingly quick response to Tommy's message, and looked at the screen obediently. At the side of the glade, there was the wall of a house, and in its shallow shadow sat three people. One was a man with a handsome face, laughing. Another was the officer with the battered old cap, tilted more than ever over his eyes to shield them from the glare of late summer while he cleaned a rifle. And the third was small, slight, with a large head of wild dark hair around a smooth face.

"A woman?" Strang asked incredulously.

"A woman," said the Colonel. "A courier. A very special courier." He lapsed into silence again, glowered at the screen, where a detail of the group by the house wall was now being shown.

Yorghis said, "Reading from left to right: Ares, the god of war; Odysseus; Elektra. Ares, we all know. Odysseus and Elektra were identified by the British officer who had seen Odysseus—but never at close hand—and met the famous Elektra, who was so close an intimate of Ares at one time."

Strang studied the detail. Coarse-textured as it was by excessive enlargement, it still held a recognizable quality. The woman's excellent profile could be noted, a long slender neck above her opened shirt collar, a noble brow. She made him think of Katherini Roilos. "Strong family resemblance."

"Especially then," said the Colonel, "when her hair was dark brown. And Odysseus—can you recognize him?"

"I can't see beyond that beard, or that tilted cap. A careful customer."

"Unfortunately, for us."

"Never seen at close hand," Strang repeated, thoughtfully.

"He kept his distance from the Englishman. Why? Is it possible that he felt he might meet the Englishman after the war? Could they have friends in common in the civilian world? He was well-named Odysseus." The Colonel was watching Strang now. "Look at his left hand holding the rifle. Do you see that heavy ring on his little finger?"

"Vaguely." And, vaguely, something stirred at the back of Strang's memory.

"Thank you, Yorghis." The Colonel switched on the table lamp. "Here," he said to Strang, "is the face design of that ring, as near as we can manage to reconstruct it. It is actually a coin, thick, uneven edge, not a circle, with a design of a man's profile and two horns. Perhaps an ancient drachma? Fourth century? The head of Alexander the Great?"

"It could be," Strang said as he studied the neat drawing of the ring's design. Its irregular edge, clipped carefully away from its original circle by some acquisitive Greek who didn't think the merest sliver of silver too small for the taking, was typical of most ancient coins. The two short horns protruding from the scalp, or from a tight skullcap covering the scalp, were a favorite device of Alexander the Great to show he was the son of Zeus.

"Alexander, the conqueror of Greece, the invader from the north," Zafiris said softly. He filed the drawing of the ring into the proper folder. "Christophorou wears no ring now. Did he wear one when you met him fifteen years ago? Such a ring is memorable to someone like you, with your interest in ancient things. You said you met him in the Grande Bretagne when it was under siege."

"He didn't wear a ring in the Grande Bretagne. Of course, the lights weren't too good then." Just candles, batteries, oil lamps. Still, there had been light enough to notice a ring like that. "Not in the Grande Bretagne," he repeated. The vague stirring in Strang's memory began again.

"Then where?"

"That night, after Christophorou and I had gone up to the Acropolis, we got back to the Piraeus road to join my friends waiting for me there. I said we had had the devil's own luck so far, and hoped it would last. He said it would: his lucky ring had never let him down yet. I only saw a glimpse of it. It was scarcely the time to stop and look. We were too busy dodging patrols and armed bands and snipers."

"How much of a glimpse did you have?"

"I only saw a ring."

"On his left hand?"

Strang tried to remember. "He lifted his hand as he spoke about his luck. . . . No, I can't remember which hand."

"Was he carrying a revolver?"

"Of course."

"In his right hand?"

"Yes."

"Was that the one he held up?"

"No."

"So—" the Colonel said, and glanced quickly at Yorghis. "Now, Mr. Strang, are you sure you didn't notice the ring was different from an ordinary signet ring?"

"All I know," Strang said doggedly, "is that he mentioned a lucky ring. And held up his left hand for a second as he spoke. Then we moved on. That's all."

"And not enough," the Colonel said, angry with disappointment. Then he recovered himself. "Yorghis," he said in lightning Greek, "we shall have to try some of Christophorou's old friends. The Englishman, Thomson, for instance. Or his family. They may know about a ring like that."

"Shall we send Elias?" Yorghis looked at the little man who was standing so quietly in the background that Strang was startled to see him.

"I need Elias," the Colonel said.

"Costas, then?"

"It will take all his diplomacy. Brief him carefully."

Yorghis nodded, locked the photographs into the box he carried. "At least, we *do* know that Christophorou wore a ring on his left hand," he said, suddenly cheerful, as he prepared to leave the room with Elias. He halted at the door for a moment. "Odysseus," he said with a sardonic smile, "Odysseus . . . Why not Alcibiades?"

The Colonel gave an abrupt laugh. "Why not?" he asked as the door closed. "But men always choose the more flattering names." Then he looked at Strang, and said, serious again, "A slow business. Step by step. Small details, such as that ring, become important. Big discoveries become of little value. Constant *bouleversement*. Yet, step by step, the climb is made. And at last, the full view. What shall we see?"

That's one view I won't enjoy, Strang thought heavily.

"It would not be such a slow business," the Colonel said, "if we had Katherini Roilos to help us."

Strang stopped thinking about Alexander Christophorou and looked up quickly as he heard the stilted voice.

"But," the Colonel said, "she is dead."

Strang sat very still for a long moment. "How?" he asked at last. "Where?"

"In the Kriton Street house. She arrived by taxi, and was observed by two of our agents, whom I had sent there, just after your telephone call to Pringle, to keep watch until reinforcements arrived. Two agents, you understand, were not enough to force their way into a house of that size and make arrests. They thought she was another of the conspirators, that they would arrest her, inside, along with the others. None of us knew, you realize, that your little witness had left Mr. Thomson's flat. When the squad of men arrived, twenty minutes later, the house was surrounded. An entry was forced through the garden door, which the girl had used.

233

There were several people inside, mostly in their night clothes, as if they had been roused from their beds. There was a man at a telephone—much confusion—a woman's voice screaming 'Traitor!' Three of our agents heard that scream as they burst into the room. The girl was dead before they could reach her, stabbed to the heart. She had been tied to a chair and—I am afraid—cruelly questioned." The Colonel's lips tightened. He stared down at his desk. "There was a woman standing over her, still screaming in anger, her hand on the hilt of the knife."

Strang stared at him unbelievingly.

"A woman called Maria," the Colonel said.

"Maria?"

The Colonel nodded.

"But Maria helped her escape. Maria—"

"—was only obeying orders throughout. The girl had come under suspicion. Her escape to Erinna Street was permitted so that she could be followed, so that her associates could be traced. The trouble about conspirators is that they must always look for counter-plots; they find it hard to believe that one girl, alone, might rebel and act. A brave girl. Not brave enough to give testimony in public against her aunt—that was the real reason she ran away, of course. But, still, very brave."

I was so sure, Strang thought, I was so sure she would get away safely. He said, "She was worried about Maria. She went back to that house to help Maria."

"That could be the reason she gave herself, and a good reason it was. But behind the reason we give, there often stands the reason we do not acknowledge." The Colonel's eyes dropped down to the two sheets of paper he was inserting into the proper folder. He was impatient to proceed with something other than Kriton Street. "Now—" he began, and stopped as he looked up at the American. "Mr. Strang," he said sharply, "the girl would have died in that chair in any case. Perhaps it was a mercy to her that we arrived so soon after she entered that house."

Strang nodded. But he couldn't get rid of his feeling of guilt. Get rid of it? It was growing with each second.

"I think you ought to know that the raid was successful," the Colonel said quickly. "Five people were arrested, including the man who stole the Kladas documents from my office. —Oh, no, not *this* office, Mr. Strang! —He is a Bulgarian, answers your description of Boris very nicely. Oh, such innocence! Such delightful ignorance of everything. But then, he does not know that we watched him hand over the stolen envelope last night just after the theft. In a coffeehouse." The Colonel enjoyed that picture. Then he went on, "This morning, such innocent tradesmen delivered the household supplies! A most successful raid." He looked at Strang and seemed puzzled. "Her death is not meaningless. Already, it is partly avenged."

"She would never have been under suspicion if I had not told Christophorou about her," Strang said angrily. "I'm to blame. I told him. Damn him to hell, I told him about the girl in *Perspective*'s office, on the ship—" His eyes met the Colonel's.

"Who else knew? Your editor in New York. Stefanos Kladas. Who else?"

"I told Miss Hillard."

The Colonel raised an eyebrow. "Do you know her so well?"

"Yes."

"I thought you only met her yesterday," the Colonel suggested politely.

"You didn't ask how long I had known her."

"Ah!" There was a slight pause, a humorous pursing of the lips. "I don't think Miss Hillard can be blamed. Who else was told?"

"No one."

"Which leaves—" The Colonel's hands dropped to the desk.

"Yes," said Strang slowly.

"So, at last, you do not find my doubts about Alexander Christophorou exaggerated." The Colonel shook his head unbelievingly. There, just when he had given up all hope of getting the American to admit his doubts openly, it had happened. Suddenly. By the death of a girl . . . Strange keys turned the lock in a man's subconscious mind.

Strang said with painful honesty, slowly, still unwillingly, "I have had my doubts. But no positive proof. And—well, it's hard to believe."

"Because a gallant stranger took you to see the Acropolis under shell fire? The romantic gesture—yes, that is always appealing."

Strang flushed. "I've sweated that nonsense out of my system in the last twenty-four hours. No. What I can't believe is—" He paused. "How could a man who saw his family forced into a death march ever join the people who seized them as hostages? That just doesn't make sense."

"He was already allied with them. You saw the photographs."

"But—" Strang fell silent.

The Colonel watched him curiously. Americans, he thought, live in a simple world of good and bad, every man considered good until he was caught, actually caught, *flagrante delicto* if possible. In a moment, he envied that world, so comfortable, so pleasant. And then he didn't envy it: too vulnerable, too easy for any dedicated enemy to smash it to pieces. Perhaps Americans did not believe in the dedicated enemy, either. Yet they admired Shakespeare, some of them at least: did *Othello* leave no sense of disquiet, was Iago simply an odd phenomenon, an unpleasant quirk of a dramatist's imagination? Some admired Aeschylus, too, he had heard: did the intellectuals who applauded the *Agamemnon* think that Aegisthus was only quaint fiction? Or Atreus himself—was his evil simply a part of barbarous prehistory? Progress made evil antiquated. Was that the assumption?

The Colonel sighed. "Must Alcibiades be understood in order to be believed? He did exist, my friend, understood or not understood. And, as you Americans say, he couldn't have cared less."

"But didn't Christophorou feel revulsion?"

"Revulsion from everything, perhaps. From the stupid democrats, who were so incompetent, or lazy, or quarrelsome, that they couldn't see danger until it swallowed them up. From the stupid fascists, who bullied and murdered. From the stupid Communists, with their obsessive hates, their blind obedience. Revulsion from all of them. Many men have felt it. Complete disillusion, bitterness, contempt. Life is absurd, meaningless." The Colonel's broad, capable hands gathered the folders on his desk into neat order, boxed them into an exact square. "But few men have followed existentialism to its logical conclusion. Which is—" The Colonel looked up and caught Strang's eye. "Ah," he said, "I see you are not ignorant of nihilism." His heavy, oval face, with its drooping eyelids, its full lips drawn into a severe line under the thick black mustache, its strong eyebrows no longer arched but knitted straight by the deep crease between them, stared impassively at the American. "I think we have one of those few, right here in Athens," he ended, his voice harshening. He scraped his chair back from the table and rose.

Strang rose, too. "There are two less now," he said.

"The Duval woman and Nikos Kladas?" The Colonel's hand brushed that idea aside. "Stalinists, both of them, with a taste for terrorism. They formed a Committee of Three with Drakon, to organize this conspiracy. It is an old pattern, that Committee of Three, with the two Communists taking over as soon as the third man's usefulness is ended. It happened throughout our civil war. But Drakon knew how they worked: he was a Communist himself then. Last night, he acted first. The sole power is now his. Why did he choose last night? Because tomorrow is the day that the first blow is struck." The Colonel turned and pointed to the map of Greece on the wall behind him. "There!" he said. "Just across that northern boundary, in Yugoslavia, the trouble will start. An assassination, and the seizing of power by the Stalinists. Then false charges, with specially prepared proof, that Greece is responsible. Border incidents will develop. And then—" the Colonel's hand swept south into Greece—"attacks. Trou-

236

ble will come from the Bulgarian border, too. From Albania. The Greek Communists are there, ready. And they will have considerable assistance, this time. In 1944, the Russians had no tanks or guns to spare." He stared at the map. "Is this why the Duval woman joined Drakon? Was this the gamble?" With his finger, he drew one last line over the map, from the Baltic and East Germany down through the heart of Europe to the Adriatic, sweeping around Greece to end at the Dardanelles.

He swung back to face Strang. "So carefully planned, this one. But its two Communist leaders are dead. And all the control is now in the hands of the nihilist." Suddenly, surprisingly, he was amused. "That is a new development, at least. In Spain, the anarchists were machine-gunned in their rest camps by their Communist comrades. They ought to have had a nihilist in charge to protect their interests. An anarchist is all emotion and no brain. He needs someone like our nihilist, the elusive Mr. Drakon, all brain, no emotions." His sardonic mood was over. Grimly now, he ended, "But the conspiracy won't succeed. Not *this* time!"

"There is still Drakon," Strang reminded him.

The Colonel reached into his desk drawer and took out a revolver. He laid it on top of the pile of folders. "Is this gun dangerous?" the Colonel asked softly.

"If it is loaded."

"Potentially, yes. But actually, no. Not until someone picks it up and puts his finger around the trigger and points it. Like this!" The Colonel picked up the revolver. "That's all right, Mr. Strang. I shall try not to shoot you." He had a smile in his eyes. Then quickly he unloaded the revolver, laid the six bullets on the table. "Now, if I were to pick up this gun and put my finger around the trigger? Yes, indeed, I'd look very very foolish. And I would be harmless. Until I found more ammunition and loaded it once more." He began loading, and then dropped the revolver back into place. "A conspiracy is very much like that gun. Drakon will pull the trigger, but the gun is empty. We have removed the bullets, Mr. Strang. The assassination will not take place, simply because there will be no one to murder. The intended victim will not attend. He will be some two hundred miles away, and his change in plans will only be announced just at the time he was supposed to die. In this way, his police will be able to draw a tight net around their conspirators."

"That should be easy. They will find them grouped hopefully in front of their radios."

"And meanwhile," the Colonel went on, ignoring that light suggestion, "we find Drakon, before he reloads."

"Haven't you found him?" Strang couldn't resist asking, and then decided to make no more small jokes. A foreigner's sense of humor was never much appreciated, somehow.

But the Colonel was receptive, this time. "That's better, much better," he said, studying Strang's face. "You must look perfectly normal when you walk along the street. You do not want your friends to ask 'What is wrong? What is he worried about?' Even expressions on a man's face can be indiscreet." There was more than a slight emphasis on that last word.

"I'll be discreet," Strang assured him. Is it time to leave? he wondered. He took a step toward the door.

"You will find your travel agent, Spyridon Makres, most dependable, now that your little Yorghis has been discharged. They were deeply shocked to hear about his activities. It's a good firm; your journey into the Peloponnese will be made simple and pleasant."

Strang looked at him. How had the Colonel guessed his plans? "I thought I ought to go and see Steve's sister," he said awkwardly.

"Of course. And Miss Hillard?"

"She was going to Nauplion."

"Alone?"

"Yes. But I'm not so keen on that idea, now."

"I think you had better tell her to stay in Athens, for this week. That would be simpler for everyone."

"Tell her?" Strang raised an eyebrow.

"Certainly." The Colonel put out his hand and gripped Strang's in a quick shake. "The Peloponnese is very beautiful in spring, Mr. Strang. The wild flowers cover the hills. A pleasant journey."

And then, just when Strang was about to open the door, the Colonel said—as if this thought had only developed now—"By the way, how did you come to be interested in nihilism, Mr. Strang? It isn't exactly an American preoccupation, is it?"

"Not exactly. So far, our delinquents haven't branched into politics." But the Colonel was still waiting for the answer.

Strang said, "Christophorou talked of nihilism."

"He did?" The Colonel had been really surprised, this time.

"Yes."

"Have you any comment on that?"

I am flattered, thought Strang. My comment?

"You have a mind that seeks explanations," the Colonel observed politely.

"Yes, even wrong ones," Strang said with a grin.

"But I am serious."

"Well, either Christophorou is so fascinated by nihilism that he can't keep it out of his conversation. Or perhaps he thought it would scare me off, make me run back to my drawing board and concentrate thankfully on pleasanter things. Or perhaps I wasn't impressed enough: I told him nihilism wouldn't work, there were still enough civilized men in the world who would reject it. So perhaps I needled him into defending it sideways."

"Or perhaps the excitement of success made him boast a little?" The Colonel pursed his lips. "We make him sound almost human." He looked sharply at Strang. "Is that your difficulty? You find him too human to be the monster I think he is."

Strang said nothing. The Colonel had made an adequate reply, in a way.

Colonel Zafiris smiled gently. "I am sure I need not remind you that Hitler and Stalin were known to kiss babies and smile on pretty girls?" The acid voice changed. "Be careful, Mr. Strang," he said softly. "Please!"

"Very careful," Strang agreed. He opened the door. Elias was waiting. Strang followed him into the dingy corridor.

NINETEEN

Strang came out of the arcade slowly, stopping to look at a window of cameras, then at a bookshop. He bought a guide to the Peloponnese, a good map of Greece, and a new edition of Cavafy's poems in translation. But he was careful to buy his cigarettes in the street outside, at one of the innumerable newspaper and magazine stands. (Elias had vanished, but if he was taking any distant interest in Strang's progress along Venizelos Street, he would approve.) He chose a couple of newspapers, too, and some American, English, and French magazines. The Greeks, he decided as he looked over the incredible display, must read as much as they talked, and drank coffee.

The sidewalk tables were filling up, although it wasn't yet noon. When the warm weather came, he had heard, they would cover Constitution Square. Considering its size, that must be the biggest concentration of café tables this side of Cedar Rapids. If I'm careful, he thought, remembering the Colonel's last admonition, I'll live to see it. In the street's clear air, bright sunshine, and general feeling of bustling rush and pleasant purpose, it was easy to smile at warnings, not ridiculing them, not forgetting them, but keeping them to a proper proportion. Besides, the most careful course to follow would be to act perfectly normally.

Today, he would pass these café tables ahead of him and cut down toward the big coffeehouse at the corner of Churchill Street. Men only. Talk and cigarette smoke. He would read, and—lost among the mass of small round zinc tables—think over those last ninety minutes. There was much, as the old Cretan would say, to think about here. Momentarily, he wished he could have a night's talk with that old boy. And thinking of the Cretan, he thought of Petros and Steve, and of Katherini Roilos.

A woman's hand touched his elbow. "You weren't going to pass me by, were you?" Caroline Ottway asked. She was wearing her jade-green earrings today, and a wistful look. A little pale, perhaps, but her soft blonde breathless charm was still gathered around her like yards of gossamer.

He was startled enough to be quite frank. "I didn't see you."

"You *are* losing your eye, aren't you? Oh, do come and sit with me! I'm all alone today."

"No Greek lesson?"

"Abandoned by everyone," she said. "I feel as miserable as you look."

"We'll have to do something about that," he told her. The Colonel was right, damn him: no serious thoughts in a crowded street. He sat down at her table—it was on the front row. He must have passed her at less than a yard's distance. He looked at her bright eyes and thought of Katherini Roilos again, and then forced himself to stop thinking.

Caroline was saying, "I'm so sorry, Kenneth. It is *really* hideous." He stared at her. "George felt grim about it all. He heard about it last night, you know. We were dining at the Pringles'." She sounded more excited than crushed. Bad news stimulated some people.

"Yes," he said. "Hideous." What was? He had at least three pieces of news that would fit that category.

"It's in the papers." She nodded to the bundle of newspapers and magazines he had laid on a free chair. "What does it all mean? It isn't so simple as it seems. Is it?"

Fortunately, the waiter was prompt today, and he could order and quite naturally miss answering. He picked up a newspaper and said, "Let's see how they treat it."

"Page one," she told him. "Isn't that significant?"

He nodded, searching, finding. DEATH OF FAMOUS GREEK PHOTOGRAPHER. He read the small paragraph, reminding himself sharply that he would have to guard against showing the truth; he must remember constantly that Steve was supposed to be dead, that Katherini was supposed to be alive.

"When did you hear about it first?" she wanted to know.

"From Bob Pringle."

"It's—it's just so unbelievable!"

And how would you know? he wondered; you never met Steve. In fact, I'd be willing to swear you were jealous of his shadow. "Is that what George says?" he asked quickly.

She looked at him sideways, green eyes still excited, and then seemed to decide he had meant that nicely. "Yes. In fact, he was so worried by the news that—well, he didn't sleep much last night. And this morning—"

she dropped her voice—"he went round to see some friends of his. Greek friends. Intelligence, I think. All very hush-hush and—"

"Then why talk about it?" he cut in. "Look, Caroline," he said very gently, "don't add to your husband's troubles."

"I?" She was hurt, indignant. "And what troubles do you mean?" she asked, curiosity overcoming her annoyance.

He dodged that neatly. "All men with pretty wives and important jobs must have plenty of worries," he said. "Come on, Caroline. Ease up on your old man. If he can't tell you about his work, don't start inventing problems for him. He's bound to have plenty of his own."

"But this visit to his Greek friends was not about *his* problems. It was about Yannis—Steve, I mean."

"He probably wants a full inquiry. Not a bad idea, either. Steve wasn't likely to commit suicide."

"There's much more to his death than all this," she declared, and tapped the newspaper.

"And how did you get that fancy idea?" he asked.

She waited until the waiter had set down fresh coffee for her, beer for Strang. Softly, when they were alone again, she said, "Last night, Mr. Pringle had a talk with George about Steve. Then Mr. Christophorou dropped in, and *he* had a quiet talk with George. Then George lay awake most of the night. He always does that when he is working out some problem. This morning, he went to see his friends. And when he came back from that visit, he started packing. He has left. For Cyprus. He would only say something about a little difficulty that had come up. He always talks understatement when he's really worried. And so I'm worried."

She was, too. Strang said more gently, "Now, Caroline—you know that's his job: to ease out any difficulties."

"I know, I know. But—" she looked at him—"he didn't think of *going* to Cyprus until he had that meeting with his Greek friends. How do you jump to Cyprus from Steve's death?"

Not from Steve's death, Strang thought; from information about a conspiracy, perhaps. He remembered, now, the jubilation in the Colonel's voice when he had talked about the raid, a *most* successful raid, on the Kriton Street house, about the captured and incriminated Boris. . . . Had some incident been planned in the Cyprus area, too? Then he shook himself free of his speculations. I'm as bad as Caroline, he thought angrily, always curious, always questioning. One thing is certain: I'll never know the full scope of the conspiracy. Neither I nor the millions of people on the outside. Only the insiders, like the Colonel, and not many of them, would ever know the full truth. But the Colonel was stretching even his knowledge when he called Christophorou a monster.

"How?" repeated Caroline, still worrying about Cyprus.

"You don't," he said, "you just don't. Unless you are Caroline Ottway." Her instinct was uncanny, he thought worriedly.

"Did you know Steve really well? I mean—"

He cut her short. "Let's not talk about Steve. Not today."

"Nor ever," she said, challenging him. "Why won't you talk about him to me?"

"Because," he said, taking off the velvet glove, "you really don't like Steve. You resent him."

"What absolute nonsense!" Her cheeks were bright with a moment's sharp confusion. Then she said in surprise, "Steve is dead. How extraordinary to use the present tense about him."

He recovered quickly. "I was talking about you. And you are very much alive." Her reaction was favorable, and he took a deep breath of relief. "I begin to think you only talk to me because I was a friend of Steve's."

She shook her head, but the retreat was complete.

"Cheer up," he said, "you'll soon be in your new apartment, and then you won't have time to invent worries over a café table."

She tried to smile, but it was a sad effort. Her eyes were too bright. "You must think me a very foolish woman," she said, looking down at her untouched cup of coffee. "But I don't really enjoy this life of wandering, of acquaintances, of living in rented furnished flats, hotels, restaurants. I had too much of it when I was young. Now, all I want is quite simple. I'd like to be able to hear my husband talk over his business, meet his friends, have a real house to worry about, and—" she hesitated, ended evasively—"everything that goes with a proper home. Isn't life funny? All I want is so simple—" She shrugged her shoulders, laughed a little unsteadily. "Or perhaps I'm just a morbid type, always wanting what I can't get." She looked at her watch. "Dear me! It's time to put in an hour on Greek verbs before lunch. I promised Yorghis to get them straight before he gets back from Yugoslavia."

"You are in no mood for verbs today. Have some sherry." Strang signaled to the waiter. "Yugoslavia? He won't be back for days. You'll have plenty of time."

"He had better be back before Friday. George and I are going to have a weekend at Delphi—probably, that is—and I'll need my camera for my own use." Then, as Strang looked quickly at her, she added, "What could I do? Refuse to lend my camera? But he can't afford one, you know. And he did want to take some photographs of the celebrations, tomorrow, in Yugoslavia. There's some terrific opening of a new highway up there—"

"He has borrowed your camera?" Strang interrupted, horrified. Her camera's serial number would be easily traced.

"Oh, I'll get it back all right. But what could I do when he asked me, so shyly, if he could borrow it?"

"You could have told him to go jump in the Aegean."

She laughed. "How could I? A foreigner? And practically a millionairess by Yorghis's count? Now don't worry about such a silly thing. Yorghis is honest."

Strang hoped he looked noncommittal.

"I do wish people wouldn't put me in the position of being unable to refuse, though." She sighed.

"If he can afford to take off on a vacation to Yugoslavia, he might have rented his own camera."

"Not on a vacation; on a job. He is interpreter for some foreign journalist." The waiter had brought the glass of sherry. She tasted it, doubtfully. "It's real!" she said in surprise.

"What did your husband have to say about the camera?" Strang could imagine what Ottway must have said, but the question served to point the conversation back in the right direction.

Caroline looked a little vague.

"You did not tell him?" Strang was dumfounded.

"Well, what with all the excitement this morning—" she began evasively.

"Caroline," he said, "you have one good habit that you had better never drop. You're the kind of girl who has *got* to tell her husband everything."

"You are joking. Surely?"

"Far from it."

"What is so wrong about lending an old camera?" She was silent and worried. At last she said, "It's all so silly. When George got back this morning from seeing his Greek friends, he was so angry about Yorghis and Evgenia Vasilika that—well how could I tell him then about the camera?"

"What did he say about them?"

"I wasn't to take any more lessons from Yorghis."

"But you are getting up those damned verbs for your next lesson."

"Just to finish the course, that's all. The lessons are all paid for."

She is in revolt, Strang thought. A week ago, she would have cut off the lessons at once. "What's the hidden fascination of a Greek verb?" he asked quietly.

Her cheeks colored. She said, "And I mustn't see Evgenia Vasilika again, either. That will be difficult. Evgenia found our new flat for us."

They really have wrapped you up, he thought as he looked at her. "Then find another one."

"You're in league with George," she said, trying to be unconcerned, succeeding only in being annoyed.

"Then I'm in good company. He is no fool."

"But he gives no explanation, no reason. I'm not a child—"

"Just take a tip from Uncle Ken: don't be so damned independent all of a sudden."

"Why not?"

"Because this is one time not to throw a rebellion. Who is more important to you? Yorghis and Vasilika or your husband?"

"Oh, don't be ridiculous!" she said, and started gathering her handbag and gloves.

"Relax, relax," he said gently. "If you can't tell George about it, tell me. You've got to tell someone, haven't you?"

"No!" she flashed at him. But she didn't rise, after all. "It is just all so *silly*. Evgenia Vasilika has been kinder to me than anyone else—taken more trouble—couldn't have been more thoughtful. It is difficult to refuse kindness, isn't it? And now I've got to tell her we don't want that flat, and I can't see her again. It's a horrible position to be in."

He asked, "And has Yorghis been helpful, too?"

She said nothing.

"How can you stand that little runt? He's on the make. Anything for quick money. What does he spend it on? Wine, women—?"

"The race track," she said. "And don't be so contemptuous. He wasn't always so pathetic."

"Yes," Strang said, "I bet he has a fine record behind him."

"He had a very good war record," she said defensively.

"Selling paper boots to the army."

"No, Kenneth! He was with the *andartes*. In the mountains. He was one of the interpreters for the British there."

"Oh," said Strang, "for the British there? And, of course, he knew your husband." So that was it: not Greek verbs, but recollections. "You really have that piece of history on the brain," he told her. "What do you expect to find out?"

She looked at him in surprise and indignation.

"I'll bet my last dollar that little Yorghis never was near your husband."

She was on the defensive at once. "He certainly was! He knew Yannis. And Sideros. And—"

"Boy, oh boy!" he said, looking away from her, shaking his head.

"You know what?" she told him icily. "You are quite impossible. I don't know why I ever bothered talking to you in the first place."

"You know why," he reminded her, his eyes watching the streams of people flowing over the broad and busy street.

"Because you knew Steve, I suppose?" she asked bitterly. But behind the fine indignation was a lurking shadow.

He didn't need to answer that. In any case, his eyes had found something surprising and delightful. He rose, a sudden smile breaking over his face.

Caroline looked at him sharply, raised her eyebrows. Then she watched him step forward to meet the dark-haired girl. Tall, slender, good skin, good features, good everything. Clothes simple; good, too, even if on the understated side. But carrying a camera; oh, you Americans! Who was she, anyway? Caroline drew off a glove, and sipped the sherry. Really magnificent eyes, she admitted as she flickered her own long eyelashes at the introduction. "Do join us," she said. "Are you staying in Athens, or just passing through, Miss Hillard?"

"Miss Hillard is taking Steve's place," Strang said, "on the *Perspective* job."

Caroline looked at Cecilia with unfeigned surprise. "I *am* impressed. But weren't you quick—getting here, I mean."

"Steve resigned last week," Strang said. "Miss Hillard arrived yesterday." He looked at Cecilia critically. "I thought you were going to sleep all day. And what will you have to drink?"

"I've just had coffee, thank you."

"Didn't you get much sleep?" he asked anxiously. She looked fine. Rested. Yet she seemed a little strained.

"Seven wonderful hours. Complete oblivion. Then I half woke. There was no sleeping after that. Naturally. There was too much happening outside my window. And so I am out, wandering." She looked at them both, a little uncertainly. "And now I think I'll wander on. Good-by, Mrs. Ottway." She rose.

"You're headed in the wrong direction for the Parthenon," Strang told her, catching her gently by the arm, coaxing her back onto her chair. "Just let me pay the check, and I'll set you straight."

"Yes," Caroline said, as she slipped her glove back on her elegant little hand, "Kenneth is awfully good at setting other people straight." She laughed very sweetly, and rose. "I have to dash. You must come to dinner, Miss Hillard, as soon as George and I get settled."

"Good luck," Strang said, rising and offering his hand.

Caroline looked at him sharply.

"With finding a new apartment."

"Yes," she said slowly. "First I must find a new apartment." Her green eyes widened, and now they were looking at him with amusement. "And perhaps a new tutor in Greek? Oh, really, Kenneth—what harm is there in a pathetic little man like Yorghis?" She looked down at Cecilia and surprised a look of recognition. "Do you know him, too?"

"If it is the Yorghis who used to work for the Spyridon Makres Agency—yes."

"Used to work?" Caroline looked puzzled.

"Well, I called them up just half an hour ago. About arrangements for my trip to Nauplion tomorrow. And they told me he had been discharged." And that, thought Cecilia, saved me a lot of embarrassment explaining I didn't want him as an interpreter. "I've arranged for a woman interpreter," she told Strang.

"But why," demanded Caroline, "why discharged?"

"I didn't ask."

Caroline looked puzzled, troubled. Perhaps the good name of the Spyridon Makres Agency had been a recommendation for Yorghis. And then, just as Strang was thinking hopefully that this might decide the question of Yorghis completely, she made one of her hundred-and-eighty-degree turns. "It seems so—so unjust," she said. Then she was walking quickly away, her head high, her heels clacking in light indignation.

"Yes," said Strang, watching her go, "so unjust. Poor little Yorghis, who needs his job so badly." He drained his glass. "Let's hope that doesn't make her rally to his defense."

"Is she like that?"

"A warm heart and a light head. It's a deadly combination."

"But attractive."

"Half of the time. The other half? I could throttle her, out of sheer exasperation."

"Oh—" That wasn't too good, she thought, and felt the little chill of despondency strike her. You had to like someone before you could be exasperated. Because when you were exasperated, you kept thinking about her (or him), worrying about her, hoping you could find what you thought was there; and so you kept trying and trying. Exasperation might be constant disappointment, but it was also a perpetual challenge. You ought to know, she told herself, remembering some of her own inexplicable perseverances. Now if only Ken had used the word "irritation," she would have felt much happier. Irritation meant mosquitoes, bothersome flies, something you smacked down or learned to ignore. "She likes you," Cecilia said. That was obvious.

Strang looked up in surprise from calculating the waiter's tip. "Yes," he said without any enthusiasm, "I'm the fatherly type, it seems."

"Oh?"

"Am I?"

"No."

"Thank you. She has got me almost believing that I am."

"Interesting technique," Cecilia observed. "Needs lots of advice, and help, and—" She paused. Dear dear me, she thought, how could I dislike another woman so quickly?

Strang looked at her. "That's it. But it's not technique, exactly. She just can't help it. She's really a sort of complicated simplicity."

No comment, Cecilia, she warned herself. But she couldn't resist saying, "She sounds a thoroughly muddled Martini."

"That's just about it," he said, and laughed, and then grew thoughtful. "If I hadn't met Caroline Ottway in a bookshop in Taormina, life would have been simpler for—" He broke off, wondering about that. Simpler for whom? Myself, certainly. If Caroline hadn't met me, I wouldn't have started worrying about Steve, or even remembering his story about the mountains; I wouldn't have heard about Sideros, or started wondering about George Ottway's curiosity in the house opposite his hotel; I wouldn't have been up in the Greek theater, late on a Saturday afternoon, trying to meet Katherini Roilos, and, instead, seeing the *Medea* sail from Messina. In fact, I wouldn't even have known Katherini was in Taormina at all if I hadn't carried Caroline Ottway's magazines back to her hotel. That simple stroll had started a chain reaction of curiosity, uncertainty, worry, doubt. And without all that, there would have been a very different first meeting with Alexander Christophorou: he would have learned quite easily that I was carrying Steve's documents. So what then? They would have been stolen before I left Taormina, and Steve would have been murdered right then. No need for any further postponement . . .

"Odd," he said, "to think what might not have happened, what did. But perhaps it was just as well my life was thoroughly complicated." Except for Katherini Roilos. Would she have been alive today if I hadn't been drawn into this whirlpool?

"Sorry," he said, noticing Cecilia's still silence. "It is always painful to try to reshape the past. It should never be done in public." He thought of Colonel Zafiris, who wouldn't approve of such indiscretion. "I had a strange kind of morning. I'm sorry." He gathered together the papers and magazines and books. He said, much more cheerful, almost back to normal, "Oh, here's a present!" He placed the slim edition of the Cavafy poems in front of her.

"For me?" She was surprised and then pleased; at least he hadn't forgotten her completely this morning, even if Caroline Ottway seemed to take more than her fair share of his thoughts. She looked at the book. It's always the way, she told herself: you meet a man you like, a man you like very very much, and he is already tangled up with someone else. Someone who is so damned obvious that she has got to wear jade earrings . . .

"But I thought you would like it," he was saying anxiously, watching her.

"I do. Very much. Thank you."

"Then where's your smile?"

She looked at him uncertainly.

"I bought you that present for completely selfish reasons," he told her. "I wanted one of those smiles you keep for thank-you occasions."

"Oh, Ken!" She smiled, a little embarrassed but mostly delighted.

"Much better," he pronounced. "You've the prettiest smile I've ever seen on any woman's face."

She began to laugh. "A smile is a smile—"

"It isn't. It's a display of teeth, a show of gums, a simper, a crack, a collection of wrinkles, a sag of double chin. And only now and again, if a man is lucky, he sees a real smile." And his heart stops for three seconds. Particularly, he thought, when there are eyes to match that smile. She was sitting quite still, holding the book against her breast, her hands folded across its back. "All right," he said brusquely, "let's find someplace to eat." He rose and gathered up her camera on his arm. "And then, we'll climb up to the Acropolis. That's what you want to do, isn't it?"

She nodded. "But you mustn't change your own plans for me. I mean—" She stopped in confusion as she saw the expression in his eyes. She rose quickly, slipping the book into her handbag. "It will be safe there," she told him, as they started toward the Grande Bretagne. She held out her hand. "Let me take the camera. It's a nuisance."

"Then why should you take it?"

She thought about that, with a new surprise. Her insistence faded. "You really have your hands full as it is."

Indeed I have, he thought. How am I going to persuade her to change her plans about Nauplion. ("Tell her?" he had asked, doubtfully. "Certainly," the Colonel had said.)

"Besides," she was saying, "I am so used to clutching a camera—"

"Independent, aren't you?" That silenced her. "You aren't the type," he told her.

"C. L. Hillard has to be."

"C. L. Hillard is strictly for the world of Mr. Lee Preston."

"Lee Preston—oh, heavens! I ought to have cabled him."

"Why?"

"To let him know I'm here and we've met, and—" She began to laugh. "He can stop worrying: everything is completely on schedule, all going according to plan."

That amused Strang, too. "I'd have taken a bet against that," he told her. "This is one morning I never expected to end with a real laugh."

She looked at him quickly, her blue eyes grave. "As bad as that?"

"No, no," he reassured her, covering up his blunder. "Not altogether. Some good news. Things are more under control than I thought. There are a lot of bright boys on this job. That's the feeling I got, at least."

And there's some very bad news, too, she thought; that is why he has been worried and tense. No use pestering him with questions. If he tells me anything at all, he will tell it in his own way, in his own good time. Probably, he is going to let me enjoy lunch, have my first visit to the Acropolis in peace, and then he'll bring up the bad news gently, sideways, trying not to alarm me. Is that the way it is? She hoped, somehow, it was. For a girl who had spent six years practicing hard to stand on her own two feet, it was surprising how quickly she had been learning to lean on a man's arm. Careful, she told herself, careful. . . . The arm is taken away, and then what? You remember. You've been through all that, once before. If you are an intelligent, sensible girl, you'll never risk all that pain again. Never. Once was enough in any lifetime.

She glanced at him. But how did you stop yourself from falling in love? Think of jade earrings. Who cares about even real jade earrings? All right, think of his faults. You can't? Then concentrate on your own: you're good at running away; it has always been the easy solution. "Tomorrow," she said, looking at the cars being loaded with baggage in front of the hotel entrance, "just about this time, I'll be leaving for Nauplion."

He looked down at her with a strange expression on his face. "We'll have to talk about that," he said. Then they were separated by one of the sponge sellers who seemed to have permanent rights on the sidewalk in front of the hotel. The sponges, strung together, covering him in a cloak of monstrous growths, bobbed and floated as he turned toward them hopefully, only his face and his feet clearly visible at either end of the swaying cocoon. "Not today," Strang said.

"Now, if he ever got caught in a heavy downpour—" Cecilia completed the vision in her own mind.

Strang's glance had paused, and hardened, just for a brief second, somewhere behind her. In the distance, walking briskly toward the hotel, was Alexander Christophorou. He hadn't seen them yet, but he would. Very soon. At his pace, they'd all meet on the doorstep of the Grande Bretagne. Strang looked at the sponges. "Choose one," he told Cecilia.

"Very good sponges," the man assured her, sensing a sale, calculating how much could be charged. The breeze whisked them up, like a bulbous ruff, around his ears.

"But I've no room in my—"

"Pick one out," Strang said urgently.

She glanced at him, asked whether she ought to poke or probe, was it color or size or what? She examined the nearest one, at least eighteen inches in diameter. "How do you pack such an object when it is wet? Or perhaps you don't take a bath on the day you are traveling?" And how long do I keep talking? she wondered. And must I really choose one of these objects? The man decided for her, by unlooping a monster and thrusting it into her arm.

"Free my right hand, will you? Thanks." Strang searched for his wallet.

She waited, hugging the slipping load of books and magazines under one arm, holding the sponge in the other, her hair whipped by the breeze from the open square over her eyes, her skirts flaring around her knees. "Help!" she said faintly, and laughed.

"With very great pleasure," Alexander Christophorou said, coming forward, freeing her arm of the books. "Hullo, Kenneth! You look as if you had been enjoying your morning." He glanced at the backs of the books. "The Peloponnese? Is that where you start?"

"I've got to get down to work sometime." The sponge seller was floating away. There was no more excuse for delay.

"Are you having luncheon here?" Christophorou was asking Cecilia. "Then why don't we all—"

"Not today," Strang said. He tried to keep everything easy and natural. He held out his hand. "I'll take the books."

Cecilia said quickly, "We have to talk over our plans, Mr. Christophorou. I'm leaving tomorrow for Nauplion, and Ken has to brief me. You know. . . ."

Christophorou looked at her for a long moment. "I don't. But I can imagine why my friend, here, enjoys his work so much." They began to walk, all three of them, into the hotel lobby, brilliantly lit, filled with sound and movement. "When will you return?" Christophorou asked Cecilia.

"Next week. Probably."

"Then perhaps—if I can get you away from your camera or from Kenneth—you'll have dinner with me?"

"Why—yes."

"I look forward to that." Christophorou glanced at Kenneth Strang. "Good-by." He shook hands with each of them, most formally. "I shall leave a note for you," he told Cecilia. He held her hand just a fraction of a second more than necessary. Then he left and went into the bar.

"One thing's for damned sure," Strang said, very quietly, "we don't eat here." He looked at her. "You aren't going to have dinner with him. Are you?"

"What else could I say?"

"You could have said no."

"And made him wonder why?"

"Why should he wonder why?"

"Because he's a most attractive man."

"You think that?" Strang stared at her. He was tight-lipped.

"He knows that. Ken," she added, looking at him in dismay, "I was only trying to help you out. You looked so—*so* grim."

"I didn't look half as grim as I felt." He looked at their armloads. "Let's dump this. And get the hell out." He started toward the porter's desk.

"We shan't need to," Cecilia said. "He has changed his mind. He is leaving." He even gave them a wave of his hand and a self-mocking explanation. "No rest for a journalist!" he told them as he passed by. But his eyes, Strang noticed, weren't smiling.

"Here is your bath sponge," Cecilia said.

"Not mine. Yours."

"Oh, heavens! I mean, thank you. What original presents you do choose. . . . Cleanliness is next to poetry?"

"That's right. *Mens sana . . .*"

"I had better leave this where it looks more natural." She turned toward the elevator, holding the enormous bath sponge nonchalantly, as if she were quite accustomed to wandering around hotel lobbies looking like an absent-minded Aphrodite with a solid piece of foam still clinging to her. "See you in ten minutes?"

"Right. I'll wait for you in the bar." He watched the elevator door close behind her.

At his elbow, a man said, "A pretty girl can carry off anything, eh?"

Strang ignored that, and went into the bar. He had always disliked people who ended sentences with "eh?" But as he ordered a Scotch and soda, and glanced around the crowd, he admitted his nerve ends were raw. If he could worry in peace, he might be less on edge. All this pretense of everything being quite normal—that was what really wore a man down. He was relieved to see no one he knew in the bar. No more pretense, meanwhile. Just some plain worrying. One thing was certain, the Colonel might murmur "Discretion!" warningly, but Cecilia would have to be told enough to put her on her guard. "To Nauplion," she had said so innocently. And Christophorou had looked at her searchingly, perhaps trying to calculate some hidden purpose, a threat or an ill-timed little joke. Then he wondered what signal Christophorou had received in this bar, or piece of information (a note concealed in a handshake: that was a specialty of his, wasn't it?) which had sent him away so quickly with that grim look in his eyes? I wish to God, Strang thought, that Colonel Zafiris would pick him up right now, and finish all this waiting. The Colonel had certainly much more information than he told me, and probably much more proof. The Greeks were never simple; they were like icebergs, one tenth showing, nine tenths hidden. What was the Colonel waiting for? I know one thing for certain: he doesn't wait without some purpose. Oh, blast them all, Strang thought bitterly, why do they make life so complicated?

As he drank his Scotch, he looked at the camera lying on the bar before him. Now what could a camera be used for, with its insides ripped out, some of these fancy new explosives expertly stuffed inside, a detonation triggered to the release? Only Yorghis wouldn't get very near any dictator to take a pretty picture with a borrowed camera; and Yorghis was not the type to blow himself up, along with fifty other people, for the sake of The Cause. Besides, preparations had been long made in Yugoslavia: a camera brought in, at this stage? Not likely. And why should a camera be borrowed and used if it was going to be blown to pieces? The serial number, the sure lead to identification, would have to stay intact. A British camera . . . In Yugoslavia? No. No purpose there. Now a camera traced to a Greek owner—that would have had some point. What if that camera never went to Yugoslavia at all? Yorghis borrowed it, Yorghis handed it over for use elsewhere.

Or perhaps I'm all wrong, he thought, perhaps I've got conspiracy and plots on the brain. Perhaps Yorghis, for once, acted quite honestly. He wanted a camera to take snapshots of pretty girls in swim suits.

Strang looked at Cecilia's camera. A revolver, he thought, could be used in a camera, and the identification not destroyed. But a revolver, when guards were around, might have only one chance of hitting its target.

Guards weren't supposed to allow more than that. No, he decided again, a revolver is too chancy for the sure thing that Drakon has been planning. He would want something with more coverage than one bullet, something more certain and more spectacular.

Good God, he thought as he noticed his reflection in the glass behind the bar, what a lot of pretty little speculations you're churning around behind that completely calm and normal face! His face, indeed, was so normal that he was shocked. What our brave-new-world scientists ought to be inventing was a thought ray, revealing everything going on inside the inhuman head. That would take care of a lot of crookery. Honest men might be able to sleep better.

A camera, used in an assassination, identifiable as belonging to the wife of an English attaché . . . Where would that stir up some really nasty trouble, setting people at one another's throats? There was no lack of places like that today, in this happy, happy world. Cyprus was one of them. And Ottway was on his way there, suddenly, unexpectedly, after a session with the Colonel this morning.

Now, if I were Drakon, how would I arrange that little operation? A batch of Greek resistance heroes and Cypriot patriots blown to pieces by a Turk in the pay of the perfidious English. Camera and Turk, of course, intact. You couldn't destroy evidence after arranging it so carefully. But what would you use *in* the camera? Or would you just use it as a carrying case, something from which you could extract a high-powered grenade and throw it? Strang felt cold sweat edge his brow at the idea he had conjured up. No, he decided, I wouldn't really make a very good Drakon. I haven't a strong-enough stomach. He paid for his drink, looked at his watch. She was two minutes late. He picked up the camera and started toward the door. In his haste he almost ran smack into Tommy, benign and ruddy as ever even after a late late night, but with a worried glint in his blue eyes.

"I was hoping to see Ottway here," Tommy kept his voice low as he looked around the room. "Tried to speak with him this morning several times. I'm sorry, Strang. I don't seem much help to you. I just can't get him on the telephone."

"I think we can stop worrying about him. He didn't need any prodding."

"He took action by himself?" The old eyes were relieved. "We should have expected that," Tommy said, a little severely. He bowed to a table nearby. "Come and let me introduce you to Madame Kontos. Delightful woman. Widow of a poet. Interested in music. Most knowledgeable. She holds the most absorbing *salon* every Sunday afternoon. You simply must see that side of Athens, my dear fellow. Come along."

"I'm afraid I can't. I'm meeting Cecilia for lunch. Another time? And thank you again for last night. I'm sorry we gave you so much trouble."

"Not at all, not at all." The genial face was clouded. "It's a very bad show, a very bad show, indeed. All around." Tommy hesitated. "I had a very odd visitor this morning."

"Oh?"

Tommy drew Strang to one side of the doorway, maneuvered him against a corner free from traffic, dropped his voice still more. "Asking questions about Aleco," he whispered.

"About that ring?"

Tommy stared for a moment, perhaps even a little disappointed. "Yes."

"Do you remember it?"

"Never saw it in my life." Then he studied Strang's tense face. "Is it so important to you?" he asked in surprise.

"Yes," Strang said. "*And* to Miss Hillard."

Tommy was worried now, embarrassed. "There was such a ring," he said slowly. "I've just come from seeing Aleco's father. That young man who visited me was leaving as I arrived. Aleco's father—well, I have never seen him so distressed. This may kill him, you know."

"He identified the ring?"

"What else could he do? Tell a lie about it?" asked Tommy angrily.

Strang shook his head. So now I know, he was thinking; no doubts, small hopes, or explanations left. Alexander Christophorou is Odysseus.

Tommy touched his arm. "This goes, of course, no farther?"

"No farther." And you and I, he was thinking, are now charter members of The Great Deceived.

"There must be some explanation, don't you think?"

Strang nodded. But not the explanation that either of us wanted.

"Ah, well—" Tommy said, leaving the incomprehensible, turning to the immediate, as he took a step away. "You will remember to bring Miss Hillard to tea some day?" he asked in a normal tone of voice, nodded to a passing friend, and moved toward the most knowledgeable Madame Kontos.

Strang stepped into the lobby. He was late. But Cecilia was later. He looked at his watch again, checked it with the clock. He had a moment of real panic, standing there in the lobby, normal faces and voices all around him, everyone safely assured, with only thoughts of food or drink or pleasant expeditions in their well-groomed heads. But just then, she appeared, coming down the last steps of the staircase that the baggage porters used.

"The elevators were packed," she said. "They kept passing my floor. So at last I gave up, and walked. Am I late?"

TWENTY

It was too early, Greek time, for the huge dining room to be busy. So luncheon was fairly quick, with several waiters in full evening dress to serve them lamb chops and coffee. "You'll need more than that," Cecilia said, looking at Strang's plate.

"I guess that drink I had in the bar ruined my appetite."

"Or something." She looked at him.

So he had to smile cheerfully and pretend he could taste the food. "About this Nauplion trip," he began, tactfully enough, once everything was eaten except the bones in little paper frills. "You're not really serious about it, are you?"

"Why not? I have to start work sometime."

"That's a good idea," he agreed. "But not Nauplion. Not for a few days, at least. Give your eye time to get accustomed to Greek light, all that sort of thing."

She didn't seem much impressed.

"You might as well wait until I can go there with you."

"But I thought you liked to work on your own. You and Steve—"

"Steve was different," he told her. "I had worked with him before. We had time to talk over our plans in New York. I knew his ideas, he knew mine. We could work alone. See?"

"I see." But there was a slight curve on a well-marked eyebrow. "If we could talk over plans, this evening, wouldn't that be enough?"

"No."

"But—"

"I don't want you wandering alone around the Peloponnese, at this time, Cecilia. Have you got that? Not alone."

His face was so set, so serious that she stopped objecting. "Yes," she said.

He took a deep breath of relief. It had been easier than he had expected, after all.

"Then," she asked, "where can I wander around alone? In Athens?"

"That was the idea, this morning. But now—"

"Now?" she wondered.

"I'd like to put you on a flight for Rome, this afternoon."

"Rome?" Her eyes widened. "You don't want me for the *Perspective* job," she said involuntarily.

"Of course I do," he said sharply. "I just want you to stay in Rome for a few days. Or Paris. Or London. Anywhere you like—"

"But Lee Preston—what is he going to say? What is anyone going to say?"

"I don't give one good damn."

"Ken," she said softly, "what I mean is this: if I went away from Greece right now, it would seem very strange. Wouldn't it? All last night, all this morning, you've been trying to keep everything looking—well, as normal as possible. We are just two visitors, with only their assignment from *Perspective* to worry about."

He looked at her. She had noticed more than he had imagined.

"I am right, you know," she said gently. "If you send me away, you might as well announce to the whole Grande Bretagne bar that you've got something more on your mind than Greek temples."

"You'd be safe, at least."

Perhaps, she thought. But he would have doubled his own danger. "Let's bluff it out," she said. "Let's keep any most attractive character from confirming his suspicions, shall we?"

Yes, she had noticed much more than Strang had imagined.

"Besides," she was saying, "how do you know that Rome or London would be any safer?"

He remembered Katherini's passing reference to her aunt's journeys abroad. The barbarians, today, had a long reach. "You have a point there," he admitted. As he signed the check, he was thinking gloomily that the battle of Nauplion might have been won, but he had lost the campaign. She was staying in Greece.

He brooded over that as she added a touch of lipstick to her lower lip without distorting her mouth or grimacing, gathered her bag and gloves together, and rose. They started the long walk to the door, in the midst of a mild clatter of plates, a polite scraping of forks, a continuous chorus in five languages or more. "Come to Sparta with me," he said. "Visit Steve's sister."

She was completely startled. Then she recovered a little. "That would seem quite normal?" she teased him.

"Completely in line," he assured her.

"I—I really don't know." She pretended to be interested in a table banked with flowers, where a Greek-American and his family were being given a welcome-back party. Her attention was caught by two elegant saris, swaying gracefully into the room, two paces behind their Western-suited husbands. "Aren't they divine—" she began.

"Plenty of wild mountains," he said, "spring flowers, blue sky, white clouds. What more does a photographer want?"

She said nothing.

"Shepherds and their dogs, peasants on donkeys, villages perched away among the crags. And there is Mistra to see, only a couple of miles from Sparta. What self-respecting photographer would miss Mistra?"

Mistra . . . "That's ruined Byzantine, not classical Greek," she protested. But she was interested. What heaven, she thought, what absolute bliss! She pulled herself up, sharply. She might not have wanted to run away as far as Rome, but she had better run farther than Sparta.

They passed through the crowded anteroom, into the crowded lobby. Strang glanced sharply back again at a neat little man, partly obscured by a group of Frenchmen. But the little man, in the unobtrusive, dark suit, had disappeared entirely. For a moment, there, Strang had imagined he was Elias. But Colonel Zafiris would hardly send Elias to watch over us, he decided. Elias had more important work to do than that. At least, he thought, I hope so.

"Yes?" asked Cecilia.

"Nothing," he said. "Let's pick up our mail and then get a cab."

She had a cable from New York, a letter postmarked Athens, a hand-delivered note in a sealed envelope. She had time to notice he had two letters, both with American stamps, both addressed in blatantly female writing. More jade earrings?

Strang stuck the letters into his pocket and helped her into the cab. He glanced around before he followed her; no, he couldn't see Elias looking into any shopwindow or dodging quickly into a doorway.

Cecilia looked back at the sidewalk, between the pleated silk curtains draped across the rear window. "The sponge sellers have gone," she said. She touched the curtains' bobbed fringe. Was this really a cab? Two-tone Plymouths, at home, were never like this: lace mats for heads and arms, a rug on the floor, a pink paper rose in a little vase fastened above the dashboard, three small framed photographs of wife and child, a three-inch doll dangling above them. Let's hope our man can drive, she thought, what with all these curtains and swaying charms and polite head turnings to talk to Ken. Nothing seemed to fascinate a Greek more than a foreigner's attempt to speak his language. But she relaxed a little as she saw the man could drive, even at high speed with his profile presented to the street ahead.

She opened the cable. It was brief: DID YOU ARRIVE? LEE PRESTON.

The letter was from Robert Pringle's wife, first name either Affie or Iffie or Effie, suggesting they all drive out to Sunium for dinner next Wednesday. Nice, she thought regretfully, but dinner parties and work don't always mix. Perhaps the Pringles would give her a rain check on Wednesday.

Now for the note . . . It was from Katherini. She read it with relief and delight. "It's from—" she began, and then looked at the driver (now telling Ken about the new cement works down toward the Piraeus, which were well worth seeing), and slipped the note into her handbag. That news would be better kept for the Acropolis.

Strang finished explaining, regretfully, that they would have to visit the cement works some other time; also Daphni, also Eleusis, also Marathon. Today—yes, all afternoon—would be spent at the Acropolis. Then he sat back, exhausted with his battle, and returned thankfully to English. "From whom?"

Cecilia handed him the cable.

One glance and, "Very poignant," he observed. "Tell him we've been busy."

"We ought to cable, though."

"And what do we tell him about Steve?"

"Yes, there's that," she said, frowning.

"Especially as Preston is probably reading about his death right now. He'll be on the telephone to us, any hour. Perhaps we better not answer any long-distance calls for the next few days. Not until we can tell him something definite."

"He's going to start fretting."

"When you have got to tell a lie, keep silent." Strang crumpled up the cable and tossed it out of the window.

"Oh!—"

"Don't worry, Cecilia. Soon we'll be able to talk to Uncle Preston without any faking."

"Soon?" she asked hopefully.

"We'll have definite news soon," he said. One way or another, he thought angrily. "I could use some good news, right now."

She looked down at her handbag and hesitated. Then she couldn't keep the secret any longer. She took Katherini's note out of her handbag. "Here is one good piece of news to go on with." Delightedly, she watched the astonishment that flickered over his face. She looked out of the window while he read the note. The shops and business houses were barred and locked. The streets were strangely quiet. Even the tables in the coffee shops were almost empty, except for a few die-hard philosophers. "What has happened? Everything has shut down."

Strang looked up from the note, abstractedly. For once, he was slow to catch her meaning. "Until four o'clock," he said at last. He said nothing at all about the note. Suddenly, he reached out and grasped her hand. He stared out of the window, seeing nothing.

Cecilia watched him, anxiously. Perhaps he didn't like the idea of her going to meet Katherini alone, this evening. But it was to be such a simple, quick meeting at the corner of Constitution Square. What could be more open? Or easier? It was only a few steps from the hotel. And all Katherini needed was a little help—money for the bus fare back to her village: two single tickets, one for Maria, one for herself. That was all.

Strang's grip on her hand tightened. He was seeing a busy corner, filled with the movement of people at the end of a work day. Darkness falling. Everyone hurrying home. Cecilia arriving at half past seven. A cab starting forward from the hotel rank, stopping beside her. A door opening, and a woman's friendly voice calling, "Here! Here!" And Cecilia going over to the car (for so many cabs looked like private cars in Athens); the woman's hand grasping hers, the voice saying urgently, "I am Maria. It was not safe for Katherini to come. Let us drive around this block, while I tell you what has happened. There is much news to give you." That was all that was needed. That was all.

Cecilia was saying, "Ken!"

He released her hand. He folded the note. "Do you mind if I keep this?" He hoped he sounded casual enough. But she still looked puzzled. So he adopted a jocular kind of tone. "One thing is definite, my girl. No Athens for you. Not alone. Not for the next few days. You're coming with me."

"You're worrying too much." She sounded fretful, she knew, but she couldn't help that.

"You still won't think of Rome?"

She shook her head.

"Stubborn, aren't you?"

"So are you."

"Yes," he said slowly, "I guess I am." He slipped the note into his pocket.

The cab made the last twist and turn in the road and drew up at an open stretch of high ground, well-paved, landscaped with trees and shrubs, lying at the foot of a broad, steep slope of hard-packed earth and out-cropping rock. Above the slope, the rock began to dominate and then, abruptly, flowed upward into a precipice, a vast encircling arm thrown around the high island of the Acropolis. The giant columns, rising from the rampart of precipices with a grace that turned solid stone into delicate movement, caught the sun's warmth and glowed, a golden white, above the cold gray rock. Everything flowed up, carrying man's eye from earth to heaven.

"I'll wait for you," the cabdriver told them, breaking the spell. He pointed to a parking space near some young trees and a booth where terra-cotta ash trays and black-figure vases were for sale. There were some tour-ists, some loiterers—other drivers, guides, the eternal post-card sellers.

Strang said, "It will be a long wait." Two hours, at least. Another cab was driving up now. But no one got out. That's odd, Strang thought.

"I'll wait," their driver said. He knew best. He flashed a bright Greek smile, white teeth against olive skin.

I doubt that, thought Strang. I must have overtipped again. He took Cecilia's arm and started back toward the other cab. "This way, this way!" his own driver called quickly, and pointed up to a wandering path which led to the admission gate.

Strang turned and retraced his steps. "Stupid of me," he said. But he had had a glimpse of the man who sat in the back of the other cab. If it had been Christophorou, he thought, I'd have smashed his bloody jaw right here and now. But it had been Elias. Colonel Zafiris was taking no chances, seemingly.

Cecilia said quietly, "The man in that cab—I saw him, back at the Grande Bretagne. He took the cab after ours. Is he following us?"

"You'd break his heart if he could hear you."

"You aren't worried?"

"Not this time." In fact, it was pleasant to feel he could relax a little and leave it all to the experts. "He is one of the Colonel's young men."

"Are we as important as that?"

"I hope not." Then he drew her around to face the Acropolis. "Let's be-gin again. Forget everything else." And forget that I just had the desire to smash the face of the man who once brought me here. Oh, forget all that, forget it! He took a deep breath. They began to climb a dusty path toward a wire fence and an admission gate.

"Forget this part, too," he told her, "and the tourists, and the guards, and the guides. Once we're through here—"

He was right. Once they were through, still following the path, they reached the end of the new, the beginning of the old. In front of them lay a series of giant steps, climbing steeply in a double staircase, up to the massive colonnade of the ancient gateway. By its side, high on its own precipice, was the Temple of the Wingless Victory, the first to be seen, always to be remembered. It was the perfect site. Everyone who approached had to look up; everyone who climbed had to walk slowly; everyone waited for the moment of seeing what lay beyond.

The whole Acropolis opened up to their eyes, a high plateau of solid rock, a vast bare sweep of sloping gray stone, uneven yet worn smooth. Once, there had been many statues and altars and sanctuaries, a multitude of offerings and memorials, a forest of marble richly decorated in color and with gold. Now, except for a few rejected fragments lying scattered around, a pathetic remembrance of things past, there were only the remains of three temples left standing—with their rows of fluted columns rising, heavy drum on heavy drum of marble, the gold and sculpture and treasures looted, the dark-red and blue painted decorations washed and faded into whiteness. The houses of the gods, the Greeks had called them.

They had been placed in no symmetrical design, but in a seemingly thoughtless imbalance. Thoughtless? It was powerfully effective, even now in this bare stretch of looted ground, spreading the temples apart, each to the edge of its own precipice, each to be studied by itself, each so different in size and arrangement, each with its own effect. The Parthenon, the largest temple, had been raised not in the middle of the Acropolis, as a methodical mind would have placed it, but to one side, on the highest slope of rock-covered ground. The rows of enormous marble columns seemed straight perfection, yet again there was imbalance to help man's eye, a careful calculation to add grace to solid strength.

Strang had become completely absorbed. Cecilia could watch him now without even risking the embarrassment of being noticed. At this moment, she thought, here is a completely happy man. Then she looked out over the precipices; down at the patchwork of houses, seamed by twisting streets, spreading over the little hills below her, scattering even around the larger hills farther away. To the southwest was the sea, shimmering in the afternoon sun around its dark islands. But this is an island, too. An island in the sky, she thought, looking back around the Acropolis, stripped of all its riches down to the essentials—the mysticism that had first built it, the vision of greatness.

She opened her bag and drew out her case of filters and her light meter. Plenty of everyday problems, though, before she could start her imaginings. These widely scattered temples, for instance. The only way to get them grouped together for the exact camera eye would be to climb that little hill opposite, to the south, a hill with green trees and a monument on the top. Here, on the Acropolis, I'll have to work with each unit complete in itself. I'll have to find the best angles for each building, the best time of day; try to give a feeling of height, of soaring. . . . There's plenty of drama, strong light and deep shade; plenty of texture, variation in color from the cold gray rock to the blended whites and golden tones of the columns; plenty of wonderful, marvelous, magnificent lines.

The canopy of blue sky was enormous, intense in color, smooth as silk. She would have to be careful of this clear air and bright sun, of the reflected light from the pillars. Very careful, too, of the human beings, moving so capriciously around, their heads tilted back, their eyes swung upward. Tourists, bless their poor tired feet, seldom looked natural. Or elegant. It was a pity they did not wear the same kind of clothes they wore back home in their own cities. "We are going traveling," people said, and started thinking of vacations, pushing *lederhosen* and shorts and sandals and beach skirts into their suitcases, as if cities abroad were places for picnics or hikes or barbecues. The Greeks, on their home ground, dressed in everyday clothes, looked real, and, strangely enough, more comfortable. If she had to have some figures in the foreground, let them be the quiet, brooding Greeks, sitting still, self-contained within their own individual islands.

Strang sat on the top step of the western end of the Parthenon, and watched her moving slowly away, circling around, standing in reflection, moving on again. For one moment, he thought she was drifting too far out of sight, and rose. Then he noticed a man, farther down the slope, rise quietly from his seat on a broken fragment of pediment—Elias it was— and follow quietly, not at all obviously. So many people were moving slowly around at random that Elias's little maneuver seemed absolutely natural. Strang relaxed, sat back on the step. At least, he thought, as he looked out once more over the Acropolis, I have had almost an hour of complete forgetfulness. And he was grateful. It was with a new decision, the bright sun pouring its warm energy over him generously, the cool spring breeze fanning away his exhaustion, that he reached in his pocket and took out the letter signed "Katherini." He rose as he saw Cecilia emerging from behind a corner of the Erechtheum portico. Quickly, he walked down the slope toward her, taking out a cigarette. Elias, he hoped, would not be far away, and this would be the closest Strang could get to him, this afternoon.

"Hello," he said to Cecilia, "how is it coming?"

"Only playing around, feeling my way, testing the film, mostly. The light is too yellow at this time of day, I think."

"I need a match," he said, and turned toward the man who had wandered into sight and was now standing quite still at the corner of the portico, admiring the procession of maidens, marble carved magically into girls' strong bodies covered by a transparent flow of silk.

"May I borrow a match?" he asked Elias politely.

It didn't take long. Within a minute, he was back with Cecilia, lighting a cigarette for her with his. "Let's go and look at the olive tree," he said. "Do you know its story?" He led her to the other side of the portico, to a stretch of sunken ground guarded by a broken wall.

"What did you give him?" she asked softly.

"Was it noticeable?"

"Not at all. But why else did you go up to him? Oh, don't worry, Ken—no one else knew that your lighter was working, and that I had matches."

He studied her face. He said, "I gave him Katherini's letter."

"Why?"

"It's a fake."

She looked at him, instantly on the alert.

"Let's sit here and talk," he suggested. It was a sunny, sheltered spot, both from the vagrant breeze and the wandering tourists. The olive tree, even one that stood on the spot where an olive tree had grown long before the Parthenon was built, and had survived as a symbol of hope when everything else on the ancient Acropolis had been destroyed by the Persians, could not compete on home movies with the Portico of Maidens or the Parthenon itself. A visitor, now, looked over the wall curiously (tourists always hopefully believed that others might lead them to a good thing) and called disappointedly to his friends, "There's only an old tree!" And then he was gone. A guard looked over, too, and seemed content that no damage was being done. Elias was walking slowly back toward the main gateway. They were alone, with the sweet smell of thin grass and dark-blue wild flowers around them, the gnarled olive tree outlined against Pentelic marble. Cecilia sat on a fragment of pedestal, Strang on a broken pillar.

"Give me the bad news first," Cecilia said. Then, as he hesitated, she added, "That way, I know that there is nothing worse to come."

"All right," he said. "I gave that letter to Elias so that he could get it to Colonel Zafiris, right away. So the woman, or whoever is going to meet you this evening, can be arrested. It won't be Katherini who is going to keep that appointment. She is dead."

Cecilia said nothing. Her face had whitened, grown expressionless. She sat very still. She could have been carved out of marble, like the maidens high behind her.

He told her what the Colonel had described to him. "That is the bad news," he said. His voice was bitter as he added, "If Drakon is only a name to cover Christophorou, then I am to blame. I told Christophorou—" He stopped speaking.

"What was the rest of the news?" she asked quickly. "What else had the Colonel to say?"

They were both silent for a little when he had ended. Then he came back to Katherini's death again. "I wondered at the time why the Colonel told me so much. Now, of course, I begin to see. There was a reason behind everything he said, everything he showed me: the fact, for instance, that Katherini was being questioned when his men entered the Kriton Street house. That was his way of warning me that they might have got some information out of her about you and me. They did, obviously." He paused. "If I had used my brains, I would have expected something like that letter." He fell silent again, wondering what else he had missed in that morning's interview.

Cecilia broke her long silence. She pushed back her hair, away from her face, then shook it free from her fingers. "No," she said, as if she had decided something, "they didn't learn much from Katherini. She wouldn't tell—"

"Look, Cecilia, they were *questioning* her," he said, his voice harshening. "Do I have to go into details?"

"She wouldn't break. Not so soon, not so quickly. She had strength, that girl."

"I know that. But even the bravest—" He didn't finish.

"Yes, I know," she said. "I've heard about such things." She frowned, fighting back her emotion. "But Katherini—she wouldn't tell them anything that would hurt us. I'm sure of that, somehow. She—" Cecilia bent her head to hide her tears. She stirred a fragment of marble with her foot. "We can still bluff them," she said determinedly. "They still don't know, exactly. If they believed we really had learned so much—" She looked around her, then, thinking that perhaps she never would have seen the Acropolis at all. But Ken is the one who may really be in danger. Why do they want to get hold of me?

"I told you too much," he said suddenly. "I wish to God you knew nothing—nothing at all."

She began removing the filter from her camera lens, and placed it in the neat little leather pocket in her case. "I'm thankful you did," she said calmly. "Ignorance is too dangerous. If the Colonel hadn't told you about Katherini, we would really have been in trouble." She shut the case into her handbag, closed her camera carefully.

"Thank God," he said, watching her, "you don't panic easily."

You're a better actress than you thought, she told herself. He helped her to rise. Nearly everyone else had left. In the far distance were only some stray students, a few solitary Greeks.

They began walking slowly toward the gateway. A vast bare silence lay around them, the deep-blue canopy stretched overhead. The western sun was stretching the shadows of the ancient gateway toward their feet. Strang paused and looked back at the Parthenon. The warm rays set it glowing gently, high on its gray slope of rock, as if a fire had been kindled inside it. Cecilia had turned to watch it, too. Her lips were parted a little, in the beginning of a surprised look of complete delight; her eyes were as blue as the sky, as radiant as the sun.

"There's something I want to tell you," Strang said.

She looked around at him. Then her eyes widened anxiously. She had never seen him look so worried, so tense.

"I'm in love with you." He caught her hands. "Will you marry me?"

For a moment, she stood very still. She could say nothing. She tried to speak. She shook her head.

"Cecilia," he said, desperate now, "you can't say no. It has got to be yes. It has got to be."

"Yes," she said slowly.

His arms went around her, bringing her close. He kissed her.

At last, he let her go. And now, as he looked at her, he could say nothing at all. He picked up the handbag and camera, which had dropped at her feet, and then they started toward the gateway. They passed through its chill shadows and came to meet the sun again at the top of the giant steps.

"Why did you say no?" he asked. That had been a bad moment, a moment of loss, complete loss: everything thrown away on a wild impulse.

"I didn't say no."

"You shook your head."

"That was sheer wonder. 'This can't be me,' I was saying, 'this can't be me.'" And it isn't, she thought: I'm the girl who was going to run farther away than Sparta.

"It is you, and it is me, and that is all there is to it."

"But it's madness." She was smiling, though. "Ken—we are *both* mad."

"Then this is the kind of madness that keeps men sane."

"But you don't *know* me. We don't—"

"Don't we?" He kissed her again. She didn't argue any more about that.

They started down the high steps, Strang leading, her hand on his wrist to steady her. "Back to earth," he was saying, descending carefully. He wasn't too steady himself. He could blame it on the dazzling light, on the steep pitch of the staircase, except neither glare nor height had ever made him feel like this before. "Take it easy," he told her, and tried to follow his own advice. He caught her by the waist at the last step and lifted her down onto the path. The two guards up at the high gateway had come forward to the edge of the portico, and were looking down with quiet interest. "We'll disappoint them, this time," he told her, and they began walking to the small office at the admission gate in the high wire fence.

Cecilia glanced back, up at the portico. "You do choose your moments," she said softly.

"Not that moment. It chose me." And that was the unexplainable truth. He had been going to wait, had he, until this trouble was over and their job for *Perspective* finished? Yes, that was the way it seemed best, last night. "I may have rushed things a bit," he admitted, "but I suddenly realized I had wasted enough time in my life." He glanced at her, to see if a shadow had crossed her face. He could be jealous of even the ghost of a memory. And that was a startling new feeling, too.

But there was no shadow, no ghost. She was looking at him, as if she had guessed his emotion. "At least," she said slowly, carefully, "we did meet before we wasted any more years." Then she looked at him with horror, "Oh Ken, we might never have met!"

And Elias, waiting impatiently in the doorway of the small office beside the admission gate, shook his head. The two guards beside the gate had been following the Americans' slow progress with sympathetic interest, but Elias, brisk from the quick telephone call he had made, could only think of all the unnecessary delay, the complications, the added danger. How strange were American reactions to a threatening note! Romantic love was one Western invention that Greece could leave well alone.

Strang halted as he saw Elias. "Back to earth we are," he said quietly. "Have a look at the post cards, Cecilia. See what competition you have got." As she went forward to the display of photographs, he picked up an illustrated guidebook from the counter at the ticket window.

Elias said, "Six o'clock in Miss Hillard's room. Six o'clock."

"In Miss Hillard's room?" That puzzled Strang.

"It is easier." Elias turned away as if to say, "Now stop asking idiotic questions and get back to the hotel as I told you."

Strang put down the price of the guidebook, and joined Cecilia. "Found anything?"

"Not yet."

"Another time, then. Come on." He took her arm and led her through the gate.

She saw something had nettled him. "What's wrong?"

"Nothing. We are just being sent back to your room, that's all." He glanced at his watch and his lips tightened. "They don't give us much time, these boys." Not much time alone, either, he thought angrily.

"But why in my room?"

"I asked that question and got very little answer." Easier for whom?

"They're probably trying to help us," Cecilia said.

"Probably," he agreed, to please her. But he was still annoyed. He never had enjoyed the feeling that his life was being arranged for him.

Then two small boys, near one of the ash-tray-and-bogus-vase booths, saw them coming and ran to wake up a taxi driver sleeping peacefully in his cab. The man stretched and yawned happily. "It was good I waited?" their driver asked. "Is very beautiful the Parthenon." And all the energy, gathered in his two-hour sleep, poured into a long discussion of the Acropolis: the foreigners all admired it; but rich and powerful as foreigners were, had they ever been able to produce anything like that? No, agreed Strang, and tactfully didn't suggest that no one in Greece in the last two thousand years had ever equaled it, either. Instead, he put forward the idea that now he had better translate all these interesting observations for the benefit of the lady. That seemed a reasonable request and was politely granted. So Strang returned to Cecilia for the remaining six minutes of the ride.

"When are we getting married?" he asked.

She looked startled. "But we've just got engaged." She began to laugh. "Right on top of the Acropolis . . ."

And we'd have been married there, too, if it could have been managed, he thought. "You didn't answer the question."

"Well—there's the *Perspective* job to finish. Isn't there?"

"Yes. But it won't get finished if you don't marry me."

"But wouldn't that be—"

"No, it wouldn't."

"But, darling—"

"It's quite simple," he told her. "I can do this job in two ways. Either without you or with you. There's no half-and-half business possible. First, you're too beautiful. Second, you're too pretty. Third, you're too distractingly lovely. So that's the choice, and there is none, because I'm not doing this job without you."

"And to think," she said, "I imagined you proposed to me because of the brilliance of my intellect." She smiled, one of her warmest and truest smiles. She reached toward his cheek and kissed it gently.

The hotel lobby was more than usually crowded. "There is a reception in the ballroom," the porter told them with lowered voice. The flowered hats were out in full bloom, the green-khaki uniforms showed their medals, young diplomats concealed light thoughts under dark suits, older men stooped under their load of boredom.

"Big guns," Strang said to Cecilia, as he recognized two faces from newspaper photographs. "No place for light artillery." He hurried her into the elevator, glancing at his watch. It was quarter of six. He took her to her room door. "I'll be back here in eight minutes," he told her, and kissed her a temporary good-by. Love in snatches, he thought wryly, as he hurried upstairs to his room. As he washed at lightning speed, changed his shoes and shirt and tie, he remembered the long lonely hours he had had to himself in Taormina. But that was only to be expected: the minute you got your girl, everything started conspiring to separate you.

He was startled to see, in the bathroom mirror, what a cheerful face he was wearing. Love, he decided, made all men look like idiots. His grin widened. All right, he told himself, it feels wonderful, but sober up, for God's sake, or you'll blast off into orbit and stay there. He prepared to leave, checking his wallet, fresh handkerchief, keys, giving a last look at his sketchbook abandoned on his desk. "Just wait," he told it, "I'll add drawings to your collection that you won't be ashamed of. I'll do the best work I've ever done." Then, just as he opened his door, with thirty seconds to get down to the second floor, the telephone rang. "Damn!" he said, started to close the door, hesitated, opened it again. He went back and picked up the receiver. The call was from Sparta.

"Waiting," he said, ready for Petros's voice. There was a good deal of crackling and fizzing, and at last a woman's voice asking "Mr. Strang?"

"Waiting," he said again.

"Myrrha Kladas," the voice said, and came in a little more clearly now. "I am Myrrha Kladas. The sister of Steve."

Strang strained to catch the distant, hesitant voice. "More slowly, please," he told her. Greek was difficult enough without a long-distance call to add to his troubles.

"Steve's sister," she repeated. "Do you understand?"

"Yes, yes."

"Please come. At once."

"At once?"

"It is urgent." The voice had strengthened.

"But where?"

"I must see you."

"Where?"

"Near Thalos there is a bridge, a path that leads to my house, one kilometer past the village. I shall wait there."

"Tomorrow? About noon?" If he left at six in the morning, that ought to let him reach Thalos by that time.

"Tonight," she said.

"But it is almost six o'clock now."

"I shall wait."

"I cannot leave until seven." Seven at the very earliest, he thought, and even that would be difficult.

"I shall wait," Myrrha Kladas said, her sad voice fading again, and, this time, into silence.

TWENTY-ONE

Strang took only thirty seconds to get down, by staircase, to Cecilia's door. She opened it, a little subdued. "I'm late, you should keep this door locked, sorry darling, there was a telephone call," he said all in one quickly gathered breath as he put his arms around her and kissed her. Then he saw that there were others there. Damnation, he thought, and closed the door and turned to face them all. Pringle, in subdued and diplomatic gray, seemed a little startled. Elias, an eyebrow raised, looked at his watch. Colonel Zafiris, resplendent in full decorations, appeared to notice nothing at all. He shook Strang's hand politely, offered Cecilia a chair with a gracious wave of his hand, selected the pink-velvet sofa for himself, and lit a cigarette.

"I have ten minutes," the Colonel said. He allowed himself a slight gleam of a smile. "Unless, of course, Mr. Strang receives other telephone calls."

It might have been a neat reminder that Strang hadn't yet apologized to anyone except Cecilia; or it could have been subtle curiosity. I'll take it as curiosity, thought Strang. "It was a call from Sparta," he said bluntly. He was too worried to be polite. "From Steve's sister, Myrrha Kladas." That got everyone's attention. Elias even stopped looking at his watch.

"Sparta—" the Colonel said softly. "By that, do you mean the town of Sparta itself?"

"I assumed it was from Thalos."

"There is no telephone in Thalos." The Colonel looked at Elias, who burst into a rush of suggestions. Elias seemingly knew the situation at Thalos. And it was his feeling that the call, for the sake of privacy, would be made from the town of Sparta itself.

"If it was a very private call," the Colonel agreed with him. And then to Strang, "Was it?"

"Yes. She said it was urgent. Wants me to leave at once. She said she would be waiting at a bridge, one kilometer past the village." He frowned. "One odd thing, though. She was talking in Greek, but she identified herself as the 'sister of Steve.' Not of *Stefanos*. Would she use *Steve?*" That was still puzzling him.

The Colonel exchanged a brief glance with Elias, and then studied the half-inch of firm white ash on the end of his cigarette. He shrugged his shoulders for an answer. Then he said, "Are you going to Thalos?"

"Yes," Strang said. He looked over at Cecilia reassuringly. "It won't take long," he told her. Cecilia tried to smile, but the worry in her eyes kept growing.

The Colonel nodded. "It would be a pity," he said, "to miss this opportunity of finding out the reason why she telephoned you. She was not very communicative yesterday morning when Elias visited her with the news we had just received of her brother's death."

Cecilia drew a deep breath. It was all very well for the Colonel to take such a cold, objective interest; he wasn't going to keep any midnight appointment on a lonely mountain road. There was open fear in her eyes. "Ken," she said softly, "may I go with you? As you had planned?" If I'm with him, she thought, he will take fewer chances. But she knew from his face what he had decided for her: it was that plane for Rome, with Pringle seeing her safely on board.

The Colonel, even if he had seemed to pay her little attention since the first moment of politeness, said, "Quite impossible, Miss Hillard. But don't worry. Mr. Strang will not be traveling alone." He signed to Elias. "Tell Spyridon Makres that Mr. Strang needs that car right away. Seven o'clock punctually at the hotel entrance. Make sure they send you a Cadillac or a Chrysler—" He noticed the amused flicker on Strang's face. "It is not a matter of snobbery," he told Strang; "it is a matter of horsepower and of weight. Our mountain roads are more easily managed in a car that will hold the curves. It is about—" he considered for a moment— "one hundred and sixty miles to Sparta from here. With a powerful car, and a driver who knows each turn on the road, you will not keep Myrrha Kladas waiting much past midnight." He nodded to Elias. "Miss Hillard may possibly not object to having your instructions telephoned from her bedroom. You would permit him, Miss Hillard? Thank you. Make all arrangements, Elias."

Elias moved into the next room and closed its door quietly but firmly behind him.

"Now," the Colonel said, shaking off the full inch of ash from his cig-arette, rising, "there seems little time left to discuss what I came here to arrange. But, after Mr. Strang's news, I'm afraid no discussion is possible. We shall just have to accept Mr. Pringle's idea of how to keep Miss Hil-lard safe."

Strang said quietly, "I hope it coincides with mine. When is the first plane to Rome? Bob, will you see Cecilia safely—"

"Ken," Cecilia said, "you know that will only double your own danger to send me out of Greece. I told you before, I just won't—" She halted, and turned away.

The Colonel looked surprised, and then relieved. "Miss Hillard is right," he said, and put out his half-finished cigarette. "One must never admit to the enemy that one is vulnerable. Or he will strike where he thinks he really has found a weakness."

Strang said, "He knows where I'm vulnerable."

"Are you sure? That note to Miss Hillard could have been a test, a prob-ing action, to find out whether she did know the name of Katherini."

Strang looked angrily at Colonel Zafiris. Then he knew that the Colo-nel had thought of several other things, too. The mass kidnaping of chil-dren, the taking of hostages, these were a part of history that the Colo-nel wasn't likely to forget. But one must never admit one's worst fears, either: was that it?

"We shall keep Miss Hillard safe," the Colonel promised him. He turned to say good-by to Cecilia. "Just one more day," he told her gently. "It isn't too much to ask of you? One day of patience, of great caution. And by tomorrow night, so much will be explained to our enemy in three little newspaper paragraphs that I think he will have no other alternative but to eliminate himself." He took her hand and bowed over it. "Entirely," he added very softly.

He gave Strang a very firm handshake. "Your driver will be Costas. Elias will be your interpreter." And then, as he foresaw an objection to that, "No, no! I cannot let you go alone. Not while I still have two questions unanswered: who made that telephone call; and if it was Myrrha Kladas, then who paid for it? She has so little money, so little of anything—" He clapped Strang's arm twice, strode to the door saying over his shoulder, "I'll see you downstairs, Pringle. We must not disap-point Mr. Christophorou, must we?" He gave a quick glance into the corridor. All must have been well. The door closed behind him.

"Did you hear that?" Pringle asked worriedly.

"He's going to the reception."

"Because Christophorou will be there," Pringle said, shaking his head.

"A war of attrition, seemingly." But who paid for the telephone call? The Colonel had made a good point: such telephone calls cost money.

"It just doesn't seem possible," Pringle said. "Christophorou—I mean. The Colonel's really tying him up with Drakon? But that's fantastic!"

"The hell with Drakon. What's your bright idea?"

Pringle, still excited by the feeling that he was standing on the verge of something really important, looked blankly at Strang.

"About Cecilia," Strang said. "And it had better be the brightest idea you ever had."

"Oh, it's quite simple," Pringle said modestly. "Miss Hillard stays at our apartment until the alarm is over. Effie will keep her company, there, all tomorrow. The Colonel will have a couple of watchdogs outside." He grinned. "And if that isn't enough to please you, I'll get a handsome young marine to come and play pinochle with the ladies."

"Very funny, very funny," Strang said grimly. "So that takes care of Thursday."

"And then you'll be back here."

"And if I'm delayed?"

"Then we'll keep Miss Hillard. Effie will take her around, show the enemy she has friends. Part of this vulnerable doctrine the Colonel was talking about is simply that you are both strangers in Athens."

Strang looked at Cecilia. "Well?" he asked.

Her eyes met his. Slowly, she said, "I'll see you tomorrow night."

"That's the girl," Pringle said. "Throw a toothbrush into your overnight case. I'll go downstairs and fraternize. I'll tell Effie it's all set. I'll come back here just before seven, and smuggle you out. Right?"

"Pack now," Strang said to Cecilia.

"But Elias is still telephoning." She crossed over to the bedroom door and knocked.

"That's okay. You won't understand a thing he is saying," Strang called after her. He turned to Pringle, who was just leaving, and lowered his voice. "Bob—there's something else. Do you know anything about marriage licenses or regulations in this part of the world?"

"Oh, I think the families still try to arrange it, and there's a dowry, and a six-month engagement, or a year, something like that."

"For foreigners, you dope. For us."

Pringle's merriment faded. "Are you serious?" He looked at Strang. "By God, you are! Well, well—" He shook Strang's hand warmly. "Full of surprises, aren't you?"

"Find out all the regulations. Get the routine straight." Nowadays, everything, everywhere, had to be signed in triple quintuplicate.

"Be glad to. That's one good piece of news today." He was still a little bewildered but honestly delighted. Nothing seemed to please a married man more than to see a holdout bachelor joining him.

"Don't spread it around, meanwhile."

"No," agreed Pringle thoughtfully. "No. Not yet." More briskly, he added, "Cheer up, Ken. Another day to wait before the ax falls. That's all. And we can all stop worrying about being vulnerable." And you are the worst off, of us all, he thought, and looked away. "I hear Ottway has gone chasing off to Cyprus."

Strang stiffened. "I meant to tell the Colonel—Bob, you'd better do it, and fast. Yorghis is heading for Yugoslavia."

"Now, now," Pringle said soothingly, "that little headache was stopped. Early this morning, just as he was leaving to pick up two journalists at their hotel."

"Did he talk?"

"Certainly. There's a big difference between being arrested for using his firm's car on false pretenses and being considered part of a lethal conspiracy. So he is clearing himself by telling as much as he knows. The people who hired him to drive them to Athens from Nauplion were Cypriots, he said, and he only thought he was being a patriot in helping them. Most disarming. But he did one useful thing, without knowing it. He directed our attention to Cyprus. There's a celebration there tomorrow, you know: general rejoicing over independence, next year."

"And did he have any camera, when he was arrested?"

Pringle looked at him curiously. "Camera?"

"The one he borrowed from Caroline Ottway to take to Yugoslavia."

Pringle's bland look had gone. "Who told you that?"

"Caroline Ottway."

"Does Ottway know?"

Strang shook his head.

Pringle's dazed moment vanished. "I'll see the Colonel," he said, exchanged a grim look with Strang, and left.

Cecilia heard the door close behind Pringle, and she came back into the pink sitting room.

Strang swung around to face her. "Packed and ready?" he asked her.

She nodded. There was so much to say, so little time. "I still wish I could come with you—"

"No," he said gently, "no." He held out his arms, and she went into them, and they stood there, holding each other, his cheek against her hair. "Later, we'll go to Sparta. Properly. We'll see it together. No one to—" he looked up with annoyance to see Elias at the bedroom door, and his voice sharpened—"keep butting in."

In spite of herself, she laughed. She drew away.

"Everything arranged?" asked Strang crisply.

"Yes," said Elias. "You will need a coat. In Sparta, a sudden freshening is to be feared." He looked at them, wondered why their faces had turned so strangely expressionless. He hesitated. He must go downstairs, for there would be some last instructions to be received from the Colonel; there always were. But they might think him impolite to leave them like this. He took a step toward the door, glanced quietly at his watch. Time was running out. "Lock the door," he told them. "Much safer. Yes?"

"Yes," said Strang.

Elias heard the key turn in the lock, and there was laughter, too. They probably thought such a precaution was stupid, but they were so careless of everything when they were together. Separate, the American was alert, a capable man, no fool—Elias had watched him this morning, most carefully; and the young lady was not one of those hysterical, nonsensical creatures—he had watched her as she moved around the bedroom, first locking up her cameras inside her largest suitcase, choosing a small one to take with her, packing neatly, decisively. But when they got together, they noticed nothing, their minds had left them, anything could happen. Westerners, he decided, were totally incomprehensible. Or perhaps the truth was that they were all a little crazy, living as they did in a child's world of indulgence and pleasure, out of touch with reality. Did they really believe that life owed them happiness?

Pringle was the first to return. He knocked gently, waited, knocked again, said, "It's Pringle" in an angry whisper.

Strang let him in. "You're early."

Pringle's annoyance melted. "Is Miss Hillard ready?"

"Just about."

"Sorry to burst in like this. But we couldn't have a better chance to slip away. Caroline Ottway came to the reception. Guess who backed her into a nice corner of palm trees?"

Strang, who had scarcely been listening, looked at him sharply.

"Christophorou. They're having a very pleasant chat."

"Good God!" Strang said slowly.

"Exactly," said Pringle. "My sentiments exactly. As for the Colonel's! I had a moment with him, by the way. Yorghis had no camera when he was arrested. Must have already passed it over to his friends. He will have a good deal of explaining to—" He turned as he heard Cecilia's light footsteps. For a moment, he stood looking at her. Every now and again, he was thinking, you see beauty like this, and it is always a new surprise, something of a shock, a paralysis. He glanced at Strang. "We'd better push off," he said, suddenly hating this job. "Ready?" he asked Cecilia unnecessarily, and took charge of her coat and small case. "Effie is bringing the car around to the door." He glanced at his watch. "We'll have to hurry. I'll ring for the elevator." He nodded to Strang and hurried out.

Strang took Cecilia in his arms. "I'll telephone you tomorrow. Stay at the Pringles' until I get back. I'll try to make it by tomorrow night."

"Take care," she pleaded. "Please, Ken!"

"I always take care." He kissed her. Soft lips, soft hair, soft cheeks, white throat. Abruptly, he let her go and opened the door. He glanced out into the corridor. Pringle was at the corner near the elevator, waving impatiently. Strang looked at her. She reached up and gave him a long kiss. And then she was hurrying toward Pringle.

Strang took a few steps after them. He halted. He heard the elevator door clang open; shut. Slowly, he turned, and walked back to her room. He went through the sitting room, into her bedroom, and stood at one side of the French windows opening onto the balcony. He waited there until they must have reached the main floor, must have crossed the sidewalk, must be in the car, before he stepped out onto the balcony. Too late, he thought, they've gone. And at that moment he saw Pringle's car, waiting down there for the traffic policeman's signal. It was turning slowly, gathering speed. He watched it until it had disappeared from sight.

He closed the windows, and looked around the room. It had become a different place. There was only the faint remembrance of roses and jasmine.

Behind him, Elias said briskly, "Miss Hillard has gone. Now we go."

Strang looked at Elias. He said, "I'll get my coat."

"At seven o'clock and ten minutes, come downstairs. Leave your key at the desk, walk out. Costas will bring the car forward, you get in. He will drive into Constitution Square, around, up. I shall meet you, then. You understand?"

"Costas—what does he look like?"

"He will look like a driver. You will know him. He searched you last night." He stood aside politely to let Strang lead the way out.

Strang said, "Wouldn't it be simpler if you just arrested Christophorou, right now?"

Elias looked horrified. Then he noticed Strang's expression. "But you are not serious," he said in relief. He raised one of his thin dark eyebrows, let a gleam of sardonic amusement enter his bright brown eyes, and gestured toward the door. American humor was crazy, too, he reminded himself. "We must wait. As you know," he added politely. He shook his head, watching Strang leave.

As I don't know, Strang thought as he went upstairs. Or rather, I do know, but I don't believe it. Sure, every contact that Christophorou makes in the next twenty-four hours may lead to wider knowledge about the extent of the conspiracy. Give no warning, arouse no suspicions, take every precaution, and wait: that's the professional point of view, but I'm no professional. I still think that one tiger within your sights is worth ten in any blasted thicket.

In his room, he did a thorough, quick job of locking everything up. His drawings and his brief case, with so many months of hard research inside it, worried him. And the worry irritated him. Quickly, he gathered coat, toothbrush, razor, map, pocket dictionary. (And, thank heavens, he had cashed that check today.)

Then, at the door, he turned and went back to pick up his drawings and brief case. He'd leave them at the manager's office.

Downstairs, he watched the manager's assistant locking his work into a cavern of a safe. He had a moment of disquiet: what instinct had made him so excessively careful? All right, it was done. He accepted the receipt, made small talk about the weather, eyed the clock, and left—exactly at eight minutes past seven—to drop his key at the porter's desk. He stepped out into the busy street, his coat with its filled pockets over his arm, the well-stocked night traveler in search of his friend. A venerable, dark-blue Chrysler eased forward, halted, and Costas, now dressed in a cheap suit much too tight for him, ran around to hold open the rear door for his client. Strang gave a stiff, embarrassed nod. Willing or not, he thought as Costas slipped behind the wheel, here I go.

Dusk came as they reached the Megara road, and then quick darkness. The broad busy highway running straight out from the city, lined by miles and miles of small flat-roofed houses, square white boxes, each set back in its own plot of Attica's dry stony earth, had ended. Now they were on a well-paved road twisting along the shore of the Gulf of Athens, past summer cottages, shuttered and silent, built at the water's edge; past long rows of barrack-like, dimly lit houses, set back on sloping fields, where the small farmers lived literally over their chicken runs. There were several cars on this road, all challenging Costas, whose idea of travel was emptiness ahead, a good engine with a powerful drive, a steady wheel under his hands, and an unbroken speed of eighty miles an hour.

278

"Better now," Elias said, breaking his long conversation with Costas to turn to speak to Strang for the first time. The sloping land was flattening out into a wide plain. Elias looked back at the cars they had passed, their headlights now sweeping away into another road. "They drive out to dinner," he added, shaking his head. "Nothing else to do but take their women to dinner." He spoke more in wonder than in envy. Then he gestured ahead. "The canal," he said, and they were running smoothly over a long bridge. Strang saw, to his right, a dark straight line of water, seemingly endless, laid deep between man-made cliffs, its spaced lights dwindling into a narrow ribbon toward the west. "The Peloponnese," Elias said softly, and pointed to the dark stretch of hills lying ahead. "Once we pass Corinth, we can make speed."

They did. The lights of Corinth vanished into the darkness behind them, and now there were only scattered groups of houses strung along the road that led through the hills, villages so small that the car had passed through the string of dim lights before it barely entered them. There was never a village so small, Strang noted, that it didn't have a room, open to the unpaved sidewalks, with a few tables and chairs where the men gathered together. He saw few women, and they all wore headcloths, the long scarves which they draped over their heads and across their mouths. It was strange to speed so quickly through these lives, glimpse the habit of centuries, see the wide curious eyes turned toward the car or a friendly arm raised, in quiet greeting, under the new electric lights. Then even the villages stopped, and there were only the vast stretches of dark hills, a wide canopy of ink-blue sky with the stars beginning to take their stations.

They swept past the lights of Argos, lying on its broad plain, and turned west toward the mountains. Thank God, the road was good, Strang thought. It twisted in sharp zigzags up a mountain's face, straining to reach the top, the sharp drop on its outer side steadily heightening. "A fine view," Elias said, pointing backward into the darkness.

"I'm sure it is," Strang said, but he was too busy driving. He never sat in a car's back seat with any comfort, but so far, Costas had refused any help; he, too, seemingly, liked being at the wheel. "God in heaven!" said Strang, as the car made almost a right-angled twist, just grazing the black-and-white markers at the edge of a precipice, only two thousand feet high.

Elias was pleased that the American was impressed by Greek road building. "Good? Ten years ago—no road like this. Just earth. No railing. No markers." He reflected a moment. "You go to Olympia someday? Then you will see what I mean," he said ominously.

I'll remember to travel by daylight, Strang told himself, as the car's headlights picked out a smashed ten-foot stretch of low railing where a driver had guessed wrong and gone sailing right out into space.

"Someone forgot to turn," Costas said cheerfully, and he and Elias burst into a fit of laughter.

Up and over the mountain, past a small guardhouse and curious soldiers, down again toward an enormous expanse of flatness stretching to farther mountains. The road was straight and easy, the moon was rising; so Costas switched off his headlights. "Saves the battery," he explained. It was a better habit at least, thought Strang, than switching off the ignition to coast down a mountain road. But the Greeks had made a fine art of little tricks like that. He tried to relax, failed, kept looking out at the vast plain of Arcadia. In the moonlight, neither nymphs nor satyrs were in sight, nor was there any sound of Pan's pipe. There was only a monotonous series of wells, wells, and rows of willow trees, and wells, and hardworked fields. Once, he saw a gypsy encampment, silent and withdrawn. Occasionally, he heard the howl of a dog.

The road curved around a sudden hill, incongruously rising from the plain, and they saw a bright cluster of lights, a glowing island in the darkness. "Tripolis," Elias said, pointing. "Petrol and food. You are hungry?"

"And a telephone call," Strang said, eying the town. After the last thirty miles of nothing, it seemed almost a metropolis.

"No time," Elias said firmly, his brows frowning.

"We'll see," said Strang. There was usually a little extra time in Greece, lying around to be picked up.

He managed to find it, too. He had got through to Athens, and talked with Cecilia for almost three minutes before Elias tapped his shoulder.

Strang joined the two men, silently, and got back into the car. Elias, still annoyed, glanced at him twice. Then, as they left the town by a white-walled street edged with mimosa trees, he twisted his head around to ask, anxiously, "She is good?"

Strang smiled. "Yes, she's safe and well." He closed his eyes, if only to be left with his own thoughts, rested his head back against the seat, felt reassurance spread from his mind down through his body. For the first time, on this strange journey, he relaxed.

Elias was reaching over, shaking his knee. Strang came out of his half-sleep and sat up quickly, looking around dazedly. The black plain had gone. Now they were on a black mountainside, following a rougher road which seemed to be running along a high pass.

"Not yet, not yet," Elias said. "But soon. A good journey, yes?"

Strang nodded. It was, he saw from his watch, almost midnight.

"About twenty-five kilometers to go," Elias said.

Roughly fifteen miles more, thought Strang. He stretched his back, put the pleasant dreams away, looked out at the wild mountainside. No lights at all. No villages. Just the rocks and night sky, and small rough fields where the stones had been cleared and piled into little thin columns that might have been markers or monuments but, in the fitful moonlight, looked more like some sad graveyard for a long retreat. "We should soon be there," Strang said.

Elias shrugged his shoulders. Then Strang saw what he meant. Costas had slackened speed to a crawl of twenty miles an hour, and even slowed below that as they approached a stretch of road weakened by a spring torrent or a fall of stones from the mountain's side. They were starting down a long decline, carefully, still in gear, this time, but with only the parking lights turned on. "Remember two things," Elias said, very seriously, "Myrrha Kladas believes that Stefanos is dead and that Nikos is still alive." He paused, hesitated, and then asked, "Do you know much about Myrrha Kladas?"

"Very little."

Elias brooded. Then he spoke in Greek. "She was fifteen when the war started, and for two years she saw more murder and hate and bitterness than an American would see in all his life. When her father was killed, she left Thalos. She went to join her brothers. These facts we do know. We also know she came back to the village in 1945. We do not know why she came back. It might have been a revulsion against the cruelties of Ares—he destroyed the political faith of many of his followers. If that were the reason, good: you can trust her. But if she came back because Odysseus had abandoned her for the woman who called herself Elektra—then, that is not good: you cannot trust her." Elias turned to look at the American. "You understand what I am saying?"

Strang wondered if he had. "I think so," he said slowly.

Elias repeated his information in English, which had become halting and difficult as he struggled with his own embarrassment. It was unpleasant to talk of such things, but necessary.

Strang was silent. Then, at last, he said, "Steve did not know about that."

"A pity. Or he would have killed Odysseus. That would have saved us all much trouble."

"Elektra—" Strang began. It was none of his business.

Elias said, "She left him, on orders, when she met the rich Frenchman after the war."

"On orders?" Now, I've got *that* wrong, thought Strang.

"On orders," Elias repeated calmly. "The Frenchman's fortune was too useful to let slip out of the party's grasp. She lived with the old fool for two years, and then—when she threatened to leave him—he married her." Elias looked at Strang. "Americans know everything about love, I have heard. Do they?"

Strang shook his head. "That was harsh discipline," he said slowly. How had Christophorou brought himself to accept it? How could a man . . . He checked his thoughts. How or why were no longer of importance. What mattered now was the extent and depth of Christophorou's bitterness and hate.

"Each tree bears its own fruit." Elias shrugged his shoulders. "And each grows according to the ground where it sinks its roots."

Except, Strang thought, a man is not a tree; a man has the choice where he will sink his roots.

Costas spoke suddenly. "How much of that fortune is left?"

Elias gave a contemptuous laugh. "Keep your eyes on the road."

"There must be something left," Costas insisted.

"Yes, safe in Swiss banks in numbered accounts," Elias said. "But one thing is certain, Madame Duval's signature is no longer needed." He sat erect, his eyes scanning the side of the road. "Slow, slow! The village is near. Is there enough moon? Then cut those lights!"

Strang looked out. They were slipping gently downhill, a rise of woods and sparse olive trees on their left, a falling slope of small patches of plowed earth and olive groves on their right. There was a broad valley, far below, a black snaking river in its center, orchards and large fields in the flat rich bottomland, and, beyond them, a wall of mountains. "Is that snow up there?" he asked, or was it a trick of the night and the moon?

"Even in June, the snow lies there." Elias smiled. "You would like to cross these mountains? Another time." He stretched his arm toward a distant point in the valley far below. "Sparti!" he said. "And here—" he touched Costas's arm, and the car eased its way to a gentle halt beside a narrow rough earth road, leading up to the left between the olive trees— "here is Thalos."

Strang said quickly, "She's waiting at the bridge, a kilometer ahead."

Elias nodded. He looked at his watch, and nodded again, this time approvingly. To Costas, he said, "Twenty minutes after we leave, drive slowly toward the bridge with full headlights. Pass over the bridge. Keep on until you reach the plain. Wait there for half an hour. Then come back;

keep your lights low. When you reach the shadow of that bank—" he pointed across the road, about sixty feet ahead of them—"draw in close. Turn off your lights. That's where we'll meet you."

Silently, the two Greeks compared their watches. Elias gave further directions: if there was no sign of the American and himself by two o'clock, Costas must drive to the police station down in the valley and telephone Sparta from there. He turned to Strang. "Are you armed?" he asked crisply.

"With a penknife," Strang said with a grin.

"Inadequate," Elias said coldly. This was no time, seemingly, for any jokes. But he didn't offer anything less inadequate. Probably, Strang thought, he doesn't think that I can be trusted with a gun, or that I'd hit anything except some harmless peasant or even Elias himself. He pulled off his coat. "You'll need that," Elias told him.

"We're walking, aren't we?" And probably crawling around on our bellies if Elias has his way, Strang thought. It was a fairly obvious remark, but Elias looked surprised, as if he hadn't quite expected a foreigner either to make such a deduction or to leave the comfort of a good coat behind him. He stepped out of the car, and slipped down out of sight by an olive tree at the side of the road. That's the wrong direction for Thalos, thought Strang, but he opened the right-hand door and followed Elias.

"Come!" Elias told him in a whisper, and, crouching low, started back along the sloping hill, following the road, keeping well under the shadow of its shoulder. When he had retraced almost fifty yards of highway, he stopped, again by an olive tree, straightened his back, looked down the road. Strang looked, too. The car was out of sight, hidden by a curving outcrop of rock. And here, too, the opposite bank was high, throwing its shadow almost as far across as their olive tree. Elias went first, slipping over the road like a ghost in the night. He signaled, and Strang followed. Then they climbed the high bank and started forward again, using the olive trees for cover, heading once more in the direction of Thalos.

Neat, thought Strang, but was it necessary? Certainly anyone who had been watching the car must have lost sight of them; but had anyone been watching? Perhaps Elias enjoyed this kind of thing. He was in a better humor, definitely; the annoyance, almost antagonism, he had shown at the Acropolis had vanished. Perhaps, again, he might think this job worth doing, interesting at least, more in keeping with his dignity than playing nursemaid to two bewildered Americans. What was his rank? Strang wondered: lieutenant, or even captain?

Elias raised a hand for caution as they reached the rough narrow road that would lead up the hillside to Thalos. Again they chose a shadowed patch before they crossed it, one by one. This may not be necessary, Strang decided, but it certainly is a good way to keep a man warm. And alert. For in spite of his secret amusement, his senses had come alive. His eyes were accustomed to the shadows now; he could hear the quiet ripple of water over stones long before he reached the stream; he could smell the upturned earth where a patch of field had been plowed between the olive trees, the sweetness of grass and wild flowers around an outcrop of boulders.

Elias's plan, obviously, was to approach the bridge from the rear. He halted as they saw the stream and a path, edging it, which must lead from the bridge on the road up this sloping hill to the Kladas house. The village must lie up in that direction, too. But from where they had stopped, Strang could see nothing beyond the dark shadowed glen which cradled the rushing stream, except a massive black curtain of hill and mountain held up against the night sky. Then Elias was hurrying on, through the sparse olive grove where each tree seemed to be fighting for its life, westward, following the course of the stream to the bridge. They stopped once more, in the shade of a tree. Elias gestured sharply with his hand, and knelt. Strang lowered himself gently onto a low boulder. Downhill, in the shadows in front of them, there were two olive trees, a sudden deepening of the stream's bed, a tangle of bushes, a cluster of rocks, and—some thirty yards away from where Strang sat—the stone bridge. There was no one there.

Strang's eyes searched for Myrrha Kladas along the opposite bank of the stream. He could see the path, some bright patches of moonlight, some black shadows, boulders and trees, but nothing else. There was a slight rustle of leaves in the night wind, the gurgling rush of water as the stream surged under the bridge toward the other side of the road to plunge on its way down the hillside. But there was nothing else. He looked at Elias, but Elias was looking carefully at the luminous dial of his watch. It had been nice timing, thought Strang. He could hear Costas bringing the car leisurely down the road toward the bridge. As the first faint beam from its distant headlights rested on the surface of the bridge, a tree's shadow, down there, came to life. A woman, heavily bundled in dark clothes, stepped forward toward the light.

Elias froze, like an alert retriever. And just as Strang was about to say "So she did wait!" two men came out of the shadows behind the woman. One gripped her arms and pulled her back behind the tree, the other chose another tree nearer the bridge. And now a third man moved from the boulder beside which he had sat so motionless and took his position behind a clump of bushes at a corner of the bridge.

Elias may have expected something odd, but he was obviously as puzzled by all this as Strang was. He drew out a revolver, thoughtfully, and watched the bridge with narrowed eyes. The two men, who had taken cover near the road, crouched down as the full beam from the headlights struck the bridge. There was no movement from the tree's shadow that hid Myrrha Kladas and the third man. The car traveled smoothly over the slight rise of the bridge and was gone.

Now, thought Strang, what the hell does that mean? There had been no attempt to stop the car. Not one movement. Elias was slipping the revolver back into his pocket, as thoughtfully as he had produced it. So he, too, had expected an attack on the car.

And then the storm broke. The man crouching behind the corner of the bridge leaped up onto the road and looked after the car. The other, at the tree by the bridge, yelled back toward the shadows, "He has gone! He did not stop! He did not stop!"

"Shut up. He'll come back!"

"He's gone," the first man reported. "He isn't coming back. He's going down." He stood well over to the edge of the road, his hands on his hips, a broad-backed figure in a heavy coat, staring into the valley.

There was a sudden stirring, and the others came out from cover. The three men clustered together on the road, the woman waited beside the tree.

A man turned toward her, speaking angrily. The woman answered sharply.

The man jumped back off the road and came toward her. She retreated up the path, just across the stream from the olive tree under whose shadows Strang and Elias lay. "You were beside me when I telephoned. You heard," she was saying contemptuously. "I gave the right directions." She halted and faced him.

The man spoke angrily. "That is right," she said scornfully, "blame me! Waste your time blaming me! He is an American. He doesn't know this road. Perhaps he did not see the signpost to Thalos. Perhaps he cannot read the Greek letters. How slow you are to think of the real reasons!"

The man was silenced.

"Why did you not let me step onto the bridge?" the woman demanded. "He would have known where to stop, then."

"Yes. And you could have warned him—"

The woman laughed. "Why should I die for an American?"

The others left the bridge and came up the path. The three men stood together, looking at the woman.

"Stupid!" she taunted them. "An American will not spend the night

285

searching for a little road. He will sleep in Sparta, and come back here in daylight. That is the practical thing. Americans are practical. They do not waste time looking for a road they cannot find in the dark." She turned and left them, walking up the path by the stream, slowly, with dignity.

The angry man took a step after her. But another caught his arm. After a little more argument, the three went back to the road, angry, baffled, straggling, as if they still had not made up their minds what to do. But when they reached it, they started down its slope.

Well, thought Strang, moving a numbed leg, if our Costas is too eager and doesn't wait a full half hour in the valley, we have another problem. He glanced at Elias. He, too, was worried. Strang pulled up his jacket collar. The cold was sharp, striking into his bones like a knife. Let's move, he thought irritably, and half rose. Elias caught his arm and pulled him back.

They heard a car, which must have been parked not too far down the road, start up with a hacking cough. At last, the motor turned over smoothly. Headlights swept over the bridge, pointing northward up the long hill. The car passed. Its motor pulled heavily, droning into a faint hum, lessening gradually into nothing.

"Now!" Elias said, rising. He started at a quick pace up the glen, in the direction of the Kladas house.

TWENTY-TWO

It was a small house, standing alone, low in spite of its two stories, nestling against the hillside as if the winter winds were still blowing from the north. Its front was in shadow, with only deeper shadows to suggest windows. They were few, and all tightly shuttered. In contrast to the dark front, the rippling tiles of the gently sloping roof seemed almost white in this moonlight. There were wide eaves, a square blackened hole which might have been a chimney. It was a peaceful house, a sleeping house, completely innocent. To one side, there was a stretch of plowed field, enclosed by a stone wall, rising steeply, ending in rough harsh boulders. And past the front door went the path, widening now, still following the stream, curving round to run straight into an earth road bordered with several dwellings.

It was something of a surprise to Strang to find the village so close. The road from the main highway and the path from the bridge were not parallel, as he had supposed: they converged into this broad stretch of bare earth, edged by a row of buildings on one side, by the stream and a scattering of trees on the other. Everything here slept deeply. Even the stream, flowing along the broad ledge of land on which the houses had grown, silenced its busy chatter to a soft murmur.

Elias had stopped, just as they had climbed out of the little glen and had come upon the Kladas place. In spite of the fast pace they had kept, they had not caught up with Myrrha Kladas. They were on the wrong side of the stream, too. They'd have to cross it, step out of the shelter of the trees, and risk that moonlit stretch of bare path before they could reach the black shadow of the house.

Elias cursed quietly as he looked across at the door, closely barred and bolted for the night. He had been so very sure that they would overtake Myrrha Kladas before she could reach it.

"Only one entrance?" Strang whispered.

Elias shrugged his shoulders. Perhaps he had not been allowed to see any other entrance on his visit yesterday. Uncommunicative, the Colonel had called Myrrha Kladas.

"How do you get across this stream?"

"Now?"

"Yes." Strang's eyes were searching the stream for some footbridge: no village let itself be cut off from its fields.

"There is Costas, too, to be considered," Elias was saying, frowning with worry. He looked at his watch. "Soon he will start uphill from the valley. Those three may be patrolling the road. He must be told what to expect."

"Perhaps they've gone back to where they came from."

"To Tripolis? And then here again, in the morning? No."

The frown deepened. The men had come from a town; their clothes were not those of peasants. Or were they staying in a village to the north? Elias sighed. He looked at his watch again. "Will she open that door?" he asked. His tone doubted that.

"Perhaps for me, if I'm alone," Strang said. "You get back to the bridge and start down toward the valley." Then, as Elias kept silent, he added, "If anything happens to that car, it's a long walk back to Athens."

Elias gave a fleeting smile. "You stay here," he said.

"No. I go over there." Strang pointed at the house.

"But those men may decide to come back. Did you not hear them arguing?"

"Then all the more reason I should be with Myrrha Kladas."

Elias looked at him.

"It's warm, over there," Strang said. "I like my comforts." He took a step away. "Where's the nearest crossing? Or do I have to swim?"

"There is a small footbridge," Elias said, pointing near them. He was converted.

"Good." Strang couldn't see the footbridge for the shadows of the trees at that part of the stream.

"Ask her—" Elias had a new set of worries.

"I'll ask her plenty," Strang said grimly. "Signal when you get back—"

But Elias was gone.

Strang waited for a few moments, admiring Elias's technique: the man melted into the shadows, moving quickly, silently. It would take him about five minutes, at that rate, to travel back downhill to the bridge. Strang glanced at his own watch. Speed was certainly needed; Costas would soon

288

be starting up from the valley. Arguments, arguments, Strang thought with annoyance; everyone wants to get his own way in this country—including me. He looked over at the silent house, glanced along the village street. All was quiet. He started toward the trees where the footbridge ought to be. It was there, all right, a couple of long planks balanced on some rocks, a simple but practical peasant's reply to inevitable spring floods. Strang crossed, carefully, his eyes concentrating on the middle of the planks. On his right, the stream gathered speed through a scattering of small boulders and then—so his ears told him—plunged into its race through the glen.

He reached the other bank, and then, past an outcrop of rock and bushes, the path. There was a small stretch of thin wood here, slender-trunked, silver-barked trees rising out of the dark undergrowth. He halted. Sheep? Had one strayed down from the hillside? For now he could smell the unmistakable, strong, heavy odor of sheep, reminding him of that mutton-fat gravy tonight at Tripolis. But there was no rustle, no movement. The sheep was dead, perhaps, carried down by the stream. He started up the dark path, soft under his feet, between the ghostly white-limbed ladies.

There was a quick movement behind him, a stronger smell of sheep. An arm was round his throat, a hand was pinning his right arm to his side, and, for a moment, he was paralyzed, pulled tightly against a filthy sheep-skin tunic. He let himself go limp, as if he were beaten; and as he felt the arm slacken a little, sure of him, he jerked his head violently back and smashed against a face. There was a grunt of pain, the arm loosened, and Strang could turn on the man. But as his left fist shot out, a second man grappled from behind, catching his elbows in a strong savage grip; and a third dark figure, a woman, raised a heavy stick and struck at his head. He stumbled forward, the man's weight now on his back. There was another blow at his head, a crashing pain followed by a wave of blackness. He tried to rise, failed, and felt the first retreat from consciousness. Complete blackness swept over, and smothered him.

The woman stood looking down at Strang. "Is he dead?" she asked, tonelessly, almost listlessly.

One of the men knelt. "You did not hit hard enough," he said angrily. Women were like that, always flinching at the last moment, always leaving a job half done.

"Which one is it?" she asked.

"The tall one, as you saw."

"There were two who were tall," she said sharply. She bent down and touched the man lying at her feet, and then drew back quickly. His jacket was of soft tweed. "His clothes are different."

"He has taken off his coat. That is all. Levadi—" he looked up at the big man with the sheepskin over his shoulders, who was wiping the blood from his nose with his wrist—"shove him in the stream!"

The woman said, "More than taking off his coat. The jacket is different. Of wool, fine wool." She knelt and touched Strang's hair. She tried to see his face through the shadows. "A stranger," she said. "A foreigner. Fetch Petros!"

Strang's eyes opened. He didn't move. His head throbbed, his throat was painful. He was lying on hard boards, in half-darkness; but he was warm, at least, with a rough blanket around him. There was the smell of a wood fire, a soft flickering light on the low ceiling. Cautiously, he turned his head. The pain stopped him. He began to remember. He lay still, trying to think, failing. From the corner of his eye, he saw a table, and two people. A woman and a man, sitting silently by the light of the fire, waiting. Then he realized his hands and feet were free, unbound; someone had put a pillow under his head; someone had wrapped him carefully in this blanket. "Hello, there!" he said slowly, and tried to sit up. The dim room swung round him, but he got his feet on the floor and kept them there. Now if he could just manage to sit this way for a couple of minutes, no sudden movements, no efforts, he might be able to raise his head, too, and look normal.

The woman exclaimed, moved to light a candle. The man came over to the bed and looked at Strang, who slowly raised his head. "How do you feel?" he asked in English.

Like the way one of those wobbly-headed, three-month-old infants must feel, thought Strang. "Fine," he said. He looked up carefully. It was Petros, grinning broadly. "Was it you who hit me?"

"Myrrha did that. Fortunately."

"Fortunately?"

Petros said, "I would have cracked your skull properly." He gave an encouraging pat to Strang's shoulder, a good-natured thump which echoed right up through the roof of his head. Then Petros sat down beside him, on the wooden platform of a bed. "In fact, you nearly ended in that stream."

"Spectacular exit," Strang said, seeing himself being hurtled in the fast-moving waters under the road and out onto the valley's slopes. He laughed. And stopped. And held his head.

Myrrha Kladas exclaimed again, this time in sympathy. She offered him a glass of water.

Petros started explaining, "She thought you were one of them. And

290

you chose the darkest shadows. She saw a man moving, but she couldn't see the man clearly. What were you doing out there?"

"Watching the bridge." The water was sweet and clean and cold.

"More?" she asked, politely, anxiously.

He said, "Please." He looked at her as she poured the water, and he wondered if this could really be Myrrha Kladas. She ought to be a woman a little younger than himself. But only her eyes, dark and glowing, were young. The skin, tanned into wrinkled leather by sun and wind, the lines at the sad mouth, the gaunt cheeks, the coarsened hair, the veined hands, all these belonged to age. She was of medium height, but she looked small: her body was so thin, stripped of all fat right down to its fine bone and muscle, that the cotton dress hung from her slight shoulders as a shapeless piece of cloth. And he thought of her father, of her two brothers, of Christophorou, who had all abandoned her in their own fashion: some women had not much to thank men for. "This water is very good," he said, and pleased her.

"Your head?" she asked politely, in turn.

"As thick as ever."

She didn't quite understand.

"As good as this bed." He rapped on the solid piece of wood, then rapped on his head, and said, "Ow!"

She laughed, her eyes inviting Petros to join in the joke. For a moment, he saw a young woman. Then her hand went quickly up to her mouth to cover it politely, shyly.

"So," Petros said, "you were watching the bridge. And who was the man who left you to go back to the bridge?" He gestured to Myrrha. "Sure, we can talk in English. She understands, although she won't speak it." He looked at Strang, his eyes narrowing. "Was he a policeman?"

"No. Counterintelligence."

"And what does that mean?"

Strang allowed himself a good Greek shrug of the shoulders. "He has gone to find our driver and car."

"They will come back here?"

"Yes."

"Do you trust them?"

"Yes."

"Hm," said Petros. "What do they want?"

"They want Steve to stay alive."

There was silence.

Myrrha Kladas said, "Are you sure of that?"

"That's one thing I am sure of."

"They do not pretend?"

"I am sure of that, too."

Myrrha Kladas and Petros exchanged a long thoughtful look. Then she said, "I believe the American."

Petros said, "We don't want any policemen around here." He pointed across the room, and Strang saw a rifle propped at the side of the door. "My friend John has a gun, too. We keep them private, hidden, you understand. For any—well—any trouble. But the police don't like guns. They take them away."

"Is John the man with the sheepskin?"

Petros laughed. "No. That's Levadi. That's *her* friend." He pointed at Myrrha. "Why don't you tell Levadi he is no longer a shepherd?" he asked her teasingly. "Or why don't you wash his coat? Or him?"

"He does no one any harm," she flashed out. "He stayed my friend when others forgot me."

"Ah!" said Petros, his eyes narrowing. "And why did they forget you? Just look at a few burned-out houses around here, will you?"

Strang asked quickly, "Where are John and Levadi?"

"Outside. On guard." Petros was still looking bitterly at Myrrha Kladas. "We expect a little trouble."

"Then you'd better tell them that my two friends are coming back here. I don't want to have them floating down any stream."

Petros stopped looking at Myrrha Kladas. He rose, yawned, and stretched. "What do they look like?"

Strang described Elias and Costas.

"And they are not policemen?"

"No!"

"Okay, okay." Petros clumped heavily toward the door.

"Sh!" said Myrrha Kladas.

"Okay!" Petros said in a softened growl, picked up his rifle, and left.

"Myrrha," Strang said very gently, "where is Steve?"

She was at the door, barring it. She turned and looked at him.

"Do you know that he is alive?"

She nodded. "Petros told me everything you told him."

But Petros would not have been sitting here if he hadn't found Steve. That was certain. Besides, there was no air of mourning in this house, no gloom. Petros would not have jeered at her, lost his temper, if Steve had been dead. And Myrrha Kladas would not be facing Strang so calmly, either, at this moment: village women took mourning seriously and were not easily comforted. "Why—why—" he began. He was having trouble with his Greek verbs. An aching head was no help at all. "Why did you telephone?" he asked with painful slowness. He put a hand over his forehead and held it there.

She looked at him anxiously. Then she said, "I speak English, if Petros is not here to laugh at my mistake. I lived in America once." As she spoke, she went to a wooden chest, found a piece of white cloth, soaked it with cold water, and came over to wrap it across his brow. "Lie back," she told him. "You do not have to pretend for me."

He lay back on the bed. He watched her lift a chair and bring it beside him. She sat down. "Now," she said softly, "we talk."

"Why did you telephone?"

"I had no choice."

"But it was a trap. I might have ended in that stream after all," he reminded her.

"No, no! When the car stopped, I was to scream."

"Then they would have hurt you."

"John and Levadi were near."

He was startled. "Where?"

"Very near. John had his rifle ready." She frowned at her hands, neatly folded in her lap. "It was the best we could do."

Then, slowly, she told him what had happened. That noon, when she came back from working in the field, she found two strangers searching this house. Levadi was still in the field. She had tried to run out, to call, but one of the men had stopped her. They came as friends, they said. Her brother Stefanos was not dead; he was alive and in hiding because there were enemies, men who had once been his comrades, who remembered that he had been a deserter. Stefanos, so they said, had sent them to find her, and to prove that, they had shown her a little diary with her brother's writing in it. Stefanos wanted to see his American friend, Kenneth Strang. Stefanos would come to Thalos tonight, and meet his friend in this house.

"You see?" she asked anxiously. "They told me I must telephone you. Because you would believe me when I said it was urgent; but you had never heard of them, and you might not listen to them. So I was to go with them into Sparta, and telephone you. At once! But I said I could not go into the big town with mud on my boots, and in my old dress from the fields. So they said they would wait for me at the road by the bridge, where their car and their driver were. You see?"

Yes, he was beginning to see.

"But then," she said, "as I went down through the little wood, I found Petros. And he told me a different story. He was unshaven, there was mud on his clothes, and he looked as if he had been without sleep, searching—

as he told me—for Stefanos. And so I believed him. For I knew him. We talked. And he made a plan. He wanted me to telephone you. How else could we bring you here quickly? But we have no money for telephones to Athens, so—you see?"

"Yes," Strang said. "You let the strangers pay for the call, and you got me out here as Petros wanted."

"But you understood my warning," she said. "And you brought friends."

He looked at her.

"When I called Stefanos 'Steve,' you understood that I had learned about the name you give him."

He couldn't disappoint her by admitting he had not fully understood. But Colonel Zafiris had understood, perhaps not fully, either, but enough to send Elias and Costas along.

"And," Myrrha said triumphantly, "how could I learn such a name if I had not been speaking to Stefanos or Petros? That was all the warning I could give. One of the men stood beside me as I telephoned." She laughed. "What money they spent! I telephoned at three o'clock, four o'clock, five o'clock, six—and there you were, at last."

"Who paid for all that?"

Her laughter died away. She sat very still. "Since I talked with Stefanos, I think I know. Odysseus—a man I met many years ago, when we took strange names and hid behind them. There was reason then. But now—he still hides behind Odysseus."

"Did he come to see you, some weeks ago?"

She stared at Strang. "Yes. About Stefanos. He wanted to warn Stefanos not to come to Greece."

"That old excuse about Steve deserting?"

"You believe he did?"

"No."

Her face softened. "No," she agreed. "But I believed Odysseus about the danger. Some people might want to have revenge. They hear one side of the story. They do not ask about the other side." She bit her lip. "I know," she said. "Once, I heard only one side. . . ."

"And so you told Odysseus where he could find Steve to warn him."

"Yes. I told him Steve would be in Sicily before he came to Greece."

He sat up slowly and swung his legs onto the floor. "Can I go upstairs and see Steve now?" He handed her the cloth from his head. It hadn't helped much, but he thanked her.

"He is asleep. I gave him a drink of herbs to make him asleep." She looked at him curiously. "How did you know he was here?"

"Why else are you all guarding this house so carefully?"

She smiled then. "Petros brought him here when I went with these men into Sparta."

"It would have been safer, perhaps, to leave him where Petros found him."

"No. He needs shelter. Care. Petros found him—"

"At the old place?"

She nodded. "Up on the hill, below the mountain ridge. There is an old castle there. In ruins. The Franks built it, many years ago."

Six hundred years ago, most probably, Strang thought, if the French knights had built it.

"And the Albanian soldiers of the Turks destroyed it," she was saying. "Every man was killed. The women were—were destroyed. The children taken as slaves. Nothing left—a few walls. A little church, without a roof." She sighed. "But not enough shelter for a man who was sick."

"How sick?" he asked quickly.

"A bullet was in his shoulder. Something here"—she put a hand over her right ribs—"is not good. He walked and climbed, over these mountains, for two nights and a day. His feet—" She shook her head. "But he is alive. And talks too much. So I made him sleep."

Strang got onto his feet. "I'll have a look. No, don't worry—I shan't waken him." He stood very still. "What was that?"

She was on her feet, her hand deep in the pocket of her skirt. "It could be the morning wind. It rises before dawn."

They stood listening. There was only silence now.

"Do you expect these men from Tripolis to come back?"

"They will come back. You are very important to Odysseus, Mr. Strang."

If so, thought Strang, he is a little late; the time to get me out of Athens was yesterday, before I could talk with Colonel Zafiris.

"I hear nothing," Myrrha said, and took her hand out of her pocket. "What made you think these men come from Tripolis?"

"Their clothes, mostly. And they traveled north. Tripolis is the nearest town in that direction."

"They have been living in Tripolis," she said. "But they do not come from there."

It was a nice Greek distinction. But he was thinking now of the timing of the telephone calls. Three o'clock was the first one. If Cecilia and he had separated after lunch—most people did, falling into the Mediterranean custom of the long rest after the midday meal—he would have been in his room for that first call, he would have been on his way to Sparta before Cecilia even came downstairs and had picked up that note signed "Katherini." And Cecilia would have kept that appointment.

Myrrha was looking at him. "There is something wrong?" she asked, sensing his tenseness. She listened. "No," she decided. "Nothing." She sat down at the table, and watched him curiously. The last flicker of the dying fire threw faint, glancing shadows over his face. But there were deeper shadows there, too, she thought. "You wonder how I knew Odysseus sent these men?"

He sat down opposite her.

She said, "I remembered one of them. He did not know me. But men do not change so much as women. I knew him. He did many things for Odysseus." She shivered. Then she said, "Levadi remembered him, too. Once, before the war, they both lived near Parnassos. That is to the north. On the mainland," she explained politely.

"And during the war?"

"They both followed Odysseus. Levadi knew my brothers, too."

"Levadi—that is a strange name."

"That is not his real name. It is the place he came from."

"Why doesn't he go back there?"

"After the war, some men could not go back."

He looked at her. "You trust him?"

"He has been here for almost thirteen years. Without him, I could not have worked my farm. . . . In the village, I had no friends. Not then. People forget slowly. But—" she paused—"they do forget. A little. There is peace here. Work and peace and food. That is all Levadi wants."

"But how did he know where to find you?"

"Oh, people find people," she said vaguely. Then she brushed aside the American's doubts. "In Greece, many people were made refugees, many left their villages, many went looking for friends, many found new places. Levadi is not so difficult to understand."

"Isn't he? You said he followed Odysseus once."

"But he rebelled," she said softly. "Like my brother Stefanos, he rebelled. Yet they are so different. Stefanos, he thinks much. He rebelled—" she touched her forehead—"here. Levadi does not think. He never questions. He feels." She touched her heart. "He rebelled, there." She closed her eyes, as if her words had struck a savage memory. She drew a deep breath.

"When Odysseus came here a few weeks ago, did he see Levadi? Did he talk to him?"

She looked puzzled. "Yes. At first, Levadi wouldn't listen. He ran up the hill, behind this house. But Odysseus followed him."

"And he patched up their quarrel, whatever it was?"

"I did not ask any questions," she said coldly. "I do not think you should ask them. It was a personal matter, between them. Not politics. Levadi was jealous, once, of Odysseus. Oh, not because of me. Someone quite different, someone who—" She halted, listening. The strange sound, breaking through the lonely night, died away. "Did you hear?"

Strang was on his feet, too. The sharp rasping call of a night bird was repeated. "A screech owl, perhaps," he said.

"Or Petros. That is his signal."

"Good or bad?"

"It is a warning. The men are coming back."

Strang said, "Look—they don't know that Steve is here, do they?"

"No."

"Then they are coming for me." They must have seen Elias and Costas returning in the car from the valley, and they had assumed it was the American still searching for Thalos. Strang pointed to her pocket. "Do you know how to use that revolver?"

Myrrha drew it out. "Petros gave it to me."

"Can you use it?" he repeated.

"I have not forgotten."

"Then bar this door solidly. Stay here. Don't open a window. If the men come here, don't let them in. Tell them you didn't let me in, either. You never let anyone inside at night. That's your story."

She watched him lift the door's bar out of its heavy sockets. "No—no!"

"Yes!" he said. "If they catch me, they won't take me far. Petros is out there. And Elias, I hope."

He edged the door open, first ajar, then a few more inches. The end of the village street and the beginning of the path lay before him. Thank God, the room had been dark; his eyes didn't have to get accustomed, all over again, to the night's shadows. He could hear no rustle, see no movements. They weren't near the house then. Not yet. He opened the door and slipped through. Behind him, the door was closed quietly. He kept close to the wall of the house, to the heavy black line of darkness under the eaves. At the corner, he stepped into the path, walking lightly through its shadows. Now, he was out of them, into the open, and he slowed his pace, as if he had no reason to hurry. He halted by the curve of the stream and lit a cigarette, as if he were wondering what he should do next. Then, he began, slowly, to walk down the path toward the woods. If there was anyone watching from the distance, they would see him clearly. If they wanted him, they would know where to find him. And if I've guessed wrong, he thought, as he approached the first tree, if Petros isn't anywhere near here, then— There was a sharp crack, splitting the night. A spurt of earth and stones shot up ahead of him, to the side of the path. He raced for the wood, dived into the undergrowth as a second shot cut the ground behind him. And somewhere dogs began barking.

He lay flat on his face, his head beginning to throb again. Someone tugged at his arm. It was Petros. "Here," Petros whispered, getting him off the path, pulling him behind a clump of bushes. "And what little game were you playing, my friend?" But he laughed softly, as if he knew. "That back of yours—it tempted them. It asked them, it begged them to shoot."

Elias suddenly appeared beside them. "A mistake," he observed in a whisper. "Now we know where that fellow is." He pointed to the field on the hillside above the house. He frowned. "But why there?" he asked himself.

"And why," Strang asked, equally puzzled, keeping his voice to a whisper, too, "don't they follow me?"

"You like trouble," Petros said. Then, as he heard a rustle near them, he gestured with his arm. "John!" he whispered, and a man rose from the underbrush and came quietly to join them. "What do you see, out there?" Petros asked him. "Eyes like a cat," Petros explained to Strang as John moved to get a clear view.

"Where's Levadi?" Strang asked.

Petros shrugged his shoulders, as he stared at the distant field encircled by its stone wall. "Around, someplace."

"Why don't they follow me?" Strang asked again, with exasperation. This was uncanny. Two shots, then silence. "Or do they think they hit me?"

"They nearly did," Elias said grimly.

Or perhaps they want to make sure I'm alone, Strang thought, and unarmed. It *was* uncanny. The dogs were barking wildly now, but the village still lay in darkness, as if it had pulled the blankets over its head, determined to hear and see nothing.

John whispered hoarsely, "Four of them!" The man who had fired from the cover of the stone wall around the field had risen. Two others were coming down from the hillside above him. They seemed to think that cover was no longer necessary. "Three are going to the house," John said.

Petros was on his feet.

"Keep down!" Elias whispered angrily.

Strang said, "Steve is in that house."

Elias stared at him.

"Stefanos Kladas is in that house," Strang insisted. "And these men know. They know. That's why they didn't come after me."

John said, "I cannot see them now. The house hides them."

Elias rose quickly, taking a whistle out of his pocket, giving a clear sharp

298

blast. From the other end of the village street came an answering whistle. Petros and John were starting up the path. Elias yelled to Strang, "Stay there! Stay there!" Then he was racing after Petros and John, and catching up with them, too. From the olive trees on the other side of the stream, men ran out and splashed through the water to the village street. And along there, a car was starting up, gathering speed to reach the house.

So I come out, get shot at, and stay here, Strang thought: the hell I do. He started after the others, halted, staring, helpless. He yelled, "The roof, the roof!" For a man was clambering up there, half crouching as he reached the ridge, half rising as he started a hobbling run toward the chimney, his right arm raised to throw. Petros and John both fired. The man's step veered; he seemed to take three running steps right down the front of the roof before he fell and clattered the rest of the way to plunge over its broad eave. His body landed in front of the house, and, a split second later, exploded into a flash of gray light, a balloon of smoke.

Strang's sense of complete helplessness vanished. He ran toward the low stone wall encircling the field, just about the point where the sharp-shooter had hidden. Petros, Elias, and John had reached the house and were fanning around it, along with the men who had crossed the stream. The car had arrived, too, screeching to a halt just as the grenade had gone off, and three men were jumping out of it to join the others. Enough men there to take care of any trouble, Strang thought. There was plenty, too; another explosion sent him ducking behind the wall. He heard the frenzied scream of a horse or a donkey, the bleatings of goats; back in the village, the dogs had gone crazy. He swung his legs over the roughly laid loose stones, and landed in the field as there was a third explosion. To his left, near the house, there was a shot, then three more, a sudden surge of men, another burst of firing, then silence.

But what interested him was the field. Up there, somewhere up there, near the top of the steeply plowed furrows, he had seen a lumbering shadow. That must be the fourth man whom the lynx-eyed John had spied. He started up the hill, and stumbled over a dog, lying wide-eyed, its throat slit. So that was why he had heard no dog barking its warning from the Kladas house. Quickly, he focused his eyes back on the lumbering shadow, now almost at the top of the field. Someone called after him; he waved, and ran on. If he took his eyes away from that shadow, he'd lose it.

It was heavy, slow travel, uphill through the field's soft earth, and ruina-tion for a careful spring planting. Behind him, Petros called again, but he went on. He was near the top of the field now; there was the low stone wall in front of him. And beyond it, a bleak beginning to a mountainside, boulders and rocks scattered over rough grass, a distant cliff face, a ridge of high peaks lined sharply against the eastern sky. Dawn was coming from the other side, a hint of green-gray behind the ragged rim of mountain, the stars fading, a cold wind rising.

Strang climbed over the wall, and then halted, his eyes searching the mountainside, while he got his breathing once more under control. He swallowed in hot, heavy gulps, feeling the saliva burn its way down his throat. He pulled his jacket collar up, the lapels over, and thrust his hands deep into his pockets; up here, the wind had an edge like a hatchet. He took a few last deep breaths, and he had steadied himself again. And then he saw the man in the bulky sheepskin tunic. It was Levadi, all right. He had stopped, near a large boulder almost as tall as he was, and he had turned to face Strang. Friendly or not? Strang wondered, noting the long, heavy stick on which Levadi, grasping it at shoulder height, rested his weight.

Strang, his hands still in his pockets, walked slowly up toward a goat path, a foot-broad, winding ribbon of worn earth. No sudden movements, he thought, as he reached it, no loud noises: just this steady plodding, up the goat path, one slow foot in front of another, eyes on that strange bulky shape that looked in this half-light like a shaggy animal standing on two human legs.

Strang halted about twelve feet away from Levadi, within smelling distance, he thought wryly, but just outside the swing of that long stave. He looked at the man, seeing his face for the first time.

"Good morning," he said, speaking in Greek, slowly.

The man said nothing, his eyes staring intently from under heavy brows at the stranger, still suspicious, still waiting for the first sign of attack.

"A fine view," Strang said, and looked briefly down over the valley. And it was a view to startle anyone. Strang had to force his eyes quickly back to the man and that stave. But Levadi had looked down over the dark valley, too, and then beyond, to the far-off giants of western mountains, their white peaks tinged with gold and mauve and pink, gleaming through the veils of soft trailing clouds. And he stood there, silent, his wild eyes watching as they, perhaps, watched each morning. For a long minute, he stood there as if he had forgotten the stranger. His hair was light in color, Strang noted, an unkempt mass of thick locks falling over the prominent brow; his features were good but coarsened, the skin ruddy with health under the layer of grime, the mouth was large, the lips heavy and slack. Now Levadi seemed to remember the stranger again, and his head swung around quickly, the eyes wary and suspicious.

Levadi spoke. It was a rough, shy voice, strangely thin, high-pitched. "You are here."

I certainly am, thought Strang. Or was that remark Levadi's idea of a question? "I want to talk to you."

Levadi's frown deepened. "You stop me, I kill you," he said. He stared at Strang's hands, still buried in his pockets.

"I came to talk." Strang took his hands out of his pockets. "I have no weapon," he assured the man. But that was a miscalculation. Levadi turned and walked uphill, with a long striding step. There was no gun to fear, after all. "Wait!" Strang started after him.

Levadi whirled around, the long stick grasped in both hands, ready to hit, if necessary.

Strang halted. "Where are you going?"

The man stared at him. "Home," he said slowly.

And where was home—a hut on this mountainside, or the ruins, far on the crest of a hill, of the Frankish castle? Then Strang made a bold guess. "This is not the way to Parnassos."

The man looked at him. "I know the way."

"But you cannot go back."

"Now—yes." Levadi smiled, the lips drawn slowly back into a wide, loose grimace.

"And Myrrha—"

The grimace on the wide mouth turned from delight to pain.

It was, thought Strang, very much like talking to a large powerful dog who might understand a few key words but mistrusted everything else. Strang said very clearly, "They tried to kill Myrrha."

There was denial in the wild eyes, staring at the American.

I've seen that face, Strang thought; somewhere, I've seen that face. He repeated slowly, "They tried to kill Myrrha."

"No. Not Myrrha. Stefanos, yes. He is a deserter. He betrayed—"

"That's a lie. He did not desert to any Germans. Sideros told you a lie. Odysseus told you a lie."

Levadi's reply to that was to raise his stick and take a step toward Strang.

"Come back to the house," Strang said. "See what they have done. The dog had its throat slit. Myrrha may be dead. You heard the—" And what was the Greek word for grenades?

"Not Myrrha."

"They lied."

Levadi leaped forward in anger, in a quick bounding run, the stick upraised and ready to strike. Strang jumped aside. And from behind him, the sharp crack of a rifle sounded, echoing, echoing along the mountainside. Levadi dropped the stick as he spun around with a cry, and fell, clutching his shoulder. He tried to rise and run.

"Stop, or I'll kill you this time," Petros yelled, clambering over the stone wall. John was following him.

Levadi stopped. Strang looked at him in amazement: he had stopped, had taken two paces back. To be killed—was that what he feared most? What made a man like that even want to live? Strang watched Levadi and wondered. The man had stopped again; he was looking across the black stretch of valley to its western wall of mountains. The snow-wrapped peaks were ablaze with colors, no longer hinted but as vivid as the fires of an opal: purple, pink, mauve, magenta, rose. The mists had drawn into soft white masses of cloud edged with a golden light. The colors shifted, deepened, mixed, paled. And then, in a moment, they were gone.

"Look at him!" Petros said bitterly, as Levadi turned to them, biting his lip, struggling with his emotion. "Tears for a sunrise! And he would have beaten out your brains on these rocks just as easily as he welcomed a dog and slit its throat. He would let a man be murdered in his bed and a woman be blown to pieces." Petros's lip curled with contempt. He raised his rifle.

"No!" Strang said sharply. "Get him down to the house!" He looked away from Levadi. The man's emotion was too painful to watch.

Levadi stumbled past him, his left hand resting on top of his head in surrender, his right arm half raised in pain. And at that moment, Strang remembered the photograph: the surrender on the slope of Parnassos; the man whose blind instinct to live separated him from those he left to die, the shepherd who wept tears of shame and followed Odysseus into the enemy camp.

Elias, his hair ruffled in the wind, his thin face tired and anxious, was waiting for them at the low stone wall. "Who's this?" he asked.

"The fourth man," John told him, his sharp eyes watching Levadi's every movement, his rifle ready.

"The shepherd," Strang said, and Elias looked at him sharply, then back at the man slipping and stumbling toward him. Now Elias was studying the face coming toward him. "Yes," he said coldly, "the shepherd from Mount Parnassos."

Levadi climbed over the wall and stopped as he saw a group of men waiting down at the bottom of the field near the house.

Elias told Petros and John, "See that nothing happens to him!"

"What? We protect him?" asked Petros.

"We need him alive." In English, Elias said to Strang, "If he will talk, that is to say." He shrugged his shoulders. "Can he talk?"

302

"He isn't an idiot. Ask him why he once rebelled against Odysseus."

Elias's eyebrows were raised. But he fell into step beside Levadi and began talking to the man. Halfway down the field, Elias waited for Strang to catch up. "It was a personal matter. Something about Elektra."

"Tell him Odysseus has killed Elektra."

Elias stared in horror. "Certainly not! Don't even say that to anyone. Not yet! I forbid you!"

"All right, all right," Strang said, and fell back to join Petros.

"It is enough to show him what Odysseus ordered to be done here," Elias said gruffly, and hurried Levadi on toward the house.

"Who are the men?" Strang asked Petros, watching the tight group that waited at the bottom of the field. Their weapons, he saw, were axes.

"From the village. You saw them rush across the stream when the captain blew his little whistle." Petros was delighted with the look of surprise on Strang's face. "What did you think I was doing when I left you and Myrrha? I went to waken my friends. We needed them, didn't we?"

"And Elias brought back no reinforcements?"

"Sure. They are on their way." Petros's smile broadened. "Arriving any moment."

Strang looked at the row of quiet little houses, and apologized to them. "When I climbed this field, I wondered why they lay so still."

"When you climbed this field, how were you so sure that I would follow you?"

"Because," Strang said, "you weren't going to let me escape—if that was what I had been doing."

Petros rubbed the scar on his brow, looked sideways at the American, and laughed softly. "There could have been a fifth man," he said, threw an arm across Strang's back and matched his step. He was still smiling broadly as they reached the group of embattled villagers around Elias and his prisoner. Strang left Petros explaining that the captain must know what he was saying, and headed for the broken door of the shed at the back of the Kladas house.

He skirted two bodies, stretched just outside the door. In the shed, where the animals had been sheltered at night, he halted. The place was a shambles, its roof torn wide by a grenade. The donkey had been put out of its misery; one goat was dead, the other would soon be. He plowed through a mass of mangled chickens to the small door that connected the shed to the house. It had been weakened by the explosion, a panel smashed to let another grenade be thrown into the downstairs room. The fireplace wall was a ruin, the rest of the place a desolate mess of fragments and dust. The wooden staircase still hugged the far wall, and there, on one of the broken treads of the lower steps, Myrrha Kladas was sitting, staring at nothing, while three women tried to comfort her. Her small face, streaked with dust, looked smaller under the bandage tied roughly around her forehead. She nursed one shoulder. She was silent, but the tears were streaming down her face leaving furrows of grime.

"Myrrha!"

Her eyes turned to him in deep despair. "They killed my animals," she said. "They killed—"

"Steve? Where is Steve?"

She pointed to the front door, wide open, the gray light of early morning stealing across its threshold.

And there, at last, was Steve.

He was huddled in a gray blanket, his feet bandaged, hobbling into the back seat of the Chrysler. Costas was already at the wheel. Behind the Chrysler was an army car, and then an open truck with a platoon of fresh-faced boys in uniform now filing out into the village street. Elias and his prisoner, still intact, were standing by the army car while Elias explained vehemently to the lieutenant in command.

Strang went forward to the Chrysler, and leaned on its back door. "Hi there!" he said. There really didn't seem much more to say.

Steve's haggard white face stared at him. Steve tried to smile, but the usual furrows wouldn't deepen round his mouth. He put out his hand and gripped Strang's.

Costas said, "He is going to Athens. Urgent business."

I can believe that, Strang thought. "But is he fit enough to travel?"

Steve said, "I am going. Ken—I've got to go."

"Fine. Just hand me that coat on the back seat, and you can stretch out there. I'll ride beside Costas." Strang put on his coat thankfully and turned up its collar. "Perishing cold by the dawn's early light," he said.

"Ken—will you do something for me?"

Strang waited. He could almost feel what was coming.

"Stay with Myrrha. Until I get back."

"I promised to be back in Athens by—" Strang began, and then stopped.

"We must leave," Costas broke in, and looked pointedly at his watch.

"Stay with her for a day, at least. Just keep an eye on things, Ken. Will you?"

Strang nodded, stepped back from the car, smiled to get that anxious look out of Steve's face. "All right," he said, and waved. Costas turned the car with an expert flourish, the eyes of the village upon him, saluted Elias as he passed and roared along the straight street in a cloud of dust.

Strang stood there, watching them go. He felt so tired, so agonizingly tired and depressed that he couldn't even make up his mind to start walking back to the house. Elias came over to him. "I am taking Levadi to Athens. There will be trouble if we keep him around here. Besides—he may decide to talk. He might be very useful."

"When he saw the house, and Myrrha—what did he say?"

Elias shrugged. "He was sorry. He was very sorry." Elias paused. Very carefully he added, "The name Elektra seems to upset him a great deal. Very strange. I do not suppose she even noticed him."

"Nor did the sunrise," Strang said. He added briskly, "Good luck, Elias! And don't leave me stranded here."

"Certainly not. I shall send a car for you, at the earliest, tomorrow." Elias shook hands very formally, and hurried back to the army car. He had commandeered a driver and an extra man from the lieutenant, too. He saluted as he got in beside Levadi. That's going to be one hell of a journey, Strang thought, as he watched another cloud of dust. He buttoned his coat to his chin.

Petros was beside him. "We'll find you a place to sleep. I have a cousin, a widower, no women to start lamenting. Some food and some sleep. Right?"

It sounded pretty wonderful. "I'll see Myrrha first," Strang said, "and then—" Sleep. And more sleep. He looked at the sky to the northeast, where Athens lay, and Cecilia. Cecilia, sweet susurrus, the name could mesmerize him into sleep, standing right here on this soft earth road, the whisper of trees around him, the murmuring stream. Then two smooth-cheeked recruits carried a body past him and heaved it into a farm cart. A girl, bare feet in unlaced boots, her long wide skirt falling to her ankles, her hair and forehead and ears enveloped in a yellow scarf twisting around her neck and over her mouth to leave only her bright, curious eyes to wish him good day, paused to stare into the cart, and then—as the two soldiers joked with her—retreated, in a fit of muffled giggles and a light hop, skip, and run, after the laden donkey she was driving toward the fields.

"Another day, another backache," Petros said cheerfully, and took Strang's arm to lead him to the Kladas house. "That's where I lived as a boy," he said, and pointed to some burned-out ruins now partly mounded over with grass, where two goats grazed. "More than half the village was stretched out dead that morning. Not a man or boy left. Funny thing, if I hadn't been away fighting, I'd have been stretched out on this street, too."

As they reached the house, Petros looked at the nasty mess of earth and shredded clothing and a single boot, lying on the path near the doorway. "If he had managed to throw his grenade down the chimney—" Petros pursed his lips, shrugged his shoulders. "Well, it's a fine dawn, anyway," he said.

TWENTY-THREE

The dawn was spreading over the sky of Athens as Alexander Christophorou came back to his apartment. He came quite openly, driving up in a taxi, ascending the steps without any haste, searching carefully for his keys, nodding to the two men who had been stationed outside the house since the police had discovered the bodies in the Drakon apartment. "What," he said, "no sign yet of Mr. Drakon?" His mock concern was well received. Anything to cheer up our gallant policemen, he thought, pursuing their entirely thankless, pointless, and useless duty.

In the hall, the smile on his lips vanished. He noticed with irritation that one of the two meager electric bulbs had failed. As his keys unlocked his door, he was thinking how very strange this all was: here was the day beginning, at long last beginning, and he felt no excitement, no exhilaration, only irritation over a faded light bulb. Strange, and yet—not strange: he was exhausted with those last six hours of meetings, of final reports, of business and discussion; of the bogus decisions appointing temporary replacements for Elektra and Sideros to the Committee; of the fake regrets concealing personal ambitions, of the search for explanations that could be used against the enemy. But it was one thing to create and use propaganda, quite another to believe it yourself. That had been the great weakness of Elektra: one month, she would help to invent, or would accept an invention knowing it was false; three months later, she believed it as an established truth. There was no future for a revolutionary in self-delusion. Leaders did not swallow the sugar-coated pills that they prepared for the open mouths of the masses.

He passed through the small entrance hall of the apartment without turning on its light, threw his coat on the couch, slumped into his armchair, stared through the windows at the half-light of dawn spreading over the city. Yes, he was tired. But mostly tired of waiting. He had lived with the plan too long. Fifteen years. Ten years alone with it—his eyes turned instinctively to the rows of books that covered a wall of his room—bringing it from seed into sapling into tree. Five years of long, bitter discussion, of sharing the theory with a selected few, of watching the theory develop into a plan, of nursing, shaping, pruning, feeding the growing organism. At last, today, the fruit was ripe. And Elektra had thought she could seize it, hand it over to men who would use revolution for their own cynical extension of national power.

Yes, that was the weakness of believing your own propaganda: Elektra and her clique had forgotten what revolution really meant. Those hypocrites, he thought contemptuously, with their talk of "revolution" and "the people," merely substituting one elite group for another, freeing people into slavery, turning the masses into an ant heap, installing a new brand of imperialism. But revolution was revolution, complete, absolute, not to be qualified and distorted by national pride, politics, or greed. What difference was there between the capitalist boss and the Communist or fascist commissar except in the carefully cultivated myths of their dogma? All of them were manipulators, parasites, exploiters. All were in search of power. And whether power was less distasteful if it was built on gold or on fanatic nationalism—that was one of those absurd questions over which only the impotent socialists, the self-congratulating neutralists would try their favorite gymnastic: the far-stretched straddle. But all of them—Communists, socialists, capitalists, liberals, fascists, Nazis, neutralists—and what a dreary bunch they were with their egos and their ids—all had one attribute in common: man's infinite capacity for self-delusion. It would be a pleasure to see them destroy each other.

Why, he wondered, was he even bothering to justify Elektra's death? (Strange how quickly he forgot Sideros: a useful man once, efficient, discreet, coldly calculating, turned into part braggart and part gigolo, Elektra's new favorite; bed and board had inflated his vanity; he had become a blunderer, an encumbrance. Sideros's handling of the Roilos affair, father and son, could have been disastrous.)

Why justify? She had earned her death. He had been expecting her treachery, or else he would not be here this morning, alive to meet this dawn. He would have been the suicide in Drakon's apartment. He had forestalled Elektra by thirty seconds. No more than that. She and her tamed terrorist had been so sure of themselves, so sure that his usefulness was over. But what he could forgive them least was their calm assumption of his stupidity.

Sitting in this unlighted room, looking out at the smug, placid street and the filtering daylight, he felt tired and cold. No exhilaration, no sense of triumph; only a vague depression, a strange sense of worry. He dismissed the feeling, as he had dismissed it earlier that evening. There was no rational explanation for it. He had not been followed. There was no suspicion. Drakon, a mere word, had vanished as easily as it had been conjured into life. Alexander Christophorou was unknown in the world of Odysseus or of Metsos. The plans were well made. The essential people were well prepared. The final reports had come in, and everything that was really important was secure, everyone in position, waiting. In Yugoslavia, a dictator killed and the old-line Communists ready to seize power (but with Elektra gone, how long would they keep it, the fools?) and direct the national vengeance against Greece who would be accused of the assassination. In Cyprus, the Western imperialists would betray the people again, conniving with a hated minority to kill the leaders of the freedom movement. From Turkey, political exiles, slipping back into their native Syria, would bring revolution and money easily traceable to America. Three small fires, to be sure. But three small fires lit beside three mountains of gunpowder did not need much wind to fan their flames. A beginning at least.

But Elektra had wanted more than a beginning. She had wanted to control the end, too. "We have offers of help, real help," she had told him. "All we have planned can be useful to them." He had replied, "And when have you been talking with them? And where?" She did not have to answer. He had known, at that moment, that she had talked with her old comrades (was she giving up her Stalinist convictions or were they moving back to them again?) and was following their orders once more. It was her chance to be reinstated in favor, to be accepted back into that comforting circle where thinking was no problem, but a set of long-established clichés. She had said, laughing, "You nihilists! You wild dreamers! Where are your armies?" But he had had the final word: "Wherever there is hate and vengeance, there are our armies. They are everywhere. Yes, even in your Russia." Those were the last uncomforting words she had heard.

He had shot her first, then Sideros. Then he had taken the handbag from her lap. She had been opening it, as she laughed, her fingers searching for the small revolver inside it, her eyes holding his. So natural, so tender had she seemed, that Sideros did not even sense what was happening. Too much bed and board were bad for a man's reflexes.

Hate and vengeance . . . Together, they formed the one force that was neither meaningless nor absurd, the only answer to life's stupidities. He rose. He might as well go to bed, sleep until noon, hear the first reports on his radio. Across the street, a match flickered near a window. He stood still, watching. A match had flickered; what of it? A man with insomnia had lit a cigarette, soon he'd switch on the light, pick up a book. But no light was switched on.

Christophorou drew to the side of his own window. Yes, there was a man over there, standing just behind the thin curtains—they moved slightly as he peered out—watching the street. In a few moments, the man would get tired of watching an empty street; he would go away. But he did not go.

Christophorou stood at the side of his window, waiting for the man to leave, timing him. His thoughts were cold, critical.

Watching me? But if Zafiris had any suspicions, he would have had me brought in for questioning. At once. Zafiris had so little to go on that he could not have afforded to leave any suspect unquestioned. So little to go on? Since the photographs and negatives had been stolen, less than little. And all the contents of that envelope, which Kenneth Strang had guarded so stubbornly, were now safely in ashes.

Kenneth Strang . . . If the American had received any information from Katherini Roilos, he had made little use of it. He had not visited any government office. No member of the Colonel's staff had visited his room. And if he had anything to communicate to Zafiris, he could not do it now. He would stay in Sparta, in close custody, until the crisis was over. He would have plenty of time to think, there; but his thoughts would incline more toward the beautiful Hillard than to anything else. To each man, his weakness.

Cecilia Hillard . . . No. The girl was nothing; a smaller question mark than Strang. There had been no response to the note signed "Katherini": The name had meant less than little to her. She and Strang could not have met Roilos, after all.

As for Katherini Roilos . . . a futile escape ending in a strange return to Kriton Street. And only three sentences spoken: "Come, Maria. We have friends. We can escape." But the fools had seized her, and she had said nothing more. In spite of questioning, nothing. Then, even as Andreas was telephoning the news of the girl's return, the police had broken into the house. Andreas had been talking about a truck which he and Sideros had followed. What truck? Andreas was under close arrest, Sideros was dead. What truck? What friends did Roilos have?

The small unanswerable questions . . . They always arose. Where was Evgenia Vasilika? She scarcely mattered, merely one of Elektra's sycophants. There would be more scandal than danger if she had been arrested. Yorghis's arrest had been for the simple matter of defrauding his employers. It was fortunate that the arrest had not occurred before he handed over the Ottway woman's camera. It had reached Cyprus yesterday, all nicely prepared, even Caroline Ottway's initials added to the leather carrying case. Ottway was in Cyprus now. Why? Part of his normal duties? Soon they would be over. Permanently. Yorghis, stupid in some things, had been clever about that. Ottway's career would never recover.

But more important than Vasilika or Yorghis or the pawns captured at Kriton Street—mostly belonging, fortunately, to Elektra and Sideros—was the question of Stefanos Kladas. The last report received said he had been taken off the *Medea,* and was imprisoned in a fisherman's hut; further instructions were awaited. The instructions had been sent yesterday, but no answer had come back. Why? Had he been executed? Or had he escaped? If he had, he was practically naked. No money. Helpless. He would head over the mountains to Thalos. Yes, he had friends there; but there was also the shepherd Levadi, who would report Stefanos Kladas to the farm Sideros had set up as a stronghold, only five kilometers north of Thalos. Levadi hated a deserter; Levadi accepted any command if he thought it came from Elektra. A simple creature, that Levadi, his hate and trust never changing. There was, too, the practical reward: a hut on one of the slopes of Parnassos, a few sheep, a dog. How easy it was to satisfy some men's dreams.

The biggest question of all was Zafiris. No one in Athens paid him a second thought: one of those honest, dull soldiers whose politeness covered their uneasiness when they faced brain power. How painful it had been to see him, in these last two or three years, dutifully attending every reception in Athens, stolid and bewildered, a tiger put to live on an iceberg. Such men would face a tank division more confidently than wit or intelligence.

Zafiris . . .

Was that his man at the window across the street? The man seemed to have gone now. Had he?

Christophorou spoke aloud. "Nonsense!" he told himself. "You are exhausted. That is why you worry. Get to bed! Sleep! Then you will not keep thinking, at this useless moment, of the small things you may have left undone. The big things are assured."

He moved through the small hall toward his bedroom, switching on its light. A scrap of paper caught his eye. It lay almost at the threshold of the front door. He must have walked over it when he entered. It was a hastily scrawled note on a small sheet torn from a diary. "Have tried to reach you all day. Telephone immediately." The signature was his sister's.

His sister? Yes. The writing was genuine. No doubt, the old man had decided to have a deathbed scene. Very touching that he should be invited to join it. And on such a day! He could imagine himself . . . He had said his good-by to them all fifteen years ago. How like his sister to insist on forgiveness for everyone, blessings for all. Nothing was ever final, with such women. And even if he did take her at her word—"Telephone immediately"—she would be angry with his thoughtlessness in disturbing the household at dawn. He crumpled the note and carried it into the bedroom to throw in the trash basket. He paused at the window before he closed its curtains. Yes, someone was standing at the window opposite; someone had just opened it a little. As if he had smoked too many cigarettes in that room? Had he been waiting there so long that the air had turned stale?

Christophorou drew the curtains closed, switched on his light. It might be just as well to make sure he had a quick exit all ready. He left the light bright in his bedroom—let any curious eyes note that!—and went into the kitchen. He unbolted the back door, and listened. Nothing. He ran lightly down the short flight of stairs to the basement corridor, taking out his keys. He would rest better—sleep was out of the question now—knowing that this door into the yard and the padlock on the gate outside were unlocked.

His key jammed in the lock. He had to struggle with it to get it out. He tried again, more carefully. It wouldn't unlock, but jammed again. Again he had a battle to pull it free.

"Oh, it's you, Mr. Christophorou!" the caretaker said in relief, her head cautiously poking around her half-opened door. "I've been that scared since last night—"

"I thought I heard a noise in the yard. But none of my keys fit. Where is yours?"

Her head disappeared. In a moment, she was back, a coat slipped over her nightdress, her feet clattering in her late husband's slippers.

"Sh!" he told her. "We don't want to give anyone any warning out there." He took the key. It turned easily in the lock.

"It's a new key," she whispered.

"Did you lose the old one?"

She looked indignant. But before she could start on one of her endless self-justifications, he entered the yard. His key for the padlock would not work, either. Quickly, he retreated back to the corridor, noticing as he passed through the yard that it had been tidied up. The coil of rope, the ladder, which had lain so long there, unquestioned, hidden behind a clutter of packing cases, had been removed with the crates themselves. Only the improvised hen house remained, with its four miserable pullets.

"No one is loitering out there," he told the woman. "Have you got a key for the gate, by the way?"

She shrugged. "The gate is never used now. What do I need with a key? If the landlord wasn't so mean, he would build a real wall." Then she dropped her voice. "He must have screamed when the police made him change the locks. Such expense!"

"Police?" He kept his voice light. "Are they expecting burglars?"

The woman said nervously, "No, no. It's those deaths. Some men were looking at the locks last night."

"What men?"

"They were here before the police came. First, there were two of them —a Greek and a foreigner with him. An American. And then a lot more came; a soldier—an officer, too. They went up the back stairs." Her eyes widened. "With guns," she whispered. "So quietly!"

"An American? That's not very likely."

"He *was* an American," she insisted. "He was telling the Greek something about that door. The Greek went into the yard, too. I heard him trying the gate. Then the others came—and they went upstairs."

"They must have been the police," he told her.

"No. When the police came later, the officer—a colonel, I heard someone call him—and his men left."

"And the American," he said. "Don't forget your American."

"He didn't leave with them. He left with a girl—"

"A girl?"

"About this height." She gestured above his shoulder. "A scarf over her head, I couldn't see her properly. But fine stockings and shoes with heels so tall and thin that—"

"How very odd," he said, to break the flow of description.

"They came down in the elevator and left with another American. His car was waiting outside for them."

"Did the police allow that?"

"Oh, yes."

"What kind of car?"

She looked at him blankly.

"Well," he said, locking the door, handing her back the key, "I am glad to see we are being so well guarded. I suppose the police have some men in Mr. Drakon's apartment?"

"They searched and took photographs all morning. They sealed the doors, and went away. But they've left two men in the street."

"Yes. I saw them." Two on the street, for everyone to see. How reassuring. Was that why they were there, so obviously? He turned away, thoughtfully.

"Oh, Mr. Christophorou!" she called after him. "There was a lady here today. She came twice. She wouldn't leave the note in your letter box, wouldn't even give it to me." There was a hint of renewed complaint in the woman's voice. "She—"

"Yes, yes. I got it all right." He ran upstairs to the kitchen door and bolted it behind him.

It could have been Strang, the girl could have been Hillard. . . . Impossible. Or had they been visiting Tommy? Hardly, at that hour. Still . . . And a colonel. And who was the other American, with a car?

Even without finding any definite answers, he did not like this at all, not one bit of it. The back entrances so cleverly made useless . . . Not one bit.

He entered his bedroom, looked at the telephone, and hesitated. His sister had refused to leave that note with the caretaker; that sounded strange. He picked up the receiver. He did not have to wait for anyone to be wakened up and come slowly to answer his call. It was his sister's voice, too, as if she had been sitting beside the telephone.

"Ah, yes," she said. "Please wait one moment."

He lit a cigarette, his eyes narrowing. Her voice had been tired, tense, but not emotional. So there was no illness in the house. And whom had she gone to fetch? Not his father, not at this hour. The old man scarcely ever would use the telephone, even at midday. But it was his father's voice, cold, impersonal, with no greeting, no first name, nothing but a plunge into a bare statement, which sharply broke the silence.

"Yesterday morning, I had a visitor. An official visitor. I was asked to identify a certain ring."

Christophorou's cigarette was crushed between his fingers. "Ring?" he repeated, almost stupidly.

"I identified it. It was my duty—as a citizen. And now, as your father—" The old voice hesitated.

Fantastic, Christophorou thought, and typical. First he informs against me, and then tells me about it. "It is your sad duty to warn me?" he asked, bitingly. How could such people ever win? Doing their smug duty in the name of so-called justice, and then helping that very justice to be evaded. They had lost even before they began to fight.

"No—to urge you to make an honorable end."

"End?" He frowned, understood, and almost laughed. "Now this is ridiculous! What ring are you talking about?" His mind was alert again.

I have that ring, he thought, I have it where they could not possibly discover it.

"You know what ring—"

"Nonsense! This whole thing is absolute nonsense."

"You will not find it so easy to persuade Colonel Zafiris of that."

"Zafiris?" He took a deep breath. "The man is a fool—you know that. Why take him seriously?"

His father said nothing at all.

"What do you expect me to do?" he asked, suddenly angered. "Blow my brains out?"

There was a pause. Then his father sighed wearily and replaced the receiver on its cradle. The cutting of the connection was final. Christophorou jammed down his own receiver.

He threw away the broken cigarette. Quickly, he began another call. They could have tapped his telephone, but he would like to see Zafiris make something out of this message. He glanced at his watch; it was almost quarter past six. Six fifteen. Allow fifteen, say seventeen minutes —that sounded better—for Xenia to phone his warning and get the cab around here. Seventeen minutes would be ample. Anastas and his cab were only three streets away, waiting for just such a call.

Xenia's sleep-filled voice said, "Yes?"

"Penelope, my dear—I'm sorry we shall have to postpone that picnic today. I'm catching a cold; grippe, perhaps. Don't worry. All I need is aspirin and a day in bed."

"You have the wrong number." Xenia's voice was wide awake.

"What? Isn't this 615-632?" He glanced at his watch as he spoke. Six fifteen, exactly.

"No." She slammed down the receiver. A good girl, Xenia. She would be running downstairs now, to the telephone in her little shop, over which she had her room. And Anastas would be here at six thirty-two.

He didn't waste time changing his clothes. But there were one or two small things he wanted to take with him. He lifted his hairbrush from his dressing table, pressed a small natural marking on its wooden back just beside the silver initials, and then pulled with a quick twist. The upper half of the brush's back slid open. There was the ring, and the keys to the Delphi house. He slipped them all into his pocket. From the concealed compartment at the back of his desk drawer, he took the small revolver that he had picked out of Elektra's handbag; a very neat Beretta, which slipped easily into his trouser pocket. Money, which he always had in reserve; a small, closely written diary, in code, which had lain carefully concealed in the base of a floor lamp; and he was ready.

315

He gave one last impersonal glance around his room, at the rows of books, his pictures, records, carefully chosen furniture. A pleasant place it had been. But possessions were like emotional attachments; they existed for him, not he for them. A man who even kept memories was a man forging his own chains.

It was now six thirty. He put on his coat and hat. He would shave and bathe and breakfast in Xenia's little flat. (She ought to have had a report from Sparta by this time.) He would wait there until the news started to break. Then he would see what remained to be done to complete this first round.

He closed his door quietly, hurried silently to the front entrance. He opened its door a bare inch, listened to the hum of the taxi as it came gently down the hill. Quite near now. He stepped out into the pale golden sunshine, nodded to the two men as he went down the steps, his movements deliberate and unworried. He took about twenty paces away from the men before he looked around, hailed the taxi, had its door open, and was inside and away.

Behind them, a car had suddenly started moving; so they, too, were prepared for emergencies. But Anastas knew his job. They turned the first corner, drove a short stretch, turned another corner, stopped by a waiting car for the brief moment it took Christophorou to make the change. Then he was speeding on, down the long stretch of street, while the car with Christophorou quickly turned around the nearest corner and seemed to be traveling leisurely back toward Dimocritos Street. It had been a very closely timed operation, but it had been well-practiced for just such a necessity. On the long, roundabout, boring drive down to Xenia's apartment, he even had time to start some rethinking about Zafiris.

He never needed much sleep, but he allowed himself three hours. Lack of it could act as a drug on the brain. By ten o'clock, Christophorou had washed, shaved, and dressed in gray flannels and a worn tweed jacket of English cut. His emergency wardrobe was proving useful at last. The thought amused him that, with those dark circles undershadowing his eyes and his hair not too carefully combed, he now looked like a slightly debauched Oxford don. But there was little else to amuse him.

There was still no news whatsoever from the Sparta area.

And a full report had now come in about the American girl, Cecilia Hillard. She was no longer to be found at her hotel. Some careful questioning had resulted in the discovery that she had left the hotel, about seven o'clock yesterday evening, accompanied by an American who was not Strang. The American had carried a small overnight case. They drove away in a private car. Further investigation had uncovered the owner of the car: Robert Pringle, an attaché at the American Embassy. The house, where he rented the third-floor apartment, had been placed under careful supervision since yesterday evening by police, or intelligence agents.

So the girl had been not such an insignificant question mark, after all. Now the caretaker's story about the American and a girl, two nights ago, slipping out into another American's car began to make complete sense. Strang. Hillard. And Pringle.

Christophorou took a deep breath. And now, too, he was remembering a telephone call from Strang, earlier on that evening, when he had been at Pringle's apartment. A harmless conversation it had seemed, an inquiry about Beaumont's address, but in retrospect, with the new facts to give a different perspective, had Strang only been covering up the real purpose of a call at that late hour? Now Christophorou recalled the report from the Bulgarian: Strang and Hillard had left Erinna Street only a short time before that telephone call to Pringle.

There it was: Katherini Roilos to Strang; Strang to Pringle; Pringle to Zafiris.

Downstairs, among her shelves of canned goods, her cheeses, her sacks of rice and small crates of vegetables, Xenia heard the frightening crash. She ran upstairs. Had Metsos fallen, met with an accident?

But Metsos was standing, quite still, near the window, looking down into the narrow busy street. His breakfast tray had been swept off the table and lay in a broken mess on the floor. "Leave it," he told her. "Get back to your shop."

She did what she was told.

Christophorou left the window and sat down in a chair. In this last week, he had been concentrating too much on Elektra and Sideros, on their attempted manipulations, their planned take-over, their secret negotiations with lip-service Communists. It was easy, now, to see his mistake. Yes, he had been too preoccupied with them. But for a good reason: they were clever, ruthless opponents who needed such concentration if they were to be defeated. If he had not done that, the revolution would have lost its truth, become merely another façade for a power that would use and then destroy him and his followers as totally as they would destroy the bourgeois capitalists. So his mistake had not been completely stupid. Nothing necessary was ever stupid. If he had not countered Elektra and Sideros, he would not even be alive this morning.

And today was going to be such a fantastic cumulation of events that Zafiris and his colleagues would find they had merely been busy counting snowflakes while an avalanche was gathering its weight to fall on them. By the end of this week, Zafiris would be back in the army proper; he would be needed there. If we leave him alive, Christophorou added to his thoughts.

And Strang? A most regrettable oversight. But who would have taken Strang seriously? Americans, by the very nature of the soft fat they collected around their brains along with all their comforts, their total ignorance of historical meanings, their delusion that anarchists were either comic little men plotting nothings in a dark cellar or misunderstood cranks —how could Americans be taken seriously in a world of real politics? One of their presidents had been killed by an anarchist. How many had troubled to find out more about the anarchist's friends, about the group whose meetings he had attended regularly in America? Had no one bothered to notice that, from the same group, other men had gone back to their native Europe, with assassination as their purpose? Had no one wondered who had planned and financed it all? Or perhaps Americans assumed that penniless men, sixty years ago, could easily afford to go traveling through Europe. The English were just as incredible. There had even been a battle with anarchists right in the heart of London itself: the siege of Sydney Street. But people had been deliciously eager to explain it all away as a fantastic story concocted for political advantage. The arsenal in the house on Sydney Street, the men who had met there constantly, the hours of violence when they were trapped, only seemed to rouse little more than a sneer at Churchill and his vote-getting mind.

Yes, the Americans and the British were alike in some things. They were surface people, skimming over past history, picking out the interpretations that pleased them, never digging deep for the truths that could warn them. When they found something unpleasant, they would forget it within six months. They even prided themselves on not remembering; forget and forgive were so much easier. They evaded serious ideas, unless they approved of them. The British put their faith in compromise, the Americans in doling out largesse; by wheedling and bribing, they thought they could avoid ever having to answer the only real question in life: Who whom? But they had never been conquered, never been occupied, never had their men carted away as slave laborers, never witnessed mass rape, never watched their children being turned into their enemies. That was their great weakness: they had merely existed while others had survived. How fortunate for the cause of world revolution, with all its varied forces remembering the bitter taste of their survivals, that the two most powerful nations in the Western clique should have had no experience in *Real-*

politik. It would not be difficult to bury them, not when they helped so obligingly to dig their own graves.

And did one of those incompetents think he could drift into my life, Christophorou thought, and wreck it? For the name of Alexander Christophorou, his convenient way of life in Athens, were now both dead. So was the name of Odysseus. Even Metsos, with its close relationship to Demetrius Drakon, was dying. But the discovery of names and identities was not a disaster; it was troublesome, annoying, time-consuming to have to build up new ones, a totally unnecessary waste of energy and planning. There was a small score to be settled with Mr. Kenneth Clark Strang.

Xenia came back into the room. It was ten minutes before noon. He has recovered his good temper, she thought, relieved. What she had to tell him would need a very calm Metsos to hear it.

"Yes?" he asked. He had the radio turned on, its volume as low as possible.

"I have something to report," she said, and glanced at the radio, which made her raise her voice more than she thought was discreet.

He looked at his watch. "Be quick then." He turned down the radio to a whisper.

"Anastas has just come in to buy tomatoes."

"Yes, yes." What idiots women were!

"He had a message from Sparta. His man there reports rifle shots and two or three explosions, up on the mountainside. Just before dawn."

"My God, the fools! Who told them to use rifles or grenades?" They would have the police searching all that stretch of mountains. In those last few months, Sideros had hidden an arsenal of weapons around that farmhouse near Thalos.

"Anastas says his man went up toward the farmhouse, early this morning. But he dared not go near it. There were soldiers there."

So they had found the farmhouse. And there went another of Sideros's ideas. Nothing Sideros had planned had gone right.

"There were soldiers in Thalos, too. Our man spoke to a girl working in the fields near the road. She said men had raided the Kladas house and tried to kill Myrrha Kladas and her brother."

He rose, looking at her sharply. Now he understood why rifles and grenades had been used. But clumsy, clumsy. Sideros and his men had always been too quick to rely on open violence.

"They were not killed. But two of our men were shot; and one was blown to pieces when he fell from the roof with a live grenade in his hand."

"What about the shepherd called Levadi?"

"He was taken away."

"And the American?" His voice became bitterly sarcastic. "He walks free, I suppose. Their bullets were too valuable to put one in his back?"

Xenia bit her lip nervously. "He is free."

Christophorou gripped the back of the chair. "Get back to your shop!"

She hesitated instinctively as she stood over the fallen breakfast tray, then retreated quickly as she saw the look in his eyes.

He turned the radio up to a volume he could hear. Two minutes to go. The small annoyances could be put aside, meanwhile. The big things were to come.

TWENTY-FOUR

Strang woke, with the afternoon sun streaming through the small window of the small low-ceilinged room to fall directly over his face. Or perhaps the footsteps at the door had pulled him out of sleep. Or perhaps he had slept his fill. He sat up slowly, rubbing his head, stretching his back, and smiled at Myrrha Kladas.

"How's your head?" he asked. Her bandage was neater now.

"A cut—that is all. I was at the top of the staircase when the explosion happened. And then I fell. Bruises." She rubbed her left arm and side.

So that was all, he thought, admiring her equanimity; two inches lower and that splinter would have blinded her. "And how is everything else?"

"It looks better. We have cleaned away the dust and broken pieces. We shall soon rebuild the room. And my neighbors will help me finish the plowing."

"So you've got neighbors now?" He got up, bending his head to avoid grazing the rough beams. There was no other furniture in the room beyond the three straw mattresses on a low wooden platform.

She nodded happily.

"Took them a long time to discover they were neighbors, didn't it?"

"But they had to wait and see," she told him earnestly. A flicker of pain crossed her face. "I could have been another Levadi."

So, thought Strang, as he followed her down the steep wooden stairs of this house which had given him shelter, into a room, barely furnished, empty of people now, Steve had accomplished much more for his sister than he had ever dreamed of in Naples. He need not worry about Myrrha: she had her friends here, after all.

"The others are still in the fields," she told him. "I came back to waken you because you said you wanted to telephone. You have a bus to catch."

"That's right." He laughed, standing at the door in the warm sunlight, feeling the strength of those ten miraculous hours of solid sleep. But instead of looking after Myrrha, it seemed as if she were looking after him. "Where is Petros?"

"He went into Sparta. There will be much talk in the coffeehouses." Her smile said, you wouldn't want to cheat him of that, would you? "The bus to Sparta passes over the bridge about five o'clock," she warned Strang.

"I'll telephone and get back as quickly as possible."

"There is no need to hurry. All is well here."

"I must telephone," he explained awkwardly. "I have to let someone know—"

"Of course." She looked surprised that he should even try to excuse himself. "Petros told me about your girl."

"I'll bring her to see you, one day soon," he promised. "Where can I wash?"

"There is water here." She gestured to a bucket filled to the brim.

"I'll just wash wherever all the men wash," he told her. Here, every drop of water had to be carried. So she took him outside and pointed to a clump of trees on the hillside. "And I'll get something to eat in Sparta," he added.

"Oh, no!"

"Yes," he said. Here, every slice of bread had to be counted. "I must not miss that bus, or else I shall have to walk all the way to Sparta. Now, you get back to your friends."

She drew the long scarf over her head and twisted it across her mouth. She clumped away in her heavy boots, the long black skirt flapping just above her bare ankles. She turned to give him a wave, a smile from the brilliant dark eyes.

He went back and found his coat, neatly folded across a chair, took out his razor and toothbrush, a handkerchief for a towel, and set out for the men's room.

He waited forty minutes for the high, narrow bus, which was less than might have been expected from the pyramid of suitcases, parcels, and baskets, covered by tarpaulin strapped over its top. For every few miles, someone seemed to get out, or come in, and the tarpaulin had to be unstrapped, the bundles carefully inspected and selected and replaced and recovered and restrapped in place.

It had not been lonely, waiting on the road. There had been an old woman, sitting on a donkey, with both feet dangling against its right flank, while her hands spindled wool at lightning speed. And a boy with a donkey practically hidden under a beehive of long thin twigs. And a man plowing the steep field near the bridge with a wooden plow and rope harness on his donkey. And a woman driving her donkey uphill, with cans of drinking water from a spring. And all had spoken to him. There seemed to be a polite formula, a duet of question and answer, after the opening agreement about the weather.

"Fine day," Strang would say.

"Fine day. Where do you come from?"

"America."

"Where do you live?"

"New York."

"Are you married?"

"No." (This drew a look of sympathy mixed with disappointment. Now there were no children to discuss.)

"You have sisters and brothers?"

"Two sisters."

"Are they married?"

"Yes."

"Where do they live?"

And so it went on, right down the line as far as his age, what did he work at, what money did they pay in America? And it ended with a look, far off into space, while the questioner considered all these mysteries. Then, with a parting agreement on the view, the heels were drummed on the donkey's flanks or the plow harness roped around shoulders, and Strang was left with the snow-topped mountains.

It wasn't lonely in the bus, either. Questions and answers, questions and answers. The Platonic dialogue was the accepted form of conversation.

Sparta was set down in the middle of the broad valley, so suddenly that one minute the bus was in the country and next minute in the town. It wouldn't be difficult to find his way around here, Strang decided. It didn't seem a large town; the dusty streets were straight and wide-edged with low white houses. The central blocks had shops and cafés and the usual newspaper kiosks. There were some trees, many peasant women with scarved heads, men in dark suits of heavy wool, and schoolboys in black-visored student caps which reminded Strang of old Heidelberg.

The bus rattled to its final stop, the passengers eased their arms free from a shoulder there or a head here, and got out. Strang followed, glad of the cool fresh air and the end of his temporary paralysis. One good thing about being so tightly packed into a bus: when it plunged downhill or around a curve, everyone tilted together. No one could possibly jolt around separately.

"Hello!" said Petros, thumping him on the back. "Looking for a telephone?"

It took a little time, but it was worth it. Cecilia's voice came through, fresh and clear. "Darling—" they both began, and then stopped and laughed. "Are you all right?" they asked in unison, and again laughed. And after that, they proceeded normally.

"Everything is fine," Cecilia assured him. "I slept and slept. And you?"

"Everything is fine. Except that I shan't see you tonight; not until tomorrow."

"I know," she said. "Bob Pringle has just been around to see Steve. They've put him in the hospital. His feet were a mess, Bob says. Poor Steve! I'll go and see him tomorrow."

"Be careful now!"

"Of course! But we can stop worrying. Have you seen the newspapers?"

"I don't think they'll hear that news out here until tomorrow."

"Then just a moment—I'll read you three little items. Bob Pringle sent this paper around just half an hour ago." There was a pause, a rustle, background voices. "Bob had three translations made for me. I still don't understand them, though. But perhaps they are really for you. Ready?"

"Go ahead." Her excitement was contagious. He gave a reassuring nod to Petros, who was lounging near him, keeping a stern eye on a group of curious children and a fringe of interested adults. Everything from bus rides to telephone calls seemed to have a communal aspect in Sparta.

She read him the three pieces of translation. The first was quite extensive. It said that the opening of the stretch of new highway now under construction between Yugoslavia and Greece had been postponed only one hour before the ceremony was to take place. Fortunately, the crowds had been dispersed before two explosions had sent a rockslide of serious dimensions onto the platform where Marshal Tito would have presided. The Marshal, himself, was in Belgrade, where a slight indisposition had prevented him from making the dedicatory speech. The explosions were, of course, accidental. But it was reported, without confirmation, that many arrests had been made in various districts of Yugoslavia, including Belgrade itself.

The second said, more tersely, that the English authorities in Nicosia, Cyprus, had canceled today's Independence Celebration, without any explanation, and had blocked off all streets leading to the cathedral. Protests from the Cypriot majority were now being made.

And the third report, from Istanbul, was very brief. The Turkish government had detained the yacht *Medea* in Smyrna harbor.

Cecilia asked, "Is that really good news?"

"The best," he told her.

"Bob Pringle says the Athens radio has been announcing these facts all day since noon. So they must be important. But it's funny—if I were back in New York, I'd probably never even give these small paragraphs a second glance. Would you?"

"Probably would never have noticed them at all," he agreed. Or, if I had, I might have drawn the wrong conclusions: more Yugoslavs arrested, the liberal element were being silenced again; the English were being stupid, once more, in Cyprus; the Turks were just naturally suspicious.

Cecilia said, "We're celebrating tonight. Champagne and the Beaumonts for dinner. I wish—" She checked herself. Why mention the impossible?

"I wish, too," he said.

She laughed. "Will you always read my thoughts?"

"What worries me is that you'll learn to read mine."

"Darling, I love you, I love you—"

He lowered his voice almost to a whisper. "And I adore you."

"That was so tender I could scarcely hear it."

He grinned. "Tender? You should see the audience I've collected around me."

"What?"

"Yes. Cramps my style a little. Can you imagine what I'd like to say to you?"

"I'll try."

"Good. We can have a demonstration tomorrow. Ask Bob to see that a car really does get out here at dawn, will you? Well, by ten o'clock, at least. Darling, my love—"

"All my love," she said.

He put down the receiver.

"All is well?" Petros asked.

"All is well." He looked at the small group of schoolboys gathered near him. "Or isn't it?"

"Oh, they're learning English at school nowadays. Wanted to hear how it sounds when the words are all strung together." He took Strang's arm. "Now what?" he asked.

"First, I'd like some breakfast."

Petros's face became a polite mask.

"And next, we'll go shopping for a donkey. Or perhaps a goat. Which will Myrrha need most?"

The frozen mask managed to keep its shape for a few seconds more, and then Petros's amusement won. "Well," he said at last, "you will be remembered for a long time in Sparta." The man who telephoned all the way to Athens to tell a woman that he loved her, who ate breakfast at seven o'clock in the evening, and then went shopping for a donkey. "Yes, they know everything about you. That was quite a bus ride you had. You live in New York, you are twenty-five years old, you are not married, you have fifteen children." The laughter rippled over his face again. He added, with just a hint of reprimand, "They believed you."

"I must have got my Greek mixed up," Strang suggested with a grin.

"*Po, po, po, po!*" Petros said.

The restaurants were easy to find. They all seemed to be long, narrow stretches of basement rooms reached by a few steps, up which billowed clouds of deep-blue smoke and a heavy smell of oil. Strang looked at the series of belching clouds along the street. "A café will do," he said. "Bread, coffee, and a hunk of cheese."

That suited Petros better for some reason. Twice, he had glanced over his shoulder, most casually. "Yes, yes. We shall go and tell John where to find us when he stops work." He led Strang up a street whose every basement seemed to be occupied by shoemakers' shops: deep-down, dark, windowless caverns, reached by a precipitous flight of steps from the narrow sidewalk, where men sat and stitched and hammered. At the bottom of the eleventh flight of steps, they found John working with three other men under a single naked light bulb. He looked up from his last, gave a restrained smile with a mouth full of nails, raised his hammer in a friendly salute to Strang, and listened to a quick brief burst of words from Petros. "That is settled," Petros told Strang, turning him around to climb up into the street again. "We'll see him later."

Then they were up on the sidewalk, in the pleasant light of a spring evening. But they called at two other shoemakers' shops before they reached the café that Petros had selected. There were only men sitting there; some indoors, some outside at the tables on the broad sidewalk, some reading newspapers, some talking in close groups, some just sitting with eyes half closed watching the people walking past.

"Sunset," Petros explained. "People stop work, and wash, and brush their hair, and start walking up and down, up and down this street, from there to here, from here to there. It's the custom. When it is dark, off they go and have their supper."

Strang watched the groups of bareheaded girls in short skirts and high heels, the separate groups of tall young men strolling past. They were a handsome crowd, lean and fit, straight-backed, heads held high, eyes direct and proud. But, thought Strang, Petros is not looking around him merely to admire the pretty girls. And why did he meet me at the bus? He kept silent until the coffee was brought, and Petros had cajoled the waiter into finding some dark bread and *fetta* for a starving American. Then Strang asked, "Petros, what's worrying you?"

"At last!" Petros said, suddenly afflicted by poor hearing. John, his leather apron abandoned, his face and hands washed, his grimy work shirt changed for a clean one, his jacket neat, his hair combed with water, made his way quietly through the tables to shake their hands.

"Ouzo for everyone and more coffee for me," Strang said, as he concentrated on the excellent peasant bread and goat-milk cheese. "You know how many to order for, Petros." Petros looked at him, and solemnly ordered ouzo for five.

When his three other friends had arrived and shaken everyone's hand, Petros began a little speech. Strang understood about half of the quickly triggered phrases—when Petros was talking to other Greeks, his words came out with the rat-a-tat-tat of a machine gun. It was something about a man, an agent for an Athens business house, who had come to live in Sparta only four years ago, who had tried to make friends and had only made people wonder. He had a fine office with a telephone, and very little work. But he wore good clothes, he ate well, his hands were white and soft from pulling money out of the air. He had a big heart and so he talked of "the people" with deep emotion in his voice; but he overworked the woman who cleaned his house, and he spoke contemptuously of "peasants." Were peasants not people?

Petros, with his circle of friends nodding their thoughtful agreement, looked over at a table where a man sat by himself. "Why should a businessman travel up to Thalos this morning? Why did he ask questions?"

Perhaps Petros saw the gleam of amusement in Strang's eye, for he looked pointedly at the American. He said, "The questions he asked were not polite. He did not ask the girl questions about herself, so he had no interest in her or her family. No, indeed. He only talked about the shooting last night in Thalos. Very cunning questions he asked. About Levadi. About strangers in the village. And when the man left, the girl thought about this. And she came running back to the village and told us. That is why I came into Sparta. That is why I met you at the bus, my friend, and stood near you when you telephoned; and that is why my friends are sitting here. Because the man saw you as you got off the bus; and he questioned an old woman who had been traveling with you;

and he has been following you ever since. Me? I am just another peasant."

Petros's smile deepened as Strang remained speechless. Petros said, "He sits over there, by himself, waiting to see where you go next. Do you stay in Sparta or do you go back to Thalos? He is wondering what should be done." Petros's lips tightened. "And here *we* sit, my friends, wondering what should be done."

"Has he many friends here?" Strang asked.

"He had three, last night," Petros said, and the others laughed. "The soldiers found their hiding place, up on the hill, not far from Thalos. The farmer, there, has much to explain. A very clever farmer; he could grow guns and ammunition among his olive trees."

Strang was still worrying.

"At this moment, my friend," Petros told him cheerfully, "that man has more troubles than you have."

That was certainly true. Strang signaled to the waiter. "Ouzo for everyone." He made an attempt to look as relaxed as the others, but he could wish that someone like Elias were around to deal with this odd situation. There seemed no solution.

"Let us get rid of him, first," Petros said, jerking a thumb toward the lonely man. "Then we can enjoy our drink."

Strang looked at Petros. "Careful, careful—" he said.

"Now, now," Petros said equally gently, but firmly, "it will not take much to deal with him. He sees you have friends. That surprises him. If you had been alone, he would have felt much braver." Petros rose. He walked slowly. He was somber and serious. The others watched with half-lowered eyelids and a strange, still smile. Petros stopped in front of the man, and spoke. There was just one sentence. Then Petros turned away and came back to his own table. He sat down, with a wave of his hand, a shouted greeting to some friends across the sidewalk. He was in an expansive mood. And the man who sat alone rose and left.

"Eh?" Petros asked Strang. There was laughter, rippling from one table to another.

"And how did you do it?" Strang asked, watching the man disappearing into the street's quickly fading light. The sunset was already over, the western rays blotted out by the high peak of Mount Taygetos. Night came quickly to Sparta, and a cold, sharp wind.

Petros looked guileless. He rubbed the scar on his forehead. "I asked him if he had forgotten Mistra." And as Strang looked at him blankly, he said, "The old ruins on the hill up there." He pointed to the foothills below the black ridge of western mountains. "A big town it was, once, hundreds of years ago—"

"Four hundred years ago," John said.

"—and it covered all the hillside. Very rich. Churches, palaces, houses as big as hotels. Then the Turks brought their Albanian troops, and— nothing! All destroyed!"

"Yes. But why should he remember the ruins of Mistra?"

"When the Germans left and the civil war was lost to the Communists, all of them here ran like rabbits to Mistra. And all the fathers, and the brothers, and the cousins of the men they had killed took after them. They were hunted through the ruins of Mistra." He pointed with an imaginary rifle, and clicked his tongue. "Like rabbits." He looked at the American's face. "Perhaps you do not understand such things? It was a night of—" he searched carefully for the right phrase.

"A night of the long knives," Strang said.

Petros nodded. "And of long memories." He raised his glass of ouzo. "The people here," he said, "know how to remember."

Indeed they do, thought Strang. That was one detail he would keep from Cecilia when he guided her through the ruined streets of Mistra. But he wondered, would I have ever been able to see Mistra if it were not for Petros and his friends? He looked at their work-roughened hands, at their grave eyes and thin faces. He raised his glass of ouzo.

They all drank, solemnly.

Then they all began debating earnestly whether it was better to buy a donkey or a goat for Myrrha Kladas. It was decided by majority vote that the goat would be better: it provided food in milk and cheese. People could lift and carry; but, if they did not eat, their donkeys would soon have no masters at all. John had a brother-in-law who would choose the right goat at next market day. He would buy it and take it to Thalos. And so, with the price paid, and another round of ouzo to seal the decision, and some supper in a restaurant where Petros's uncle was cook, and a return to Thalos in an old rattletrap of a car driven by one of Petros's cousins, the evening passed pleasantly if—toward its end—a little hazily.

By ten o'clock, with most good people indoors if not in bed, they were traveling up between olive groves and small clusters of houses, until at last they branched off the highway to follow the earth road that led to Thalos.

The village was peaceful, reassuring; a snug, safe, placid place, resting from its labors. Petros's cousin left them at the beginning of the village, by a small church with its cluster of miniature domes. They began walking along the straight street of darkened houses, sleeping quietly beside the gentle flow of water. Petros said softly, "I can go back to Athens tomorrow. All is well here."

329

"I can give you a lift."

"No, my brother will bring the truck. We have a load of shoes to take back." Petros halted, looked at a few clusters of stones where a house must have stood years ago. "You have not spoken of Katherini Roilos."

"She is dead."

Petros looked at the remains of the house in front of them. He thought for a long moment. Then he turned away, saying nothing, and they walked in silence to his cousin's house.

Just after dawn, Petros left. By six o'clock, the village was fully awake and starting on the day's work. Petros's cousin and his two young sons were embarrassed but pleased as they received Strang's thanks, and clumped out of the house toward their field. Strang dressed and went to wash and shave, and when he came back into a street almost deserted except for a few very young children and two old women, he found Myrrha Kladas waiting for him.

"I have brought you some breakfast," she said, and uncovered a plate of bread and cheese and olives.

"Where did you sleep?" he asked her.

"At home."

"So you are getting things back into shape?"

She nodded. "When will Stefanos return?"

"In a few days. They put him in the hospital. He will soon be fit again."

She frowned worriedly. "I need another week to get the house ready. He would not like to see it now."

Strang shook his head in wonder. Everything was indeed all right when women started worrying about their house cleaning. "He will probably be a week in the hospital," he reassured her. "Don't stand there and serve me breakfast. Sit down, and have some, too." He had a suspicion that the food had been saved especially for him.

"No."

"Sit down and eat," he told her.

"It is not the custom."

"It is with me. I never eat unless a pretty girl sits opposite me."

She stared at him, and began to laugh. She sat down, though.

"That's much better," he said, and offered her a roughly made open sandwich, which she refused, and finally accepted a little nervously. She ate it hungrily. Between bites, she would look at him as if she wanted to break out into laughter again. It was a silent but merry meal.

"You are what Petros said you were," she told him as she finished the last crumb of bread.

"And what's that?"

She wouldn't tell him. She sat, with her hand up at her mouth, politely covering her smile, but her eyes were glancing bright. "A pretty girl," she said, and began to laugh once more.

Then she fell silent. "Once," she said softly, "I was." Her face changed. "Odysseus said I was." Very quietly, she added, "What will happen to him?"

Strang lit a cigarette. "Arrested. Tried." He shook his head over the revelations, the disclosures that were going to shock more than Athens. It would be a grim and horrible business, hurting the innocent in order to catch the guilty.

"Arrested? No. He is too clever. Even if they catch him, he will go free. He will take their words and twist them and throw them back in their mouths. They will never convict him." She was sure of that.

"And if they can prove he killed Sideros and Elektra?"

She stared at him.

"Sideros and Elektra are dead," Strang said. "Yes, they are dead. I saw their bodies."

Myrrha kept staring at him. "He killed my brother?"

Strang nodded. "You had no love for Sideros," he said, a little startled. "He has brought nothing but disaster to you."

"No love," she agreed. "But—" She struggled with her emotions. "Who knows of this? I have heard nothing about it."

"Very few, as yet. But I thought you ought to know."

"So he killed Elektra," she said slowly. "He had his revenge."

"Revenge? It is more a case of power politics, I think."

"That, too. But revenge . . . I know Odysseus. He must always win. Even when he loses, he must win."

And that, thought Strang, was quite an apt definition of revenge. It brought a slight shiver to his spine, though.

"You look unhappy," she said. "Did you know him?"

"Once, I thought of him as a friend."

"He probably was your friend, when it suited him. He was always—" She struggled for the right words.

"Sincere even in his insincerity?" he suggested.

Myrrha's thoughts had glanced on to something else. "Will he be hunted?" she asked.

"If he tries to run—yes."

"You think he would kill himself instead of running?"

Strang hesitated. "Perhaps. A trial would be a hideous thing for his family." And for you, too, he thought, looking at her unhappy eyes. You

331

would have to stand in a courtroom and identify him. What would the newspapers make of you, poor Myrrha Kladas? "He might at least spare them that."

"He spares no one. He will not kill himself. If he is caught, he will laugh. His trial will create much argument, much distrust, much hate. He will admit nothing. He will say he is an innocent man, that the law is unjust. There will be protests, demonstrations—" She broke off. "Once," she said, "I was taught such things, how to help organize—" She stopped again. She rose and went over to the window, and looked out at some bitter memories. "But he will not be tried. He will escape," she said, her voice heavy with foreboding.

"This time, I think not."

"This time, any time, yes! And do you know why? He plans. He plans even for failure. And so he is always ready. That is his secret. He plans."

"Look," Strang said a little impatiently—the infallibility of evil was one myth he wasn't going to increase by believing in it—"roads will be blocked, all airports and harbors watched, and towns and villages will look for him. There will be a house-to-house search in Athens. I tell you, he has got men against him now who are as determined as he is. He is in big trouble, Myrrha. Big trouble."

"He will not stay in Athens. He will not be so stupid as to try to leave Greece. Not at this moment."

"Then where will he go?"

She turned away from the window, and came back to him. "When Stefanos escaped, where did he go to hide? Into strange country? No. He came to the mountains and hills he knew best. And that is what Odysseus will do. He will go to Parnassos. He knows all the slopes, all the hills around the mountains. When he was a boy, he spent many summers near Delphi. He spent two years in that area, fighting against the Germans. Once, they searched for us. Almost six weeks, they searched. Day and night for six weeks. And we never were discovered. He had a house there, a small wooden house hidden by trees. When a German patrol came along the road, a villager warned us and we slipped away. We stayed in a hut on the hillside, too, and when the Germans were near, a shepherd would give warning. There were caves to shelter us, forests, even the tombs of the Old People. But we never went away from that district. It made Odysseus laugh to think of Ares and his men scattering far to the north for safety, some retreating back to the Pindus mountains and beyond, while he and I stayed near Parnassos, and were safe."

"There is one difference, though. Then, he was fighting the Nazis, so the villagers and shepherds helped him. But now, he is fighting them."

"Do they know that?" she asked, with her strange sad smile. "Levadi —what did he know?"

From outside, came a woman's voice, calling.

"I come," Myrrha called back. She picked up the empty plate and its cloth. "You will visit us again, someday?"

"Yes. I'll bring my girl with me, next time."

"A Saturday night," Myrrha said, her face brightening, "is a good time to come here. There is singing. Sometimes, the men dance." Suddenly, she looked at him gravely. "Tell Stefanos that all is well. There is nothing to worry about now. Not here." Then her heavy shoes clattered over the doorstep, and she was hurrying to join the other woman.

He stood at the door and watched them walk, with their steady stride, along the village street toward the Kladas house where other women waited for them. He heard the shouts of greeting, some laughter. Indeed, he thought, there was nothing to worry about now. Not here.

Unexpectedly, that last remark from Myrrha Kladas began to haunt him. Not here. Then where?

The car, much to Strang's surprise, arrived early. He rose from the church steps, where he had been sitting in the sunshine, surrounded by a cluster of new friends: eight small children, three silk-bearded goats with sloping yellow eyes and soft-sounding bells, two great-grandmothers, a completely toothless old gentleman, the village priest, who had just come off his field where he had completed a four-hour stretch of plowing. Their questions died away as they all stared solemnly at the large car slowly drawing to a stop.

Strang went forward. Costas, he saw, again to his surprise, was driving. Elias was with him. And Elias was wearing officer's uniform. Why? Strang halted. Two of the children running after him, bumped against his legs and fell. Automatically, he reached down and pulled them to their feet, still looking at Elias, who was coming toward him, slowly. There was no reason for Elias to be here; he was more needed in Athens. There was no need, Strang thought again, unless he brought news so bad that he had been given the job of breaking it. Strang said, "Is she—"

Elias looked at him quickly. "Not dead," he said. "Miss Hillard is not dead." He turned on the children. "Go home," he shouted angrily, "go home!"

"What—" began Strang.

"I shall explain to you in the car. We shall drive at once back to Athens. Where is your coat?"

"What has happened to her? For God's sake—"

"She is being held as a hostage."

Strang gripped the other's arm.

Elias said, "Please—please, if you would let me explain how it all happened." He drew his arm free. "It would not seem so bad if you would let me explain."

"Seem?" Strang said savagely, and turned away. He walked over to the car, and stood there, his hand on its door, unable to get in, to move, to act, to think.

"I'll get the coat," Elias said, and left. And I must explain to him, he was thinking, that it was not our fault: there was no carelessness, no stupidity; and we have some leads, many ideas; it is not hopeless. "Where did the American sleep?" he asked one of the children, and followed the boy to the house. Some doors away, he saw Myrrha Kladas, who must have heard the car and come out to wave good-by. She was looking along the street, toward the American. She broke into a run.

"What is it? Something has happened to Stefanos?"

"No. To the American girl."

"What?"

Elias took the coat which the child had brought him.

"Tell me," Myrrha insisted, "tell me!" She hurried beside him back to the car. "Has Odysseus killed her?"

"No."

"He is free?"

"Yes. But he won't escape." We know the car he used, Elias was thinking; we have traced him as far as Thebes. That is not much, but it is better than nothing. He is traveling north. But the borders are being patrolled. He won't find it so easy to get across. Not so easy. "He won't escape," he repeated as if he were persuading himself.

"What happened to the girl?"

"She was seized last night."

Myrrha grasped his arm and stopped him. "A hostage," she said. "That is his old pattern. A hostage. He will bargain his way free. And he will go. But the girl?" She looked at Elias. "You know, and I know, what has happened to hostages."

"Be quiet!" Elias said angrily. "Have we not troubles enough without—" He glanced toward the American. "We will find her," he said, his mouth tightening, shaking off her hand from his arm. He started walking.

"Then search Parnassos, all around there, every wood, every hillside, every hut, every—"

"Parnassos . . ." Elias halted and stared at her.

334

She stood still. "I—I do not remember well enough. Ask Levadi. He knows all that country. He knows it even better than Odysseus."

"We shall ask Levadi. But I am also asking you. Now. Come over to the car. We can talk about it, quietly, there."

"But it is so long ago."

"And have you forgotten?"

Myrrha Kladas looked toward the car, at the American.

"There is no time to lose," Elias reminded her brusquely. "Tell me all you can remember about that district. What were Odysseus's special hiding places? Where did Odysseus take you, for instance, when you disappeared for many weeks?"

Myrrha stared at him. Then she glanced quickly over her shoulder.

Elias turned and called to the curious women, who had come following Myrrha along the village street. "Go back to your work. I must talk with Myrrha Kladas—about her brother Stefanos, who is in the hospital in Athens and cannot talk for himself."

Myrrha Kladas looked at Elias again. "Thank you," she said, softly. She walked over to the car. Elias, having routed the gaping children, hurried after her. She was saying to Strang, "I shall tell all I know. Perhaps it will help."

"It may, indeed," Elias said with a burst of renewed confidence.

Strang listened to their quiet voices, to the steady flow of Greek, the question-and-answer game now played with deep earnestness. Gradually, his attention began to focus, gradually his mind began to work. From that deep plunge into the black abyss of complete despair, of utter helplessness, he began to climb back. Hope lay in action, not in surrender. We'll find Cecilia, he kept telling himself. I'll find her.

He forced himself to stop seeing her face, hearing her voice; for, remembering her, he was lost. He must become as cold, as calm, as quick-witted as Elias. He must know the facts, and think into them, and around, and over them. Man's mind, not his emotions, was his strongest shield, his sharpest weapon.

The talk had ended. Myrrha Kladas stood back from the car. "Thank you," Strang said very quietly, and got in. Elias saluted the slight black-clothed figure, and followed Strang. The car swept round and left the group of children, surrounding Myrrha, laughing, waving. She raised a hand, to give Strang one last small sign of friendship. The car went bumping and swaying down the rough little road between the olive trees toward the main highway.

Elias leaned over to speak to Costas. They would stop at Tripolis; he would telephone Athens from there, this new information might change some plans. There was a hint of excitement, of triumph, in his normally restrained voice. Then he sat back, beside Strang, and waited.

As the car finished the long climb up the mountain's side and started down toward the high plains of Arcadia, Strang sat more erect, searched for his cigarettes, looked squarely at Elias. "All right," he said, "tell me."

Elias accepted one of the American cigarettes, although he disliked them, and the proffered lighter. He noted that the American's movements were as controlled as his voice. He gave a nod of relief and approval. "It was daring. It was simple. And it was well planned," he began.

TWENTY-FIVE

Yes, it had been daring, simple, and well planned. And the setting, yesterday evening, in the Pringles' apartment, although Elias could not know that, had been most helpful, too.

Cecilia had put down the receiver, and stood looking at it, with the smile Ken's voice had brought still curving her lips. Strange how a voice could make you so happy, words which were spoken by millions and millions of people but which, in that one voice, became unique. So this wasn't spring madness or a dream, she told herself. It might still be unbelievable, but it was real: I love this man and he loves me, and don't ask me how it happened because I can't tell you—it just happened. Like that. And that's all. That's all and that's everything.

"Well, is he all right?" Effie Pringle asked. After three years of marriage, she could allow herself to be entertained by that dazed look on her guest's face. "Would you arrange this bowl of flowers for the center of the table? Fanny is late. I think I'll start camouflaging some court bouillon for the fish." Oh dear, she thought, with only Fanny to clean every morning and to come in when she's needed for little dinners, I do get overambitious with my menus.

"It's just seven o'clock," Cecilia said encouragingly. The Beaumonts weren't expected until half past eight, which meant nine. Dinner wasn't until an hour later than that, at least. But Effie Pringle wouldn't be comforted.

"Heavens! Fanny *is* late. I hope another grandchild hasn't caught whooping cough. It seems that women don't really know what involvement is until they have grandchildren," she said gloomily. But being two months pregnant was a stage in life that made you feel such involvement

337

was almost upon you. Morning sickness and evening worry . . . She rounded up some of her old cheerfulness as she left for the kitchen. "You know," she called back, "you're an awfully calm person to have around. You look so cool and unperturbed. I wish I could learn that trick. Oh God! Where did Fanny put those bay leaves I bought yesterday?"

That was the setting: a long, dreary day ended; the serious tensions gone, the siege lifting; trouble no greater now than a misplaced bay leaf; the apartment, a charming little place of green and white, adequately lit at last by the peaceful gold of evening; dark-red ikons, bright-pink flowers, champagne on ice; Bob soon to arrive home and have fuller details cajoled out of him about all the secret excitement that had been going on in the world outside. And Cecilia, purposefully calm to keep Effie from fretting (she had been told so little that she had been imagining a hundred possible disasters, all ending in Bob's transfer from Athens), now relaxing, now forgetting her own forebodings. All was well, nothing had happened to Ken, he would be back in Athens tomorrow, she was the luckiest of women, she was the happiest of women.

The telephone rang. "It's for you, Effie," Cecilia called.

"Oh, no! Don't tell me Bob has got stuck at the office and won't be home until ten! Not tonight!" She came running to the telephone, a look of comic resignation already forming on her face. As she listened, she seemed to crumple. "Yes," she kept saying, "yes," her voice becoming smaller and smaller. With an effort, she said, "I'll come at once." She put down the receiver, staring at Cecilia unbelievingly. "Bob—" she said at last—"Bob was hit by a taxi. They have taken him to the hospital."

So Cecilia was alone in the apartment. "No," said Effie, when Cecilia had wanted to accompany her to the hospital, "you stay here. Someone has got to be here to explain to the Beaumonts. I'll telephone you and let you know how Bob is. No, darling. I can get a cab easily by myself. I'm all right. Keep that door locked. And I'll call you."

The door was locked. It was almost eight o'clock. The sunlight had gone from the room. And Cecilia drew the curtains, turned on some of the lights, turned off the gas under the court bouillon, and worried about Bob and Effie. Perhaps Bob had not been badly hurt, perhaps he would be fit enough to be brought home. She tried to comfort herself with perhapses, but all she could think about was Effie standing, her face taut with worry and anguish, beside the telephone.

It rang again. And again it was a call from the hospital. It was a typical hospital-nurse voice, so very calm, detached, making bad news sound like a railway timetable. Mr. Pringle was seriously injured. An operation

338

was necessary, immediately. Mrs. Pringle was in a very distressed state. Would Miss Hillard please bring some night clothes for Mrs. Pringle? Mrs. Pringle would have to stay at the hospital, possibly for the next twenty-four hours. Here was the hospital address. It was easy to reach— just beyond the British Embassy.

That was all. A precise, abrupt, businesslike call. Cecilia found a night dress, a robe, a toothbrush, soap, handkerchiefs. She took one of Effie's larger hatboxes, emptied its garden-party straw hat onto the bed, jammed the things she had collected inside it. Fanny still had not arrived. So she scribbled a note for the Beaumonts, explaining what had happened. Then she pulled on her coat, grabbed her handbag along with the hatbox, left her note balanced on the outside door handle, and ran.

The self-service elevator was too slow. She kept on running down the stairs. The man on guard in the hall would go with her to the hospital. (There had been two on guard last night, but since early this afternoon, one was all that had been necessary. There was another on guard some-where in the rear of the apartment house, checking all the deliveries by the service entry.) But when she reached the hall, it was empty. So the man was no longer needed, she thought, and felt relieved, too, at that idea: the all clear must have been sounded.

(But the man, at this moment, had just been summoned to the telephone in the shop across the street: an emergency message from headquarters, so he had been told, which kept him fuming over their care-lessness as he waited for the connection, stupidly broken, to be re-established. And Fanny? She was blissfully standing in line to see a new American movie. She had received a note from Mrs. Pringle at six o'clock saying that the dinner party had been canceled.)

Cecilia stepped out onto the sidewalk. There was a taxi, starting for-ward from its parking place. She signaled, and went to meet it. "Do you speak English?" she asked the driver. He nodded. So she opened the door. From the sidewalk behind her, a woman seemed to think the taxi had stopped for her. "I'm sorry," Cecilia said firmly, and got in. She pitched forward with a scream that ended in a gasp of pain. The blow on the back of her head had been quick, neat, and sufficient. The woman stepped in, closed the door smartly even as the cab drew away and a man came running out of a shop across the street.

Two passers-by stopped. "Was that a scream?" one asked. "And what is that man yelling about?"

"Look," said another, stopping at the curb, "someone has dropped a hatbox!" And, too late to do any good, a small, inquisitive crowd began to gather.

TWENTY-SIX

"You see," Elias was asking anxiously, "it was well planned?"

They were speeding, Costas at the wheel, Elias finishing his story, Strang saying nothing, along the straight road across the vast plain toward Tripolis. Willow trees and wells, wells and willow trees, long rows of women bending their yellow-and-red-scarved heads over long rows of dark furrows. "I see," Strang said. "But that is all you know about Miss Hillard?" A note left for the Beaumonts mentioning a telephone message from the hospital; a hatbox dropped at the side of the street; a taxicab disappearing into the maze of evening traffic—was that all?

"Yes. But you understand that the agent on duty went across to the shop only because he was told the emergency call came from the office of Colonel Zafiris. Such a call could be of greatest importance."

"Yes." But it had been a fake, like the telephone call to Cecilia.

"He did see the taxicab—its type, its number."

"Yes." But the cab had been abandoned three blocks away in a quiet square. Had Cecilia been unconscious? How else had they lifted her into another car?

Elias said, "I think you did not understand, perhaps, the importance of that number. It was the same cab that helped Christophorou escape." Elias thought, perhaps he has not really listened to anything I told him, except about the American girl. He sighed. "Please!" he said sharply. "Even in the best of plans, there is a small mistake—so small that it seems of no importance, a loose thread in a piece of cloth. But if we can find two, three loose threads—each so small that, by itself, it means nothing— then we begin to find the color, perhaps even the pattern of the cloth. It takes much work, much patience, but we begin to see—"

"And time?" asked Strang. "Much time?" He tried to keep the bitterness out of his voice. It was no one's fault, he had to remind himself. He looked at Elias's frowning eyes. The Greek was upset, too; he was troubled, deeply troubled, behind that cold, grave face. Strang said more gently, "Perhaps I missed something important at the beginning of your story. Would you repeat it?" And this time, Strang thought, I shall listen with my mind as well as with my ears. Perhaps there was more to Elias's account of the events than an attempt at justification, a parade of explanations. Elias shrugged his shoulders, and began all over again with unusual patience.

The taxi, which Christophorou had used to make his sudden escape from his apartment yesterday at dawn, had been an American car of 1958 design, long and big and two-toned in the colors of green and white. After a long wild chase around Athens, it had vanished near the open market not far from the old Turkish bazaar. The whole area had been searched by the police, every garage, every yard, every shed, a considerable undertaking; and there, in a little street off the market square, a small garage had been found with three cars, one of them a green-and-white American Plymouth. But its number was not the one they were searching for, and it had no license as a taxi. Moreover, as the owner of the garage was at work on this car, and swore he had been working on it for the last two days, and as five other taxis of similar design and color were discovered in other garages in other parts of Athens, the police could only make out a report of what they had found, giving the description and license plates of the three cars: one green-and-white Plymouth, out of order, front bumper damaged; one blue Renault; one gray Fiat.

Checks, of course, had been made on all the roads leading out of Athens. That afternoon, about four o'clock, a blue Renault had been one in the stream of traffic that had been checked at Eleusis. It was driven by a woman. Passed through the examination point, it had taken the road to Thebes. It halted some five kilometers farther on, at a café beside a bus station. The driver of the next bus to arrive from Athens noticed that one of his passengers, a peasant seemingly, had left the bus at that stop, although his ticket was still good for some kilometers ahead. The bus continued on its way to Thebes. On one of the hills, it was overtaken, and then passed, by a blue Renault, its one occupant a man. The bus driver was sure it was the same man who had left his bus at the café where he had seen a blue Renault waiting, although the man had now taken off the ragged old coat which he had worn in the bus. Who ever heard of a peasant not taking full benefit of his paid bus fare? Who ever heard of a peasant driving a good car? The bus driver, alerted perhaps because of the check on traffic back at Eleusis, reported what he had noticed at the next small town, and gave the Renault's number. It was the same Renault that had been noticed in the small garage near the old market quarter of Athens.

The Renault was traced as far as Thebes. It had been noticed in Pindar Street just after six o'clock by a group of young men at a coffeehouse; they had admired its speed. And a young boy had seen a blue car leave the town as he drove his father's donkey home from Thebes. The car had stopped on a quiet stretch of road, on a bridge over a hillside stream. A man had got out, dropped something into the ravine below him, driven away to Levadia. The boy was sure of that. Standing on the heights of Thebes, he had watched the car take the long, lonely stretch of road, over the flat marshlands and plains which stretched to the north. Then, curious, he had climbed down to the stream, and searched, and searched. But he found, to his disappointment, nothing he could use. It was only a small round cylinder of metal, with pretty markings on it. He had taken it home to see if his father could find some use for it.

But farther to the northwest, at Levadia, the car had not been seen. (There were rumors, of course, but they had only wasted time and energy.) It was possible that, in the failing light and early darkness, it had skirted Levadia before the alarm had been raised, and was now far to the north.

At Athens, that evening, as soon as the Renault's number had been reported and recognized, the small garage had been revisited. It was now empty. All three cars, and the owner, had vanished. So a search was started in Athens, too, complicated by the darkness, by the rush of late-evening traffic. The green-and-white car, again pretending to be a taxi, again with its false number, had picked up Miss Hillard. It was found abandoned, opposite the Church of St. Dionysios, near the Swiss and Argentine legations. Its license plate linked it to Christophorou; its damaged bumper linked it to the garage and the other cars. After intensive questioning, the police discovered that a gray car, with a diplomatic label stuck on its rear window, had been parked just at that same place for about ten minutes that evening. One elderly servant had noticed a cab stop beside the gray car; people and some luggage, she thought, had been transferred, but it was dark and she had not been close enough to see clearly.

Now, the search was on for the gray Fiat. But all these details, which could be recited in a matter of minutes, had taken time to be unraveled, put together, made into a sensible pattern, for there were some people who had been too helpful: they would say anything, when questioned, rather than admit they knew nothing. So the Fiat must have had an hour's full start before the alarm went out. And it must have taken another, less usual, route to the north, traveling by the eastern road, which swept over the hills above Marathon, curving past Tanagra, to turn westward to Thebes.

There, it had taken a rough country road to skirt the town, and had almost been stopped by two local policemen. Both were injured, one critically. The car, running without lights, had come at them out of the darkness, swerved round the small farm cart drawn partly across the road, jolted over a corner of flat field, and come back onto the road again. It had not been seen after this incident near Thebes.

So both cars had vanished. Only one thing was certain: both the blue Renault and the gray Fiat were traveling north. It had been assumed that they were heading toward Bulgaria. (Albania was difficult to reach: the road was mountainous, and dangerous with spring rains. Yugoslavia, obviously, was hardly to be considered.) But now—and Elias allowed himself a certain touch of self-congratulation—the escape might be taking a different pattern. It could be possible that, from the cars' point of disappearance, just south of Levadia, the Renault and the Fiat were circling westward to the Parnassos area. There, Christophorou might plan to stay hidden for several weeks, until it was safer to travel toward one of the borders. That, ended Elias very somberly, was something to be considered most seriously. That was what he would report back to Athens when they reached Tripolis.

"How big is this Parnassos area?" Strang asked.

"Altogether?" Elias considered. "It is a district, not just one mountain," he explained. "There are villages to be included, too. Let us say less than six hundred square kilometers."

More than two hundred square miles. Strang's moment of hope vanished. "God in heaven!" he said softly. He tried to imagine the vast stretch of Parnassos, twin peaks surrounded by a bastion of other mountains, all of them forming a huge mass of rock sloping into steeply falling hills, with ravines, gorges, high meadows, torrents, caves, precipices. Some of its lower slopes edged into forests, others were bare hills, others halted in a broad ledge where a little village could perch—as at Delphi—and then continued their plunge down wooded cliffs to the floor of a valley far below. He tried to remember the odd details he had collected about Parnassos when he had been making notes on Delphi for his work. It was a place of violent storm and earthquake, of constant mists veiling the upper slopes, of eagles soaring over the deep clefts. No one, unless he was a suicidal maniac, climbed the peaks without a guide, and a fully trained guide at that. So Christophorou would be nowhere near the peaks themselves; nor on the open mountainsides, nor on the barer hills. His hiding place would be somewhere among the ravines and caves and torrents and forests of the lower slopes. "Parnassos," said Strang, slowly, bitterly, "the home of the Muses."

"Ah," Elias said, "the Greeks never called it that. It was the foreigners, the Roman poets who came to Delphi and saw the Temple of Apollo there, who said Parnassos must be the home of the Muses. But they did not understand Parnassos."

True enough, Strang recalled now. Parnassos had been the mountain consecrated to Dionysus and the Maenades, the wild Bacchantes. It had been the place of secret initiations, of savage orgiastic rites, of wild pagan ceremonies. The ancient Greeks had understood the symbolism of nature and the elements too well to make Parnassos the home of the Muses.

"It is strange, is it not," asked Elias, "that such a lie becomes accepted as the truth? But then, in life—" he shrugged his shoulders.

"Yes," agreed Strang, and he thought of Alexander Christophorou, and of Myrrha Kladas's prophecy. "What kind of lies will Christophorou think up for his trial?" he asked. "If you catch him, that is."

"Plenty," Elias said. "But we have proof, now, that he killed Sideros and Elektra. That farmer's boy near Thebes—it was the silencer to Christophorou's revolver that he found."

Strang did not look impressed.

Elias said quickly, "It was especially designed. We traced the maker by his markings. His records say that, four years ago, it was ordered by Mr. Alexander Christophorou."

"Christophorou will say the revolver and silencer were stolen."

Elias smiled. "Of course. But we also have found the locksmith who made two keys for Christophorou: one for the back door into the yard, one for the padlock on the gate. The locksmith had to visit the house to take the correct impression for his work. We found him by questioning the caretaker who used to live in that house two years ago. Also," Elias said with great satisfaction, "we have at least two witnesses who know the man called Demetrius Drakon. We have two other witnesses who know the man called Odysseus. And they will all point to Christophorou and say, 'That is the man.'" Elias was silent for a moment. "But it is strange, most of all, that the death of a man and a woman who lived on lies should make people tell the truth. We would have found no witnesses against Christophorou if Sideros and Elektra had not been murdered."

"You will have to catch him first." Strang remembered Myrrha Kladas's words. He took a deep breath. "Pringle?" he asked. "How badly was he hurt?"

"Not much. He leaped aside. A cut on his leg. Perhaps concussion. Nothing serious," Elias said cheerfully.

Strang was silent for a long moment. And then the question which had lain at the back of his mind rushed out. "Will they hurt her?"

"I think," Elias said slowly, "that Christophorou wants to hurt you. He is a man who knows how to hate. But he is also a most practical man. If he finds he cannot escape, he will use the American girl to make a bargain. We give him his freedom in exchange for her." Elias shrugged his shoulders. "That has happened before. Last year, we caught six spies who had come secretly over the Bulgarian border. Bulgaria offered us some of the children who had been kidnaped, ten years before, in exchange for the six Communist agents. They were valuable men. What could we do?"

"What?" asked Strang, his face suddenly white.

Elias looked at him in surprise. "We got back more than two hundred of the children," he said. "April, 1958, they returned. After ten years . . ." And now he had his own bitter thoughts.

He sat in silence until they entered Tripolis. As they drove up the long straight street of whitewashed walls and yellow mimosa trees, Elias pointed and said, "Costas will take you to that café. You will eat, both of you. I shall join you when I have telephoned Athens. It may take a little time."

Strang looked at him.

"Yes, you will eat," Elias said severely, as the car stopped and he got out. "You are sick with worry. To make your body sick, too, will be of no help to us. That is an order! I am in charge here." He drew himself up to his full five feet four inches. He added, gently, "We may hear better news. We have had our share of bad luck. It is time for the good luck to begin."

"You're an optimist," Strang said wearily.

"How else have we survived?" Elias asked, quite simply, as he left.

They did hear better news. And it was, as Elias was quick to admit, entirely due to Cecilia herself. "She has not lost her head, that girl," he said. "She thinks. She does not give in. She has the will to fight. And that means hope—for all of us."

Strang nodded. It was strange how two small objects, a lipstick in a crumpled empty pack of American cigarettes, could raise up just enough hope to change the face of this journey. It was no longer a useless rush across the Peloponnese toward Corinth, and then on to the mainland of Greece. It had become something urgent, purposeful.

345

As they came down the twisting, turning road from the last of the mountains they had to cross, and gathered speed on the long highway across the Argive plains, Strang reached over to tap Costas on the shoulder. "Time to take a rest," he said. "I'll drive now."

TWENTY-SEVEN

A lipstick, a crumpled empty pack of cigarettes . . .

The idea had come to Cecilia after the car had jolted around a farm cart, had jumped across a corner of a field. There had been two men beside that farm cart. A scream would have been useless, because the roar of the engine and the screech of brakes as the car had accelerated and skidded around the cart had drowned out even the shriek of "Anastas!" from the woman who sat in the front seat beside the driver. But I could have thrown something out, Cecilia thought, if I had had it ready, if I had been able to open the window in time. That way, they would have known I was in this car. Because if people are guarding this road, then there is a search for someone. It may not be for me, but there is a search going on. And when a search is going on, even small things are noticed. But I missed the chance, I missed it. When we came on that farm cart, I was still too bewildered to think of anything, still feeling too sick and frightened, still trying to remember what had happened.

But the sickness had almost gone now, the dull ache round her head did not matter any more, and the sense of helplessness, which the blackness of the night, the speed of the car, the two voices talking an unintelligible language had made so complete, had left her. People are searching this road, she thought, and the hideous feeling of total loneliness began to vanish.

The woman looked around as Cecilia moved into a corner of the back seat, and raised her hand. She had a revolver. That was only to give her authority, Cecilia decided; if they were going to kill me, they could have done that back in Athens.

"I need some air," Cecilia said slowly. They had not spoken any English, perhaps they didn't even understand it, but she repeated, "Air," as

347

she wound down the window about six inches. The woman leaned over and aimed a sharp blow with the revolver barrel at Cecilia's wrist. She pulled her hand back in time—the blow only grazed her fingers—but she gave a little moan and let her head rest, quite helplessly, against the side of the open window. The woman tested the handle of the door to make sure it was securely locked. She watched Cecilia with suspicion, but as the man spoke to her, she turned away to reach for a map and a small flashlight. Perhaps the speed of the car made her feel that Cecilia was safe enough. Or perhaps the fright she had had, back at the road block, had made her feel a little sick, too. At least, the window stayed its few inches open, blowing a welcome stream of cold night air into the suffocating warmth of the car.

They are not sure of the way, Cecilia thought. Certainly, the man and woman were engrossed by the road ahead. They kept looking to their left. Perhaps there was a small branch road near here, Cecilia thought. She drew around her the blanket that had covered her when she lay unconscious on this seat. The woman gave a quick look round, said something in Greek, and pointed to the window. Cecilia shook her head. "I feel sick," she said. "Very sick."

The woman turned back to her map at a question from the man. A small, intense argument started up.

Under the cover of the blanket, Cecilia drew her bag onto her lap. She opened it. Her fingers found her comb. Useless: anyone might own a small brown comb. A pack of American cigarettes: that was better. She emptied the cigarettes into her bag. Someone finding cigarettes in place might just smoke them and think nothing more than that he had made a lucky find. But what was needed was a strange find—something to puzzle, to be talked about. She found her lipstick—that, too, was American. It would weight the empty pack nicely. Desperately, she closed it inside, folded the top over, pressed the metal foil together. The woman looked around again. Cecilia's eyes were half closed. She wondered if the woman could hear the sudden quick beat of her heart.

"Ochi, ochi!" the woman said angrily, as the man slowed down at a rough road. The car regained its speed. So they were searching for a branch-off, Cecilia thought; and perhaps the next opening would be the right one. That is where I'll have to drop this little package. If I can just get my hand up, near the opened top of the window, if I can just . . . She raised her hand to her head and let it rest there.

The man's eyes looked up for a moment, studied Cecilia in the rear-view mirror. But he seemed satisfied. His eyes went back to the road. The woman was pointing ahead, talking quickly. The car slowed, turned to the left. Cecilia's hand dropped the neatly packaged lipstick as the front wheels bumped over the first ruts of the side road.

The woman had turned to look at her, perhaps thinking she might try to open the door as the car's speed slowed on the rough surface. Cecilia didn't draw her hand away. She kept it at the side of the window as if she were holding it there to steady herself from the jolts. Her head drooped against her arm, her eyes half closed. She actually did feel a return of the nausea. Her hands were trembling. Then she felt the attack of fear pass over and leave her. The car had not been halted; no one had got out to search. And now, instead of fear, there was a growing excitement. It was extraordinary what a small piece of resistance could do for one's morale.

What next? she wondered, as her hands began searching blindly in her bag again. There was Ken's book—the Cavafy poems—but she wanted to hold onto that, somehow. Even touching it was a comfort. And besides, she couldn't tear out pages without drawing attention to herself. She had to keep up the illusion that she was weak and thoroughly tamed. And pages would blow away in this open road with the first touch of a breeze. It had to be something heavy enough to fall straight, and lie. Her compact was the next choice, a difficult one, though, for it was not easy to hide in the palm of her hand. She would have to wait for the right moment. It came, about half an hour later, when they left the rough road— it ended as it had begun, in a series of deep ruts of hard-dried mud—and the jolts were so bad (the man had not eased up sufficiently, in time) that even the woman on the front seat bounced around like a ping-pong ball. She turned her head to look at Cecilia just one second too late to see the compact disappear. She spoke urgently, as if she sensed something was wrong. Or had she heard the sound of the compact smashing on the road? The man swore and put on the brakes. The car stopped, and the woman got out and walked back along the road, her flashlight sweeping across it like a brush.

There was a falling sensation inside Cecilia's stomach. Please, she prayed, oh please let the woman think that the noise was only a loose stone cast up by the wheel. Suddenly, the man called a warning. There were, Cecilia saw as she glanced back, the lights of a car far behind them coming along the highway which they had entered. The woman had not yet reached the intersection. She gave one last sweep of the flashlight, turned, and ran back. She climbed in quickly, speaking reassuringly, rapidly, and glanced around—as the car leaped forward into high speed— angrily at Cecilia. She had found nothing, it seemed. But she leaned over and closed the window.

Well, thought Cecilia as she drew a deep steadying breath, it had been a nice little game while it lasted. She pulled the blanket more tightly around her shoulders—the draft from the opened window had almost frozen her in the last fifteen minutes—and pretended to be falling asleep.

She listened to the two voices, talking, talking. She wished she knew Greek. Anastas, the man was called. And the woman had a strange name. It sounded like Kseneea. Cecilia puzzled over that. Not that the names mattered to her—except as a little proof that the man and the woman were so sure of her, now, that they were talking freely. Xenia? Anastas and Xenia. Where were they taking her? What part of the country was this? South or west or north or east? Outside, there was nothing but the lonely highway, running between dark fields or dark hillsides; inside, the two strange, unintelligible voices.

Cecilia's small moment of triumph left her. Oh, Ken, she thought, Ken . . . She felt hot tears sting her eyes. She bit her lip, and forced herself to stop crying. Tears were of no help, no help at all. Ken would be looking for her; so would all the others. But no one could help her if she let herself be blackmailed by fear. Not tears, but anger. Not fear, but determination. These were the answers. She might have little hope, but at least she was not going to think her way into despair.

The car drove on through the black, anonymous night. And as she rested, with her eyes closed, she thought of Ken and what he would do if he were here, dear, darling, stubborn, determined Ken. He wouldn't yield one inch. He wouldn't accept the fact that he was helpless. He would resist, and go on resisting. He'd say, "Damn your eyes, all of you!" And so shall I, she thought. That is all I can do, meanwhile. That is one thing they cannot stop, unless they kill me. They cannot stop resistance.

So she rested, for there was nothing she could do while the car traveled at this speed. But when it stops, she thought, I am going to be one of the most unhelpful, most intransigent, most ornery prisoners that these two barbarians have ever snatched. From her handbag, she began, carefully, slowly, to transfer every useful little object she could find into the pockets of her coat.

For the last twenty minutes or so, the car—without lights—had been traveling steadily uphill, a long, gradual curve between bare hills. There was moonlight and clouds, a sky not altogether clear, throwing strange shadows over the desolate countryside. Yet the road seemed smooth, a first-class road. By day, there would be several cars traveling along here. But, now, nothing. Not a house to be seen, far less a village. Abruptly, the road swept round to the left. The car stopped. Xenia put away her map. She turned to Cecilia, the revolver very evident. She opened the door and got out, gesturing impatiently to Cecilia to follow. Anastas still sat at the wheel. He must be leaving them here.

"Out!" Xenia said impatiently, and spoke some last directions to the man. So she knew a word or two of English, Cecilia thought. She pulled herself, very slowly, out of the back seat. The weaker she looked, the better. She sat at the open door of the car, feeling the road under her feet, wondering if she had enough strength in her legs to run. But the woman, although she was talking to Anastas, was watching. Cecilia pulled the collar of her coat up around her neck and her handbag over her arm, plunged her hands into her pockets. She did not have to pretend she was cold.

In front of her was a gently rising meadow, wide and deep. To one side, a stream, with its melancholy ripple. On the silvered grass were small trees, perhaps fruit or olive trees, their gnarled and twisted branches making grotesque patterns in the moonlight. At the top of the meadow, rising above it, there was a huge band of dark shadow: a wood or a thick grove. Behind that, gleaming coldly—and then darkened into an abyss as a cloud drifted over the face of the moon—was a precipice of rock. Above that, was a jagged patch of stubbled shadows, a hillside with sparse trees; still higher, there rose the bold slope of a mountain. She could not see the peak, even when the light cloud floated free from the moon, and the silvers and blacks and grays all took sharp shape once again.

"Come!" said the woman, and grasped her right arm.

Cecilia rose. Her legs were cramped and stiff. But any impulse to run was checked not only by the woman's paralyzing grip but by the lack of cover, down here by the road. Behind her, across the road, there was only a bare hillside, open, no possible shelter. She would have to reach the woods above the meadow before there was a chance to reach a hiding place. Suddenly, she froze, and so did the woman, as the wild barking of a dog tore the silence to pieces. It came from some distance away, higher up, but the hillsides and precipices, which rimmed round the amphitheater of meadow, funneled the frenzied far-off sounds down to the road. The barking ended. Then came two long howls, lengthened by a ghostly echo. Wolves? Were wolves still to be found here? Or perhaps it had been a shepherd's dog, disturbed by a prowler. Remembering what she had heard about the savage dogs that guarded the lonely flocks of sheep in Greece, Cecilia did not envy the prowler.

The woman was staring up at the mountainside. Cecilia dropped to her knees as if her legs were weak. She took her left hand out of her pocket to help her rise, while the woman tried to jerk her to her feet. She got up, slowly, her hand leaving her small key wallet on the ground, her foot covering it lightly as she stood and faced the woman. From the car, the man's voice called a question impatiently. The woman laughed as she answered, and pulled Cecilia off the road, onto the silvered meadow. The car started quickly, gathered speed, and raced along the road to start climbing again.

Across the meadow there was a goat track, not a bare path, but a narrow ribbon of grass worn down by small neat hoofs. Cecilia walked slowly over it, her right arm twisted behind her waist, the woman at her heels, the hard mouth of the revolver digging into her ribs. Well, she thought, they must be understaffed or else I wouldn't be here, alone, with this woman. And where had the man gone? To some place where he could hide the car? Where he could report that his mission was accomplished? I don't quite follow this routine of theirs. Where am I being taken? Why? But better not think of that, better to stage another little stumble, now that the road was ten yards away.

She staged a perfect one, falling forward on the cool damp grass, almost pulling Xenia down with her. Again she had to take her left hand out of her pocket to help her rise. "I need two hands," she told Xenia faintly. The woman released her arm and stepped back at once, the revolver well aimed. Very very slowly, Cecilia began to rise. This was going to be difficult. On her knees, she looked quickly up at the mountainside. "What was that?" she asked. "The dog?"

Xenia listened, too. Cecilia stood erect, her foot hiding what she had left there: the key, with its metal label numbered and "Grande Bretagne Hotel" in large letters across its face. Swiftly, she moved beside Xenia, hoping her body would block all sight of the key lying on the path. Her eyes held Xenia's. "There was something up there." She pointed to the woods.

Xenia was watching her. "You are afraid?" she asked. "You are afraid the big dog will come and eat you?" She laughed, but not too convincingly.

And you are not unafraid, Cecilia thought, as she kept looking at Xenia. Thank God, the woman was too busy studying her face, waiting perhaps for some rapid movement, expecting some trick, some attack. Then she gestured with her revolver toward the part of the wood that lay near the stream. At the edge of the trees, in a sheltered corner of the meadow, Cecilia saw a square of rough stone wall and, beside it, a small lean-to. At that moment, the wild barking began once more. It sounded near, now; much nearer, certainly.

"Quick, quick!" screamed Xenia. Cecilia did not need any prodding this time. In spite of high heels, shoes sodden by the heavy dew into paper slippers, she could run as quickly as Xenia. Her arm was no longer being so tightly held. Was this the time to escape? But another series of deep harsh barks, much much nearer, made her decide that Xenia—meanwhile—was preferable. She did manage to get her notebook out of her right-hand pocket, and throw it back, to the side, as she ran. Then she was pulled through the door that Xenia had tugged open, and they were both inside the hut. Xenia barred the door, and they stood, their heads almost touching the thatched roof, in a room no more than ten feet square, with the moonlight streaming through the spaces between the vertical, stripped branches that formed three of the walls.

"Why, it's a wickiup!" said Cecilia. She looked at Xenia, standing in moonlight stripes before her, and felt a moment of triumph. She laughed softly. "If that animal is half the dog he sounds, he will chew this place to pieces in no time at all." She saw the angry face, distorted still more by the bars of moonlight, staring at her. All right, all right, she thought, don't blame me because you felt so frightened. She looked now at the striped floor. It was of earth, of course, not particularly clean earth; but the hovering, rancid smell of sheep was faint. There was a lot to be said for so much ventilation. She moved over to one wicker wall, and tested its seemingly fragile strips with the palm of her hand. They would hold.

There was no furniture, just a low pile of twigs and thin branches against the one wall of rough stone opposite the door. Cecilia kicked the pile with her foot and waited to see what would run out. Nothing did. Even the mice had deserted the shepherd's hut. She tried the bed of twigs. They were perhaps less uncomfortable, if a little noisier, than the earth floor.

"Quiet!" Xenia whispered angrily. She was listening to the soft padding of the dog around the hut. There was a clatter of stones as he leaped on top of one of the sheep-pen walls.

Cecilia moved silently to one side of the hut and stood close to a slotted opening. In front of her was the long stretch of meadow sloping gently away, and part of the road, white in the moonlight. And near the hut, not more than thirty feet away, she saw a small black patch lying on the grass. It was her notebook. She stared at it in despair. Xenia had only to step out of that doorway and look down toward the road, and she would see it. She would search the rest of the way across the meadow and find everything, everything . . .

"What are you looking at?" Xenia asked sharply, and took a step toward her. But the dog leaped down from the stones and ran out on the meadow. He turned to face the wicker wall, his massive muzzle pointing, his long fur rising around his thick neck, a deep growl beginning in his huge chest, working its way slowly up into his throat, barking out from the yawning jaws. Cecilia flinched back from the sound. Xenia had retreated to the door, making sure of an exit if this enormous animal came lunging through the thin walls.

Strangely, there was only that one bark. The dog still faced the hut, but he was silent. There must be someone with him, Cecilia thought. He is waiting for a signal. Someone? Not anyone that Xenia had expected, certainly.

"He is still there," Cecilia said, and hoped that would keep Xenia at the door.

"Sh!"

"Oh, don't be silly! The dog knows we are here." The growl started again.

"You fool!" Xenia said in anger and alarm.

A man came into sight, now, walking with a strange loping gait around the hut.

Cecilia said loudly, "Dogs have to get accustomed to people." The man stopped, just behind the dog. He was short and broad-shouldered, bundled bulkily in a ragged sheepskin vest. His wild head of hair turned slowly from side to side, his eyes searching the trees. His heavy boots were almost standing on the notebook, but he had not looked down. "If he hears our voices," Cecilia said clearly, "he may calm down." The man stared at the hut. He held a large stone ready in his raised right hand, the other gripped a long, thick stick. Then he relaxed. He still glowered at the hut, but his throwing arm fell slowly to his side. He rested his weight on the long stick, as the expected enemy was not found. He even looked down at the notebook. Quickly, he picked it up, studied it for a moment with a frown.

"How else," said Cecilia, "can he know that I have only the friendliest feelings toward him?" She raised her voice. "Hello, out there! Hello, boy!"

"You fool!" cried Xenia and rushed over to silence her. The man moved away, quickly, in his strange silent lope. The dog waited for a last long moment, and bounded after him.

"Fool!" repeated Xenia again, and struck hard with the butt of the revolver. Cecilia saw the upraised arm, and tried to dodge the blow. She succeeded, mostly. The blow glanced onto her shoulder; but she let herself fall, and she did not try to rise. This, she thought, as she clenched her hands to keep from crying out with the pain, this is where I now start some passive resistance. I'll lie here until I damned well please to get up. I'll walk no more. I'll just lie here and wait. She kept her eyes closed and lay quite still. What misery this is, what complete misery, she thought. Why didn't the shepherd come into the hut? Why don't I know the phrase for "Help me!" in Greek? But at least the book was no longer lying

354

out there. And the shepherd? Perhaps he had already lost his curiosity and had cast the notebook aside as he climbed back through the wood. Or he might light his fire with it. Sheltering in his hut, up on some high meadow, he might sometime remember the strange voices he had heard. Yes, she thought bitterly, and talk to his sheep about them.

She wondered if all the other things she had scattered around would be picked up by people as slow-thinking and cautious as the shepherd. If so, they would all be useless. Useless. She had had a nice little game to keep her mind occupied; that was all. Oh, Ken! she thought. Ken . . .

The moment of despair was gone. No, she thought now; even if it is useless, it isn't a game. It is a battle, a small battle. And by scattering the keys and the notebook and the compact and the lipstick in the cigarette package, I won five small victories. Important to no one, perhaps, except to myself. But isn't that still something? Isn't that—in this misery—isn't that everything?

She was too cold, too hungry, to fall asleep. She watched the bars of shadows across the floor broaden and swallow up the stripes of moonlight. The night sky was dimming. Once it is daylight, she thought, I can see where this hut is, where the trees begin, where the precipice lies. There is no use in escaping blindly. People die just as easily on a cliff face as by a bullet from a gun. The dog will have work to do, once the dawn comes, guarding the sheep from straying over the ravines on this hillside. The shepherd must have two dogs, of course: he would never leave the sheep penned within their stone walls for the night, up on the higher meadow, without some guard. Let's hope there's enough work to keep two dogs busy, high up on the mountainside, a good two miles or so from here; and I'll keep that distance between them and me. If I could just get into the shelter of those trees, and circle back toward the road. Yes, it's the road I much reach. . . . It's a first-class road; good roads aren't built to lie idle; there must be some cars, or mail buses, or trucks or carts with supplies.

And now the hut was plunged into deep black-gray shadow. The dark hour of dawn had come. If the woman were asleep, or almost asleep, Cecilia thought, perhaps I could slip out into the trees. She tried to stretch her numb legs. But even as she tensed her muscles, the woman moved from the bed of twigs over to the door. Cecilia heard it being unbarred. She tried to rise, but before she could pull herself up from the earth floor, the woman had stepped outside and closed the door. So Xenia had not liked being locked up in a small dark hut where she could no longer see her prisoner. That was a quick retreat, Cecilia thought. I suppose I should be flattered.

The door would be barred from the outside. But she rose, and moved stiffly over to test it. Barred it was. She tried to see through the wicker wall. Xenia was standing a few feet away from the door. She was looking up toward the wood. It was too dark to see the expression on her face. But she was angry. She was saying something under her breath. Her clenched fist struck her thigh twice.

So something had gone wrong. This is not according to plan, Cecilia thought. It can't be: we are far too near the road; daylight is coming. But how stupid I am, not to realize that things can go wrong for them just as much as they go wrong for us! Someone had once said that the whole art of winning was by outlasting the enemy, even by one minute.

She began rubbing her numbed arms and legs. Walking was impossible inside this small dark room, so she bent and stretched her body, and rubbed, and stretched, until it felt less like a slab of marble. As her eyes became more accustomed to the half-darkness, she lifted her handbag from the floor and began searching inside it. She took a cigarette, but before she struck the match, she hesitated. She looked at the wicker walls, the thatched ceiling, the bed of dried thin branches. She put the cigarette and match folder into her pocket; it was much wiser not to remind Xenia that she possessed any matches. She could hear the woman stamping her feet, blowing on her hands to keep warm, outside. She might come back into the shelter, such as it was, of the hut, once the light was strong enough to let her watch her prisoner in safety. What was more, they wouldn't be staying here, once dawn came; the road was too close.

Cecilia began to tear out the sheets of the Cavafy poems, quietly, carefully, crumpling them slightly. She pulled some of the branches away from each other, trying to make a deep nest. She pushed the crumpled paper, lightly, between the twigs she had torn apart, working as quickly as she could. It was a difficult job. She was not quite finished when she heard the far-off sound of a light engine. It was coming nearer, nearer. It stopped. She laid a branch lightly over the top of the fire nest, hoped it would disguise the paper, thrust the few remaining sheets into her bag, and crossed over to the wall from which she could see the road. Anastas was walking obliquely across the meadow, pushing a motorcycle.

Xenia ran to meet him. They stood talking, in low intense voices, almost at the spot where the shepherd had quietened his dog. Xenia was scolding and complaining. Anastas was worried, angry. He gestured at the hut, at the road, at the lightening sky, as if he were saying, "Well, we have to move. And don't blame me!" Then he silenced Xenia by taking a flat round loaf from the inside of his coat and thrusting it into her hand. He left, still angry, walking over to some bushes at the edge of the wood. He searched. He must have found a hiding place for the motorcycle, for he walked back to fetch it. He wheeled it over to the chosen spot and pushed it out of sight. He walked around the clump of bushes, studying it from every angle. He was satisfied. He turned back to the waiting Xenia. And now it was he who was scolding, pointing up to the mountains, making a sign for her to hurry.

Cecilia didn't wait any longer. She crossed to the bed of twigs, struck two matches and dropped them down among the paper. She struck two more, dropped them, picked up her bag and ran to the door as she heard Xenia pulling its outside bar loose. As the door opened, she stepped outside, almost onto one of Xenia's feet. "I must wash," she said, and started past Xenia toward the stream. Xenia caught her wrist. "I must wash," Cecilia insisted, and pulled the woman toward the path.

"Not here!" Xenia told her angrily. "Later, later!" But she didn't enter the hut. She walked beside Cecilia, still holding her wrist with one hand, the loaf of bread with the other. The man was waiting for them by a large plane tree at the edge of the wood, his revolver ready. He gestured up toward the mountainside, impatiently.

Cecilia glanced back at the meadow. The road was empty. There wasn't a house or a farm in sight, anywhere, on these bare sloping hills. The little thatched hut leaned against its gray stone wall, innocent and peaceful in the still light of dawn.

Xenia jerked her arm, and she began climbing the little path that led up through the wood. The man followed them. There was no talk, now. I'll walk, Cecilia decided, until we are far enough away from the hut so that the trees blot it completely from sight. And then I won't walk. I won't walk one yard. She wondered if the paper had caught at all, or had the matches only flared and died away? Even as she worried, she felt sorry for the little hut. There it had been, lying at the edge of a peaceful meadow, offering refuge, wishing no harm on anyone; and for its kindness, it was sent up in flames. Someone had built it carefully and well. Some shepherd would remember the shelter it had given him when he had been driven off the hills by bad weather.

The path through the woods veered to the left as it climbed steeply up the hill. And at last, the trees thinned out and Cecilia could see a gray hillside of rough fields, with scattered boulders and a few small trees and bushes. It seemed endless, cold and bleak under the half-light of early morning. This is where I stop walking, she thought. There is no place to hide on that hillside: I must keep near the trees.

"You wash here!" Xenia told her, and pointed to a shallow pool, where the small stream, tumbling down from the heights, rested, too, before it went cascading through the wood. Boulders sheltered the pool from the hillside. And the path, once it crossed the flat steppingstones of the pool, divided into two narrow tracks, each finding its own way on to the hill. They looked equally uninviting: the lower one disappeared behind the boulders; the upper one branched steeply, more directly up the hillside. I'll stay close to the wood, Cecilia decided. But where did the sun rise? Where are we now?

They were guarding her carefully. While Xenia hacked the black bread into thick slices, the man watched Cecilia, his revolver held ready. He talked. He was angry. Perhaps, thought Cecilia, he is disappointed. Something is still wrong. But what is wrong for them is right for me. Listening to the voices she could not understand, she sat on a boulder, looked down over the treetops toward the valley, waited for the moment when the sun would rise high enough to be seen.

Xenia took over the watch, choosing a seat opposite Cecilia to face the hillside, keeping a cautious distance of about ten feet between them. The man folded up the map he had been studying, made some last bitter comments, took another slice of bread, and crossed the shallow pool by its flat steppingstones. Cecilia could hear his feet clattering and slipping on one of the paths up the hillside behind her. He had left them, she decided, not out of tact but of necessity. Perhaps he had to explore the two paths and decide which was the better one. Perhaps, she thought in a surge of wishful hoping, he felt almost as lost as she did.

She washed, ate her slice of bread, and waited. Xenia moved when she moved, always keeping the same distance from her. Cecilia could neither draw farther away nor come nearer than those ten or twelve feet. When Cecilia came back to her boulder, Xenia took the same seat again to face the hillside. They waited in silence. It was a long, long wait.

At last, Cecilia saw the sun coming out over the woods. So that is definitely the east, she thought. And now I know that the hillside stretches to the north and the west. And down there, south, is the meadow and the road we traveled last night. Southeast, to be accurate. That is where Athens lies. But where can we be now?

She studied the woman, who was chewing at her second slice of bread, her revolver still carefully ready. How much hope lay there? Cecilia wondered, and found very little. Xenia was a thoroughly discouraging type.

She was probably not much older than Cecilia, almost the same height, but broader, heavier. She could have been handsome, something pleasant to look at, for her features were not ugly, her eyes were large, her hair thick and intensely black. But her mouth never softened, her dark eyes concentrated on her job. No wit, no humor in those eyes, no sympathy, no gentleness. They only held a strange mixture of aggressive intensity and impersonal coldness. She was the educated, dehumanized female, the dedicated machine. How do I get any information out of her? Cecilia wondered. "What has happened to your friend?" she tried. The woman ignored her.

Cecilia reached for her handbag, the woman's eyes following her movements. "I have no gun," Cecilia said.

"We know that." The voice was as cold and contemptuous as the eyes. She watched Cecilia comb her hair. "Now put on your powder and lipstick," she said derisively. "Make yourself pretty for them."

Cecilia finished combing her hair. "Them?" she asked.

The woman ate her slice of bread.

Cecilia said, "Have you been doing much kidnaping recently?"

Xenia stopped eating and looked at her.

"Or did you have enough practice with the children?" Cecilia kept her voice gentle. "What a magnificent experience that must have been for you! How many thousands of them, actually? I heard that it was almost fifty thousand who were kidnaped and taken out of Greece. Did you take some of them by this route? Did they cry much? Did they weep? You must have had a busy time, wiping away their tears, telling them they should be glad they had been stolen from their reactionary parents. Who wants a father or mother, anyway?"

The quiet voice had, at first, deceived the woman. But now she rose, staring at Cecilia. She mastered her anger. "You are politically uneducated," she said contemptuously. "It is useless to talk with you. You would not understand liberation. You do not—"

"Oh, I am being liberated, am I? Ever since you hit me on the head and shoved me into a taxi, I have been liberated? And how ungrateful of me, not to appreciate it."

Xenia's eyes narrowed. "You make a joke. Tomorrow, you will make no jokes."

"No?" Would she really use that revolver? Cecilia wondered. The sound of a shot would carry on this hillside. She wouldn't want that; I would. But then, she might hit me. She'd like that; I wouldn't. If I did not want so desperately to live, now that Ken— She looked down at the valley, trying to stare the sudden tears away. Yes, I'd take the chance of being hit, she decided, if there was anyone near enough to hear the shot. But the little stretch of white ribbon, the curving road, was empty. The hills around it were still and silent under the early-morning sky. This country reminded her of the loneliness of Wyoming, of the rise and fall of the foothills leading up to the Big Horn, of nothing but mountains and forests and overwhelming sky. "Where shall I be tomorrow?" She managed to smile. "Dead?"

"We are not criminals."

"That's nice to know. Where shall I be tomorrow?"

Xenia brushed a crumb from the sleeve of her coat. "I do not know," she said, coldly, casually. And that, thought Cecilia, is the truth: this woman does not know and she could not care less, and she believes she is not a criminal. A chill, far sharper than the shrewd mountain air, struck through her. "So you are just delivering me over, like a package? To whom?"

Xenia did not bother to answer. She glanced at her watch, then up at the hillside in front of her, then back at Cecilia. "Why do you look down at the road?" she asked with open amusement. "There is no car there. It is too early. And no one could see us here. No one."

"You gloat so nicely," Cecilia said. "You have such endearing traits."

"Say good-by to the road," the woman said. "Say good-by to everything!" But she could not see the first wisps of smoke, darkening, thickening, a thin black column rising above the treetops near the meadow.

Cecilia looked away. A column of hope, she thought. Even if, at this hour, there was no one to see the blazing hut, someone would find its ashes later. And, suddenly, she remembered the unexpected side to the loneliness of Wyoming. How often as she had ridden through empty countryside had she come around some trees and found a man fishing in a creek; or on a high meadow, near a stream, there would be a little cabin; sometimes, in a draw, she would find a solitary cowhand searching for strays; on a hillside, a Basque would be sitting at his wagon door, watching his sheep. Here, she thought quickly, there are shepherds, too. Even if the one I saw last night has moved on with his flock, this morning, there may be others. There may be a peasant going to work in his fields, a woman fetching water from a spring, a boy gathering wood. I may not hear or see them, but they exist all the same. A man with short sight would not see those two eagles, far to the west, circling slowly in the sky. Yes, she thought, this country is no more lonely, no more unexpected, than Wyoming. This woman had almost shocked her into hopelessness; the cold, disinterested eyes had almost mesmerized her with despair. But now, as she looked at the distant eagles soaring over some hidden valley, her heart rose, too.

"Stand still!" Xenia said angrily, nervously. She sensed a change. She couldn't understand it. But her caution doubled.

Cecilia, bending down to take off her shoes, only rubbed one ankle as her reply. A pity, she thought, that there was such a stretch of open ground in this clearing; the nearest trees were thirty feet or more away. The course of the stream was no help, either. After this pool, it plunged down between boulders in an unpleasant drop through the wood. There was the hillside behind her, of course, with its outcrops of rock, large boulders, no doubt some gullies and its own sudden precipices. But the man was somewhere up there. And, besides, she did not want to run uphill. She wanted to get down, down to the road.

"It is better," the woman said, relaxing as she approved of such unexpected good sense. "The shoes are useless on the hills." She looked at the high heels and found them comic. "Put them down! Here!" She pointed to a boulder near where she stood.

Cecilia moved slowly over, staring beyond the woman's shoulder. "There's smoke rising, down there."

Xenia had been expecting some trick. "Some smoke rising!" she mimicked.

From the hillside, behind Cecilia, the man called out. Cecilia glanced around. Anastas was not near the two paths which had diverged at the boulders on the rough field near her. He had come back by a higher, easier route and he was now standing on the hillside itself just above the wood. From there, he had seen the smoke rising. He was pointing, as he began to scramble down toward the trees.

Xenia had looked toward the valley as he called. For a moment, she stared down at the rising column of black smoke. And in that moment, Cecilia moved. She smashed the heel of the shoe into the back of the woman's neck, and sent her sprawling. She tried to pick up the revolver; but from the trees came the man's shout, a shot. She turned and ran. There was only one way to run, after all. Toward the paths at the boulders.

A second shot rang out, but she was already dodging behind the first boulder. Which path now? Which path? Instinctively, she chose the one on her left, the lower one, the one nearer the valley. She kept on running. Her luck was holding. The path was good, a narrow trail of worn grass, easy on her feet.

And then she knew it wasn't so good. It was only a goat track, narrowing as the ground on her left began to fall away more steeply. One slip—she looked down at the fall of hillside, now developing into a precipice, and stopped running. The man wasn't even bothering to chase after her on this path. He knew what lay ahead.

She drew against the steep bank on her right, regaining her breath and her sadly splintered confidence. She would have to go on. There was no going back. The man, she thought, makes mistakes, too: he is now regretting the two shots he fired. She remembered his heavy build, his plodding walk, his sallow face; he wasn't accustomed to scrambling around a hillside. His wits might not be so nimble here as they were when he was arguing over a coffee table back in Athens.

She started along the narrow trail, less than two feet wide, which now curved around a rock face. She took that carefully, not looking down. Halfway, she realized for the first time that she was still holding a shoe in each hand. She waited until she was past that jutting face of rock before she paused to slip the shoes into her pockets. And, unexpectedly, the trail relented. It swerved away from the edge of the precipice and climbed uphill. She increased her pace.

But she was also out in the open, away from the rocks and the boulders which had sheltered her. She looked back along the hillside, toward the wood. The man was following the upper path, still some distance away, but in clear sight. As he saw her, he began a slow run, stumbling, as if his morning's exploration had already exhausted him.

She ran, too, abandoning the trail which was now climbing straight uphill toward the higher path which the man was following. She cut across the hillside, westward, soft grass under her feet, blue wild flowers to cover her ankles. She struggled up the last slope of the hill's shoulder. Her thoughts came in gasps like her breath. Over there, just over that shoulder, perhaps there were trees, a wood, someplace to hide.

But when she reached the hill's shoulder, there was no wood, only a vast country of high meadows and far hills. Immediately in front of her, cutting down the hillside in a jagged furrow, was a deepening gully. There was no way across except by the path, higher up on the hill. She looked down at the gully, almost a ravine at this point; and then she glanced back over her shoulder. The man had gained slightly on her as she stood here, fumbling for breath, for a clear thought. He was still keeping to the path; he knew she would have to climb back to it to cross the gully.

Could I manage to reach the path up there ahead of him? she wondered, and knew it was impossible. She looked at the deep gully once more, cutting her off from the meadows. Over there, might be safety. In the distance, she could see a movement: black sheep, white sheep, a flock of them grazing. There was only one way for her to reach them. Quickly, she started down into the gully.

She ran where she could, scrambled where she couldn't, and let herself slide when there were bushes to break her descent. As it became more difficult, she slowed her pace, held on to the branches to lower herself to each new level. The ground was dropping away steeply now, but it wasn't a precipice. Not on this side. Across the deep bed of the narrow stream, it was a different matter. There, a giant bite had been taken out of the high bank, clean and neat, leaving only sharply ridged rock. The farther she climbed down, the worse the other side looked. Its scattering of bushes, growing into its clefts, had made it seem not impossible from the top edge of the ravine; but from below, looking up at that wall of rock . . .

She stopped where she was, and let herself fall beside a clump of bushes, her breath tearing her body, her heart pounding up into her ears, her legs suddenly trembling and helpless. She stared up at the wall of rock. I'll never manage it, she realized. Never. She lay back, staring up at the blue sky, and she wept.

TWENTY-EIGHT

Still keeping to the path, the man, Anastas, reached the rough bridge over the gully. He was as much out of breath as out of temper. He stared down the length of this wild, abandoned place, the stream bed deepening as it ate into the ground, its banks rising higher until the gully had been transformed into a ravine. There were bushes down there, straggling dwarf trees, falls of sharp-edged rock, boulders worn smooth by winter torrents.

Where did he begin to search? It would take four men to scour that ravine, block its exits. He decided to stand and watch. There must be a movement, sometime. Let her think he had gone away, and she would move. Move, he told her under his breath, move!

He waited for thirty minutes, thirty silent minutes, long long minutes. But there was no movement. He could see not one sign of her, hear not one stone dislodged. Cursing her, he started down into the stream bed. He was sweating inside his heavy coat. The sun was warm down here. He was thirsty and tired and depressed. If everything had only gone according to plan, the girl would have been off their hands before dawn came. Xenia and he could have left the hut on the meadow as soon as he arrived on his motorcycle. By this time, they would have been as far north as Thessaly. He could really travel on that machine.

He searched for twenty minutes and he still had not covered more than a quarter of the ravine. It was obvious that if the girl was still here—he was beginning to doubt that—she could even shift her position and take cover where he had already searched. One man was useless on this job.

Then he saw Xenia, standing up on the path at the plank bridge over the gully, watching him. That's right, he thought as he wiped his brow with his sodden handkerchief, loosened his collar still more; she will stay up there and give me advice. He left the ravine and scrambled back to the bridge.

"She isn't there?" Xenia asked, her eyes searching the ravine.

The question annoyed him.

"You saw her go in?" Xenia insisted.

"Yes."

"Where?"

"If I knew that exactly, I'd know where to find her. There is a rise on this hill slope, perhaps you'll notice. It hid the ravine, didn't it? So it hid her as she went in."

"Perhaps she went right down the ravine, and out by the other end."

"Yes," he said, "right over a precipice."

"Then perhaps she's stuck on that precipice."

"You climb down and look," he suggested.

Xenia ignored that. The pain at the back of her neck was almost gone, but she had one of her blinding headaches now. It would last for hours; they always did. That bright sun, the glare from the rocks, were no help, either. "We shall have to search," she said doggedly, closing her eyes wearily.

Her air of martyrdom annoyed him. "Impossible!" He looked at his watch. "One man is useless on this job."

Her eyes opened, and she turned to look up at the crest of the hill. "Where are the men? Did you find them?"

"They are there. In the cave, just around the other side of the hill. They are resting. They had a long walk last night."

"And did not finish it," she said angrily. "If they had come down to the hut as they were told—"

"How could they? There was that shepherd and his dog searching—"

"Frightened of a shepherd and his dog? You men!"

"Not frightened. Cautious. They cannot afford to be seen. There isn't a peasant for miles around who wouldn't go running to the police." He stiffened as he looked at a ledge on the high cliff wall of the western side of the ravine. "There's something!" he said, and pointed.

Xenia shielded her eyes. She laughed. "It's a sheep," she said, "it's a dead sheep." She turned away, her eyes blinking the strain out of them, the headache tightening its iron band around her brow. "Go back to the cave and make them come down here."

"Make them?"

"They have got to help us search."

"They won't come down here in daylight. It's too open. They might be seen." His patience was shortening rapidly again. "Look, Xenia, I tried to get them to come as far as the wood. What do you think I was doing all that time I left you and the girl alone at the pool?"

"They wouldn't come?"

"Not until dark. Do you think they want the police tracking them back to their valley? A raid?"

Excuses, she thought, always excuses. "How many are there?"

"Two. A man and his son."

"Is that all?"

It's quite enough, he thought. She hasn't seen them. I have.

She said, "Go back and tell them—"

"Go yourself!" He never wanted to see them again. They troubled him. They lived in absolute freedom, a communal life, everything shared. Idyllic? He remembered their faces, the eyes that had studied him. Absolute freedom did strange things to some men. Men? They were animals. Not proud or noble animals, either; just . . . Quickly, he corrected his heresy. Those outlaws never had the chance to practice absolute freedom properly. They were free only in their miserable valley; and even there, they lived with fear, keeping constant watch, ready to abandon their huts and run to the mountains. How many raids had they survived in the last fifteen years?

"Where is this cave?"

"Xenia, don't be a fool."

"On the contrary," she said coldly. "If we don't find that girl, do you realize what we must do?"

"Get out of here at once." We should have left hours ago. The girl was probably as dead as the sheep.

"We go back to Metsos and tell him what has happened. He has to know what has happened." As he frowned, finding that an unpleasant and dangerous complication, Xenia asked anxiously, "You did see Metsos last night when you left the car at the house near Delphi? He had arrived? He is all right?"

"He is safe enough." There were three trails onto the hills from the back of that house; a clear view, in front, of the road by which any danger would come. A well-placed house. Yes, Metsos was safe enough. Safer than we are, he thought, and a sight more comfortable.

"You gave me a fright, for a moment," she said angrily.

"He is safe," he repeated. "But the road to the house is no longer safe by daylight, for us. There are villages. We would be noticed. They must have heard the motorcycle, this morning. If they see it, now—"

"Anastas, the fool!" she said derisively. "What makes you think we can even risk going back for your motorcycle? We may have to walk. Yes, walk! And the sooner we get rid of that girl, the sooner we can start." She turned to climb up the hill.

"Don't go!" he told her. And I'm damned if I do much walking. I hid the motorcycle well. I'll find it. But soon. I must find it soon.

She looked down at him. "What has happened to you? These men are friends of Metsos. They listened to his message, didn't they?"

"Because he offered them something for nothing." And he didn't see Metsos visiting them himself.

She said coldly, "They are free men, Anastas. Since when have you become frightened of free men?"

"All right," he said, angry now. "Have your own way. But don't waste any time. And keep under cover. There are shepherds over on the meadow, to the west."

"Shepherds!" she said derisively. "Are you afraid of them, too? Don't worry. I know how to keep my head down. You keep yours! Watch that ravine!" She left, making for the scattering of stunted trees that lay under the crest of the hill. From there, she would follow a sheep track through them, over the shoulder to the other side of the hill. He tried to imagine the scene: Xenia laying down the law to the lawless. She would have a long climb for nothing. They would do things their own way, not hers. In their world of free men, women did not give orders. For a moment, he almost smiled. He wondered if he should have told her to keep a distance from them, her revolver ready but out of sight. The men might take a fancy to it.

He waited impatiently, staring down at the ravine, searching its sides carefully with angry eyes. The girl was not here, he told himself again, and persuaded himself completely. Xenia had been the fool to waste time like this. He would have to climb up to the cave and hurry her away. But I'm damned, he thought, if I'm going back to the Delphi house to tell Metsos. I'll telephone him from Levadia. My orders were to get out of this district as soon as the job was finished, and stay out. Well, the job seems to have finished itself. What does Metsos do when he faces a reverse? He cuts his losses and gets out. And plans to fight another day. The trouble with women was that they never knew when to get out. They kept on and on.

He cursed Xenia, the ravine, the American girl, that eagle planing overhead. He watched it uneasily. It was still flying at a great height, but it seemed to be circling round and round over the same spot. Could it actually see the sheep lying on that ledge of cliff? He liked the ravine less and less. Time to leave this place and find Xenia. And then he saw a shepherd, standing quite still, watching him from across the ravine, leaning on his long staff.

Anastas looked up the hill. No sign of Xenia, damn her. But, up there, was the shepherd's dog, a huge brute even from this distance, pointing toward the crest of the hill. Xenia would have to choose another way down. She would. Xenia would walk through a gate of fire if she could report back about it to Metsos.

He watched the shepherd coming slowly along the top of the ravine. Soon, Anastas thought, he will be near enough to see my face clearly. He turned his head quickly away, hesitated, started along the hillside path back to the shelter of the wood. It was the only intelligent thing to do, he kept telling himself. Xenia? She would be already there, waiting impatiently, angry because she couldn't get the men to show themselves by daylight on this hillside.

But Xenia was not waiting near the pool.

I'd better make sure of that motorcycle, he thought, while the wood is still quiet. He began to run down the shaded, silent path. At the last trees, he halted and listened. No sound at all. He came through them slowly, stopped behind a huge plane tree, looked cautiously out on the meadow. The hut was a glowing heap of ashes. Three peasants were grouped beside an olive tree, watching in silence. That was all: the quiet meadow, three silent peasants. Let them try to stop me, he thought: a woman, an old man, a boy. Let them try!

They watched him, motionless, making no effort to stop him at all. He reached the bushes where he had hidden the motorcycle. It was still there. Then two policemen closed in, one from each side.

The shepherd came slowly along the top of the ravine. He watched the man in the dark coat stumbling over the path toward the wood. A frightened man. What is frightening him? Foreigners are strange people.

He whistled to his dog and brought it bounding back down the hillside. "What do you smell up there?" he asked the dog. "What angers you? Yes, yes, I'll go and see. Later. First things first." He dropped his stick and began to climb down the cliff toward the sheep. There was still a little life in it. Kneeling by the sheep, he looked up at the eagle with a toothless grin of triumph. The giant stretch of wings made its last circle. It rose into a current of air, and turned to float away across the valley.

From his high perch on the cliff, he saw—down there, hidden behind a clump of bushes—a color that his eye had been trained to notice. The color of natural wool. His heavy eyebrows knitted in a puzzled frown. Not a sheep. A woman. Why does she lie there? Is she dead? No. She moves. She

368

sees me. A foreigner. She does not belong to this valley. Strange people, these foreigners, from the towns and the city. Crazy people, stupid. And their women are the craziest of all. Like the women in the hut last night. They come, in a car. They wait for the sun to rise, so that they can climb the mountain. Every summer, they come. Women dressed like men, bundles on their backs, climbing the mountains by all the wrong paths. For what? So that everyone must stop his work and search for them. Crazy and stupid and selfish.

He stared down at the other bank of the ravine. This one is very quiet, she does not scream or cry out, she needs no help. A strange foreigner. She is resting. She chooses a nice warm place in the sun to lie on the grass and watch the sky. She is not so crazy, this one.

Slowly, gently, he hoisted the sheep over his shoulders. "Keep still, keep very still!" Slowly, slowly, he clambered back to the top of the ravine, to the green grass and the flowers of the meadow, the sheep's little bell sounding sweetly with each step he took.

The dog was waiting obediently beside his staff, but it whined as it looked up the hillside toward the crest. "First things first," he told it sharply. A good dog, brave and willing, but it has much to learn.

He set out across the meadow, the sheep stirring on his shoulder as it sensed it was safe. He put it down as he neared the scattered flock, watched by his brother and his brother's dog. It felt so safe, it even tried to run on its shaking legs, which made him laugh. His eyes swept over the flock: sixty-five white, forty-seven black. All there now. He leaned on his staff, listening to the tinkling bells as the sheep grazed safely over the blue-flowered meadow.

His brother limped over to talk. "The dog is restless."

"It smells their trail again."

"Where are they? I see nothing."

"Perhaps they rest in the cave."

"They wait for the sun to set. Why? I do not like this. They come too near." Yesterday, in the village, there was talk of two wild men, two bandits, seen wandering on the hills. There was no talk of anything stolen, this time; no talk of violence. But those men were not to be trusted. They did not wander out among honest people without a reason. "We guard the sheep well tonight," he said slowly.

The shepherd frowned at the hill. "First, we see if they are in the cave."

"They have guns," his brother warned him. "Twice, this morning . . ."

The shepherd nodded somberly. He left his brother and began the long walk back to the hill. If the bandits are there, as the dog believes, I go down to the village for help. Eleven years since they have come hunting so near this valley. That time, they steal three sheep. They kill a farmer. They take his wife. The soldiers go after them. Seven days and nights of searching. Five caught and punished. But they are like rats in an old wall. Always one or two who slip away, find another place to nest. They never have enough sense to stay there, to leave other people alone. "We do not want them here, eh?" he asked the dog as it led him over the shoulder of the hill to the shallow cave at the edge of the forest. "They steal and kill too much."

For a long time, the shepherd lay watching the cave. He could hear no sound. There was no movement. Frowning, he studied the forest which began close to the cave and then slipped downhill to a desolate valley. Beyond the valley were hills and mountains, and between the hills and mountains were valleys which he could not see. A wild and lonely land. Beautiful. Peaceful. As peaceful as this hilltop. He looked again at the cave.

He rose, releasing his grip on the dog's neck, letting it run free. It bounded toward the cave, and stopped, whining. He followed, still cautious, crouching, one sharp stone in his right hand, two more thrust inside his shirt.

The cave was empty.

But the dog is right, he thought, as he saw the signs of men on the dusty earth floor. He dropped the stones he carried, and spat for good riddance.

The dog was worrying at the edge of the forest now. He called it back. He stood, leaning on his staff, looking over the long northward stretch of trees. Then he turned away, and spat again. "We sleep tonight," he told the dog, and they went back toward their meadows.

Curiosity took him wandering past the ravine's edge to look down at the bushes. He held the dog by its long heavy hair, tugging and cursing until it stood obediently quiet. She was still there. This foreigner would not come disturbing his sheep, annoying his dogs. It was all he asked of any stranger. He crashed his stick over the dog's head when it almost lunged away from him, and made it pay attention enough to follow him back to the flock.

"They are gone," he told his brother.

"Did you see them go?"

"Perhaps," he said, evasively, "they go through the forest back to their own place."

His brother stared up at the hill for a long long time. "Is it a trick?" he asked, at last. "They hear the dog. They see you. They find someplace else to hide until it is dark."

It was an unpleasant suggestion. The shepherd thought about it. He looked at the grassy knoll where he had hoped to spend the rest of the afternoon. He looked at his brother. "We must tell the police," he said reluctantly.

His brother nodded. He rubbed his bad leg to show he could not walk so quickly nowadays.

"Stay here!" the shepherd told his dog. "Keep your mind on your own business!" He left them both, grumbling to himself, and struck across the meadows to the west. It would take an hour to reach the little trail that would lead him down over the western hillside to Arachova on the Delphi road. The afternoon would be over before he got back to his knoll, and the warm sun gone.

Cecilia had wanted to call to the shepherd. But a call, a wave, might bring Anastas and Xenia right back to the ravine. At least, she thought, lying quite still, watching the wild head of hair making the large head larger even from this distance, he is keeping one of his eyes on me. The other, thank heavens, must be restraining that dog.

It was the same huge black monster she had seen last night. It stood more than waist-high to the shepherd, and looked fully his bulk. An amiable beast, no doubt, provided his master chugged at his neck and cursed in his ear. But this was hardly the day when her nerves were strong enough to climb up the ravine, walk over the meadows, and join the shepherd's family circle. Because if Anastas or Xenia arrived, and could talk Greek when she could not, the shepherd might even believe the story they had no doubt concocted and let them take her away thinking they were her friends. She would do better to lie here, keeping quite still, and let this heavenly sun relax her body. She was hungry and thirsty and tired and frightened, but—at last—she was warm. Perhaps, now that the shepherd had vanished, a little lightheaded, too, with relief; that last glimpse of him kneeling on the top of the ravine, looking over, reminded her of Notre Dame Cathedral somehow.

The silence of the hills surrounded her again. It had been a long time since she had heard any voices, or Anastas's fumbling footsteps crashing around the gully up there. She doubted if Xenia would give up the search so easily, though. That woman was more terrifying than the savage dog.

I'll wait here, she decided, until the sun is almost set. Then I'll have to move quickly, back toward the woods, before it gets so dark that I'm lost all over again. In the dusk, I'll reach the road. I wish I weren't so scared. I'd be less afraid if I knew where I was. That's silly, I know, but if I only knew where this hill was, what valley lies far over to the west, where I can see the two eagles circling high in the sky, I'd feel a little less lost. Well, I shan't be lost if I can reach the road. Ken, she told him, you've got to be there, you've got to be. . . .

TWENTY-NINE

Kenneth Strang reached the meadow by the road in the late afternoon. He got out of the car, stretching his shoulders, exchanging a quiet nod with Costas. Between them, they had made good time. "Record time," Elias acknowledged, forgetting—in the excitement of their arrival—the qualms he had endured in silence during their wild ride onto the mainland and through the hills toward Parnassos. He made his way quickly to the two cars parked ahead of them at the meadow's edge.

Strang waited, looking around him. It seemed as if a small field headquarters had been set up at this point. There were three uniforms—army, or perhaps police—and two grave-faced civilians grouped around one car. A little distance away, there were a few interested spectators—two old women sitting on donkeys, a girl guarding a small herd of silk-bearded goats, some children.

There must be definite news to have brought us here, Strang thought. At Corinth, Elias had been told to head for Levadia. At Levadia, he had been told to take the Delphi road. And here they were, still about fifteen miles away from Delphi, with not a village in sight. Behind him were bare hills, through which their road had traveled. In front of him was the beginning of the Parnassos slopes, which stretched west and east and up as far as he could see: a pleasant meadow, with a stream at one side, a wood climbing behind it onto a steep hillside; more hillsides to the east; and to the west, high above the Delphi road, a buttress of precipices, meadows, more hillside. God, he thought in despair, if this place is where they brought her, where do we begin to look? Grimly, he eyed the wreaths of gray-white mists that blotted out the topmost peak. Were they lifting? Or were they settling lower?

Elias came back, followed by a man in police uniform. "They are ex-

373

pecting Colonel Zafiris immediately." He looked pleased for a moment. "We got here before him."

"Why here?"

Elias spoke to the policeman, who produced a key wallet and a hotel key. "You recognize these?"

Strang took them. He nodded.

"The key wallet was found, at the side of this road, by a farmer on his way to Arachova. The hotel key was found halfway across the meadow, just after the hut over there was discovered to be on fire." He pointed to a heap of black ashes beside a gray stone sheep fold. "The wallet was found at half past six. The fire was seen, much later, by a boy and his sister, herding goats. The boy went to Arachova for help. The girl stayed here, and one of her goats tried to eat the hotel key. The police came, just after ten o'clock. They searched all around, found a motorcycle hidden behind some bushes. When its owner came out of the woods, he was detained. Naturally. He had a revolver. Two bullets had been fired." Elias paused, trying to search for nonalarming words. "The girl with the goats said she had heard two shots while she waited for her brother. She couldn't say where, exactly. But the shots may mean very little." He looked away from Strang. "The man who was detained for questioning has a very simple story. He was traveling to Athens. He stopped to rest in the wood. He saw a man running away from the hut—a rough shepherd, he thought. Then he saw the hut was on fire, so he followed the man. He tried to stop him by firing twice in the air. That is his story. And he does not change it."

Strang said bitterly, staring up at the hillside, "Do men carry revolvers when they travel to Athens?"

"No. And when men travel by this road to Athens, they must pass through Delphi and then Arachova to reach here. No motorcycle was heard or seen in Delphi. Yet one was heard, just before dawn, passing through Arachova. Interesting." Elias took the wallet and key from Strang, and looked at them for a moment before he handed them back to the policeman. "These things, by themselves, seemed not important—just strange little events, until—"

"What action was taken?" Strang asked sharply.

"At first, as I was saying," Elias reminded him, "there seemed no action that was necessary. But Colonel Zafiris put the Parnassos district under a special alert after I telephoned from Tripolis, and the strange happenings here began to fit into a pattern."

"Yes, yes," said Strang, trying to control his impatience. Elias and his patterns . . . The hell with them. Where is Cecilia? "Who is out searching?"

374

"Two parties. Local men who know this terrain well. The wood has been searched, the hillside above it, too. They are now working over the hill slopes, there." He pointed to the east. "That seems more likely than to the west." He pointed to the open hillside above its sweeping buttress of precipices.

"Why?"

"There is more cover to the east. That is what the kidnapers want. Also, there is a good path; some huts; some summerhouses, now closed. Remember," Elias said gently, "they are not climbing along any hills blindly. They are taking her someplace. So we must search all the huts and the houses. You understand?"

But Strang kept looking up at the western slopes. "What's there, above the precipices? After that open hillside—what?"

Elias turned to the impassive man who waited patiently beside them, listening to a conversation of which he could not understand one word. Now, as Elias spoke in Greek, he was delighted, and gave a long, detailed, and enthusiastic answer.

"High meadows," Elias reported back to Strang. "No houses, no villages. Shepherds have just taken up their flocks, there, for the spring. Later, they will go to higher meadows, farther to the west. They—"

"Shepherds?"

"The kidnapers will keep far away from the shepherds. They do not want to be seen. Besides, shepherds do not like people very much. That is why they are shepherds." As Strang said nothing, but simply looked up toward the meadowland lying beyond the precipices, Elias added, "This search is extremely difficult. The searchers cannot call out. It might be dangerous for Miss Hillard, if the rescuers could not reach her before—that is to say, the kidnapers might take very stupid action if they thought that they were being tracked—what I mean is that—" Elias stopped, completely defeated in the battle of truth against tact. It would be so easy, he thought unhappily, to get rid of any evidence quickly on these hills. Didn't the American understand that? "If only the man who came out of the woods would talk!" he said angrily.

Strang's face looked suddenly ugly. "Where can I see this son of a bitch?"

"He is locked up in Levadia. Colonel Zafiris is probably talking to him, at this moment."

"I'm going up that hillside," Strang said, and pointed to the west.

"Wait until Colonel Zafiris arrives. Then I shall go with you. It is not wise for one man—"

"I'll manage. Ask your friend if there is only one path. If there are several, which is the quickest?"

"Wait for one of the search parties to come back. It is not wise for a stranger to go near the shepherds. Their dogs are—" he shrugged, and then admitted the fact—"savage. Sometimes, quite wild."

"Have you a gun you could lend me?"

Elias looked worried. He spoke to the policeman, who looked even more worried. Elias said to Strang, "If you hurt one of those dogs, the shepherds may hurt you." He kept glancing toward the road to the southeast that led to Levadia, Thebes, Athens, as if he were willing Colonel Zafiris to appear. But there was no car speeding along between the bare hills. From the opposite direction there were only two rustic types, coming leisurely down the hill from Arachova.

"Okay," Strang said, and began walking toward the burned-out hut, where the path into the wood seemed to begin. Behind him, he heard Elias call. He didn't look around. The call turned into a shout, two shouts. He turned, almost at the little heap of charred ashes, and glanced backward. Elias was sprinting after him, the police officer was waving his arms wildly.

His first impulse was to go right on, into the wood. But he waited, as Elias let out another yell. "A shepherd!" Elias called, and pointed toward the man who was now talking to the policemen. "News—"

Strang hesitated, looking back at the growing group. Everyone was crowding around the wild-haired man, who stood leaning on his long shepherd's staff.

"Or," said Elias, regaining his breath, "he would not have left his meadow and gone down to the village. Or walked here—" He took Strang's arm and urged him back.

News? Strang wondered. He wouldn't let himself count on that. Yet the word "news" had a magic quality. News . . .

The group was silent around the shepherd. He was pointing to the western hill slope, talking in short phrases. Strang could not follow the man's dialect.

"What is it?" he asked in frustration. Everyone could listen and understand except himself. "Elias—"

Elias said, "He came to tell the police that two outlaws—brigands, he calls them—are on that hillside."

"And Cecilia—"

"One moment," Elias said, listening intently. You could not hurry this shepherd. He had come to tell about brigands and that was what he would talk about until his message was complete. Either he would describe today as he had seen it or he would become bewildered and start repeating his story, thinking that his listeners were the stupid ones. The shepherd was looking at the hut now and saw its ruins. He stopped speaking altogether. Then he let out a cry in anger, and began speaking again. He pulled a small book from inside his shirt.

"He says people were there, last night," Elias translated quickly. "He found this book near the hut. He heard two women talking. Climbers, he thought they were."

Strang knew Cecilia's notebook at once. He reached for it. But the shepherd would not give it up.

Strang said in very slow Greek, "Did you see the women today?" He pointed up to the hillside. "Women?" he asked again.

The shepherd held up one finger.

Elias began questioning him. The man seemed surprised. What was all this excitement about a young woman? She was safe enough. He answered Elias gruffly, and went back to his story about the two brigands wandering so far into peaceful territory. *That* was something to worry about.

Elias said to Strang, "There is a young woman up in the ravine. Alone. She is safe."

"What ravine?"

"Between the hillside and the western meadows."

Strang turned and ran.

"Wait—" called Elias. "It may not be Miss Hillard. There were two women—" But nothing was stopping Strang now. It was Cecilia, he knew. It was Cecilia.

It was easy to follow the path through the wood, and where it forked—one spur to the left, one to the right—it was easy to choose the trail that mounted to the west. At the cascading stream and its little pool, he hesitated between the two tracks that diverged at the boulders. He chose the higher one; it climbed over open ground, it would give him a better view. He started up it as he heard men's voices from the wood behind him. He didn't wait for them to catch up with him. High up on the hillside, he paused to gain his breath and loosen his collar and tie. Then this inexplicable sense of urgency drove him on.

His eyes could see no one on the side of the hill. She must still be in the ravine. Safe, the shepherd had said. But how did the man know that? He must have taken an hour or more to walk to Arachova, another hour or so, perhaps, to tell his story and be sent to the policemen down at the roadside meadow. Safe . . . Anything could happen to a stranger on this hillside, once she was off the path. Anxiety and urgency, that was all Strang could feel. He couldn't even explain them. And that, itself, drove him on.

Ahead of him, he saw a gully. Was this the ravine? A shallow place, shallow enough for the path to cross onto the meadows that sloped away on the other side. He stopped, breathing hard, looking down the gully. It twisted and deepened, deepened dangerously. It must end at the precipices he had seen from the road. His anxiety returned. And then he heard a dog barking, barking wildly, far down the ravine.

"Cecilia!" he yelled. "Cecilia!" He began to run.

It was still too early to leave, Cecilia had thought. The sun was well over to the west, the shadows from the steep wall of the ravine had fallen across the stream's rocky bed and were moving up to where she lay on the other side. But the light was good. She would be seen very easily if she came out of cover. She had heard nothing at all, neither feet on stones nor far-off voices, for several hours. They must have gone. Yet she couldn't believe that the woman had given up the search. Anastas, perhaps. But Xenia, no. In the last extreme, Xenia wouldn't hesitate to shoot—if she could be sure of killing. Not as a criminal, Xenia would say. Simply as a matter of necessity, which—in Xenia's cold-eyed world—justified everything. It hadn't been any touch of compassion, Cecilia realized now, that made her throw me a slice of bread, or allowed me to drink from the stream, or kept her from drugging me in the car, or let her leave my legs and hands unbound. It was necessity, her kind of necessity: I had to be able to walk. Did Xenia really have so much contempt for ordinary people that she thought they'd walk, at the point of a gun, so despairing and lost and hopeless, right into their own graves? But then, Xenia had not known I wanted so very much, more than I've ever wanted, to live. She chose the wrong day. . . .

Sharply, Cecilia looked up at the sky line to the west. Above the rim of cliff opposite, there was the dark shape of the dog. It was racing now, uphill, toward the shallower banks of the gully.

Where's the shepherd? she thought, as she rose in sudden panic. See where the dog is going first, she told herself. It may be only on the trail of a fox. But, no, it was crossing the gully at the path, turning to run down this bank of the ravine.

She moved quickly, over the bed of the stream to the steeper side of the ravine, to the cliff she had thought she could never manage. Her hands felt desperately for every possible fingerhold. She pulled herself up, her fingers searching, her body straining, her feet bracing themselves against every small ledge. A stone slipped and clattered into the stream bed underneath. She dragged herself up another stretch of cliff. Now she could hear a strange, eager whining. Suddenly, something hit the rock below her and fell back. There was a yelp of pain, an angry bark.

She tried to take one more step upward, and couldn't. She hung on where she was. At least she was sure of this ledge on which her feet rested. She must not look down. Desperately, she stared at the gray rock streaked with coarsely mottled veins of gleaming crystals. The dog jumped again, and fell back. Not a friendly animal, she thought, and knew she had overcome her paralyzing terror: she was frightened sick, she could climb no more, but at least her mind was functioning again. She laid her cheek against the cold rock. She heard one more leap, one more thud against the cliff below her feet, and the wild barking filled the whole ravine like the early spring torrents. If I can just stand on this ledge long enough, she thought, the shepherd will come. Or Xenia? No, Xenia would not risk coming near that dog. But she could see me here; she would wait; she could—

"Cecilia!" It was Ken's voice. "Cecilia!"

Or was that only what she wanted to hear? The barking came in waves, lapped at her, tried to pull her backward into the surge of hideous sound. She pressed her body to the rock, closed her eyes, tried to close her ears, and hung on.

Strang, as he ran and jumped down the sloping side of the ravine, saw the dog leap and fail again. Each time, as it landed back on the harsh, dried bed of the stream, it yelped with pain and rage. He picked up a couple of stones, a fallen branch from a stunted tree. It would be useless; it felt rotten even to his touch, but it looked better than nothing.

He moved instinctively. He threw a stone hard, struck the dog's flank. The dog jerked around to face him. He ran at it, shouting, the branch raised to strike. The dog hesitated. For a long minute, they faced each other, the dog's growl beginning to rise with its mane. Then, as he watched it, ready to throw the second stone when the dog charged, he heard a yell behind him, an avalanche of curses. The shepherd came rushing down the bank of the ravine, and the dog stood still. With a whine, it turned and in a limping run tried to escape the blows that fell around its head. The shepherd had it by the neck, pulling it away from the ravine, cursing, pulling.

Two policemen, and Costas—with his revolver ready—and the shepherd's friend from the village came clattering down the bank toward Strang. He snapped the stick he was holding in his hand and threw it away.

"I hope," said Costas, white-lipped, "he beats its brains out."

Strang walked across the bed of the ravine. "Cecilia!" he called, gently. She didn't move.

"Cecilia—" She has frozen, he thought. She can't even turn around.

379

Her voice said, as if she were a great distance away, "Ken! I can't—I just can't—"

"Then don't move! Just stay there. We'll get you. Darling, just hold on!"

It was a short climb, only twelve or fifteen feet above the base of jagged rocks. While the others grouped underneath to break any slip, Strang pulled himself carefully up over the face of the cliff. He found an easier way than Cecilia had taken, but he hadn't a hundred and thirty pounds of dog at his heels. He reached the ledge where she stood, and moved sideways along it until he could reach out and grasp her wrist. "That feels good," he said.

Slowly, she turned her head to look at him. Slowly, she nodded. She even managed a smile.

"This way," he told her. "It is much easier. Your right foot a little toward me. Now your left. Face the cliff. Keep the flat of your other hand against the rock. That's the way. You *chassez* very prettily, Miss Hillard."

She laughed a little, and then caught her breath sharply as if even a laugh might topple her backward. But would he be talking so lightly if this were not easy? She listened to his quiet, confident voice, to his funny little remarks, and her confidence came slowly back. His grasp on her wrist was gentle and yet firm. Her thighs were no longer rigid, her feet were obeying her mind at last. "I'm all right," she said delightedly. "Ken— I'm all right!"

"I'll go down first, just beneath you." He let go of her hand slowly. "I'll guide your feet onto the ledges. Right?" Now he was below her. He said, "I'm going to grip your right ankle—steer it—see? There! The foot has got a good grip on that ledge. There's room for another. That's the way. Only two more efforts like that, and then— That's the way." At last, he could stand on a boulder at the base of the cliff, and reach up to catch her waist and lift her down beside him. He stood looking at her, his arms around her.

Now, all the joking was over, the light, easy voice had gone. He said, the strain showing naked in his eyes, "Oh, God! Cecilia—" The tight voice broke. "Oh, God!" he said again, and buried his mouth in her hair.

They were pulled apart by three quick shots. "The signal," Costas called to them from the opposite bank, his revolver still held up above his head. "I let everyone know she is safe."

Which was, Strang considered, a polite but practical way of jogging them all into motion out of the ravine. He picked Cecilia up and carried her across the rocks and the gravel to the other side.

"I left my coat," Cecilia said. "Up there, by those bushes. That's where I lay—"

He set her down on a boulder. "Don't walk. We'll carry you and get your feet attended to, at once."

"Poor feet!" Cecilia said. "They were all right until that last dash across the ravine." There had not been much time for picking and choosing her way then.

He knelt to look at the cuts and scrapes.

"Oh, it isn't too bad," Cecilia said cheerfully. "Blood always makes things look worse than they are." She laughed. "It's extraordinary how brave I am when you are around, Ken."

He kissed her, caught Costas's polite but impatient eye, and went to get her coat. Her shoes were over there, too. He paused for a moment, as he picked them up, and looked at the bushes that had sheltered her. From whom? He had a lot to learn.

He returned, and wrapped her inside the warm cashmere. It was cool now on the hillside. The sun had not much more than another hour to travel before it slid behind the far mountains. And from the east, the gray-white mist was thickening, lowering slowly. The two policemen and the man from Arachova had left. He saw them climbing quickly, far up the hill.

Costas noticed his surprise. He said, "There is a cave up there. They go to see it before the light is bad. The shepherd said the bandits—" He paused, looked at Cecilia, and said nothing more. "We carry her. Yes?"

Strang looked at him, looked back up the hill toward the hidden cave. His lips tightened, and he nodded.

By the pool, at the top of the wood, they halted. Strang bathed her feet gently in the cold, clear water. He moistened a handkerchief and wiped the dust and tearstains from her face. She had not spoken at all since they had climbed out of the ravine. But now she said, "They have gone? They really have gone?"

"The police caught one of them. A man. He was trying to get his motorcycle out of some bushes—"

"Anastas. That was Anastas. . . . But wasn't the woman with him?"

"No, darling."

"Alone? He was alone?"

"Yes." Strang smoothed her hair, and kissed the questions out of her eyes. "Forget them both," he told her. "Let's concentrate on us."

She nodded and tightened her grip on his arm. But as they left the clearing and started down through the woods, she looked back for a moment. "I never thought Xenia would give up the search so easily," she said slowly.

"Now—" Strang warned her, gently.

She laughed, and kissed him, and watched the worry leave his face. She settled her head against his shoulder. She had never known anyone could feel so happy as this.

Down near the road, the clusters of people had thickened. One search party had returned, several more children had arrived out of nowhere; there were two more cars strung along the edge of the meadow.

Elias hurried across the grass to meet them in a bustle of energy and excitement. The Colonel had been here; he had stayed until he heard the three shots; then he had left for Arachova, where he was setting up headquarters; the house had been traced; it was a matter now of moving quickly, of throwing a cordon around it and pulling it tight.

"What house?" Strang asked. He was amused, in a way, that their arrival on the meadow was causing so little excitement. The girl was safe; everyone was delighted, but there were other things to think about. The police officer was talking earnestly to some of the search party, no doubt about the reported appearance of two sheep-stealers, marauders, outlaws, what have you, on the hills. The peasants had grouped around a tall, powerful man with light-colored hair. Who was that? Levadi? He was so washed and brushed that Myrrha Kladas would scarcely have recognized him.

"The house near Delphi," Elias explained. But that seemed to mean little to Strang, so he added quickly, "The house where the Roilos father and son hid when they got back from Yugoslavia."

"Oh—that house!"

Elias glanced at him, and dropped the subject. "Your friends are waiting," he said, and pointed to a car. "There is a comfortable hotel at Delphi where you can sleep tonight."

"Delphi? No, not tonight, Elias. We are getting back to Athens."

Elias looked at Cecilia, then at Strang. "Athens is at least three hours away. Delphi is thirty minutes, perhaps less."

"I'm taking Miss Hillard nowhere near that house on the Delphi road."

Elias said quietly, "There will be three Americans and three Greeks to make sure she is safe. Besides—" he shrugged—"in a few hours, we all stop worrying. Perhaps, even now, he is caught."

Christophorou . . . "He is in that house?"

"We think so. A Renault car passed through the hill town of Arachova yesterday evening. It never reached Delphi. Early this morning another car was heard traveling through Arachova, but not through Delphi. Then the motorcycle—"

"Yes," said Strang, "it's all part of a pattern."

"Exactly," Elias said, most seriously.

"We are still going to Athens." But his voice was that of a completely exhausted man. Bad-tempered, pigheaded, he admitted to himself angrily; stuck with one idea, too tired even to make a simple decision. Now that they were almost at the cars, he could admit he had just about ten more paces left in his legs. A hot bath, food, sleep. "Is there a good doctor in Delphi?" he asked.

"Miss Hillard's feet will be all right tomorrow," Elias promised.

Like hell they will, thought Strang. But the sooner they were treated, the better.

He recognized one of the men standing beside a car, who was starting forward to meet them. "Hello!" he said to Henry Beaumont, and couldn't conceal his surprise. "What are you doing here? Come to excavate some ruins?"

"Just rallying around," Beaumont said cheerfully. "Someone had to drive for old Pringle. He insisted on getting out of bed and coming here." He looked at Cecilia and smiled. "I'm the man who almost came to dinner. Beaumont." He thought of several things to add, and then didn't. Instead, he turned back to his car and got the travel rug and his flask of brandy. "She's fine," he told Pringle. "Much better than we expected. Strang doesn't know it, but he's all in."

And so they drove, along the hill road to Delphi. "We'll telephone Effie from the hotel," Pringle said. "She can bring up some clothes for Cecilia tomorrow."

"And my camera," Cecilia said.

"What did I tell you?" Beaumont asked, with a wide grin. "Miss Hillard will be up, nursing you both, tomorrow."

"But this is the place to look through a viewfinder," Cecilia said. She pointed to the vast semicircle of ruins, of broken monuments and columns, rising tier by tier from the roadside up their steep, wide hill. In the dusk, the golden-white pillars were pale ghosts, picked out by the dying rays of the sun, dominating the darkening valley until the last moment of light. "Oh, Ken!" She grasped his hand more tightly.

Beaumont pointed to a dark high pinnacle of stone precipice, rising to one side of the remains of ancient Delphi. "They used to throw the blasphemers from that peak," he said amiably.

"That," said Pringle, "is what I like about classicists. Full of beneficence and uplift." He looked back at the precipice. "You know," he added softly, "the Greeks might have had something there." He was silent as the car curved around the road and climbed into a straight little village street of stone houses, wood balconies, and sloping roofs, perched along the edge of more cliffs. He turned to Strang, eased his leg with a quick grimace of pain, and asked, "You noticed his house, four miles back or so?"

Strang nodded. At least, he was thinking, I saw the army cars drawn up on the road. I saw radio antennae, I saw a truck, some soldiers. And up on the hillside, I saw a house with closed shutters. A pleasant vacation house, it had looked, abandoned until June came along.

"My bet is that he saw them coming up the road, and took to the hills," Pringle said gloomily. "But he won't get far. Zafiris has got troops lined out in a wide circle. They will draw closer and closer. It is just a matter of time." He noticed Strang's face. "Stop worrying, Ken. Christophorou has got other things on his mind now. The hunter hunted—" He liked that idea. "He doesn't even know that you found Cecilia. Nice going, Ken. Very nice indeed." Then his face changed. "We all weren't so lucky," he said softly.

He remained silent as they drove through the village. At its far end, where the road ran free of houses, the hotel stood by itself, alone with its magnificent view. As he got out of the car, Pringle, balancing his weight on a heavy walking stick to favor his injured leg, said in a low voice to Strang, "Ottway caught it."

"What?"

"Yes." Pringle glanced back at the car, but Beaumont was talking to Cecilia; she couldn't hear them. "In Cyprus. He was at a café table, watching. A tourist passed by, with a camera slung over his shoulder. Ottway recognized the case—there were even initials on it. C. O. As brazen as you like. Ottway reached for the man, and got a knife in the belly. Died last night." He paused. "They found an ingenious kind of grenade inside the camera. Enough to blow up ten resistance heroes making patriotic speeches."

Strang and Pringle looked at each other. "Yes," Pringle said grimly, once again. "Exactly." He limped away, slowly, painfully, toward the hotel doorway.

Strang lifted Cecilia out of the car. Beaumont was saying, "Well, well! For once, I don't have to worry about reservations. It looks as if we were expected." Around them, five sets of bright smiles had materialized, five pairs of sympathetic eyes and helpful hands. And at the corner of the building, there were two spruce and observant Greeks waiting along with old friend Costas. They made a most comforting trio, against a background of lonely, darkening hillside and far, black mountains.

Strang said, listening to the faint gentle sounds coming from the hillside, "What's that? Bells?"

"Sheep bells," Cecilia told him. "I'm an authority on them now." And she laughed. "Oh, Ken, it's good to get back to our own life again!"

He held one of her hands against his lips for a moment. "Tomorrow—" he began, and then stopped, and then thought: two hours ago, there was no tomorrow; two hours ago, I came blankly up against the minute where I was drawing breath; and everything beyond that was covered in thicker, colder mist than Mount Parnassos.

"Tomorrow will be a heavenly day," Cecilia said, looking at the last glowing embers of a dying sunset. The bells had drifted away. The falling hills, the valley far below, lay silent and still.

Strang nodded. But some of us were not so lucky; and he thought of George Ottway.

THIRTY

Next morning Strang awoke from the best night of sleep he had had in a week. He went out on the little balcony of his room to say good morning to the valley. One sight of the view, and he stood paralyzed. I suppose I saw scenery yesterday, he thought, but then I wasn't particularly receptive: every prospect pleased and only man was vile. Now—he looked over the folding, rising, falling hills above the deep valley that led to the sea— now, I'm even juggling around quotations again. It had been a long time since a line of verse had bobbed up in his head. A good idea, after all, he decided, to come here and sleep and awaken in such peace.

On a distant pasture a shepherd was surrounded by a gentle sway of small bells; on the rough road, leading to nowhere namable, ambling as leisurely down the hillside as that donkey with its side-saddle load, was a long-skirted woman climbing back toward the village; on the stone terrace beneath this small row of balconies, two men were sitting in the sunlight, talking quietly. Strang leaned over to make sure who they were: Costas and a friend. He relaxed as quickly as he had tensed up. Every prospect pleased, and not even man was vile.

The windows on the next balcony had all their blinds tightly drawn down. Cecilia was asleep. She was well guarded. She was safe. He took a deep breath of thankfulness, and went back to dress and order breakfast.

He slipped out of his room before the food arrived to check on the corridor of this small, low wing of the hotel. He found the second of Costas's friends sitting on a chair beside Cecilia's door, talking in a low murmur with one of the pink-cheeked, dark-eyed maids.

"How is—" he began, and then hesitated to use Cecilia's name. He had been too tired to remember, last night, what name had been used for Cecilia's safety. Smith? Brown? Something like that . . .

The maid opened Cecilia's door cautiously, glanced in, gestured to him to see for himself. He entered quietly, stood for a moment in the darkened room. Yes, she was asleep. She was well guarded. She was safe. He could give the maid as broad a smile as she gave him, when he closed the door slowly behind him. *"Poly kala!"* he said softly to the man and the woman. Fine, *va bene*, okay. Indeed it was.

Indeed, everything was. Even his appetite had come back. He ordered a second helping of scrambled eggs and two more pots of coffee. And now the sun was high enough to dull the cool edge of the mountain air; he sat over several last cups of coffee on the little balcony outside his room, enjoying the pleasures of waiting without worry. He was high on a sloping hillside with one of nature's most startling views unrolled, mile on mile, before him: blue-shadowed mountains beyond red-flowered fields; a narrow wooded valley plunging deep between steep-sided hills toward a distant glimpse of sea. That, he remembered as he looked long at the far tongue of blue water, was how the ancient Greeks used to come to Delphi. They landed from ships, in the bay down there, and walked the miles up the valley toward Delphi, perched above them on its hillside. When Cecilia and I start work here, he thought, I'll get down to that valley and catch the first glimpse of white columns as they rise, high above the olive groves, against their background of rock.

We're in business again, he told himself. It was a good, a good and wonderful feeling. Before yesterday, before those last four or five days, had he ever really known how lucky he was? He lit another cigarette, poured the last few drops of coffee into his cup, and surrendered his body to the gentle sun, his mind to the spell woven by shapes and colors. This was an hour of complete and absolute peace.

It was almost half past ten—angrily, he glanced at his watch—when the drone of a truck, of several cars shattered the stillness around him. They were coming from the village, on the road that lay behind the hotel. He rose, waiting at the edge of the balcony, looking along the hillside until they'd come into sight, praying that they would continue on their way to vanish behind the far arm of the hill. It was a truck filled with soldiers, only one car following it. The others must have stopped at the hotel. And now—barely three hundred yards away—the truck and the car stopped, too. The soldiers spilled out, spreading into a long thin line, fencing in the hillside above them.

He moved quickly through his room into the corridor. The man outside Cecilia's room looked up in surprise at his sudden appearance. Strang opened her door. She was still asleep. Everything was all right. He nodded to the man as he closed the door and went to the next room. This was

Pringle's. Strang glanced at his watch again. Pringle must be awake by this time. He knocked.

"Who is it?" Pringle asked sharply.

"Strang."

The door was opened by Elias.

"Good morning," Strang said cheerfully, but his heart sank. Whenever he saw Elias, there was always some blow to be expected. That was the way things seemed to work out, with Elias. "You are looking much better," he told Pringle, who was sitting on his bed, his wounded leg stretched out in front of him.

"You look good yourself," Pringle said. "How's Cecilia?"

"Asleep."

"That's fine."

"Yes." Strang looked at him pointedly. "And what's the news?"

Pringle rubbed his knee thoughtfully. "Mixed," he admitted frankly. Elias had walked over to the window and was looking at the balcony outside.

"Christophorou is on the loose?"

"I am assured," said Pringle, a thin smile playing around his lips, "that he is just about to be caught."

"That's comforting." Strang's voice was tight. "Have you any cigarettes left, Bob?"

"You take the news better than I did," Pringle said. "Why doesn't Christophorou admit that he has lost completely and blow his brains out? That would save everyone a lot of bother."

Strang raised an eyebrow, and lit one of Pringle's cigarettes. Elias, tired and troubled, looked around and nodded his agreement to that.

"All right, all right," Pringle said—he was, if anything, a gentle-minded man—"but the bastard tried to have me killed. This damned leg keeps reminding me of that. And of Ottway—"

"And of Cecilia," Strang completed for him grimly. "And of Steve. And of Myrrha Kladas. And of Katherini Roilos." Christophorou had chalked up quite a personal account. The total ran high. Much too high. "So," Strang asked Elias, "he is running free, somewhere out on that hillside?"

Elias was so exhausted, so weary, that his English had almost deserted him. "He is running hard. Very hard. Last night—" He looked at Pringle. Perhaps the situation had started to spin wild and there was no longer any pattern for Elias's mind to put together. He raised his hands in complete frustration. "You tell him," he said in Greek. So Pringle told the story.

Yesterday evening, when Zafiris had reached the house on the road to Delphi, Christophorou had already left. There were signs of a hasty departure. A fire was still burning in one room; food was on the table. ("You break my heart," Strang said.)

From behind the house there were several trails leading to the hill. These had been followed. The shepherd Levadi had taken Elias and a search party to a climber's hut, high on one of those trails. Again, Christophorou had been on his guard; he had slipped into the darkness as the squad of men approached. Later that night, the dogs from the meadows to the east had given tongue. Levadi had said that the dogs would keep Christophorou to the western side of the meadows. He wouldn't risk crossing them when the shepherds and their dogs were on the alert. ("That," said Strang, "isn't hard to believe.")

By dawn, there were several search parties circling around the area. Christophorou had actually been seen once. More important, he had seen them. He could guess, now, the extent of the search. ("And give himself up?" asked Strang bitterly. "That's a sweet hope. Nihilists expend everything and everyone except themselves. They are the indispensable men, without whom the world might try to live almost happily. Besides, think of their superior brains! They can outwit all of us, can't they?")

Pringle looked at him. "You're a deceptive kind of guy, Ken. I believe you hate him even more than I do."

"I am not competing," Strang said harshly. "All I want is some peace to live my own life again." He remembered the troops deploying along the road behind the hotel. He said to Elias, "So he is somewhere near Delphi?"

"Yes. He is waiting."

"For what? For darkness?"

"For Colonel Zafiris to promise him a safe-conduct out of Greece."

"That's rich, isn't it?" Pringle asked. "And in exchange, Christophorou will have Miss Hillard released and returned safely to Colonel Zafiris. Isn't that magnanimous?"

Elias said in a surge of anger, "He lies. And he knows that he lies. He could not set Miss Hillard free once she was delivered to the outlaws. They take, they do not give back. They obey no God, no laws, no man. He knows that! He lies!" It was the first violent outburst from Elias that Strang had seen. Then the Greek took tight control over his emotions once more. "He sent the message two hours ago. He gave it to a boy who was herding goats on a hillside near the stadium of Delphi."

"The ancient stadium?" Strang was incredulous. "Just above the Greek theater?"

"As near as that," Pringle said. "I think he rather enjoyed that touch. He must have looked down over the theater, and the temple below it, and all the sanctuaries below that, right down the Sacred Way to the road, where he could see the patrol passing along. At least, he told the boy to take his note down to the soldiers."

Elias said, "So now he waits. Hidden. There are many hiding places above Delphi. He waits until noon for our answer." His lips tightened at the impudence of such an ultimatum.

"And how do we give that?" Strang asked.

"We have brought in more troops. We have encircled this whole area. We shall go in after him."

Strang almost smiled. That was certainly one good answer. "I meant —what did Christophorou suggest?" After all, Christophorou thought he was calling the tune.

But Elias had, obviously, no more interest in any of Christophorou's suggestions than he would have in considering the rights of a smallpox virus to live. So Pringle said, "He expects to see Colonel Zafiris climbing up the Sacred Way to the Temple of Apollo. Zafiris is to stand by the columns for five minutes—"

"In prayer and meditation?" Strang suggested.

"—and then return to the road. This will be the sign to Christophorou that his proposal has been accepted. Zafiris will also, at noon, call off all search parties, send the troops away. By sunset, Cecilia will come walking, free and unharmed, down from the hillside above Delphi into the theater." He looked at Strang, and laughed. "Imagine him expecting us to swallow such nonsense!"

Strang wondered if they might not have been forced to swallow it if Cecilia had not escaped. If they had been desperate, they would have clutched at every faint hope, persuaded themselves that probabilities were possible, that gambles were necessary risks. Besides, the time element was clever: Christophorou had only asked from noon until sunset to make good his escape. If he had stretched his request until tomorrow, set Cecilia's reappearance at dawn or at noon, questions might have arisen in the minds of even the most wishful thinkers. "Six hours—where could he get out of Greece in six hours?" Strang asked. "He must walk, mustn't he? He hasn't any car, I hope."

Elias looked at him quickly. "We found both cars at his house. There is only one way he can leave. By the sea. To the south is the Gulf of Corinth, a walk of two hours. Less than that for a man who is running hard."

"So that's why the troops are strung along this road?"

Elias nodded.

"I suppose he will wait to see if Colonel Zafiris makes his little pilgrimage?"

"I doubt," Pringle said, "if Christophorou would miss that."

"I wonder if he has a rifle and a telescopic sight?"

Elias said, "When seen, he had no rifle. But he will have a revolver."

"He won't be close enough to use that." Colonel Zafiris wasn't to be shot at then. Just humiliated. A Greek would prefer a bullet. "If he can see Zafiris clearly on the east side of the Temple of Apollo, he must be lying somewhere up on the twin precipices to that side of the amphitheater. How does he get down from there?"

"By the gorge between them. It leads to the road. There will be many tourists there between twelve and one o'clock."

Pringle said, "The buses from Athens will be parked all along that road. Once he is across it, he just keeps climbing down through thick groves of olive trees into the valley below. No, no! You'll have to do more than station men at the bottom of the gorge, Elias. You'll have to go up and gouge him out."

"Yes," Elias said gloomily. He was thinking of the tourists, of Saturday at Delphi. "There will be shooting." And Delphi was a holy place. Even if pagans had built it and worshiped there three thousand years ago, it was a place where man had brought his fears, his worries, and had gone away comforted. "Shooting . . . In Delphi," he said slowly, heavily.

There was no joy, anywhere, in this undertaking, thought Strang. "Where is the shepherd Levadi?" he asked. "He could climb that gorge, get close to Christophorou without any shooting—"

Elias looked most unhappy. "He disappeared. This morning—just at dawn. We cannot find him."

Pringle said, "I don't blame him. One sniff of his own mountain air, and I bet he is high-tailing it up to the Levadi pastures to join his friends among their sheep."

"It's too early in the year for shepherds to be there," Elias said. "It is a summer pasture."

Strang said, "Find the best peak near here from which he can watch the dawn rise, and you'll find him."

"We haven't time—" began Elias, the literal man.

"We haven't much time for anything." Strang looked at his watch, and rose. "Does Levadi know that Miss Hillard is in this hotel?"

"No. We have told everyone she returned to Athens, last night. We also say that she was one of a small party of mountain climbers; and we have explained the troops on the hillsides by saying they are on spring maneuvers. We thought it safer for all of you if people did not talk or wonder."

"Would Levadi join with Christophorou again? He once followed Odysseus, even when his mind rebelled against it." Strang thought of the photographs he had seen in Zafiris's office three days ago.

"His *mind?*" Pringle asked, startled. "Do you know he wouldn't believe there had been an amnesty after the civil war, until he actually stood and listened to the peasants, yesterday, by the roadside? Until that moment, he still believed he had to live hidden away in Sparta, not even using his own name, to stay free and alive."

"Then he had much to think about as he sat and watched the dawn rise over Parnassos," Strang said. "A pity, though, he couldn't tell Christophorou that Cecilia had been carried safely down to the road, yesterday. That might have shaken Christophorou a little. More than a little. He might even have made a rash move." For the great problem with Christophorou was the man's confidence, the brain that was so sure of everything, working calmly, contemptuously. Danger? Christophorou never objected to that. He enjoyed it. But to be made ridiculous, with his message to Zafiris? "He can bear hate, but not ridicule," Strang said slowly.

"Let them hate, provided that they fear," Pringle said. "Yes, that's his motto. He would make a very efficient tyrant."

Strang stood, hesitating, making his decision. He said, "Why don't we tell him that Cecilia is free? That he hasn't any bargaining power? That he has trapped himself by his own mind?"

"And how do we tell him?" Pringle asked, unimpressed.

Strang said to Elias, "You are sure that no one in the village knows that Miss Hillard is here?"

"No one. And even here, the servants do not know who she is. We have tried to keep everything—"

"Good. Bob, will you sit out on your balcony for the next hour or two? Have you a gun?"

"A most undiplomatic question." Pringle's voice was light, but his eyes were uneasy.

"Elias, tell Costas and his friend to keep on the alert. Also the man guarding Miss Hillard's door. I have a plan. But first, I've got to be sure that Miss Hillard is safe here."

"Look, Ken—" Pringle began, as Elias nodded and left the room.

Thank God, thought Strang, that Elias does not need long explanations. But Elias understood all about *philotimo.* "Have you a gun?" he asked again.

392

"Yes."

"Use it, if necessary. And don't let your eyes leave the hillside. Right?"

"Ken—"

"Don't worry. I'm no hero. Didn't you hear me make sure Christophorou hadn't a rifle?"

"What's the idea?" Pringle asked sharply.

"I climb up—not Zafiris—to the Temple of Apollo. I look happy, unconcerned, all the time in the world on my hands. Would I look like that, would I even be there if Cecilia had not been found? He will get the message."

Pringle stared at him. He nodded. "And then what?" he asked worriedly.

Strang considered for a moment. He grinned. "I'll ask the Oracle," he said. "She spoke from the Temple of Apollo, didn't she?"

Elias opened the door. "We leave now?"

"That's right." Strang looked back at Pringle. "Get out on that balcony, for God's sake."

Pringle pulled himself from his bed. "Damn this leg," he said. "I'd like to be there." He opened a drawer and found his revolver. He checked it. "When will you be back?"

"When you see me. If Cecilia wakens—"

"Yes. I'll give her your love. I'll also tell her to stay inside her room. No deep-breathing exercises on the balcony."

"Look after her, Bob," said Strang, and left the room. It was eleven twenty by his watch. "Just a moment," he told Elias. There were two men, now, outside Cecilia's door. The chair was gone. He nodded to them, opened the door, and stood in the darkly shaded room. Cecilia had scarcely changed her position since he had last looked in. Her head lay sideways on the pillow, one hand upstretched, the other resting on her shoulder. He stood for a moment, looking at her. Then he went out, pulling the door gently closed.

Ancient Delphi was only a mile, perhaps less, away from the village. "Is that car of ours still outside?" he asked Elias.

Zafiris looked at Strang, then at his watch. They were sitting in Zafiris's car, drawn up under the shade of an enormous plane tree on the road below ancient Delphi. Strang felt the calm appraisal, but he kept his own eyes fixed on the amphitheater of ancient ruins which rose, layer on layer, up the side of the hill above them. Very near to them on this road was the stream rushing down the gorge between the precipices on

393

the eastern side of the amphitheater. Ahead of them was the entrance, the first flight of stairs in the Sacred Way, climbing between the sanctuaries, the half-fallen columns of small temples, the pedestals of statues, the monuments, until high up, in the center of the vast arena, it reached the ruined Temple of Apollo. Above the temple, at the topmost rim of the amphitheater, was the theater. Beyond that, stretched along the sky line, hidden by trees and bushes, was the ancient stadium where the athletes had competed. And then—hills, the slopes of Parnassos, wild country, savage and beautiful. As if, Strang thought, the men who had built Delphi had felt that civilization was only one side of a hill carved out from the wilderness.

Zafiris said, his eyes scanning the curve of rocks and bushes around the top rim of the amphitheater, "He knows how to take cover. There are small caves up there on the precipices, clefts— You have noticed how many colors there are in the stone around here?"

"Could he escape to the north?"

"No. Nor to the west, nor to the east. We have men all around there. And two helicopters. The search is thorough, and therefore slow." His heavy face, its muscles sagging with exhaustion, its lines deepened with worry, turned to the road where the first tourist bus had drawn up. "Added complications," he said. "This is not the place I would choose to hunt any man."

"That is why he chose it, perhaps."

The Colonel nodded. He spoke, almost to himself. "He lies up there, quite still, watching, calculating. He expects we will agree to his terms. But if I do not walk up there, he will simply wait until darkness falls. He will be rested, by then. He needs that rest. He is no longer a young man; last night was a greater effort than he had expected. He has lived in cities, in comfort, for fifteen years. At this moment, he is exhausted. He has overestimated his physical powers. All men do. Men's legs give out before their brains. Yes, he will wait for darkness, I think."

"And then the odds would be mostly in his favor," Strang said. Christophorou would be rested; he would be confident, laughing at us all, thinking he had turned us into something inhuman, something as calculating as he was, something willing to abandon Cecilia in order to get him.

"Yes, darkness would favor him. I would need a long, closely drawn line of men, each of them sure of his way on a mountainside at night. There are not enough old guerrilla fighters in the villages to form that line. The troops are young, good men, doing their military service; but this terrain is strange to them, and it is exceptionally difficult country indeed."

"Civilians, like me," Strang agreed tactfully. "I couldn't guarantee to see anything on a dark mountainside until the split second that might be too late. That is all Christophorou would need: that moment of surprise, of indecision. He knows those hills, that mountainside. All he needs is some rest, and his confidence."

"Yes."

"Then let me jolt that confidence. It may be the only grenade we can throw at him."

"A grenade? It may be an outsize bomb." The Colonel's eyes glanced at his watch again. "We have little time to make a good decision."

Strang said, "You have decided. Why don't you give me the go-ahead signal?"

"Your plan worries me."

"What else can we do? Close off Delphi, send away all the tourists, make a frontal attack right up those cliffs, flush him out of cover? I still think we can goad him into moving. He has already wasted enough time. And for what? For a last laugh at us all." Christophorou was going into exile, picking up the remnants of his organization, planning anew, drawing confidence from that last laugh. It would keep him going for years. "Some men thrive on that kind of victory."

The Colonel nodded.

"So that is why I'm walking up to the Temple of Apollo," Strang said quietly. "I am going to wipe that last laugh right off his mouth."

Zafiris said slowly, "You have thought a lot about this man."

"Too much." Strang opened the door of the car. "We have more to do, all of us, than keep worrying about him," he added as he stepped onto the road.

"You are determined?"

"Is there a quicker way to let him know that he has failed?"

"And that we laugh at him?" The Colonel considered for a moment. "Ridicule is a good weapon," he admitted. "But then what?"

"We'll let nature take its course." Strang closed the car door.

That, thought the Colonel, is what worries me. He looked at Strang. "Good luck," he said.

He watched the American walk toward the open approach to Delphi. No gates. No railings to shut off the excavations from this road. Four more buses were pulling in, under the shade of the trees. The Saturday crowds were beginning to flow in straggling groups toward the entrance. Problems, plenty of problems. Colonel Zafiris turned abruptly from thinking about them to taking action. He got out of the car, and gave Yorghis quick instructions. All bus drivers were to make a careful check of their returning passengers; all agents, except Elias, to watch every group of visitors coming back from their tour of Delphi; one squad of men to be stationed at the foot of the gorge, another on the opposite side of the amphitheater near the path to the museum; a platoon must be spread, even thinly, along the road itself; Elias and two men were to follow the American. Everything must be done quietly, circumspectly; no obvious fuss or trouble. It would not do to alarm the visitors; or—he looked up at the cliffs and then let his eyes sweep round the rim of hillside, still and silent in the warm noonday sun—the wily Odysseus. He could almost smile at the ill-chosen name, except that a well-founded depression accompanied his amusement: every Christophorou was a very great hero to himself. His last gesture would be a self-assertion. It would be as destructive and as meaningless as he had made his life, the ultimate victory of the Absurd.

Zafiris's eyes were now scanning the whole amphitheater of mounting terraces and ruined walls, of marble steps and broken monuments. A few people were wandering around by themselves or in pairs: students and scholars. The other tourists kept near their own groups. There was one collection of them from the first busload, high up, near the theater. They had begun at the very top, with the stadium, and were working their way down. The later busloads were still clustering around the treasure houses on the lower terraces. He saw Strang, climbing up the oblique slope of the Sacred Way; he was out in the open clearly visible, a man strolling between ruined foundations, stopping to look at a fallen pillar here, a broken pedestal there. The American halted, and turned to look back at the view. He seemed to be a man with nothing on his mind except the beauty of Delphi. At this moment, he had addressed some remark to the guide who usually stood up on that slope, waiting to conduct any visitor to the temple above it. Then the American turned away with an easy wave of his hand, a polite refusal perhaps, and climbed on.

Zafiris said to Yorghis, "You're in command here."

"Sir?"

"You know what to do." The Colonel crossed the road, choosing a small path that led toward the gorge at the side of the amphitheater.

"Alone, sir?" Yorghis said, running after him.

"You stay here. Take charge." He began walking briskly. He would not go up into the gorge; he would only use this path to get quietly into the amphitheater. He would make his way cautiously between the eastern excavations, circling up around their perimeter. This was neither a natural nor an easy approach, but it let him climb possibly unnoticed until he chose to be noticed. We'll give Christophorou a choice, he thought with some pleasure: a little division of attention, a conflict in impulses, might turn the last gesture into nothing.

Strang felt the warm sun beat into his spine as he walked slowly up the last incline and reached the base of the temple's eastern steps. The Temple of Apollo, he thought, looking up at the massive pillars on their high platform of stone, and he forgot the eyes that might be watching him from the towering cliffs or from the hilltop. He climbed up to the level of the temple floor. What a site, he thought, what a perfect site for a temple to the god of the Sun. He felt that old, wonderful quickening of astonishment and delight. There was amazement, too: so much had been destroyed, by pillagers and plunderers, by malice and greed, by violent earth tremors which had torn open wide fissures; and yet, the vision had survived. The greatness of man's imagination still held fast.

Quite automatically, he began to study the proportions of the temple. And then he came back to the eastern portico. He leaned against a column at least six feet in diameter; a small insignificant man, he thought, as he looked at the view, down over the Sacred Way. Yet, small and insignificant men had conceived and built this place. He began to reconstruct the magnificent scope of their ideas, the fantastic total of beauty and strength, all carefully planned within this half-circle of hills and precipices which was flung around Delphi like a protecting arm. Only to the south, to the sun, the cupped arm lay open. There, the ground sloped steeply down, down past all the man-made terraces where the man-made monuments and treasure houses had stood, down beyond the little road, into the deep, narrow valley. And across the valley was a noble rise of hills to lead man's eyes back to the sky, to the sun. The builders of Delphi had put their heart into their work, from the choosing of the site to the last careful fluting of a column. What lies in man's creative work comes from his heart, he thought. The mind, by itself, is not enough.

"Hello, up there!" a voice called. "And what's your verdict?" It was Beaumont, standing down on the path and looking up at him with an expression of real pleasure to see another enthusiast sharing his addiction.

Strang could only shake his head in wonder. Praise would even be an impertinence.

"Now, that's the right response," Beaumont said. "But don't you see the busloads arriving? Time for us to start thinking of lunch. How's Miss Hillard?"

"Fine. Just fine." Wait until Cecilia sees all this, he thought. I want to see her face when she does. That would be just about perfect. The girl, the

397

place, long peaceful days . . . He glanced up at the hillsides around him. "Where have you been all morning?"

"I always like to spend some time up in the theater."

"Reading Euripides?" Strang asked, noticing the book in Beaumont's hand.

"Oh, well—" Beaumont was a little embarrassed. And then they both laughed.

"I've discovered why the Greek dramatists had to be good," Strang said. He glanced up the hillside again. Yes, the movement that had caught his eye was not imagined. There was someone up there, by the topmost rim of the theater. But it was not Christophorou. Strange way to move, though: from cover to cover, among the bushes and wild shrubs, carefully, quickly.

"Why?" asked Beaumont.

"Competition. Your audience sat up there and looked over this view. You would have to be good."

"Better than good," Beaumont agreed, looking back at the theater. "He's still up there!" he said in surprise. "He has been giving a good imitation of a mountain goat, all this morning. And he is as wary, too."

"Who is he?"

"That shepherd from Sparta."

"Levadi?" The figure had vanished behind some boulders. Yes, it could be Levadi. He looked as if he were making his way across the excavations toward the eastern boundary of cliffs.

"I saw him up on the cliff, two hours ago. When I wandered up into the stadium, he was disappearing behind some trees. What is he looking for—missing sheep?"

"Look—" Strang said very briskly—"why don't you head down toward the road, Hank? And tell Elias that Levadi is here. I'll join you in five minutes or so."

"Something wrong?"

"No. Just unexpected. Tell Elias that Levadi seems to be stalking something."

"What?" Beaumont was worried.

Strang stared at the base of the cliffs. He could see no more movement. "Go on, Hank!" he urged. "Get down there, fast. But don't look as if you were hurrying." He gave a short wave of his hand and raised his voice. "See you over a long, cool glass of beer!" He turned away from the perplexed and troubled Beaumont.

"All right, all right," he heard Beaumont's voice say testily, and Beaumont's feet went clattering down the Sacred Way.

398

This, Strang told himself, was scarcely the moment to remember that the path got its name from the sacrificial offerings that were led up here to be given to the gods. He did start moving (slowly it was true, but still, moving) away from this exposed position at the east end of the temple, and put a six-foot diameter of cylindrical stone between himself and the cliffs. He shook his head in wry amazement; so we all thought Christophorou was hiding somewhere high on the cliffs because, obviously, the best hiding places were up there. But Christophorou might have decided that the obvious was the less safe. Call it impudence or daring—and Christophorou had plenty of both—but it was just possible he had come down into the amphitheater of Delphi itself. In that case, he must have hidden—judging by Levadi's direction—among the excavations over at the eastern side. But why?

Strang moved again, between a row of columns, letting Christophorou know he was still there. Why? he kept wondering. And then he found the answer: a large group of tourists, about thirty of them, were descending from their visit to the theater. There, thought Strang, is the best escape route of all: thirty people, mostly strangers to each other, wandering slowly, sometimes straggling, sometimes thickening into a concentrated group around the young woman who was their guide and culture-dispenser. He watched them as they listened to her (tourists were a most respectful audience), waiting patiently as she switched from an explanation in English to one in French, to one in German. At last, they flowed downhill again, the usual lingerers lagging, the usual independents straying farther off the path.

That was the escape route, he suddenly knew: join the tourists, wander with them, be packed into a bus, exclaim that you were sorry you had become separated from your own group (don't we all?) and that it didn't matter for the five-minute drive into the village of Delphi for lunch. And from the village of Delphi, you climbed down into the valley far below and headed for the sea. You abandoned all the slopes of Mount Parnassos, all the obvious hiding places to the north. You let the search parties climb and clamber. You found a fishing boat, perhaps even a decrepit foreign freighter at one of the little ports along the Gulf of Corinth. All you needed was money and confidence.

Confidence? Had Christophorou still so much of that? Strang moved quickly back to the temple's entrance, his eyes now fixed on the eastern slopes of the amphitheater. The group of tourists was going downhill. A man hurried to catch up with them. He saw Strang watching him. He halted. Then he began walking again, less hurriedly, more naturally. The delay had been slight, and yet it was disastrous. For the gap between him and the last stragglers had grown too big to be closed without drawing attention. He was out in the open, too, away from the cover of the ruins of the Roman cisterns. Now he was clearly seen, a solitary figure, Alexander Christophorou. He looked toward the temple once more. He looked at the receding group of tourists. Run after them? Scramble over fifty, sixty feet of littered marble and limestone?

No, thought Strang; that, he will not do. Retreat back into his hiding place? Not that, either. I have seen him and he knows I have seen him. He will come here. Yes, his anger is so great that it has become a rage that destroys even himself. And me. I asked for it, thought Strang, and I'll get it.

Outwardly, he didn't move. There was a moment of dismay, of frankly admitted fear. But he stood his ground, watching Christophorou advancing steadily toward him. And Christophorou was watching him. No, thought Strang, I'll not give you the pleasure of seeing me dodge and run, you son of a bitch. Eighty yards, seventy yards, aren't you close enough yet?

"Odysseus!" The sudden command rang clear across the hillside. Christophorou halted abruptly, swung around to face it. Colonel Zafiris was walking up toward him.

The revolver in Christophorou's hand was no longer hidden. He looked back at Strang, looked again at Zafiris. And then the huge bulk of Levadi rose from behind a broken wall on the terrace above and leaped down on him.

It was quick and silent.

Strang saw Zafiris reach the body and look down. He did not kneel. He stood, looking down. Levadi had drawn slowly back along the side of the terrace from which he had jumped. From other levels of the amphitheater, Elias and two men were converging quickly on the little group. The few tourists who had halted to look vaguely around were being called together by their clock-conscious guide. Far down the Sacred Way, Beaumont had stopped to turn and stare.

Strang left the temple, and made his way slowly toward Zafiris. He stopped, first, beside Levadi. The shepherd's face was white and set. An unpleasant gash drew a scarlet line at one side of his brow; the blood dripped over his eyelid and he kept wiping it away, angrily, with the back of his huge clenched hand.

"Here!" Strang said quietly, and gave him his remaining clean handkerchief.

Zafiris came forward now. "Neck broken," he said briefly, and gave a passing glance at Levadi's good left hand. He looked at Strang. His dark eyes studied the American for a long moment. "I am glad there was no shooting in this sanctuary." He gave an unexpected smile of relief, one that almost chased the exhaustion out of his face. "Now, we can sleep. The nightmare is over." He clapped Strang briskly on the arm, and turned to walk down to the road.

Strang watched him go. Then he said to Levadi, "Why don't you?" He pointed to the hills behind Delphi.

Levadi stared at him.

"Who will stop you?"

Levadi looked at Elias. He looked at the hills. He looked at Christophorou, lying so still against a bed of broken marble. "He will kill no more," Levadi said. He looked back at the hills.

Strang turned to walk a little distance away. Levadi might follow his own impulse more easily if no one was watching him.

Elias came over to join Strang. "Who told him to leave?" he asked, looking up the hillside after Levadi.

"He's already spent fifteen years in exile," Strang reminded him.

Elias considered. "Too much," he said, "too much for the death of a traitor." He looked away from the hillside. Mentally, he filled up his report. "Accidents can happen. People should not walk across this ground without watching where they put their feet. It is dangerous, here, not to pay attention."

"It certainly was."

Elias put out his hand and shook hands warmly, much to Strang's surprise. "Time for you to go. I wait here. Soon, everyone leaves for lunch. We shall get the body down to the road then. No trouble, no notice, no fuss." Elias added softly, "How he would have hated that!"

Strang walked down the Sacred Way. Beaumont was waiting for him. "You had me worried, there," he told Strang.

"I had myself worried," Strang admitted.

"He is dead?"

"Yes." Nemesis played by a shepherd, Strang thought.

Beaumont took a deep breath of obvious relief. "Not that I know very much about the man. Still, from the little I did learn—well, I think we can do without his kind. One of our poor world's terrible simplifiers, wasn't he?"

Strang nodded. "The most deadly of all barbarians," he said.

Beaumont looked at him curiously. "What happened, up there? It was all so quick—" And I hope it wasn't what I thought it was. . . .

"Later, Hank. Later. Let's walk back to the hotel. Do you mind?"

"No," Beaumont said politely, all visions of cool beer and an early luncheon vanishing. "The village will be crowded with tourists at this hour, though."

"People aren't such a bad prescription, at this moment," Strang said. Just ordinary, everyday people, in search of a little culture, some food, and sheepskin rugs.

Pringle, limping heavily, met them outside the door of the hotel. "Zafiris sent word," he told them. "My God, it's all over. It's all over!" He put his hand on Strang's shoulder, his grip heavy with excitement. "What happened?" he wanted to know. "What happened, Ken?"

Everyone, thought Strang wearily, wants to know what happened. The nightmare was ended. That was all he could feel now: release. Release and thankfulness. But he couldn't talk about it. "Later, Bob," he said. "Later." He looked around him. The truck and the soldiers had gone. The hillside road, stretching toward the mountains in the west, was empty. Here, by the door, cars were parked, a bus; some drivers stood around, smoking and talking. As in the village, everything was delightfully normal.

"Well," Pringle said cheerfully, hiding his disappointment, "it seems as if I don't have to do any more sitting out on a balcony with a gun in my pocket." He could laugh now, at that memory.

"Is Cecilia still asleep?"

"No. She awoke just after you had left."

Strang turned quickly to enter the hotel.

"She's fine, Ken," Pringle assured him. "Effie arrived with some clothes for her. I have a spare shirt for you. Fifteen neck?"

Strang gave his first smile. "Thanks, Bob." We are certainly back to normal, he thought, as they entered the lobby.

"Steve Kladas telephoned you, by the way."

"How is he?"

"Pretty good. Quite his usual self again, I'd say."

"I doubt that," Strang said with a widening grin. "A long-distance call? Or did he reverse the charges?"

"He's anxious to see you as soon as you get back to Athens. He wants you to persuade Lee Preston to run a series on Frankish castles. Kladas thinks he could do a good job on that. Not a bad idea, actually."

"Not bad at all," Strang agreed. He even laughed.

"We thought we'd start back to Athens around four. How does that suit?"

"Fine—if I can find that car I'm supposed to have hired."

"Zafiris sent it back. Also, Cecilia's handbag. One of the search parties found it, up near that pool at the top of the woods. It had been kicked behind a boulder. They probably hadn't much time to hide it carefully."

"What about the woman?"

"Xenia?" Pringle shrugged his shoulders. "No trace," he said.

Beaumont took Pringle's arm to help him down a flight of steps. "You make a fine Byronic figure," he told him. "Let's limp toward the bar, shall we? See you later, Ken!" When Strang left them, he said very quietly, "There was a moment, back in Delphi, when I didn't expect to be able to say that to him again."

Strang knocked on the door of Cecilia's room. No guards, any more. The bright-cheeked maid glanced into the corridor, nodded approvingly, and went back to her work.

"Come in," Effie Pringle called.

Cecilia was sitting in a chair drawn up near the French window, her feet—in soft silk slippers—propped up on a stool, her camera beside her unopened, her face turned tensely to the door. As she saw him, life came back into her eyes.

"She has been worrying her head off," Effie told Strang. "But there's no more need for that, is there?" She looked at him and then at Cecilia. "Of course not," she answered herself. There were only the usual little worries left, and they were almost a pleasure, by contrast. "Is Bob still hobbling around? He isn't supposed to walk much on that leg. I'd better—" She picked up her handbag. They hadn't heard one word she had said. So she left. She could not help thinking of Caroline Ottway, who no longer had anyone to worry about.

Cecilia looked at him, her eyes wide and blue and beautiful. She did not ask what had happened. She simply smiled and held out her arms. She laughed as he knelt beside her and caught her in his, a little laugh that ended in a sob. He kissed her lips, her eyes, her lips, her cheeks, her lips. Then he drew back, holding her hands, looking at her eyes as if he could see through them deep into her heart. This is the real world, he thought, the only world that makes the innocent dream come alive.

THE
VENETIAN
AFFAIR

Printed in the United States of America

To Eliot and Keith with love

THE VENETIAN AFFAIR

ONE

Two men sat in a darkened room. Outside was the blare of traffic grinding its way through the brilliant heat of the last day of August. But here in this room, the closed window, the drawn Venetian blinds kept noise and glare to the street. Here in this room, guarded by two locked doors, New York was forgotten.

The two men ignored the spasmodic screech of the dentist's drill from his adjoining room: it was only a jagged part of the blurred background of sound; an annoyance, like the still, stifling air within these four safe walls. One man was talking, the other listening, both concentrating on every spoken word. They had exactly fifteen minutes to conclude their business.

Then the one who was talking would leave by the door that would take him to the service stairs: although he was the one in command, he was dressed in gray shirt and trousers appropriately soiled and wrinkled from a day's work, his electrician's toolbox lying beside a silent electric fan on the bogus mahogany of the dentist's cheap desk. The other looked like a businessman, not too affluent but eminently respectable; he had removed his gray jacket, hung it carefully over the back of his chair, slackened his dark-blue tie, loosened his white collar. When he left, tightened and buttoned up once more, he would unlock the door into the next room, pass the empty dentist's chair, not even glancing at the white-coated man who would be staring blankly out of his window, enter the waiting room, with its huddle of patients concentrating on their own problems. As he closed the front door behind him, he would leave the white-clad receptionist saying "Next please!" with the same crisp boredom she had dealt him only twenty minutes before.

The man who was dressed as an electrician was middle-aged, thin-faced, and angular. He had a voice as smooth as the palms of his hands. It was an educated voice, cool, deliberate, held low, but stressed by urgency. "This evening, you will leave from Idlewild. Your destination is Paris, as you learned from the plane reservation that Thelma delivered to you at noon. There was no difficulty when you met Thelma? No one interested in your movements; in hers?"

The other shook his head. He spoke for the first time. He was a man in his late fifties, thickset, short, with muscles running to fat. Either he found it cooler to sit on the edge of his chair or he was exceedingly deferential. His voice, too, was low, a little hoarsened by the tension of this meeting. "I followed instructions. I walked into the Zoo from Central Park South. I reached the seal pond fifteen minutes before noon. No one followed me. I went into the cafeteria, quickly got a cup of coffee and a sandwich, paid for them with the exact money I had ready. I carried my tray out to the terrace. Thelma was sitting at a table, finishing her lunch. She left, and I took her table. I pushed aside her tray to make way for my own. Under the tray was the envelope with the reservation. I spent half an hour on the terrace. No one was interested in me. No one followed Thelma."

"And no one followed you?"

"I saw no one."

The cool voice sharpened. "Not even the man we call Bruno? He was watching you."

The thickset man moistened his lips.

The other relented. "He kept at a distance. He reports that no one followed you."

The thickset man smiled weakly, dabbed his brow gently with a folded handkerchief, felt his stomach muscles relax again. If they had kept an eye on him when he picked up his flight reservation today, they must also have had someone guarding him when he was collecting his passport yesterday from Bruno in the Museum of Modern Art. So he was in the clear, ready to leave as soon as he got back to his hotel and changed his clothes. He looked at his watch. Half past three. No time to waste.

"This is what you take to Paris," the gray-uniformed man said. He had opened his toolbox and drawn out an envelope. It was a medium-sized opaque envelope, unaddressed, sealed, not much bulkier than if it contained a three-page airmail letter. He threw it across the desk.

The thickset man picked it up, weighing it automatically in his hand, and frowned.

"Unfortunately," the cool quiet voice continued, "its contents cannot be made into a film or a microdot." There was a thin smile on the thin face. "And so we must use you."

The thickset man lifted his jacket and inserted the envelope carefully into a zippered inside pocket. He made no remark.

"You are wondering why we did not use diplomatic channels?" The cool voice had sharpened. It was on the defensive. It disliked even unspoken criticism.

"It would have been simpler."

"On the contrary. This whole operation must not be connected in any way with our embassies in Washington and Paris. Or with any of the consulates. Or with the Mission to the United Nations. No connection whatsoever. That is of highest importance, only second to the importance of the envelope itself. It has taken us four months to prepare that envelope. Only three people besides myself know what it contains."

The thickset man used his folded handkerchief again. Patches of sweat were spreading over his white shirt.

"Actually," the cool voice went on, "we could have sent this envelope by mail. It contains nothing illegal. But we could not risk having the envelope opened by mistake, or being delayed. Its value, incalculable, lies in its surprise. So we send it by safe hand."

"I will take care, great care."

"That is why I chose you," the electrician said sharply. "Because—although there should be no difficulties at Orly; they pay little attention to anyone's baggage—it must be hidden. No risk of discovery, I repeat. You understand?"

The man nodded. He eased his collar open still more. "And after Customs?"

"You will hand the envelope over at once to an intermediary. He will be waiting for you just outside the arrival hall at Orly."

"Identification?"

"We have made that as simple as possible for you. And certain. He met you three years ago, when you arrived in Zurich. Remember him?"

There was a nod. "The meeting will be easy. There won't be any —any delay."

"There won't be *any* mistake." The thin man uttered the word the other had hesitated over and left unused. "You know each other. You know the method to follow."

"As at Zurich?"

"Why not? It was successful."

Again there was a feeling of hesitation.

"Yes?" The quiet voice was impatient. It didn't even wait for the answer. "It is perfectly safe to let you work together once more. He has been kept out of sight, inactive, for almost two years. Just as you have been kept inactive for the last fourteen months. Both of you have changed your names, your occupations, your countries, your lives. Two different men; except you know each other by sight. To help your eye find him quickly, he will wear a blue shirt and a yellow tie. His hair has become white, and slightly longer. We have told him that your suit will be brown, your tie green, and that you have begun to wear glasses. Is that adequate enough?"

The thickset man ignored the hint of sarcasm. He nodded, rose, put on his jacket. "Thelma—and Bruno—you are sure of them?" He was looking at his watch again. The room was suffocating him.

"Quite sure. They know nothing except that they were asked to help you escape to Europe. Tell an American comrade that he is saving a hero of the revolution, and he will come to the rescue at full gallop on his white horse."

And now they both smiled. On Americans, they agreed completely. They were the professionals, with only contempt for the amateurs.

"You leave first," the electrician said. "I have this fan to fix." He pushed its socket into an outlet. Its slow whirr began, and mounted into an overwhelming whine. "I make a good electrician," he added, but there was no one left to enjoy his heavy humor. The door into the dentist's workroom had closed noiselessly: nothing less than a crash or a shout could be heard over the high falsetto of that damnable contraption. Still, he was grateful for the current of air even if it was stale, even if the sudden coolness was only an illusion made by motion. He waited for five minutes, thinking of the man who had left him. A reliable man, instincts excellent, senses alive, quick wits. Today he had seemed less at ease, overcautious. It could have been the heat: he had felt it badly.

The five minutes were over. The electrician lit a cigarette, caught up the toolbox under his arm, and opened the door into the back corridor. By the time he sauntered into the street, his friend was already in a cab heading south to Pennsylvania Station. There he would take another taxi, then another, and drive to his hotel, the third hotel he had used in the three nights he had spent in New York.

The electrician stopped, almost at the corner of street and avenue, to look at the window of a small delicatessen. Parked cars, moving trucks, bareheaded women with groceries in their arms, screaming children gathered around a fire hydrant hopefully, a bulldozer ending its day's work on the site of some old brownstone houses, workmen in sleeveless singlets and helmets, a pneumatic drill, glare, heat, noise, total confusion. But he was almost sure that no one was following him. He lit another cigarette, timing the traffic lights at the corner. At the last possible second, he turned away from the overcrowded window with its red neon sign, loped swiftly across the avenue just before a four-lane stream of traffic came rushing down on him. No one could follow him now.

He hurried along the crowded sidewalk to the subway entrance. A good operation, he thought with some satisfaction, and it would succeed for one simple reason: the enemy did not know it even existed. Success always lay in surprise.

And failure, too. Although at that moment, surrounded and protected by a sweltering mass of the enemy, he gave it little thought.

TWO

Bill Fenner settled himself comfortably in the plane. There was plenty of space on this flight. It was almost the end of summer, the last day in August, when most people's vacations were over. But it was also the end of summer in a year, 1961, that had produced its crop of alarms. The Wall in Berlin was nearly three weeks old, voices from Eastern Europe were alternating from cold to hot, memories of shoe-thumping and outshouting at the United Nations were still alive. So the average tourist must have decided that life was simpler at home, this year, where he didn't have to depend on strangers or cope with a foreign language if a real emergency blew up in his face. There had been a lot of quiet cancellations. And the plane, ready to take off from Idlewild, was less than half filled.

The other passengers on the flight to Paris were either young enough to be unencumbered with wives and children or determined enough on pleasure—the kind of tourists who would be found climbing Vesuvius on the day that smoke was already forming over the crater; or they were businessmen, soberly optimistic; or they were lone travelers, like Fenner himself, with a job of work to do. At least, he thought, as they waited for take-off, there will be no crying children on this flight, no nervous old ladies fretting about the weight of their luggage, no neighbor crowding my elbow.

Not that Fenner was an antisocial type. He had spent the afternoon over a long luncheon at the club with three of his old friends, who, like himself, had begun as journalists some thirteen years ago, but had since diverged into book publishing, magazine editing, politics. Bill Fenner had stayed with the New York *Chronicle,* and for the last six years he had been its drama critic. Which was exactly what he had wanted to be in the first place: it was the job that would keep him alive, mentally and physically, pay the rent and stimulate his mind and—in the great moments of theater—stir his soul. And in a few years, he would reach his second objective: the play he intended to write.

It hadn't altogether worked out that way though. Perhaps the critical mind was too analytical, too pragmatic, for the creative to be bold enough to assert itself. Here he was, on his way to France for a four-week vacation combined with a job of writing. A play? Not on your life. Two articles for the *Chronicle*'s Sunday edition on the French national theater, a starter for a book on the European theater, which might be ready by the year 1967. God help me, he thought, perhaps I'd better never begin those articles.

What's delaying us, anyway?

It was hot on the waiting plane. The air conditioning wouldn't start until they were two thousand feet up or more. He glanced at his watch. The man across the aisle was doing the same thing, only more intently. Like Fenner, he was traveling alone; a sturdy individual, with a solid chest expanding into fat under his heavy brown suit, and a red round face looking redder by the minute above his tightly knotted green tie. He was middle-aged. (Fenner, fully thirty-seven, was kinder about other people's advancing years than he once had been.) And in no mood for any talk, thank heavens. For he had glanced across at Fenner, eyes sharp behind his horn-rimmed glasses, and looked quickly away. His fingers tapped on his arm. Nervous about flying? But who wasn't?

Fenner glanced through the window. Two late-comers were joining the flight, looking as cool in their crisp white shirts and neat blue suits as if the hot sunset outside were only an evening mirage. Fenner concealed a smile: he knew the type well from his cub-reporting days, when he had been sent to haunt the law courts. They could give evidence as expertly as they had trailed a suspect. What was taking them to Paris—an extradition case, some federal offender who might now start wishing he had not jumped bail? Serious business, certainly, or the plane wouldn't have waited. The delay had been only six minutes, but to those who were impatient to leave, each minute had seemed endless.

The smiling hostess was performing the usual ritual of take-off with a gentle prompting here, a helping hand there. The man across the aisle seemed adept at air travel, after all. He was already secure in his safety belt, and was setting his watch forward. He certainly wasn't going to be caught unawares by a sunrise only a few hours away. He will eat a large dinner, Fenner surmised, go soundly to sleep, wake up looking efficient, while the rest of us, having had a nightcap or two, and read, and talked, will be just about thinking of bed by the time we arrive. With that he dismissed the man in the brown suit, a pretty dull and harmless fellow, and began to look through a copy of *Réalités* to get some French phrases rolling on his tongue again.

Across the aisle, the man in the brown suit (who considered no one harmless) studied Fenner quietly until dinner arrived. Despite the heat of the day and the tensions of waiting at Idlewild, he had recovered something of his normal appetite. He ate quickly, greedily. In his youth, he had starved often enough in Odessa to make him appreciate any free meal. (He was, his nicely faked passport said, Mr. Albert Goldsmith, naturalized citizen originally from Frankfurt, resident of Newark, New Jersey, and an importer of ladies' handbags.) Just as he had finished his steak and was eying the blueberry pie appreciatively, one of the efficient-looking men whose late arrival had delayed the flight six long agonizing minutes chose to walk through the cabin, glancing (an automatic habit) at his traveling companions as he passed. He only wanted to chat with someone he knew in the forward section of the plane. But he stopped Mr. Goldsmith's appetite cold.

Mr. Goldsmith did not panic. He was too experienced for that. His mind stayed alert, his thoughts were quick-darting but intensely rational, his face remained as placid as ever. Only his digestion betrayed him: the food he had eaten coagulated into a heavy, solid lump in his chest. Even the return of the brisk stranger with the photographic eye to his own seat didn't help Mr. Goldsmith. A false alarm? Yet no alarm in Mr. Goldsmith's profession could be treated as false. He sat quite still, planning emergency countermoves, elaborating his new identity so that his Mr. Albert Goldsmith was more than a fake name. If there had been any suspicion about him, surely he would have been stopped as he entered this plane. No one knew of the contents of the envelope except the man who had given it to him that afternoon, and three others. And none of them, if they had been arrested, would talk. If they could have been interrogated by the Gestapo or the old NKVD, he might have good reason to fear. Logically, he was not afraid. Illogically, he was worried. His instincts would not be quietened. He felt threatened. By what?

He did not sleep, even with his raincoat safe under his hand. He felt cold—the air conditioning was as great a curse as the heat had been— yet beads of sweat kept gathering on his brow. A tight band seemed laid across his chest. Indigestion, he thought, it was just indigestion. He sat still, his hand gripping his coat, while his mind held firmly to one comforting thought: at Orly, it should not be too difficult. There was a long walk, yes, but no delays, few formalities. And in the entrance hall his contact would be waiting.

· · ·

At Orly, the two brisk men in their neat blue suits were the first to leave the plane. They were joking, laughing, bright as two polished buttons. Bill Fenner left more slowly, admiring their resilience. He watched the narrow stream of passengers trail after the stewardess, the pretty one who swung her hips a little, toward the right entrance in the huge building of shining glass. Stiff legs in crumpled clothing began to pick up pace as the fresh morning air washed night-tired faces. Fresh, but tinged with the kerosene smell of jet planes. There was a long line of them, drawn up neatly, beautifully angled, exactly spaced. A nicely welcoming honor guard, thought Fenner. Good morning to you, too, gentlemen!

He let the others pass him. Each was determined to be the first out of the giant airport and on the road to Paris. But he could enjoy stretching his legs, this feeling of release from a tightly sealed bullet. There was no hurry: no one meeting him, no urgent conferences, no brief stay into which Chartres and Versailles and Montparnasse had to be jammed, no plane connections to make, no wife to add to the worries of transport and wrong accommodations. This was one time, at least, when the solitary bachelor had an advantage. He was the casual observer, the disengaged, free to wander, free to do as he liked when he liked. Except, of course, for that little errand Walt Penneyman had given him. He might as well clean that off his plate this afternoon, oblige Penneyman by sending the facts he wanted, and retire into a long lazy weekend before he even started his own work. An odd kind of errand that Penneyman had assigned him. Yes, "assigned" was the word; Walter Penneyman was part owner, part editor, and total energist of the *Chronicle*; he had given Fenner his first chance at journalism, nursed him through that bad patch of his life just after Korea, when—

His thoughts were knocked aside as someone, passing him quickly, lurched against his arm. It was the man who had sat across the aisle from him. Extraordinary thing, Fenner thought, that some people can have the whole width of an enormous airfield to walk over and still manage to collide. The man's white face looked at him without a smile. Did he think Fenner had blocked his path purposely? "Excuse me," Fenner said. The man walked on rapidly, almost too much in a straight line to be natural. Was he drunk? Had he spent the night nipping from a flask? He had been slow at coming out of the plane, but he was putting on speed. He stopped to put down the small case he was carrying, shifted his coat to his left arm, picked up the case with his right hand, and was off again. And don't look around at me, Fenner told the departing back, I'm not following you: I'm just going where we're all going. Well, where was I— oh yes, Walt Penneyman. . . .

An odd assignment—an interview with a professor named Vaugiroud, whose interests were entirely political and had nothing to do with the theater. It would be simple enough, something that Fenner would have treated as routine six years ago, when he was a foreign correspondent, but now—unusual. As odd, in fact, as Penneyman's urgency yesterday morning when he had asked Fenner to look in at his office. "You're leaving for Paris tonight, Bill? You're just the man I need." It was always flattering to be needed. Besides, this Vaugiroud character sounded like an interesting type.

He stepped into the glass palace and smiled for the little hostess, who waited worriedly for the last one of her flock. "That way," she showed him, pointing to the cluster of people ahead. He had his passport and landing card all ready, so she forgave him. "The luggage will be examined when it reaches the arrival hall," she told him. Now he saw that her worry was not about him.

"Baggage will be opened?" he asked her in surprise. That wasn't usual at all.

"It won't take long," she said soothingly. "A formality."

The well-trained nurse, he thought. If she knows, she is not telling. Nor was the welcoming committee, waiting patiently in the vast stretch of light-colored wood and glass with the slightly jaundiced eye that French officials keep for those who have time and money to waste on travel.

Fenner's luck was in. He saw his suitcase and weekend bag traveling smoothly along on a moving belt, and signaled to a blue-smocked porter. They were quickly placed on the counter. *"Vous n'avez rien à déclarer, monsieur?"*

Fenner shook his head, produced his keys. "Excuse me," he said to the passenger standing beside him, and moved a couple of feet for elbow room. It was the man in the brown suit, who had been in such a hurry and now was waiting for his luggage. He didn't look well, Fenner noted: he was no longer energetic and businesslike; he was almost listless, withdrawn into some overwhelming worry—he hadn't even noticed he was standing in Fenner's way.

The French officials were serious-faced, silent. The innocent tourist was probably the least of their problems this bright and pleasant morning. Algiers and generals in open revolt had put the peaceable traveler into proper perspective: someone not necessarily likable, but not inimical either. Yet, Fenner noted, the quick fingers examining his luggage were extremely thorough; the eyes glancing over him were equally searching. What interested them?

420

Nothing, so far. The Customs official saw just another American in a dark-gray suit, blue shirt, dark-blue tie; neatly cut brown hair, gray eyes, well-marked eyebrows, bone structure of his face noticeable and pleasant, an easy smile. He was fairly tall, thin, relaxed. He had a raincoat over one arm, a bundle of newspapers and magazines under the other, a hat which he preferred not to wear, and nothing to declare. Nothing? the sardonic French eyes seemed to ask: no failures, fears, frustrations? "And what is that? In the pocket of your raincoat, monsieur? Thank you. Ah—" An eyebrow was raised in pleased surprise. "You are an admirer of our Comédie-Française?"

Fenner nodded. As it once was, he thought, and as it may be again. But he didn't risk saying it. This, he felt, was not the year for plays upon words or double meanings. Beside him, he heard a hiss of breath—or was it a slow sigh of impatience?—from the man in brown. His suitcase had arrived. He leaned on it heavily. His face was set. "Are you all right?" Fenner asked him. He got no answer. Just a look that told him to mind his own business and get on with it.

"In French," the Customs official observed. He smiled. "You are preparing yourself?"

"That's my homework," Fenner agreed, and jammed the small, thin edition of Le Misanthrope back into its hiding place. He dropped his coat on the low counter and began locking his cases. He glanced at the impatient stranger beside him as if to say, "There now, I'm hurrying, can't you see?" He looked more closely. This man is ill, he thought worriedly: he won't admit it, but he is ill. Fenner caught the eye of the Customs official, and nodded toward Mr. Goldsmith's white face. "Where can I find a glass of water?" he asked.

The Frenchman pointed to a gendarme who was patrolling the background in quiet boredom. "He will show you." And then, to Mr. Goldsmith, "Would you like to rest? Please sit down over there." He turned to a woman whose bracelets jangled as she searched for her keys halfheartedly, hoping her sweet smile would save her the trouble. "Open everything, madame."

"No," Mr. Goldsmith said angrily. "No, I am first." And indeed, he had his suitcase unlocked.

At that moment, three short and violent explosions burst savagely into the quiet room. Everyone jumped. Two of the officials ducked automatically. The woman with the bracelets screamed. Fenner spilled the water he was carrying. Mr. Goldsmith, after a violent start, stood rigid. The gendarme, the least perturbed—either he had been the first to realize the explosions were outside on the street or he had become accustomed to such disturbances—noticed Fenner's accident. Quietly, he himself brought another cup of water for the man who stood at the counter. "Le voici!" he said crisply, tapping the man's shoulder to draw his attention.

Mr. Goldsmith's head made a slow half-turn. Suddenly, the ridges of agony on his face were no longer controlled. He moaned and slipped to the ground, his eyes staring with incredulity at the ceiling.

"We shall take care of him. Please continue!" the gendarme told Fenner and the woman, and signaled to the nearest porter to help him lift Mr. Goldsmith away from the counter. Fenner obeyed: the order made good sense; those who had been cleared were to move out; those still to be examined were to stay where they were, under the official eye. A little commotion like this one would be made to order for any smuggling. So he looked around for another porter.

The Customs official was repeating "Everything to be opened, madame!" The woman recovered herself sufficiently, bracelets jingling with haste, but first, as her gesture of sympathy to the poor man who had collapsed almost at her feet, she lifted his raincoat from the floor and placed it neatly on the counter beside some luggage.

Mr. Goldsmith's eyes watched her. He tried to speak. He shivered. He managed the word "coat."

"His coat!" the gendarme said to one of his helpers. "He wants his coat over him." The porter moved quickly to the counter—the woman was anxiously explaining the contents of several plastic jars; the Customs official was opening them carefully—and seized a coat lying near the sick man's suitcase, bringing it quickly back to throw over the inert legs. Mr. Goldsmith was quite helpless now, his eyes closed, one hand feebly clutching the edge of his raincoat as if it comforted him.

Fenner had found a young and agile porter. "Over there," he said, pointing. "A brown suitcase, a brown bag, and a raincoat. That's all." The porter darted ahead of him, toward the counter. There, the Customs official was looking dubiously at the contents of a jar, trying to reason out why one woman could need so much face cream for a two weeks' stay in a city that had practically invented cosmetics. The woman was saying anxiously, "It's *only* night cream, the kind I *like*. I didn't *know* if I could get the same brand—" She paused helplessly, watching a penknife gingerly testing the opaque, heavy mess. She paid no attention to the porter, who collected two pieces of luggage and a raincoat with great efficiency and speed.

Mr. Goldsmith was being placed on a stretcher. A doctor, a nurse, an attendant surrounded him. The gendarme, back on normal duty, saw

422

Fenner hesitate and look in the direction of the little group. "Please proceed," he told Fenner, pointing toward the exit. The porter was already there, glancing around impatiently, hurrying on as Fenner started after him into the giant entrance hall, glass and more glass, people and people, arriving, leaving, waiting, searching, talking, looking.

"Want a lift?" a voice asked at his elbow, and laughed.

Fenner swung around. Mike Ballard? Yes, Mike Ballard. Fenner recovered slowly from his several surprises. First, he hadn't expected anyone to meet him, and most certainly not Ballard, whom he had known only slightly in New York before Ballard had come over to work under Keir in the *Chronicle's* Paris Bureau. That was four, if not five, years ago. Secondly, Ballard had changed. He had added a bulge to his waistline, a jowl to his square-shaped face, and removed a couple of inches from his thatch of dense-black hair. His dark eyes were satisfied, his mouth was soft-lipped and relaxed, he smiled readily. An easygoing type was Mike Ballard, who—judging from his clothes, and they were the third surprise—had come to appreciate the finer arts of dressing as well as the food and wines of France. The fourth surprise was simply that Ballard was not the type to drive all the way out to an airport to meet an early-morning arrival unless something pretty special was involved. For Ballard, since Keir's heart attack last spring, was now acting head of the *Chronicle's* Paris Bureau. Also, Ballard liked his comforts. "Expecting someone important?" Fenner asked with a grin.

"You," Ballard said, administering the fifth surprise. "What kept you so long in there? Come on, this way. Where's your porter?"

"He guessed the wrong direction, I think. He's over there, just beyond that character in the yellow tie."

Ballard waved his arms, but the porter didn't notice. Fenner started briskly after the man, gave a whistle that stopped the porter in his tracks. It also made several other people look around sharply. Only the man with the yellow tie paid no attention; he didn't even halt his steady pacing. The porter, quick to cover his miscalculation, headed back toward Ballard, whose arm was still signaling. "There's a hired cab waiting in the parking lot across the road," Ballard told him. To Fenner, as he returned, he added, "Seemed easier than bringing my car. I don't drive so well at this time of the morning—not after last night's party."

"You're taking too much trouble," Fenner said. It was the usual polite formula, but he meant it. For the last hour he had been looking forward to arriving in Paris. By himself. He didn't need a conducted tour. All he wanted was to drive, alone, to his favorite hotel on the Left Bank, with a guaranteed view of the Seine from the balcony of his old room. And there he had planned to bathe leisurely (unless a shower had been added since his last visit), shave, and enjoy a second breakfast with the morning sunlight on the trees outside for company. Now he would have to invite Ballard for breakfast, and listen, and talk. He would be lucky if he didn't find his whole day arranged for him.

"No trouble," Ballard lied gallantly. "Besides, someone had to steer you to the right hotel."

"I've got a hotel."

"Not any more. It was bombed yesterday."

"What?"

"Secret Army stuff. Oh, it was bound to spread to Paris. We have had bombs and machine-gunning in the provinces all summer. It was bound to spread. I got you a room at the Crillon."

"Thanks. But isn't that a bit rich for a drama critic's blood?" Certainly too steep for his pocketbook.

"Not after I got a phone call from the old man yesterday, telling me you were coming over."

"From Penneyman?" Fenner gave up counting surprises, this morning.

"Well—he was on the phone about something else. But he mentioned you. Told us to let you have free run of our files if you needed them." There was a look of speculation in Ballard's side glance. "So I figured your expense account was good. Also, I hadn't the time to go shopping around for hotels last night."

Fenner felt churlish. "Sorry I gave you so much trouble." He still couldn't find a reason for it though. "Thanks a lot."

"My pleasure." They had crossed the broad, handsome road. "There's my driver, willing and waiting." And the porter was already stacking Fenner's possessions in the front seat, eager for his tip, impatient for another job. (Ballard had the money out, brushing aside Fenner's arm reaching into his pocket.) "Besides," Ballard said as they settled themselves in the small taxi and were off, "someone had to come out here and identify the pieces."

"What pieces?" Fenner asked absent-mindedly. He was marveling at the speed with which they were negotiating the cloverleaf that led them onto the expressway.

"Yours. There was a bomb threat against Orly this morning. Didn't they tell you? No, I don't suppose they would. I bet they searched the baggage pretty thoroughly though. They always do that when they're jumpy."

"There was a moment when we all jumped," Fenner said with a smile.

"The three explosions? Just a truck expressing its opinion. A plastic bomb has a real bang to it." He shook his head, and his grin faded. "It was bound to spread," he said. "The damn fools."

THREE

Once they entered the new expressway to Paris, the journey promised to be quick and direct until the immediate approaches to the city were reached. But Ballard's conversation, even if it was headed in one direction as determinedly as this *autoroute,* had as many crossways and detours as any old-fashioned road. It was loaded with questions, asked and unasked. Fenner resigned himself to the inevitable and roused himself from his pleasant after-arrival lethargy. Ballard, after several hours of sleep in a comfortable bed, was expansive. He always had been a compulsive talker: silence worried him.

"How long are you staying?" he asked suddenly.

"In Paris? Probably only a few days, at first. I'll return by mid-September for a couple of weeks."

"That's wise. Not much theater to see in Paris right now. What are your plans?"

Fenner answered as briefly as possible. He had had to explain all this so often in the last few weeks—vacation plus research, plus articles, plus future visits to other countries, plus other articles—that it had become a standard routine. It now embarrassed him to have to listen to himself.

Ballard was smiling, but not so easily as he usually did. "Come off it, Bill. You don't have to tell old Mike all that theater stuff."

"Theater stuff," Fenner said, "is my business."

"You were a newspaperman long before you were a critic."

"Meaning?"

"What story are you after? This Secret Army Organization? Doesn't old Penneyman trust me to handle it?" Ballard was smiling broadly.

Fenner's astonishment gave way to perception. Was this the reason why he had been met at Orly? "I'm after no story. All I'm interested in is a book. Eventually."

"Wish I had time to write a book."

"Yes, that's all it takes."

Ballard glanced at him quickly.

Fenner was studying the invasion of suburban houses, glimpsed briefly before the expressway burrowed more deeply between its high banks. "Am I wrong, or didn't there use to be a lot of woods around here?" That would turn the conversation nicely, he thought.

"There are still plenty of forests around Paris," Ballard said defensively. "We've rented a place out on the Bois. You must come and visit us when Eva and the kids get back from Brittany."

"How many do you have?"

"Three. Four in December."

"Busy man."

"Too busy to take a vacation this year—there's a lot to handle at the office, with Keir sick."

"How is he?"

Ballard shook his head, pursed his lips. "Old Penneyman had better stop hoping." He hesitated. Then, "Keir has been off the job since April. When is Penneyman going to admit that Keir is never going to get back on it?"

"When Keir admits it, probably. Heart attacks aren't always the end of a man's career. Relax, Mike. You're in line for the job when it's declared vacant. By the way, there was a case of heart attack, or something pretty close to it, at Orly this morning. Fellow just folded up—"

"In line for the job—" Ballard laughed briefly, bitterly.

Fenner kept his eyes on the cars they were passing.

"Or perhaps he just likes to keep me dangling," Ballard added, but genial again, as if to sweeten his criticism of Walter Penneyman.

Fenner moved a cramped leg. "He likes Keir a lot," he said uncomfortably. "Keir isn't old. If he makes a good recovery, he could go on for another fifteen years at least. If he were ditched now, he'd probably be dead in six months."

"Sure, sure," Ballard said. He lapsed into unusual silence. When they reached the Porte d'Italie and the beginning of the city proper, he came to life. "Cut left as soon as you can," he told the driver, "and get onto the Boulevard Raspail." But the driver had his own ideas of a quick route. Ballard didn't argue. He laughed and shook his head. "We'll take almost as long to reach the Place de la Concorde as we took to get here," he predicted. "By the way, did you see Walt Penneyman before you left?"

"Yes."

Ballard's gloom returned.

Fenner said, "But he didn't talk about Keir. Or the Paris office. He is making a speech next week in Washington, and that's filling his mind." But as he spoke he began to wonder why Mike Ballard had not been given the job of visiting Professor Vaugiroud. Or perhaps it wasn't an important-enough assignment. "I have a professor to visit—"

"I've told my secretary to give you all help with the addresses of people you have to see. I'll be out of Paris for the weekend."

"Belgrade?"

Ballard shook his head. "I've got a man there covering that neutralists' conference. Nothing important is going to happen anyway. It will be a nice long weekend with not one screaming headline in sight." The prospect pleased him. He slapped Fenner's knee. "Even the acting head of the Paris Bureau has to get off the chain now and again. Right?"

Perhaps . . . and perhaps not. It depended on how much the acting head wanted to be head.

"So old Penneyman is giving another speech in Washington. What's his subject this time? Don't tell me—I can guess." Ballard struck a pose of upward and onward. "The freedom of the press depends on its integrity!"

"Something like that."

"He never gives up, does he? He was harping on that back in April, when he flew over here for two days. Two days—imagine that—for Paris! I thought he was going to give all of us heart attacks. I'm just getting the office back into shape now."

"I'm not following you."

"He didn't tell you?" There was a look of relief in Ballard's eyes. "Oh, you know—the Great Rumor of April. CIA urging French generals to revolt in Algiers. Remember?"

"Oh yes. That was the rumor an Australian journalist flattened out for us."

"Not quite. He just forced the French into admitting that they had no evidence at all."

But the rumor had been allowed to run wild, gathering momentum, a nasty piece of international suspicion that could have been disastrous. "So Walt Penneyman came over himself to see what it was all about?"

"Found out nothing, of course. None of us could. If he had paid attention to my reports, he could have saved himself a journey."

If Ballard imagined that Penneyman had lost interest in finding out, he couldn't be very much in Penneyman's confidence. It was just as well,

Fenner decided, that Mike Ballard's garrulity had interrupted his remark on Professor Vaugiroud. "Well," he said, "Walt Penneyman has always been a great Francophile. You can't blame him for being upset when his favorite foreigners seemed to be spitting right in America's eye."

"Oh," Ballard said with a laugh, "it would have all ironed out anyway." And he really believed that. It made crises easier to bear, perhaps. Certainly it made life simpler. "Walt Penneyman fusses too much. Well— here's the hotel. I'll see you in, and if you ask me to stay for a cup of coffee, I won't refuse. Can't wait long, though. I've got to clear some things up at the office and catch a plane by noon. No, this is mine!" He had his black crocodile wallet out with a flourish. Changed days, Fenner thought as Ballard paid their driver, changed days from New York and Ballard's dogged news coverage over at the United Nations when he had always looked as if he needed a good square meal, a haircut, and still more information. "Don't worry about your luggage," Ballard was telling him. "This place really takes care of its guests."

Fenner repressed his amusement. Was he just the New York country boy come to town? He gave a last look at the Place de la Concorde, with its sea of cars flowing in a steady surge, their chrome and glass flickering like the ripple of small dancing waves in the early sunlight. The man-made sea with its man-made roar, he thought: I'll probably end up as a true country boy on a Vermont farm.

"There's no place like it," Ballard said at his elbow as they crossed the broad sidewalk, newly watered and swept. He looked around at his adopted city with proprietary pleasure. "Ever think of coming to work here?"

"No."

But Ballard didn't quite believe him. He is coming up for that cup of coffee, Fenner thought, just to make sure where I stand with Penneyman. How do I make it clear that I've no interest in his job without showing him I know the real reason why he met me at the airport? This called for more tact than he felt capable of mustering after a night journey. Besides, he was handicapped by a qualm of memory: Walt's words, yesterday, at the end of their meeting. "You used to be good at finding the threads of a story, Bill. Never feel the itch to get back to international politics again? No? Well, enjoy your trip. Call me as soon as you've talked with Vaugiroud." He had thought nothing of that casual question at the time. Now, it had taken on more meaning. So had the Vaugiroud assignment. Was Walt Penneyman trying to make him feel that itch again?

"There's no place like it," Ballard was repeating.

"It has its points," Fenner agreed, his eyes following two pretty girls for a brief but adequate moment. Two very pretty girls, neatly cinched at the waist, dark hair piled high, slender legs under floating skirts.

Ballard said, "I'm old-fashioned in one thing: I still prefer blondes. By the way, did you know your wife was living in Paris?"

Fenner's step hesitated. Then he went in through the giant doorway, past the elegant waiting rooms and the colonnades and the elevators. Behind him, Ballard greeted someone in the lobby, stopped to speak. Fenner had finished all the usual routine at the reception desk before Ballard rejoined him.

"Sorry about that," Ballard said awkwardly.

"I had no trouble. You laid it on well."

"About Sandra, I meant." There was no malice, only curiosity glancing out of his dark eyes. "I thought I'd better tip you off, in case you ran into her."

"It wouldn't matter if I did. And," Fenner added pointedly, "it is eight years since she was my wife." He moved toward the elevators. "I may go bankrupt, but I'll do it in comfort," he said as he looked around him. Soft rugs underfoot, soft air, soft voices. Deceptive. "Everyone looks so damned important. Are they?"

Ballard wasn't to be sidetracked. "You know, I've often wondered why Sandra left America. I know it's none of my business, but—"

"That's right," Fenner said with a quiet smile. "It was no one's business. What about that coffee? And I need a shower and a shave." But both elevator doors were now closed.

"Look"—Ballard was glancing at his watch—"do you mind if I take a rain check? I've just met a man who has some good contacts with the Quai d'Orsay. He's waiting for me." He nodded toward a room near the entrance. "You know how it is, Bill."

"That's all right. Thanks for delivering me intact."

"Use the office whenever you need it. I'll be back on Monday. And the Embassy is across the street"—the old smile was back again—"just in case you need to take refuge."

"From a bomb, or Sandra?"

Ballard looked at him. "You don't have to worry about Sandra. She has no hard feelings about you."

Wasn't that generous of her? "That's kind of her."

"No, believe me. I was at a party last night at her place—she has a big apartment out on the Avenue d'Iéna, been living there for the last three years—"

"That's nice." Glutinous word, "nice," applicable all the way from rice pudding to sun tans.

"She entertains a lot, you know. Not theater stuff—she's given up the stage—only politicians, diplomats, a few journalists, that kind of thing—"

"Policy-making level," Fenner suggested. That sounded like Sandra, all right. Poor Ballard, didn't he know what he was getting into?

"Not quite," Ballard said modestly. "But an interesting bunch." He dropped his voice. "She's the very good friend of Fernand Lenoir."

"Is she?" And who was Monsieur Lenoir, who rated a dropped voice? Fenner looked at the returning elevator. "I'd better take this one," he said. "We can't keep the Quai d'Orsay waiting, can we?"

Ballard held his arm, his voice hurrying. "Sandra and I had a little talk last night. She had some pretty nice things to say about you. In fact, she—"

"Now," Fenner remarked and freed his arm, "that really is worrying news." Sandra at her sweetest was Sandra at her most dangerous. "I'll call you," he told Ballard as he stepped into the car. From the background, one of the assistant-assistant room clerks, with Fenner's room key in his hand, moved forward to join him.

"Any time," Ballard said, "any time at all, Bill." He looked disappointed, as if he still had one more question to ask. Or perhaps he was disappointed in Fenner, the man who had never appreciated such a sweet and generous woman as Sandra Fane. The name, Fenner reflected as he came out of the elevator and followed his guide through half a mile of carpeted corridors, had been as bogus as her life, and as carefully planned. He wondered how long Sandra had stayed in Czechoslovakia? All of the five years between her quiet exit from America and her descent on Paris? Perhaps she had changed. People did. But Sandra?

The clerk hurried ahead of him with the key held ready, an elderly maid with folded towels over her arm moved out of a pantry to appraise the new arrival discreetly, a door opened and a waiter pushed a breakfast cart into the corridor. A young woman followed it, calling back to someone in the room, "All right, I'll have the sketches ready for you by noon."

"No later, honey," a querulous female voice reminded her.

"No later," the girl said calmly. "Thanks for the breakfast." She closed the door, shaking her pretty blonde head, almost blocked Fenner's path as she adjusted a large black portfolio to fit more comfortably under her arm, said "Excuse me" in her charming voice, glanced at him with large gray eyes, and walked quickly away toward the elevators. It seemed unfair, Fenner thought, that anyone as young and decorative as that should have to be so crisp and businesslike at half past nine in the morning. A waste of natural resources.

His room was comfortable and handsome. There was not much view— a side street, with some small cafés and shops topped by two or three stories of nineteenth-century façade now converted from private homes into offices and dressmaking workrooms—but there was a shower, in a bathroom as large as his bedroom in New York. His suitcase and weekend bag were placed on luggage racks; his raincoat was already in one of the huge wardrobes. He tipped the elderly porter, thanked the room clerk, locked the door, and began throwing off his clothes. He ordered breakfast to be sent up in half an hour, and felt pleasantly efficient. The shaving lights were excellent. The shower worked. He even burst into a brief aria from *Tosca*.

He breakfasted in the bathrobe the hotel had so obligingly provided, the warm air floating in from open French windows along with the grind and shriek of buses and cars. If it hadn't been for them, he might have fallen into a pleasant sleep: the beds were as soft as everything else in this hotel. He opened his suitcase and began dressing. Fresh clothes made a new man. He even decided he would call Professor Vaugiroud and arrange an appointment for—well, not for this morning; that was being too damned efficient. This afternoon would give him time to collect Vaugiroud's remarks, simplify them into basic points, and cable them to Walt Penneyman. It was only the beginning of the day in New York right now. He had at least twelve hours before he need call Penneyman and tell him the information was on its way.

He lit a cigarette (the last one in this pack, he noted with a touch of annoyance), found the telephone number that Penneyman had given him, and got through to Vaugiroud with only reasonable delay. Professor Vaugiroud spoke good English, if a little impatiently. "Yes, yes," he said as soon as Fenner had identified himself. "I had a cable last night to tell me to expect you. Is Mr. Penneyman ill?"

"No. He just could not get away himself."

"I am sorry," Vaugiroud said with marked disappointment.

"He was, too. Could I see you this afternoon?"

"Where?"

"Anywhere you like. And whenever it suits you."

Vaugiroud thawed a little. "Come to my apartment at four o'clock. You have my address."

"Yes."

"At four, then."

So that was that. Fenner looked thoughtfully at some of the other addresses in his notebook: most of them he would have to see toward the middle of September, when they were back at work in Paris. There were only three—one a director, another a playwright, one an assistant to the Minister of Cultural Affairs—whom he knew well enough to be able to visit even while they were on vacation. He had their invitations in that folder in his suitcase. He could reach them easily by telephone. No, he decided, today I relax and walk around Paris. I've got to find another hotel anyway, or else I'll have to cut my vacation to a week. For like most Americans abroad, well-dressed, educated, seemingly carefree millionaires from the land of giveaway, Fenner had to keep an eye on his traveler's checks.

He got out a map of Paris and tracked down Vaugiroud's address. It was across the Seine, not far from the Sorbonne, where Vaugiroud had once taught Philosophy. It would make a long, but pleasant, walk among some of his favorite streets. He might even revisit the bullet hole, unless they had plastered it over, although he had still seen it—and the other bullet holes from a Nazi sniper—on his last visit here, in '58. It wasn't every tourist who could look at a wall in Paris and say, "And that was the bullet that nearly got me." My first visit to Paris, he thought, just ten days before the Germans left. He looked around his elegant and peaceful room; and he shook his head slowly.

He rose to find another cigarette. There should be a couple, at least, left in the pack in his raincoat pocket. As his hand touched the coat, he had his first suspicion. He pulled the coat off its hanger, and the suspicion was a fact. It wasn't his.

There was no identification mark, not even the usual label at the back of the collar. He dug his hand into the deep pockets to find some scrap of information, but there were only two folded sheets of blank airmail paper, as if someone had meant to write a letter and never got around to it. And that was all.

He looked at the coat again—same color and same shape, but many raincoats were. Only the texture of the fabric was different. Hell and damnation, he thought, this takes care of my morning. I'll have to start telephoning around. Where do I begin? He stared angrily at the coat, at his shattered plans. One of those efficient prize packages who shuttled luggage in and out of this hotel must have mixed up—no, possibly not. It could have happened back at the airport, with that other efficient prize package of a porter. And Fenner's attention had been wandering; first, with the man who had collapsed; second, with Ballard's unexpected appearance; third, with Ballard's constant stream of questions; fourth, with talk of Sandra.

He cursed himself for an idiot, sighed wearily and telephoned the baggage porter downstairs.

Had any guest returned a wrongly delivered raincoat this morning? No one had.

Would the porter check and find out? The raincoat would have to belong to someone who had arrived or departed around half past nine.

The porter could tell him that right away. There had been several early departures this morning before eight o'clock, and some arrivals around ten o'clock. Only four people had had their luggage moved between nine-fifteen and nine-forty-five. One was Monsieur Fenner, the other three were ladies. He would investigate further if necessary.

"No need, thank you," Fenner said. He was sure in his own mind, now, that the coat had been picked up by mistake at the airport. He had put it down, after jamming the book back into its pocket—yes, that was the last time he had touched it.

The scene at the airport came back to him. The man next to him had had a raincoat, hadn't he? Yes, coming back from that abortive expedition for water, he had seen the man collapse and the coat fall with him. . . . There had been a coat thrown over his legs when they tucked him on the stretcher. So that's how it happened. . . .

He had better start calling Orly. He would probably have to use French, so he must get his story brief and clear. It would be better still to be able to use the man's name: that simplified all explanations. There must be some identification on the raincoat; people did not travel around without identification. Fenner searched the edge of the sleeves and the pockets. No label, no inked name on any part of their lining. But this time, as he thrust the blank folds of airmail paper back into its pocket, roughly, annoyance growing at every defeat, his knuckles felt something. There was a slight thickness between the pocket's loose lining and the heavier lining of the coat itself. A very slight thickness, of cloth possibly, from some hidden welt or seam. He pulled his hand out quickly, with exasperation at his own time-wasting. His impatience had added to the delay: a thread, loose in the pocket's lining, was snagged around the stem of his wrist watch. He tried to free his watch, but it was well caught. He tried to snap the thread, but it was strong, of nylon possibly: he would end by pulling off the stem of his watch. Cut it loose? Easier, in his annoyance, to try to break the thread at its other end in the pocket. It didn't belong to any seam, this thread; it had been drawn out of the lining material itself. So he tugged at it with a quick, firm snap. The thread ran along the lining for a good three inches, and the material parted in a neat line.

There you've done it, he told himself angrily. Then he looked in amazement at the two gaping lips of cloth. He hadn't pulled at a thread; he had opened a secret kind of zipper. His watch was still firmly trapped by the

434

end of thread. With the coat over his arm, he went into the bathroom, found his small folding scissors in his shaving kit, and cut his watch free. After all that trouble, he felt he was owed a look at the secret pocket. Inside, lightly held in place with Scotch tape, was an envelope. It was unaddressed, opaque. There was something inside, not heavy, not bulky; smooth and firm.

Fenner walked back into the bedroom, threw the coat on the nearer bed, and ripped the envelope open. He was angry and he was troubled. The incredible secrecy of the pocket was much too professional a job for a normal person to have planned. The man in the brown suit had been either a very clever criminal or a canny lunatic.

Fenner's first reaction was embarrassment. He never liked handling someone else's money. All that secrecy for a few dollar bills? He counted them—there were ten—thinking of the complications ahead of him. When he called Orly, he would have some explaining to do. Or would the currency-control people be interested? Ten bills of—he looked again, thinking his eyes had added zeros and a comma. My God, he said to himself. "My God," he said aloud. In his hands he held ten bills, each worth ten thousand dollars.

FOUR

Fenner recovered from the shock. A hundred thousand dollars carried in a raincoat? Of all the crazy places—why not in a money belt hidden around a man's waist? Beyond that first reaction, he did not waste any time trying to fathom the implications of this puzzle for himself. There would be plenty, he knew. He wanted someone else to start on that, someone, too, who would take the ten monstrous bills safely into keeping. Even the thought of a hundred thousand dollars lying on his dressing table was more than disconcerting.

He put them out of sight in the envelope, replaced it in the coat (damn him for an idiot: why hadn't he kept his eyes glued on his luggage like some first-time-abroad tourist, and saved himself this trouble?), hung the coat in the wardrobe once more. He had better start telephoning Orly.

But would they believe him? They would begin by thinking that he was some kind of crank. Perhaps he had better take the coat all the way back to Orly. The idea depressed him. What a damned waste of time, what a— If only he knew someone at the Embassy—no, the Consulate: that was the right place to inquire about this, so that it could be handled for him by the proper people in the proper way. Besides, it would be easier on his temper to be able to explain in English. This was going to take a lot of explaining, he thought gloomily. Surely Mike Ballard knew someone at the Consulate, who'd know someone, who'd know . . . The roundabout approach could be the quickest one.

So his first call was to the *Chronicle*'s Paris office, which was a general headquarters for the collation and distillation of news reports gathered mostly from European sources. (It had been established just before the war, when suspicions were aroused that one of the big European news-gathering agencies had sold out to the Nazis. Today, with the wire services doing a reliable job, it might have been disbanded, but the *Chronicle* maintained it as possible insurance. Walt Penneyman had very firm ideas about news: he wanted not only accuracy, but accuracy double-checked, with no opinion-molding additions or subtractions in the presentation of facts.)

But Mike Ballard was not in his office. His secretary was French, and well trained. She was precise on all the information Fenner did not need, vague on the details he wanted. Monsieur Ballard had already left to join his friends. They were flying in a private plane. No, not from Orly. He would not be back in Paris until Monday afternoon. He would telephone tomorrow and on Sunday, of course, to hear any urgent reports. Could she give Monsieur Ballard any message from Monsieur Fennaire?

No, Monsieur Fennaire had no message. "But," Fenner added quickly, "if he is calling for news reports, who is collecting them?"

"His assistant, Monsieur Spitzaire."

"Spitzer?"

"But yes. André Spitzaire. You would like to talk with him?"

"But yes."

André Spitzer was French, too, and a sharp journalist. It was something of a triumph, Fenner reflected as he put down the receiver, to have managed to extract a name that might be able to help (or advise, at least) without having actually satisfied Mr. Spitzer's probing curiosity. Fenner had begun by explaining that he wanted someone at the Consulate who could deal with a problem involving an American citizen and French currency regulations. Oh, nothing serious, but urgent. No, no, nothing to do with any black market—did the Consulate have a specialist in that, too? (Laughter on the phone.) Yes, he wanted a specialist in French currency regulations, currency control. Oh, not currency control at any particular place, just currency control.

It was only then that Spitzer admitted he didn't know anyone, personally, at the American Consulate. He could, of course, make inquiries, and let Mr. Fenner know in half an hour? If Mr. Fenner could be more explicit, it would be much easier . . .

Fenner resisted the reply that he could make inquiries, too. "Does Ballard know anyone at the Consulate?" A name is what I need, he kept telling himself, just a name I can reach directly without having to explain all the way up, from information clerks to secretaries to assistants of assistants. A hundred thousand dollars brought so secretively into France was not exactly his idea of telephone conversation.

"No, only at the Embassy."

"Who?"

"Well, there's a press officer named Dade, Stanfield Dade. And there's—".

"That will do. Thank you. Thanks a lot."

Stanfield Dade. He remembered the name. He remembered its owner from the days when Dade used to haunt the long corridors at the U.N. A tall young man, thin, with glasses and a Haavad Yaad accent? That was eight years ago. Would he remember him? Anyway, remembered or unremembered, Fenner had the name he needed.

Stanfield Dade was eventually tracked to his desk. There was someone with him, for Fenner heard background voices as Dade came onto the phone with a sharp "Who is this?" Fenner was terse and urgent. He identified himself, didn't pause when Dade said in better mood, "Oh yes. And how are you?" but rushed on with his story. Dade kept saying, "Yes, yes," with growing impatience, until Fenner reached the final discovery. "Money? In an envelope? Was it much?" Dade was jolted into attention.

"I'd say yes." It would keep me comfortably alive for at least ten years, Fenner thought wryly, but then, I don't play in the Miami-Vegas circuit.

"Well—" Dade was bemused. He paused. "I was going to suggest that you contact the Consulate, but—" He paused again. "And this envelope was really well hidden?"

"Definitely."

Dade turned his head away, spoke to someone, muffling the receiver as he began, "It's very odd, you know—" Soon he was back again with Fenner. "What did this fellow look like?"

Fenner described the brown suit again.

"He arrived at Orly just after eight this morning?"

"That's right." What goes on here? Fenner wondered.

"Please hang on." The line became silent, with Dade's hand completely smothering the receiver this time. Fenner waited patiently, but gloom and annoyance mounted: this was one hell of a way to spend his first morning in Paris. Then Dade was on the line again. He sounded soothing, like a family doctor who feels his first job is to get the patient calmed down. "Fenner, there's someone here who may be able to advise you. He knows more about this kind of thing than I do. Half a second—"

A stranger's voice spoke from Dade's office; a quiet Midwestern voice, possibly competent. "Mr. Fenner? You have a problem, I hear. I think, as far as you are concerned, it is mostly with the Lost and Found at Orly. And there isn't much the Consulate could do about any American taking currency out of the U.S. There are no restrictions on that. How much did you say the amount was, again?" The voice was so innocent.

Fenner half smiled. He was beginning to feel really assured about the competence of the unemotional voice. "Too much to be carried in dollar bills. A bank transfer would have been simpler."

"It's in an envelope?" The voice was slightly incredulous.

"It's in an envelope."

"Do you think you could drop over here for a few minutes? Bring everything. Ask for Dade's office."

"Yes, I could do that. I'd feel better, though, if I could hire a Brink's truck to get me across the street."

There was a short silence. "In that case, I'll come over and see you in your room. Let's say around noon?"

"I'll be here. Whom do I expect?"

"Someone who is five feet eight, hair light, eyes blue; gray suit, brown tie and shoes. The name is Carlson. Okay?"

"Fine." Fenner grinned. "I'll keep my door barred and bolted." He heard Carlson laugh. "And could you have someone contact Orly? I really would like to get my own coat back."

"We'll make a try," Carlson said. "See you!"

A cheerful type, Fenner thought with relief. And careful. He arrived exactly at twelve o'clock, too. His manner matched his voice, but Fenner had a feeling that he had been examined, classified, and catalogued all in the time that Carlson shook hands, walked briskly into the room, said "Let's get rid of this" as he pushed the breakfast cart into the corridor, and locked the door. He didn't waste a gesture or a word. He took a chair with its back turned to the windows, so that Fenner faced the light. He might be around forty, Fenner decided, and added a few notes of his own to Carlson's description of himself. Medium height, but solidly constructed. Fair hair, thinning away from a high brow. Blue eyes, pale, certainly clever, but highly amused at this moment. Clothes not expensive, but quiet and neat; the brown shoes good, expertly polished, no high gloss, just the rich gleam of carefully honed leather.

"Doubtful of me?" Carlson asked. He sat easily in his chair, one ankle over the other knee.

"Just curious. You look more like an ex-Marine than State Department."

"I'm neither." Carlson looked at him with disarming frankness. "I'm attached to NATO. Just spending a few weeks in Paris." He hesitated briefly. "My job is Security."

"No official connection with the Embassy?" Fenner asked, worriedly. He wanted someone who could take responsibility, start things moving.

"Oh, the Embassy has given me a temporary corner in someone else's office. You could say that I am attached there. Meanwhile. On a special assignment from NATO." Carlson grinned. "Not specific enough? All right. I go around making sure that everyone has burned the trash in his wastebasket. Just a general errand boy and go-between. Is that better?"

I'll settle for that, Fenner decided. A lot of going-between may be necessary before the problem of this coat is solved. So he pulled it out of the wardrobe, and handed it over. "I hope you are also a puzzle-solver. Frankly, the only reason I can see for carrying a lot of money in a raincoat would be to hand it over to someone else in a public place, easily and quietly."

Carlson let that pass. He studied the coat. "When did you first realize this coat wasn't yours?"

"About twenty of eleven, when I went searching for a cigarette."

Carlson nodded, as if he found that reasonable, and fished out his pack of cigarettes for Fenner. He tossed it over. "Keep them. PX rates. I can afford to be lordly. And when did you discover the envelope?" Carlson was drawing out the two blank sheets of airmail paper.

"I think they're a blind," Fenner suggested. "If anyone was making a quick search, these sheets would distract his attention from the secret pocket—it's just underneath—"

Carlson looked at him, raised an eyebrow. "When did you say you discovered the envelope?"

"Later. You see, when I found the coat wasn't mine, I checked with the porter's desk downstairs. No dice. I thought I'd telephone Orly, and I started searching for some clue to the owner. My watch caught on a thread inside that pocket. I pulled. It held. And—well, I wrenched at it."

"Forceful." Carlson examined the opening that had come apart with the wrenched thread. He ran his finger along its edge; his eyes were thoughtful. "That was just about eleven?" he asked casually.

"Five minutes past, to be exact."

"And you called Stanfield Dade at eleven-twenty-five."

Fenner couldn't help admiring the technique. He explained what happened in that gap of time.

"So that's how you got Stan's name—from Spitzer?" Carlson was amused. "He was sure you had remembered him. Set him up for the day." He had taken out the envelope from the concealed pocket, and looked at its ripped flap. "You were getting madder by the minute, I see." He nodded as if he sympathized thoroughly. "What did you tell Spitzer, by the way?"

"Nothing about the envelope. Or the coat."

"Congratulations. Spitzer likes to know." And then, at last, Carlson drew out the ten bills. His eyes opened wide; his face muscles froze.

"I was waiting for that moment," Fenner said with a wide grin.

"Did it come up to expectations?" Carlson picked up one of the bills.

"I've heard of them, but these are the first I've seen. Queer feeling, isn't it, to handle a year's pay in one small piece of paper?"

Fenner pointed his cigarette at the bill's engraved portrait. "Who was Chase? If Washington is on a one-dollar bill, Lincoln on a five, Hamilton on a ten—you really are slipping down the ladder if your head is only worth ten thousand."

"Salmon Portland Chase," Carlson said crisply as he replaced bills and envelope in their hiding place. "Civil War Secretary of the Treasury, and a good one. He had a bankrupt country to prop up." But he was thinking of something else. "May I use your phone?"

He called Dade. "Definitely interesting. And very professional," he reported. "Yes, I think the Embassy should take charge until we can find out more. . . . No, no, it isn't consulate business: our American citizen here isn't in any trouble." He grinned across the room at Fenner. "Don't worry. I'll take the responsibility. After all, the brown suit may tie in with what Rosie told me this morning. You just alert the Treasury boys and Rosie. Do that for me, will you? Tell them I want to see them right away. . . . In your office, why not? Just say we borrowed it. I don't give a damn where we meet as long as it's as soon as possible. . . . Sure, tip off the French if that makes you feel better: get Bernard; he doesn't think all Americans are morons. . . . Fine. Do that now, will you? And save time. Yes, we'll be with you soon. The quicker we get this little package back onto U.S. territory, the happier I'll be. I've got a feeling it should never have left there."

He glanced over at Fenner, who was staring at the raincoat as if he could strangle it. "By the way, did you get any reply from my call to Orly?" He listened intently. The news did not please him. "In that case, telephone Bernard first of all. We'll need him." He ended the call.

"Well?" Fenner demanded.

"No coat at Orly. The man took it with him."

"He *left?*"

Carlson nodded. "Nothing is ever made easy for us, is it? I thought we had him nicely wrapped up in bed. But no, he recovered enough to refuse to be sent to any hospital. He rested for almost an hour, and then wandered off, declining all help except for a porter. Last seen following the exit arrows."

"He's crazy. He'll be dead within a week."

"Perhaps that doesn't matter so much as his job," Carlson said softly. He seemed very far away from this green-and-golden room.

"Is it as important as all that?"

Carlson's frown deepened.

"So he didn't notice the exchange? Damnation, I was hoping he would."

Carlson said, "He's too smart not to notice. But he wouldn't ditch your coat. He needs it to find out who you are. Once that's done, he will find out where you are. He wants his own coat back, intact."

"That's going to be difficult." Fenner took a deep breath. "How do you get me off this hook?"

"That's why I'm standing here, wasting time," Carlson said sharply. "The process is known as creative thought."

"He's a sick man," Fenner suggested. "He is in no shape to play detective."

"His friends may be in very good shape."

"If it's any aid to your attack of thought, there's no address in my coat. No telephone numbers. No notebook."

"No name?"

"My initials. And the maker's name, of course. Nothing in the pockets except cigarettes and a lightweight edition of a Molière play with some notes I was making in the margins. I'm hoping to see a production of it in Avignon. But none of that would tell very much." He looked at Carlson hopefully.

"It tells something. An American who is interested in the French theater. . . . One inquiry at Orly, with a good excuse behind it, will soon add a name to your initials. It isn't a totally unknown name, either. They could find it in one of the *Who's Who* series in any reference library. Next step, the *Chronicle* office. And so—to here."

"A bit awkward for me," Fenner admitted. He liked the idea less and less. "Let's hope he's working alone, with no one to run errands for him."

Carlson's eyes measured Fenner. "I'm going to give it to you straight. If he is alone, he will hire some help. You're in for trouble, friend, unless—" His eyes brightened. He picked up the coat and handed it to Fenner. "On your way out, you are going to stop at the porter's desk to pick up your passport. Tell him not to worry about your lost coat—"

"Like hell he is."

"Because it must be at Orly. So you're taking the wrong coat back and getting your own."

"I can answer that one: he will offer to send a boy out to Orly."

"You have to identify it, haven't you? And be identified? That's why you want your passport. It fits, doesn't it?"

"It fits," Fenner had to admit. "But supposing this fellow and his friends or his hired help go chasing out to Orly?"

"They will. So we'll get the coat out there, after we have finished with it."

"It won't be exactly as they expect to find it. What then?"

"At Orly, they will learn that the Sûreté arrived and confiscated the coat. My friend Bernard is very adept at arranging that kind of thing. In fact, I think he would like one of them to go chasing out to Orly. That would give his boys someone to follow."

Carlson opened the door. "I know it isn't brilliant," he said as Fenner still hesitated, "but can you think of anything better to get them off your back?"

Fenner couldn't.

"Well, what's worrying you?"

"The scene at the porter's desk. I'm no actor." I'll play it loose, keep it brief, he decided. Perhaps the porter will fall for my story.

"You'll do all right," Carlson told him. "Just use the Method."

The baggage porter accepted Fenner's offhand remarks with the impassive, drooped eyelids of a man who saw no other sensible course. Carlson was at Fenner's elbow. "Come on, Bill, we'll never make that lunch date," he was saying with all the sharpness that a very old friend, almost family, could be allowed. "Yes, we'll need a taxi," he told one of the doormen, "for Orly."

As they stood on the sidewalk, a girl came out of the hotel. *The* girl, Fenner saw. She was now wearing a gray linen dress, straight, sleeveless, and simple. Her hands, in short white gloves, were carrying her large black portfolio. She glanced at the two men and looked away, far far away, across the stretch of traffic toward the trees of the Champs-Elysées. "Punctual as well as pretty," Fenner observed. "She had her sketches all finished by noon, I see."

"You know her?"

Fenner shook his head. "Should we offer her this taxi? Better still, share it?" He grinned at the nervous look in Carlson's eyes, and climbed into the cab as the doorman announced their destination to the driver, and the driver announced in turn that he would have to make a detour—one-way streets and don't blame me. He repeated his self-clearance in basic English. A cautious man, this Frenchman, with not much trust in foreigners' comprehension.

"Then detour around by the Faubourg-Saint-Honoré," Carlson said. His French was fluent and authoritative, even if the accent was still Midwest. "I have to buy some shaving cream." He glanced back at the girl. "For a moment, I thought you meant it," he told Fenner.

"I did, but this isn't the day for it." In fact, this wasn't his day at all. "I've got an appointment at four. Unpostponable. If I miss it, I'll never get another." That much he could tell from Vaugiroud's voice on the telephone.

"You'll get there," Carlson promised. They had traveled about five hundred yards, and were now in a narrow street with smart shops. The driver was slowing up in front of an English apothecary, and looked around for approval.

"Fine," Carlson said, and paid the man, overtipping handsomely to calm his grumbles about their change in plans. Their visit to the shop was brief. After that, they retraced their route, nicely mingling in the lunchtime stroll of clerks and salesgirls, until they had almost reached the Embassy grounds. "The side entrance is easier," Carlson said, and guided Fenner expertly, quickly. "This won't take long. Just tell your story. Play it straight down the middle. Keep out the jokes. Sign it, and that's that. No sweat."

"It won't take long?" Fenner asked blandly.

"Not for you. You'll be out of all this in an hour."

"In one way, I'm sorry. I've got my feet wet, and the water looks inviting."

"You're an ungrateful son of a gun," Carlson said with a broad smile. "I've been spending the last half hour scrubbing you clean. Stay clean, dammit. Don't waste Auntie's efforts."

FIVE

Carlson's efforts were certainly impressive. Fenner had a small, quiet room to himself, with old acquaintance Dade keeping so much in the background that he was practically a crack in the plaster. There was a stenotypist tapping noiselessly on a small machine that obediently sucked in every syllable and spewed out a continuous sheet of paper covered with compressed symbols. It was a magic palaver, Fenner thought, fascinated by its speed. Sometimes it seemed as if the machine were even ahead of him. "Beats Indian sign language, any day," he observed to Dade when the stenotypist left to have fair copies made. Dade smiled faintly. Perhaps he was hungry. Perhaps he wished he could have been in the other room, where four sedate and thoughtful men had gathered. "This will soon be over," Fenner reassured him.

"You know," Dade said with some reproach, "this is not really my line."

"Sorry, but I didn't know anyone else to call around here."

"Oh, that's all right. It has been a devil of a day. Carlson has been digging into my files all morning, my chief is still on vacation, and now this envelope business. Haven't got one stroke of my own work done."

Fenner commiserated with him, tactfully. Dade might really be upset if you took his crying-towel away from him. Fenner made a mental note—he did this periodically in order to tighten up the weak strands in his own character, of which, he was convinced, he had too damn many—never to complain aloud, never to enjoy complaining. "How's the family?" he tried. Everyone had a family, except him.

That launched Dade. He was talking quite happily about German measles and French poodles when the stenotypist returned. He and Fenner read over the copy of the statement (Dade caught a misplaced comma), and Fenner signed.

"All clear?" Fenner asked. "Thanks a lot, Dade."

"We must have lunch someday."

"We must do that." Fenner opened the door and almost walked into a heavy-set, dark-haired man with a beaming smile.

"Just got you in time," the newcomer said. "Hi, Stan!"

Dade said with marked coldness, "Hello, Rosie!" but whether it was for the form of greeting or for Rosie, Fenner couldn't quite guess. "Did you receive my earlier message to you, this morning?"

"Sure, sure. Don't fret. I'll listen to her if she calls me. What's her name?"

"I didn't get it," Dade said stiffly.

Rosie looked hard at him. He turned to Fenner. "For you," he said, "I bring good news." He handed over a slip of paper. "Don't wait for us, Stan. We'll show each other out."

Stanfield Dade and the stenotypist left. "So he didn't get the name," Rosie said pleasantly as the door closed behind them. "Well, that's one way of keeping yourself clean. Cautious son of a." Rosie was amused by some thoughts of his own.

The note, which Fenner was reading, was equally cheerful. *Coat problem solved. Told you, didn't I? Auntie.*

"I'm Frank Rosenfeld," the dark-haired man said. "Can you talk to me for two minutes? Then I'll conduct you to the street. Quietly. No use disturbing the masterminds at the front gate: what never came in can't go out." He observed Fenner looking at him. "Carlson warned me that you're curious. All right, I'll tell you and save time. I don't belong here at all. I come from the big bad world outside, and Dade doesn't approve of me or it."

"On special assignment from NATO, too?" Fenner tried.

"Do I look like a military type?"

He did not. "Then you are CIA?" persisted Fenner. He wanted to know exactly who was going to talk with him for those two minutes.

There was a slight inclination of Rosenfeld's head, but no direct answer. His smile broadened, splitting his face into two camps: below, was a rounded jaw line, a full underlip, a chin with a marked cleft; above, was a sharp nose, clever brown eyes, a remarkable brow. He said crisply, "I've read your statement. My particular interest is Mr. Goldsmith—the little man in the brown suit. Describe him as exactly as you can. Take your time to remember. Exactly."

Fenner did all that.

"Good. That tallies." He offered Fenner a cigarette, lit it for him. He seemed to be making up his mind. "Let me explain a little," he said at last.

"I had word from New York last night about Mr. Goldsmith. So this morning, bright and early, I had someone out at Orly, just to keep Mr. Goldsmith in sight. But he didn't show. My friend waited for almost an hour. He made some tactful inquiries, and heard that our man was ill, would probably be taken to a hospital. He telephoned me. By the time he got back to the first-aid station, Mr. Goldsmith had walked out. My friend was too far away to catch up or get the taxi number. But he did see that there was someone helping Mr. Goldsmith into the cab. I'm telling you about this slip-up for one reason. Did you see, among the people waiting to welcome their friends in the entrance hall at Orly, a man with white hair and a yellow tie?"

Fenner thought back. "Yes."

"Close enough to describe him?"

Fenner considered. "In a way. I wasn't looking much at him—I was trying to get my porter's attention. I remember thinking he was a pretty cool character, not easily jolted or startled. That was strange, come to think of it. He looked like a painter, or a poet. An amateur artist with some money of his own—you know the type."

"I know the color of his clothes—blue shirt, yellow tie, gray suit. And that they looked fairly expensive. And that his white hair was long. But what about his eyes, features, complexion?"

"Eyes blue; features blunt and blob-shaped; complexion very sallow."

"Are you sure?" Rosenfeld was dubious of the quick answer.

"I remember saying to myself, 'Well there's a chap who not only matched his shirt to his eyes, but his face to his tie.' Then I didn't give him another thought."

Rosenfeld was amused. "Just one more question: what is blob-shaped?"

"Sort of—well, a pin-cushion effect. The opposite of taut, tightly drawn. Sponge under the skin instead of bone."

"Thanks. I get the picture. Where did you learn to use your eyes?"

"It's my trade. When I sit in a theater, I have to look as well as listen. But tell me—this character in the yellow tie, why does he interest you? Was he the friend who helped Goldsmith into a taxi? That's not in the tradition, is it?"

"Tradition?" Rosenfeld's eyes opened in bland astonishment.

"If he was waiting to contact Goldsmith, they should never have seemed to meet at all. At least, that's the way I thought those things were worked."

"You go to a lot of movies, too, I see."

"How to be successful in espionage without really trying—just break the accepted patterns?"

"Not funny, my friend. And who said this had anything to do with espionage?"

"Are there other forms of international understanding?" Fenner asked with mock innocence.

Rosenfeld smiled amiably.

Surely the two minutes are almost up, Fenner thought. If he left now, he could have a decent lunch before he saw Vaugiroud. He looked at his watch, and rose. Rosenfeld made no move. Fenner tried some sympathetic talk to ease old Rosie toward the street. "I don't think you should feel too upset about losing Goldsmith. The mistake was in New York."

"Oh?"

"Why did they let him leave? Easier for everyone if they had stopped him at Idlewild."

"On what grounds?"

"They don't know what his business is?"

"No."

"But surely they must know who he is, what he is?"

"Not even that."

"In that case, why alert you to keep an eye on him?"

"Well," said Rosie, with his sharp brown eyes gleaming, "you know how stupid we all are."

Fenner smiled. "That must be the explanation."

Rosenfeld offered him another cigarette. "Since I've answered your questions—well, some of them at least, didn't I?"

Fenner nodded and took the cigarette.

"I'd like you to answer a few of mine," Rosenfeld ended. "Fair enough?"

"If I can answer them."

"Sit down. This will only take a couple of minutes. Did you ever hear of a man called Bruno?"

"Bruno what?"

"Just Bruno."

Fenner shook his head.

"Or of a man called Geoffrey Wills?"

"No."

"Who sometimes used the name of George Williston?"

Fenner's eyes went cold.

"He was a very close friend of your wife's ten years ago." Rosenfeld was lighting his cigarette carefully. "In fact, they both belonged to the same group."

"I was in Korea," Fenner said. "She had many friends I knew nothing about."

448

"But you did meet Williston?"

"For five minutes, one night. I had the pleasure of throwing him out of my apartment. Him and three others."

Rosenfeld raised an eyebrow.

"Not physically. I just told them pretty forcibly to get out, and stay out."

"Why?"

"Not my type," Fenner said briefly. "A man has the right to decide who is to be invited into his home and who is not. Hasn't he? That's one freedom of choice that hasn't been taken away from us yet."

"A Constitutional right," Rosenfeld agreed. He rose and paced around the small bleak room, as if he were marshaling his thoughts with each even step. "The next question—I hope you'll answer it—did you come to Paris to see Sandra Fane?"

"I didn't even know she was here until Ballard told me this morning."

"Sorry—I just thought—well, after all, there isn't much going on in the theater here at present."

"People connected with the theater are still going on," Fenner reminded him angrily. He mastered his irritation. "I haven't seen Sandra since the night I told Williston to leave."

"Were they having a meeting of some kind in your apartment?"

So Rosenfeld knew about Sandra; more, probably, than I do, Fenner thought. "You might call it that."

"With *you* around?" Rosenfeld was amazed.

"I was supposed to be covering one of those late-night emergency sessions at the U.N.—I had just got back, the week before, from Korea—but I went home at ten o'clock. I felt I was coming down with an attack of grippe. And the emergency session was getting nowhere—" He halted. He was remembering the long dark hall of the apartment, the sound of subdued voices from the living room at its far end. He was standing there pulling off his coat, cursing the idea of a party and people to face, feeling the ache in his bones and his tight throat, wondering if he could slip unnoticed into the bedroom and fall asleep. He needed Scotch and aspirin. He went to get them, quietly, just outside the living-room door. There was one voice speaking, clear, authoritative. My God, he thought, ready to laugh, someone's giving an imitation as his parlor trick; Sandra has developed a strange taste in entertainment since I've been away. But the parlor trick went on and on. My God, he thought, no longer ready to laugh, and what's this about germ warfare, what's this about arranging protests and demonstrations? The voice ended its instructions, and it was Sandra who was talking the same vicious nonsense, with a seriousness, an intensity he had never heard before. He came out of his trance. He could see, even now, the startled faces staring at him in the doorway; and Sandra, reverting automatically from the agitprop activist into the fluttering hostess. "Darling, but how wonderful! You're just in time to hear us read Act Three of George's new play. George Williston—my husband. And this is Jenny— Why, Bill, Bill! Bill, these are my friends, will you shut up?" The sweet hostess words had ended in a shout of anger, but he finished what he had to say. And so began the Grand Exit. Followed by the Great Quarrel. That lasted until three in the morning. It was more than a quarrel: it was, in the unguarded heat of Sandra's anger, a revelation.

And then he had left, his body shivering with fever, head throbbing, heart sick. He spent one day in a hotel, four days in a hospital. When he returned to the apartment to pick up his clothes, it was empty. Sandra had gone. On orders, he thought bitterly, like everything else in her well-controlled career. He had been a useful name to cover her real life; he had become a positive handicap, perhaps even a possible danger.

"Well," Fenner said, "I suppose we have all been fooled one way or another at one time." He mustered a smile. "Yes, I've met George Williston."

"He was in Paris last April for a very brief visit," Rosenfeld said smoothly. "He met Mrs. Fane—that's what she calls herself, these days—at a café over on the Left Bank. It could have been an innocent meeting, from Mrs. Fane's point of view. Perhaps he was trying to pull her back into her old life again; perhaps she was refusing, and chose to meet him far away from the Avenue d'Iéna to save herself embarrassment. The truth is, she's a question mark. She's been living a perfectly normal life since her escape from Czechoslovakia." If, Rosenfeld added to himself, being the mistress of a French government official with private means and a wide circle of friends could be called a normal way to live.

Fenner said nothing. Not even the use of the word "escape" had aroused his interest. He looked at his watch.

"But Williston is no question mark. He hasn't changed his aim in life. So that is what makes the meeting with Mrs. Fane important. Was it real business or was it only an attempt at business that failed? The answer is essential, because of her—of her influence over a certain Monsieur Fernand Lenoir. He's an important guy."

"Another blind idiot?"

Rosenfeld looked nonplussed. But he wasn't defeated. "Won't you even think of accepting her invitation?"

"What?"

"She sent you one last night, by way of Ballard. Didn't he pass it on?"

"He never got the chance. I cut him off when he started talking about

Sandra." There was complete disbelief in Fenner's eyes. "She'd never invite me—"

"But she did. Stanfield Dade was there at the time. She was talking to Ballard and him. About you."

"Then she's just using me again." The words had slipped out. He cursed himself under his breath.

"Perhaps. Perhaps not. There's one way we could find out. That would answer the question about her meeting with Williston, too."

Fenner stared at him. "I hope you are not meaning—"

"I'm meaning this. People who reform have anguish and remorse. Right? They feel better if they can give an honest apology to those they have hurt the most. Right? She would talk to you, more than she would talk to anyone else. She would feel she owes you that. Why don't you see her?"

"No."

"But you could be doing her a good turn."

"I'm doing her no kind of turn, either good or bad."

"Look, she proposed seeing you. Why don't you—"

"No," said Fenner quietly. "And no, and no." If Sandra had wanted to see him, it was more likely for quite another reason: she could very well want to gauge how safe she was with him in Paris. She was a much more devious and intricate character than Rosenfeld imagined.

Rosenfeld was saying, "Oh well, it was worth a try. But I'm still curious why she talked about you to Ballard. Either she wants to say she's sorry—she was the reason you ended your career as a news correspondent, wasn't she?"

Fenner studied the leaves in the garden outside. Some were beginning to shrivel at the edges into the first hint of autumn.

"Or," Rosenfeld went on, "she wants to know where you stand. You could do her a lot of damage. Not many people know her history; and you know her better than they do." He noticed the look in Fenner's eyes. "Yes?"

"Oh, just making a mental apology. You're a smart boy."

"Sometimes not smart enough." Rosenfeld wished he had never brought up the subject of Sandra Fane. "Well, let's go. Thanks for the two minutes. They stretched a little. I'm sorry." He paused with his hand on the doorknob. "How's your memory, by the way?"

"At times, it can be very bad. I just can't remember a thing you were talking about. How's that?"

"That's fine." Rosenfeld opened the door. "I'll escort you across the frontier. When you reach France, turn right. You'll be back at the Crillon Bar in no time."

At the side gate, Fenner looked at his watch and decided he would have to settle for a short lunch, after all. He had lost his appetite, anyway. He said good-by to Rosenfeld. They went separate ways.

Fenner crossed a busy narrow street to a small café with a red-striped awning. He was thinking gloomily that the past was never over. As long as you lived, you carried it with you. It shaped your life: what you were, today, depended on all you had seen and felt and heard yesterday; and what you now accepted or rejected would mold your tomorrow. We are, because of what we were. . . . Shall we be, because of what we are?

Let's try some will power, he told himself, and blot out the ghosts that came rising up this morning. It has worked before, giving long stretches of blessed anesthesia. No good in remembering the hurt and the misery and the damage that was done you: that only nurses your bitterness, and you inflict hurt and misery and damage on yourself. Just remember enough never to be vulnerable again: total forgetting could be as self-destructive as complete remembering.

He settled at a small zinc table outside the café. He disregarded the traffic, the heat, the arms brushing past, the unsuccessful sandwich and the bitter coffee. Will power, he reminded himself wryly, was sometimes necessary for the present as well as for the past. But a small cluster of typists from the Embassy turned his mood. They were young and pretty, trying to be chic and worldly. Their chatter held pleasant no-meaning, more amusing, actually, than most first acts he had sat through this last season. Their laughter won. The traffic became friendly bustle, the heat was tempered by a small breeze, the passing faces were varied and intelligent, the second cup of coffee tasted better. Patient coming out of shock, he told himself almost cheerfully, and could smile. He would sit here and enjoy the Paris sun until it was time to move toward the Left Bank and Professor Vaugiroud.

Only a few streets away from Fenner, in a small restaurant without any outside tables, Neill Carlson was having his third cup of coffee. The place was almost empty: the customers, mostly Frenchmen, had been leaving steadily for the last half hour. He finished reading *Figaro*, slung it back on its hook on the brown paneled wall, took down *Combat*. As he was returning to his isolated table, Frank Rosenfeld joined him.

"About time," Carlson said. "Another five minutes, and I'd have to leave."

"Went back to the office," Rosenfeld explained. "I got a face-to-face description of yellow-tie that was worth sending out."

"So?" Carlson was curious.

"But that was about all I got from Fenner." Rosenfeld broke into a description of his mother-in-law's visit to Paris in July as the waiter approached for his order. An omelet and coffee, Rosenfeld decided.

"You didn't do so well?" Carlson asked when they were left alone again.

"I don't know."

Carlson looked puzzled. "He didn't strike me as an evasive type."

"He wasn't. He answered my questions. And he had a few of his own." Rosenfeld grinned. "Wanted to know if yellow-tie was the friend who had helped Goldsmith into a cab."

"Reasonable deduction, seeing you were asking questions about yellow-tie."

"Then he suggested their meeting wasn't in the tradition, was it?"

"Well, he's a critic. They like to cast doubts."

"He's a bit of a comedian, too. Suggested how to be successful in espionage without really trying."

"How?"

"Just break the accepted patterns."

Carlson laughed. "He might have something there."

"Yes," Rosenfeld admitted. "That open contact and departure was a bit startling. I was beginning to wonder, this early morning, if Goldsmith wasn't just a harmless soul being met by a patient friend. Kind of comic, when you think of it."

"Not for Mr. Goldsmith. It must have been a quick and agonizing reappraisal on his part. He couldn't pass on the wrong coat. Contact needed for explanation, and some reorganization."

"That's what worries me. This business must be pretty important to make him act with such speed. He's a sick man."

"No ideas as yet?"

"Just speculations. And you?"

"Just speculations. Give us all time, Rosie."

"Do we have it to give?"

"Well, the other side is stymied, too, meanwhile. How do they replace those ten bills? It must have taken them weeks to collect them, using carefully chosen people to ask for them at their banks. The Treasury boys can trace them: the banks make a note of that kind of transaction."

"Glad to hear someone can get results."

"You've made a start yourself. You've got an adequate picture of yellow-tie. Bernard's files over at the Sûreté may be of help on that—they're pretty complete on the Communist underground."

"If Bernard will co-operate."

"He smells another of those one-for-all-and-all-for-one situations. Sure, old Bernie will co-operate."

"At least," Rosie said, "I made certain that yellow-tie isn't going to be forgotten by Fenner."

"You think he may be in danger?"

"If this business is as urgent and important as I feel it is, anyone involved is in danger."

"He's back to his own life again, seeing his friends in Paris, going to theatrical parties, talking about Molière and Anouilh and Beckett. His involvement is over."

"Certainly," Rosenfeld said, "he isn't going to let himself be involved with Madame Fane."

"Your suggestion fell flat?"

Rosenfeld saw his waiter approaching. "Flatter than a jalopy's tire running on its rim." He began talking about the Grand Canyon's pitted walls. The omelet was served, and the waiter left, surrounded by Hopi Indians taking refuge in the Canyon's holes from a Navajo raiding party striking across the Painted Desert.

"So," Carlson said, "he just clammed up when you started probing?"

"About her, yes. He did say he had met Comrade Bruno. Not as Bruno. Nor as Geoffrey Wills. George Williston was the name he used on the night Fenner threw him out of the apartment."

"Dear old Bruno-Wills-Williston," Carlson murmured, "what would you do without him to lead you to such interesting people?"

Rosenfeld laughed. "You know, that's one question Fenner forgot to ask: why didn't we nail Williston if we knew he was such a bastard? But I agree with you; he has his uses."

"New York will be preening itself on following that hunch. Bruno suddenly turned aesthete, visiting the Museum of Modern Art, standing a long time in front of *Guernica,* very close to a quiet man. Meaning? Nothing. Quiet man unknown, innocent visitor; Bruno just an admirer of Picasso. But next day Bruno turns animal lover, walks in Zoo, seems to be keeping friendly watch. On whom? Same quiet man. Quiet man now interesting. Becomes more interesting when he jigs around town, takes three taxis to get to his hotel from a dentist's office only a few blocks away." He noticed Rosenfeld's deep gloom. "Didn't I get your story right?"

"You tell it better than I do," Rosenfeld said sourly.

"All is not lost, Rosie. After all—"

Rosenfeld said, "Yes, they had a good hunch in New York. They tipped us off. And we missed." He pushed his plate aside. "Never thought a French omelet could taste like a piece of flannel."

"After all," Carlson persisted, "the man wasn't half so interesting as the envelope he carried. And you've got that, Rosie, my boy."

"Through pure luck. Where's the credit?"

"Everything is luck and unluck. We get the credit when we use them properly. The only thing we can't deal with is the bullet that flattens us out. Stone dead hath no fellow."

Rosenfeld's brooding face looked up. He almost smiled.

"What would you rather have? Someone tailing the puzzling Mr. Goldsmith all over Paris? Or the envelope in good hands?" He had Rosie's frown ironing out. "Well—your little ray of sunshine is about to depart and tend to his own business. Sometimes I wish I were back in West Berlin. Bloomers are made there, all the time, but no one has to be cheered up."

"I see your British contacts in West Berlin have enlarged your vocabulary, anyway. Yes"—Rosenfeld brightened visibly—"that was a real fast-blooming bloomer about the Wall. There ought to have been advance notice on that. Why not, I wonder?"

"It was left lying in someone's in-tray too long," Carlson suggested. He wasn't so amused, but he had old Rosie back to normal.

"They missed you, I guess. When do you return?"

"Soon."

"Oh, you've got everything sewed up on your film producer?"

"Yes and no. I've found out a lot. But it's not enough."

"Who says so?"

"I do. There's something deeper—"

"What? I thought you did a pretty good analysis in depth. You know him better than the men who made out his life history for him."

"Perhaps there's a lot they don't know either."

"You mean he is really a big wheel?"

"If I could find out his real name, I could answer that."

"You can't trace it?" Rosenfeld was astounded. "That really makes him very interesting."

Carlson nodded. "I'll bequeath him to you, once you get the problem of Sandra Fane worked out. By the way, how much did you tell Fenner?"

"A certain amount, to enlist his co-operation. But it wasn't enough, obviously." Rosenfeld frowned and shook his head. "He won't talk, though. He has learned to keep his mouth shut. Don't worry about that."

"So what's worrying you about him?"

"I'm just hurt," Rosenfeld said with a broad grin. "He doesn't take us seriously." He pulled a note from his pocket. "Fenner slipped this into my hand when we said good-by. He thought you'd want it back, so that you could burn it and save yourself extra work in searching Dade's trash basket tonight."

455

"Indeed?" Carlson's usual quick phrase deserted him. He took the note he had sent Fenner about the coat. He rose, saying, "Keep in touch, will you? I'd like to know how this puzzle ends."

"I'll keep in touch," Rosie promised. "And thanks for the help."

"Thank our critic," said Carlson wryly, and departed.

Rosenfeld glanced at his watch and called for his check. Time to get back to the office and be waiting for that woman's telephone call. Who was she? Dade might have told him. He must have known who she was or else he wouldn't have given her Rosenfeld's number. People had odd ways of figuring out the limits of their actions: I'll give Rosie's number because this may be important; but if she changes her mind—as women do—and doesn't call Rosie, then let's leave her anonymous, and Rosie can't try to reach her. And if that was the way Dade had figured it, the woman must be pretty important, too. For Rosie, happily married, didn't go around trying to telephone women unless they were interesting. And "interesting" in Rosie's vocabulary did not mean glamorous.

SIX

Bill Fenner took a taxi to get him across the Seine and along the stretch of tree-lined quays that marked the river's left bank. He got out near the Ecole des Beaux-Arts, was tempted to loiter among the bookstalls across the street, even sit under the coolness of the green leaves and watch the sun-speckled water swirl past the Louvre's gray eminence. But there were only twenty minutes to Vaugiroud: ten minutes of walking; ten minutes of margin to find Number 7, Rue Jean-Calas. So he turned to his right, and headed south on a street that was long and narrow and, more importantly for his purpose, remarkably straight.

It led him, at a good quick pace, past a sprinkling of antique shops and small studios where art objects were displayed or made. Here and there a bakery, with the sweet warm smell of new loaves; little bookstores to remind man that he did not live by bread alone. And everywhere were the people who lived or worked in this quarter: craftsmen out of their workshops for a breath of air; students with books or portfolios of drawings; thick-waisted housewives clopping along in heelless sandals; thin-legged, button-eyed children, carrying pikes of bread as tall as themselves; two sculptors in clay-smeared smocks; girls with alert faces, fine eyes, tight skirts, loose sweaters, wild hair combed by the winds and washed by the rains. He crossed the Boulevard Saint-Germain, broad and busy. Shortly, he ought to branch off to his left, following a twist of side street which—if his map was accurate—would lead him into the Rue Jean-Calas. His map was correct: there was Vaugiroud's entrance just ahead of him. And he had five minutes to spare.

Fenner strolled past its huge doors, sun-seamed and rain-scrubbed. Like the house itself, they belonged to the eighteenth century, when they no doubt led to a porte-cochere, perhaps even to an interior courtyard. They stood closed; the windows above and around them were silent. There was no row of name plates, no indication of how many apartments now lay behind those doors. Fenner walked on, and reached the end of the short street. In front of him there was a small cobbled expansion, which someone had called a square: Place Arouet. It was more of a breathing space, to trap some sunshine, before another little street closed in with its walls of gently decaying houses. All around was the peace of age and forgetfulness, a sense of quiet resignation and retreat from busier streets and a noisy boulevard only a few minutes away.

There were few people in the Place Arouet. Two old men, carefully dressed, had paused to talk in their late-afternoon saunter, a boy jolted over the cobblestones on a bicycle, a car was parked on the shaded side of the square near an antique shop. At the café opposite, marked by four zinc tables under a faded green awning, there was a man comatose over an unfinished drink. It would be pleasant to join him and have a long cool beer: but perhaps not, Fenner decided. The café lay on the sun-drenched side of the Place Arouet. It would be hot under that awning. The man who sat there must be a Finn enjoying a late-summer sauna.

Fenner, his eye on his watch (Professor Vaugiroud's voice, this morning, had been too brisk for unpunctuality), retraced his steps along the Rue Jean-Calas. He pulled the old-fashioned bell, and heard its weak jangle echo its echo, dying, dying into a distant tremor. As he waited, he glanced briefly back to the Place Arouet. The man at the café table was visible from this doorway. He would certainly know Fenner again. But what else had a man to do, who had finished his newspaper and hadn't armed himself with a book and had chosen to sit at a lonely little café, except look? Yet, Fenner thought, I could have sworn he was dozing like a dog in the sun when I stood at the corner of the square. What brought him back to life?

One of the doors half opened. A woman, her short and heavy body covered by a tight black cotton dress, her bare feet thrust into flat-heeled scuffs, looked at him inquiringly from under a dyed, dried fringe of hair.

"Professor Vaugiroud?" he asked.

The door stayed at its forty-five-degree angle. She was middle-aged, sad-faced, distrustful.

"He is expecting me. At four o'clock."

Her sharp brown eyes studied him.

"My name is Fenner," he said clearly. Was his French as difficult to grasp as all that?

She looked over her shoulder quickly, and she scolded someone. "Get back to your work!" She waited, the lines in her face deepened by her annoyance, and at last she swung the door fully open to let Fenner step inside. The depths of the building encased him in a short but massive tunnel, with an entrance to a staircase on either side. Ahead was a shadowed courtyard with a cluster of old bicycles around a covered well, ivy climbing around dark ground-floor windows, a few scraps of clothing drying on a sagging rope. The woman had closed the door behind him and barred it. She was at his elbow, pointing to the staircase entrance on the left. "One flight up," she told him, voice brisk but pleasant enough. She noticed that he seemed fascinated by the courtyard. "Everyone except the professor is away—place is empty until the classes start again—my husband—" She looked at the bicycles, shrugged, and said nothing more. She nodded recognition of his thanks, her eyes looking past him into the courtyard, and clopped off in her loose slippers. As he entered the staircase hall, he could hear her voice, changed back into sharp anger as she called to the child who provoked her so much. Then there was only the sound of his footsteps on the elaborate wooden staircase. Above him, from a small crown of window in the ancient roof, the light and heat streamed down.

A door opened as Fenner reached the second-floor landing. A small man, slight of build, dressed in a neat light-gray suit, cocked his head to one side as his deeply set brown eyes studied the American. "Mr. Fenner? You are punctual." The voice was precise but melodious. "That way!" Professor Vaugiroud raised his walking stick and pointed. Fenner walked through the small hall, jammed with furniture, toward an open door. Behind him, Professor Vaugiroud snapped a bolt into its socket and followed him with a good attempt at speed in spite of his dragging right leg.

The room they entered was a surprise. It looked across the Rue Jean-Calas to the sun-baked houses opposite, but here, on the shadowed side of the street, it was cool. It was airy, light. And it was, in comparison with the crowded hall, almost empty. Large, high-ceilinged, bare-floored, it contained only a large table (serving as a desk), three chairs, a couple of practical reading lamps, a telephone, a small radio, and books. Books everywhere, covering the walls, climbing to the carved scrolls of the ceiling. A filing cabinet was tucked into one corner of the room, a narrow bed into another. It was a neat place, with its piles of magazines and newspapers stacked in orderly fashion on the lower bookshelves. Even the clutter on the desk had a certain logic in its arrangement. Professor Vaugiroud was a busy but well-organized man. Perhaps, to be effective, the two attributes had to be closely married.

He was also an agile man, even with his disabled leg. He had moved quickly to the desk, leaning heavily on his walking stick, and seemed to be absorbed in selecting some papers. He must be almost seventy, Fenner guessed. His hair, thick-thatched, was white and carefully brushed, but one lock insisted on hanging free over his brow. His thin face, with its long nose and strong chin, magnificent eyes, high forehead, gave the impression of alert intelligence and considerable will power.

"Satisfied?" he asked Fenner, looking up with an abrupt smile. "Does Walter Penneyman's description fit me?" His English was fluent and accurate, but strongly accented.

Fenner decided to be equally brusque. "Yes. And here are my credentials." He searched for the note of introduction in his pocket. Vaugiroud took it, but he seemed more interested in studying the American as Fenner moved over to the near window. Fenner glanced at the desk as he passed it, stood at one side of the opened window, looked down at the end of the Rue Jean-Calas and the beginning of the Place Arouet.

Fenner was both embarrassed and amused. On the desk there had been three old copies of the New York *Chronicle* neatly folded back to the drama page. One had a reasonably accurate photograph of Fenner, taken along with other New York critics at the Tony Awards last year. There was also a copy of *Who's Who in the Theatre*. Fenner could imagine Carlson saying: "See how easy it is?" (Come to think of it, Carlson might have been the man to interview Vaugiroud. He would have known how to get this conversation started, at least.) I'll let Vaugiroud make the pace, Fenner thought: he may have decided he doesn't want to talk with me at all.

"Something interesting in the Place Arouet?" Vaugiroud asked.

Fenner shook his head. The café tables were empty. Just as he was about to turn away, he noticed a small tilted mirror fixed on the wall outside the window at his elbow level. He drew a few paces backward and bent his head to see into the mirror. It reflected a stretch of sidewalk in front of the house entrance. "Useful gadget," he remarked as he watched the man who had sat at the café table now standing below, close to the gateway, facing it. Even as Fenner looked, the man stepped back from the door, stared up at the windows above him, turned abruptly away. Instinctively, Fenner drew aside: the man's quick glance had seemed a real confrontation. Then he relaxed, remembering he was invisible from down there. The man might be interested in him, but Fenner had seen more of the man than he had seen of Fenner. Fair hair, light-colored eyes, a strongly boned face with snub features, bluntly handsome, tanned deeply, powerful shoulders under a blue summer shirt. It was a flash impression, yet deeply etched into Fenner's mind: he wasn't accustomed to seeing such menace as the man's eyes had shown in that brief moment.

Vaugiroud had noticed Fenner's face, and he was puzzled. "Very useful," he conceded, and waited.

"Can you hear the doorbell up here?"

"Not always. Age has dulled its tongue. You seem worried, Mr. Fenner."

"No." Not worried, just on edge. This morning's events were still with him, seemingly. He was tired, of course. Last night's sleep had been broken. When you were tired, everything was exaggerated. In his normal senses, he would never have seen a pair of curious eyes and read menace into them. Had the man actually been talking to someone inside the front doorway? Or was that just imagination, too?

"But not at ease. I am sorry. If I can entice you away from the limited view offered by that window, I shall offer you this chair. Let me find you a cigarette." Vaugiroud looked vaguely around like a typical nonsmoker for the small box of dried-up cigarettes that he kept for visitors.

"I have my own, thanks." But Fenner took the hint, left the man in the process of crossing the street—good strong shoulders and muscular body, Fenner noted, but below average height—and sat down.

Vaugiroud laughed unexpectedly. "I had expected to be distrustful of you, Mr. Fenner; not to be distrusted by you."

"Far from that, sir," Fenner said, smiling, forced into an explanation. "I was only puzzled by a man loitering outside."

"He followed you here?" Vaugiroud asked quickly.

"Of course not."

"How pleasant to be able to say 'Of course not' with such complete certainty."

"Let's say I am reasonably sure. He was already sitting at a café table on the square when I arrived."

"People do sit at café tables."

Fenner nodded and lit his cigarette.

"You think he is watching this house?"

"Perhaps."

"That's always possible, of course," Vaugiroud said evenly, but he limped over to the window and looked toward the Place Arouet. "A fair-haired man in a blue shirt?" He frowned. "We shall let him swelter at his table," he said, and came back to face Fenner. "I have long since ceased to worry about things over which I have no control."

"You have no control over your concierge?"

Vaugiroud eyed him sharply. "I trust Mathilde." That was final. "Now let us begin. First, I have a few questions." Politely, but skillfully, he set

461

out to discover some information about Fenner: could a drama critic, dealing with a world of make-believe, be a serious student of international politics? Fenner had often been probed by experts, but Vaugiroud was the master-prober of them all. Why, wondered Fenner in half-amusement, must he be so sure of me in his own mind? What has he to tell me that makes it so important for him to be sure?

"You must forgive my curiosity, Mr. Fenner," Vaugiroud said, noticing the look in Fenner's eyes, "but you have me at a disadvantage. Walter Penneyman no doubt told you something about me, but he had no way of telling me very much about you."

"Except that he sent me here."

"Trust me, trust my friend?" Vaugiroud seemed amused. "Yet we do not always like the friends of our friends. How far do we trust people if we don't like them? Or, conversely, trust too blindly if we like them? Human emotions, Mr. Fenner, are scarcely a reliable basis for any accurate judgment."

"So I have learned," Fenner said abruptly. His face tightened, became guarded.

Vaugiroud sensed he had touched a nerve center. This was the difficulty in trying to talk with strangers. Even with people you knew, there could be hidden gulfs of experience which you discovered unexpectedly, one foot ready to plunge over just as you caught your balance and took a step back to safer ground. "My curiosity was not aroused by any distrust of you," he said quickly. "I only wondered about your capability for this special job. You see, I cannot talk freely unless I know I am going to be taken seriously. There is an attitude, among some people, of thinking that anything dealing with clandestine politics or conspiracy is—well, either cheaply sensational or comic."

"I think I've learned something about the hidden face of conspiracy," Fenner said stiffly. "It has its comic aspects, sure. But I don't confuse them with reality any more."

Vaugiroud had been watching Fenner carefully, listening, sensing. Suddenly he nodded, pulled the desk chair around, sat down, manipulating his damaged leg with skill, managing to hide a grotesque clutch of pain. "I have several facts to give you for Mr. Penneyman. How do you propose to get them into his hands?"

"He suggested I should cable the main points. In code, of course."

Vaugiroud rejected that idea with a shake of the head. "Your code is meant for brevity, not secrecy. This information must be handled, meanwhile, with—shall we say, discretion? Because there are two parts to my information. The first is a report for Mr. Penneyman. The second is an

462

analysis, made on the basis of the facts I discovered for him, which could be of interest to Washington. He has friends there? I thought so. I want him to get this analysis, this memorandum, into official hands. The memorandum is not for him, you understand? It goes far beyond the facts I gathered for the report he wanted."

"Have you tried sending this memorandum to Washington through our Embassy here in Paris?"

"How? I don't know anyone there personally. Do you think they would send someone to listen to me? Or would he listen to me if he did come? Another—as you would say—another crackpot professor. Might that not be his judgment?" Vaugiroud almost smiled. "It is never easy to gather such information, but it is sometimes still more difficult to communicate it to the proper authorities."

Fenner, remembering this morning, could agree. "I know someone at the Embassy—" He stopped. Would Carlson be interested enough to find the proper authorities? "You have two problems of transmission. First, the report for Walt Penneyman; second, the memorandum for Washington. I can deal with the first. I'll make a breakdown of its main points, and get it over to Penneyman at once."

"How?"

"I'll try to persuade my friend at the Embassy to send it by diplomatic pouch. You have no objection to letting him see what he is sending?"

"None. But the memorandum?"

"It could travel the same way. Provided, of course, it really is urgent. Someone at the Embassy would have to check that, of course."

"Of course." Vaugiroud was not too enthusiastic. "But will they send it quickly, or will they spend weeks in verifying my facts? Of what use is a warning of danger if it is not made before the danger arises?"

"None, except to produce a fine crop of gloom, breast-beating, ashes on the head, and a general state of despondency." Danger, wondered Fenner: how the hell did anyone analyze danger? Was Vaugiroud one of those crackpot prophets, after all? No, not from what Penneyman had told him.

And Vaugiroud, as if he could share all Fenner's mixed emotions, asked quietly, "Do you trust me enough to believe me, Mr. Fenner? That is important, you know. What do you actually know about my life? Or don't you?"

"You were once a professor of Moral Philosophy, and lectured at the Sorbonne." Fenner glanced at a bookshelf where two volumes had caught his eye: Vaugiroud—*Man's Search for the Divine*. "You resigned during the Nazi occupation and"—Fenner glanced at the crippled leg—"became active in the Resistance. At the end of the war, you changed your interests from Moral to Political Philosophy. You are at present working on *A Social History of Violence*. You also write analytical articles on power politics. You live alone"—Fenner avoided looking at the photograph of Vaugiroud's wife on the desk: she had died as a hostage during the Nazi occupation, Walt Penneyman had warned him—"and you haven't left Paris in the last sixteen years." Fenner hesitated. He had also been warned that Vaugiroud disliked visitors, except his own friends and old pupils, and that he had—from some of those friends and old pupils, now highly placed in their professions—developed one of the best amateur intelligence services in Western Europe. But he thought he could omit that. "That's about all, I think."

"Enough, I suppose. But how meager one's life becomes when it is reduced to its basic facts." Vaugiroud shook his head ruefully. "And the last, most complete, reduction is on one's tombstone: a name, two dates. This man was born, and died. And few ask why." His voice dropped away; his sharp, intelligent face became a sculptured head brooding over his own grave. Then, very much alive, he quickly picked up from his desk a sheet of paper covered with fine handwriting and a batch of newspaper clippings. "Well, here are the items that Mr. Penneyman would like to see. I have called this report the *History of the Planted Lie*."

Fenner looked sharply at Vaugiroud.

"Last April, Walter Penneyman came over to Paris. He was worried about the truth or untruth of certain current newspaper stories dealing with our Generals' Revolt in Algeria and the alleged backing of that revolt by your Central Intelligence Agency. I was interested, too. Why?" Vaugiroud had not yet handed over the report. He waited for the answer.

Penneyman had been interested in the responsibilities of the press, Fenner knew. But Vaugiroud? "Possibly it's the same reason that made you change from the study of ethics to power politics. Your experience in the Resistance, perhaps?"

Vaugiroud was pleased with the answer. "You are half right. My conversion was a little earlier than that, though. It happened on the day I stood and watched the Nazi tanks roll down the Champs-Elysées." He paused. "I had always a questioning kind of mind. But that day I wept. I had no answers. How could this be happening? How did an enemy break you down before any real war began, so that all your military protections became useless? How did he weaken you, separate you from your friends, divide opinions, destroy your morale and your purpose? I have been trying to find the answers ever since. I gave up my work, my search for the Good, and turned to analyzing the Evil." He looked down at the report he held in his hand. "I have learned several things: without knowing what is menacing us, we cannot protect our safety; in 1940, it was too late for any answer except remorse, and misery, and hidden resistance; in 1935, we could have saved ourselves that agony. For the basic reality of power politics is always this: who is going to control your life—you or your enemy? There is no evasion of that question. If you ignore it, you have lost."

Vaugiroud's voice hardened. "If we were sheep, or pigs, it would scarcely matter who shaped our history. When a sheep, or a pig, can eat and sleep and procreate, it is satisfied. It cannot even imagine tomorrow. But we have more to demand of our lives than that; and more is demanded of us. Unless, of course, we have become two-legged sheep. Or pigs." He checked his rising anger. "Ah, well—" He shrugged his shoulders. "These are the times that try men's souls, Mr. Fenner."

"And character," Fenner said quietly.

Vaugiroud's eyes, watchful and probing, were suddenly satisfied. "Character—an old-fashioned word nowadays. But still a good one." He handed over the report for Walt Penneyman.

It was in French, very closely written, precisely detailed. Fenner read it carefully, condensing, selecting the main points that were the skeleton of the report. In brief, it began with the date of the Generals' Revolt—April 22, 1961. Within a few hours a story was circulating that the Central Intelligence Agency of the United States had instigated and aided the revolt against France. Within a few days the story was printed as uncontrovertible fact in the Roman newspaper *Il Paese*. Immediately, *Pravda*, Tass, and Radio Moscow were quoting *Il Paese* to Europe and the Middle East. By April 27, the London *Daily Worker* was denouncing America. A non-Communist French newspaper followed suit. So did other French papers. So did some officials in the French government, who talked cautiously, with shrugs and pursed lips, to foreign journalists. The news was even beginning to be accepted by some friends as well as enemies. The storm was rising to hurricane proportions. Americans protested their innocence, but how do you prove innocence? Even the usually accurate, and conservative, newspaper *Le Monde* could begin an attack on the CIA with the damning phrase "It now seems established . . ." But it wasn't. An Australian newsman, reporting for a British paper, challenged a French official at a public luncheon, and the French government issued a statement that no evidence had been discovered that could support the story. The report became what it always had been, a planted lie.

As Fenner finished reading, Vaugiroud handed over the sheaf of newspaper clippings. "Verification," he said. And it was impressive. Vaugiroud had gathered every report from all the European newspapers that had joined in the attack.

"Damning," Fenner conceded. And damnable. Even at this distance, with the lie nailed to the floor, he felt a surge of cold anger.

"As a Frenchman, I find it painful."

"Was that the reason you did so much work on this report?"

"Partly, yes. And partly because I could not make any deductions unless I gathered the facts first. From them, I have been able to make some suggestions in this memorandum"—he reached for a small pile of closely written pages—"very lengthy, I'm afraid: so much documentation, references, additional facts. And names." He hesitated. "You see," he went on, "I learned more than I expected to learn when I first started on that report for Walter Penneyman."

Fenner looked with some awe at the pile of manuscript. His French wasn't as good as all that. This would take him several hours of concentrated work. Still, he was eager to see what Vaugiroud had written. He held out his hand, and then drew it back. "Sorry," he said.

"You are interested?"

"Definitely."

Vaugiroud didn't pass over the memorandum. He said, "It would be safer for you not to see it, Mr. Fenner. But I can tell you, very roughly, at least part of it. So that you can judge if it really is worth all your trouble in helping me send it to Washington."

Fenner hid his disappointment. Even Vaugiroud's phrase "safer for you . . . Mr. Fenner" had aroused his curiosity still more: any information that was dangerous was usually worth knowing. As a onetime newsman— He caught himself sharply. Had Walt Penneyman been right? Was the old itch to know all about a story still there? He said, "That's fair enough."

"The memorandum is divided into four sections. First, the purpose behind the planted lie. Second, the means and methods used to spread it. Third, the reason for its failure. And fourth—the next attempt."

Fenner stared. "You think they will try something like this again?" The question had been jolted out of him.

"I don't think. I know," said Vaugiroud very quietly.

"You *know*?"

"I know that an act of violence is being planned right now. I know that it will take place soon. I know that the same propagandist is already preparing the campaign against America."

"You don't know time or place?"

"Obviously not. Or else you wouldn't be sitting here listening to me.

Instead, I would be talking to some Intelligence officers from NATO, or some of the international experts from our own Sûreté."

"Sorry. That was a damned silly question of mine."

Vaugiroud was mollified by the frank statement. "Why shouldn't they try something like that again?" he asked, pointing to the report for Penneyman. "It was a brilliant success, except for one omission. Next time, they won't make that mistake."

"What was it?"

"They did not provide evidence."

"Evidence? A letter, some kind of signed document? But that would have been a forgery, and forgeries can be disproved."

"Disproof takes time. For the last four years, the Russians have been fabricating several letters and memorandums which could have caused serious trouble for the West. Fortunately, our governments had the time to examine them, exchange proof with each other of the falsity of the documents."

"How did they get that time?"

"No headlines in the newspapers, Mr. Fenner," Vaugiroud said with a tactful smile. "The documents were examined and checked, very quietly. I don't expect you will approve of that. But it did save several unpleasant misunderstandings between the NATO allies. Looking back at last April, I now think we were very lucky."

Fenner said thoughtfully, "The revolt broke so quickly, I suppose, that there wasn't time to manufacture evidence?" He could imagine the added effect of some bogus correspondence between a French general and the CIA being published in *Il Paese*.

"They did very well as it was. But if they could have produced some definite evidence—such as a large sum of American dollars found in a general's luggage or house or deposited in his bank account—what then?"

Fenner, who had been lighting a cigarette, looked up quickly.

"That amazes you, Mr. Fenner? Surely you've heard of planted money? What could be more definitive than a large amount of foreign currency? Oh, I grant you that, given time, we could disprove our guilt. But will we have time?"

"Do *they* have time to manufacture our guilt? There are constant crises, God knows, but—like that Algerian revolt—they can break unexpectedly for both East and West. Unless, of course—" Fenner stared at Vaugiroud "—unless they manufactured a crisis, too. Prepared everything, knew what to expect, and exploited it. To the hilt."

"To the hilt," Vaugiroud agreed. He smiled like a professor who was delighted with his pupil's efforts.

467

Perhaps the interview could have ended with that. But Fenner wouldn't let it. He was interested. He wanted to learn, to know. He was still a newsman, still the man searching for answers. He forgot about time, about his own plans for the evening. And in that moment of sitting back, of lighting another cigarette to replace the one that had gone out, of framing his next sentence most carefully, he changed the whole course of his life.

"So you know," he said, "that a crisis of some kind, an act of violence, is being planned. But how?" We've been doing some sharp deduction, he thought; we have made several acute inferences, but neither deduction nor inference was knowledge, actual knowledge. "You're a trained philosopher. You don't use the word 'know' meaning 'think' or 'expect' or 'feel.' Right?"

Vaugiroud nodded gravely. "I have seen three terrorists meet regularly, twice a week, for the last month. Two weeks ago, they were joined by one of the most skillful Communist propagandists in France. I know enough about these men, their politics, their past history—" He had become deadly serious. He pointed once more to his report for Walt Penneyman. "You read, in there, about the minor officials connected with our government whose gossip helped to make the foreign journalists so bewildered about America. Their connections gave a special significance to any hints or criticisms they passed around. You understand?"

Fenner nodded. Gossip about an international crisis was only speculation if it came from a grocer or bank clerk. But from anyone connected with a Foreign Office or State Department, gossip might seem inside information.

"For that reason, I was alarmed by that crop of rumors last April. So were several of my friends who are in government service themselves. Granted that our national pride was badly hurt by the army revolt, granted that some officials at the Elysée Palace were only too willing to hope for a scapegoat, there still remained the question: did those minor officials who gossiped really believe what they were hinting? Or were they only repeating what had been dropped very skillfully into their ears? If so, by whom? It took time and patience and tact to find out. My friends did find out. The so-called information of the officials concerned could always be traced back, eventually, deviously, to one source. To one man and his own small group of intimates. He is in a position of trust. Not important, not policy-making level. But he is a man, in government, with a wide circle of friends and acquaintances, and many contacts. I have his name. Here." Vaugiroud's fingers tapped the memorandum on his lap. "It has a special significance for me. Because I knew him once. Under another name, of course." He paused. "I have been searching for him for sixteen years."

Sixteen years. Since the end of the war, Fenner thought.

468

"Today," Vaugiroud went on, "his politics seem nicely left of center, liberal without being rabid; always admirable, always acceptable. But I knew him when I was in command of a special unit of the Resistance working here in Paris. He was known only as Jacques. He was a Communist, very able; he fought bravely, risked much. A capable and intelligent young man, interested in psychological warfare. I made him my second-in-command. I trusted him. And so, on August 11, 1944, eight days before the liberation of Paris, I found myself in Gestapo hands." Vaugiroud looked down at his crippled leg.

"Jacques denounced you to the Nazis?"

"He informed secretly."

"Why?"

"The end of the Nazi war was in sight. That was the time to eliminate any Resistance leaders who would oppose any Communist attempt to seize power. He was acting under orders, of course. It was part of the pattern, at that time—like the arms and the money they were beginning to steal and hide."

"How do you know it was Jacques who informed?"

"If there were only five people called to a most secret meeting, and four appeared, and the fifth man did not, but the Gestapo did; and if in subsequent examination of these four, the Gestapo's questions all centered around the special business of that meeting; if only two people knew about the exact business, myself and Jacques; if the Gestapo showed no interest in the fifth member of that small group; if Jacques made no immediate move to alert other Resistance units about our arrest so that they could have us traced or make an attempt to help us; if Jacques abandoned us completely, assumed leadership of my section, replaced the four of us with men of his own choosing—" Vaugiroud's quiet voice didn't finish his long but damningly clear sentence.

"If you only knew him as Jacques, how did you find out who he really was?"

"Life plays its jokes. I searched through Paris for sixteen years, and never could trace him. Then, two weeks ago, he walked into a café to meet a very odd group of men. It's a small restaurant not far from here, just off the Boulevard Saint-Germain, where I lunch each day. He did not recognize me, for two reasons: I have changed a great deal, physically; and I was supposed to have died under Gestapo examination. That was one rumor I have allowed to live."

"And he never knew your real name, or your background?"

"Just as I never knew his. It was a security measure that all our unit shared. It was supposed to mean some safety for our families." He looked at the photograph on his desk. "Life also plays cruel tricks. She was arrested because she was the wife of Professor Pierre Vaugiroud, who was believed to be working with the Free French in London. She never told them that—" He broke off. His face became as lifeless as his voice.

Fenner searched desperately for another question. "What happened to the three others who were captured with you?" he asked sympathetically, drawing Vaugiroud away from that blank stare of grim memory.

"Two died. One stayed barely alive, as I did. The Americans freed us. And a year later—when we were fit enough—we came back to our own identities, Henri Roussin and Pierre Vaugiroud. We both had the same purpose: find Jacques. But he had dropped out of sight long before we were released from the hospital. I began to think that the Communists had transferred him to another city, another country. Or perhaps he was dead. Until two weeks ago—" Vaugiroud began to smile "—when Jacques walked into the Café Racine, which Henri Roussin owns. Jacques is now affluent, handsomely dressed, very confident in manner; a man of position, most respectable, restrained. But he is recognizable. He has aged normally, unlike Henri and myself." Vaugiroud paused. "How old would you say I am, Mr. Fenner? Frankly?"

Fenner hedged. "About sixty-five or so, I guess."

"You are being too polite. Even so, you add eleven years to my age."

Fenner was shocked into silence.

"So," Vaugiroud said, "once we found Jacques, it was easy to discover his present name. It was a double shock for me, I must admit, when that same name was given to me a few days ago as the source from which all rumors flowed."

"He is the propagandist you spoke of?"

"Yes. And the three men whom he joined for luncheon in the highly respectable Café Racine are the terrorists."

Fenner was startled. A highly respectable restaurant?

Vaugiroud did not hide his amusement. "They have been meeting twice a week since the beginning of August. My friend Henri makes a point of knowing his patrons. Most of them are regular visitors—lawyers, professors, judges. These three terrorists seemed very much the same type, well dressed, circumspect, interested in good food. One was a wine merchant, another a retired industrialist, and the third a film producer. But after Jacques met them, we naturally took a closer interest in them."

"Three rather unlikely terrorists." Were they really that? Fenner couldn't help wondering. The word had such supercharged emotion attached to it. Vaugiroud was really floating off the beam there. Why did good men who uncovered twisted politics seem to develop some twist of their own?

"Unlikely? They have money, brains, international contacts, intense convictions, ruthless ambition. The wine merchant is a staunch sympathizer with the Secret Army Organization. The industrialist subsidizes an activist group of right-wing nationalists. And the man who is now a film producer, a propagandist for Communist causes, a naturalized Frenchman, was previously—to my own knowledge, eighteen years ago—an organizer of Communist militants. His work was most secret, and so important that Comrade Jacques took abnormal risks to help smuggle him out of France back to Russia. I saw him only once, briefly, by accident. I didn't remember him until Jacques came into the restaurant. Seeing them together struck some distant memory, brought it to life. Of the four men at that table, he may be the most dangerous. . . . Yes, they are terrorists, for they are the arrangers. They are as guilty as the men who bomb, and kill, and destroy. I believe they are more guilty; because it is their planning, and their money, that can turn vicious impulses into a concerted pattern of violence. They have the means, and purpose. In the most cowardly sense of the word, these four men *are* terrorists. Do I make myself clear?"

"Quite clear." And I apologize: it was I who was wandering off the beam. Only, Fenner thought, only—

"Yes?" Vaugiroud had sensed his puzzlement.

"I suppose they couldn't be arrested, or questioned by the police?"

"On what grounds? For having luncheon together? For having political connections? They've hidden themselves well, Mr. Fenner. My friends and I have had to dig deeply to find out what I have just told you. Even I, until a few days ago, was merely puzzled, interested, worried. It was only when the man Jacques was identified as the source of anti-American propaganda last April that the warning bell sounded for me. I knew then that the threat was real. And I knew the purpose of the threat. But until I know its actual shape, all I can do is to gather facts about these men, analyze, suggest." He passed a hand over his eyes. He added wearily, "And hope that my warning is taken seriously."

"Well, they're not lunching together to finance a new movie, that's certain," Fenner said bitterly. There was a real threat in their meetings. But what? Their objectives must be far apart. What could have brought them together? A fascist and an extreme nationalist sitting down with a hard-shell Stalinist and a hidden Communist propagandist. An unholy alliance. But it had happened before. They'd use each other. Their ends justified any means.

Vaugiroud was looking at him, a little startled. "You know, that is exactly the reason they give for lunching together. Whenever Henri or one of his waiters is near their table, the talk is all about the costs of film making."

Could that be the reason, after all? No, Fenner decided slowly. "A very smooth act," he said. Too damned smooth.

"Like the meeting between Jacques and his old comrade," Vaugiroud said. "They pretended they were strangers. It was the retired industrialist who introduced them, invited Jacques to have lunch with them." That amused Vaugiroud briefly. "Very smooth, as you say, Mr. Fenner. As smooth as the lie that Jacques is now preparing against your country."

"We are again their target?"

"Again and again, until America is eliminated from Europe. I have shown you what could have happened if that last lie had succeeded. America would have been isolated, pilloried. Properly fanned, that fire could have burned out NATO. Or do I exaggerate?"

Fenner shook his head. Distrust, dissension, denunciations. Bitterness, anger, complete disillusionment with all those who had taken so much help from America, and yet, when we needed friends, had been so willing and eager to believe the worst about us. "We would have been pushed back into isolationism," he said. "NATO would have had its back broken."

"And without NATO, what protects Western Europe? Without a peaceful Western Europe, what protects the growth of the Common Market? And without the Common Market, how could a United States of Free Europe ever develop? And that, Mr. Fenner, is their ultimate target. The Communists think far ahead. The dream of a United States of Europe is the nightmare of the Communist world. They have preached that Western capitalism is doomed, ready for burial; a system breeding wars and economic cannibalism. A collection of prosperous and peaceful nations in Western Europe would be the complete rebuttal to all Communist theories. Who would believe them then?"

Well, thought Fenner, here is a definite disciple of Monnet. Here's another Frenchman who thinks in terms of people instead of nationalities. "The Communists would find their ideas outmoded. They might have to renounce Lenin as well as Stalin," he observed with a smile. Even if Vaugiroud was a Common Market enthusiast, his basic argument was valid. If the Communists feared the prosperity of West Berlin so much that they built a Wall, how much more would they fear a prosperous and peaceful Europe?

"They may be forced to do that," Vaugiroud said soberly. "But before that, they will fight us every step of the way, with every psychological weapon they can find. They don't intend to lose."

Fenner rose, glancing at his watch. "I may just catch my friend at the Embassy. May I use your telephone?"

"You trust him?"

"Yes."

"How well do you know him?"

"Actually, I only met him today."

"Today?" Vaugiroud stared incredulously.

"Yes. He is with NATO. Some kind of security branch, possibly Intelligence."

"Did he tell you that?"

"No. Just my guess. He is attached to the Embassy, meanwhile. I saw him there."

"Alone?"

"No, no," Fenner said patiently. He restrained a smile. "There were other Embassy people around who knew him. He wasn't an impostor. Shall I telephone?"

Vaugiroud did not answer. He rose, painfully, placed the memorandum on his desk, and walked over to the window. "If there were any careless talk, any casual handling of that memorandum, then our enemy might learn we were interested in their activities. I do not believe in warning our enemy, Mr. Fenner. Much wiser to make him feel secure, secure enough to be bold, to make one mistake. One, Mr. Fenner, is all that is ever needed." He looked along the street. The furrows on his brow deepened. "Is your friend a careful man?"

"Surely he wouldn't hold down his job if—"

"Wouldn't he? You really trust him a great deal on one day's meeting."

"I trust you. Is that foolish?" And you trusted me; a little, certainly.

"I hope not." Vaugiroud smiled. Then the smile vanished. He drew back slightly from the window. "I think you were right about that man in the blue shirt," he said very quietly.

"He's still there?"

"He is restless. Bored, perhaps." Vaugiroud watched the man strolling along the street again. The stranger's face came into focus.

"Perhaps you haven't had enough visitors today to please him." Fenner started toward the window.

Vaugiroud's upraised hand stopped him.

"Is he coming to check on me again?" Fenner asked jokingly. "He probably thinks I've made an exit through a back basement."

"He checked on you? How?" Vaugiroud asked sharply.

"With Mathilde at your front entrance. I thought he might be finding out my name."

473

"Why didn't you tell me?"

"Well—it seemed a silly idea at the time: sort of jumping to conclusions." Vaugiroud turned away from the window, his face set in worry. "Would you telephone your friend at the Embassy and ask him to come here?"

"When?"

"Now."

Fenner made no comment. He moved back to the desk, glanced at his watch again, registered the fact that they had lost four minutes by all that hesitation, hoped that Carlson would still be in his office at half past five, and began the intricate job of telephoning. There were, of course, various stages of waiting. He used them to continue talking to Vaugiroud, holding his hand over the phone. There were several questions that puzzled him. "Is it possible that Jacques did recognize you in the Café Racine?"

"I am sure he did not. Otherwise, I would have been watched before now. This flat would have been entered and my papers searched, to let them know how much or how little I know."

"And then what?" This man, Fenner thought, may be in greater danger than he admits. He takes it all so calmly. "Would they kill you?" he asked sharply. "Would they go as far as that?"

"I should certainly be very careful in crossing any streets," Vaugiroud admitted, and smiled. Then the smile became bitter. "Monsieur Fernand Lenoir, secure in his career, could hardly tolerate anyone who could identify him as Jacques."

Fenner stared at Vaugiroud. "Yes," he said into the telephone. "I want Carlson. No, I don't know his first name. Carlson. That's right. Tell him it's Fenner. And it's important." He looked back at Vaugiroud. Fernand Lenoir and Sandra Fane and the pleasant parties on the Avenue d'Iéna . . . That had been a calculated indiscretion on Vaugiroud's part, slipped in as skillfully as a hypodermic. Why? Because Vaugiroud knew that he had once been married to Sandra Fane? Or because Vaugiroud wanted to establish Lenoir as a name to be remembered if, someday, he wasn't too careful in crossing a street? At last, Carlson's voice came over the telephone, and Fenner was speaking with a new sense of urgency.

"This is becoming a habit," Carlson told him. He sounded far from enthusiastic.

"It's urgent."

"Again?" Carlson asked, and groaned.

"Did I disappoint you this morning? This may be still bigger news."

"You do get around, don't you?"

"I've got a new angle on those people Rosie was asking about." And

474

Fenner had Carlson noting down Vaugiroud's address without any more protests.

Vaugiroud said, as Fenner put down the receiver, "That was very expeditious. And remarkably cryptic." The unasked question hung in the air.

But I can be discreet, too, Fenner thought. He said, "Carlson will be here at six-forty-five. I'll wait until he comes." He grinned and added, "I know how you like proper introductions."

"I find them reassuring," Vaugiroud said dryly. He pursed his lips, frowned. "Perhaps you should be waiting downstairs at a quarter to seven, and let your friend enter?"

"Of course. Anything to keep Mathilde from finding out his name. I don't think Carlson would like that."

"Not Mathilde. Her husband is the one who should perhaps be kept ignorant. Was he in the courtyard when you arrived?"

"Someone was there. Out of sight. I thought it was a child."

"No children. Her husband is problem enough. Nothing he does is ever successful. You saw the bicycles? He lost his little repair shop, asked me to let him work in the courtyard until the other tenants come back." Vaugiroud sighed. "It is always the small request that turns out to be the greatest nuisance. Constant visitors, all explained as clients. If he had as many clients as that, I don't think he would ever have had to give up his shop. One thing, Mr. Fenner. When you do leave, you may see him. Mathilde won't be there; she goes out in the late afternoon for her daily shopping. Pay no attention to him at all. And if that man in the blue shirt is still out in the street—do not even look his way. Let him think you have never seen him. Will you do that?"

Fenner nodded. He didn't quite follow Vaugiroud's reasoning, but that was something he could puzzle out later. The quiet voice again amazed him. He said, "You take all this pretty calmly."

"How else?"

How else, indeed? "If I could borrow a corner of your writing desk and some paper, I might start working over the material for Walt Penneyman." He might even have his notes complete to hand over to Carlson for dispatch by the next diplomatic pouch.

My first evening in Paris, he thought, as he settled at the desk and tested his pen.

It was with some amazement that he heard Vaugiroud's voice from across the room saying, "Mr. Fenner, it is twenty minutes to seven."

SEVEN

Bill Fenner left the Rue Jean-Calas with mixed, but pleasant, emotions. There was relief for a job that was over—his report for Walt Penneyman was in Carlson's hands; satisfaction in the way he had convoyed Carlson upstairs, briefing him abruptly on Vaugiroud's past, leaving Vaugiroud's present to be discovered from Vaugiroud himself; and some plain, unabashed glee over his own nicely timed departure. He had waited beside the window for a few minutes after his introduction of Carlson, just long enough to see the curious stranger, sitting once more at the café table in its cool evening shadows, begin to rise and stroll toward the Rue Jean-Calas. Fenner's hasty good-by might have startled Vaugiroud and Carlson if they hadn't been too busy sizing each other up like a pair of circling judo experts, but it got him down the stairs in a quick run to make sure he would be gone before the stranger could reach the house. In the courtyard, darkening rapidly, he had glimpsed a hefty, sausage-eating type in a tight gray suit which had never seen work more arduous than opening a beer bottle. And paid no attention. He had stepped out into the street well ahead of the man sauntering toward the doorway. And paid no attention.

So here he was, no one following, duty done, free. Carlson could handle all the worries from here on out. The fading light of September's first day was broken by the bright splashes of the Boulevard Saint-Germain, just ahead of him. The bookstores and shops were closing, but there were plenty of cafés in all shapes and sizes. This was the time to be meeting a girl; beautiful, of course, and intelligent, naturally; with taste and a sense of humor. Too much to hope for? These things rarely came together in one pleasing package. The intelligent ones were usually too old, the beauties' conversation lasted about fifteen minutes, the ones with taste tried too hard, the ones with humor knew it, alas. My God, he realized, I left out the one ingredient that matters most: honesty, just some decent, reliable, plain old-fashioned honesty. Didn't you have enough of the pretty little finagler, all open innocence, all hidden purpose? And then he wondered wryly, who was he to demand so much anyway? How much would a woman see in him? How much did he deserve? Not so much, he decided, not so much at all.

His speculations about a girl, the girl who always waited just around the corner or in the next room, had begun with a smile and ended in bitter memories. He needed a drink to get the sour taste out of his mouth. Besides, coping with Vaugiroud's French for the concise translation he had sent Penneyman had been an arduous hour. He stood at the edge of the broad boulevard, nineteenth century driving its straight way through the maze of ancient streets, debating where he would have that drink. For here the cafés had their own hard core of constant patrons drinking and talking in chosen groups, while the visitors wandered in to look at the captive poets and would-be philosophers, and went away after an inadequate dinner but at least with another coup notched on their tourist tomahawks. Fenner wondered, as he hesitated, if his eyes had not really been searching for a café called Racine. ("Not far from here," Vaugiroud had said.) It wasn't in sight from where he stood, so he gave up, crossed the boulevard, turned left, deciding to play the complete tourist and head for the Deux Magots, where the existentialists had established their original beachhead. But before he reached the heavy gray stones of the medieval Church of Saint-Germain-des-Prés, the only relic of its green meadows in its name, he saw—just off the boulevard, at the corner of a side street—the sign Café Racine above a quiet little restaurant. Again he hesitated. His job with Vaugiroud was over, but his interest was still alive. One minute he was telling himself it was no longer any of his business, the next minute he was crossing the side street to reach the two long window boxes of prim marigolds that flanked the Racine's open doorway. The narrow sidewalk held no room for outside tables, but, as he realized when he stepped over the threshold, this was a place that took food seriously.

There was a pleasant paneled room in front of him, with a large central display of remarkable cold dishes, cheeses, fruit, over which a large fan revolved slowly. Around the walls were well-spaced tables, covered with white linen, only half filled at this hour. The lights were bright in unshaded globes. Plenty of polished brass, but not an inch of chromium, he noted. Only two women were in sight, and they were both middle-aged, carefully coiffured and dressed, listening with small, correct smiles while their husbands discoursed airily. This was a man's restaurant, most definitely.

No one paid any attention to him except Madame, who sat on a high chair at an old-fashioned desk to one side of the doorway. "Good evening," he said, aware of her careful scrutiny.

"You wish a table, monsieur?"

"Eventually."

"Ah, you are waiting for someone?" She was the quick, clever type who always knew what you wanted before you did.

"Yes." For a glimpse, at least, of Henri Roussin. It was a safe answer, true enough, not committing him to anything.

She gestured to the other side of the door, where the corner opposite her held a group of marble-topped tables against a background of newspapers, each hanging from its wooden spine hooked onto the wall like a medley of medieval banners. Yes, this was the waiting-place, Fenner decided, where strangers warmed cold feet with a tepid *apéritif* until courage was recovered and they could ask if one of those empty dining tables might not possibly be granted to a mere foreigner? He selected a chair that faced the room. Madame's powers of remote control had summoned an ancient waiter, but that was the extent of her interest. She was back to business, checking accounts, concentrating. She was a thin, small-boned woman, about thirty-five, dressed in subdued gray, with intense black hair, pale lips, thick white skin, deep shadows under her sharply observant eyes.

The waiter took his order, showed no visible signs of shock when he was asked to bring a Scotch and soda. He even suggested ice. So some Americans must wander in here occasionally. Fenner felt less of a stray Martian, lit a cigarette, studied the room, with its small islands of complete self-absorption. There was a preponderance of gray and white heads, of double-breasted suits, of lapel decorations. Solid citizens, all of them. There was a mild clatter of heavy silver as some threw themselves into the serious business of eating, a hum of talk from those who waited for food to be cooked. Voices were low, although clear-pitched, brilliant; faces were quiet, clever; gestures were controlled but expressive. Intelligent citizens, too, but preoccupied with themselves: not one knew, or cared, what was going on around him. Just the place, thought Fenner, for a clandestine meeting. All you needed was a double-breasted suit, a long haircut, and drooping eyelids.

Where's my drink? Fenner wondered, reaching overhead for a newspaper. And where is Henri Roussin? Madame was watching him again, and then—as he had looked over at the desk—not watching. He began to read, but could give the paper little attention. The puzzle that had drawn him to the Café Racine was unexplained: if Vaugiroud was being observed, Roussin would also be under suspicion. Yet there was no one here who seemed to be interested in anyone else, except Madame, and that was possibly an occupational disease. I am not going to snitch any newspapers, he told her under his breath as he looked up and saw the curious eyes glance away from him; in fact, I'm just about to leave. But now, from the back of the restaurant, was *Monsieur le propriétaire* himself, emanating.

He was a large man, Henri Roussin, an impressive testimonial to his chef. He moved slowly along the row of tables, a small bow here, a few words there, his head always turning to one side as he paused to speak. Quite naturally it seemed, he came toward Fenner. "You have not been served, monsieur?" His voice was half muted, hoarse, as if it were strangled in his throat.

Fenner nodded toward the arriving waiter. He forced himself to keep looking at Roussin politely, tried to banish the shock from his eyes. Roussin's face carried the traces of his war. Once, they must have been hideous. Surgeon's clever fingers had worked hard, but there was still a disfigured look to the right side of the face in spite of its carefully disguised scars: an overneatness of the ear, its lobe gone, a drawn smallness of the eye; the side of the jaw oddly fallen. His thin gray hair had its long strands brushed carefully over a bald welt, the continuation of a puckered furrow of white flesh that ran from the misshapen ear up over the brow onto the scalp. "Here's my drink," Fenner said awkwardly, glad of an excuse to drop his eyes. He studied the one small cube of ice that had been allowed him.

"Monsieur would like a table?"

"Eventually." Fenner was pleased with that word; his French accent sounded better this time.

"You are waiting for someone? I shall arrange a table for two?"

Fenner said, "Well—I'm not sure—"

Roussin watched him with amusement. "Or perhaps you came to see me, Mr. Fenner?" he asked in English. As Fenner stared up at him, he added, "I'm sorry I was not here when you arrived. I was in my office, speaking on my telephone."

Fenner grinned. "With Professor Vaugiroud? So he called you to expect me. But how did he know?"

"To be exact, he did not telephone. I called him. When we were talking, he mentioned you."

"And described me pretty accurately."

"The professor is always accurate. He notices the essential details. That signet ring on your left hand, for instance; the blue shantung tie; the small lapels of your dark flannel suit. It wasn't difficult to identify you."

"But how did he know I was going to drop in here?"

"He did not know. He only thought what he would do himself if he were you. It was a brilliant guess, don't you think?"

"Are all his guesses as good?"

"Usually, yes."

"Sometimes wrong?" Fenner asked jokingly.

"Not in recent years."

"Not since August 11, 1944?"

It was Henri Roussin's turn to stare. The quick dark eyes in the half-dead face widened for a shocked moment. He recovered. With a smile, he said, "You had an interesting talk with the professor, I see. Excuse me—" He turned away to greet two men who had entered the restaurant, delivered them into the care of a waiter, stopped at the desk to speak to Madame, and returned to Fenner. "Will you have dinner with me, Mr. Fenner? My table is just over there."

Fenner looked across at the table. It was the nearest one to Madame's desk, separated from it by a tactful screen of potted plants. "I'd like that very much. But another night. I have a telephone call to make before dinner."

Roussin took that as a rebuff. "You are welcome to use the telephone at the desk," he said stiffly.

"This is a call to New York. If you aren't too busy, why don't you sit down, and we can have a drink together?" Fenner glanced over at Madame.

Roussin noticed his look. His manner had eased again. "No one would be astonished if I did. In fact, they might be astounded if I did not. I like Americans. I like to practice my English. And I like to sit down. These habits are well established. Also, I have already dropped a hint that you were recommended to dine here by one of my old English friends who now lives in New York. So we have much to talk about."

He pulled a chair to face Fenner, and lowered his enormous bulk carefully. All his movements were calculated and slow.

"I have a feeling," Fenner said, "that Madame does not like Americans as much as you do."

"True. We disagree about most things."

"Difficult." Fenner was embarrassed.

"Ah, you think Angélique is my wife? Not at all. She is my sister-in-law. A widow. Her husband was killed in Algiers."

"Oh, one of those OAS attacks."

"No. By the Algerians, in 1958. In an ambush. He was a soldier."

"And that makes your sister-in-law anti-American?"

"That is part of it. She thinks you forget about atrocities unless the Rightists commit them. The other part? Simply that I like Americans."

Does Angélique take opposite sides just to feel she is at least that much independent? Fenner wondered.

"After all," Roussin was saying, "I owe them my life. And they salvaged enough of my face to let me come back into the world. Seventeen years ago, they found me." He fingered his right cheek thoughtfully. "I was more like a lump of hamburger than a man. I never forget the words I heard from the American soldier who first saw me. 'Holy Christ!' he kept saying, just those two words over and over again. There was a very encouraging sound in the way he spoke them—with awe and admiration—as if he were pinning medals on my chest. Most flattering. I began to feel that by simply staying alive, I had triumphed. And so, I decided not to die. What man wants to be cheated of his medals?"

"Yet, in one sense, you have cheated yourself."

"That was necessary. I might not be alive to talk with you tonight if the true story of these injuries had been known." He tapped the damaged side of his face. "A bad car accident in a London blackout. I spent the war years in England, didn't you know? Later, when all danger was over, I returned here to inherit my father's restaurant. On the whole, I am considered a lucky man—one who has arranged his life very comfortably, except for a silly accident."

Fenner was beginning to like Henri Roussin. "So that's where you spent the war. I'll remember."

"Please do," Roussin said very quietly, all the humor drained out of his eyes. "This deception is not a joke that the professor and I have played all these years. We had a purpose."

"I know. And you hooked your fish."

Roussin showed frank shock for the second time that evening. Then he narrowed his eyes, studying Fenner's face. "And how did you extract so much information from the professor?"

"Does he let anyone extract anything, unless he wants them to?"

Roussin nodded his agreement on that. "Now I would like to do some extraction. Why did you come here? It did not puzzle the professor. But it puzzles me."

"Oh—just checking on the story I had heard. It becomes a habit with newspapermen."

"And how could I help you to check on the story?" Roussin asked with mock concern. "Shall I point out the table where we hooked our fish, and caught three minnows as well?"

"Minnows—" Fenner repeated the word, searching for some way to turn Roussin's distrust back to amiability once more. "You don't think they are important?"

"To me? No." Roussin's eyes were hard. "First things first. That is my way. My main interest is the man who was the cause of this." Once more his hand went up to his face. "The professor is a philosopher. He thinks mostly of the future. But I am a practical man: I find the past enough to think about."

"So you don't always agree with the professor's ideas?"

There was a pause. "Common Market? European unity? Nonsense! But what are friends for, except to enjoy disagreement? All day, with my guests, I have to agree, agree, agree. It is a relief to disagree. A necessity, perhaps. What are friends for if they can't help?"

Fenner studied his drink. He said lightly, "I guess I'm almost a friend. At least I'm disagreeing with you."

Roussin laughed, a strange, strangled gasp heaving out from his massive chest. "We might be very good friends. Indeed, if I show you the table where one of our minnows is sitting at this minute, will you answer a question I would like to ask you?"

"Right now? I thought they only came here at lunchtime."

"Right now," Roussin repeated firmly, watching only Fenner. "The pattern is broken. Interesting? I do not think our film producer has merely developed a taste for my cuisine. He has postponed ordering. He is waiting, I think." Roussin was enjoying himself. "He arrived only two minutes before you did. In fact, before I went off to telephone the professor about this strange development, I wondered if you might not be following him."

"What?"

"But the professor reassured me about you."

"What worried you?" Fenner asked sharply.

"You could have been on either side: his or ours."

"Watchdog or bloodhound, is that it?"

"Exactly."

"Where is he?"

"Four tables to your right, Mr. Fenner," Roussin said, still keeping his eyes on the American's face.

Fenner looked casually around the room. A well-dressed man, with receding red hair and a handsome profile, sat at the fourth table. He was studying a menu, sipping a glass of wine, looking remarkably at ease. "A most affluent Communist. What's his name?"

"You are a very inquiring journalist, Mr. Fenner."

Yes, thought Fenner, I had better stop being so interested: I am letting myself become too involved in something that goes deeper and farther than Walt Penneyman's assignment. "Thanks for the reminder," he said dryly. "It's none of my affair."

"Most wise. But before you put all this out of your mind, you still owe me an answer. Why did you come here?"

"Let's say I was trying to find an answer to a question of my own."

"And that was?"

"Who told Jacques that Vaugiroud and you are still alive?" Fenner asked very quietly.

"Jacques—" The name jerked out under Roussin's breath. "So the professor even told you that? He must trust you."

And perhaps that's the reason why I've been worrying about him, Fenner thought. "He is being closely watched."

"So I heard," Roussin said quietly, grimly.

"He is not the man to be panicked by the threat of danger."

"No."

"So he must have recognized some real danger."

"When?"

"This evening." When he so suddenly reversed himself about a telephone call to Carlson.

"Is this a guess, Mr. Fenner?" Roussin asked shrewdly.

"What we call an educated guess. I was given the impression that he felt time might be running out, and that he had better make sure that others knew about Fernand Lenoir."

"Yes," Roussin said slowly. "If Lenoir knew who we were— Yes, there would be real danger for both the professor and myself. But he does not."

"You are sure of that?"

"With this face? With my story about London? I don't even look the right age. I was twenty when the Gestapo caught me. Do I look thirty-seven, Mr. Fenner?"

Fenner shook his head. "I still think Lenoir knows."

"Someone told him? Is that what you have been trying to say? No one could tell him. No one."

Fenner said nothing. Perhaps, he thought, I've said too much. Roussin was angry.

"No one," repeated Roussin. "For the simple reason that the men who worked with me in Paris during the war have died, either then or since. Jacques himself is the only survivor, besides the professor, of those who knew me; and he believes that the Gestapo finished me." Roussin studied Fenner with impatience. "Do not blame me for any carelessness. I learned English to prove I had spent the war years there. I even go back to

London every autumn for a week's holiday to see my wartime friends. I leave, in fact, for this year's visit on Monday." The impatience turned to annoyance. "I am not an indiscreet man, Mr. Fenner."

"I didn't think you were."

"Then why blame me for this real danger?"

"There's no blame—"

"Yet you came here thinking you would find the answer to your question. You could have found it in the Rue Jean-Calas. And why? The professor has drawn danger upon himself. All those intellectuals who come to talk with him, all those anti-Communists, anti-fascists, anti-OAS, anti-this, anti-that—"

"Anti-totalitarian," Fenner suggested quietly. "That sums it up."

Roussin paid no attention: the exact meaning within a phrase did not seem important to him. "They have made many enemies for themselves. Why are intelligent men so stupid? It is enough to be clever, and live. Politics! Can a man eat politics, sleep with politics?"

This, thought Fenner, is where all rational discussion ends. Nothing I could say would either impress or change Roussin. His link with Vaugiroud is an emotional one—an old comradeship, loyalties based on danger and sufferings shared. Nothing wrong with that, as far as it goes. But with Roussin, it can't go much farther. He hasn't the mental equipment, clever fellow as he is, to grasp half the implication of Vaugiroud's ideas. No doubt Roussin hates Communists because Jacques was one. When he looks at Jacques, he sees the traitor who caused death to his friends, torture for himself. But Vaugiroud—he sees Jacques not so much as the man from the past who deserves punishment, but, rather, as a clear and present danger that must be fought for the sake of the future. "Well," Fenner said evenly, "it's possible that Professor Vaugiroud believes that men who have learned something about power politics have a special duty to share that knowledge."

Roussin turned his head to eye the clock above Angélique's desk. "Almost eight. The beginning of a very busy hour. The tables will all be filled by nine." He rose to his feet. "I shall reserve one for you, just in case you decide to stay. My private office is at your disposal if you wish to telephone New York. Meanwhile, let me order that other drink. With more ice this time?"

"Thanks," Fenner said, and had to smile.

Roussin snapped his fingers impatiently for a waiter. He dropped one last thought before he turned to the door, where some newcomers had entered. "Look around you, Mr. Fenner. The professor is being watched.

484

But who is watching me?" And then he was moving away, welcoming the arrivals, checking Angélique's list of reservations, a very perfect host.

True, thought Fenner, no one here seems to be watching anything beyond the aphorism on his tongue or the food on his fork. Except Angélique. Perhaps that was part of her job. But why that sullen stare at Roussin's back as he led his guests toward a table? Had he corrected her for some mistake? Not in front of any customers, Fenner decided. As he watched her, she looked sharply over at him. For a brief instant, he could see the tense look on her face, something more bitter than angry, before she even became aware of him. Her expression changed, falling back into its pattern of frown and suspicion.

What was her trouble? Widowhood? Dislike of a job handed out by her husband's brother? Or resentment that this restaurant had been inherited by her brother-in-law, who was alive because he had not been a soldier in Algeria? The French had a strong sense of possession and property. Whatever Angélique's feelings were, she barely hid a seething contempt for the world around her. There's a volcano here, Fenner thought, about to erupt.

The waiter brought him his drink, and—from one extreme to the other —a bowl of ice. The old man hovered around anxiously, emptying the ash tray, making sure that monsieur had the right newspaper. "Everything's fine," Fenner was reassuring him as another guest arrived—a tall man, distinguished in dress and manner, dark of hair and eyes, thin-faced. He gave Angélique a pleasant good evening, received a smile in return, looked around for Roussin, who seemed much engaged with a recent batch of arrivals, quickly set out for his table by himself. Angélique's voice sharply summoned the waiter: "Auguste! Conduct Monsieur Lenoir to his table!"

The old man hurried after Lenoir into the dining room, catching up with him in time to pull out a chair. It was, of course, at the fourth table on Fenner's right. So that is Jacques, he thought, and gave a good pretense of being absorbed by his newspaper. It was hard to believe that anyone so well groomed, so well dressed, with such a pleasant smile on his intelligent face could be anything else than what he wanted the world to believe: a man of honorable career, a foreign-affairs specialist or perhaps a press officer or a confidential secretary, with government security and private means to cushion him comfortably against the sharp edges of life. Fenner had to smile at himself. If those two men talking so quietly at the fourth table had been poorly or carelessly dressed, gaunt, white-faced, intense of eye, bitter-mouthed, would he have been asking himself if Vaugiroud's information could be true? The nihilists of the mid-twentieth century had taken a lesson from confidence men: merge, and you'll be accepted; be accepted, and your battle is half won. No one bought the Brooklyn Bridge or the Eiffel Tower from a man who looked like a crook. And then his amusement changed to amazement. When he had seen Lenoir, he had immediately remembered Vaugiroud. Only now did he think of Sandra Fane, who entertained so successfully for Lenoir in his apartment on the Avenue d'Iéna. I really am cured of Sandra, he thought, and relief swept over him like a cold clean draft of fresh air.

The doors shook against their anchoring chains in the sudden gust of wind from the street. There was a muted ruffle of drums from the sidewalk. Rain? Fenner looked up at the high window. Rain it was, a thundering downpour. The newest guest had just managed to arrive in time to save her blonde hair and smart black dress. Yes, Fenner thought approvingly as she hesitated within the entrance, you're as neat and pretty a piece of honey cake as I've ever seen, but don't be so scared, my pet; I know how you feel, but they don't chew you into actual pieces; Angélique at the desk is not old Cerberus himself even if— My God, it's the girl I saw at the Crillon!

She stood there, one short white glove smoothing back a lock of hair that the wind had blown wild, hesitating, looking at the dining room. Her eyes swept around to Fenner. There was a spark of recognition, a smile of relief. She came toward him, ignoring Roussin, who was looming up with unusual speed, her hand outstretched. "I am so sorry to be late," she said, her gray eyes pleading from under dark lashes, the smile on her lips widening as he rose to meet her. "Have you been waiting long?"

EIGHT

"I am Claire Connor," she said in a low voice as she took the chair that Fenner offered her. Color was high on her cheeks, her eyes were embarrassed, but otherwise she seemed perfectly natural. She pulled off her white kid gloves, frowned briefly at three rain spots, and said she would prefer Dubonnet. He ordered, talked, and gave her time to catch her breath again. The color subsided in her cheeks, her eyes could meet his, her pretty hands (no nail polish, no rings) were relaxed as he lit her cigarette, she even laughed. But a shadow of worry, of strain still lurked in her eyes.

"Please forgive me," she said when the waiter had come and gone.

"My pleasure." Indeed it was. Close up, her skin was as flawless as he had thought, with a touch of color in her cheeks to give it life. The eyes were large, darkly lashed, warm. Chin and nose and cheek and brow were all molded by some master hand. Fair hair had been piled high to crown her finely shaped head. Her lips—yes, pretty lips that knew how to smile. "And don't explain," he told her quickly. "In fact, you were just the explanation I was needing. Madame at the desk has stopped wondering why I am here."

"Is she the wondering type?"

"That, among other things. My name is Fenner, by the way. Bill Fenner."

"I know. I read your reviews, Mr. Fenner. They tell me what I'm missing by living abroad."

"You haven't missed much in the last year. So you live in Paris?"

"Off and on." She glanced back to her own thoughts. "Actually, I have been doing some work for the *Chronicle* in the last month."

"I'm in luck. Small worlds aren't usually filled with colleagues that look like you."

"But that was only a temporary job—an emergency. I was filling in."

"You got the drawings finished in time?"

She looked a little startled. "You actually noticed—"

"That large portfolio was very impressive."

"Just some illustrations from the latest Paris showings."

I might have guessed that, he thought. Her simple black dress, sleeveless to show slender tanned arms, her pearls at the neck and on her ears, her smooth fair hair once more in perfect place, were all part of the pattern of the fashion world.

"The man who usually draws them for your fashion editor went for a weekend to Switzerland and fell from an alp. Broke his shoulder. So Mike Ballard thought of me."

"Very knowledgeable fellow, Mike Ballard."

"Fashions aren't really my line," she admitted. "But half the battle of getting a job is just to be there. Like Everest."

"What is your regular job?"

"I work for Historical Design and Decoration. It's a New York firm. They sent me to Europe three years ago. I've been here ever since."

"And off and on in Paris?"

She smiled. "Yes."

"Well, I'm glad I met you in an on-period. Or are you off again soon?"

"For a little, perhaps. It depends on what the clients in New York want. I have to travel around a good deal."

"I'm not really following you. What do they want?"

She laughed. "Designs and decorations."

"You mean someone wants her dining room to look like the Taj Mahal, and you go flying out to India?"

"Now, now," she said gently. "Some of our best clients are hardheaded businessmen. They need exact details of certain designs—a ceiling in a Roman *palazzo*, a mosaic floor in a Venetian church, a paneled wall in a French château, an arrangement of seventeenth-century fountains, an eighteenth-century staircase. They have an idea, and no time to travel. We find what they want. Usually, that is. Sometimes ideas seem wonderful in New York but—" She shrugged her shoulders.

"You sound like an enthusiast, anyway."

"Except when some occasional Marie Antoinette wanders into the New York office, all ready to play milkmaid. Usually it's the swimming pool that brings out the silliest in women. Last month, a lady from Texas wanted some designs of Hadrian's villa—the part that lay around *his*

488

pool." Claire Connor smiled and added, "The nymphs' shrine, she meant."

"Never underestimate the power of an oil well."

"Or what you can save in taxes if you claim depletion."

"So you chased off to Rome and sketched madly?" And I bet, he thought, that her pretty mouth was drawn into that strange little curve of disapproval—not unpleasant to see, but a little unexpected. The age of twenty-five or so (how old was she?) was not usually so critical of the silly season or aesthetic blasphemy.

"No. We talked her out of the idea. She settled for a Japanese tea-garden effect. We didn't have to send anyone to Japan. That's file nine: standard procedure, nowadays."

"But you didn't tell her that? My, my, what deception!"

The long eyelashes flickered. There was a sharp little intake of breath, and then again that wonderful smile. "But beneficial," she insisted. "Our client has taken up flower arrangement and boulder placing. She may become contemplative in the cherry-blossom season. Husband much pleased."

Fenner grinned. "Where did truth end and fantasy begin?"

She opened her gray eyes wide. "What is a story without some embroidery? Just a little, here and there? And you didn't let me finish."

"That," he agreed gravely, "is unforgivable. Please finish."

"I can't! I've lost the pace."

"It was something about her haiku poem for her next barbecue," he prompted.

"Oh yes . . . She began it well enough. 'Peaceful is evening among charred embers.' But she is running into trouble with the end. Can't get the poem into seventeen syllables."

"The next thing you know, her husband will be asking you for a full-color design of an authentic sixteenth-century padded cell, the kind of place they kept for little princes when mama and papa came from a long line of first cousins."

"Perhaps that's what we should have designed for her all along. In fact, I think it could become quite a standard item. There's a need for it nowadays."

"Not only for ladies with wild dreams of grandeur," he agreed, and glanced at the table where Lenoir and his friend were talking. They didn't seem exactly happy with their conversation. Lenoir wasn't even pretending to order from the menu which lay at his elbow. "You'll have dinner with me?" Fenner asked Claire Connor, whose eyes had followed his glance.

She hesitated. "I wish I could—"

"I have a table."

"But—"

"Oh, come on! You blow in here with the wind, all dressed to celebrate the end of an assignment, and then you won't stay. You aren't going to leave me to eat alone, are you?" His tone was joking, but he was mystified. Beautiful girls in smart little black dresses did not go out to dinner by themselves.

"It isn't really like that, you know."

"Isn't it?"

"Well—"

"You have another date? Just my luck."

"No. At least—not exactly—"

He smiled. "You just put on your prettiest dress to run around in the rain."

She looked at the white kid gloves, her small black silk bag. "I got all dressed up for a party. But I changed my mind."

"That's my fault, probably. I sat here conjuring you up. And you arrived."

"It was the fault of the party."

"Food or people?"

"People."

"All of them?" he asked, amused, still puzzled.

"One of them." She gave a little laugh. "When you are faced with certain situations, the only way to deal with them is—run."

"I thought you were a little breathless when you came in here."

"And I had to choose a restaurant like this! If it hadn't been for you, I'd have retreated right out into the rain." She looked around the tables. "Not a woman in sight."

"Two most respectable ladies," he corrected her.

"Firmly attached. Like their hats. Think of all the cafés on the Left Bank where I could have slipped in by myself, ordered an omelet, and not even raised one eyebrow. And I had to choose this one!"

The lady does protest too much, he thought, his interest growing. "I still wish you'd have dinner with me. I'm sure they make wonderful omelets here."

"Sacrilege," she said. "If we don't spend three hours over dinner, we are barbarians. And that's the reason I can't have dinner with you. I just haven't got three hours tonight. I haven't even got two. I've an appointment at half past nine. That's less than an hour away."

"Back to business so soon?" But she wasn't going to have dinner with him, that was certain. He couldn't keep the disappointment out of his voice, and his disbelief.

That upset her a little, somehow, as if she were being ungracious. "Please forgive me. I wish I could spend the evening with you. I really do." She hesitated. "The truth is that I'm leaving for Venice early tomorrow. I'll be away for a week perhaps. Will you still be here when I get back?"

"No. I'm leaving Paris on Monday. I don't get back until the middle of the month, perhaps later. Will you be here?"

"I don't know." She looked at him quickly. "Honestly, I don't."

"Historical Design and Decoration keeps you busy."

"Yes," she said bleakly. She tried to smile.

"Have another drink, anyway."

"I think I'd better leave." She glanced at the dining room. The gentle smile on her face was still there, but she had become, very suddenly, a thousand miles away.

"I know who you are," he told her, watching her profile. "You're a Greek girl from the fourth century. Scopas saw you walking past in the market place."

Her gray eyes had been startled for a moment. And then they relaxed. Her smile widened. She said softly, "You make it very hard for me to leave." She rose. "If I don't, I'll—" She shrugged her shoulders, held out her hand, as he rose, too. "Thank you, Mr. Fenner."

"I'll see you to the door, at least."

"You'll give the waiter apoplexy."

Fenner grinned and dropped twelve new francs on the table. "That should hold him." Roussin was coming toward them, he noticed. And at the fourth table against the wall, Lenoir was on his feet, still talking eloquently. The red-haired film producer was arranging and rearranging his fork and knife, his eyes cast down, as he listened. Abruptly, he cut off Lenoir with a wave of the hand, and it was he who was now talking. Around them, other tables were complete islands of self-absorption.

"Where do you live, Miss Connor?"

"Just across the Seine. Oh dear, have I lost a glove? No, here it is—"

"Let me take you there." That was one way of getting her address.

Her pace quickened as they reached Angélique's desk. Outside, the heavy thundershower was over, leaving the dark street hosed-down, clean, glistening under its lights. "It really isn't far," she said. "There's no need. I've been enough bother to you for one night."

"Mr. Fenner!" Roussin's voice called quietly.

Fenner half turned. Behind him, he heard a murmured "Good-by," and the light staccato of slender high heels. He swung around again. She had left.

"Mr. Fenner!" Roussin's voice was urgent enough to stop Fenner dead.

Angélique, he noted, was well within earshot. He forced the annoyance out of his voice. "I'm sorry we can't stay for dinner tonight," he told Roussin. "Another time." He took a step toward the door.

"Perhaps I may have the pleasure of having you as my guest for luncheon tomorrow? Is twelve o'clock too early? That allows me some time for my friends before most people arrive."

Lunch with Vaugiroud? Fenner wondered in amazement. Surely Roussin wasn't being serious.

He wasn't. It was only an excuse. For, without being obvious about the little maneuver, he had managed to turn his back to Angélique. He dropped his voice, spoke rapidly. "A message has just come. Mr. Carlson will be at your hotel. Eleven o'clock. Tonight." More normally, he added, "Please give my apologies to the charming young lady for detaining you. I am sorry that tonight has been so busy. Excuse me." He turned away, to bow politely to another departing guest. It was Monsieur Fernand Lenoir, hurrying out with a crisp step, a pleasant smile for everyone, a man of grace and good manners, healthy, happy, and wise. The perfect picture of a discreet and successful man of affairs, Fenner thought, and followed it out into the street.

He could see no sign of Claire Connor. The interchange with Henri Roussin had taken only a matter of seconds, but it had been long enough for her to vanish in the darkness. At the corner, he halted and lit a cigarette to give himself time to study the boulevard. It was crowded and hopeless. There were several pretty blonde heads, many little black dresses. For a minute, he watched the busy traffic, the swarm of people hurrying to make up for the delay of sheltering from the heavy shower of rain, and saw his hopes for a most promising evening disintegrate.

Monsieur Fernand Lenoir, he noticed, had found a taxi. Fenner watched it speed away, thinking gloomily that there was one man who knew where he was going. From the side street behind him, where the Café Racine lay, a gray car came swiftly, turning the corner sharply to take the same direction as Lenoir's taxi. Well, Fenner thought, Lenoir may know where he is going, but does he know he is being followed? The idea amused him. His gloom began to lift. Sure, his evening was shattered, but it had not been planned in the first place. He had better find a cab, himself, and return to the Crillon, let the porter there deal with all the palaver of making a call to New York. After that, a quick supper in the bar, and back to his room by eleven o'clock for Carlson. He'd be half asleep by that time, in any case: this had been a long, long day, and not one of the most restful, either. It would be pleasant to wake up tomorrow and think about his own interests, for a change. Good-by Professor Vaugiroud, good-by Roussin, Lenoir and quiet film producers. And good-by to Claire Connor. That, at least, he regretted to say. She was only a mirage, he decided: a dream shining out from an expanse of desert, thirty minutes of delightful hope, and then nothing. Good-by Claire.

But through the rest of the evening, at odd times, she would keep coming back into his mind. Mike Ballard must know her address. And there was that firm, too—Historical Decoration and Design. Or Design and Decoration. She would be back in Paris some time, wouldn't she?

Not good-by at all, he decided over his cognac and coffee. You just gave up too easily there, he told himself. And felt better.

NINE

Eleven o'clock found Bill Fenner, relaxed in pajamas and dressing gown, ready for bed the minute he got rid of Carlson. He wasn't disappointed in Carlson's punctuality. "Hello," he said as he opened the door. "And where have you been? You're five seconds late."

Carlson, looking at Fenner's clothes, had his own question. "What's the idea? I didn't know drama critics went to bed before dawn."

"I've had a hard day. And what's *your* idea? Out with it. Then I'll pitch into that bed and not move an eyelid until noon."

Carlson took the most comfortable chair. He needed it. He said, a little gloomily, "Your raincoat never showed up at the airport."

Was that all? Fenner wondered. "Oh, it's here. It was left at the porter's desk at five o'clock. An exchange was proposed, but our story of returning the other coat to Orly was passed on. Did anyone try to pick it up there?"

Carlson nodded. "A man tried to claim it around seven o'clock. But alas, alack, it had already been impounded by the Sûreté. Which must have made his telephoned report, back to Paris, a little on the somber side."

"I thought that would have made you cheerful."

"It would, except for one thing. Mr. Goldsmith's friends have traced you to this hotel. So my job is to get you out of here."

"What?"

"That's right. Get dressed, pack, and pay your bill. We're moving you out."

"But—"

"You were going to look for another hotel, weren't you?"

"Sure, but I haven't got around to finding one."

"I have a friend who has lent me his apartment. You'll like it there. It

494

has a view of the Seine and Notre-Dame and all the rest of the American dream."

"Look—" began Fenner.

"I'm looking. At your safety, friend. Get cracking, will you? I've had a hard day myself."

Fenner stared at the blue eyes that were meeting his with the hardness of cold fact behind them. He began peeling off his dressing gown. "I suppose you've already arranged for a car to meet us at the front door?" he asked with some annoyance.

"That's right," Carlson said blandly. "At eleven-twenty-five, to be exact. Step on it, Bill."

Fenner began to dress. His brows were down, his mouth in a straight line.

"Thank God," Carlson said, "you are not the arguing type."

"I can be. But you wouldn't be here if you hadn't a good reason."

"Several good reasons. Bill, why the hell did you have to go and see Vaugiroud?"

"Aren't you glad I did?"

"From my point of view, it was fine. But from yours—well, Goldsmith and his coat were trouble enough for one day. Add Vaugiroud and that setup over on the Rue Jean-Calas, and you really could be in double trouble. Somewhere tonight, my friend, you are being discussed pretty heavily."

Fenner knotted his tie, brushed his hair, and began packing. "So you think that the ten-thousand-dollar bills may connect with Vaugiroud's idea of fabricated evidence for the next big lie?"

"I didn't say that," Carlson said.

"Well, I'm saying it."

"To me only, I hope."

"Look," Fenner said, amusement returning, "whoever is concocting fantastic plots to shake the West into pieces hasn't much time to worry about one drama critic who wandered on stage at the wrong moment. Besides, I'm off stage now."

"I'm just making sure that you'll stay off." Carlson rose and began checking closet and drawers. "And don't use the word 'fantastic' too lightly, Bill. The only time to laugh at conspiracies is after they have been smashed."

"Then you are taking Vaugiroud seriously?"

Carlson didn't answer that. He moved into the bathroom. "All clear here," he called. "Lucky you didn't spend much time unpacking."

"Well," Fenner said, refusing to be diverted from Vaugiroud, "that's a relief. I began to wonder after I left you at Rue Jean-Calas if I had acted too quickly."

Silence from Carlson.

"I took a chance on calling you. I wasn't shown the memorandum. He just briefed me."

"How much?"

"Just enough, I suppose, to get me sufficiently interested to help him. Say—shouldn't I have called you? I thought you were the expert on that kind of thing."

"Thank you," Carlson said dryly.

"Well, seeing you're so communicative—was your visit worthwhile?"

"Interesting."

"No real value?" Fenner asked worriedly. All that trouble for nothing. "I didn't say that."

"You don't have to be so damned cryptic."

"Bad habit," Carlson agreed. He closed the last wardrobe drawer. "All clear? When you pay your bill, give them American Express as your forwarding address. Say you're spending the weekend with a friend if they seem puzzled by this quick departure. At twenty-four minutes past eleven, start walking out. I'll be in the lobby, keeping an eye on you. The car, at the front entrance, will be a dark-blue Citroën. The driver will be dressed in tweeds, and has gray hair. I'll be just behind you. And the minute you are in the car, I'll join you. Right?"

"Right." Fenner moved over to the telephone to call the desk, hesitated. "Shall I tell them I'm checking out, or do I just surprise them?"

"Best keep to the usual procedure."

"That's what I like about life with Auntie: everything is so nice and normal."

Carlson's tired face relaxed into a grin. He closed the door quietly.

The blue Citroën sped quarterway around the Place de la Concorde, then branched off into the Champs-Elysées. Within a few hundred yards, it stopped near some trees sheltering the driveway to a restaurant, once a private villa, which stood discreetly withdrawn into its own grounds. Quickly, Carlson and Fenner climbed out with the luggage, and crossed over to a gray Renault that was waiting under the trees. Before Carlson had slipped into the driver's seat with Fenner beside him, the Citroën was continuing on its way, up the broad avenue lined with trees and park and restaurant gardens, toward the distant neon lights of the Champs-Elysées' busier section.

Carlson waited. He let a few cars pass before he swung the Renault out of the driveway, and followed the Citroën leisurely. He was gently humming *Get Me to the Church on Time.*

"I'm most impressed," Fenner said. Far ahead, the Citroën had become only one of a weaving pattern of taillights. He was still irritated by the supercaution. "All this split-second timing just for me?"

Carlson stopped humming. "It isn't as comic as you think. Or will you wait, before you take this thing seriously, until you're picked up by one of Kalganov's boys, hauled out to a quiet house on the outskirts of Paris, given the electric treatment so they can find out how much Vaugiroud does know?"

Fenner was shocked into silence.

"I am not playing wild hunches, Bill. There was a guy in the lobby whose eyes popped when he saw you were checking out. He made a quick dash to a telephone, a very quick call, and another quick dash outside just in time to note the Citroën driving off. Fortunately for us, taxis are scarce at this time of night. Since honking was banned, I guess cab drivers have lost some of their incentive. Anyway, our eye-popped friend couldn't quite reach us by the time we changed cars. A taxi did chug past at full tilt, though, before I switched on our engine." Carlson began humming again. This time it was a neatly ordered snatch of Bach.

"And who the hell is Kalganov?" Fenner asked angrily, transferring his annoyance onto the strange name.

Carlson finished humming the last line of *Sheep may safely graze.* "Soothing," he said. "Encouraging, too. Just kill all the bad wolves, and you can eat in peace." Ahead of them was an avenue of giant movie houses, neon lights as bright as day, broad sidewalks with innumerable cafés and tables and people gawking at the slowed automobiles. So they swung left from the Champs-Elysées, and traveled gently through quieter, residential streets in a leisurely detour back toward the Seine.

"Who is Kalganov?" Fenner asked after a silent five minutes.

"A name to remember," Carlson said briefly. "Not to repeat, not to say aloud, just to remember."

"Was Kalganov your business in Paris?"

"And not to ask questions about, either," Carlson told him sharply. "Sorry, Bill—I've got a lot on my mind. I've been spending the last hour talking about Kalganov. It's a name that has haunted many of us for years. There isn't an allied Intelligence unit that hasn't been interested."

And in the last hour, Kalganov was no longer a name but a man, to be found right here in Paris? Fenner studied the small smile on Carlson's lips. "Is he another of those terrorist types?" he asked most innocently.

Carlson's smile broke into a laugh. "That's about it," he said noncommittally. "By the way, how much did Vaugiroud tell you?"

The question was not as idly curious as Carlson's voice made it. It had purpose. Two purposes, Fenner decided: one is to find out what I know, the other to get me off the subject of Kalganov. I've had a quiet warning about that name—why else the calculated indiscretion on Carlson's part? All right, I'll tell him what I know. That may be the quickest way to get back to Kalganov. Any man who thinks he could forcibly kidnap and question me is slightly more than a name to remember, as far as I'm concerned.

Fenner began his answer. He kept it as brief as he could, but factual. Carlson listened intently. By the time they had crossed the Seine, and were heading back to the old center of Paris, the story of Jacques who became Fernand Lenoir was completed. "I still don't know how Lenoir got away with it for all these years," Fenner ended.

"Not too difficult. He has always been Fernand Lenoir except for the three years he worked as Jacques in the Resistance. All he had to worry about was any ghost from that period of his life returning to haunt him. He thought there were none."

"He was born Fernand Lenoir, built up his life as Fernand Lenoir?"

"And a very pleasant life, too."

So Lenoir was not the puzzling Mr. Kalganov. "Does the same go for his friend the film producer?"

"Robert Wahl? He is a very different pattern from Lenoir. He wasn't born here. Didn't grow up here. He arrived in 1946, a survivor from a Nazi concentration camp in East Germany."

"Whose records are all in Russian hands. No family, I suppose?"

"All died in the camp."

"Where was he born and brought up?"

"Leipzig, supposedly."

Also in Russian hands, Fenner thought. "No questions ever asked?"

"As far as many Frenchmen are concerned, a man's life only begins from the instant he arrives in Paris. Besides, he was clever enough to work his way into the intellectual camp. He was interested in writers, started a little magazine."

"That takes money."

"His family had money. Deposited safely in Switzerland, it seems. And everything he touched seemed to make just enough to let him branch out farther."

"One of those lucky guys."

"One of those well-provided guys."

"Subsidized?"

"Must have been. Wahl's projects weren't as successful financially as people think."

"So he began with a little magazine—" Fenner waited. No response. He said jokingly, "You know, I could find out all about his career, as far as my friends in Paris know it."

Carlson shook his head. "I bet you would, too. All right. First, the magazine; a few years later, a small radio station; after that, controlling interests in two provincial newspapers; next, two short films with excellent photography and despairing themes; and now, he wants to make another movie. Scene: American Zone in West Berlin. He has applied for our permission. He has even sent us a copy of the shooting script to show us the story is nonpolitical, harmless."

"West Berlin? Why didn't he choose East Berlin?"

"That is what interested us. We knew Wahl was far to the left. That's no secret. He doesn't like Americans. That's no secret, either. And there are several anti-American Leftists among the French intellectuals: that's their normal conformity. Only, why should one of them choose to make a film in West Berlin?"

"Perhaps," Fenner said, with a grin, "he is a reforming character. Wants to make up and be friends."

"We thought of that. We also knew that if we refused him without adequate reason, we'd have his friends chanting about American intolerance and hysteria."

"So you came to Paris to find out more about Robert Wahl?"

Carlson nodded. "And kept running up against the same blank wall. Even non-Communists would say, 'Yes, he is obviously in sympathy with the Communists, perhaps he is even a party member. But that isn't against the law. Besides, you know our Communist intellectuals: they talk ideas, make propaganda, but they aren't militant. They may be annoying, but they are harmless. They want peace, not war. They quote *Izvestia*, but they weren't trained under Beria. They don't torture or kill.' Yes, that was always the reaction. Robert Wahl was honest because he did not disguise his opinions. He was sincere. Therefore, he was pure in heart." Carlson's laugh was brief and bitter. "Not trained under Beria! My—" He concentrated on the curve of Seine, its black waters gleaming in golden streaks under the lights edging its banks.

"So until Vaugiroud identified Wahl today, he was in the clear?" That was a depressing thought.

"Not quite," Carlson said sharply. He spoke like a man who had done a good deal of work and saw the credit being taken from him. "I had already made out a report against his project in West Berlin. My reasons were valid. Not based on his opinions, either."

"On what, then?"

"You want to know everything, don't you?" Carlson was amused.

"Not everything," Fenner said, very gently. "Just enough to flesh out the skeleton. If Wahl is as dangerous as Vaugiroud implied—I'd like to know what league I'm playing in."

"You aren't playing in it any longer."

"Who is to decide that? You or Robert Wahl? You know, his name is familiar." Then Fenner remembered, at last, the article that the honest and sincere Mr. Wahl had written. On Cuba. And one some years ago, when Fenner had been interested in the Far East, on Indochina just before the French back out. "He travels, doesn't he?"

"He gets around," Carlson said. He glanced sharply at Fenner: how much did he really know? Was that only a harmless question about Robert Wahl's travels? "We'll make a little detour here," he said, and swung the car away from the Seine. At this moment, he was a sorely tried security officer, whose own hard-earned triumph of the last few weeks had consisted of a detailed study of Robert Wahl's journeys abroad. Their reasons were always admirable: a search for new talent among foreign writers or actors; original backgrounds for movies (which never got made); material for travel articles; attendance at some international conference. But Wahl's visits abroad, when examined closely, formed a disquieting pattern. He arrived in a time of mounting crisis, and just after he departed there had always been some unexplained troubles added to the general strain: riots which erupted violently, bombings, assassination attempts. Situations always deteriorated after Wahl came on the scene, whether it was to attend a student peace conference or give a series of lectures. This could be coincidence, Carlson had noted in his report. But regularly occurring coincidence deserved closer examination. Until that was made, he advised against any visit by Robert Wahl to West Berlin. Period. Triple period, in fact.

"Lot of detours," Fenner observed caustically. And the biggest one, so far, had been around Kalganov. "If we make a left turn here," he suggested humorously as he looked out at the busy boulevard, "we can drop in at the Café Racine for a nightcap."

"No more visits for you there, my friend," Carlson said warningly. "And we'll postpone that left turn for another block. I'm taking you to the Ile Saint-Louis. Any objections?"

"Not to that."

"To what?"

"To being kidnapped." Fenner's grin was wide. "Even one of the best views in Paris won't compensate for a locked door."

Carlson looked shocked. "We're only keeping you safe—"

"Sure. That's easier than telling me what's going on."

"Do you really enjoy making my life miserable?"

"At present," Fenner said, "mine is no sweet-smelling bed of roses."

"It could be worse."

"I planned it quite differently. This, Carlson, is my first night in Paris."

"And this is my last," Carlson said quietly. "Helluva way to celebrate, I agree." He was smiling though. Fenner's complaint had been more cheerful than he had expected. Fenner would co-operate, he was sure. Fairly sure. But how much more will I have to tell him to keep him quiet for a weekend behind a locked door? Of course, it could be less time than that. The too long and happy career of Robert Wahl might be ending even now. The quiet hunt was on. Bernard, at the Sûreté, and his men were on the job. "You were only going to spend it sleeping. Alone, too. You can do that just as well here."

Fenner looked around him with sudden interest. They were driving onto the peaceful island of Saint-Louis, turning into a placid street edged on one side by tall houses, silent and proud, and on the other by the quick dark current of the Seine. Across the waters lay a second island, where Notre-Dame rose with flying buttresses into the pale glow of a young moon lazing over a cloudless ink-blue sky. "Except," he told Carlson, "this is the kind of place where a pretty girl should be more than a dream."

"You'll find everything else. Running water, electric lights, all modern comforts, monsieur will be happy here; cheap at the price." He stopped the car, handed Fenner a key. "Top floor, front. Marked 4A. You can't miss it."

"Concierge?"

"Expects you. Won't be visible. I'll get the car parked away from here. See you in ten minutes." As Fenner looked at him, he added, "Just want to see you tucked up for the night. I take my kidnapping jobs very seriously. Hey, don't forget your coat!" He threw it over Fenner's arm. "You'll find the Scotch in the first cabinet in the pantry." There was a small salute for a laden Fenner, and the car moved off, smoothly, into the quiet and gentle shadows.

More than running water had been added to the apartment on the top floor. There was an efficient kitchen, a gleaming bathroom, a well-stocked pantry. A clutter of small cubicles had lost their dividing walls to form a pleasant living room with three windows and a view toward

Notre-Dame. The room had low, simple furniture, books and pictures on white walls, white rugs on polished wood floor, white roses in a green bowl on the desk. Fenner raised an eyebrow and removed his luggage, quickly, into the bedroom at the back of the apartment. It was marked by simplicity, comfort stripped down to the essentials, a place to sleep deeply, with no intrusions except from the closet (cleared for his use and the only one left unlocked) which had a haunting scent, faint, delicate, lingering. Behind the shower curtain in the bathroom, he found a flowered cap, a charming piece of rubberized froth, forgotten on a faucet. The man who lived here had good taste in women as well as in pictures. But white rugs? Fenner raised his eyebrow again.

The Scotch, however, was authentic. There was ice, too, in the refrigerator. Standing at an opened window, looking at the view, he was a reasonably contented man.

TEN

When Carlson arrived, Bill Fenner was still standing at the window with the living room in darkness. "Another admirer of the old lady, I see." He groped his way expertly to a chair. "She'll still be there tomorrow," he suggested.

Fenner had a last look at Notre-Dame, switched on the lamp at the desk, and pulled the white tweed curtains together. "Big and black and impressive. The proportions never seem quite right, and yet there's something about her. . . . Why didn't they add the spires, I wonder?"

"Spent too much on the gargoyles."

"A couple of centuries to put together, and still here after eight hundred years."

"That's how to build," Carlson agreed. "None of that planned-obsolescence stuff about her."

"Nor was there for St. Paul's or Cologne," Fenner reminded him.

"She was lucky. At a price though."

Which is still being paid, Fenner thought. He poured two man-sized drinks in outsize glasses. "Hope your friend doesn't object to having his Scotch vanish."

"We'll replace."

"Who is he?"

"An illustrator. Good guy."

"He does all right."

"You like it?"

"I wouldn't mind having an apartment on this island myself—" Fenner stopped. "Was that why you chose this place? So that I'd stay put for a couple of days without much kicking or screaming?"

"You might as well be comfortable."

"Look, Carlson—"

"Neill is shorter. Saves the breath."

"I'm not staying put."

"Give me that drink, Bill. Thanks. Well—" He raised his glass. He began drinking, thirstily.

"Here's to the good guy," Fenner said shortly.

"Here's to all of them, wherever you find them," Carlson added between two long draughts.

"You sound pessimistic about the human race."

"Only about its future. It has been that kind of day." Carlson finished his drink, refused another, and relaxed in his armchair. He was letting his exhaustion show now, and didn't care who saw it. "Sorry to keep going back to Vaugiroud. But how much did he actually tell you?"

"You heard it all in the car."

"All? Come on, Bill, I need to know."

"Everything. It wasn't too much, was it?"

"No. But Robert Wahl may not believe that. We'll have to think up some safe explanation for your visit to the Rue Jean-Calas and pass it around." He paused. "You see, Wahl is definitely interested in Vaugiroud."

"That was Wahl's man, was it—the one who was watching the house?"

"Yes. I had a good look at him when I left Vaugiroud."

"In that case, he had a good look at you."

"A calculated risk. And it paid off. I wanted a close-up of that face. It was the one chance I had, so I took it. Why not?" Carlson was smiling it off. "I'm leaving Paris tomorrow." And they'll be under arrest, he thought, bless their clever little minds.

"Was his face worth that risk?"

Carlson studied Fenner thoughtfully. At last, he said, "I'll make a bargain with you, Bill. I'll tell you what I can, within certain limits, if you will stay here quietly for a couple of days. Will you?"

"That's a hard bargain."

"It's pretty soft, actually. You could have been hidden for those two days in a back room of some dreary small hotel where the plumbing doesn't work and the view consists of a brick wall."

"Hidden? Damn it, Neill, you're taking all this too seriously."

"That's better than taking it too lightly."

"I'll keep my mouth shut. I'll attend to my own business. Isn't that enough?"

"You go wandering around, and you know what? You'll be just the man to run into one of Kalganov's boys, on the street, in a bar, at a museum—which they use frequently, I assure you."

"They wouldn't know me; I wouldn't know them."

"If you met the man who was watching Vaugiroud's house?" Carlson had scored there. His exasperation faded.

"So he is Kalganov's man, too?" Fenner asked quickly. "Then Kalganov and Wahl are one and the same?"

Carlson only looked at him blankly.

"Who is this Kalganov?" Fenner asked. "What kind of a man—"

"You really are trouble prone, Bill," Carlson said quietly. "That's one sure thing about you."

"I've been trouble prone since I decided I was going to major in French at college."

Carlson was mildly amused. Or perhaps he needed another of his detours. "And didn't you finish college?"

"Eventually. On the G.I. Bill. But first, my weakness for French landed me in North Africa as an interpreter, and got me promoted to Paris before the Germans pulled out. Someday, you must let me show you my bullet hole. Oh, it's not in me. It looks much better decorating a corner building on the Place Saint-Michel."

Carlson had a new look of interest in his eyes. "What were you, in that war? OSS?"

"You might call me an expendable contact man. Strictly minor jobs, but seldom a dull minute."

Carlson showed some quiet astonishment. He seemed relieved, too, and thoughtful. "You didn't tell Vaugiroud you had been working with the French Resistance."

"With *his* record? My few days in Paris, even with a bullet hole—" Fenner shook his head. "That proves two more things about me: I know when to fall flat on my face; and I can keep my trap shut."

There was a deliberate pause. Then Carlson said slowly, "I'll tell you about Kalganov. After that, I don't think you'll argue about staying here for a couple of days—until he and his contacts are safely locked up. Here is what we know about that name. He has used many others at various times, but this is the real one." And Carlson's unemotional voice began pulling the facts out of a well-remembered file.

Alexei Vassilievitch Kalganov, born in Kiev, 1917; taken to Belgrade in 1919 by *émigré* parents; his father an ex-general turned taxi driver. Early years unrecorded. By seventeen, he was taking part in Balkan politics —blowing up bridges, derailing trains, shooting at cabinet ministers. Two years later, he added some ideology to his anarchism and went to Moscow. He had specialized training there, and was sent to Spain—not to fight, but to liquidate. From there, he went to Marseilles and learned how to organize. He went back to Moscow in 1944, traveling through Paris, with a Resistance group (subsequently eliminated) helping his escape. He worked with Beria for a couple of years, in the Ukraine, in eastern Poland. And then he became untraceable.

It was thought he had been liquidated with Beria. Except, in recent years, there were hints of the name Kalganov—from a couple of defectors who had been trained in assassination, from a few of the terrorists who were arrested in some of the disturbances he had possibly organized. Kalganov was, perhaps, dead. Yet the name persisted. Since 1946, it had become a rumor, a myth, a threat, a hidden menace.

Carlson ended. And frowned. "In 1946, just before he disappeared, he stated that he had killed over two thousand people. Two thousand and twenty-nine, to be exact. And don't think he was boasting. Those were the days of the grand massacres. I guess the anarchists and socialists he liquidated in Catalonia, at the end of the civil war, accounted for half of them. And the Free French he finished off, when he was trusted by the *maquis*, added some more. And the Ukrainians, and Poles—" Carlson's frown deepened. "Let's have another drink," he said.

As it was poured, he went on, "Today I learned two interesting facts from Vaugiroud: he identified Wahl as a terrorist who was secretly passed through Paris in 1944, en route to Moscow; he recognized the man watching his house as Robert Wahl's chauffeur. So after I left Vaugiroud, I paid a visit to my friend Bernard, over at the Sûreté. He has been interested in Kalganov ever since those murders in the *maquis*. He has collected a file of photographs—men who have been known to work with Kalganov."

"And none of Kalganov himself?"

"What do you want to do—make our job easy?" But Carlson had made some discovery from the Sûreté files. There was excitement in his eyes, in his voice. "The man who watched Vaugiroud's house is one of Kalganov's men, all right. His name is Jan Aarvan. And that's the boy I want you to avoid, Bill. So you'll stay here. Right?"

Fenner nodded. A bargain was a bargain. Carlson had answered his question. But he still had others to ask. "So Robert Wahl is Kalganov?" *And I wasn't so far wrong,* he thought.

"Possibly."

"Only possibly?"

"Deductions and coincidences don't make a case. But—" Carlson smiled —"this is the first opening in that blank wall. Thanks to Vaugiroud."

"And to calculated risks."

Carlson turned aside the compliment by saying briskly, "We'll have to concentrate on Robert Wahl. When we catch Kalganov, it will be for a crime that Robert Wahl has committed. So far, Wahl hasn't made any mistakes." Carlson thought over that. "So far," he repeated, more optimistically.

"Have you any idea what he is planning now?"

Carlson only looked as ignorant as possible. The briefing session was over. "It certainly isn't just handing out leaflets, organizing pickets." He glanced at his watch and rose. "I'll push off. I probably won't see you again, so—"

"Where shall I leave the apartment key?"

Carlson looked at him sharply.

"I'll stay here for a couple of days—no good adding to your ulcers—but I'm pushing off, too."

"Where?"

"I'll be wandering around the provinces for the next two weeks. I'm doing a couple of articles on the French national theater. I won't be back in Paris until mid-September. Does that make you feel better?"

"No."

Fenner said in amusement, "Hey! Let's keep things in proportion, Neill. Kalganov hasn't taken over France."

"You'd be surprised how much backing he can command from ordinary party members, who won't know what they are doing, or why they are doing it, but who'll obey. Without one question. They're fighting a war—"

"Look, you don't have to exaggerate to make me realize they're a well-organized bunch—"

"Exaggerate? That would be impossible with men like Kalganov. They are hard realists, in the same sense as the top Nazis were realists. Their aim is total victory. And if they speak of total victory, they are at war. Or aren't they?"

"I'm not arguing with you on that. But, at present, they are—well, partly leashed."

"Are they?"

"Or at least marking time."

"And they'll halt smartly—on whose command?"

"They do take orders. That's what you said yourself, wasn't it?"

"Sure," Carlson said wearily, "they all take orders. All the way from soft-sell, sweet-talk boys who bloom in the open right down to the hidden things in the undergrowth like Kalganov, they all take orders. That, Bill, is what depresses me."

He worries too much, Fenner thought. He's losing his sense of balance.

He will end up not even seeing real peace when it's offered to us. "Relax, Neill, relax. After all, the masters have been talking peace. At Geneva, for three years. They've been getting nowhere fast, I admit, but the thing to remember is that they haven't walked out of the conference room. They are still talking. No bombs exploded for three years. That's my point. There's always some hope while there's talk."

"Only if the two people talking mean the same thing in the words they use. Peace, for instance. There's peace in Hungary, according to the Communists. But who wants that kind of peace? Bill, when both sides have agreed on an exact meaning of an all-important word, such as peace, and start talking from there—I'll not only relax, I'll be able to resign and go back to Iowa, where there's a small-town newspaper I once edited. And on Sundays I could stretch out in my favorite spot under an apple tree I used to know, and I could look up at the sky and say, 'Peace, you're wonderful!'" Carlson's voice had lost its edge. He laughed at himself, at Bill Fenner. "You civilians! You hear an army man worrying aloud about the Russians, and you immediately think he is some jaundiced militant, trigger happy. He is just as much a civilian as you are, only he has probably been reading the documents that don't get published."

There was a slight inclination of Fenner's head. "Okay, okay," he said soothingly.

"Here's one little item that will be published, however. Tomorrow. In headlines right across the front page. The Russians, while still talking at Geneva, have exploded a bomb."

"*What?*"

"You heard me."

"They've broken the moratorium?"

"Smashed it. This bomb is only the first of a planned series. There's another being popped right this minute. It takes several months to prepare a series like that. What price talk?"

"My God—" Fenner's anger was rising.

"Exactly how I felt," Carlson told him. "Remember that piece of fakery, will you, when you are dealing with the Kalganovs in this world?"

"I've had some experience with them," Fenner reminded him sharply. Perhaps that had been his whole opposition to Carlson in the last half hour: the feeling that Carlson might have studied Communist techniques, but he himself had experienced some of them, first hand, and nothing made up for all the bitterness and anguish of a personal betrayal.

"You haven't. Kalganov is a different type from your ex-wife's friends in New York. He isn't George Williston, alias Geoffrey Wills, alias Bruno."

Fenner could only stare blankly.

"In New York, your wife had two other names, also. Didn't you know?"

Fenner rose. He shook his head. He walked over to the desk, then to a bookshelf, then to a picture.

Carlson's quiet voice, flat and unemotional, followed him. "Kalganov makes George Williston look like a toy balloon you can buy at the Central Park Zoo."

Fenner said slowly, under control again, "What about Fernand Lenoir? Is he another Williston, or is he in Kalganov's league?"

"Kalganov wouldn't lift a finger to help anyone like Williston. So, judging from today's interest in Vaugiroud, Lenoir is Kalganov's man. Kalganov protects his own to protect himself."

Fenner came back to the group of armchairs. "Sandra has really moved up," he said bitterly. "Or gone far down."

For a moment, Carlson hesitated. "You did divorce her?" he asked.

"She divorced me." A small smile played around Fenner's lips. "For desertion. In Mexico."

"You went down there, I hope?" Carlson asked in alarm.

"I sent a lawyer to represent me."

Carlson relaxed. "Then it is legal."

"Quite final." Fenner's voice was final, too.

"I'm glad of that. Especially now." He added, as if his words had sounded too ominous, "Desertion? Of all the damned impudence!"

"I did walk out."

"Into a hospital."

"You pick up a lot of information, don't you?"

"Just an old newspaperman, like yourself." Carlson remembered something. He sat down again. "I'll just have a last cigarette. Sit down. Relax, Bill."

What's next? Fenner wondered. He sat down and lit a cigarette, too.

"Mike Ballard met you at the airport. How well do you know him?"

"Just off and on. What's wrong?"

"Nothing as yet."

"You mean he's enjoying Sandra's parties too much?"

"He is clean politically. Honest enough, that way."

"Then what?"

"Well—he is laying himself wide open for blackmail."

"How?"

"He has a family which he seems to love. He has a career that he likes. Yet the idiot has set up a mistress in an apartment in Paris, with the money that he has made on the stock market by following Lenoir's friendly tips. Could you warn him—tactfully?"

"Me?" Fenner had to laugh. "He thinks I am here to take over his job." And no wonder Walt Penneyman has been worrying about the Paris office. "Good God—Ballard isn't even in town this weekend. He didn't expect any news to break. Left everything in charge of André Spitzer. Let's hope Spitzer can handle it—or else Walt Penneyman will really start his own bomb explosions."

"Spitzer will handle his report on the French reaction to the breaking of the moratorium exactly as Lenoir would like him to. Play it down, muted key. Show no alarm, suggest understanding for Russia's mistrust which makes her sometimes so 'difficult,' drop a reminder of Hiroshima, pull out every psychological stop in the organ accompaniment to the neutralists' hymn."

"Does he think Walt Penneyman is a fool?"

"No. He knows that Penneyman, like the rest of us, will be shocked and bewildered. And angry. Angry, too, with the French, who—from Spitzer's report—seem to equate Soviet Russia and the United States as two similar nuisances. By the time your New York office gets in other reports from Europe, and starts evaluating the news properly, Spitzer's suggestions will have entered into a lot of subconscious minds. Second reports from France, however corrective, won't entirely blot first impressions out of some minds. And in Spitzer's creed, every little helps."

Fenner nodded. He had seen that happen before. It was one of the nightmares of newspapermen: the dishonest source, the unsuspected twist. The Nazis had been expert at that. There was one major news source in Europe that had scarcely recovered yet from that duplicity. "How the hell did Spitzer ever edge his way into the *Chronicle?*"

"Ballard needed extra help, and Lenoir recommended Spitzer. He has an enormous capacity for work. Most obliging, and no complaints. So promotion came. He is now second to Ballard. He also introduced Ballard to his mistress. What you might call the generally useful type."

"He will be out on his ear after his handling of today's news."

"Will he send it under his own name?" Carlson asked with a most disarming smile.

Of course he wouldn't. He would send it under Ballard's name, with the friendly pretense of covering up his boss's absence. And Ballard would either have to stand by the report or give himself away.

"Where is he this weekend? Could you reach him?"

"I'd have to ask Spitzer for his address," Fenner said. He swore under his breath. "Damned if I don't spike Comrade Spitzer's little gun."

"How?" Carlson was suddenly and most cheerfully interested.

"I'll cable a report to Penneyman myself, say Ballard's in bed with grippe—"

"Sweet Mademoiselle Grippe," Carlson said reflectively.

"You're recovering fast." And Carlson did look more like the Carlson of that morning.

He said, "It's pleasant to spike a gun now and then. Perhaps that's all we can do: keep spiking, until they get good and tired of loading." Carlson thought over that. "Yes, when our policy is to prove that defense is superior to attack—a most original policy, which would certainly have lost us the American Revolution—the only thing we can do is to keep spiking, call their bluff from the big to the small, let them get away with nothing, wear the bastards down. Bill—thank you! You've put life in these old bones. You've inspired Carlson's Doctrine of Peaceful Persuasion, or Coexistence without Burial." He watched Fenner searching for some writing paper in the desk drawer. "You really are going to cable Penneyman?" he asked delightedly. "What authorities have you interviewed, Mr. Fenner?"

"What authorities has Spitzer interviewed?"

Carlson's old grin was back in place. "Well, you could guess the official French reaction easily enough: De Gaulle vindicated in refusal to hold conferences with Russians. As the old Cross of Lorraine proverb runs, 'He who sits in a bed of poison ivy will sleep facing down for a month.' *Vive la France! Et les pommes de terre frites!*"

"You just go home to bed and leave me to work out a short cable to Penneyman."

"And how are you going to send it? The transatlantic wires will be crowded out."

"All right; stay. And take the cable with you. You have ways and means."

"It seems to me I've been doing a lot of work today for Walt Penneyman and his New York *Chronicle*. What would a Congressional committee say?"

"It could be that a Congressional committee may owe him a vote of thanks."

"He certainly started something when he asked Vaugiroud to analyze a planted lie," Carlson conceded, and wandered off in the direction of the bathroom as Fenner sat down at the desk. By the time he came back, Fenner had finished wording the cable. It was brief: Ballard was ill and could not make a full report until Monday; Penneyman was to disregard any substitute report meanwhile which did not emphasize official French justification of De Gaulle's policies or did not credit the French people with the same shock and outraged concern that all free men must feel everywhere.

"Discreet," was Carlson's comment as he pocketed the message. "Can't do anyone any harm except Spitzer." He started on his way to the door. Casually, he looked at Fenner; most casually, he said, "Talking of discretion—does this project of yours on the national theater have to deal solely with France? There are other national theaters in Europe, you know."

"That's for next year, and the year after that. I'm an optimist, it seems. Even in spite of tonight's news—" Fenner shrugged.

"I'm with you there. Keep on planning: it's one form of survival. Provided we keep on spiking those guns, too. But frankly, do you have to stick closely to your plans? Why not switch to England this year? Or Greece? September's a good month there. Sea is fairly flat; sky is cooling off. Or what about Sweden? Have you seen the girls in Stockholm?"

"You sound like a travel folder."

"I can't be a very good one. No interest, Bill?"

Fenner thought of a slender girl with fair hair that fell softly over her brow at the brush of a breeze. Would she wear a little black dress and short white gloves when she sat in the Piazza di San Marco? Whatever she wore, he'd know her. He said, "I wouldn't mind a trip to Venice."

Carlson's slow walk halted. He stood very still. "Venice. Why Venice?" His voice was guarded.

"I like it. September's a good month there, too. The tourist invasion is just about over; the Fenice opens up." He was almost talking himself into a visit to one of his favorite places. He grinned, and clamped down on the idea. "Next year, with luck," Fenner said. "I've planned out this September too well to change now."

"And if you had slipped coming off the plane and broken your leg? What would have happened to your darned plans then?"

Fenner's answer was to clap Carlson's shoulder reassuringly. "Again, where do I leave that key?"

"Anywhere you like. The door's self-locking." Carlson held out his hand. "Good luck with your book."

"Good luck to you. And thank your friend for putting me up for the weekend. I'd like to have met her."

Carlson looked at him.

"Blue-edged writing paper in the desk drawer with blue-lined envelopes, flowered cap behind shower curtain, a scent of jasmine and roses in the closet that took several months to build up. Elementary, my dear Watson."

"Elementary, hell. You are at least high-school level. I guess old Rosie was right about you."

"And what did Rosie have to say?"

"You'll find out if you don't take my advice and clear out," Carlson said blithely. "I tell you, Bill, there are times when the only way to deal with a threat is to run."

The phrase had an echo of Claire Connor. Fenner's thoughts were too easily pushed in her direction. He was both amused and disturbed by that admission. It seemed as if everything she had said, everything she had done—the simplest word, the smallest movement—had struck deep into his memory.

"What's wrong?" Carlson asked.

"Relax, Neill, I was just thinking of the Café Racine."

"I told you before, and I meant it: keep clear of that place. Keep clear of Proprietor Roussin." Carlson guessed Fenner's thought from the unexpected shock in his face. "No, no," he said quickly. "Roussin isn't the one who betrayed Vaugiroud's past. It's the woman, Angélique, who told her fascist friend, the industrialist, who told his new Communist friends about Roussin and Vaugiroud."

"But how did she learn?"

"From her late husband, Roussin's brother. Vaugiroud's unit helped him to escape to North Africa in 1943."

So Roussin had thought that the secret between him and his brother was buried in his brother's grave. "You'd better warn Roussin," Fenner said.

"Vaugiroud is going to do that tomorrow."

That was best. Roussin was not an easy man to persuade.

Carlson was saying, "So you know why I've been losing my sleep over you. Angélique is watching every contact Roussin makes. What do you think she has reported about you, sitting alone, waiting for Roussin to talk to you? No more of that, Bill. Leave—"

"She has reported that I was waiting for a girl."

"And when the girl didn't turn up? Nice going, Bill, but not good enough for Angélique."

"But the girl did turn up."

"You *were* meeting someone?" Carlson's eyes were wide. He had a smile of relief spreading over his face.

"Not exactly. But a pretty girl did join me. Most enthusiastically, I might say, although I'm still wondering why. It would look perfectly natural, even to old hawk-eyed Angélique."

"You have the devil's own luck."

"The trouble with the devil's luck is that it doesn't last long. Instead of a pleasant evening with a beautiful blonde, I've been talking with you."

"Well, well." Carlson was at ease again, his hand reaching to open the door. "I'm glad to hear she was beautiful—while she lasted."

"You saw her today. Outside the Crillon. Remember the girl I wanted to give a lift—"

"Yes," Carlson said, looking at him, "I remember."

"But I saw her first. Remember that, too."

Carlson half smiled.

"She's a pretty high-powered little package in her sweet little way."

"She is, is she?" Carlson shook his head. "I still think you'd be safer in Copenhagen. By the way—Rosie may drop in to see you."

Fenner came out of his dream. "Why?"

"Heaven knows. He has, as they say at Harvard, his own thought processes. Just keep refusing all his bright ideas, and you'll get that book written." He opened the door abruptly to cut off any further questions. "See you, someday. But not too soon, I hope." He looked out at the landing, nodded, gave Fenner a broad grin and another handshake. The door closed gently, surely, and locked automatically.

Bill Fenner went slowly to bed—ten minutes spent wandering restlessly through the apartment; five minutes at the window with its view; some scattered minutes opening his suitcase to free his clothes from creases, searching for toothpaste and hairbrush—not only because he was so exhausted that every movement had become the semiparalysis of a dream, but also because his mind, tired as it was, raced and jumped. He had plenty to think about. Carlson had told him far too much. Why? To impress him enough to lie low, clear out? Carlson wanted that, obviously. Or had Carlson been following orders to put him in the picture as much as was feasible, to give him some ideas to sleep on, to prepare him—for what?

At two o'clock he gave up, stripped off his clothes, fell into a bed that was nicely firm and yet yielding. Linen sheets, no less, ice-cool, smelling of sunlight and clover. Bliss, he thought, the kind of bliss that women think up when they put their minds to it. The owner of this apartment had the right ideas for living, certainly. For a few moments, he wondered what she looked like. Brunette and fastidious, as cool and smooth as this pillow . . . And then there was the beginning of a deep slide, steady and gentle, down into the dark caves of sleep.

ELEVEN

Far away, a small bell rang. And kept ringing. Nearer, louder, nearer, until it echoed at his ear. Fenner came out of his deep sleep as smoothly as he had entered it. Time to wake anyhow. It must be noon. The narrow strips of sunlight stretched from the shuttered window across the floor, a golden ladder pointing to the chair with his tumbled clothes. God, I was tired last night, he thought, as he stretched his spine. The phone rang again on the table beside the bed. As he reached for the receiver, he was astounded to see that his watch said only ten o'clock. He had gained two hours on this day, after all. "*Ici Fenner. Parlez!*"

"You amaze me," Frank Rosenfeld said. "Such geniality at this hour! Had breakfast?"

"Not yet."

"Then I'll bring the *croissants,* and you put on the coffee. Fair division of labor." In spite of the sociable phrases, Rosie sounded sharp-set. He hadn't slept so well, obviously; or, he meant business. He must have telephoned from around the corner, for he arrived in less than five minutes, neatly dressed in a dark-gray suit and a crisp white shirt, *croissants* in a string-tied parcel dangling from one curved finger, an amused smile on his amiable lips, a quick all-over glance from his sharp brown eyes. First they took in Fenner, who had just had time after the brief telephone call to pull on pajama trousers, start the coffee percolating, open shutters and curtains. "Had a good eight hours, I see," Rosie said approvingly. His eyes traveled around the cool, shadowed living room, which faced west toward the towering walls of Notre-Dame, and rested on the vase of white roses. "A House of York sympathizer?"

Fenner hoped he had hidden his flicker of astonishment. It never was very flattering to let a man see you had underestimated him. And why shouldn't an Intelligence agent be interested in history? He helped its shaping, one way or another, just as the soldiers who won, or lost, a battle helped to decide the kind of future their country would face. "She has everything cosily arranged. There's a small table for breakfast set up at the bedroom windows."

But his remark led nowhere. Rosie did not even seem to hear his reference to a woman, far less explain her. He glanced in at the sunlit bedroom, discarded it, and returned to the cold living room. He settled quite definitely in a green armchair by a coffee table, well away from the windows, and began opening the parcel of *croissants*. "These are the best in Paris," he said. "But why the hell haven't they got around to inventing paper bags?"

Fenner relinquished his hope for a pleasant breakfast in front of an open window filled with September sunshine. (The owner of this apartment and he shared some tastes in common, it seemed.) He pulled on his pajama jacket and dressing gown, poured the coffee, found some sugar (she used several American brands, he noticed from his search among the cans on the pantry shelves), and hoped he would be at least granted a peaceful half hour. He disliked any kind of serious politics before his third cup of coffee. Until then, back in his New York apartment, he looked over the theater, book, and sports pages of the *Chronicle, Times,* and *Tribune.* And with food inside him, he felt fortified enough to face the news of the day with all its puzzles and frustrations, alarms and excursions.

Rosie was human, apparently. He allowed Fenner the recovery space of two excellent *croissants* and two cups of strong coffee, chatting affably about the recent governmental reprimand to the Comédie-Française for spending elaborate production on nitwit plays—a situation that the advocates of state-supported theater had never imagined could develop. It had been that anomaly which had first amused Fenner, interested him in writing about national theaters. His own views were objective: he would find out the facts, the good and the bad, and set them down without any covert attack or special pleading.

"You'll be damned by both sides," Rosie predicted.

"There's always a middle ground, where reasonable men can argue."

"Must be nice," Rosie said quietly, watching Fenner light his cigarette, "to have reasonable men as your opponents."

At last we're getting down to business, Fenner thought. But Rosie was approaching it gently (and when it comes, Fenner thought again, it will be like a bucket of ice water). He lit his own cigarette thoughtfully. "It's a world pretty far removed from what you dipped into yesterday."

Fenner agreed on that. "I prefer my own world," he admitted. He smiled and added, "I'll stay with it."

Rosie shot him a quick, hard glance. "Can you? Can anyone? Sometimes, there is a matter of priority. In a time of crisis, we may find precious little left of the world of art if we don't pay attention to the world of power politics."

Fenner could agree on that, too. "Civilization is a perishable commodity. But still—"

"Still what?"

"Life is short; art is long. That's one way of looking at it."

Rosie exploded. "Long? If an implacable enemy, proud, hard, can force his ideology on art, how long will it live—as we know it? He has got to change it, pull it down to his level. How else can he maintain his authority? He won't allow himself to be shown inferior. If he can't usurp and change a civilization over which he has managed to seize domination, he will be forced to destroy it. What would happen to the freedom in our world of art if we lost this war of power politics?"

I've really stirred up old Rosie, Fenner thought. Surely he doesn't think that I don't know what is at stake. Or has he met so many who ignore it that he has got to assume I may be one of them? And why doesn't he want me to be one of them? What does he want me to do? But I'm not ready to hear it yet; not until I know still more about Rosie. Yesterday he was a quick-witted guy with a droll tongue. Today, even if he is trying to reach me by talking about things that interest me, he is really concerned. About what? Does he really believe what he is saying—he is not just a man who likes the mystery and hidden power of his job? "It would be the first freedom to go," Fenner agreed. "Yet your implacable men, proud and hard, don't win in the long run. How many political systems have come and gone since Sophocles wrote his plays? You can still read them, sometimes even see them produced. But where are the fanatic power groups that thought they had a grip on the world by its throat?"

"How many plays did Sophocles write?"

"About a hundred."

"How many exist today?"

"Seven."

"And the others lost, destroyed?"

"Most thoroughly."

"Like most of the plays by Euripides and Aeschylus, or the poems of Pindar."

Fenner looked at Rosie with interest. He smiled. "You win," he said. "Art is long, provided the barbarians don't get their hands on it."

517

"And it's the educated barbarian who is the worst: he knows what to destroy. A bunch of illiterate Vandals come blundering in. They'll destroy anything in sight, but what is hidden may escape them. But the educated barbarian knows what to search for. He knows. That's my point, Bill. He is selective in his destruction. He knows what must be destroyed if he is to hold power. He—" Rosie's intensity slackened as he looked at Fenner. He frowned. "When did you stop disagreeing with me?" he asked. "Or didn't you disagree?"

"I tried hard."

"You're a son of a."

"That's right."

"You've wasted three whole minutes by my watch."

"Not wasted, I assure you."

Rosie took a deep and audible breath. He shook his head slowly, a smile growing on his lips. "All right," he said, "we can get down to business. I saw Neill Carlson after he left you, this early morning. He sent your message to Walt Penneyman, all right. By telephone, actually. Cable will follow as verification."

"Whatever did he have to say to Penneyman that made him telephone?" Fenner was alert.

Rosie concentrated on lighting another cigarette. "I did the talking with Penneyman. I've met him. Last April, to be exact, but that little story will have to wait. At the moment, let's concentrate on you. I have been thinking about your situation."

"And it isn't good?"

"From my point of view, it's perfect."

Fenner's amusement ended. "Carlson didn't like it."

"Oh, Neill and I don't always agree on methods. Besides, he feels sort of responsible for you."

"Why? If I hadn't handed over the money to him yesterday, there would have been someone else." But not someone, perhaps, whose judgment I trusted enough to put him in touch with Vaugiroud. Strange in a way, Fenner thought, how Carlson and I got on so well, and so quickly: a rare thing, too, the older one got, and all the more pleasant for that.

"That's how I see it. You did get involved. Of your own free will. Didn't you?"

That was going rather too far. "The money in Goldsmith's raincoat hadn't much to do with my free will."

"But after that?"

Yes. It was true enough. "One thing led to another."

"It always does. That's why I'm here. You've guessed that, of course."

518

"What are you trying to do? Recruit me?"

Rosie was shocked. "Good heavens, no. There's just a small assignment which you could handle."

"Why me?"

"First, you've learned quite a lot in the last twenty-four hours. Carlson put you in the picture, more or less. I don't have to spend valuable time on arguing about Communist conspiracy. Right? Second, you're a newspaperman—"

"Once upon a time, only."

Rosie shook his head. "Once upon a time and always. You know that. So does Walt Penneyman. You'll find a cable from him waiting for you at the *Chronicle*'s office suggesting that you interview two of the prize neutralists returning from the Belgrade Conference on their reactions to the Russian bomb tests. That will take care of André Spitzer's curiosity about your change of plans and hasty departure."

"And where do I interview the returning neutralists?"

"Oh, they are making quite a jaunt of their visit to Europe. Some will recover from their labors in Rome, Athens. And two—so a rumor says —have decided to relax in Venice. I heard you didn't dislike the place."

Venice . . .

"Yes," Rosie said, "that's where you'll find your story. It's big. It's so big, in fact, that Penneyman would certainly not object if you hadn't time for any interviews."

"You'd let me write that story?" Fenner was disbelieving.

"It will be written about. That's for sure. You might as well have first crack at it."

"So it isn't something that's top secret." Or even minimum secret, Fenner thought: Rosie wasn't exactly the type to let anything out of his private files unless it had descended to the common-knowledge level.

"At present, it is highly top secret. It will be for the next week. After that—it's anyone's story. I'm giving you the chance to be able to write it first." He rose, stretched his shoulders, walked over to the window.

Fenner waited, but Rosie was keeping his silence. "Go on," Fenner said.

"Not until I know if you are interested."

"How can I be interested until I know what you are talking about?"

"Were those three minutes wasted, after all?" Rosie asked slowly.

Fenner shook his head. "Far from it. If you ask me to do anything for you, I know that you aren't using me for some quick little advantage of your own. I am not a labor-saving device. I'm not just a lucky opportunity, either, to help someone get a promotion. And here is something for *you* to know: I may do this job, but not for you or your department; not even for your whole organization. I may do it because I just like Americans to be able to go on living their own kind of life. That's why I'm listening to you."

Rosie had walked slowly back to face him, his eyes never leaving Fenner.

"Also," Fenner said, "if I go to Venice, it won't be for the sake of any news story. So you don't have to use that as bait. Just tell me what's at stake. If I can help, I'll do it. If I can't, I'll say no. Will you risk that?"

Rosie said slowly, "Yes, I believe I will." He sat down again. "I'll lay it on the line, Bill. You may not like part of this story, but hear me out, will you? The stakes are high. The highest, in fact. An assassination of the head of a Western state. It's planned for next week."

"An assassination? Who is to be removed—De Gaulle?"

"Quick to guess, aren't you?"

"He's an obvious target, at this moment." And now the meeting of Secret Army backers with Communists at a quiet luncheon table in a respectable restaurant began to show its threat.

"Only at this moment?" Rosie asked wryly. Grimly serious, he added, "This moment is enough for us, anyhow. It's our problem. Definitely."

"But if you know of any attempted assassination—"

"Oh, that? I alerted the French as soon as I heard about it. The assassination will fail, this time."

"Well, what's worrying you?"

"We've been implicated. The United States and Britain will be blamed." Rosie looked like a man whose doctor had just told him he wouldn't last a week.

"Implicated?" Fenner took a deep breath. "So Vaugiroud was right. They've manufactured evidence?"

Rosie came out of his black thoughts. "You saw part of it yesterday morning," he said grimly.

"The money?"

"In most traceable bills. Anyone in the States who asks for a ten-thousand-dollar bill at his bank must register—it's a safeguard against any attempt at income-tax evasion."

"So ten people registered—"

"All of them Americans."

"What are they? Not Communists—they don't register so easily."

"Not Communists. Just ten gullible Americans. Rich sympathizers, perhaps, who could be easily persuaded to back a cause. Or people who were paying blackmail; or contributing to some quick-money scheme; or following the instructions of a confidence man. They wouldn't know that any of these approaches were being directed, remotely but definitely, by a Communist—a foreigner sent into the States specially for this mission. It must have taken his organization some months to gather the cash."

"Well, they haven't got it now."

"No. They'll have to substitute something else—a hundred thousand dollars deposited in the bank account of the man who hired the killers."

"Couldn't that deposit be proved a fake?"

"It is less conclusive than an envelope of ten-thousand-dollar bills being found in the man's own home," Rosie conceded, "but difficult to disprove unless we had time and a reasonable climate of opinion. Which we won't have. Lenoir has attended to that."

"How?"

"He will publish two letters to prove that the Americans subsidized the Secret Army to assassinate De Gaulle, with the British acting as go-between."

"The letters could be proved a fake, too." If we had time, Fenner thought worriedly, if we had no screaming headlines.

"One is real."

"*What?*"

"It dealt with quite another subject altogether. It will be taken out of context. And it will lend itself, very neatly, to misinterpretation."

"To aiding and abetting an assassination?" Fenner was incredulous.

"It will be used that way."

"And what damn fool handed the Communists that triumph on a golden platter?"

"He isn't a damn fool. And the triumph wasn't handed to them. They planned it that way."

"Who wrote the letter? Was he American, or British?"

"He's a good Intelligence officer, no fool, far less a damn fool. It could have happened to any of us. In fact, from now on, I'll never write a discreet letter again with any pleasure."

"But this one must have been written to one of the conspirators," Fenner objected. "Otherwise it wouldn't be much use to Lenoir's plan."

"They thought of that, too."

Fenner could only shake his head. "Then we've had it," he said softly.

"We'll see about that." Rosie's lips tightened. "We'll make a damned good try—"

"What man in any Intelligence service would write to a Secret Army sympathizer, and confidentially at that? Surely—"

"He wrote in reply to a wine merchant called Trouin, an authentic businessman with right-wing politics, whose Algerian imports were folding. So Trouin had been closing down two of his European outlets—one in London, one in Warsaw. For that reason, late in July, he visited Poland briefly. And in Warsaw, he picked up some highly secret information. When he came back to Paris, he wrote a letter to the British Embassy. He gave them the information, and he also made a request for the Pole who had told him that information. The Pole wanted to defect on his next secret mission into the British Sector of Berlin. Would the Brits keep his defection secret until his wife and child could join him? They would have to leave all possessions behind them, of course, so would the Americans help him and his family to start a new life in the United States, where he wanted to settle? If the answers were in the affirmative, Trouin would be willing to act as the intermediary. Considering that this Pole was a high-ranking officer in the Polish Secret Service working with the GRU—the Red Army Secret Service, that is—the British and Americans were interested."

"I take it that the piece of information was accurate?"

"Both accurate and valuable. The British Embassy passed the letter along to their Intelligence, who checked everything. The piece of information was real. There is such a Polish officer in Warsaw, who has been sent, twice, on spying missions into West Berlin. Trouin's business visit to Warsaw was authentic. The note paper came from Trouin's office, the typewriter used was Trouin's own portable, the signature seemed genuine. Now, of course, we know it was probably a very clever forgery."

"How?"

"Trouin had asked for an appointment—the place and time to be chosen by the British agent who would meet him discreetly and hear the details about the Pole's plan to escape. Everything had to be arranged with great secrecy and precaution—Trouin even gave a poste restante address for the reply to his letter. He did not want any telephone call to his home or office. The reason for that was obvious: complete security. He had to visit Warsaw once more, quite soon. He didn't want the Russians to learn he had been in communication with the British."

"So the appointment was made, and Trouin didn't turn up?"

A small gleam, perhaps of approval, sparked in Rosie's eye. "You've got it."

"And Lenoir got the British reply at a poste restante."

"That's right."

"And the Brits felt no alarm when Trouin didn't show?"

"He could have had a bad scare or an attack of cold feet. That happens, you know: people do chicken out of situations like that. The secret meeting with a British Intelligence officer was supposed to be yesterday morning. The Brits were going to give Trouin a couple of days to calm down, before they tried approaching him again. Their involvement seemed little enough: just a letter suggesting the time and method of meeting for discussion of his problem. It also assured him that he could report to his friend that all his conditions had been accepted, and the Americans would co-operate fully; he would be given every assistance, with the utmost discretion."

"When did the alarm sound?"

"Last night."

"After Carlson had learned from Vaugiroud that the wine merchant was more than ultraconservative?"

"Partly that. Partly—well, I picked up some extra information, too, yesterday evening." Rosie fell silent: discussion on that point was barred; meanwhile, at least.

Fenner was tactful. "A very double-crossed conspirator," he said, returning to Trouin. "I suppose, when the British reply is published, it will be used with some other letter—not about a man defecting from Poland, but dealing with something really damning."

"That's the plan. The letter about Warsaw will be destroyed: its purpose was achieved in getting a reply out of the British. In its place, Lenoir is substituting a real beauty. I haven't seen it, but I can guess. It will make the British officer who wrote to Trouin look as if he were the intermediary between Trouin and the Americans. The hundred thousand dollars deposited in Trouin's bank account will appear to be the purchase price of an assassination." Rosie took a deep breath. "Neat, isn't it?"

"If I were you," Fenner said slowly, "I'd nail Trouin right away. If he sees he is the sacrificial goat, he may bleat. Come to think of it, I'd nail them all."

"We tried that. Last night. The Sûreté sent men to arrest Wahl. But he walked out of the Café Racine just five minutes after Lenoir, and disappeared completely. It's my guess he has left the country. Trouin had already left—yesterday afternoon. His friend the industrialist is somewhere in Spain. And Lenoir is on the vacation he has been planning for some weeks. They are, in fact, all out of the country."

"Sudden alarm?"

"Only in Wahl's case, perhaps. The others had made their arrangements in advance. This was a scattering by plan."

"And you haven't an idea where any of them can be found?"

"We know where Lenoir is."

"Have him picked up."

"It isn't as simple as that."

"How?" Fenner asked sharply. Then he eased his voice and smiled. "Or is that none of my blasted business?"

"It could be your business in Venice," Rosie said, and wiped the smile from Fenner's face. "I want you to go there. But before you give me an answer on that, there are some things you should know. You see, this concerns Sandra Fane. Now, now, hold on, hear me out!" Rosie's hand was up, like a traffic policeman, pacifying, bringing order. "We are in debt to Sandra," he told Fenner, "we owe her something."

Bill Fenner stared at the serious face opposite him. "She's lying to you, Rosie," he said warningly.

"I don't think so."

"She never defected. No one who defects can live such a cosy and carefree life as she does on the Avenue d'Iéna. Especially a defector like Sandra. She was important in the party. She still must be. Or she wouldn't be working with Lenoir. She may even be working with Wahl—Kalganov himself, isn't he?" For Rosie hadn't mentioned Kalganov by name.

Rosie nodded. "I believe Wahl is Kalganov. But we've no factual proof, have we? We need someone like Sandra who could identify him for us."

"She wouldn't! Stop kidding yourself, Rosie."

"She has already given me a lot of information. In fact, without her help, we wouldn't have been able to fit the pieces of this puzzle together. I met her yesterday evening near the children's puppet show in the Tuileries."

"She really did defect?" Fenner asked slowly. It was a complete reversal of his guesses.

"No. She is defecting *now*. Next week, to be exact. In Venice. She needs help, a lot of help—"

"Look," Fenner said, "I told you yesterday, and I meant it—I'm not going either to help or to hinder Sandra Fane." He rose abruptly to his feet. "I don't want to see her. Ever. Not even from a distance."

"Why?" Was he still in love with her? Rosie wondered anxiously. Some men could take an awful beating and still be afraid of asking for more.

"Because," Fenner said, with a rush of truth, "I have felt like a bigenough god-damned fool without being reminded of it all over again. She never married me for love. Did you know that? Oh, she liked me. That was lucky, she told me on that last night. I hadn't been repulsive. Most fortunate for her. She had been told to marry me. Get that, Rosie? On orders. For political advantages. I was on my way up, in line for news editor at the *Chronicle*. I could be manipulated. I could be useful." Fenner's voice halted. "No, Rosie, don't keep reminding me of that sleazy little bitch."

"I must."

"No!"

"Hear me out, Bill." Rosie's voice was sympathetic. "Just hear me out, will you?"

Fenner's lips closed tight.

Rosie's mood changed. He began to laugh. And as Fenner looked at him angrily, ready to walk out, Rosie said, "I was just remembering the way the Communists even put sex to work for the revolution."

"That's funny as hell," Fenner said savagely.

"Sure. But it's true. They have a School for Seduction in the Soviet Union. Special Intelligence agents take a course there. They have lectures and practical demonstrations. There's one instructor who shows the class how to make love to seven consecutive women without even staggering. He teaches mind control. It's useful, too, when a student is ordered to make love to a beautiful woman—mustn't enjoy it, might become involved; or to some old bag of lard—no flinching allowed. So they graduate, come out into the big simple-minded world, with a diploma in how to make a woman and influence people. Seduce some women thoroughly, and you've got them: they'll do anything in return—even to borrowing documents, searching files, reporting on their husband's work. That's the theory. In practice? It has worked." Rosie shook his head. "In fact, it has been one of the minor headaches for Counter Intelligence in non-Communist countries. But it also gives us a laugh, now and again. Especially when I think of that instructor. A dedicated man." Rosie's hilarity broke out again, and this time Fenner almost smiled. Rosie noted the improvement, the easing of tension. "Clinical and cynical, and oh, so earnest!"

Fenner shook his head, began to laugh in spite of himself.

"Picture of two men discussing an impending threat to Western unity," Rosie said when their laughter died away. There was no amusement in his eyes, though. "Will you hear me out, Bill?" he asked quietly.

Fenner nodded and sat down. He noticed, then, that he must have upset the ash tray when he had risen. "Clumsy beggar, I've ruined her white rug, damn it!" He picked up the stubs and burned matches, tried to blow the gray ash away. By the time he had finished, he could face Rosenfeld again quite normally. "Go ahead," he said crisply. "But I still don't think Sandra is being honest with you. It's a trick, Rosie. She has fed you some information, yes. But it could be the old confidence game: you hold my money and I'll hold yours."

"I am going to tell you exactly what happened. After that, you can judge. Fair enough?"

"Fair enough."

"Well, it was this way—" Rosie said, and began the story of his meeting with Sandra Fane.

TWELVE

The story, itself, began at Sandra Fane's party on the night before Fenner arrived in Paris.

She had invited Stanfield Dade, along with several other attachés of various embassies, and had asked Mike Ballard to persuade him to accept. Sandra was an expert hostess, with five minutes neatly devoted to each of her forty guests. It was perfectly natural that Dade was given his quota of conversation. Only, what she had to say to him was unexpected. First, she emphasized that it was confidential. Next, she said a friend of hers—an American woman—needed help. The friend was a Communist, on an important mission in France. The friend wanted to get out of the party, get out of Europe. Would the Americans be interested enough to help? In return for their help, Sandra's friend would be willing to tell them something of great interest. Would Dade give her the telephone number and name of anyone who could help her friend? She asked him to think over this—he was speechless with astonishment, actually—and because she must leave him to speak to another guest, he could quietly pass her the name and telephone number later in the evening, when she was talking to Ballard. She left him with the same bright smile with which she had talked—gaily, expressively, but with her voice carefully lowered, a contrast which impressed Dade so much by its technique and desperation that, after an hour of brooding inwardly, he decided to take a chance. Or rather, to let Frank Rosenfeld take a chance; what was there to lose, except the hope of valuable information, if this defector turned out to be less interesting than Sandra Fane had so quietly implied? So when Sandra and Ballard were chitchatting, he had joined them. And when Sandra asked Ballard to bring her another glass of champagne, Dade had given her Frank Rosenfeld's business name and his firm's telephone number.

. . .

"So there's Act One of our little drama," Rosie said to Fenner. "The exposition, you would call it. Any comment so far?"

"Only that Sandra was always her own best friend," Fenner said wryly.

"Ah!" said Rosie, eyes approving. "You jump ahead of me. I didn't find that out until the next day. Dade sent me a cryptic message; he's a cautious man, doesn't like involvement, just warned me I might get a call sometime from a woman who needed help in escaping from political entanglements. But I was too busy with Mr. Goldsmith's arrival and disappearance to pay much attention. There was nothing urgent in Dade's message."

"He didn't think the woman could be Sandra herself?"

"No. Remember, she is generally supposed to have already defected."

"And he doesn't question that?"

"His not to reason why; his but to do, up to a point. Which was me."

"And when did you get her call?"

"The first one reached my office just after noon, while I was at the Embassy, meeting you. No name was left, only a message that the woman would call again at four o'clock. I was to make sure to be there, because she had to put in the calls from a public telephone. She had vital information to give me. My secretary said the woman sounded urgent and capable—she could mean business. So I was in my office just before four o'clock, cursing Dade for dragging me away from the Goldsmith problem, but curious, too. Information, even if it isn't as vital as its donor thinks, may still be interesting. But as soon as this woman's voice began talking to me, I knew she was someone important. Because, although she was asking my help, she was giving me orders. She couldn't get away from the habit." Rosie laughed softly. "I was told where to meet her, and how. She asked my height and weight and general description: and what was I wearing? I was to carry a newspaper, a copy of *Time*, and a rolled umbrella. Just before five o'clock, I was to stroll around the open-air puppet theater in the Tuileries Gardens, choose a path among the trees in a direction away from the Rue de Rivoli. She would follow me. I was to hire a couple of seats under a tree, and as soon as the attendant was paid and moved away, she would join me. I was to meet her alone. Tell no one. Have no one watching, so that he would not attract attention to us. If I thought I was being followed, I was to read *Time*. If I was sure it was safe, I was to read my newspaper. And I would easily recognize her from her photograph in our files." Rosie enjoyed that bit. "She has a sense of humor."

That's something new, Fenner thought. But her way of flattering—that had always been peculiarly Sandra's. Even Rosie had been pleased that his powers of deduction were not underestimated. "Where did you find a rolled umbrella?" Fenner asked.

"I called in at the Embassy and borrowed Dade's," Rosie admitted. "Forgot to tell him. I guess he wouldn't like having even his umbrella involved."

"You're too hard on him."

"Why not? If everything turns out well, he'll get all the credit."

"Will he?"

"He'll take it anyway, in his memoirs. He is one of those now-it-can-be-told guys, and wasn't-I-right-all-along?"

Fenner laughed. "Okay. So there you were, with a rolled umbrella, strolling among the neatly spaced trees. Background of children playing, nurses gossiping, mothers comparing clothes and manners, wandering couples holding hands, older people renting chairs to rest their legs for a blessed hour." And the time was almost five o'clock, and Vaugiroud and I were talking.

"Not bad, not bad at all. Just add some spotty sunlight, distant shrieks of laughter from the open-air Punch and Judy show, two chairs nicely protected by several prim trees, and you've got me waiting, reading a newspaper. She didn't take long. It was Sandra Fane, all right, although I didn't recognize her until she had almost reached me. She was dressed in black, unrelieved; and she wore no jewelry, no make-up. That makes a big difference in her type. She was just a white-faced, faded blonde with no eyes or lips. A ghost in mourning."

"She'd have make-up and earrings in her purse, all ready to doll her up once the meeting was over."

"No doubt. She did say she was on her way to an art-gallery opening, where she'd meet Fernand Lenoir. Cool customer," Rosie said admiringly. "Our meeting was fairly brief, no more than thirty-five minutes, but her thoughts were well organized. She didn't waste any time. And she had several surprises to deal out. Several . . ."

Sandra Fane had begun with a very direct question. "How," she asked, in a low, calm voice, "could I get back to America?"

"Take the first plane." Rosenfeld wasn't even troubling to be polite: he might admire her technique, but he hadn't any sympathy for her problem.

"You know it isn't as easy as that."

"Perhaps not, but your chief difficulty will be in leaving the Avenue d'Iéna. Or is your friend Lenoir behind this idea?"

"No. Could you help me reach America?"

"Why should we?"

"I'm getting out. I'm no longer a Communist."

"Since when?"

"I've been thinking about it for the last six weeks. I was supposed to have quit the party three years ago, when I came to Paris. It was only a cover story. You knew that, didn't you?"

"Why are you deciding to leave, just at this time?"

"Two reasons. I'm getting in too deeply, the kind of thing"—she looked at him frankly, her blue eyes pale and tired under the uncolored eyebrows and lashes—"that I never have been involved in, don't want to be involved with."

"Turned squeamish?"

"And also," she said, ignoring that, "I have been recalled to Moscow." She had kept her voice calm, but her eyes looked away. Her hands tightened on her bag. Their knuckles, under the black gloves, would be white.

"When do you leave?"

"Next week. From Venice, where Fernand and I are supposed to be on vacation. He has engaged a suite at the Danieli. The plan is this: he will be out of France when the assassination takes place; then return at once to Paris to take full advantage of the situation."

"What assassination?" Rosenfeld asked quickly.

But she wanted his promise first. She had merely ensured he would listen to her. "Will you help me escape from Venice? I leave Paris tonight with Fernand. I'll spend this weekend with him; and on Monday, I escape. Monday evening. The assassination attempt is late in the week. That's how I've calculated it. Because Fernand plans to return to Paris by next Friday. He must be here as soon as the assassination is a *fait accompli*, but not before."

"What assassination?" Rosenfeld repeated.

"I am not in their confidence."

Like hell you aren't, Rosenfeld thought. "Who are they aiming at? De Gaulle?"

"Perhaps. Their plans are big enough for that."

"When? Where?"

"I don't know exactly. I'll know by Monday. I can tell you then."

She knows all right, Rosie thought. She is safeguarding herself, wants to establish that she isn't guilty of conspiring to assassinate. He restrained his impatience, his shock and excitement. He shrugged his shoulders. "You haven't left us much time to arrange an escape. It will take some planning. You are important to them: they won't let you just walk out."

"I know. That is why I ask you for help. It is the only way. I would have asked you before, except"—and the pale lips half smiled—"I had nothing to bargain with. I have no illusions. If I buy help from you, the price will be steep. Ordinary information would not be enough—not to get the kind of immunity I want."

"No one could promise you complete immunity."

"But if I make this gesture—surely I'll be given some consideration? I am thirty-five. By the time I am fifty, perhaps even before, I shall have a new name, a new life. Some quiet, some safety . . . I'll have earned that, I think."

"So far," he reminded her pointedly, "your information isn't worth much. An assassination, with no date, no place, and a big perhaps around the victim's name."

Quickly she said, "I know who has planned it. I know who is implicated. Why else do you think I'm being recalled?"

"You know too much?"

She dodged that answer. "Once it is over, Lenoir doesn't need me to do any more entertaining for him. He has other plans." She looked at him. "Are you interested in helping me?"

"As you said, ordinary information will not be enough. Why did you wait so long before you contacted us? An assassination isn't planned in a week." Not even in a month. Not this kind of job, obviously.

"I told you. I needed bargaining power."

"Show me it."

"Are you interested in helping me, if I do?"

"Yes."

"Can you persuade Washington to be equally interested?"

"I think so."

"The escape and transport to America could be arranged—even at such short notice?"

"Yes."

"I'll take your word," she said softly. "And you have mine. I'll tell you what I know, what I can do for you. And you'll do your best for me. A bargain?"

Rosenfeld nodded.

"The assassination is to be entrusted to the OAS. It was planned by Robert Wahl, a naturalized Frenchman, a Communist. He is supplying money—in American dollars, a large amount but easily handled, which came into the country this morning. This will be used as part evidence of American complicity. The other part is being provided by Fernand Lenoir, also a Communist, in the shape of a letter that will implicate the British and the Americans."

"A letter?"

"It will look like part of a correspondence between Trouin, a wine merchant and secret backer of the OAS, and a British Intelligence agent named Holland. That correspondence exists: I have brought copies of Trouin's letter and Holland's reply, so that you can check with the British on my story."

"And the implicating letter that Lenoir is concocting?"

"It will be substituted for Trouin's letter. It will appear to be the letter that received the British reply."

"And where is this fake letter?"

"I shall have it for you in Venice." Something almost amused her. "I shall have the original fake itself."

"How can you be sure that Lenoir will take it there?"

"Why else are we vacationing in Venice? There he will meet several of his prize neutralists, some of his pet pro-Communists. As soon as the news of the assassination breaks, he will show them two letters: the one he invented and the British reply. He will show the originals, and give them copies for publication." She smiled. "Lenoir's 'original' will certainly be in Venice. I know. Now about my escape—"

"First, what about that money you mentioned? Has it been delivered to you?" Rosenfeld asked, interested in the shape of the lie he expected.

But she was telling the truth, at least in this. "There has been some delay. It was to have been delivered at my apartment by my masseur, who visits me regularly. Instead, it will be handed to me, this evening, at an art-gallery reception for a new showing of pictures which"—she pulled back her glove and glanced at her wrist watch—"I'll attend, after I leave you and spend half an hour in the Métro." Her sense of humor was returning with her confidence. "How I am going to miss dodging back and forth in the subway just when I have perfected the art! In Venice—"

"You're way ahead," Rosenfeld cut in, and brought back her tense look again. "Is Lenoir going to be at this art gallery?"

"I meet him there. Then we leave for Venice."

"Taking the money with you?"

"No. Fernand Lenoir will see that it is hidden in the wine merchant's private safe."

"And the wine merchant?"

"He doesn't know. And when it's found, he may have already committed suicide. Of course, that's only a guess—I don't *know.*"

That's right, Rosenfeld thought: you know nothing about any form of murder. Bright girl, aren't you? "Who is delivering the money to you at the gallery?"

"The owner. His present name is Anton Mehr." She spelled his second name carefully.

"What does he look like?"

She said impatiently, "He is of no importance. White hair, blue eyes, yellow complexion. Liver trouble. He worked for many years in French Indochina."

Rosenfeld studied his hands. Blue eyes, yellow skin, and a blob-shaped face, I bet. "Why don't I have the Sûreté pick you all up at the gallery? Right there and then? That's one simple way of arranging your escape from them."

"Yes. You would get Mehr, Lenoir, and the money. And me. But you would not get the letter. You would not get Wahl. You would never get him. One warning, and he would disappear, go underground, work from there. You would not stop the assassination. You would not stop other money being used—oh, it would take a less dramatic form, perhaps a bank deposit in Trouin's account—but it still could be dynamite when used with the fake letter asking for one hundred thousand dollars as expenses." She knew she had made a good point there. Very quietly, she added, "You need that letter, don't you?"

"You can't hand it over now?"

"If I could, I'd walk away with you. Wouldn't I? So it has to be Venice. Here is how I escape. I stroll into the Piazza San Marco on Monday, just before half past six. And you will have someone waiting there for the letter. You must send someone I know, someone I might stop and talk to, quite naturally, without arousing any suspicion. I have three names to suggest: Mike Ballard, who would do it if you promised him first rights to the story; your little moon-struck blonde, who has come to my last parties with various attachés attached—she's on your team, isn't she? The one whose husband was killed in Indochina some years ago? She always was a straight-down-the-middle little patriot. Oh, don't look so worried—I didn't share my suspicions with Fernand Lenoir, who finds her delightful but stupid. Why should I, when I might need her help someday?"

"Uh-huh," said Rosenfeld noncommittally. "And the third suggestion?"

"My ex-husband, William Fenner, who is in Paris and might be persuaded. Not because of me; because of America. He has a quiet sense of patriotism, which once I found amusing. Now, I see it as—well, a little touching, too."

"His beliefs seem to have lasted longer than yours."

Her eyes stared at the empty path lying between the trees. Then, abruptly, she said, "Have one of them meet me. On Monday. In the Piazza, at Florian's Café at half past six. We meet, we talk briefly. I pass the letter.

533

When I start to leave, your other operators, the serious professionals, can pick me up. There will be several around, I'm sure." She smiled. "But how they do it, how they get me out of Venice—that I leave to their ingenuity. They can appear to intercept me, kidnap me, arrest me—anything that seems most convincing. I don't care. Do you agree to all that?"

"Agreed. We'll get you out. But what about the time and place of the assassination attempt? Will you pass that along with the letter?"

She looked at him, amused.

"You may not have that information?" he insisted. The Sûreté would want this most of all. They'd have their agents in Venice, if they could be sure of that. The Italians would help, too: they never approved of foreign conspiracies being hatched on their soil. The British were already in, of course, with that reply of theirs to Trouin— My God, thought Rosenfeld, I am actually believing her.

"I shall have it. I give the letter to the amateur help. But the other information can wait—for the professionals."

"Once you are safe, you'll give it to us?"

"Is that unreasonable?" She lifted his magazine, pretended to look at it, laid it on her lap.

"No. You are a very cautious woman."

"I have to be."

"You seem to be taking a very big chance today." He glanced around at the trees, at the other chairs within seeing distance.

She opened her handbag as if she needed her handkerchief. "I had a lot of last-minute shopping for my vacation. Even Wahl's men lose their quarry between the beachwear and lingerie departments. Besides, his best man of all is on another job this afternoon." Her fingers pulled out two letters from her bag, slipped them quietly between the pages of *Time*.

"Wahl doesn't trust you?"

"Robert Wahl is much too important to trust anyone."

"Thanks for that tip. Who is he, actually?"

"I may even tell you that, someday."

"When you reach America? And we deposit twenty-five thousand dollars in your new name?"

"And a passport to match the name. I shan't bother America very long. Or in any way. I have had my dream. I have had my beliefs." She closed her eyes wearily, the lines at the sides of her mouth deepened, her lips drooped. "Robert Wahl does not know that I have learned about my recall to Moscow. He intends to catch me off guard in Venice, no doubt. So he does not expect trouble from me. And don't you make him expect trouble! Keep the French from gossiping about an assassination plot. Stop the

American leaks and the English hints. Handle this with the greatest care. If you don't, you will never see me on Monday. Robert Wahl will make sure of that." She rose. "Don't forget your magazine," she said. She walked away, a fragile woman dressed in unrelieved black like so many Frenchwomen in mourning, taking her late-afternoon stroll under the shade of the trees.

Rosenfeld let her drift out of sight before he rose and sauntered away in the opposite direction. He did not forget his magazine. He almost forgot Dade's umbrella, though. He didn't waste any time on returning it to the Embassy. He had much too much to do. Besides, it did rain, that evening.

"Well?" Rosie asked, after he had given Fenner the main points of that meeting.

"She is hiding a lot."

"She is safeguarding herself."

"You think she will tell you Wahl's true name, for instance?"

"Yes. And more quickly than she plans. We can bargain, too. The French might just be willing to drop extradition charges against her if she can identify Wahl as Kalganov. He is the man we all want to get."

"Extradition—she hadn't thought of that."

"Oh yes, she had. She took care to give the impression that she is not one of the actual conspiracy."

"Is she?" Fenner asked.

"Of course she is. Wahl, Lenoir, Fane; Committee of Three. If she hadn't been recalled, she would still be with them. And don't ask me why she has been recalled. Wahl's responsible, I think. It may be some personal clash between them. And if he *is* Kalganov, he certainly has the power to have her silenced permanently. These people live in such a surrealist world. . . ." Rosie shook his head. "Well?" he asked again.

Fenner had risen. He moved restlessly around the room. He stopped at the desk and looked at the clock. Ten past eleven, he noted. He could feel Rosie's impatience reach across to nudge his shoulder. "You can't send Ballard."

"No. His mistress would have the story out of him before he could turn on the pillow. Bed is a place where men let down their defenses."

"Sandra Fane didn't know about that mistress, obviously."

"Nor does she know the girl was recruited by Lenoir."

"Anything else that Sandra slipped up on?"

"No. We've checked her story. Anton Mehr, for instance, is the man who met Goldsmith yesterday morning. And Lenoir did join her at Mehr's art gallery, as she said he would. He arrived in good spirits, but—after a telephone call around twelve minutes past seven, just the right time to let a report about a missing coat come from Orly—he left in a decidedly grim mood. He even let Sandra find her own taxi. He changed his, three times, and eventually arrived at the Café Racine. He stayed there, briefly, just long enough to tell Robert Wahl the bad news. No ten-thousand-dollar notes. Scratch play one, start play two. When he left, he went straight to Le Bourget, where Sandra was waiting for him with their baggage. She had plenty, too."

"It would have seemed simpler to telephone the Racine."

Rosie raised one eyebrow.

Fenner reconsidered quickly. "He knows Angélique is not a trustworthy type?" And there would be new instructions to receive, perhaps, before leaving for Venice. Fenner remembered the way Wahl had had the last word. "He took a risk, though."

"How much risk did he actually take? People saw him and Wahl chatting together. Did anyone know what they really were, or what they could have been talking about?"

Fenner shook his head.

"Risk develops when people have some idea of what you are, and why you are there. If they don't know, they may be puzzled. They may even be suspicious. But they can't start adding two and two. And that is what counts; knowing the exact factors that make the correct total." Rosie looked at him with a touch of humor. "That works for our side, too."

"You're saying that you think I could risk going to Venice?" Fenner asked with a grin.

"Yes. But it's up to you—"

"Like hell it is. The choice is between me and some little blonde, charming but stupid. Good God, you can't send her, Rosie, even if that stupidity was only a bit of play-acting for Lenoir's appreciation."

"You want to go?"

"That question should be, do we really trust Sandra?"

"We have to. We want the letter. And we want Sandra Fane. She's the only person who could, and would, point to Robert Wahl and say 'That's Kalganov!' So, you see—" Rosie threw up his hands.

"Well, we can't have any moon-struck blonde sitting alone at Florian's, like a pretty little pet lamb staked out for the wolves." Here goes sweet Sir Walter with that damned cloak of his again, Fenner thought morosely. "Who is she? Sandra's counterpart, but playing on our side of the fence?"

"No more than you are Lenoir's counterpart," Rosie said with sudden and real anger. "Have you ever betrayed a friend, or even an enemy, to the Gestapo? Nor would you."

I suppose I deserved that, Fenner thought. "I apologize to the lady," he said stiffly.

"She's someone who got caught up in this whole business by a quirk of fate. She's like you, in many ways. Her life would be much more comfortable if she hadn't listened to me." Rosie sighed. "Come on, Bill—what's your answer? Yes. Or no. Definitely."

"I thought I said yes."

"Just wanted to be sure. And you didn't have to worry about our little pet lamb of a blonde being staked out alone at one of Florian's café tables. No, as I see it, you and she are going to be sitting there together."

"What?"

"Eliminates some of that risk we have been talking about. The two of you are having a week together in Venice. Reasonable?"

"If I'm having a week in Venice with a girl, I don't want it reasonable."

"Now, now," Rosie said, good humor returning, "and after we've planned such a pleasant little jaunt for you!"

"You sound like Carlson."

"I don't think so. She's his girl."

Fenner raised his eyebrows. His smile was forced. "My luck, as usual."

"About money," Rosie said, ending the topic of Carlson's girl. "You'll have an expense account. Seemingly from the *Chronicle*. So first thing you do is call at the Paris office and find a cable from Walt Penneyman with your Venice assignment. Drop a small remark that it's the right place to combine business and pleasure, and start phoning for reservations for two, on the train this evening—there's the Simplon Express, which leaves at seven-twenty-eight. Also telephone the Hotel Vittoria in Venice for two rooms."

"And will I get them? Venice is still pretty crowded."

"You'll get them," Rosie said most definitely, but didn't explain. "You do all that from the office, and call this number, too." He handed over a slip of paper. "It's hers. Tell her, again within earshot of Spitzer, that you've got a surprise for her—a week in Venice, and she can start packing. You'll pick her up in time to catch the train."

"Why by train?"

"What is cosier than a private room on a train? Or would you prefer a quick flight surrounded by strangers?"

"You can stop leering, Rosie. You know this will be no damn picnic for any of us."

"No. But—as far as you two are concerned—we've kept it fairly easy. All you have to do—"

"—is wander around Venice together, have a drink at Florian's on Monday evening, meet Sandra, get the letter, wait for Carlson to contact us. Nothing to it." Fenner's voice was bitter. "I wish to God this girl wasn't being drawn into all this. I can handle this alone. Why involve her?"

"It's safer this way. Believe me, I've given that some thought." Rosie's voice came out of its momentary gloom, and turned humorous. "She'll act as a restraint on you. No daring improvisations if you are responsible for her."

"I'll stick to instructions," Fenner promised grimly.

"Good. Play it safe. Take no chances. If you are baffled, do nothing. Let us solve any problems."

Fenner nodded. "What's the girl's name?"

"Langley. Mrs. James Langley. Her husband was killed eight years ago—"

"Yes, so I gathered."

"You've a sharp ear," Rosie said approvingly. "I hope you can remember everything I told you, until Monday evening. Afterward, I want you to forget everything just as completely. Can you?"

"I've had some training in the art of forgetting," Fenner reminded him. "How much does Mrs. Langley know about this mission?"

"She knows a good deal about Sandra Fane and Lenoir. She has heard of Wahl. She knows that a man called Kalganov was responsible for the terrorism in Saigon when her husband was killed. She knows nothing about the money, or Goldsmith. About Vaugiroud? Possibly his name, but little else. She knows about the letter, but not about its contents. In fact, she knows just enough to understand that something of major importance is at stake."

Rosie had kept a lot from her. "You trust her?"

"Completely. I wish we could have told you as little, but you forced our hand. You're a hard man to persuade, Bill."

I wonder how much he kept from me, too, thought Fenner. "Why is she doing this for you?"

"Why are you?" Rosie hoisted himself slowly out of the comfortable armchair. "She is doing it, not for me, not for Carlson, not for anyone. She has a concern, as the Quakers say. A concern about the shape of the future. She has seen a heartbreaking sample of Kalganov's work. She doesn't believe that there is any peace for the rest of us as long as the Kalganovs are loose." Rosie paused. "You know, in spite of Sandra's sneer, there is still a lot of quiet patriotism around. The Kalganovs may be in for a surprise. . . . They won't bury us so easily."

"Where do I meet Mrs. Langley?" Fenner asked, a little quietened.

"Here. About six o'clock?"

"Here?"

"She lives here, when she doesn't move out for a night to help a stranger in trouble."

Fenner recovered. "Full of surprises, aren't you?"

"Let's say, when things break naturally, it is a pity not to use them."

Meaning? Fenner wondered. That he had spent the night in Mrs. Langley's apartment, that it would be logical to take her to Venice? "It's hard on her," he said, disliking the role he was helping her to play.

"Appearance is *not* reality. That's how she feels. Just you remember that, too!"

"All right, all right. What do I do with the letter when Sandra hands it over?"

"You won't have it long. Someone will contact you at once. Someone you know. Saves time, saves tension."

"And mistakes."

"There will be no slip-ups. Don't even let yourself think of that. Remember Sandra's guess: we are going to have plenty of professionals in the background. Carlson insists on being among them."

"Sort of expected he wouldn't be too far away from his girl. Well, that's about everything." Except for my doubts about Sandra's good faith, but they have possibly become a conditioned reflex. "I'll get shaved, and start thinking of lunch."

Rosie held out his hand. Its grip was encouraging. "Just stick to the script and Act Three will end happily ever after."

"What happened to Act Two?"

"It began in the Tuileries and ended on the Ile Saint-Louis."

"You should write a play someday. I'll review it."

"Thanks for the warning. By the way, have that lunch before you call at the *Chronicle*'s office. Penneyman's cable will certainly be there by this time, but we'll give Mr. Spitzer a little time to digest it."

Fenner paused at the bedroom door. "As a matter of fact, I do have an invitation to lunch at noon. At the Café Racine, mine host's table no less, with Roussin and Vaugiroud."

"You aren't serious?" Rosie was shocked. He looked as if he had been struck by the hideous doubt whether Fenner was really the man to send to Venice. Then he saw Fenner's smile widening, "Don't *do* that!" he said testily.

"Oh, it will be a pretty grim luncheon, anyway. I suppose Vaugiroud has already warned Roussin about Angélique."

"We left that to him."

"A difficult job. This is one day they won't enjoy their daily bread. In France, that's a crime."

Something caught Rosie's attention. He swung around. "How often do they lunch together?"

"Every day."

"At the same table? It's a fixed date?"

"Yes. Twelve o'clock prompt."

"Go and shave," Rosie said. He headed toward the telephone on the desk. "Can you remember Vaugiroud's damned number?" he called, his voice sharp with worry.

Fenner shaved, showered, and dressed quickly. But Rosenfeld had left by the time he came back into the room. There was a note propped against the clock. *His telephone doesn't answer. Will call him at the restaurant. Have a nice vacation. Bring me back a pigeon.*

Fenner burned the message, reminding himself wryly that he was behaving in the very best tradition. While he was being security-minded, he might as well memorize Mrs. Langley's telephone number and get rid of that slip of paper, too. Also, he would call the *Chronicle* on some pretense, and let Spitzer tell him that there was a cable from New York waiting to be picked up. That was better than walking in, asking, "Has a cable by some chance arrived?" This was a game not too difficult to learn, he thought. A game? A game in deadly earnest. A vacation in Venice that was grim business. A girl constantly beside him who wasn't his. How the hell had he walked into this upside-down world? His first mistake had been to play the good Samaritan at Orly, to leave his raincoat unattended. If he hadn't gone rushing off for a glass of water, there would have been no Carlson, no Rosie, and only that wish-I-could-help-you good-by to Vaugiroud.

And no problems, no cause and effect, not one thing leading to another . . .

Where, he wondered suddenly, would Venice lead?

THIRTEEN

So he had picked up Penneyman's cable at the *Chronicle*'s small office
—one large room, one private cubicle, and a switchboard—where two diffident women and one plump-faced boy were keeping Spitzer dutiful but
not enthusiastic company on a bright but bomb-shocked Saturday afternoon.

The cable was good. (Fenner even wondered if Rosie's fine hand had
not carefully sprinkled the chosen pieces of information over the text; if
Carlson had not signed it in Walt Penneyman's name.) It was clear and
exact. First, congratulations on persuading Vaugiroud to write a piece on
the Common Market for the *Chronicle*'s Sunday, October 15, edition.
Proposed length (three thousand words) and rate (seven hundred dollars)
agreeable. Next, could Fenner fit a trip to Italy into his existing schedule
for two interviews (five hundred dollars each, plus simple expenses) written in his old U.N. style? Subjects: two rival neutralists returning from
the Belgrade Conference, recharging their batteries in Venice on Monday. Topic: the Bomb. Spitzer, a thin-faced, intelligent-eyed man, with
a large forehead and a small chin, must have read the cable, but he pretended appropriate interest and surprise. Play it loose, Fenner reminded
himself. Sure, he agreed with Spitzer, this shot his immediate plans to
hell, but you know Walt Penneyman, always thinking up some job for
little hands to do, besides—once the idea was suggested, it began to have
possibilities. After all, Venice. With expenses.

So he had made the call to the number Rosie had given him.

The conversation, even if somewhat one-sided, wasn't too bad an effort.
A woman's voice answered, but he hoped it didn't belong to Mrs. James
Langley—too flat, too routine, not even bothering to return his enthusiasm.
"Look, darling," he began softly, "remember that talk we had last

night? . . . I know you said Avignon was too hot at this time of year. . . . No, no, I'm not trying to make you change your mind about Avignon. What about Venice? . . . Yes, I thought you'd like Venice. Sure, I'm brilliant. . . . I'll set it up at once. I'll collect you around six—okay? Yes, honey, I remember you don't like to fly. We'll go by train. There's no rush, is there? . . . Oh, about a week, I'd say. Can you manage that? . . . Yes, I love you, too, darling." And the woman's noncommittal voice said, "How nice." Spitzer, head bent over some copy, looked up casually. "A week in Venice?" he asked with thin amusement. Fenner grinned like a happy idiot who had just settled a very smart deal. "On an expense account, too," said Fenner. That was the phrase that would really twist the hook into Spitzer's gullet: wasn't the weakness of capitalists their constant thought of money money money?

So he had made the train and hotel reservations, too, growing cheerier by the minute.

Spitzer was making some work for himself with a blue pencil when he received the biggest shock of the day. Even Fenner, in the middle of his call to Venice, faltered for an amazed moment when Mike Ballard walked in. Ballard was haphazardly dressed, a green cotton-mesh shirt with white stripes, no tie, a natural-colored linen jacket (crumpled at the back), faded red trousers, loafers on his feet. His temper was foul. He scowled at Fenner by way of greeting as he marched to Spitzer's desk. "Why the hell didn't you call me? The Russians start exploding bombs and you don't even pick up a telephone," he began, and went on with increasing vividness.

Fenner completed his call and drifted over to the two men. "Nice beach?" he asked with a grin, looking at Ballard's clothes.

Ballard was studying a copy of Spitzer's report to New York on the Soviet bomb tests. He snapped, "That's where I've come from. Heard the news at eleven. Caught the plane with ten seconds to spare. Now I feel like a refugee from a circus. What are you doing here?" He was eying the cable, with Penneyman's name clearly visible, that still lay casually on Spitzer's desk.

"Picking up a cable." Fenner reached over and lifted it.

"Venice?"

"That's right."

"Why there?"

"I don't think it's any of your damned business," Fenner said gently.

"Isn't it?" Ballard asked, after a startled pause. He went back to reading Spitzer's report. "No good, no good. Scrap it!" he told Spitzer angrily.

"It went out, this morning. I did my best. I thought—"

"You sent this garbage under my name?" Ballard demanded.

"Good-by, chaps," Fenner said, and made for the door.

"Hold on, Bill." Ballard followed him quickly. "What is all this about Venice?"

"Do you want to read it again?" Fenner handed him the cable.

Ballard waved it away. "It is my business, you know," he said, no longer aggressive but openly worried. "And why send you to see this Vaugiroud when I'm here?"

"But you weren't, Mike. Don't worry. I covered up for you."

"And took the Vaugiroud assignment," Ballard said bitterly. "When did Penneyman telephone about it? Yesterday morning?"

Fenner dodged a lie. "You had already gone. So I told him you had grippe, wouldn't be on your feet until Monday." He glanced definitely at Spitzer. "It's a good out for you. Every way. Use it."

The idea had begun to glimmer in Ballard's eyes. He said, mollified, "Who is this Vaugiroud?"

"A retired professor of Moral Philosophy."

"How did Penneyman hear about him?"

"He's an old World War II buddy."

"Oh, one of those." Ballard relaxed visibly.

"Have a nice weekend with your typewriter," Fenner said, leaving. Ballard grunted, stripped off his jacket as he headed for his private cubicle, and threw the two women into a frenzy of work as he yelled for the boy to get coffee. Spitzer, bent over the copy he was checking, looked like a man who had miscalculated and didn't know how.

So all that was over, the first steps taken, no retreat possible. Fenner studied the last hour's performance from every angle as he walked briskly down the broad and spruce Avenue de l'Opéra. On the whole, good. His credentials had been established. Strange how a little evasion here, a little play-acting there, had changed the accounting of his thirty-odd hours in Paris. He hadn't actually liked that skirting of the truth, so why should he be enjoying this feeling of petty triumph? He could almost hear Rosie's probable comment: "Petty? What's petty about Robert Wahl's plans? What's petty about the smallest success against them? And another thing —drop that word 'triumph,' even if you use it ironically. Especially when you use it ironically. Cut out the comic heroics and concentrate on survival. And it's not only *your* survival I'm talking about, either. You know what's at stake."

Yes, I know what's at stake, Fenner thought grimly. Even Vaugiroud, ethics and all, must have put philosophical questions of right and wrong aside in his resistance to the Nazis. How had he equated argument and action? Strength in one could mean weakness in the other. Carlson had guessed something of this conflict in Fenner: that explained, perhaps, why he had wanted Fenner out of this whole business. Yet Rosie, who was in several ways a less sympathetic character, had disagreed with Carlson: did he see Fenner less clearly? Or more deeply? Let's hope it's the latter, Fenner thought: I like feeling flattered as much as any man. And if I laugh at cloaks and daggers, I don't laugh very much at treason, stratagems, and spoils.

He suddenly realized that he was striding down the avenue looking like a man with a fixed destination ahead of him. Not good, that, he warned himself with mock seriousness. He eased off his pace, stopped now and again at the shop windows, some smart, some cheap, glanced casually at the more interesting faces that passed him, as if he were enjoying a normal walk through Paris. The streets became more crowded as he reached the Louvre. He thought of dropping in—he had the theory that the only way to see a museum was in brief visits, no longer than an hour each, when you could choose what you felt like seeing and spare your mind wild indigestion: whoever ate his way through a menu from top to bottom, missing no dish? But he recalled Carlson's hint, much in line with the shenanigans in all the espionage movies he had attended: museums were excellent meeting places for agents. So—with another touch of levity—he kept himself clear of suspicion (if he were being followed) by skirting the old palace and sauntering across the Seine. He could imagine Carlson's shake of the head, telling him he was doing the right thing but with the wrong attitude. Fenner's jocularity turned into quick and complete depression.

He was not too far from the Ile Saint-Louis, but there were almost two hours to kill before he met Mrs. James Langley. Had that voice on the telephone really been hers? Perhaps that was why he felt so damn depressed. With that voice at his elbow, even Venice would be ruined. If he had to share Venice with a woman, he'd like her soft-spoken, laughing, interested; and, at very least, agreeable to look at. I've become too much of the successful bachelor, he thought, wanting everything just my way. Master of my fate, captain of my soul? Like hell I am!

He stopped at a couple of the bookstalls on the quay to find out if he was being followed. (See, Carlson? I'm learning.) He reasoned that he could expect that from now on: his movements would be checked just to make sure that they'd tally with the story that had been built up around him. But after fifteen minutes of looking at battered books, old prints, and bargain seekers, he felt sure that no one was interested in him at all. He

walked farther into the Left Bank area, still more convinced that he
wasn't being followed, beginning to wonder if Carlson's caution had not
been excessive, a sort of occupational disease. He came to the Boulevard
Saint-Germain. There was no breach of security in walking along it, in
the direction of the Boul' Miche, where he could have a beer and relax
before he headed for the Ile Saint-Louis. There was no breach of security,
either, in glancing down the street where the Café Racine retired so
modestly from the busy traffic of Saint-Germain. Today it was a crowded
corner, jammed. And quiet. Fenner halted abruptly, became one of a
group pressed together, staring across at the Café Racine.

The restaurant's front had a jagged gape. There had been a fire, too.
Blackened stone, dark water deep in the gutter, smashed glass on the sidewalk, the acrid smell of disaster still hanging over the quietened little
street. Policemen were on duty; some firemen were walking in and out of
the ruined restaurant. All action was over.

"Terrible, terrible," the woman beside Fenner kept repeating. "The
filthy pigs. Assassins! Two children dead. They lived on the floor upstairs."
She saw she had caught a listener. She was normally a fat, jolly woman,
but anger and excitement had turned her into a hoarse phonograph. She
had seen it all. Been walking along this street. Poor little innocents. Their
mother had just left them to buy some olive oil at the shop around the
corner. Some women didn't even know how to keep house, nowadays,
running out of olive oil—

"What happened?" Fenner asked abruptly.

"A fire. And the two little—"

"How did it start?"

"A bomb. Then the fire. Spreading. I saw it as I walked along the street.
I could have been struck by flying glass. It was terrible. They lived on the
floor upstairs—"

Fenner turned away quickly from the grim evidence of smoke-stained
walls, of smashed and blackened windows, leaving the woman in search
of a new listener. The bewildered face of an old man caught his attention.
It was the waiter who had served him yesterday in the Café Racine.
"Auguste?" Fenner asked, catching the thin, frail arm.

Auguste looked slowly around, with no recognition. "Terrible," he said,
"terrible . . ."

"What happened?"

The old man shook his head slowly, as if he still couldn't believe it.
"Both dead," he said at last. His white hair was soot-streaked; his threadbare alpaca jacket was smeared and stained. One sleeve was charred.

"I know," Fenner said. Did terrorists never think of two children when they packed their ideals into a bomb? All and everything for the cause, including two children. "Did anyone get hurt in the restaurant?"

"Both dead," Auguste repeated dully. "Monsieur Henri. Madame Angélique. Both. They were at his table. The bomb was there. I had just left." The red-rimmed, watering eyes looked at Fenner. They still could not understand his escape. The others were dead; he was alive.

"Was there no one else at the table?" Fenner asked quickly.

"The professor had left, too. To talk on the telephone. He was at the desk. Madame Angélique's desk. And she was at the table. Monsieur Henri was talking to her." Auguste sighed. "And so they are both dead."

"Was the professor hurt?"

"An arm broken. A little burned. He tried to reach Monsieur Henri. They took him to the hospital. Three waiters, too. No guests were there. It was early, you see. Twelve o'clock. I had just left to fetch a bottle of wine—" Again the white head was shaking, slowly, wonderingly.

"No good standing here," Fenner said. "Come away. Where do you live?" I'll get Auguste into a taxi, he thought, and deliver him home: he has lost the will to move.

But Auguste would have none of it. He drew his thin shoulders, almost angrily, back from Fenner and resumed his staring at the Café Racine, his eyes dull again, not seeing, only remembering that he, counting the months to his own death, had stayed alive today. All right, Fenner thought, I shan't cheat you of your miracle. He left the old man, then.

So Wahl and Lenoir had silenced Henri Roussin. And if Rosie hadn't telephoned, they would have silenced Vaugiroud, too. And Angélique —she had been expendable. So were the two children who had nothing to do with anything. . . . Fenner's shock gave way to anger. It deepened with his sense of personal failure. Somehow, he ought to have warned Roussin in time. Even Rosie came in for a touch of blame: why hadn't he got hold of Vaugiroud before he had left his apartment? But Fenner's recrimination collapsed: it certainly wasn't Rosie's fault; he hadn't known Vaugiroud's daily routine; he hadn't known about any bomb. He had only followed an instinct, a suspicion, when he had telephoned Vaugiroud. "It's a fixed date?" Rosie had asked unexpectedly. Now, Fenner knew just how worried he must have been. And there I was, Fenner thought bitterly, not realizing what danger could really mean, just thinking of it as a big vague threat, even making light reference to Roussin's invitation to lunch— Good God, I could have been there when the bomb went off!

. . .

He reached the Ile Saint-Louis almost twenty minutes early. He hadn't stopped for any beer—he had forgotten about it, in fact. He unlocked the door, and stepped into the small recess that formed the entrance hall. The white-and-green living room was softly bright in the afternoon's sunshine. There was a grouping of suitcase, overnight case, red handbag, near an armchair where a dark-blue cashmere coat had been thrown along with a pair of white gloves. So Mrs. Langley was already here, and ready to go. She was in the bedroom, for he heard a door close sharply, and then, "Who's that?"

"Bill Fenner," he called back. "Sorry if I frightened you." Stupid oaf, he thought, I ought to have rung the bell.

"That's all right," she said, coming into the room, high heels tapping lightly. He knew the voice, even knew the footstep, before he saw the fair hair falling softly over her brow and the large gray eyes looking at him hesitantly from under long black lashes. The smile on the rose-pink lips was uncertain. "My name really *is* Claire Connor Langley. I hope that answers your question."

He recovered himself. "One of them." He tried to smile. "When are you which?" She was wearing a light-gray suit with one of those stand-away necklines that emphasized a slender neck.

"Professionally, I use Claire Connor." She noticed the slight lift of his eyebrow. "By profession, I mean an illustrator and designer," she added severely.

He looked at the small automatic she had carried into the room. "A new type of pencil? Splatter effect, perhaps, in the Pollock manner."

"Oh, this?" She laughed, embarrassed. "I was just getting it out of a closet. I keep it in a hatbox." She crossed over to the armchair and picked up her large red handbag and slipped the automatic inside. "You think it's pretty silly, don't you? Perhaps it is. But it's a comfort, too. Especially when a door was unlocked twenty minutes before I expected anyone—no voice, just a man's footsteps."

"I don't think it is silly at all." And he meant that.

She shook her head in mock wonder. "Neill Carlson will never believe it." She noticed his face more closely. "Is something wrong? Did anything happen to you?"

"Just an initiation. My first terrorist bomb."

"Near you?"

"No, no. I only saw the results. But I could have been there. If Carlson and Rosie hadn't told me to keep clear of the place, I—" He paused. "It was the Café Racine. Roussin and his sister-in-law—"

"I heard about that on the radio. An OAS bomb, wasn't it?"

547

"Not OAS this time. At least, I think not."

"They'll get the blame, anyhow."

"Four dead—two of them just kids, burned alive—"

"Don't," she said, "don't keep thinking about it." The gray eyes seemed to have darkened. Then she brushed aside the invasion of grim memories. "You look like a man who needs a quick shower and a long drink." She glanced at her small wrist watch, compared it with the clock on the desk. "We have plenty of time." She adjusted her watch and wound it. "Did you collect the tickets?"

"No." And blast me, he thought, for not remembering. "We'll pick them up at the station."

"That will cut down our time. I think we better take only twenty minutes here. Can you manage?"

"If you fix me that drink." The Gare de Lyon wasn't far from here. "Aren't we going to be a trifle early?"

"It's nice to look around and see who is traveling with us," she said. She was already in the pantry, pulling out an ice tray. "I really am sorry for last night. Truly. You see—"

"Forget it," he said, and headed for the shower. Last night . . . This wasn't the same girl at all. This wasn't the helpless little blonde that had been blown into the restaurant. This was someone who needed no help, capable and cool. This one would check her watch, see that they got to the station on time; the other one invented fanciful and funny stories. Which was the real girl, he wondered, or were they two sides of the same girl? Whatever she was, she had made sure of one thing: the fireproof asbestos curtain had been definitely lowered between them.

"Hell!" he said, as the cold water turned to scalding.

"All right?" she called through. "Cold runs hot and hot runs cold. Faucets are marked wrong. Sorry! And it wasn't a lie, last night—about going to Venice this morning. I really was. But the plans were changed, and I—" She gave up. The hiss of water blotted out her voice. She went back to pouring the Scotch, making it a good stiff drink. He needed it, on every count.

She placed the glass on the bureau outside the bathroom door, selected a fresh shirt and socks from his suitcase, folded up his pajamas and last night's tie, and packed them away neatly along with his other clothes. The water had stopped hissing. "All clear," she called, and went back into the living room. She was waiting at the telephone when he came to join her. She picked up the receiver. "I'll just let our taxi know that we are ready to leave," she told him. She was still keeping her role of capable secretary. But, he noted, she had added a pair of pearl earrings, and a gold pin to her jacket.

"Our taxi? This is service."

"Shall I say we'll be downstairs in five minutes?"

"Fine." He carried his luggage into the room as she telephoned. He was still thinking about the carefully arranged taxi. He remembered the pistol, too, so innocently hidden inside her handbag. "Are you expecting trouble to begin so soon?"

"You never can tell." She looked around the room, checked windows, drew the curtains. She propped a note she had written for the concierge against the clock.

"I'm pretty sure they didn't follow me," he remarked, picking up her coat and handing her the gloves. "Can you take your overnight case? I'll manage the rest. Ready?" I can be casually businesslike, too, he thought.

"They didn't need to follow you. They knew you were collecting me here. Spitzer would tell them."

"And from here on we can expect to be followed?"

"Or to have a check made on our story. They have to know whether this trip is what we say it is." She hesitated, but added nothing more. There was the faint pink of embarrassment on her cheeks. She avoided his eyes.

"We'll make a good pretense. It won't be hard—not for me."

She looked at him. There was the beginning of a soft smile on her lips. "You have forgiven me for last night?"

It really worried her, he thought, and was somehow pleased by that. "We start afresh," he told her. "In future, we tell each other the truth. Right?"

"Yes." She suddenly relaxed. Even her voice changed from polite worry to warmth, hinting at laughter. "That will be a pleasant change—to have someone who can tell me all the truth, quite frankly."

"Doesn't Neill Carlson?"

Her large eyes widened, guessing and a little amused. "Now, Bill," she said gently, "how can he?" Her eyes became thoughtful; she half sighed. It might have been for Neill Carlson.

He opened the door. "Well, here we go. Good luck to us."

We'll need it, she thought. But she smiled and said, "We'll manage."

FOURTEEN

At the Gare de Lyon, in spite of the usual hustle and bustle and small delays, they had almost half an hour to spare. Tactfully, Fenner said nothing. Their luggage had been hauled through the windows of their adjoining compartments and stowed as far out of reach as possible; the blue-smocked porter, inclining an eyelid as a thank-you for a generous tip, had huffed away to pastures new and other sheep for the shearing; the *wagon-lit* attendant, either a Frenchman who spoke brilliant Italian or an Italian who spoke impeccable French, had shown them how the lights went on and all the mysteries of the concealed cabinets. He also had presented them with several forms to fill in detail for the two invasions—one just after midnight, when the Swiss passport control would board the train, the other for Italian Customs officers at three-fifteen in the merry morning.

"Shall we write these up while the train is stationary?" Fenner asked. "Or do you want a stroll?"

She wanted that stroll of inspection. So they walked back down the long platform, slowly, arm in arm. "Sorry about my train fever," she said, "but this is pleasant, isn't it?"

"Comforting, too?" he teased her, looking at the large red handbag slung over her arm.

She nodded, pretending to study the length of the train with admiration. "I always like to know the worst."

"That saves you from nasty surprises?"

She smiled. "Sometimes." She gestured to the train. "Look at our tame monster, getting up strength to pull us over the fields and forests of France, push us through the mountains of Switzerland and spill us out on the plains of Lombardy." She seemed only to be talking for him, an astonishingly pretty creature whose complexion attracted other women's eyes like a magnet, while their men, after an appreciative stare, would turn their speculation on Fenner. Listening to Claire, he was thinking that this would not be exactly an unnoticed journey. Perhaps that was the idea, perhaps that gave them a small margin of safety: who could imagine that any man traveling with this girl had anything on his mind except her?

"Help me talk, Bill," she said pleadingly.

"But I like listening to you."

"Don't make me more nervous than I am!"

"You, nervous?"

"Tell me the worst play you saw last season. And why."

"That would take exactly thirty seconds. What about turning back? We're pretty far from our base." Talk about the theater when he himself was so damned nervous by this open-view walk? It was all he could do to keep his mind on the crowded platform. Left to himself, he'd have been skulking in his own compartment, reading, with the door firmly closed. Which possibly would have been the wrong thing to do. Their role was complete unawareness, wasn't it? The happy travelers . . . Like the hundreds around them, installed in their places, standing at their windows to enjoy the rush of those who still struggled with suitcases and porters on the platform, or to call to the rolling food trolleys for sandwiches and drinks, stretching out their arms, snapping their fingers. Babel of tongues, of wheels, of excited talk, of darting movement.

And at that instant he saw Jan Aarvan. The man was standing at a crowded window, laying in a supply of ham rolls and red wine from a trolley below him. He was reaching down, too engrossed in being served before his neighbor to notice Fenner's recognition. When he looked up, the food in his hands, Fenner was walking on at the same strolling pace, talking, smiling down at the girl beside him.

"We could turn back," she was saying.

"Walk on," he said quickly. "Just another carriage or two."

"You saw someone?"

"I think so. Wahl's chauffeur. He doesn't look quite the same. His hair is darker, cut shorter." But that intent face, caught off guard, had been the same one Fenner had seen glancing up at Vaugiroud's house yesterday. There was the same bone structure, the same powerful shoulders, the same heavy neck. Now he was dressed in a mid-blue suit, neat white collar, neat tie, to make him look like a *petit fonctionnaire* traveling to visit his family back in the Jura, or a country lawyer from Provence who had been on a business trip to Paris. There were a hundred like that on this train.

"He must have spent an hour with his barber this afternoon," she said lightly.

"If that's Jan Aarvan, he's a wanted man. The Sûreté—"

"Let them take care of it." A shadow of worry flitted over her face. She forced a laugh, as if he had made a funny remark.

"We do nothing?"

"Nothing."

"What about using a telephone? Getting a message through to the Sûreté, or to Rosie? That would let them pick up Aarvan somewhere along the line—before we reach the border."

"No," she said. "I wish we could, but—no. He might see us. One of his friends might see us. No, Bill, that isn't the kind of risk we take."

She was right, of course. "Better get back to our own car." They turned and started the long walk forward to the Venice section. "He's waiting for us to pass," Fenner reported.

"Waiting for you to recognize him," she said in a low voice. "He is testing you, Bill." And then, when they had walked a hundred yards or more along the platform, she said, "Congratulations. I couldn't even tell from your eyes which was his window. You are sure he didn't notice you the first time?"

"Quite sure. I caught him at a vulnerable moment. He likes his food." But perhaps, as Dr. Johnson maintained, a man who does not mind his belly will hardly mind anything else. "Cool customer, isn't he?"

"Cool and quick." And I missed him, she thought with sharp annoyance. I saw no one who looked in the least like Jan Aarvan as he appeared in Inspector Bernard's files. Poor Neill, wasting all those good hours this morning on briefing me! Either my eyes are failing or that was a very old photograph of Jan Aarvan. No wonder the man is so confident. "Cool, quick, and confident. That has always been his reputation." She added, encouragingly, "Don't worry—I saw Neill and Chris. Separate, of course. We aren't traveling alone."

"Who is Chris?" And where had Neill Carlson been? Damn, thought Fenner, I missed him: my eyes must be failing.

"An Englishman. Neill's friend. He's in NATO, too. He has been on leave in Paris for the last three weeks. He—"

"Look out, Claire!" Fenner pulled her aside from the headlong charge of two empty luggage carriers.

"So it's to be Claire," she said. He has forgiven me. "I thought I was going to be the nameless one." She smiled and climbed up the steps to their *wagon-lit*.

The attendant was there to help. His indignation about the carelessness of the porters who drove the luggage carriers seemed excessive, but perhaps it was one outlet for his annoyance over two workmen in crumpled overalls who were elbowing him aside as they climbed off the train. The attendant brushed the sleeve of his neat, dark-blue uniform with marked emphasis as he went to Claire's compartment to switch off and on the lights. He shrugged. He repeated the performance in Fenner's room. "All perfect," he assured Fenner.

"What was wrong?"

"The electricians were checking the lights. Always at the last minute—"

"The lights seemed all right to me."

"I know," the attendant agreed wearily. His thin, sallow-skinned face was both tired and annoyed. "Seemingly there was some complaint. They wait all day. They remember their job just as I wanted to make the beds ready. It is always the same with these workmen. Always at the wrong time, always at the last minute."

Everyone loved a good grumble, Fenner thought. But he was grateful to the electricians that the beds had not been made ready for the night. Claire and he could at least have a couch to sit on until dinner. "Let's wait in here," he suggested to Claire, pointing to his room. "This is the time I miss the good old Pullman parlor car."

"First service is very soon," the attendant hinted, dark eyes worriedly calculating the number of beds he had to prepare. "And the dining car is very far away."

"And I am hungry," Claire said, unexpectedly taking the man's side. "I'll just freshen up, Bill. See you in two minutes." She went into her own compartment and closed its door. It was actually four minutes before she reappeared. She looked a little disappointed, but, as far as lipstick and smooth hair went, very much the same.

They began the long walk to the dining car, past three first-class sleepers and seven second-class coaches, through swaying corridors where people stood at opened windows. Wandering through the train were several tight blue suits, which gave Fenner several false alarms, but the man who had watched Vaugiroud's house (Kalganov's man, Carlson had said) was keeping out of sight, probably chewing on his hard-crusted sandwiches, preparing to sit out the night like so many others in the crowded compartments. Except in the *wagon-lit* section, there wasn't an inch of spare room on this train. Fenner couldn't see Carlson, either. If Claire did, she gave no sign. As for friend Chris, there were several Englishmen in view. And Italians, and Swedes, and Americans, and Germans, and people talking a strange language which might be Serbo-Croat, for the forward section of the Simplon Express would eventually reach Zagreb. And because the make-up of the train was carefully planned to let its different sections drop off at various stages in its journey across Europe, Fenner wasn't too surprised when they entered a freight car, half filled with crates and sacks, where the train's wheels rattled and clattered frenetically under the jumping wooden floor. One of the sliding panels of the side loading door had been left open to let the cold air whistle in. Practical refrigeration, Fenner thought. He halted. This deserted car made as good a talking place as any. It was the nearest they'd come to privacy on this train.

Claire had stopped, too. She was looking at the opened panel just ahead of them. "Do we have to pass that?" she asked in horror.

He nodded, steadied her with his arm as they lurched together, bent his head so that she could hear him against the background of creaks and clatter and groans. "Electricians?" he asked softly.

"Perhaps they were. Perhaps not." They were jolted together. She caught her balance, laughed, tried to smooth down her wind-blown hair. "Rough journey, isn't it?"

"Seriously, Claire—" he began worriedly.

"I did try to find if they had concealed anything in my compartment, but I hadn't enough time. We'll find out when we get back."

"Will we?" His worry was growing. Microphones and midget recorders were easily installed nowadays, but how did you find them without tearing the place apart? "How long could any small recorder run? A couple of hours?" But how could it be turned on, when they arrived back in Claire's room? Or was it fed through to the next compartment? Why bother to speculate, anyhow? He just did not know one damned thing about the working of any supersecret recorders, except that they were miniature, powerful, and fantastically ingenious. Only the very best would be good enough for Kalganov and his boys—of that, he was sure.

"I've no idea how these things work. They do, though."

"But you know what to look for?"

"This morning, Neill briefed me on several little tricks that could be played on us. Don't worry, Bill. If we think any gadget is tucked away somewhere in my compartment, we'll just have to play up to it. That's all."

One false word, one giveaway phrase—he looked at the large gray eyes so close to his, and he felt fear for this girl. And he thought of poor old Carlson—he couldn't have enjoyed himself very much this morning.

"Don't worry about me," she said, guessing at the look on his face. "Please, Bill!" Doesn't he know, she wondered, that I was sent to get him safely to that café table on the Piazza San Marco? Wisely, she didn't tell him. And it was a pleasant feeling to have someone beside her who thought he ought to be responsible for her.

"Why did they have to send you?"

"Because no one has to explain to me what a man like Kalganov is. Or means. Or can do."

"You think that he—"

She touched his arm. "Later," she said, and looked back to the carriage they had passed through. "We can talk seriously in Venice."

"They'll think up some way of bugging our rooms even there," he said gloomily.

"Well, they can't eavesdrop on *every* gondola." And with a smile, she drew away from him as three other passengers came laughing and lurching into the freight car from the corridor. "Oh Lord," she said in dismay, looking at the open doorway, hesitating.

He took a firm grip of her wrist, felt the cold rush of air whip around them as he led her past the five-foot stretch of gaping wall. Outside, the darkening fields rushed along. Some thoughtful trainman, he noticed, had fastened a chain as a handgrip across the opening in case anyone staggered too much at a curve in the line. "It's safe enough," he told her reassuringly, thinking of the return journey.

She tried to laugh at herself as she smoothed her hair back into place once more. She was glad to hear a high-pitched squeal from one of the passengers behind them. "I suppose that's the trouble," she said, pointing to a wooden crate stamped *Pont l'Evêque* over which a faint smell of cheese hovered.

Fenner grinned. "If that door wasn't left open, none of us would be able to face any dinner. How's your appetite?"

"Still good. How much farther?"

"We're almost there. Roast lamb, I think?"

It was an excellent dinner, too. Only the French could prepare and serve five courses on a fast-moving train. There was no choice: the menu was set. And so were the diners. Those who arrived late would have to wait for the second sitting. Claire and Fenner sat next to the window, facing each other, sharing the table with a solid Frenchman and his silent wife, who followed their conversation with as much critical attention as they examined the texture, size, and taste of each course. Perhaps they were interested in the sounds of a strange language. Or perhaps it was an overwhelming shock for the voluble French to discover that foreigners could enjoy conversation, too. But even if they did understand

English, they certainly didn't understand any of the light talk, wild gambits, happy *non sequiturs* that flowed so freely between Claire and Fenner.

Fenner was having the best dinner he could remember. It wasn't just the effect of good food and pleasant Beaujolais, or even of the smooth cognac sliding down so benevolently with his coffee, that made him raise his glass to her. "A thousand years!"

"A little optimistic. Even the head Lama in Shangri-La didn't last as long as that. In any case, a thousand sounds much too wrinkled."

Fenner's eyes had flickered toward a man who was coming down the aisle between the tables. It was Neill Carlson, ignoring Fenner completely, looking like a man who had enjoyed his dinner and was on his way forward to his own carriage. "Well," Fenner said slowly, "there is *She,* isn't there?"

"Who?" She caught sight of Neill Carlson's back. "Oh, *She?* Rider Haggard's *She?*" Neill had run into a traffic jam at the doorway, where the second shift had already started to line up for its dinner. An attendant was telling them to go away, without much response.

"She lasted two thousand years, give or take—" He studied the small glass in his hand so that the man in the blue suit, who was following Carlson from the rear of the car, might not notice he had been seen. Fenner's lips went dry. "Give or take a few years," he ended.

Claire had sensed something worried him. She smiled brightly, said, "You know, I always thought that was the silliest of titles."

"*She?*" Jan Aarvan was coming nearer. "Why?"

"Imagine being a critic who is very sensitive to grammar—"

"As what critic is not?"

"And his wife says, making sweet dinner conversation, 'What good books did you review today, darling?' I suppose that someone does call a critic darling, now and again—"

"And he replies, 'None, as usual.'" Jan Aarvan, passing their table, almost collided with a hurrying attendant and halted.

"Will you please stop the obbligato? This is one story I am going to finish my way. He says—oh dear, let me get this right—" Neill Carlson was now making his way with difficulty through the doorway. The attendant had lost his argument with the second sitting: the hungry people were determined to wait there.

"He says that?" Fenner asked, smiling broadly. Beside their table, Jan Aarvan was lighting a cigarette, leaving slowly.

Claire shook her head. "Our sensitive critic says with a shudder, 'Pour me another drink, honey. I've just had to write three thousand words about *She.*' And his wife, who went to Vassar, raises her eyebrows and says gently, 'About her, darling, about *her*. And I think you have already had one drink too many.'"

Fenner drained his glass, even if it was sip-worthy cognac.

"Was it as bad as all that?" she asked. She let her eyes rest on the massive blue-clad back of a brown-haired man who was pushing his way through the waiting crowd at the door. He was in a great hurry, whoever he was. Abominable manners, she thought: the sharp-elbow-and-shoulder-aside type.

"On the contrary," Fenner told her, signaling for the chief attendant wandering up the aisle with his cashbox tucked under his arm, "you were superb."

But I didn't ask about me, she thought. And are we leaving? She concealed her surprise, finished her coffee with some difficulty, for the train was gathering tremendous speed, reached for her handbag and lipstick. And she wondered at Bill Fenner's growing impatience as the chief attendant added, made a mistake, added again, apologized, counted the change with great exactness from his little tin box. Monsieur Solidity and Madame Silence rose to let them pass. "Not at all," the Frenchman said in perfectly good English. Madame was still too shocked by the tip Fenner had added to the bill to say anything.

"It was only fifteen per cent," Fenner reassured Claire as they eased themselves past the group at the door.

"I wonder what he made of our conversation? I could have sworn that he couldn't understand one word we were saying. Which only goes to prove—" She smiled at him.

"That all foreigners are crazy." But from the quick look he gave her, he showed that her point was well made. He opened the door that led to the freight car. Someone had turned on the lights, obligingly—two bare small bulbs swung from two cords. The wooden floor jiggled and jumped; the rattles and creaks, the shrieks and groans had multiplied. "Glad we didn't have dinner here," Fenner yelled at her ear. "Not much hope for the soup." He took a firm grip of her arm.

Claire nodded, averted her eyes from the black yawn of night at the opened door, shivered as the cold wind whipped bitterly at their shoulders. Why this hurry? she wondered. But he didn't stop to explain. They walked more slowly through the interminable corridors: it was almost as if he were looking for someone, trying to keep it unnoticeable. Twice they stopped and looked out at black walls of hills rising steeply, and still he didn't talk. The corridors were becoming empty. Most people were settling in for the night. The compartments' lights had already been dimmed, some were even turned off completely. This was no good, she decided:

we can't worry separately. And we can't risk any real talk in our rooms, either. As the train roared out of a long tunnel, she stopped by one of the open windows, grasped its brass rail, let the wind tear her hair to pieces. "Where do you think we are?" Outside, she could see black masses of trees, black stretches of fields, black ground steeply sloping. Here was a downward stretch, and the train, released from the hills it had traveled through, was running free into a valley. The noise of wheels was lessening. One could talk without raising one's voice.

Fenner looked at his watch. It was almost ten o'clock. "We are due at Dijon in twelve minutes." It was a one-minute stop. No one got on or off the train there. "Come on, Claire, only two more cars to go."

But she didn't move. She rested her head against his shoulder. They were just a romantic couple looking out at the rushing night. She looked up at him, saying blithely, "Sorry. You'll just have to get used to this." Her mood changed. Quietly, she asked, "Is something wrong?"

"Carlson was being followed." He slipped an arm around her waist. His voice was equally low.

"Does he know the man?"

"Yes. And the man could recognize him, too."

"The man in the blue suit, with the powerful shoulders?"

"Yes."

"Aarvan?"

"That's right."

She bit her lip. "Can he connect you with Neill in any way?" If so, she thought, our mission is over.

"He saw us visit the same address, but he didn't see us together."

"Do many people visit that address?"

"Yes, I suppose so." Vaugiroud must have a constant procession of ex-pupils and friends.

Beginners always worry too much, she thought. She said gently, "Then there is no definite link. We haven't been spotted. Forget it, Bill."

"But why should he be following Carlson so openly?"

"He could have been trying to see if Neill had any contacts on the train. One word, one small sign would have been enough. Chris was just two tables away from us, you know: the well-tailored suit talking Italian like mad to some Milanese friends. He didn't blink an eyelid as Neill passed him. And you didn't either."

Claire could be right, he thought: Jan Aarvan might have wanted to note any sign of recognition between Chris, or us, and Carlson. And yet—he kept remembering Aarvan and the way he had followed. Fenner stared at the black countryside, dark shadow piled on darker shadow, outlines suspicioned rather than glimpsed, swirls of treetops eddying into a thick mass of night. "I just can't figure it out," he said slowly.

"Don't try." It was meant to encourage him. "Let Neill figure it. He will." She smiled, thinking of Carlson. "Someone's coming," she said, and drew still closer to him.

It was an elderly shirt-sleeved man, suspenders undone and flapping. He crushed past them, with unsteady legs and sleep-heavy eyes. "*Scusa, scusa!*" he said irritably, and lurched on toward the lavatory.

"Night traffic begins," Fenner said. "Let's move." The train's speed was tapering off.

She nodded. "When you next see Aarvan, point him out. Talk about shoulders, if he is close to us. I'll get it." As a woman, clutching her tweed coat over her slip, poked her head into the corridor and hesitated, Claire raised her voice to normal again. "You're right—it's chilly. I suppose we ought to start thinking of sleep, like everyone else."

"Forms to be filled out," he reminded her.

"Oh, heavens!"

"Sh!" said someone angrily from a darkened compartment.

The brakes were on. The express was beginning its long slide into the station of Dijon as Fenner left Claire in her compartment. "See you in five minutes," he told her. "I'll get those forms. And a nightcap."

"Yes, darling." She smiled as he glanced sharply at her. You never know, her eyes seemed to say as she gestured comically at the four small walls around her.

He entered his own compartment, and pulled up the window shade. The station was modern; the platform was long and broad, brightly lighted. He forced his window down from the top and looked out. Neither Carlson nor Jan Aarvan appeared, so they were both still on the train. But three men, waiting quietly on the platform, caught his eye. They were dressed in civilian clothes; they carried no bags, not even a brief-case. And they were the only people on that long platform to board the train. They moved in a tight little group, as if they knew exactly what they wanted. Well, thought Fenner as the minute's stop at Dijon was over, it seems as if someone did get a message to the Sûreté from the Gare de Lyon. He pulled down the shade, thoughtful, but somehow re-assured by his guess.

Claire had made good use of those five minutes. He found her stand-ing on her bed, the pillow pushed aside, reaching up to one of the heavy brackets on the wall just under the high luggage rack. She gave him a smile of triumph. She had found what she had been looking for. But what do we do? he wondered. He suddenly felt useless and stupid, just standing there speechless.

Claire moved silently back from the luggage rack, and lowered herself carefully to sit on the bed. "Darling, how wonderful, you did find your flask! I'm completely refrigerated. It wouldn't really be much fun to arrive sneezing in Venice."

"Better put more clothes on, honey."

She gave him an indignant look, and said nothing. Let him get out of *that* one, she thought.

"You have the prettiest legs, even when they are turning blue. Here, drink this—" He stepped over her shoes and reached for the tumbler on the washbasin.

"Bill—please—stop that! How can I drink if you— I'll spill it, Bill. Bill!" She began to laugh.

Perhaps it was the astonishment on his face that amused her so much. Her laugh sounded merry, carefree, happy. All is jollity, he thought grimly as he went on pouring the drink. Silently, he offered it to her. She shook her head. So he swallowed it himself, and looked bitterly at the bracket, high on the wall, above the pillow. I'll yank it out from its hiding place, he thought, and let us talk naturally. No, I can't do that either: it's the proof of our innocence. Who was going to listen to its recording, and judge? Robert Wahl? Fernand Lenoir? Lenoir was the expert with words, wasn't he? Damn him, damn them all, damn—

Claire had caught his hand, tugging at it gently to bring him back to the present. "Dear Bill," she said quietly, and she wasn't acting.

He sat down beside her. "Claire, I've been thinking about us."

"Don't! Just let's enjoy ourselves—"

"Yes, that too. But when Venice is over, what then?"

"What then . . ." she repeated, at a loss for words.

"Would you throw up your job and come back to New York? With me?"

She stared at him, her gray eyes widening. She had almost believed him. Why, she thought as her alarm subsided, he can act my head off! "Bill, you promised me—you said you would give me time. That's why I'm going to Venice with you." She glanced up at the hidden microphone. "You know that, darling."

He said nothing.

Again she felt that strange alarm.

He was smiling. "Yes, I know. I'll wait."

"And no more thinking about us?"

"Just occasionally."

"Kiss me, Bill." She was lighting a cigarette. She offered him one from her case.

He pushed it aside, took the cigarette away from her lips, tossed it into the hand basin, and kissed her. Her body went rigid; she tried to push him away, but he kissed her long and hard. "There!" he said softly, as he let her go. "Feeling warmer, honey?"

She just kept looking at him. He was very careful not to touch her again. "Hell!" he said. "I've just remembered—we've got these forms to fill out. Come on, my pet, duty before pleasure. Sit up and start reading the questions."

"Must we do it now?"

"Now," he said firmly. "Or do you want to be stuck at the border in a black chiffon nightie? It would be much admired, but—"

"That's what I like about men," she murmured, pulling her gray wool jacket neatly into place, "you can always depend on their taste: it's so catholic. All right, darling. If I tell you the facts, will you be the recording angel? Claire Connor Langley—is there room for all that? Born: May 20, 1933, Sheridan, Wyoming. Father and mother: John and Agnes Connor. What next? Heavens, they want just about everything. When did I leave the U.S.? When was my last visit to Italy? Why am I going there? Oh dear, would they accept the truth? For the purpose of making up my mind."

"You'll have to be more specific than that."

"What's that you've written? Pleasure."

"Well, isn't it?"

"I also have a little job to do."

He looked up, shook his head even if he was amused. She enjoyed sailing close to the wind, this girl. "I thought you were leaving your work behind, just for once. Don't tell me a client wants a copy of Saint Mark's horses for her front gate in Beverly Hills?"

"My client is a very impressive and well-known magazine, Mr. Fenner, and it wants some details on the upper hall of the Scuolo di San Rocco. Do you know it? It's the large building put up by the Venetian guilds, decorated by Tintoretto, just to show that the trade unions could keep up with the Doges."

"Sounds a pretty big job to me."

"Darling, don't look so upset. This is only a small assignment: it won't take long. I have just to make some suggestions, as a guide for the photographers who will be arriving in October. Of course, if the Editorial Brains like my ideas, that could lead to something bigger— Bill, please don't look

561

so depressed. You have a job to do in Venice, too. How long will your interviews take?"

"Not so long, once they are arranged."

"You see? Arranging them might take you two or three days. And what would I do meanwhile?"

"Just sit around and look beautiful, my pet. Besides, Penneyman has probably made most of the arrangements. His cable sounded as if everything was all laid on."

"You used to do some good interviews," she said. She was serious again. "You know, I think Mr. Penneyman is trying to entice you back into news reporting."

"Could be. But I have a book I want to write."

"Why don't you write a play?"

He stared at her.

"You could, you know," she said.

He tried to laugh the idea away. "And what shall it be—comedy or tragedy?"

"That's the problem, isn't it? You're essentially an optimist, Bill. But you wrap yourself in pessimism."

"Just an old cynic," he agreed.

"No, no. Not that. You are a romantic with your guard up against the realists."

"Just an old, battered, beaten-up idealist?" he asked with a grin.

"Do you always underrate yourself, Bill?"

"I think I've overrated myself with you. I ask the prettiest girl I know to come jaunting in Venice. And what do I find? Does she want to be kissed or cajoled? No. She's too busy analyzing my psyche."

"Darling," she said softly. "I'm just helping you fill out forms. Oh, let's finish them, shall we? And after that's over, we can—" She yawned.

"Don't fall asleep!"

"Of course not," she said drowsily. It was a good act, a nice prelude to his departure, a reasonable explanation for the microphone when all sounds ceased. "Where do I sign? Oh Lord, so many places. You know, Bill, there's one aspect of the population explosion that has no solution."

"Only one?"

"Where are they going to file the forms that everyone will have to fill up?"

"There's always outer space," he suggested, trying to concentrate on his own answers. Date of birth: December 17, 1923. You're old, Father William. You're thirty-seven, and she is twenty-eight.

"The brakes are going on," Claire said. "Another station so soon?"

562

"Probably Dôle. There's a six-minute stop here. Would you like some hot coffee?" He was already on his feet. The train gave one last lurch and came to rest.

"It might be one way to keep me awake," she said with a low laugh, and made a comical face up at the hidden microphone. Fenner was smiling broadly as he entered the corridor: that's the idea, he was thinking, don't let the beggars grind us down.

The attendant blocked the door to the platform. He wasn't enthusiastic about anyone leaving the train. There was no food cart in sight; the station café was distant and possibly closed. Fenner didn't argue with these suggestions: he had a good-enough view of the platform from the door. Some people got off, some got on; a few people in more countrified clothes still sat on bulging suitcases, hugged paper parcels, waited for other local connections. Two policemen in dark-blue uniforms walked smartly along the train. Abruptly, they halted, as if they had seen someone at one of the carriage doors, and climbed on board.

The attendant had been watching, too.

"Looks as if somebody is going to be arrested," Fenner said hopefully.

The man shrugged his shoulders; his white, tired face was blank. Perhaps he was unwilling to admit to any foreigner that anything could be wrong. He stared along the platform. The policemen did not get off.

"They're traveling with us," Fenner said, taken aback as the train's wheels started moving again.

The attendant said, "You'll have no trouble, monsieur. If you hand me your documents and passports, I shall answer any questions. You will not be disturbed at the frontiers, either."

That was as close as Fenner would get to an admission that the train might be searched. "Thanks," he said. "You're going to have a sleepless night."

"The documents are all ready?"

"I'm just completing them. You'll have them in ten minutes." Fenner went back to the compartment. He was making no more guesses about the Sûreté having been alerted just before the train left the Gare de Lyon. If they had been, wouldn't Jan Aarvan have been hauled off the train at Dôle? After all, plenty of criminals traveled: trains and liners and airplanes carried them. Ordinary travelers forgot that. There could be others on this train who were wanted by the Sûreté. "Disappointment," he told Claire. "No coffee. Our attendant wouldn't trust me out on the platform. He has lost some passengers that way, I gather. And I've got to get these forms ready."

If he was disappointed, she thought, it wasn't about the coffee. What is puzzling him? But she sighed deeply and said, "Red tape is very hard on romance."

"Shan't be long, honey." He began printing his name, et cetera et cetera. Red tape was strong on et ceteras.

Claire let the magazine she had been reading drop on her knees. She curled her legs under her thighs for warmth, pulled over the pillow to soften the hard wall for her shoulder blades. She yawned again. She had never been more wide awake.

She watched him as he worked on the small folding table near the window. Intelligent eyes, lips serious in concentration, a well-shaped head; no flabbiness, either physically or mentally. The movements of his hands with paper and pen were neat and capable. Capable—yes, he was all of that. She remembered Rosie's words when he was persuading her into this trip: "Fenner is all right. I wouldn't send you with him if he wasn't on the beam. Just get to know each other before you arrive in Venice, so as you'll feel natural. No strain. You can't be stiff or stilted. Don't worry, Claire, he's a dependable guy." Yes, Rosie had been right: she could always work with someone she liked, someone she trusted. She had liked Bill from the very first meeting. (That would have startled Rosie. It had startled her.) Now, on this strange journey, she was learning to trust him. Or why should she be feeling more confident? We'll make a good job of this little assignment, she thought happily. Little? Only her part in it was small, and so was Bill's. How many others were converging on Venice, each with his own job to do? Add up all those assignments, big and small, and the sum total must be enormous. And all this effort, which she could sense but not see, all this for one letter? A letter, one faked letter—could it really pack so much possible destruction within one page? Rosie had told her the minimum, naturally, but there was no law against thinking. The letter was only one part of the problem; why else would the French be interested? Why else was Rosie asking for the Italians' help? And the English were involved, too. This was going to be quite a party in Venice. A surprise party. That was the only chance of success, Rosie had said: complete surprise. Keep them unsuspecting, she told herself, and glanced defiantly at the bracket overhead.

"Oh, *darling*," she said, "you are taking for*ever*."

"Won't be long, pet." Fenner seemed a little amused by the warmth of the interruption. "Just four last questions, damn them."

"What was the color of your grandmother's eyes?" she asked sleepily, still looking at the concealed microphone. And what do you make of that, Comrade Lenoir? Lenoir and Wahl: psychological-warfare expert and organizer of terrorism. A very complete combination, a real threat. Yes, much more than a letter must be involved. This was something really big. Not that size mattered when it came to threats against peace. Even the smallest could grow. . . . Again she remembered Rosie's words: "Nothing is negligible, nothing—if it can shift the delicate balance of peace." He wasn't making a phrase to win some votes or impress a television audience. Old Rosie believed that. So did Neill and Chris Holland. So did Bill Fenner —or he wouldn't be here. And so must I—or I wouldn't be here, either.

She looked back at Bill Fenner. He was reading over the four sets of forms with a strange smile on his face, as if to say, "How the hell do I get into this kind of situation?" What did he really think about her? Someone who made this kind of journey quite nonchalantly? Regularly? Some kind of a sublimated nymphomaniac, treating life as the great and gay adventure? Heavens, she thought in distress.

Fenner turned his head to find her watching him, with her cheeks flushed, her eyes troubled. "Finished," he said. "I'll hand everything over to the attendant. He will deal with the—" He rose, and let his voice change. "Claire! Claire—wake up!"

Had she been waiting for this cue? The worry, certainly, vanished from her eyes. "I'm all right, Bill—all right, really—" Her voice drifted away.

He wondered if they had play-acted themselves into a corner. How was she going to lock her door once he left? And how did he say an adequate good night? She was leaving it all to him, this time: no more invitations to a kiss. Just as well. When he kissed a girl like Claire, he stopped all pretending. "Good night, Claire," he said gently. He ruffled her hair, raised her hand to his lips. Just a gentleman of the old school, he thought wryly, and kissed her hand twice. Then, on impulse, he added, "Mes hommages." His eyes were serious. So were hers. He remembered to switch off the main lights as he left.

Claire cautiously slipped off her jacket and skirt. That was all she could risk. She'd have to go to bed half dressed. She couldn't risk any sounds of washing or brushing, either. She was fast asleep, wasn't she? I'll look awful tomorrow, she predicted as she slid carefully between the sheets. Her handbag was close to the pillow, luckily. Her hand searched quietly and found the small automatic. It reassured her, at least, about the unlocked door. Strange how people who thought they knew you understood so little. "Steel-lined nerves," Neill Carlson used to tease her. And Rosie, in a moment of weakness, had told her that her strongest asset was her calm competence. Even Bill Fenner had said, "Mes hommages," as if he had been saluting her. But this, she thought as she slipped the automatic under her pillow, is the real me: someone who is doing a job because it's necessary, because she can do it; someone who feels so frightened that she is afraid to admit it, even to herself. Except now and again, in the lonely hours. The hours like those that stretched ahead of her, as cold and bleak as the mountain air whistling against the window.

FIFTEEN

Venice welcomed them with blue sky and high clouds, little trails and folds and careless gathers of white silk draped high above the fresh breeze that blew in from the Adriatic and set the waters of the lagoon dancing in the morning sunlight. In the Grand Canal, the ripples slapped at mooring poles and jostled the black gondolas, nudged cellar walls and dared to mount the green-stained steps toward a palace door.

It was a city of contrast. Colors were bright, yet soft: gamboge, yellow ocher, raspberry, terra cotta were bleached into gold, pink, russet; faded, muted, and streaked. Shapes were large and bold, yet decorative, even fragile. Solid walls of high houses rose out of the canal; balconies and windows were carved and fretted, fluted and laced. Stone floated on water.

Bill Fenner, high on the narrow terrace that linked the four topmost rooms of the placid Hotel Vittoria, was waiting for Claire. Directly below him, five floors down to the Grand Canal, was the small landing stage that formed the front, and slightly swaying, approach to the hotel, where they had arrived this morning—Claire, white-faced and tired, saying, "Just give me a couple of hours, Bill, and I'll start appreciating like mad." She hadn't even looked at the view from this balcony; no doubt she had done what she had promised herself—dropped into bed and fallen asleep. She had insisted she would join him by eleven. It was now fully half past, but there wasn't a pleasanter place to pass a Sunday morning than a terrace over the Grand Canal. There was sun on his face, a gentle breeze. He had breakfasted heartily; shaved, showered, read the papers, and dressed leisurely. And as he watched the busy waterway below him, the worries of last night receded into better proportion. (But, he reminded himself, he had slept well on the train.) He hadn't seen Carlson, or any Englishman who might be called Chris, in the Venice station, but it was unlikely that all four of them would arrive together. More probably, Neill Carlson and Chris had got off at Milan, and would travel here by bus or local train. As for Claire and himself—they had two days to wait. Tomorrow evening the mission would be over, and they could relax and enjoy themselves. Or would Carlson collect Claire as well as the letter? I may never meet her again after tomorrow night, he thought bleakly: she may vanish out of my life as quickly as she came into it. We'll see about that, he decided, we'll see. . . . He stared down at the Grand Canal.

New-looking motorboats, brightly varnished, swept across the path of water-buses, the *vaporetti*, crammed fore and aft with Sunday travelers. Delicately balancing gondolas, in deep mourning for their lost Republic, moved with the grace and majestic silence of black swans. There was much maneuvering, no slackening of anyone's speed, hoarse calls of warning from the gondoliers, the rushing sound of water sliced through by the heavy fast-moving *vaporetti*, the roar of a brash engine cutting into power. Across the canal, there were seventeenth-century buildings—a customs house, a large-domed church; and a sixteenth-century palace turned business office, but so restrained, so appropriately faded and gently restored that it was hard to tell from the other Gothic palaces housing museums or real *contessas*.

He heard Claire's light step and turned to meet her. The three other people who sat on the terrace were noting her arrival with interest. The middle-aged German couple, who sat over their late breakfast at a small table just outside their bedroom's French windows, stopped all conversation and watched her with unflinching curiosity. The obvious Englishman, passing fifty, gaunt-featured, gray-haired, his long thin body draped at ease over a wicker chair, stopped reading and seemed to be only admiring the balustrade's boxes of trailing geraniums and sprightly verbena. "Observed and approved," Fenner told Claire, taking her arm and leading her to his small corner of the terrace.

"Venice?" she asked. She looked as if she had slept a solid eight hours and spent two more in dressing.

"You." He studied her openly. Her eyes were rested, her skin glowed. She was wearing a blue linen dress, a light blue that matched the Venetian sky. Her legs and arms were bare, tanned, slender. Pretty feet, he noticed, in flat-heeled sandals. Hair brushed smooth, a neat golden cap on a neatly shaped head.

She laughed and played down his compliment. "Oh, the shower worked, the bed is comfortable, and we have a view. Last time I was here—the only other time, in fact—I had a narrow window facing a line of laundry strung over a small canal."

"The one with the squeezed oranges floating in it?"

"And melon rinds. And a nest of gondoliers just underneath my window. They talk all the time, did you know that?"

"About moonlight and pretty girls—"

"No. About the price of gondolas, new housing developments, and rheumatism. And if curses could sink anything, all these newfangled motorboats would be on the bottom of the canal." She looked over the balustrade, up the grand curve of water, then down its sweep. Her eyes rested on the little island of San Giorgio, rising with Palladian balance from the shallow waters, and she fell silent.

"I agree," Fenner said, watching her face. "Sky by Tiepolo, vista by Guardi, foreground by Canaletto, all set to music by Vivaldi."

She glanced at him, catching him off guard. "What else were you thinking about as you stood here so quietly for the last twenty minutes?" She smiled. "I looked out twice. You were watching the canal and thinking—?"

About you, and Venice, and you and Carlson. He said, "About Venice."

"What about her?"

"She's the aging beauty who comes to breakfast wearing all her jewels, a lace turban covering the pins in her hair, powder uneven, bright lipstick, a flow of silk and velvet to disguise her arms and thighs."

"But her hands and feet are still elegant."

"Yes. And her profile is magnificent."

"Wrinkles, though, which she can't disguise. Wrinkles from laughter and tears. She has had plenty of both."

"Why should she hide them? On the contrary, she wears them proudly."

"Besides," Claire said, "her eyes outshine the candles."

"Candles at breakfast?"

"Behind half-closed shutters? Naturally."

"Naturally." He looked down at her. Their laughter faded.

"At this moment," she said, quickly glancing back to San Giorgio, "there's an anti-candle man who is planning to fill up the Grand Canal with concrete, and run an eight-lane highway right down to Saint Mark's Basin."

"In that case, we had better wander out and enjoy Venice while we can." Certainly the others on the terrace had staked their claims. The Englishman was settling back to read: he had propped his feet on one chair, and covered another with a clutter of newspapers. The German couple had expanded their beachhead with chairs for their legs, too.

As they walked along the narrow terrace to Claire's room, she was asking, "What about your interviews?" Her voice was casual, clear.

"They arrive tonight."

"Heavens—when did you find that out?"

"I telephoned the Danieli when you were testing the shower." And possibly some other things, too, he thought, such as the existence of automated eavesdroppers. From the gaiety of her mood he could guess she had found nothing to worry her so far.

"So we have today to ourselves?" she asked delightedly.

"And most of tomorrow. I'll try to see them tomorrow night."

"That means you'll be writing on Tuesday. Wednesday, too?"

"We'll have the rest of the week to ourselves." Shall we? he wondered. I can make a damned good try.

"I shan't keep you waiting," she promised him as they reached her room. "I'll get my bathing suit and meet you in two minutes at the elevator." She reached up and brushed his chin with her cheek. "Appropriate?" she murmured.

"Two minutes," he said, smiling, and freed her arm. He turned and began the walk past the Germans and the Englishman to his own room. So they were going out to the Lido and find themselves a few square feet of free sand? It was hardly the way he had planned their first afternoon in Venice. Still, the journey across the lagoon was short, and packed with enough panorama and local color to keep him happy. And two people could be very much alone in a crowd.

The German couple were talking once more—about prices and qualities of decorated leather wallets. Their comparative shopping was driving the Englishman away: he was gathering his papers together, with a pained look and excessive neatness as if to remind the voices of the trouble he had taken to establish himself comfortably. But the voices, delighting in being left in possession of the terrace, only surged louder. They even followed Fenner into his room. He closed the French windows quickly.

His swimming trunks were somewhere at the bottom of his suitcase. He found them under a folder of correspondence: letters from two producers, three directors, a playwright, several actors—all of them working in the French theater, some of them introduced by American friends, others who had become his own friends during their visits to New York. He closed the folder. Letters from another world, he thought. Man was an adaptable animal: he might curse and complain about having the pattern of his life broken up, even temporarily; but within a couple of days, he could be so immersed in his new problems that the old projects became something postponable, to be dealt with once the present urgency was over. And there, relegated to the bottom of a suitcase, the folder lay like some pathetic waif with dumb reproving eyes. He locked up the case securely, shutting away his own life, and left. First things first, was all he allowed himself to think.

As they dropped their keys at the hall desk, the assistant manager came over to ask if their rooms were satisfactory. He was a smooth and pleasant-faced Italian, correct in dark suit and English accent. Anything, he assured them, to oblige Mr. Stephen York: delighted that Mr. York's friends found their rooms comfortable; what a pity that Mr. York couldn't make his usual visit to Venice this year for the Lido film festival; Mr. York always liked that terrace; please give Mr. York his good wishes when they saw Mr. York.

Fenner looked at Claire. "It's a most likable terrace," was all she said.

"And it will be less crowded tomorrow," the Italian assured her. "The honeymoon couple is leaving—"

"Honeymooners?" Claire stared, and then recovered herself.

"—so you will have the terrace to yourself, except for Sir Felix Tarns. He is—" The assistant manager froze, smile in place, eyes immediately veiled to hide his embarrassment. He bowed to the tall thin man in well-cut, fine-checked tweed who was passing them on his way through the long dark hall toward the distant front entrance, where the sunshine rippled in, over polished floor and gleaming brass, from the canal. The Italian retrieved his balance. "He is a very quiet gentleman. It will be as if you had the terrace to yourselves." He bowed and left. He looked as if he would like to mop his brow. Sir Felix Tarns was certainly a most quiet gentleman.

"Quiet but quick," Fenner observed. "It didn't take him long to slip into his sharp tweeds, knot his old school tie, and get down here." I've seen him somewhere, Fenner thought. Some place. Where, when? Then the name and the face came together. United Nations, debates over Korea, 1953. Sir Felix had come over to New York as one of those free-lance observers who were going to write a series of articles, give some lectures to finance their visits. The professional journalists paid little attention to them. Fenner's memory of Sir Felix was dim. But at that time Fenner had discovered plenty of trouble in his own life. Trouble . . . why did he associate that word with Tarns?

Claire was standing very still. "Was he interested in our reactions to Stephen York?"

"He was leaving his key at the desk, just behind you and the assistant manager, for a full minute." But interested in us? Fenner felt a touch of annoyance. There she goes, he thought, slipping back into Carlson's world. "By the way, is Stephen York—"

571

She didn't seem to be listening. She had glanced along the dark, gleaming hall to the square of sunshine at its end. For a brief second, she studied the black silhouette of Sir Felix. As he stepped onto the moored platform outside, very much the austere admiral on a swaying deck waiting for his boat to come alongside, she said quickly, "Let's look at the gondolas."

So they walked along the stretch of silent carpet to the front entrance, past empty chairs and writing tables and flowers in polished brass vases and a solitary man who was reading peacefully. His eyesight is better than mine, Fenner thought, or perhaps he is the type who only glances at a magazine's pictures. Even so, there were better glancing-places in the hotel than this hall, lit only by a scattering of subdued lamps on the writing tables.

"What about Stephen York?" Claire asked as they approached the shimmer of reflected light from the canal.

"Is he a friend of yours?"

"No such luck!"

"Come, Mrs. Langley, don't tell me a woman of your mature judgment is impressed by a film star!"

"Come, Mr. Fenner, don't tell me you think the only great actors belong in the theater." As they stepped out into the glare of sunshine, she asked, very softly, "So he isn't a friend of yours, either?"

"No."

"That's interesting, isn't it?" But meanwhile, she seemed more interested in Tarns.

"Who is he?" Fenner asked, as Sir Felix, sitting erect on a small black leather armchair, floated away, his gondolier shouting a hoarse warning to two workmen in a heavy unpolished gondola filled with vegetables. For a split second, it looked as if Sir Felix and the zucchini might become a very mixed salad marinating in the Grand Canal. But, with strenuous back-oaring the gondolas scarcely grazed, drew apart, the two workmen now expressing their view of the situation. Everyone, from the terraced bar nearby to the balconies above and around, watched the scene with amusement or admiration. Only Sir Felix, Fenner noticed, paid no attention whatsoever. We should be flattered, Fenner decided, that he had paid any attention to us at all. Claire could have been right.

She hadn't answered his question. Instead, she had placed a hand on his arm as if to steady herself as one of the water-buses, a large steam launch with its captain's wheel amidships under its small funnel, cut quickly down canal toward a pier and sent the hotel landing stage rocking gently. The man who could read so blissfully in the shadowed hall had come out to see the fun, too. He was standing near them, a pink-cheeked, round-faced little man, smooth and well fed, neatly dressed in a sedate brown suit, innocuous enough, blinking disapprovingly at the workmen's exchange of oratory with the hotel doorman. "Let's get a motorboat," Fenner said, and signaled.

"No," she said quickly.

"But a gondola will take a couple of hours," he reminded her, making an exaggerated guess if only to sound authoritative. Who was in charge here, he'd like to know? "Or do we swim?"

"Please, Bill." Her eyes were pleading. She smiled for the doorman. "Later," she told him. "I've forgotten something." She turned back toward the hotel. "I've forgotten my sun-tan lotion," she said to Fenner. "Isn't it stupid of me?"

"Yes."

"Oh, Bill—"

"You could always buy some out at the Lido. If we are ever going to get there."

"Of course we are. But I like my own special brand."

There was no answer to that. He followed her, still annoyed. The hall was empty except for the cluster of people at its far end near the porter's desk. "What's the bright idea?" he asked her quietly. "We walk out, we walk back in." And I feel like a damned fool who can't even hire a motorboat.

"Well, we found out two things."

"Did we?" Carlson's girl, he reminded himself, in Carlson's world.

She restrained her excitement. "That was a private gondola. Didn't you notice the special uniform of the gondolier, the throne effect of its chair, the polished brass coat of arms? So it was sent here specially for Sir Felix. And he kept it waiting."

"Likes to show his authority, no doubt."

"Perhaps. Or perhaps he was delayed on the terrace. Why did he have to waste time up there, hurry his dressing to get down here, waste more time at the desk?"

"Must have found our conversation fascinating."

"You aren't being exactly helpful." Her small sense of discovery ebbed.

"But aren't we beginning to exaggerate?" He was smiling. His voice was gentle. "Really, Claire—" Sir Felix Tarns, after all . . . "I can't see him snooping around."

"When he does," she said with marked coldness, "it is called perceptive observation."

Fenner had to laugh.

"I am not being funny. And I am not being silly," she said.

"Well," he said with maddening equanimity, "what was the second thing we found out?"

There was a short, but marked, silence. A spot of brilliant carmine stained each cheekbone, faded to delicate pink as it spread over the fair skin. "Him!" she said abruptly, not even looking over her shoulder to confirm her guess. "Little Mr. Brown Suit is back at his post again. Isn't he?"

He was. "It is possible," Fenner tried, "that the gondoliers' shouts drew him outside. Perhaps he hoped to see a really bang-up accident."

"Perhaps, indeed," she agreed. She halted at the porter's desk for her room key. "Shan't be long," she told Fenner. The delicate flush had vanished. But her eyes were too bright, almost close to tears.

Fenner stared after her. What did I do? he asked himself, retreating behind his own defensive wall. But he knew damned well, and the cigarette he had lit tasted like straw swept from a barn floor. It was possible, he justified himself, to exaggerate conjecture and suspicions. All shadows were not necessarily sinister. Last night, on the train, he had gone through a couple of hours of supercaution, clothing mystery with more mystery. Let's keep our balance, let's not invent worries, he told himself, glancing again at the distant figure in the brown suit. The man was probably dozing gently, or just staring vacantly into space while he waited for Sunday luncheon to be served in the dining room.

Four minutes went by. Five. At last, Claire stepped out of the elevator, carrying a camera, a white sweater, and sun-tan lotion as her excuses. She looked calm and poised, and was smiling charmingly. "And this time, I remembered my camera, too," she told him. "I couldn't find any film, though. I can buy that on our way to catch a water-bus. Do you mind?"

"Wouldn't a motorboat be simpler?"

"But not so much fun." The gray eyes held a hint of alarm, as if they feared he was going to start arguing again. So he stopped trying to take control. He went along, with no comment. A *vaporetto* it would be, jammed to the gunwales with a couple of hundred other people. With marked politeness, he offered to carry her camera; and with equal politeness, she accepted and offered to put his swimming trunks along with her things in her oversized handbag. "That's much better, isn't it?" she asked, with a small smile dawning at the back of her eyes.

It was. He would no longer feel like an idiot parading through Venice with plaid swimming trunks dangling from one hand. "Do you always think of everything?" he asked. She had possibly been right about the man in the brown suit: he had left his chair, at least, and was sauntering down the hall toward the porter's desk.

"I wish I could." Fleetingly, the strained look of worry appeared on her face; just as quickly, she banished it, and resumed that calm, oblivious-to-everything exterior.

He took her hand as they approached the large, ornate back door of the Vittoria. It was his way of saying he was sorry. She looked up in surprise, and smiled. He had chased some of the worry away, at least. "I wasn't much help to you there," he admitted. "Was I?"

She laughed in her relief. "You did let me get my own way," she reminded him. Kicking and screaming, she thought. What had made him so ornery all of a sudden?

"Do you get your way with every damned man you meet?"

The large gray eyes widened. The pink lips parted as if to speak, closed in a firm line.

"I am sorry," he said, ashamed of the resentment that had slipped out into the open and betrayed him. She was Carlson's girl. He kept forgetting that. He had forgotten it at dinner last night. He had forgotten it on the terrace high above the Grand Canal. But now they had come down to the ground floor, and he was being reminded of Carlson constantly. The hell of it was, he liked Carlson. If he didn't like him, it would all be simpler. "I am sorry," he said again. "I guess things just seem out of my control." And that is not the way I like them, he thought, not one bit.

They were passing through the small courtyard that lay at the back of the hotel, a square of worn paving stones surrounded by the tall walls of other houses. He noted the chipping plaster, the streaked colors, under the heavy ropes of wisteria. Board shutters, unpainted, bleached into greenish brown, closed the silent windows away from the world as the buildings themselves enclosed this courtyard. The only exit was by a narrow crevasse at one corner, dark even by daylight, leading them between more high shuttered houses. "I never knew a place that could be so crowded and yet so private," Claire was saying. She looked around her, and upward, as if measuring the safety of this alley, and halted. She spoke in a low quick murmur. Fenner bent his head to catch what she was saying. Here we go again, he thought, as he slipped his arm around the soft, yet firm waist. And I wish to heaven she wouldn't use that perfume, either.

Claire was saying, "When I went back to my room, I telephoned Neill. He had given me a number where I could check with him if necessary. But he hasn't arrived yet."

"He may have stayed in the Rome section of the train. Perhaps he is flying here this evening," Fenner said, to drive away the frown of anxiety over her eyes.

"Perhaps. Or perhaps he had someone to see in Milan. Anyhow, I wrote a note for Chris and asked him for some advice. We'll leave the note at a camera shop. It's quite near—"

"Are you sure of that camera shop?" It seemed an additional risk to Fenner.

"Rosie gave me that address for any emergencies."

"You think we have an emergency on our hands?" He was startled. But grave.

"I don't like the rooms we've been given. Perhaps Rosie arranged them, but I don't think so. I just want to be sure we aren't sitting in a pretty little trap."

His arm tightened around her. Someone had just stepped from the court-yard into this dark passage. The footsteps faltered, stopped. "This might be the time to drop a nice, brotherly kiss on your brow," he suggested. And did it.

"And I can laugh coyly, like this." She had a very pretty laugh, even when it was pretense. She hates this as much as I do, he thought suddenly, and felt an enormous relief. She drew away, raised her voice back to normal. "Darling, not here! Someone will see us—" She looked around, as women do.

"Just a man lighting his cigarette," Fenner said with male nonchalance. They walked on, close together, their shoulders almost brushing the house walls on either side of them, much to the relief of the man in the brown suit who seemed to be having so much trouble with his matches. Claire was pointing out a wrought-iron decoration around the lamp on the wall overhead. That was what she loved about Venice: the small ordinary things made into little works of art, tucked away in hidden corners, not even demanding attention, just there to be seen by accident. Behind them, Fenner heard the slow footsteps begin again.

Abruptly, the narrow alley ended. They were beside a canal, walking under a *sotto portico* for a short distance, then out into the open. Ahead of them was a busy Venetian street that crossed the canal by a gentle slope of bridge, a main thoroughfare all of twelve feet in width, lined with shops, above which flower boxes and shuttered windows rose to three or four tight stories. There was a feeling of lightheartedness, of gaiety, in this stretch of sunlight and movement. And the only sounds in the city street were those of voices, of lightly pacing feet. "At this moment," Fenner told Claire, "your anti-candle man is planning to introduce a fleet of Vespas. What's a street without gasoline fumes and the roar of exhausts?"

"Only Vespas?" She dropped her voice. "We go across the bridge, Bill."

The brown suit was very close to them now. Fenner went on talking. "Oh, that's just the thin edge. Once he conditions people to being pushed to the walls, he will bring in cars—small cars, at first, of course—and people can retreat to the roofs. It's the technique of gradualism. Accustom people to retreating, and you can not only push them to the walls, but they'll even begin to believe that climbing across the roofs is really much better than strolling along a street."

She was amused until she thought about it. "That really isn't a joke," she said gravely.

"Not when you think of the Communists." Let's give Brown Suit a bolt and a jolt, he thought. "They really are much cleverer than the Nazis. Hitler's patience was too easily exhausted. He wanted everything all at once: a thousand-year Reich in ten years. But the Communists think of politics as the art of the impossible: just take everything in thin slices, little by little."

"The art of the impossible . . ." she repeated slowly. "Like getting away with bomb tests while you sit at a disarmament conference. You know, Bill, I wish I could listen in to your interviews tomorrow. What do you expect from your neutralists—a retreat to the wall?"

"They are already up on the tiles."

"Will they give you a real interview, or will they just hum a little song to themselves?"

"They'll play it safe by putting on a performance, the holier-than-thou act, black is white and white is black, and gray isn't tattletale. After all, they're the kind who are always polishing their Public Image. Do you think they would pass up a chance to get free advertisement in the *Chronicle?*"

"They may wish they had," she murmured, "once you get through with them."

"If my interviews get published," he said as he remembered that they were entirely the brain children of Rosie. He had forgotten that. Here he was, discussing two ambitious, second-rate politicians as if the *Chronicle* wanted to publish their polished clichés. Well, he thought, when Rosie picks a cover for me, he picks a good one: he has even got me believing in it. He began to laugh.

"That's a good sound," Claire said. They had halted on the crest of the bridge. From here, they could look right down the narrow strip of water, edged with houses, all the way to the Grand Canal. Just below them was a mooring place for gondolas, where their owners polished and scoured their black, gleaming craft from sharp Viking prow to curved stern, talking in hoarse, amiable shouts as they worked. "Can you see the man in the brown suit at all?"

The gondoliers had certainly seen them. "Gondola, gondola?"

"No thanks," Fenner called back. "He passed us when we were discussing Communists," he told her.

"And now he is waiting for us to pass him?"

"Shouldn't be surprised. He is fascinated by a camera shop just across the bridge."

"Oh dear!" Claire said, keeping her eyes fixed on the distant sliver of the Grand Canal.

"Gondola, gondola?" came the renewed invitation. One of the gondoliers was even waving his arms wildly, in hopeful enthusiasm, looking at Claire with a wide smile.

"No!" Fenner hoped he sounded definite enough this time. "Our shop?" he asked Claire.

"It would have to be, wouldn't it?"

"I have a feeling you can cope," he told her, smiling. "I won't even offer a suggestion."

She said quickly, "You'll have to take full charge later. But at present —well, there was so little time before we left Paris—while Rosie was talking with you, Neill was briefing me. That's the only reason—well, you see how it is?"

She was so anxious for him to understand that he felt—pleased, relieved, reassured? There was a strange mixture of emotions, certainly, in his reaction. He smiled, mostly at himself, and nodded. "By the way, what made you so interested in Sir Felix Tarns?"

"Chris Holland will tell you about him?"

"I'll be meeting Holland?"

"That's the idea of our message." She glanced casually toward the camera shop. "He is still there. We'll just have to risk it. Let's—"

"*La biondina! La biondina!*" the gondolier shouted, waving his arms still more wildly.

Claire halted and looked back at him.

"*La biondina!*" he called up to her, with absolute certainty.

"Zorzi!" Claire said, and waved back.

"Well, well," said Fenner, "and did Giorgio teach you that ripe Venetian accent?"

"Gondola, gondola?" The appeal was directed to Fenner as keeper of the purse.

"Later," Fenner told the broadly smiling hawk-face looking up at him.

"Tonight? When the moon is up?" Giorgio shouted. "I wait here. What time?"

Fenner looked at Claire. "Ten o'clock?"

She nodded. She was as delighted as if he had given her a Christmas present all wrapped in shining paper and bright ribbons. She looked nine years old at this moment.

"Ten o'clock," Fenner called down.

"I wait here," Giorgio shouted back, and saluted nonchalantly.

"And so he will," Claire said as they left the bridge. "We had better keep that promise." She was still very much Alice-in-Wonderland. "Imagine! *Imagine* Zorzi remembering me! It's three years since I was here."

"What really astounds me is the fact that you remembered him."

"Would you forget that old sea raider's face?"

Perhaps not. But it wasn't the answer Fenner had gone fishing for. "Old? He's younger than I am, I bet. He hasn't reached the age of discussing rheumatism, has he?"

"Only the first twinges." She may have guessed Fenner's feelings, for she smiled and said, "I hired him for a week, last time I was here."

"Opulent."

"It was the cheapest and quickest way to explore the little canals and back waterways. I was sketching all the decorations—windows, balconies, doorways, lanterns—that caught my eye. There was a Venetian phase in Grand Rapids, that year. My first assignment abroad. Zorzi thought I was crazy at first. Then he began to think I was really in earnest. That pleased him. He's a true Venetian."

"Remembering some of those smaller canals, I'd say you really suffer for the sake of your art."

"Oh, I had some luck with cool weather. And a large bottle of Eau de Cologne helped." She was smiling at the memory. Quietly she said, "Remind me to buy some film, will you, Bill?"

"And after that, I shut up. Right? No suggestions, I promise." The brown suit seemed glued to the Kodachrome window. "He is going to have a front-row seat for the next act. Want to postpone it?"

"We haven't the time. Let's show him what innocent travelers we are. Don't worry, Bill"—she was really encouraging herself—"it will be simple enough if we just follow the rules."

They almost passed the display windows. Fenner stopped, catching her arm. "What about that film you need?"

"Why, Bill—I nearly forgot."

They brushed past the waiting man and entered the shop.

SIXTEEN

Neat Italian cursive over the shop's entrance told them it was owned by V. Arnaldi. It was small, dark, but authentic. On either side were two glass-topped counters, displaying filters and light meters in considerable profusion. There were shelves of Leicas and Rolleiflexes, all bargains at the cheap Venetian price; stacks of varied film; many excellent photographs showing how you could do it, too, if you got up at six in the morning or lived in a city without people. There was one assistant, very young and very martyred, who obviously disapproved of the prominent notice in four languages stating that this shop was open for business every day, all day. For this was a bright, warm Sunday, when reasonable places were either firmly closed or at least putting up their shutters for a pleasant three-hour lunch.

"I need some thirty-five-millimeter color film," Claire said in English. "Seven rolls of K135-38."

The boy stared at her blankly. Fenner sympathized with him. Claire had asked for a film with thirty-eight exposures, and there was just no such thing.

"*Uno momento,*" the boy said, jolted out of his apathy. (He wasn't stupid, Fenner decided; just bored.) Quickly he went to a curtained door at the back of the shop. A chair scraped, a limping step dragged on the wooden floor; and a white-haired man appeared, wiping his mouth from an interrupted dinner. His movements were slow, deliberate, calm.

"Mr. Arnaldi?" Claire asked.

The proprietor nodded, his eyes as blank as the boy's had been. Outside, a second man had halted beside the brown suit, to look at the window's display.

Claire repeated her request, with a slight emphasis on the seven. Arnaldi listened placidly, but he had noted the tightening of Fenner's lips as he watched the street. The man in the brown suit was moving on; it was the other, a thin man, much younger, who was coming into the shop.

"Certainly," Arnaldi said as the man entered, and selected three boxes of standard K135-36 film from the shelf behind him. He placed them in a neat pyramid on the counter in front of Claire. "Anything else today, signorina?"

"No thank you. That's perfect." Claire relaxed visibly as she looked at the three boxes. So Arnaldi was the right man to deal with, Fenner decided, quickly changing his mind about mistakes. "I think I'll load the camera here," she said, holding out her hand for it, smiling reassuringly.

Fenner gave it to her, tried to pay no attention to the strange man who had walked over to stand beside them instead of choosing the other counter. Perhaps he was lonely, wanted company, the Coney Island— Brighton Beach type. Why wasn't he out at the Lido? That should suit him perfectly. "Need any help?" Fenner asked.

"Have you ever used a Stereo-Realist?"

"No," he lied gallantly.

Claire began examining the camera's back. "I ought to have brought that book of directions," she said, half to herself.

Mr. Arnaldi was trying to serve the newcomer, but the man was in no hurry. He wanted a yellow filter; he needed time to choose one. He looked down, vaguely, at the boxes displayed near Claire. He liked to work close, this fellow: he was missing nothing.

"A filter for what camera?" Arnaldi was asking patiently.

The stranger hesitated for a fraction of a second. "Leica," he said briefly. His eyes flickered over the three boxes of film that Claire had bought, still lying on the counter. "And I want some of these." He picked them up.

"Here!" began Fenner, ready to put on an act of indignation. But Claire was unworried. She was much more preoccupied with the back of her camera, which seemed to have stuck.

Arnaldi took quick command. "That film is not made for a Leica," he told the man. "You need—"

"I have other cameras."

Arnaldi's expression did not change. He merely reached to the shelf for three more yellow boxes, and stacked them into another pyramid before Claire. He drew out a pencil, opened a drawer for a piece of paper, and began calculating the cost. "I shall be with you shortly," he told the man. "My son will help you meanwhile. Luigi! Show this gentleman the yellow filters." He pointed his pencil at the other counter.

Luigi's boredom vanished. "Over here," he insisted, and led the way quickly. The man hesitated, looking down at the filters beside Claire. "Not for a Leica," Luigi told him firmly, and drew him, still holding his prize of three boxes, to the other counter.

Claire said, "This has got stuck again. I had it fixed only last week. Can you help?" She handed over the camera to Mr. Arnaldi, who placed it flat on the counter, lifted its back just enough to extract a folded slip of paper, which disappeared into the open drawer. He had the camera closed and locked even as he pushed the drawer shut.

"I am sorry," Arnaldi was saying all through this small operation, "the back of your camera is not working properly. I am afraid you will not be able to load it here." He shook his head.

"Let me try again," Claire said, taking it from him. "Imagine walking through Venice with an empty camera."

"Frustrating," Fenner agreed.

"Oh, I'm sorry," Claire said to the stranger, who had come back to stand beside her. "Am I in your way?" Then she laughed delightedly. "Look, I've managed it!" she told Fenner, freeing the back of the camera, holding it up in triumph.

"Next time, you'd better carry a hammer as well as a book of directions." He reached for his wallet—he was good for that, at least—while Claire started to load the camera right under the stranger's inquiring nose. The man's suspicions were dying down. He watched Claire's fingers, his interest shifting to gadgetry.

And what kind of a man is this? Fenner wondered. He is about my age, about my height, dressed in a gray suit and white shirt. Shoes and tie are not my taste. Apart from that, he might be another version of me or my friends. His face is just the ordinary face of an ordinary man, a mixture of small worries and pleasures, hopes and disappointments, a few simple longings, several deep frustrations. Yet his business is far from ordinary, and so is his power. If Claire or Arnaldi has made one small slip, he can destroy us all: an adverse report to the men who hire him, and that might be the last mistake any of us would ever make. Does he do this for money to buy a gray suit, pay his rent, get promotion? Or does he call himself dedicated: everything, anything for the cause? Complete obedience, blind belief? . . . Possibly he would think of me in the same way: I'm an American, he would reason, so I do what American interests tell me to do. But he is wrong there: I am not in the middle of this fantastic game because I was given an order by Rosie or anyone else. I am here because my beliefs are shaped by my own thoughts; and a man's thoughts are shaped by his conscience. That is what gives me my orders, and I may damn it to high heaven, but I'll listen to it. That's why I'm standing here. Can he say the same? Did he really choose Kalganov's way—the bomb that burns two children to death in an apartment over a restaurant? Or is he a totally ignorant man, a know-nothing who'll lend himself to anything? Or—even more depressing—would he enjoy seeing hate and dissension spread over Western Europe; would he gloat over anarchy?

"All ready," Claire's soft voice said at his elbow. "You look depressed. I'm sorry I was so slow—"

"No, no," he reassured her quickly, and smiled. "Just hungry, I guess."

"Would you like to lunch here?" she asked as she fastened the camera back into its leather carrier.

"And forget the Lido?"

"It doesn't really matter. . . . I just thought some sun and sea would iron out the travel creases."

Was that a hint? He took it as such. "They probably would. We can dine at Quadri's tonight, or perhaps we might try The Resuscitated Louse. You know it?" They said good day to Mr. Arnaldi. The man in the gray suit was watching them carefully, his interest again bleakly calculating, reverting to duty either hired or dedicated.

The boy Luigi darted to open the door and bow them out with a brilliant smile. He could guess from the way they were talking so easily, from the quiet look in his father's eyes, that the difficult customer had somehow been defeated. There he was, complaining about the price of the film he had wanted so badly and which—in any case—wouldn't fit any camera he was likely to use. He wasn't even waiting to choose a filter, either. Hurry, hurry, hurry, Luigi's mocking eyes told him as the man left. He would almost be too late to follow the Americans. Or was he going to follow them? No, he looked as if he would be going to pass them over to a woman who had been window-gazing at the shoe store across the street. A very dull-looking woman she was, dressed in blue: not chic, not young, not beautiful.

"Luigi!" his father called quietly. He was sealing an envelope. Luigi came back into the shop. "Take this to Pietro," his father said. Luigi placed the envelope carefully inside his jacket pocket. He didn't need to be told to be quick and careful, or to leave by the back door that led into a wandering alley, or that the envelope contained an urgent message. He had learned all these things even as a child of seven, before he and his father had managed to escape from the Yugoslav zone of Trieste.

He didn't need to be told about Communist control, either. His mother, two uncles, his older brother . . . Even at seven, you remembered that.

"Simple," Fenner reminded Claire as they joined the stream of pedestrians outside Arnaldi's door. "Did we follow the rules?"

"With a few improvisations," she admitted. "There are always complications."

"I suppose," he said too gravely.

"One follows one's instinct, that's all."

"*La biondina* is not quite the helpless little blonde that Zorzi thought she was, is she?"

"I can be very helpless, very silly, very stupid. Why do you keep worrying about what I am and what I am not?"

Why indeed? She was Carlson's girl, he reminded himself. He forced a smile and a light voice. "The trouble about *la biondina* is that she brings out all my protective urges—and she couldn't need them less."

"Doesn't she?" Her voice softened. I know what's really troubling him, she thought: he wonders if I am another Sandra Fane, even if I am on the other side, his side. But I'm not. I am not Sandra. I have never hurt any man the way she hurt him. I have never pretended love, or used it. How do I prove that to him? I can't. And I don't. Because I'll probably never see him again once we have finished this job. He'll be back to his own life, and I to mine. They overlapped for a few days. That's all. She sighed.

He glanced down at the large gray eyes watching him so sadly. This was no way to spend their short time together, he told himself. "I take it all back, Claire. You look as lost and bewildered as any tourist."

"I am."

"This way—if we *are* trying to find a pier." He held her arm, guiding her into a narrow *calle* that led to the Grand Canal. He glanced briefly over his shoulder as they turned the corner. He saw a Hindu girl in six yards of floating sari walking the usual two paces behind a paunchy, splay-footed husband; a couple of clear-eyed, fair-skinned Swedes stepping out bravely; a group of sauntering Venetians, carefully dressed; a dour-faced woman in blue; three English students, needing a haircut, in stained and uncreased flannel trousers; a collection of Austrians with rucksacks and *Lederhosen*; a French couple in loose shirts and flopping sandals; heads, and more heads, bobbing and floating along in the human tide. Useless to worry, he decided. "I'll always remember our theme song in Venice," he told Claire.

"And what's that?" She waited expectantly. She was beginning to know him.

"*I wonder who's trailing us now . . .*"

She burst into a peal of laughter, then silenced it to something more restrained, with a hand at her lips. "I made the ladies jump," she said, and looked at three proper Venetians in hats and gloves.

"You and Papa Haydn." She has forgiven me, he thought in relief as he watched the delight on her face. He has forgotten Sandra Fane, she was thinking happily.

SEVENTEEN

The water-bus was crowded. Claire and Bill Fenner had to stand well for'ard, but nothing could dampen Claire's high spirits—not even the fine spray from the prow of the ship cutting through the lagoon's blue water, nor the salt breeze tangling her hair, nor the squeeze and jostle as more passengers were gathered up at other miniature piers. She loved it all. "It's like traveling on the open back of the old Paris buses, where you swing and sway through narrow streets. I always feel there ought to be music playing—Offenbach done with a rush—something that sweeps along and hurries your heartbeat."

"You're a strange girl." He was thinking of her elegant white room, restrained and remote, under the shadow of Notre-Dame. "Difficult to please, but easy to amuse."

She laughed. "I have that out-of-school feeling. We took our first examination, and I think we passed."

"I don't see our examiner around," he said quietly.

"Oh, there will be someone else." She glanced casually over the little ship's passengers. Venetians plus ten other nationalities; you name them, we carry them. "Shall we make bets on him?"

"It could be a she this time," he said very quietly, and then remembered Rider Haggard and grinned widely, in spite of the solemn-faced woman in a dull-blue dress who had been edging forward toward them. Will she really try it? he wondered in amazement, and was answered as the woman plumped a hip down on a fraction of a seat near them. A patient Italian lifted his small daughter and her dog onto his lap, and the woman's second hip secured her position.

Claire's amused eyes met his, looked back at the widening lagoon as their water-bus now headed out to the long, low sand bar called the Lido.

"This is the way to travel. It would be a pleasure going into the office at eight every morning if you could think of sailing back again at five."

"Beats the Lexington Avenue subway, any day," Fenner agreed, watching a liner floating in from the Adriatic, a towering bulk easing its way along the marked channel toward the Giudecca Canal where the heavy ships could dock. A large freighter was already there. He could see its yellow funnels jutting up in the distance among the red tiled roofs like two fat periscopes.

Claire was saying, almost to herself, "Pink-and-white palaces, silvered towers and golden domes . . ."

"Rising like Venice from the foam."

She laughed again. "At this moment," she told him, "I am really and truly happy." She said it with a kind of wonder. He looked at her and fell silent. He was far from unhappy himself.

Beside them, the solemn-faced woman stared straight ahead in deepest boredom.

From the Lido's lagoon side, they took a taxi across the narrow island to its Adriatic shore by way of its main street, an odd mixture of Cannes and Atlantic City with a hint of Miami. There, they drove along an interminable esplanade of trees and gardens, lined on one side by hotels the size of Pennsylvania Station, on the other by an endless stretch of cabins and bathhouses that blocked all view of the beaches. Fenner could imagine them, one after another, each with its blanket of bodies.

"Don't be so depressed," she told him with amusement. "You look like *Death in Venice.*"

"How do you know I'm depressed?" He thought of the white sands along the lonely eastern dunes on Long Island, miles and miles of them, with only the thundering waves for company.

"Because you get politer and politer. Cheer up, Bill. We're going to the end of the line, so far out that most people give up. There's a beach there that's only three quarters filled, usually. It's just beyond the Excelsior."

"Is that good?" he asked morosely. It was one of those enormous hotels, mink-lined and gold-plated.

She dropped her voice, even if their driver was screened off by glass from them. "A small canal runs in from the lagoon just behind the Excelsior. There's a private landing place. Very useful for a quick exit."

"When?"

"After we have had our swim and lunch. Around four, or four-thirty."

"And the swim and lunch? Any reason for them? Or are they just an innocent diversion?"

"Establishing our sweet, pleasure-seeking characters," she said, and giggled. She glanced past the pleated silk curtain covering the cab's rear window. "I think our lady in blue had to take a taxi, too. I hope her expense account is as ample as her hips."

"I wonder what she looks like in a swimsuit."

"That really should cheer you up," she said, sharing his vision.

They stretched out on the milk-chocolate sand, and talked. About themselves, mostly. There was no one near enough to hear them. The lady in blue kept at a distance, perhaps only interested in anyone they might meet. She sat, fully dressed, with her shoes and stockings off, near the bathhouse where they had rented cubicles for their clothes. But the doors of the cubicles were solid and strongly locked, and the owners of the bathhouse—a smiling Venetian couple, scoured by wind and sun, as fresh and clean, in their sparkling white clothes, as the wooden buildings—were dependable watchdogs. Claire was sure of that. "Which solves several problems," she told Bill Fenner when she joined him on the beach.

"Yes, I wondered what you were going to do about your Little Comforter," he remarked, and stretched his spine luxuriously on the warm sand. "There isn't much room left for it in that swimsuit." It was a white *maillot*, as perfect in its cut as the body it molded. He stopped looking at her, rolled over on his elbows, and glanced at the people around them. Their nearest neighbors were a pleasant Italian family: a black-haired man devoted to his three children, a gentle-faced wife who smiled on all of them. Next came three French girls in bikinis; four young boys throwing a rubber ball around to develop their minds; two older men who were having themselves spaded into the sand, with only their heads left popping up from their anti-rheumatism caskets. "All shapes and sizes," he said. "What does your instinct say, Claire?"

"We can relax." She arranged her white towel beside his, and lay down.

"That's a pleasant change."

"Our guardian lady watched to see if I used the telephone at the bathhouse. I didn't. I talked to no one. No one talked to me. She seems pacified. So"—Claire stretched herself happily—"we relax and wait."

"For what?"

"A message. I told Chris we'd be here. The rest is up to him."

"If he doesn't get in touch with us?"

"That means there are no additional instructions. We just spend the day enjoying ourselves."

"Enjoying?" He glanced briefly at the woman in blue.

"That won't last forever. Once they feel sure we are harmless, they'll call off the bloodhounds. By tomorrow, we'll be free of them."

"We had better be." He was thinking of tomorrow evening and a table at Florian's Café, of Sandra handing over a letter. "Did Rosie calculate we'd raise all this interest? I doubt it." Rosie had made a mistake, he thought gloomily.

"Yes, he did. And we are raising less interest than any of his agents might. We aren't in any files, Bill. Two complete unknowns, you and I. That's why Sandra chose us. One reason, at least. The other—well, she will see us at once. Makes identification quick and sure. Saves her a lot of strain."

"Did Rosie know we met at the Café Racine?"

"I told him."

"And he saw it as the beginning of a good cover story," Fenner said bitterly.

"Well, it was, you know," she said quietly. "Are you sorry I met you there?"

"No."

"Truly?"

"Truly," he said, smiling at the feminine word.

She relaxed again. "I'm sorry about the way it happened though."

"It had a certain mysterious charm."

"You couldn't figure me out?"

"You made no sense whatsoever," he told her.

"I was pretty shaken," she admitted.

"Were you following Fernand Lenoir?"

"In a way—yes. You see, Neill and I were going to have a last-night dinner together. I was leaving in the morning for Venice on the San Rocco job I told you about. Neill was about to go back to Berlin. Then Neill was called out, on some emergency, around six o'clock—"

After I telephoned from Vaugiroud's flat, Fenner thought.

"—and he asked Chris to take charge of me until he was free. So you see, I *was* all dressed for a party."

"I see."

"But Chris had a small job to do—he had to drop in at some art gallery briefly. I waited outside in his car. Then Lenoir came out of the gallery in a very great hurry. And so did Chris, and we followed him. To the Café Racine. Do I begin to make sense?"

Fenner nodded. "Chris didn't want Lenoir to see him again, and so he sent you."

589

"No, that was my bright idea. And it would have been a blunder if I hadn't met you. You saved me, Bill."

"He shouldn't have let you take that risk," Fenner said angrily.

"I didn't give Chris much time to argue. And it did seem so simple—a little Left Bank restaurant, lots of crush and bustle, men *and* women." She smiled, remembering the formal Racine. "I was going to wait five minutes for a friend, and then leave. Five minutes is long enough for a girl to wait, isn't it?"

"Long enough for a pretty girl to wait."

"So that's the way it was."

"Chris Holland is British Army, isn't he?" Attached to NATO, Fenner remembered.

Claire nodded. "You'll get along. He's a humorous type. Like Neill. They've been close friends for years. Met away back in the days when. That kind of thing."

"And they work together?"

"Not actually. They came to Paris on separate assignments. But somehow everything seems to be overlapping. There's a slight emergency, I think. Have you any idea what's—"

"Where does Rosie stand?"

She smiled at the way he had dodged her uncompleted question; and let it go. "Rosie sells refrigeration plants, didn't you know? He is a deep-freeze specialist. Very appropriate for the cold war—keeps things at safe temperatures." Her little joke pleased her. She waited for him to share it, add to it. "No comment?" she asked.

He was looking at her, wondering again. He tried not to ask her the question that puzzled him most. Then it came blurting out. "How did you get into this kind of work?"

She sat up, dusted the sand off her shoulders.

"Sorry," he said.

"Do you really want to listen to the story of my life?" she asked with mock concern. But her eyes held real surprise.

He thought of Neill Carlson. "I suppose it's none of my business."

There was a flicker of disappointment in the polite little smile. "I suppose not."

There was a small silence. Then one of the bikini girls strolled past in Grand Duchess fashion, seeing nothing, aware of everyone. Some French girls always walked as if they were coming down the runway at the Tabarin, Fenner thought. "All she needs is a three-foot stretch of ostrich feathers on top of that little pinhead," he said. There was reaction, too, from the neighboring Italian family: the pretty wife, scandalized, drew her bathrobe more closely around her in silent protest; the man, intrigued but embarrassed, devoted himself hastily and too emphatically to his three children. The four handsome boys lost interest in catching and throwing. Even the distant lady in blue seemed startled out of her boredom into stiff-spined contempt.

Claire was saying, very softly, "I just can't believe it. . . ." She was on her feet, slender and lithe. "Come on, Bill," she urged him, clear-voiced, "let's test the water." She picked up her cap, tagged his shoulder and ran, laughing as he picked himself up and raced after her. They overtook the bikini girl, swerved past her, reached the calm sea. They waded out into the warm shallow water, beyond the shrieks of the bobbers and dunkers, avoided the little paddle-bicycles, the flotilla of water wings, and still were only waist deep. "Just a few minutes here," Claire said, as she stopped beside a group of young men, "before we swim out to the raft."

He smothered his amazement. Claire, he had discovered, did nothing without a reason. He ducked away from a shower of water—the bikini girl had somehow become entangled with the group near him. She had suddenly come to life, Grand Duchess turned *gamine*, as she splashed back at two handsome hairy-chested Italians who scooped water over her. She was fair game, Fenner thought as he watched the running battle. Miss Bikini decided to retreat, turned and fell with a little shriek, came up beside Fenner, gasping as if she had taken a high dive from a twenty-foot board, floundering in panic. He reached out and caught her arm. "Steady, there!" he said.

She regained her feet, pushed her seaweed hair away from her eyes, seemed to thank him briefly, and really let her two admirers have a full swipe of water. Masculine guffaws, swirls of feminine giggles, amused voices, a babble of general jollity. And where was Claire? He saw her white-capped head already half-way to the raft.

They reached it together. He hauled her up beside him. Claire caught her breath, looked back toward the beach where the sea battle had reached gigantic proportions, with splash-reinforcements joining in from all sides. Wading at the water's edge, skirt held up with one hand, shoes and handbag safely clutched in the other, was a lonely figure in dull blue.

"And what had Miss Bikini of 1961 to say?" Claire asked softly. They were alone on the raft, but there were other swimmers around, and voices carried very easily over water.

"Half past four. Take the Hotel Vittoria boat."

"So Chris did get my message," Claire said thankfully.

591

"Who is his friend, do you know?" Fenner counted three swimmers who were definitely heading in this direction.

"I thought she was a filing clerk in Inspector Bernard's office, yesterday morning. At least, she brought photographs for me to study. I didn't know she was studying me."

"Well, that's co-operation." Fenner was impressed.

"Must be quite an emergency," she said thoughtfully. "Rosie really has pushed the panic button. What do you—"

"Look out for boarders," Fenner warned her as two men and a woman came to join them on the raft. And then, swimming up to hoist himself on board, too, was a dark-haired man who had been floating peacefully nearby. He apologized pleasantly to Fenner as he stepped, dripping, over his legs to reach a vacant space. Close up, the face was handsome, with bold blue eyes and strong white teeth displayed in a friendly smile. His shoulders were massive, his torso firmly muscled, his neck strong and thick.

"That's all right," Fenner said not too enthusiastically, and went on talking to Claire. She had not recognized Jan Aarvan at all: the photograph in Inspector Bernard's file could not have been either clear or recent. The man's hair was darker than it had been on the Simplon Express. But the eyes were the same hard blue, the nose and cheekbones were of the same blunt cut, and the same speculative expression was still there to remind Fenner of the face glancing up at Vaugiroud's window. Stop thinking about him, Fenner's instincts warned him: go on talking to Claire, or listen to the discussion behind you about the cost of water-skiing, but don't think about Kalganov's man stretched out so peacefully just three feet away. This was certainly not the time to warn Claire; just let her talk on, he thought. She wouldn't stay long here anyhow. Their use for the raft was over.

"I'm hungry," she said suddenly. "What about lunch?"

They dived, and swam until they grounded. As they waded ashore hand in hand, he said very quietly, "I wanted to talk about your shoulders on the raft, but I didn't want to see them stiffen."

She got the allusion. She pulled off her cap and shook her hair loose. "He will know us again, all right," she said worriedly. "He's very confident, isn't he? You could feel that, even as he lay there. I thought he was one of those lone superwolves." She paused. "I'm glad you didn't talk about my shoulders. He's the animal who can sense—" She didn't finish. She tried to smile. "What would you have said about my shoulders?"

"Oh, something conventional—the prettiest shoulders I've seen today, even when slightly broiled. But I like them rare. With mustard."

"They can't be!"

"We'll know tonight, just around dinnertime. I hope you weren't thinking of wearing an orange dress, Mrs. Langley?"

She was laughing, which was a good way to walk up the beach, past the rows of private tents where darkly tanned people lay and looked all day.

As she picked up her towel, she was back to worrying again. "He stared straight at you, Bill—" She bit her lip.

"And I stared right back at the gobs of water he was sloshing around. Okay?"

"Good," she admitted. She rubbed the back of her head where her hair was wet. "I suppose a man would do that."

"Completely authentic," he assured her, "when ladies are present. Alone, I'd have said, 'Hey you, watch where you're putting your so-and-so feet, you such-and-such!' Stop worrying, my pet. You're just a hungry girl. How do *scampi* and some chilled Soave Verona sound?"

She was smiling again. "Find them for me," she said, and went to dress.

He did find them, by asking the advice of the bathhouse couple, whose cousins—it just so happened, Italian-style—ran a small garden restaurant behind the beach. Half of its little tables were empty by this time, allowing them privacy, at least. Underfoot was hard-packed earth floor; overhead, a trellis of vine leaves with colored lights waiting (mercifully, thought Fenner) for evening gaiety. The checked tablecloths were clean, and the fish—straight from the Adriatic onto the charcoal grill—excellent. Greatest triumph of all was Claire, who thought he was a magician to have pulled this place out of his hat, and Fenner, bronzed by the sun and strong sea air, incredibly refreshed by a warm-water swim, felt relaxed and even-tempered for the first time in twenty-four hours.

As they drank the bitter black coffee, he settled back to watch the sunlight spilling through the leaves over Claire's golden hair. "There is only one thing for you to do," he said quietly. "Get out of all this business. Marry Neill and take him out, too."

The gray eyes under their long dark lashes looked up in astonishment. "I'll get out, when I finish this job. But Neill?" She was half puzzled, half embarrassed.

"He was a country newspaper editor before he was a soldier."

"Go back to that?" She shook her head. "He would develop ulcers wondering what really lay behind the headlines." There was a long pause. "And marry him? Why did you say that?" Her eyes dropped to the twist of lemon peel she had picked up.

"Well—you're his girl. Aren't you?"

Again she fell silent. Under the sun-kissed skin, a soft glow spread over the beautifully molded cheekbones. She said, "Neill didn't tell you that."

"No."

She looked up again, in relief. "So it was—" She halted out of caution, although their nearest neighbor was four tables away.

"Our deep-freeze expert," Fenner conceded.

"He would." The embarrassment had cleared from her face. She smiled, treating it as a joke.

And was it only a joke, Rosie's little invention to keep Fenner's mind from wandering off into romance when hard business had to be dealt with? "It isn't true?"

Claire hesitated. "I don't know," she said slowly. "At least—" He was looking at her, unbelieving. "Why do you ask?"

It was he who hesitated now. He had known this girl, apart from seeing her twice in the distance and one brief meeting on Friday evening, exactly twenty-one hours and fifty minutes. A very concentrated twenty-one hours and fifty minutes, it was true. He was thirty-seven, practically touching thirty-eight; a veteran of several wars, declared and undeclared; a man who thought he knew, at last, the direction his life was taking. Not the kind of man, his friends would have sworn, who would be tripped up by a pair of sparkling eyes. But these had him sprawling. He told her the truth, however impolitic it might be. "Because your answer is important."

She didn't ask why. She was neither amused nor flustered nor embarrassed. She simply repeated, "I don't know." She noticed the expression on his face. "You can scarcely believe that, can you?"

"Not in you. You're a woman who has a mind, and uses it."

"My mind tells me that—I'm bad for Neill."

"Bad for him?" He shook his head. "How?"

"I've known him for about six weeks. I saw him a lot. He could relax with me, trust me. . . . But now he talks of getting out of the army, of giving up his work in Intelligence, of returning to Iowa." She was worried, unhappy. "Because of me, Bill."

He agreed with Carlson: it would be a hard life for any woman to be married to a man in his profession. "Nonsense," he said very gently. "Carlson wants to get back to Iowa."

"To that apple tree?" She shook her head. "We all talk that way, now and again. We mean it for a month. And then?" She sighed. "No. Men like Neill are needed—here, in Europe. He knows that. He would begin to feel like a deserter. That's no good. No good at all. Some men could argue themselves into believing that life owes them their own pleasure. Not Neill."

"You have told him all this?"

"Yes. We had a small fight over it yesterday."

"Who won?"

"Who wins in a quarrel with someone he likes? We both lost something." Her head drooped. "The truth is that he is one of the kindest men I've ever met. And I can't bear to hurt him." And the truth is, she told herself painfully, you can't really be in love with Neill Carlson or else you'd have married him right away, whatever his job, wherever he worked. And the truth is you might have drifted from affection and trust into love, into marriage, if you hadn't met Bill Fenner on Friday evening. How could one short meeting with a stranger have had any meaning at all? It had none. Except that it made you uncertain. And if you are really in love, there is no uncertainty: there must not be, or else your marriage would always be vulnerable, a gamble. . . . She looked up at Bill Fenner. I should hate this man, she thought, for having destroyed my pleasant drifting dream. Yet I don't.

"But you don't marry anyone out of a sense of obligation," Fenner said worriedly. "Do you?"

"I don't know—I don't even know that, any more."

"Claire—"

"What time is it?" she asked quickly.

"Quarter of four. If we leave here by four-fifteen, we should have plenty of leeway."

"Ample," she agreed. She stared at her fingers. They had shredded the sliver of lemon peel into a yellow pulp.

"More coffee?" he asked. He took her hands and wiped their finger tips with his handkerchief. "And this time, we'll ask for several twists of lemon." He signaled to the waiter.

She had to smile. She was relieved, too, to retreat away from her painful moment of truth. "How is our theme song?"

"The lady in blue is still with us. Far behind you, trying to make a plate of spaghetti last a full hour. No more interest in our conversation, apparently. I don't think she even expects us, now, to meet anyone. We have wasted her day."

"How nice!"

"But of course if we concentrate on her, we might not notice anyone else. That could be the idea, couldn't it? It's pretty silly the way she has kept haunting us—too obvious."

"You catch on very quickly."

"Slowly," he corrected. "I only thought of it."

"You are doing beautifully," she told him gently, "for a man who lost his raincoat only two days ago."

"You know about that?"

"You look startled. Too startled," she reminded him. No one could hear them. But they were certainly in clear view of at least fifteen people.

He put his hand over hers as it lay beside her coffee cup. "As startled as if you had just promised to go back to America with me?"

She tried to draw her hand away, then—as his tightened—she let it lie under his. "You *are* doing beautifully," she told him again. "This looks perfect."

"You aren't blushing enough."

"I'm a hard case."

"Are you?"

"Not with you, it seems. I shouldn't have let that slip—about your coat."

"How did you learn?"

"I wanted to find out how you got mixed up in all this."

"Why?"

She tried to evade that, and didn't succeed. "Because, oh—just because I was interested." She fell silent, thankfully, as the waiter brought another pot of *espresso* and left.

"I told you I wasn't good for Neill," she reminded him. And in quick defense of Carlson, she added, "He didn't say too much. Just a phrase about meeting you in search of a coat. But there was a report in one of the Paris newspapers yesterday that the French had tracked down a currency smuggler at Orly—at least, they were in possession of his coat, and an arrest was imminent. Didn't you read about it?"

He shook his head. "I didn't get around to reading many newspapers yesterday. And I wish you hadn't."

"Why?"

"The less you know, the safer you'll be."

"And what about you? Or is it all right for men to know, and be placed in danger?"

"Yes."

"You are looking much too serious," she said, her eyes glancing at the rest of the garden.

"I am serious." He uncovered her hand, held it, looked at it, at last released it. "You worry the hell out of me."

"I wouldn't have been sent here if I had to be worried over." She tested the drip coffeepot, and poured carefully.

"How did you get mixed up in all this?" he asked her.

"Two reasons. I knew Sandra Fane long ago in New York. And Frank

596

Rosenfeld knew me in Indochina. Two separate little points in my life which traveled a long long way until their lines crossed, here in Venice."

"You knew Sandra—?" He broke off. Their young waiter was returning with some strips of lemon peel.

"We both had small parts in a Broadway play. I was the little maid who brought in the breakfast tray to a glamorous screen star and opened her bedroom curtains each morning. I looked out at a blank backstage wall and the tired face of a stagehand, and spoke my immortal line: 'It's going to be a lovely day, Miss Julie.'" The waiter was clearing away the dishes. He'd be back for the glasses and wine bottle. "She was the disapproving secretary who found Miss Julie on the terrace in Act Three. Suicide. Oh, it was a very pregnant play, filled with deep inner meanings about the empty shell of success." Here came the waiter for the glasses and last crumbs. "It ran for two months—that was in 1951, when you were in Korea, weren't you?—and by the time it ended, I decided my brain was being turned into cream cheese. So I thought I'd try art school instead. And then I met Jim Langley" (and fell in love, really in love, she thought) "and we got married and went out to Indochina. That was in 1953."

The waiter had left. But Fenner still remained silent. He concentrated on melting a lump of sugar in his coffee cup.

"I didn't know Sandra well. She was older, mixed with a different crowd." She paused, wondering if he was even listening.

"I guess she did," he said. The white sugar turned brown and crumpled slowly. "So—when Rosie heard you were going to one of her parties in Paris, he asked you to talk to her, find out whether she had changed politics." Insistent boy, old Rosie.

"How did you guess?"

"He asked me to do the same thing. What did you find?"

"I thought she was putting on the best act of her life. I was wrong—obviously."

"I wonder."

"You mean you don't think she is honestly defecting?"

"I think she's quitting the party because she has no other choice left." He shook his head. "That was the last small hope I had. That one day she'd make a clean and honest break—something she needn't be ashamed of." He looked up and saw Claire's expression. "For her own sake," he said. "Her life is hers to arrange. Her conscience is her job, not mine. And thank God for that." He drank the coffee, a bitter brew.

"You never tried to reason with her, persuade her?"

"We were together four weeks after we were married in 1950, and there seemed nothing much to argue about, then. After that, I was away from

New York a great deal. On assignments. Alone. She couldn't leave the theater—all these great dramatic roles discovering bodies in Act Three. Or she had to go on tour. Or appear in country stock. She even tried Hollywood. I was actually glad of that long stint in Korea. And when the *Chronicle* brought me home—well, we had a fairly cross-purpose week together before the final break came. I blamed myself for having given her such an empty marriage. I think I would have reasoned with her, tried to persuade her, argued and explained and—" He broke off. From this distance, he could smile at such innocence. Innocence or ignorance? "But she had left. For good. And I was spared a lot of wasted breath. You just can't reason with any dedicated missionary."

"You think she still is?"

"Let's put it this way—she's been quarreling with a bishop, or archbishop. She's leaving her church, but she has still got her religion. She sees us as the benighted reactionaries who'll give her refuge. She'll use us for protection. She has a will to live. Because if she doesn't live, she never can make that comeback, someday, somehow, into her church. When there has been a change in bishops, of course. Communists have patience. We count in months; they count in years." He looked at Claire. "Too cruel?" he asked her.

"You ought to know her better than most." Claire was shaken, though. "You're saying that a conversion out of necessity is not real, not honest?" And when he nodded, she asked, "Did you tell this to Rosie?"

"No. You're the only one I've ever—" He broke off, forced a good imitation of a smile, and went back to Rosie. "He knows a lot about people, that guy. And Communists are people—a pretty mean type of people at that, unless one admires liars and traitors, or the kind of man who keeps silent when his neighbors or family are carted off to torture or execution. As has happened. By the millions."

"I still think Rosie would be interested."

"Anything I tell him would sound like someone in high school analyzing Spinoza. Very worthy, but not exactly contributive to the cause of advanced scholarship. How did Rosie come to know you, by the way?"

"By the way?" She almost smiled at his careful casualness. And then all hint of amusement vanished. "By way of a bombing—a terrorist bombing of a café in Saigon where Jim was killed." She frowned down at the checked tablecloth. "We had been married just five months."

"This was a political bombing?"

"Yes. But those who were killed and mutilated were just ordinary people—all Vietnamese, except for Jim who was waiting for me to meet him at the café." She raised her eyes. "I had chosen the meeting place. We were going furniture-hunting. There was an inlaid table I wanted him to see—it cost more than we had planned—before I bought it." Even at this distance of eight years, there was self-reproach in the simple words.

Fenner said, "Claire, please—"

"I have to tell you. Briefly. Because it is the main reason that brought me into all this business. That bombing killed Jim and four men. It crippled three children and two women. It wounded nine others. I saw them—I saw them all." She paused, hurried on. "So that was what one bomb meant, thrown from a passing truck. No one seemed to know who was responsible. I kept asking who and why, and got no real answers. People were very kind and gentle. But their sympathy was driving me numb with despair. Because everyone seemed so helpless and ignorant; and the bombings went on. So did the anti-American propaganda. No one knew how the rumors spread, but for a time they were believed by people who ought to have had a little more faith in us. They whispered that the Americans were responsible, that we were trying to undermine the French, intimidate the Vietnamese, blame the Communists because we always blamed the poor Communists. Jim's death, you'd think, might have ended the rumors, but it was whispered around that there had been a small slip-up in American planning: they hadn't warned Jim to keep away from that café on that day at that hour. It sounds ridiculous, doesn't it? Yet at the time, the results of that propaganda weren't ridiculous at all. They were deadly.

"So Rosie appeared in Saigon. And he came to see me along with some friends—he was called Frank Rennie then. It was just a sympathy visit. Poor old Jim, poor little widow. It wasn't much of a success. I think Rosie knew why. He seemed to understand that kindly platitudes were no answer at all to my questions. Look, Bill, when a man dies, we try to learn what caused his death, don't we? That's the law in civilized countries, isn't it? And here were civilized people who were shocked and sorry but didn't even know why bombs were being thrown or who had paid and organized the terrorists. Most of them didn't even link the bombs to the anti-American propaganda: they thought the propaganda was only silly talk and no one who really knew Americans would believe it; they thought the bombings were the foolish work of dissidents or madmen on the loose, or a matter of local gangsters trying to shake down the café owners. Except Rosie. When the others left that afternoon, he stayed for an hour. He explained the propaganda campaign and the bombings, all part of the same story being built up around us. Americans were aggressive and ruthless and stupid, who'd turn any crisis into a war. In Korea—but, you remember all that—"

"I remember." A lot of us remember, he thought. We don't all push history into limbo.

"So Rosie made sense. And that was what I needed. Sense, not sympathy. Because that's the only way to stop men like Kalganov. You'll never stop them if you don't know, or won't admit, that they exist. It's knowledge and action, not sympathy and kind words, that will save us from Kalganov's world."

"Rosie actually told you about Kalganov?"

"Not directly. I didn't even know Rosie's job—I thought he was just another businessman visiting Saigon." She smiled and added, "But one who used his brains."

"So he didn't recruit you there?"

"Heavens, no. He just helped me when I needed help. I got a grip on myself and went back to New York and art school. And later, much later, when all the facts had been discovered, he sent me a newspaper clipping about the bombing. The men who threw the bomb from a passing truck were irregulars—bandits calling themselves soldiers. Their war lord, no politics, had been paid for the job. The men who had paid him were Chinese, no politics, who themselves had been paid by other Chinese, who were Communists, plenty of politics. They did it because they were instructed. And who gave them orders, planned everything? A man called Kalganov. He was the only one who wasn't caught."

"He had protected himself pretty well, I must say."

"That's his way. Usually his name doesn't appear in print. In fact, that's the only time I ever saw it. So Rosie and his friends came very close to him."

"And when did Rosie get in touch with you again?"

She laughed. "He *isn't* a sinister old spider, Bill. We met in Paris, as Americans do. When he asked my help, I gave him it. I have seen the enemy, and what he's willing to do to get what he wants. And that's why I'm here. Not because of my own memories, but because of what I learned. That bomb was a threat to all of us—not just a personal tragedy for me. Do you see?"

He nodded.

"If I could help, in the smallest way, to upset any Communist conspiracy—" She stopped, laughed off her tightening emotion. "Let's say I declared war on Kalganov a long time ago. It's my way of fighting for peace. Peace through active discouragement of all peace-breakers."

"Kalganov may need more than active discouragement to end his career."

"His record is black enough. That will take care of him."

"So all we have to do is catch him." Fenner was smiling.

"Not us! That's a job for the professionals. Neill or Chris or some of Rosie's agents. Or perhaps the Sûreté—"

"You think he's in Venice?"

"You saw Jan Aarvan."

"And that means Kalganov is here?"

"He won't be far behind."

"Protecting himself as usual," Fenner suggested. Very casually, he added, "Was Robert Wahl in Saigon around the time of the bombing?"

She stared at him. "Yes," she said slowly. "He was going to make a film out there. But it came to nothing. Bill—"

But he hid his rising worry by glancing at his watch and saying briskly, "There's just time to put on some lipstick and pay the check."

"Heavens!" said Claire, noticing her own small watch and the emptied restaurant. There were only three customers left, far distant. Even their blue ghost had vanished. "Whatever happened—oh, I know, I was explaining myself. Briefly." She smiled at herself, and searched hurriedly for a powder puff and lipstick in her bag. Carefully, she outlined her lips in soft pink. "My nose is going to peel," she told him.

"It wouldn't do anything so indelicate." He watched her, and all her neat feminine motions. She was even remembering to gather their swimsuits from a nearby chair, shaking her head over their dampness, deciding to carry them.

"You're the strangest mixture," he told her. She was ten, twenty different women. Enough to keep a man chasing them all his life. Infinite variety. Poor old Carlson. Poor old Mark Antony, too. "Come on, Cleopatra." She looked up, charming and wide-eyed. "Let's go, my little front-line fighter for peace," he said, and draped her soft ridiculous cardigan around her sun-tanned shoulders. "And give me those blasted swimsuits."

They walked up a sheltered path, a tangle of vines and rough pergola, toward the main road, passing the restaurant's bad-weather dining room, which now lay neglected. They were alone except for three barefooted, bronzed children, who chased long-legged pullets in and out of a kitchen door.

They were almost at the street. "Drop something," he told her. The cardigan slipped off her shoulders. He halted, took a step back to where it lay, shaking it as he picked it up to free it of dust and a withered leaf. She hadn't looked around. "Our friend in the brown suit has joined us again. He must have been in the dining room." They had fallen into step, arm in arm, the cardigan slung through the strap of her red handbag. "Are they trying to scare us into a false move?" Either these people were damned well organized or he was crediting them with too many brains. "Jan

Aarvan, for instance—" (how had he managed to be floating around on their part of the swimming beach?) "—was he also on the water-bus we took? I didn't see him. I was too busy watching the woman."

"It doesn't matter," Claire said as they came out into the street. "As long as Aarvan didn't feel either of us recognized him, it doesn't matter."

Fenner noticed two taxis waiting near the lane's exit. "How convenient," he said, and looked at the street, a long straight line stretching for miles, edged with gardens and bathhouses and hotels. It seemed uninhabited, except—a little distance away—for a small group of ex-bathers and sun-worshipers waiting for a trolley-bus to start back into town. Claire looked at him with brief alarm, and relaxed. They weren't going to take any too-convenient taxi. I can let Bill take charge, she thought thankfully; and the feeling of reassurance, of safety, which had fallen over her like a soft and silken cloak in that dusty, vine-shaded lane, was wrapped around her again.

One of the taxis moved forward. Its door was open, as inviting as its driver's wide grin. "Taxi, taxi! Very quick, very quick!"

"He'd make a successful playwright, that one," Fenner observed as they walked on, the taxi cruising gently behind them, "emphasizing the obvious, repeating everything twice." The man's face had been remarkably untanned for someone who lived on this wind-scoured, sun-baked sand bar. No doubt he had quick ears, a good memory, too. And he knew English. I may be oversuspicious, Fenner thought, but— He looked at Claire, who was letting him handle this completely. "No thanks," he called to the taxi, which had drawn alongside again.

The bus ahead of them would leave any minute, and among the swarm of passengers climbing on board by the rear door, he saw a woman dressed in dull blue, her somber face not at all amused by the good-natured jostling around her. Better avoid the bus, he thought. But the taxi was creeping along, cajoling. Its driver would certainly keep following, if only to wear down their resistance. The Excelsior was only a few minutes away. Fenner could see it, even from here, along that stretch of empty road. The woman in the bus would notice them get off, but she could hardly follow them as blatantly as that. At the moment, she was the lesser of two dangers. "Run, Claire!" he said, catching her hand. They sprinted wildly, and reached the bus as it moved slowly away from the curb. He swung her onto its step, and scrambled after her as the bus went into high speed. "And you can run," he told her, regaining his breath.

"You can pull," she said, breathless herself. She looked back at their line of flight. The insistent taxi had given up. Or perhaps it was waiting for further instructions from the other cab, which the man in brown was entering. "You can guess right, too," she told Fenner as he found some small change for their short ride. There was no need to search for a seat. They'd leave at the next stop.

Which made the blue lady's reactions all the funnier. First she had been startled: was *she* being followed? Then she had become suspicious: they must be meeting someone on this bus. So she moved to a side seat near the front, uncomfortable as it was, from which she could watch everyone with that blank, stolid gaze. And just as she was settling, dutifully, at her vantage post, the bus swerved toward the sidewalk for its next halt.

Claire and Fenner slipped off quietly by the rear door, their exit blurred by the rush of oncoming passengers crowding into the aisle. They crossed the street toward the lagoon, walking smartly. "We've got one minute left," Fenner said. He glanced along the road. The two taxis were still standing together, some five hundred yards away. Quickly, they started forward. "Not a chance," Fenner told them under his breath, as Claire, much amused, and he, feeling pretty good, came into the anchorage.

It was a sheltered place—a large and glorified swimming pool, Fenner thought—with a few highly polished motorboats drawn close to one edge. Their owners were not grouped together, talking and scouring, as the gondoliers had been. They wore natty tweed jackets, correct collars and ties, nautical caps at a jaunty angle on good haircuts, and a proud look. "The jet pilots of the lagoon," Fenner said with a grin. "And which is ours?" He didn't wait for Claire's guess, but started toward a boat, lying a little apart, whose owner seemed only interested in lighting a cigarette. "Hotel Vittorio?" Fenner called to him.

"Right here," the man said, and waved them casually on board. He was a young, dark-haired Italian, with interested brown eyes even if the manner was cool and nonchalant. Amidships, there was the usual glass-enclosed cabin with pleated curtains, sashed and befringed, giving privacy. A good deal of privacy, Fenner realized as he handed Claire through the small front door and ducked inside after her. There was a man sitting in one of the neat red leather armchairs. From the jetty, the cabin had seemed empty.

"Fasten your seat belts," the stranger said as the engine roared, the boat curved sharply toward a narrow tree-lined canal, and they were jolted wildly together. "Hello, Claire. You've had a pleasant day in the sun, I see."

"Hello, Chris. Where's Neill?"

"I like boat rides, so I am here. And is this Mr. Fenner? How do you do?" The English voice was cold. "I'm Holland."

EIGHTEEN

There was tension in the small cabin. Claire glanced anxiously at Chris Holland, as much as to say, "Come on, make one of your funny remarks. I've talked you up. Don't let me down!" But the Englishman was making no further remarks at all. He shook hands briefly, lit another cigarette. He was, in spite of his concentration with his lighter, studying Fenner critically.

Of course, Fenner remembered, I was Rosie's choice for this little expedition. Neill Carlson had been against it. No doubt Holland was, too. In his phrase, but in my New England accent, I am the bloody amateur who clutters up the landscape. So I'll keep quiet, he decided, let Holland talk; and if I have to talk, I'll do it in short questions and not flat statements. The opinion of an amateur was not worth too much around here.

Fenner settled himself comfortably in the chair opposite Claire. He lit a cigarette, too, and studied the Englishman in turn. An amateur could do that, at least. Christopher Holland was of medium height, weight, and age; his features, even, pleasant, but unremarkable; his hair, neatly cut, well brushed, graying brown; eyes, an indeterminate mixture of gray and brown, but certainly observant; lightly tanned, unlined skin; his clothes of brownish-gray mixed tweed, worn most casually. A medium kind of man in every way, Fenner thought, one you'd scarcely notice in an empty street, and quickly forget. A man without worries or troubles, you would guess, even meeting him as closely as this, until you noticed the ash tray beside him, filled with half-smoked cigarettes.

Claire was reporting. "They are definitely interested in us, Chris. We have been watched and monitored ever since we left Paris."

"One minute—" Holland said in his quiet, even voice. They were zooming into the lagoon, two scimitar-shaped waves curving up and out from the boat's sharp prow. He slid open the rear door's panel. "Dammit," he bellowed, "what's the rush, Pietro?"

Pietro grinned cheerfully. He had had his flying start. He eased the speed of the boat and shouted back something that blew away in the wind. Holland shook his head, closed the door again.

"First," Holland said, "let's talk about the message you sent me. Your rooms are no good. No good at all. Change them." He was looking at Claire. Claire looked at Fenner.

"So Rosie did not book those two rooms on the terrace?" Fenner asked.

"No. He arranged for two rooms on the second floor, no connecting balcony with any other rooms. Also, two of his men have rooms on that floor, close by. We've been outmaneuvered"—he smiled, thinly—"by film producer Wahl, who could very safely use the name of Mr. Stephen York."

"Are they friends?"

"Not at all. But it was safe to use York's name. He is making a picture in deepest Africa. We checked." Again there was a touch of acid amusement. "Wahl was never known for his lack of impudence."

"Wahl," Fenner said reflectively. "Not Kalganov?"

Holland was startled, certainly less diffident in manner. He looked at Fenner thoughtfully. "We don't know that Wahl *is* Kalganov, do we?"

"Where is Wahl?"

"Switzerland, they tell me."

"Not Venice?"

Holland's quiet stare asked for an explanation.

"Claire thinks Kalganov is in Venice. We saw Jan Aarvan today."

"Where?"

"On a raft." Fenner relented and grinned. "About a couple of hours ago, or more."

"You are sure?" Holland looked at Claire for confirmation.

"Bill recognized him. I didn't. Really, Chris, that's an awful photograph in Inspector Bernard's files. Aarvan has thinned down, for one thing. And he must be fifteen years older."

"Also," Fenner said, "he is dyeing his hair. It was brown yesterday on the train. It's almost black today. Miracles of modern science. When I first saw him, from Vaugiroud's window, he was blond. How is Vaugiroud, by the way? His arm was broken, I heard."

"You must introduce me to your sources," Holland said. "They sound more accurate than mine."

"Is he all right?"

"He is all right. He escaped the second attempt on his life, too."

"There was *another* one?"

"We can talk about that later." Holland stared at his cigarette stub, let it drop into the ash tray with distaste. His thoughts had drifted onto something unpleasant. He tried to pull them away from it, said, "Now, about your message, Claire—" He was half lost in his own thoughts again.

Claire looked astounded. She exchanged a puzzled glance with Fenner. "Yes," she said, "I was beginning to wonder if it had fallen flat on its funny little face. There were three questions in it. We haven't even finished with the first one. Rooms to be changed. How? That isn't easy, without warning Comrade Wahl that we are suspicious."

Holland said, a little sharply, "That's your problem, old girl."

"I'll take care of it," Fenner said quietly. "What was the second point in your note, Claire?" The sooner Claire's note was dealt with, the more quickly he'd learn about Vaugiroud. There was something wrong. That, he could sense.

Claire was watching Holland curiously. "It dealt with the coat of arms on the gondola that collected Sir Felix Tarns."

Holland was in control of his thoughts again. He even produced an unexpected smile. "You described the coat of arms as either a crocodile rampant or a sea horse sitting on its tail, with either a thin pineapple or a fat palm tree in support."

"Well," Claire said, "I only had a quick glimpse. You know how gondolas float away."

Fenner looked at her blankly. He hadn't paid any attention to the coat of arms. He had been too busy thinking, as they stood on the Vittoria's landing stage, what a damned silly piece of nonsense it all was, following Tarns out there.

"Crocodile and palm tree," Holland was saying, "the most useful piece of information we've had today." He seemed to enjoy the expression on Fenner's face. He explained, with some slight amusement, "We lost Lenoir and Fane last night, after they arrived at Lido Airport. Their launch behaved very much in the way that Pietro is steering our boat at present: most erratic, very difficult to follow. They vanished somewhere in Saint Mark's Basin; never docked at the Danieli, where we expected them to stay. And since then, there's been a bloody flap. Not a clue where they were until"—he gave Claire a nod of approval—"your crocodile and palm tree reached us. After that it was easy, of course."

"Of course," said Fenner. "A crocodile and palm tree, after all."

"It's the coat of arms of the Longhi family, who own a retiring little palazzo known as Ca' Longhi just off the Grand Canal," Holland clarified. "It was leased for the summer—the Longhi family is down to one survivor

606

and none of the cash it made in Near Eastern trade three centuries ago—
to an American, who calls herself—" He broke off, and then murmured
apologetically, "I'm afraid she went back to using your name, old boy."

"What?"

"Yes. Mrs. William Fenner. She has almost as much impudence as
Wahl. Or perhaps it was another of his comic touches. I suppose her old
passport was easy to bring up to date for the agent who leased the place,
last May. So, crocodile and palm tree saved us a lot of time, a lot of investigation."

"You'd have tracked down Ca' Longhi—" Claire began. She was taking
her small triumph well, Fenner thought. There hadn't been even a flicker
of an eyelash in his direction saying "See?"

"Yes," agreed Holland. "With some co-operation from the Italians, we
would have. But even with all hands on deck, Ca' Longhi might have
taken a full day's work to uncover. Instead, we could set up a close watch
on the place early this afternoon. Most rewarding. There has been a series
of visitors for Fernand Lenoir since our noble Sir Felix left him at half
past two." Holland's voice was icily contemptuous for that one reference.
He dropped Tarns there. "It seems as if the briefing session has begun at
Ca' Longhi," he said, watching Fenner.

"Already?"

"Yes."

"I don't get it," Fenner said worriedly. Sandra would deliver the letter
and make her escape, tomorrow evening, well ahead of either the attempted assassination or the big lie. She had told Rosie that the crisis could
be expected by Friday. And here was Lenoir, meeting his contacts today.
"I'd have thought the later Lenoir left that briefing session, the safer for
them all. Or is he just preparing the ground before he starts planting the
lies?"

"Frankly," Holland said, watching Fenner with growing interest, "I
don't get it either. Unless—as you say—the ground needs a good deal of
preparation. Tell me, how much do you think we can trust Sandra Fane?"

Fenner hesitated. He phrased his answer carefully. "At present—I think
we can."

"But in the long run—not at all?" Holland asked quietly. He was a sharp
character, Fenner decided. The question had been only rhetorical: the
unspoken agreement spared Fenner an answer. Strange, he was thinking,
that Claire is the only one with whom I've discussed Sandra quite willingly. He looked at Claire, and Holland noticed it. (What have we here?
Holland wondered: whatever it is, I don't think I like it; nor will Rosie.)

Quickly, he said, "About that third point in your message, Claire: the man in the brown suit. Not to worry. He has been noted. So have the others. We have marked them all, once they showed an interest in you."

Fenner was amused. "So we've been watched by your experts, too?" To Claire, he said, "You know what we are? A couple of lambs staked out for the tigers."

Holland almost smiled. "Cheer up, chum. You've been very useful. Rosie sends his thanks."

"Is Rosie *here?*" Claire asked, suddenly grave.

"Arrived an hour ago."

"But why—"

"Rosie wants you both to play things very loose indeed. No strain. Just get through the next twenty-four hours as normally as possible. Leave the problems to us. Except the change of rooms. You'll do that right away?"

"First thing," Fenner assured him.

"Good. I remember, in Budapest, we had the same situation. Bloody balcony connecting several rooms. We lost a good man that way." He glanced out through the glass panel in the cabin's rear door, opened it, signaled to Pietro, who, if he couldn't make high speed, had at least been having a merry time criss-crossing the lagoon's Sunday traffic, mingling and disentangling skillfully from various groupings of boats. "Ten more minutes and then up the Giudecca Canal," Holland shouted. "Drop me at San Sebastiano."

Pietro nodded, shouted back cheerfully. Holland shut the door, pulled its curtains securely together. In fact, Fenner noted, all the windows around Holland were thoroughly screened.

"We are getting close in," Holland said. "Keep together, you two. Don't look at me. Look as if you were chatting only to each other. Any further problems?"

Fenner shook his head.

"Then we can talk about Vaugiroud." He would make as good a bridge passage as any, Holland thought. His voice became quite emotionless. "Just around noon yesterday, when that bomb went off in the Café Racine, Vaugiroud's flat was entered and searched. Rather violently. The concierge says her husband allowed a man to go upstairs to the flat. She thinks it was the same man who loitered in front of the house on Friday afternoon. Her husband has been arrested; so far, he is sticking to his story. He swears he allowed only a telephone repairman to go upstairs. Once we get Aarvan, of course, and have a little confrontation scene, the husband may decide it's wiser to tell the truth."

Holland pulled a folded sheet of newspaper out of a jacket pocket.

He unfolded it slowly, spoke rapidly. "So, with all this attention on Vaugiroud, we expected there might be another attempt on his life. We announced he was being transferred from one hospital to another, and sent out an empty ambulance to make that journey. A truck smashed into its rear. Truck driver jumped, was caught, pleaded brakes had not worked properly. Ambulance a mess."

"I hope its driver jumped, too," Fenner said to Claire.

"He is one of our very best jumpers," Holland said dryly. "Here's the newspaper story. We thought it a good idea to announce that Vaugiroud had been killed. Saves us a lot of bother in the next few days."

"Where is he?"

"Much hidden." Holland handed over the unfolded sheet to Fenner, and Claire changed her seat to read, too. "It's from the early-morning edition. Rosie brought it with him. I circled the paragraph for you."

"Vaugiroud's friends are going to be in an uproar," Fenner said, after he and Claire had read a brief but highly vivid account of the accident.

"For a few days," the calm voice said. "There will be a retraction, a plea of mistaken identity, a blushing apology and general thanksgiving."

"And what does the poor journalist do who wrote these immortal lines? Cut his throat?"

"He was overdescriptive for a man who didn't arrive on the scene until the two bodies were taken away," Holland said coldly. As Claire looked at him, he added, "Keep your attention on Fenner! And for bodies, read dummies."

Claire addressed Fenner obediently. "What's wrong?" she asked frankly. Chris was usually good company, with a string of bright remarks. He could turn any situation, however grim, into comedy. Normally, he would have taken Bill's gruesome joke and expanded it to something really hideously funny. "Chris—" She was inexplicably, and deeply, worried.

"I circled another paragraph, too," he said, "on the next page."

Fenner turned over the sheet quickly. He heard Claire's sudden gasp as she saw the ten lines of close type, headed FATAL ACCIDENT ON PARIS-ZAGREB EXPRESS. She drew back from him, her body rigid. Fenner stared at the lines. He knew, before he read them. He knew, and he didn't want to read. But he read.

Last night, Emile Daubenton and Jean Lacordaire, cousins, both from the village of Darcey, discovered the body of a man lying beside the railway line over which the Simplon Express had passed less than one hour previously. From the contents of his pockets, the man has been identified as John McNally of New York City, traveling to Milan. It is thought that M. McNally slipped, or fell, from the express, about eleven kilometers east of Les Laumes, as it traveled at highest speed before starting the ascent through the Côte-d'Or. M. McNally was traveling alone, and his tragic accident was unobserved.

Claire's face had bleached white under its sun tan as she watched Fenner. At last she said, "It's about Neill, isn't it?" She held out her hand for the paper. She read it, her face masked; and when the reading was over she let the sheet of newspaper drop. She rose, looking at neither Fenner nor Holland, abruptly opening the small door that led to the prow of the boat.

"Let her be," Holland's quiet voice said, stopping Fenner as he rose, too. Claire was sitting, numbed and still, on a wooden bench, her body half turned away from the cabin.

Fenner came back to his armchair. The two men faced each other grimly. Holland said, "We have been able to calculate the time of Neill's death: I glanced at my watch when I saw him walking through the dining car, and the engine driver could give us the exact time the train passed eleven kilometers east of Les Laumes. It's a lonely spot, just before the line starts climbing the Côte-d'Or hills. If it hadn't been for a couple of poachers taking a short cut along the rails, we'd still be searching for Neill." He paused, frowning down at the spilling ash tray.

"When was he killed?"

"Soon after he left the dining car. Who followed him into that goods van—did you see?"

The freight car, with its opened side door, with the cold wind rushing past . . . "Jan Aarvan."

"You are sure?" Holland asked quickly.

"Fenner nodded. "Didn't you recognize him?"

"From where I sat, I could only see his back. I didn't know he was on the train. Neill had made no contact with me at all. That was our arrangement: raise no suspicion, no alarm. It seemed safer—for everyone."

For us, Fenner thought, for Claire and me and our innocent journey. But not for Neill Carlson. "He must have warned someone that he had seen Aarvan. I noticed some plain-clothes police board the train at Dijon."

Holland nodded. "Neill did get a message through to Rosie, just before the train pulled out of the Gare de Lyon. He told Rosie to alert the Sûreté that he would be waiting for its agents on board the train at Dijon. He could identify Aarvan for them." Holland frowned again. "I saw them get on the train. And wondered. And could do nothing—not even identify myself." He looked at Fenner. "Jan Aarvan didn't know you had recognized him?"

"I think not."

"I hope not," Holland said softly. "Be alert, will you, Fenner? At any other time, I'd be amused by the situation. Of all the people we've got here in Venice, you're the only one who could pick out Jan Aarvan in a crowd without any hesitation." He remembered Claire's remarks about Aarvan. Worriedly, he asked, "When did you tell Claire about Aarvan?"

"When we were well clear of the raft. I'm not such a fool as that, Holland." He looked toward Claire. "I'm not going to leave her alone out there," he said, and started to rise.

"Wait—what are your plans for this evening?"

"A drink at Florian's around six-thirty. Then dinner at Quadri's. At ten, we take a gondola ride with an old friend of Claire's—his name is Zorzi. He parks his gondola at the bridge near your camera shop."

"Zorzi," Holland repeated. "I'll let Rosie know." He glanced out of the window. "Better bring Claire inside before we start cruising up the Giudecca. And take a look at the Soviet freighter that is docked there. She's supposed to sail on Thursday." Holland studied his hands. "She has been loading all day."

"You think Sandra—" Fenner hesitated. A clever act put on for Rosie's benefit in the Tuileries. A trick, a trap? "More lies?" he asked quietly.

"Not altogether. There must be some truth in her warning. Why else would Aarvan want to stop Neill from reaching Venice?"

Yes, there was that. But couldn't Sandra tell the whole truth, honestly, just once in her life?

"Aarvan—" began Holland, and stopped. He was beginning to sound emotional, and that wouldn't do, that wouldn't do at all. We'll get him yet, Holland thought, we'll get him. He stared impassively ahead.

"How did Aarvan murder Neill before he threw him off the train? With a bullet in the back?"

Holland's quiet mask slipped. He looked at Fenner. "Yes," he said, watching the American with a new respect.

It would have to be a bullet, or a knife, in the back. Carlson hadn't been the type to be pushed off a train, Fenner thought as he stepped through the door to reach Claire.

The motorboat was leaving the lagoon, making one last sweep around the small island of San Giorgio before it cut up the Giudecca Canal. He took Claire's hands between his and sat down beside her. She had been crying silently, sitting so still, her face turned blindly toward the roofs of Venice. "Come," he said gently, "back into the cabin. You'll be frozen." She didn't seem to hear him. "Please, Claire," he said very softly. At that, she looked at him, the tears ignored. When he pulled her to her feet, she didn't resist. He steadied her with his arm firmly around her waist, and she didn't notice. The broad waters of the Giudecca stretched before them. At its long quay, backed by antique houses, he could see the liner safely docked. And beyond it, a freighter, large, clean, efficient. And it was still loading.

He brought Claire into the cabin before they reached the freighter. Holland, making ready for his quick exit, only signed his approval. He had shredded the sheet of newspaper, and dropped it along with his cigarette stubs into the canal. His hand was on the rear door, his eyes watching the quay. "Change those rooms," he reminded Fenner again, as his parting word.

Fenner nodded. Whatever had happened in Budapest had really seared itself into Holland's mind. "Does Sir Felix shoot people in the back, too?"

"He does everything short of pulling the trigger. That," Christopher Holland said bitterly, "would be against his principles." His eyes were still on the quay. The freighter was safely passed.

I'll take that warning about Tarns, Fenner thought, watching the freighter, too. Claire noticed nothing. She hadn't even heard their voices.

As the boat curved around into a small canal, Holland pulled the door open. "Good-by," he told them, "good luck!" He was out. "Quick as you like!" he said to Pietro as he climbed onto the broad stretch of quay. The boat backed into the Giudecca, pointed to the lagoon again, gathering the speed that delighted Pietro. Chris Holland was already out of sight.

They swept around the island of San Giorgio again, and entered the Grand Canal, slowing down for the increased traffic. Fenner looked at Claire anxiously. He couldn't bring himself to remind her that they'd have to land in a few minutes, all smiles and general jollity, a happy couple returning from an afternoon in the sun. "There's the Vittoria," was all he said.

She nodded, opened her handbag, stared at a small mirror, combed her hair. Her normal color had partly returned to give some life to her face. The pitiful bleached look had gone. She added lipstick. She looked up at him. "Will this do?" she asked bitterly.

"Very well," he said gently. He remembered to pick up the swimsuits. Nothing else left, except his five cigarette stubs. "Ready?" he asked, and handed her out of the cabin.

"I'll go straight to my room, do you mind?"

"No you don't. You stay with me. I'm going to have the rooms changed immediately. We pack together. We keep together." I can take a warning, he thought. And Chris Holland gave me several in his own quiet way.

"All right," she said, capitulating. "Now," she added, watching the crowded hotel terrace as the boat eased broadside against the floating landing stage, "we smile, and smile and smile." Oh, God!

The assistant manager was just about to leave. He looked at the two sun-reddened faces and the damp swimsuits. "Did you have a pleasant day?" he began politely, wondering what had brought this handsome couple to his office.

"Marvelous," the lady said. Mrs. Langley, that was her name; a widow. And so young, so beautiful. Life was sad.

"It's about our rooms," the tall American said.

The assistant manager stopped looking at his clock. "Is something wrong?" And he must not be late, he thought worriedly. This evening he was entertaining his bank manager at his house.

"Not wrong. But not exactly right, either."

"Please?"

"There must have been a mistake."

"How—a mistake?"

"About Mr. York telephoning—"

"His secretary telephoned me. This morning. From Zurich."

"Yes, yes, I'm sure he did. But he didn't telephone you about us. There must have been some mistake in the names. I'm afraid we have these rooms on false pretenses."

The assistant manager's English failed him. "*Prego?*"

"We don't know Mr. York. When you spoke to us this morning, I assumed he was a friend of Mrs. Langley's. She thought he must be one of mine. It was only when we were on our way to the Lido that we discovered neither of us knew Mr. York."

The assistant manager relaxed. He could even glance at the clock again. He said gaily, starting to shepherd them to the door of his office, "Ah, it is all a little comedy of errors? But if you like the rooms—"

"They are excellent." The American was standing his ground.

"In that case, what is there to worry about?"

"Two things. First, Mr. York's friends will expect to have these rooms when they arrive."

The assistant manager's dark eyes drooped tactfully. There had been no mistake about the names, he told himself. What was behind all this? "And secondly?" he asked.

The American lowered his voice, spoke with considerable embarrassment. "I'm afraid these rooms will be too expensive for me. I did, you know, book two rooms from Paris yesterday afternoon. I think they'll suit my expense account."

The assistant manager's eyes opened wide. So there was the true explanation. Film stars were lordly and impulsive creatures, but they forgot that their friends' expense accounts rarely measured up to theirs. "In that case," he said, "let me see if your original rooms are still available. One second, please." He picked up his telephone and made contact with the reception desk. There was a sharp volley of rapid Italian. The assistant manager was the winner. He replaced the telephone, eying the clock, and said, "If you will go to the desk, Mr. Fenner, they will be able to help you, I think."

"Thank you," the American said briefly as they left. But then, to be embarrassed, in this way, in front of the beautiful Mrs. Langley did not help any man to be voluble in his expression of gratitude. The assistant manager followed them at a tactful distance, in a thoroughly good humor: so there were some Americans who had to worry about money, too.

"Neat," Claire said, after Fenner had arranged the transfer of rooms at the desk, and they were on their way to remove their possessions from the terrace view.

"Easy," he told her. "All I did was to lose face." It was little enough, he thought grimly. That ought to make them believe our story, even if nothing else does. How much *is* believed, by this time: all the story we have so carefully built up around ourselves, half of it, none of it? Are all our precautions quite useless? If so, we are in a completely comic situation bound for a tragic ending. We shall have as small a chance as poor old Neill Carlson.

"I'm coming in while you pack," he said as they reached her room. She's going to break down again, he thought worriedly, she's really going to let down every guard this time. He closed the door behind them. "Claire!" She was standing at the French windows, looking out on the terrace, seeing, hearing nothing. "Claire," he said, coming over to her. She turned to him blindly, and he put his arms around her, holding her closely. He could feel the silent sobs racking through her body. He held her like that, saying nothing, letting the seconds slip away while he kept his arms tightly around her.

She took a deep, steadying breath. "It's my fault." She tried to wipe away the tears with the back of her hand. "He is dead. It's my fault."

"No."

"But it is," she cried out. His assignment in Paris was over, she thought

614

in anguish. He was going back to Germany. "He didn't have to come to Venice. He wouldn't have come if I hadn't been here. He wouldn't—" "He would have," Fenner insisted. He glanced around him worriedly, wondering if some visitor to Tarns's room this afternoon had been able to come in here and plant another of those hellish contraptions to trap their words. So he didn't risk speaking what he wanted her to hear: Neill Carlson had known what was at stake; he had come to Venice for the same reason that Chris Holland was here. More was involved than a letter, or Sandra's escape. Much more. "Believe me, Claire!" he said. "Please believe me."

Claire saw his glance, his worried eyes. She heard the intensity of his voice. And she left her private world of regret and remorse, and came back to reality. She nodded. "I believe you," she said at last. "I'll start packing." Her eyes, too, searched the room quickly. And then they met Fenner's. "All right," she said, "let's get this job finished."

"We'll finish it," he said quietly.

NINETEEN

Two men sat in a darkened room. Outside was the shadowed stillness of a narrow canal threading its cold, black way between the high walls and barred windows of quiet houses toward the warm glow of sunset on the broad and bustling Rialto. But here, in this room, the drawn shutters cut off the distant sounds of life. Here, behind locked doors, Venice was forgotten.

The two men were on board the Simplon Express. They listened to the rattle of its wheels, to the voices of a man and a woman talking happily, clearly audible except when the brakes screeched to give warning of a curve ahead on the railroad track. They might have been sitting in a neighboring room of the sleeping car, with a connecting door left ajar to let them overhear Claire Langley and William Fenner discussing themselves in between filling out details in Customs declarations.

They listened intently. They were both men in their middle forties, obviously affluent by their excellent clothes and careful grooming. One was Fernand Lenoir, dark-haired, tall, thin, with the diplomatic manner, now permanently established even if it was far from natural, of a government official whose career depended on politeness to his equals and deference to his superiors. The other was shorter, more heavily built. His brow was heightened by thinning reddish hair, which had receded in an even line; his face, blunt-featured and broad, was sallow and coarse-skinned, unprepossessing from a close front view—the eyes were small, closely set, clever-quick; the mouth was wide, thin-lipped, determined—but in profile, with the expression lost and only the strong bone structure showing, it could be called handsome. He was a man of many names, many interests, and one ambition. For the last fifteen years he had been known to most people as Robert Wahl.

616

Robert Wahl . . . Naturalized Frenchman, a clever writer turned subsidized businessman, with money made in publishing and in radio, and, in recent years, a small but valuable reputation as an original in the film world. His real name? Alexei Kalganov, a name that existed more in top-secret files than on people's tongues. His face had appeared only twice in print. The first time was in a photograph taken at a May Day celebration in Moscow when Kalganov had stood third from the left behind Stalin, and the foreign experts on Soviet affairs had wondered for four days—until another international crisis had sent them prognosticating in wider fields—whether this unknown (identified by Tass as an agricultural expert named Shakhov) would be a rising star in the variable Russian firmament. The second appearance was in a photograph, highly unauthorized, hastily taken by a Freedom Fighter in Budapest, of a group of smiling Soviet officials clustered around a benevolent Mikoyan, with an oversized tank as appropriate background. (Kalganov's hand had instinctively covered the lower half of his face. He was the only one in the group to be unidentified. The Freedom Fighter was arrested and shot that same day.)

Even Fernand Lenoir, who had been working under his direction as far back as 1944 when Vaugiroud had been marked for liquidation— an intransigent bourgeois intellectual who would always rally to any resistance, a potential leader who must be eliminated with the Nazi retreat—never mentioned the name of Kalganov. Or addressed him as Kalganov. It was an identity he guarded, like the neolithic men who hunted and fought and died as Running Wolf, Sitting Bear, Bird-in-the-Grass, but whose real names were kept hidden to give them secret strength, to protect them from their enemies. Kalganov would have been the first to scoff at religious superstition, but he clung to the practice of supersecrecy as the first law of self-preservation; and in this he was not far removed from those he sneered at. Only in the form of his self-perpetuation did he differ from those who aimed, by their deeds, at a Happy Hunting Ground, a Paradise beyond this life: his deeds, if successful, would be the shaping of history, and that was something which could never be undone. He would have his own kind of immortality.

Lenoir rose impatiently. They were coming to the end of the recorded conversation. "Good night, Claire," the American's voice was saying, *"Mes hommages."* After that, there would only be the interminable sounds of a train, its passengers silenced by sleep, climbing its way up toward Switzerland. Lenoir moved to turn off the machine. "That's all," he said.

"Leave it!"

Lenoir's hand hesitated and stopped. He didn't show his annoyance. He lit a cigarette, and walked around the room, stretching his shoulders. Gold and cream and faded green—the room's elegance was a piece of the past, like the dust-smeared candelabra and the chipped teardrops of the crystal lamps; a place only fit to be rented to some antique-crazy American who had replaced the English as upholders of what was finished and over. Still, it was a strongly built house, well silenced, remote from the busy little streets and square behind it, yet central enough to be useful.

"Keep quiet!" Wahl commanded, and listened intently to a sound track recording the nothings of an empty night journey.

He is always thorough, too thorough, Lenoir thought. A virtue, of course. But does he never become bored with his virtues? Lenoir studied Wahl's expressionless face. Never, he decided. He moved with his crisp step toward the room's communicating door, heavily ornate with late Renaissance panels and tarnished silver handles. He unlocked it quietly and slipped through into the adjoining library, where Sandra was at work. He closed the door gently behind him.

She was sitting at the large writing table, transformed—with a portable typewriter, a bright light, scattered sheets of paper, inks and pens—into an island of efficiency in a sea of high-backed chairs, dim lamps, and ornamented bookcases that reached the painted ceiling. She looked, as she glanced toward him, a little tired. She pushed her glasses up onto her brow. In her plain black dress, sleeves rolled up, bracelets and rings and earrings in a discarded heap near an overfull ash tray, her hair twisted behind her ears, a cardigan over her shoulders to protect her from the damp chill in the air, a pair of white cotton gloves on her hands, she was far removed from the elegant hostess in Dessès chiffon of only three nights ago. Now she was the efficient and most private secretary, completing the final piece of top-secret work. The last, in every way. Perhaps he should be glad that Wahl had turned up in Venice: let him break the news of her recall. "You look cold. Why don't you light the fire?"

"I have tried. It smoked. Why don't we have the furnace turned on? Or does it smoke, too?"

"Heating in September? You have still kept some of your American habits, Sandra."

"In July, this place could feel like November. Oh well, I'll soon be finished here—just checking the copies of the letter. You wanted seven in all?" And if he counts them, how am I going to explain the eight copies I've made? But he didn't, and she talked on to distract his attention. "Five

618

for the men you meet today, and two for your pet neutralists. When do you see them?"

"Tomorrow. Is this the original letter?" He stretched out his hand to pick it up.

"Careful!" She lifted it with her gloved fingers. "I'll hold it, while you read."

"It looks very good," he said with real pleasure. "You notice I placed the main emphasis on the Americans, making the English more of a go-between. The style is just right, don't you think?"

"It could be the wine merchant himself. How do you like his signature?"

"Most authentic. You would have made an excellent forger, Sandra." You've given me enough practice, she thought.

He had a criticism, of course. "The type jumps a little."

"It's Trouin's own typewriter, isn't it? If it jumps, it jumps."

"So typical of him to tolerate the imperfect."

"I hope he hasn't discovered it's missing." Carefully, she laid the perfectly faked original on the desk before her.

"No more than he noticed the missing sheets of his writing paper. He was too busy preparing to leave for Switzerland."

"How did you borrow the typewriter? Bribe or make love to his secretary? Or was it stolen by a cleaning woman?"

He joined in her laughter, without much humor. "You must not pry out all my little secrets. Actually—it was very simple."

"You're too modest, Fernand." That pleased him and brought real warmth to his face. "It's a brilliant idea. I just hope this sheet of Trouin's writing paper has at least one sample of his fingerprints."

"I can assure you it has. You've been very careful with it?"

"Didn't take off the gloves once. Let's finish this job. I'd like to see the original safely in its envelope, just in case anyone is forgetful enough to pick it up without gloves. If it's spoiled, we are out of luck. Completely."

"I gave you three sheets of his writing paper," he said sharply.

"I had to destroy two. The signature wasn't good enough," she lied most innocently. "I don't think much of the type of nib that our wine merchant likes to use. It's too soft."

"Typical," Lenoir said. He was still annoyed.

"When does he commit suicide?"

Lenoir stared at her, forgetting nibs and two wasted sheets of paper. "You know, Sandra, you really are indiscreet at times."

"Only with you, darling." Her blue eyes were large and sad. "You used to enjoy my little jokes."

"This is hardly the time for any joke."

"Especially when it hits on the truth."

"Sandra!" he said quietly, warningly. He glanced at the door to the sitting room.

"Oh, forget it," she said wearily. She pulled her glasses back in place, not caring how she looked. "Shall I fold the original in three, or does Trouin usually quarter his letters?" She had lifted the letter again, studying Trouin's embossed letterhead across its top. She noticed Lenoir's second glance at the connecting door. "This is *your* department, Fernand. Isn't it?"

"Yes. But Wahl will insist on seeing the letter."

"Did he bring gloves?" She was half laughing.

Lenoir made a gesture of impatience.

"Too bad. He will just have to read one of the copies. You don't supervise his work. Why should you let him interfere with yours?"

Lenoir looked at her quickly. Her face was as expressionless as her voice.

"What's he doing now?" she asked.

"Listening to a recording."

"Oh!" She shrugged. "How shall I fold this letter? In three? Or four?"

"In three." That was Trouin's custom. He watched her fold the sheet most carefully, and search for the two envelopes she had addressed, one long, one square in shape.

She chose the long one. It looked as if it had been handled, crushed in a pocket. "I managed to get plenty of finger marks on this, all untraceable, I hope. You'd better destroy the other one, Fernand. You'll find matches over on the table by that red velvet chair."

"You are remarkably thorough," he told her, taking the discarded envelope over to the fireplace. He studied its typed address: Major Christopher Holland, Paris 6e, Boulevard Raspail, Hotel Saint-Denis. "Yes, we'd better get rid of this."

She talked on in the same light voice. Adroitly, she slipped the original under a box of carbon paper, picked up one of the copies and folded it silently, inserting it into the long envelope. "I suppose you can explain why there was no postmark? That may be the one weak point."

"Not so weak. The letter was intercepted before it could be mailed." He cursed quietly. "The matches are damp."

They ought to be, she thought grimly. She said, "Oh, everything is damp around here. I don't know how these books survive." Her fingers trembled on the long envelope she had just sealed. "Try my lighter." She reached for her handbag, placing it beside the box of carbon paper.

She opened it, searched inside with one hand. With the other, she slipped the original out of its hiding place into her bag. She snapped it shut.

"These matches are useless!" Lenoir exploded as the third one flared and died.

"Here's the lighter," she said, bringing it to him.

I really shall miss her, he thought. I have come to depend on her a great deal. That wasn't good, of course. That could be the reason she was being recalled. "It's all right," he said, striking another match. Yes, he was being disciplined more than she was. It was Wahl's way of reminding him who held the power. The idea displeased him. He frowned angrily.

"Wouldn't this be quicker?" she asked, holding out the lighter. He will begin to realize I dampened those matches, she thought anxiously.

"It's all right," he told her sharply, and the match, miraculously, flared and caught. The envelope curled slowly into black tissue. Once the address was destroyed, he dropped it into the fireplace and ground it into dust with his foot. "Where's the original?" he asked, excessively efficient now, avoiding her eyes. Quickly, he skirted the heavy armchairs and reached the writing table, pushed her handbag aside and picked up the sealed envelope. He pointed to the seven copies. "Better get them into envelopes, too," he said as he crossed over to a wall of bookcases.

She came back to her chair, and as she sat down again she felt her legs tremble for a brief moment. She dropped her handbag back on the floor and began folding the copies. She didn't look at Lenoir. She could hear him swinging open three bogus shelves to reach the wall-safe behind them. It was part of the Ca' Longhi furnishings, to match the heavy inch-wide bars on the downstairs windows and the huge bolts on the doors. The Longhi family must have been almost as security-minded as Fernand, she thought. That was why he had chosen to rent this hideous place. No garden, or terrace; just thick walls rising at the junction of two canals, one big, one small. The main entrance was on the dreary little canal, with slimy steps to reach the massive, nail-studded door. And at the back of the huge house, two more doors equally sturdy: one leading into a street so narrow and shadowed that even Fernand had joked about an assassin's lane; the other opening into a small square with flagstones uneven and tilting and the surrounding houses so covered with cracked and stripped plaster that they seemed to be sinking, too. And let's not forget the washing, she reminded herself, strung out from windows: all our neighbors' nightshirts and underpants. Venice . . . She began sealing the letters, angrily. She felt cheated. Venice could be so many things, and she had been given its worst for her last few days.

"I know what happened to the Longhi family," she said, sealing the fourth envelope. "They all died of galloping consumption. I'm chilled to the bone. What about setting the dining room on fire to get some warmth into these walls?"

Lenoir was smiling as he turned away from the safe and swung the bookshelves back into place. Quickly, the smile vanished. Coldly, he said, "The Longhi clan? Bourgeois capitalists adopting the trappings of feudalism. Twice damned, my dear Sandra. Their death was merely a matter of historical inevitability: the self-elimination of the obsolete."

I know who has just come in, she told herself. She forced herself to glance up casually. Robert Wahl stood just inside the room. Everything he does, she thought angrily, is for an effect. Can't he enter a room normally? We are supposed to be his friends. Friends? No, we are his comrades. His behavior is correct. For comrades. Eternal distrust, hidden faces, smothered voices. Comrades. How bitter I have become, she thought as she watched the man who had made her bitter. She wished, suddenly, she were eight years younger, filled with hope and belief. There had been rapture and excitement eight years ago, lifting, sustaining. . . . The worst thing I ever did was to leave America: I would still have been a good Communist if I had stayed there, happily drugged with my hopes and beliefs that were never put to the real test. But here in Europe, I was promoted. I met the elite group, the gray eminence behind the commissar's chair. And hopes have been replaced by fears. Beliefs are tortured ghosts haunting every waking hour, driving me back. Back to a new beginning? Shall I find it in America? Probably not. It will be enough if I can stop fearing.

Robert Wahl said nothing. He walked over to the desk, picked up one of the unsealed copies, read it—Fernand dancing attendance, explaining that the original was locked safely away, all under control, everything according to plan. Oh shut up, Fernand, just *tell* him and stop excusing yourself! And she looked at Wahl and she was pleading, silently, "Give me back those eight years." Aloud, she said, "Good evening, Comrade Wahl."

"So punctilious?" he asked. "And very busy, I see." His eyes noted everything, even the little heap of jewelry on the table. "You do act your part, Sandra. A most efficient secretary."

"I hope so," she said, with marked modesty.

He let the copy fall, drift back onto the table. "When you have finished, please come into the next room," he told her. The smile was as meaningless as his "please."

She nodded, and went on with her work. The two men left, Fernand casting a look over his shoulder that told her quite plainly, "And no more jokes!"

Strange, she thought, as she cleared the table, pulled off her gloves and straightened her sleeves, fastened her jewelry in place again, strange that I seem to make so many bitter jokes nowadays. Because when I lived in America, and had my hopes and beliefs and paid my dues and did what I was told, I never made any jokes at all. That was one of the things Bill used to tease me about: no sense of humor. Perhaps I ought to be grateful to Wahl and Fernand and all those others—in Czechoslovakia, Moscow, East Germany—for one thing at least: developing a sense of humor in me, even if it is sour. She picked up her handbag to find a comb and her powder box. From the drawer of the writing table, she drew out the folded map of Venice she had placed there carefully that morning. She slipped it into her opened bag, seemingly searching for her lipstick as her fingers inserted the letter deep and safe, into the map's fold. She colored her lips with a bold red, closed her handbag (the map looked innocuous), slung it over her forearm nonchalantly. She gathered up the little bundle of seven envelopes with seven copies of Fernand's masterpiece. I'm ready, she thought as she went toward the connecting door. What have they been discussing, those two? Me, no doubt.

Yes.

"I'm going to miss Sandra," Fernand Lenoir had begun. And regretted his frankness. So he qualified his regret. "She has been useful in many ways. Why don't you trust her?"

"Because she cannot be trusted," Robert Wahl told him shortly, and left it there. The full answer was, "Because anyone who could betray her country, as she has done for fourteen years, could betray us, too." But he couldn't give the blunt truth: Lenoir was in the same category—a Frenchman who worked for Soviet Russia. That was something these people never understood: no matter how well they worked, there was always that initial stain of treason, recorded deep in the memories of those who had to work with them. All was grist for the mill; but the mill separated the wheat from the chaff.

Lenoir felt the silent criticism emanating from the small, sharp eyes. That had been a mistake to ask why she wasn't trusted, a dangerous error. He, working so closely with her, ought to have been the first to become suspicious. "I only asked to see if your reason coincided with mine."

"You don't trust Comrade Fane either?" Wahl asked smoothly.

"Recently—well, she is too restless, too cynical. Paris has been bad for her." He paused, phrasing a tactful denunciation which would not be marked permanently against him, in case Sandra's rehabilitation in Moscow's purer air might even set her over him at some future date. "It is an unsettling place for those who do not belong there." As I do. And he looked at Wahl.

"Only temporarily unsettling, we hope. The role she played, these last three years, brought her into contact with our enemies. They have been sympathetic, admiring. Her vanity is inflated. Very dangerous. Her judgment is not as detached as it once was. Life has become too soft, too pleasant. Weakening."

"Yes, I've felt that she was forgetting the realities of the situation. In fact, I had prepared a report on her behavior, but it's hardly necessary now."

"Why?"

"Well—your report to Moscow must have covered all my points."

"No doubt. Still, I would like to read them. You would see the development of her deterioration more closely than most."

"You'll have that report." He could write it late tonight. Denunciation must be firm, tempered with sadness over the falling from grace, with hope for quick and complete rehabilitation. That should cover every possibility: past, present, and future.

"How much have you told her in this last week?"

"Only the necessary. No more than that."

"You placed that letter in the safe yourself?"

"Of course."

"Its signature is completely adequate?"

"It is practically authentic." Lenoir was becoming impatient. "I hope everything else goes as well," he said pointedly. Not one compliment about the wording of the letter, not one small admission of its excellence.

"I hope so, too," Wahl murmured with ironic modesty.

It was one of the little habits he had adopted in the West. It irritated Lenoir: the tone of voice was wrong, the smile unnecessary. Wahl's subtleties lay in a different sphere. Lenoir looked at the machine still lying on the table at Wahl's elbow. "Did you find anything remarkable in the rest of the journey?"

"Fenner never returned to Langley's room."

"You seem surprised." And I could have told you that. I listened to a quick run-through of all three recorded wires this morning. The only part worth slowing down to hear was at the beginning of the second wire, an hour of talk between ten and eleven last night. The rest— Lenoir shrugged at the waste of three precisely timed microphones. He allowed himself a touch of sarcasm. "The girl fell asleep. That does happen, you know."

"But does an American give up so easily? Was he aware that they were being recorded? If so, this was an excellent plan to guard their tongues."

Lenoir heard the library door open behind him. "Sandra can tell you more about Fenner's love-making than I can."

"Come in!" Wahl said. She had halted at the sneer in Lenoir's voice. Stupid pig, Wahl thought, he has warned her. Damn all those clever Frenchmen; they can't resist the right tone of voice at the wrong time. "Come in, Sandra, we need your advice. Sit over there. I am going to play a little recording for you. It was made last night. On a train. Listen!" She nodded, handed the envelopes to Lenoir, took the chair opposite Wahl. He turned on the machine, watching her face. Into the quiet room came the sound of a door opening, a man's voice (distant, blurred) saying, "See you in five minutes. I'll get those forms. And a nightcap." The door rattled shut. Movements and rustle and a sighing yawn.

Sandra Fane waited patiently, obediently, conscious of Wahl's eyes. Lenoir was restless. And at last, there was the sound of a door opening, closing. A woman's voice welcomed the man with "Darling, how wonderful . . ."

Sandra's eyes widened. Could that be Claire Langley? And the man answering her—yes, that was Bill Fenner. She let an amused smile lift one corner of her mouth, raised her eyebrows slightly. Wahl motioned abruptly for silence, for attention. And he kept watching her. At last, the voices ended. There was nothing but the rhythm and rattle of the hurrying train.

Lenoir glanced covertly at his watch. It was half past six. He had two more men to see this evening—the Roman newspaperman, then Mike Ballard. He would have to snatch a bite to eat in between these appointments: Ballard would need careful handling—that unexpected return to Paris yesterday, and the quarrel with Spitzer raised new difficulties. Still, he could be handled. He was the fish that was hooked but had to be played carefully before he could be gaffed and netted. After that, there was the final co-ordination of his story, and the report on Sandra to write. She was losing interest, now, in the steady pounding of train wheels. Wahl was still listening intently. Lenoir wondered at his infinite patience.

Wahl switched off the machine. "Et cetera, et cetera," he said lightly. He was pleased. He looked at them both and smiled. "That was the most important part of the whole recording." And as both of them kept silent, he added, "Because, *if* their whole conversation had been a performance, if there had been no black nightdress, no attack of sleep—" he paused for emphasis—"that was the time, once Fenner had left her, for the Langley woman to prepare for bed and lock her door. There was a slight rustle, I thought, but it stopped. Not enough to explain any undressing. Possibly she was turning in her sleep."

Lenoir sat corrected. Sandra looked at the emerald on her third finger. So Rosenfeld had sent not only Fenner, but Claire Langley with him. Rosenfeld had taken her seriously, that was certain. She almost sighed in relief. She studied the deep green of her ring: how much would it bring her?

Wahl said, watching her, "Does your ex-husband sound quite natural?" She looked up at him, openly amazed. "Really—" She shrugged her shoulders. "I haven't seen him in eight years. I'm no longer any judge—"

"But from your memory of him?"

"He is interested in Claire Langley definitely—for the next few weeks."

Lenoir glanced at her sharply. Could she be jealous? There had been a touch of the cat's claw there.

"Would he have let you fall asleep?" Wahl insisted.

Lenoir said, "Sandra is not the type to fall asleep."

"I am serious!" Wahl warned them. "Answer me, Sandra."

"It would depend on his mood," she said evasively.

"Was he impulsive about women?"

"It's eight years—look, I haven't been following his career."

"When did he meet this woman?"

"I've no idea."

"Not in New York then?"

"He could have met her there. It has been eight years—"

"So we've heard," Wahl said sharply. "You knew her in New York?"

"Yes."

"Her politics?"

Sandra could smile. "Politically immature."

"Why did you invite her to your parties?"

"She came with a friend from the British Embassy."

"You had no suspicions about her?"

"Why should I? She's one of those ornamental girls without a notion of politics."

"You once gave that same appearance, my dear Sandra, when you first lived in New York." He studied her with cold eyes. "So she accepted your story in Paris. How?"

"She asked the same polite questions that everyone asked, and I gave the same sincere, sad answer. It was all part of my return to the West."

"Did you ever think, or feel, that she could be possibly working for American Intelligence?"

"Langley?" Sandra looked amused. "She is totally brainless. Of course, that might be a recommendation for the CIA to pick her."

Lenoir was smiling. "Not altogether brainless. She holds an important job as a designer. Spitzer sent me a report—"

"That's merely being artistic," Sandra cut in. "Since when did either of you credit artists with brain power?"

"True," Wahl said, "but what did Spitzer report?"

"Her firm is completely legitimate. She heads its European branch, lives in Paris. Spitzer tells me that Fenner stayed at her flat on Friday night."

"Does she have many visitors? And who?"

"There hasn't been time to check on the details of her life in Paris. Spitzer reports she is a widow. Her husband was killed in Saigon. In 1953."

"Langley." Wahl was searching his memory. "James Langley. Yes, I remember." What he remembered did not please him. "There was an investigation, a very close investigation." Too close, he thought. That newspaper report with his name boldly printed . . . What was the name of the CIA man who had leaked Kalganov to the press? Rennie. Frank Rennie, a so-called businessman. He had known Langley's widow. Yes, they had become friends. . . . "So," he said pleasantly, aware that Sandra and Lenoir were watching him curiously, "you found nothing that puzzled you in that train conversation?"

Sandra said, "The only puzzle was that you should have been interested in those two."

"Indeed." He half smiled. To Lenoir, he said, "And Fenner?"

"We've checked his movements since he arrived in Paris. There are explanations and reasons for all of them. Still, he could be a very clever operator. The girl is harmless, I think. But he may be dangerous."

Sandra Fane was aware of Wahl's eyes on her face. Were his ears as quick? Had he heard the missed beat in her heart? "Bill Fenner?" She began to laugh. "Bill as an agent of the CIA?"

"Or Military Intelligence. Carlson was seen at his hotel."

"With him?" she asked in alarm.

"They both left the Crillon on Friday evening about the same time."

"Together?" Sandra's heart missed a second beat. Stupid, stupid fools. Wahl did not answer that.

"Not exactly," Lenoir said. "We can't be sure though. That is the trouble with Fenner. We can't be sure of anything about him. Did he intercept the money? Or was the exchanged coat a completely innocent mistake? I'm inclined to think it wasn't—"

"Perhaps you are inclined to read too much into his actions," Wahl said coldly. "There is no room in our work for emotions." He looked angrily at Sandra Fane. Had she thought she would safeguard herself by making Lenoir fall in love with her? Yes, it was time for her to be disciplined. Did she guess what he was thinking? For she had turned pale. She was sitting too still.

Sandra recovered herself. "What's this—about the coat and the money?" She asked Lenoir, "Do you mean Fenner was there when the money disappeared at Orly?"

"It was his coat that was exchanged with Goldsmith's."

She stared at him. And I had to choose Fenner as my contact in Venice, she thought: I had to suggest his name to Rosenfeld. This time, she couldn't control her laughter. This time, it was real. It pealed on, and on, uncontrolled, uncontrollable.

Wahl raised his voice. "Stop that! Stop it!" Was the idea of Fenner as an Intelligence agent so absurd? "This is no time for hysteria," he said acidly, well aware that Lenoir was as startled by her outburst as he had been. She was not a woman who behaved like this normally. Yet the laughter was normal in the sense that it was natural, unpretended. She had not been acting; of that, he was sure. He rose and crossed quickly to where she sat. She got control of herself. She opened her handbag and searched for her handkerchief to wipe the tears of laughter from her eyes. Her fingers touched the map, and the thought of its contents—of her careful plans and calculated risks, of Rosenfeld seeking out Fenner at her suggestion, Fenner the natural suspect for the master of suspicion now standing over her—set her laughing once more. Wahl struck a smart blow at her cheek. There was a sudden silence, ended by the snap of her handbag as she closed it.

Lenoir was saying indignantly, "I see nothing comic in my remark, Sandra."

"But you do not know Fenner as she does," Wahl said thoughtfully. "Have today's reports come in yet?"

"There was nothing in them."

"Let me see them."

Lenoir left the room. Wahl sat down again, pulling his cuff back into place.

Sandra Fane was rubbing her cheek. "What has gone wrong, Comrade Wahl?"

He stared at her. "Nothing. All is in order."

"But why are you worrying so much about Fenner and Claire Langley? I thought Venice was to be a place where we could wait safely until the Big Bang went off."

"We do not need flippancy."

"Just a circumlocution. In case," she was smiling, "Bill Fenner has installed a microphone in this room."

"You take this too lightly, I think."

One could never tell, she thought, how this man would react. She had been wrong, there, to joke about Fenner. "No," she said quickly, seriously, "I am worried."

"Why?"

"Because you are."

"Very sympathetic of you." From sardonic irony, he passed to outright challenge. "But perhaps *your* mistakes are really the cause of your worry?"

"Mistakes?"

"Such as sending the gondola that belongs to the Ca' Longhi to pick up Sir Felix Tarns today. Was that necessary?"

"He—he expected it," she said weakly. "Last spring we sent the gondola for him. He assumed—" Her eyes turned thankfully to the door, to watch Lenoir's return.

"He assumes too much. Pamper his vanity, yes—but not when it could endanger this house. That was a very foolish, a very stupid mistake. We pay for his hotel. Let him pay for his own transportation." He took the two sheets of paper that Lenoir held out to him. "Is this all?"

"My condensed notes," Lenoir explained.

Wahl glanced down the page. He pursed his lips. "Sir Felix thinks they are two simple-minded Americans. That almost makes me believe they are as clever as I thought they might be." He read on. "Nothing much here," he conceded. "No contact with anyone except the gondolier—who is this Zorzi?"

"Just a gondolier who knew the girl from a previous visit. He offered them a ride, but they were going to the Lido—"

"I can read. So"—he turned the page—"they are planning to hire his gondola tonight? At ten."

"That was too openly discussed to be significant."

Wahl said nothing, read on. "No contacts at all. Completely absorbed in each other," he observed. Then he saw something that really impressed him. "Aarvan says that Fenner showed no sign whatsoever of recognition." But he didn't like the way they had run for a bus and refused his taxi. Or the way they had left the Lido by motorboat before they could be followed. He read those items aloud, interspersed with his own opinions on stupidity. "And what's so funny about that?" he asked Sandra Fane sharply, catching her off guard.

She rallied quickly. "It's all so normal. If a bus is leaving, you have to run for it. And why take a taxi for the few blocks to the Excelsior?" She couldn't tell whether this suggestion was accepted. A bigger furrow was gathering on his brow as he read the last item on Lenoir's report sheet.

"So they changed their rooms, did they? Too expensive—" He rose abruptly, and swore.

"That sounds the truth," Sandra said. "Fenner isn't a rich man. And his expense account from the *Chronicle* wouldn't keep Fernand in shirts. It's just as I told you: he is—" She flinched as Wahl turned on her, stood looking down at her. And so she changed her tactics. "Oh, why don't you get rid of him and save all this argument? You are wasting time, Comrade Wahl."

Lenoir agreed. "One call to Aarvan, and this problem would be solved."

"And create a bigger problem for ourselves? Perhaps needlessly? For the next twenty-four hours, we do not want any more violence. Nothing to stir up the Venetian police—so far, we have broken no Italian law. And as for our other opponents—they have no idea that I am in Venice. Or that Aarvan is here."

"They know I am here," Lenoir said worriedly. "That is no secret."

"They don't know this address. And what could they possibly have against you? Nothing. You had no connection with the bombing of the Café Racine. Or with the American's death on the Simplon Express."

"Why did Aarvan have to—" Lenoir began.

"Carlson was an Intelligence agent much too interested in Robert Wahl. He was also much too interested in Aarvan. He had to be eliminated for our safety. Just as Vaugiroud and Roussin had to be eliminated for your safety, my friend." He looked pointedly at Lenoir, reminding him of an assignment in 1944 that had not been properly finished. "You are needed in France. We have spent too many years in establishing you there to let anything destroy you now."

Lenoir nodded. He had no more criticisms.

"And so, Fenner's death would certainly cause us more trouble than it's worth. Unless he threatened our safety, of course. I don't think he can. Not for the next twenty-four hours, at least. And that is all that matters."

Twenty-four hours? Sandra's mind groped for an explanation.

"One more day is all we need," Wahl said quietly.

"You mean—" she began, and couldn't finish.

"We are ready, aren't we? The longer we wait, the greater the danger. So I have moved our timetable forward."

Lenoir's eyes were brilliant with excitement. He couldn't resist saying to Sandra, "You see why we worked so hard today?"

Wahl silenced him with a sharp gesture. He made the announcement himself. "The assassination will take place tomorrow evening as De Gaulle leaves Paris for his country house. I saw Trouin in Zurich last night. I had him make the telephone call to Montpellier to give the signal to his friends, who have been waiting there for the last two days. They are, at this very minute, en route to Paris. Separately."

Sandra Fane's mind went completely blank. And then it raced madly along on its own train of thought, while she sat calmly smiling. Tomorrow was Monday, the day she had chosen to meet Fenner in the Piazza San Marco. Tomorrow evening. Tomorrow. Dimly, in the background of her crumbling hopes, she was aware of Lenoir's anxious questions about Trouin, the go-between, the man who knew them. Vaguely, she heard Wahl's impatient reassurances: Trouin's bank account was swollen by a hundred-thousand-dollar check; Trouin's suicide would be staged at the time of the publication of the letter, with Major Holland's supposed reply; and Trouin's friend the industrialist would not return from his vacation in Spain. But there was one thing that worried Wahl, and that was Lenoir's story about the interception of Trouin's letter to Holland. He wanted it altered.

That brought Sandra out of her half-attention. "Altered?" So he was finding some excuse to look at the original letter.

"It is inadequate."

"What?" asked Lenoir indignantly. "It's excellent."

"Your present story, Fernand, is that you were much perturbed by the American backing of the Generals' Revolt last April in Algeria; that you had heard rumors of Trouin's connections with American and British agents which aroused your suspicions; that you arranged to meet him casually at a small restaurant; that you came away from that meeting with your suspicions increased; that you hired a detective to watch him and make contacts in his office; that one of those contacts, a secretary, intercepted a letter on Friday just before it was mailed—the address made her suspicious; that your detective sent this letter to you in Venice; that you decided it ought to be turned over to the Sûreté but, just as you were telephoning Paris, the news of the assassination came through."

"And what's wrong with that story? Within a week, I don't think any questions will be asked at all. That is the great advantage of victory: those who win can write the history books."

Were they so sure of victory? Sandra wondered. They must be strong to speak so confidently. How many years had Wahl planned for such a complete take-over? Dismay attacked her; she felt new doubts, a sense of stupidity. I've chosen the losing side, she thought bitterly. I threw everything away in one small mistake. I thought that Wahl had over-stepped his authority, that his ambition would be disciplined, that, as a Stalinist and Leftist opportunist, his days were shortening. They will be, if he fails: he will be disowned, denounced, recalled, sent to Mongolia or the Arctic in some minor job. But if he produces a *fait accompli?* It will be called the inevitability of history. It will be accepted; his methods will be ignored. And he will be a hero of the revolution.

Wahl was repeating, "It is inadequate. It would seem that either your detective delayed in sending the letter to you or that you delayed in calling the Sûreté."

"I can explain the delay—a matter of embarrassment that a hired detective went far beyond my instructions and actually intercepted—"

Wahl was deeply amused. "Always the gentleman, Fernand. In that case, you will like my suggestion: your detective photographed the letter in Trouin's office, and sent you the negative of the film. You needed time to have it developed. And in this way, no explanation will be needed."

"And the letter itself?" Lenoir asked.

Sandra Fane kept her face calm, but interested. As she should be. Wahl was watching her. Stay out of this discussion, her instinct warned her.

"I shall send it to Paris tonight, and have it placed in Major Holland's hotel room. The Sûreté will discover it there."

"But Holland?" Lenoir objected.

"He is away for the weekend. The English habits are ingrained."

"Leaving the letter behind him?"

"Leaving it very safely concealed. You wouldn't expect him to travel with it?"

"It's a good idea," Lenoir admitted slowly, "but it's a big job. If I were in Paris, I would have reliable help to photograph the letter, develop the film. Here? We'd have to do it ourselves." His resentment grew. Everything had been perfect. Why had this change to be made? "And all Sandra's typed copies will be useless. We'll need prints to distribute, won't we? And we can't let the letter leave for Paris until we are sure the prints are clear."

Sandra said nothing at all. Clever, clever Wahl, she was thinking: he wants to see the original letter. He wants it out of the safe, and into his own hands. For a moment, she almost abdicated: everything was lost, not only escape, but life itself. She almost opened her handbag and drew out the map; almost said, "Here is what you want, Comrade Kalganov."

"Any objections, Sandra?" Wahl asked.

I won't give up my life so easily, she thought. "None. It will be a lot of extra trouble, but we can do it—if we work all evening."

"Sandra!" Lenoir said. "You know I can't—"

"We've been trained for this kind of job," she told him. "It's only a matter of time. We have the equipment and the supplies."

"You know that I—"

"You could manage it if you started work on it right away."

"I have two appointments," Lenoir said in rising anger.

"You can cancel them." Her voice sharpened, too.

"Impossible!" he exploded. "I must see these men tonight, and you know that!"

She stormed back, "I can't do this job alone. I'm willing to work all night, if necessary, if Comrade Wahl wants the letter treated his way—"

"Not," said Wahl, breaking into the argument, "to the point of having you two quarrel about it." He looked at Lenoir. "That was scarcely your diplomatic best."

Lenoir's thin face flushed. "Sandra," he said severely, regaining control of the situation, "there was no need to scream at me."

"I'm sorry." Her voice was still on edge. "I'm tired. You know that. I've been chained to that damned desk all day."

"*All* day?"

"Most of it," she snapped back. Lenoir was completely silenced this time: his eyes were childlike in their astonishment. She waited, thinking, I have given Wahl his cue: will he use it, will he tell me that I obviously need a vacation, a sea voyage? Or a nice trip by plane? Let him tell me, she willed: I have to know what time I have left, what I can plan. I'm fighting for my life. At least, I made a point there, and Wahl has taken it: I do not seem to be afraid of having the safe opened, the envelope taken out, the exchange noticed; and he has dropped his suggestion, his bright little idea to interfere and check and probe. He has his instincts, this man: he feels something is wrong. And he is searching. Attack and retreat, that was his technique to confuse and frighten. He has retreated about the letter. Now he is going to attack again. But even if my nerves are at snapping point, I still have enough control left to seize a small advantage, to avoid a definite danger: my instincts are as good as his. We are well matched. Beside us, Fernand—who is the most brilliant man I have ever met, more intelligent than this clever animal opposite me— is stupid and slow thinking. He hasn't sensed yet that I have made him look as if he were the one who did not want the envelope opened. For a split second, she had the vision of getting rid of the letter in her bag by slipping it into one of Fernand's suitcases: the fleeting idea amused her. Generously, she smiled at Lenoir. "I am sorry, Fernand. I was not complaining. Can't I be tired—just a little?"

Wahl said slowly, as if she had left the room, "Sandra is worrying too much. She needs a rest. A change of air. There is a ship sailing from here—a pleasant voyage through the Corinth Canal, the Greek islands, to Istanbul." He paused. "And to Odessa." He paused again. "Sandra will sail on it. Tomorrow morning at eight. From the Giudecca."

"Tomorrow morning?" Her voice faltered. She looked at Lenoir, who avoided her eyes. "Hasn't my work pleased you?"

The telephone rang. Lenoir jumped to his feet. "I'll take the call next door," he said. "And put these safely away." He lifted the seven envelopes, and hurried from the room.

"My dear Sandra," Wahl said, "your recall is in no way a reprimand. It will lead to promotion." He watched her carefully. "Don't you want to return to Russia?"

"It's—it's just so unexpected."

There was no doubt of her blank astonishment, numbed shock. Wahl was well pleased. We'll have her safely on board before she realizes all the implications, he thought. "I think you should leave here when it's dark. Around midnight."

Tonight. Leave tonight . . . She could only stare at him.

"There will be a motorboat waiting for you at the canal door. Twelve o'clock. You will be ready?"

She nodded. Lenoir had returned to the room. She looked down at the emerald ring. I have until midnight, she was thinking. Until midnight.

Wahl was asking Lenoir about the call. It had been a report on a brief conversation between Fenner and Langley in her terrace room at the Vittoria. "Nothing very much," Lenoir judged. "The girl was very upset about some other man. I've given orders to stop watching them. We are wasting our—"

"Upset?" Wahl asked quickly. That was always a vulnerable time. "Did you make a transcript?"

"Of course." Lenoir handed over a few scrawled sentences. Wahl frowned over them.

"A lover's quarrel, perhaps," Lenoir suggested.

"As meaningless as most," Wahl agreed. Who didn't have to come to Venice? he wondered. Who wouldn't have—if it hadn't been for Claire Langley? Whose death was her fault? Death. Had she known Carlson? If only we had time to check on all her past history, he thought. "I'll take this with me," he said, pocketing the piece of paper. "I must leave. The gondola is waiting?"

"For the last hour. But that's quite usual in Venice."

"And it isn't your private gondola," he told Sandra, smiling. He patted her shoulder. "My congratulations. And a very pleasant journey."

Congratulations? On the promotion he had dangled before her? She could have struck these smirking lips. "Good-by, Comrade Kalganov," she said. He stopped, looked at her, his face frozen for one brief instant. Then he was walking to the door, his arm around Lenoir's shoulders. They were talking of other matters.

"She took it very well," Lenoir remarked as they went down the curving sweep of grand staircase into the dark, flagstoned hall.

"Just treat her normally. Keep her calm. Arouse no animosity. Women have long claws."

"She'll give no trouble," Lenoir assured him.

"I wish we could say the same for that American newspaperman, Ballard. I thought it was rash of you, Fernand, to bring him to Venice."

"Not too rash. He tried to discharge André Spitzer yesterday. So I had no choice. I had to make direct personal contact with him. Don't worry, Robert. I know how to approach that type of man."

"It might help if Aarvan were to make the first approach, so that by the time you see Ballard tonight, he would be more—malleable. At least you would know what to expect from him. If he is totally intransigent with Aarvan, I would advise you do not see him at all. We'll deal with him."

"All right. But you had better tell Aarvan to contact him at once. He is staying at the Danieli."

"I know. I have already told Aarvan to keep an eye on him." Wahl's smile was disarming. "By the way, I may need one of your attic rooms, with a strongly shuttered window. Someplace where we could keep a guest hidden until tomorrow evening?"

"Who?" Lenoir was still annoyed with Wahl's interference in the handling of Ballard.

"Fenner's little friend. That should immobilize them both for the next twenty-four hours, quietly, efficiently."

"Quietly? He will go to the police—"

"He will not. Because if he does, he will never see her again. He will be so informed."

"I don't like this—"

"She will never know where she was held, or who was her host. Instruct a servant to guard her room. That's all you have to do. *You* keep out of sight."

"But how—"

"I shall make the arrangements."

Lenoir stared at him. There was no arguing with Wahl in this mood. What had he against this girl?

"That terrace room at the Vittoria would have made everything simpler," Wahl was saying, "but there are other means. Expect her some time after ten o'clock. By the canal door. Don't worry. Just keep out of her sight and hearing."

They had been talking quietly in the center of the round hall. Now Wahl moved toward the door that opened on the narrow street, picking up his coat and hat from a chair.

"This way," Lenoir said, pointing to the door that led out onto the canal.

"I shan't use the gondola. It has waited too long."

"As you wish." Strange man; I shall never know him, Lenoir was thinking as he followed Wahl across the stone floor and between the pillars that circled the hall. Suddenly, he felt alone. Without Sandra, he would be very alone. "Do you really think that Fenner and Claire Langley are dangerous?" he tried.

Wahl only shrugged his shoulders. He opened the door slightly, and listened. "I am making sure that they won't be. That is all." He looked out into the small, narrow street, sadly lighted by one lamp placed high on a far corner wall. "Cats," he said contemptuously, as shadows stirred and snarled to defend the food they had found in a black doorway, "cats and cold spaghetti." He glanced back at Lenoir. "I may send Aarvan to question the girl," he said softly. He pulled his hat well over his brow, turned up the collar of his coat, and stepped into the night. He walked quickly along the narrow *calle*, past the shuttered windows, still and dark. The cats were silent again.

Lenoir closed the heavy door. Strange man . . . He had walked in the direction of the canal, after all. Had he some other gondola or motorboat waiting for him? He trusts no one, Lenoir thought. Not even me?

The cats snarled, and two men in a darkened ground-floor room were sharply alert. Through the inch-wide crack of shutter, two pairs of eyes watched a man leave the Ca' Longhi. When he had passed, only an arm's length away, one of them moved carefully over to a telephone. His voice was low, English. "Gino? Roger here. Unidentified man has just left. Hat pulled down. Dark coat, collar turned up. About five feet six. Weight around thirteen stone. That's right, solid construction but light on his feet. Proceeding toward the canal. You'll pick him up at the bridge." He put down the receiver.

"Will they?" his companion asked. His voice also was low, but American. "Listen!" The roar of a motorboat was funneled along the little *calle,* and receded.

American and Englishman both cursed softly.

"Slippery beggar, whoever he was," the Englishman said. He made his way back to the window. "Any guesses?"

"We didn't see him enter. Must have been there before we got here. That's a long time."

"He sounds important. A motorboat waiting, ready to leave at high speed. Most illegal. The Gondoliers' Association will disapprove."

"Sounds like Wahl," the American said gloomily, "but he is in Switzerland." They settled into boredom again, to wait for the next visitor to Ca' Longhi.

Lenoir locked and bolted the heavy door before he hurried back upstairs. He found Sandra still in the sitting room. She hadn't moved. There were no tears, he noted in relief, no imploring eyes. "I must pack," she said, becoming aware of him. She rose, drawing her cardigan around her, cradling her handbag in her arms. "Or would you take me out to dinner for my last night?"

"You can't be serious!" He was aghast.

"Why not? You and I are known to be in Venice. Weren't we supposed to appear together, to look as if we were on vacation?"

"That was the plan." He emphasized the past tense. But within this last week there had been discovery of Vaugiroud, Roussin. Even Carlson's presence on a train that could take him to Venice had sounded an alarm. Perhaps needlessly. Still— "Be sensible, Sandra! I begin to see why Wahl wanted you recalled."

"Do you?" she asked, and paused at the door.

He frowned, puzzling out her hidden meaning.

"Strange," she murmured, "how everyone who can identify Kalganov is eliminated. Vaugiroud and Roussin. Carlson. They knew, didn't they?"

"Nonsense," he said stiffly.

"They are dead, aren't they?" She looked so wide-eyed and innocent, standing there at the door. "Is Kalganov so important? To whom? I'll tell you: he is important to Kalganov. That is his own private personality cult. You know, *he* could be recalled—for Leftist deviationism."

"Shall I tell him that?" he asked bluntly, and hoped the threat would silence her.

"But you couldn't, without mentioning his real name. You haven't done that once, to his face, in the three years I've known you. Stay clever, Fernand, and keep alive." She laughed unsteadily. "Good night. Or shall I see you again?"

"I have much to do," he said. "Good night, my dear."

He is afraid to see me again, she thought, afraid to listen. "Please try. It's our last evening together." She smiled and was gone. Good night and good-by, she thought. She climbed the stairs toward the bedroom floor, her face white and haggard.

She heard the echoing clang of a doorbell: Fernand's first visitor. That would give her at least an hour. Until half past nine. She had no plan, but time was more precious than any plan. First, get her coat, money, jewelry. Get away from this house, get out of Venice. She was on her own: Rosenfeld and all his schemes would have to take care of themselves. The hell with him and everything else. On the floor below her, she heard Fernand coming out to greet his visitor. An effusive welcome. Yes, this meeting would last a full hour; the stranger must be important. She wasted no more time, but quietly moved into her bedroom, quietly closed the door, quietly locked it.

TWENTY

At the Hotel Vittoria, Bill Fenner unpacked and surveyed his new room. There was not much of a view, but it was a comfortable place, all the more so because Claire was safely next door, and close by two of Rosie's men were installed. So Chris Holland had said. And that compensated for the dull courtyard outside, with its tightly shuttered dead windows.

He had a shower, shaved, and dressed slowly. There was no need to hurry. Claire needed some time to steady herself and be able to face the Piazza San Marco. She had insisted on keeping to his plans for the evening, and he hadn't argued with that. It was important, he knew, to establish the custom of having a drink at Florian's; even more so to stick to the timetable he had given Holland. That was a kind of insurance, he felt. He wondered, as he chose his best blue tie to add some newness to his stand-by dark-gray flannel suit, how many men and women were keeping an eye on their wanderings. "We" was a word that Chris had used constantly. Who were "we"? British and French, as well as Americans? Italians, too? Whoever we are, he decided, we have a comforting sound.

You've come a long way, he told the grave, worried face in the looking glass as he knotted his shantung tie neatly, a long way, indeed. You didn't find Holland's order to change rooms one bit comic or unnecessary. You just acted on it: and your only question is "What did happen in Budapest?"

I wish, he thought as he turned away from the glass to find his jacket, I wish that Claire would develop a howling cold, something to keep her safely in bed and out of all this. Damn Rosie for sending her along. Yet without her, I'd have been lost. In every way.

He checked his pockets. It was twenty-five minutes past six. Time to

639

move. He glanced around the room again, wishing that Sandra had chosen this evening for the meeting instead of tomorrow. Even the idea of another day's waiting was becoming intolerable.

The telephone rang. He thought it would be Claire, letting him know she was ready. But it was a man's voice. "Bill?" it said quickly.

"Speaking."

"Look, can I drop around and see you?"

It was Mike Ballard's voice. Fenner said in astonishment, "What the hell are you doing in Venice?"

"I flew in an hour ago. Look, Bill—"

"I'm just going out."

"This is so damned urgent—"

"You can't talk on the phone?"

"No." Ballard heaved a worried sigh.

"Why don't you join us at Florian's? We'll be at a table there, in ten minutes or so."

"Who'll be with you?" Ballard was anxious.

"Claire Langley."

"Just the two of you?" Ballard asked in relief.

"Yes."

"Sorry if I intrude—but I'll take your suggestion."

"You can take it for half an hour. Then get lost," Fenner said cheerfully.

"Thanks, Bill," Ballard's voice said earnestly. "Thanks a lot."

"It probably was a mistake. But I was caught at the end of a telephone, and couldn't think of an excuse," Fenner told Claire as they walked toward the Piazza. "He sounded so damned pathetic with that sigh of his." But there was no doubt that Ballard had made himself a useful topic of conversation. Claire had done her best to look normal: she was as smartly turned out as ever in a softly flowered dress of blues and greens, with her blue coat draped over her shoulders; her hair was perfect, brushed high yet neat, gleaming, smooth; her skin glowed, her make-up was skillful— there was no sign left of her violent tears; her eyes were clear and brilliant. This time, Fenner's admiration was not only for her beauty. He wondered a little, though, if this outward calm could last. It would not if she had really been in love with Carlson.

They made their way through a crowded little street filled with the sound of high heels and soft footsteps, with Sunday dresses and freshly pressed suits taking their small frills and furbelows for the weekly family stroll. (Walk a little, stop a little, talk a little, a pleasant evening to you and to me and to you, here we are all washed and polished, no work today, no worry, a man can saunter along with the richest of them and be proud of his own.) They squeezed through a cohort of families, and at last had some free space for talking.

"A mistake?" Claire asked quietly, still thinking of Ballard. "No. I don't think we'll drag him into any danger."

"I meant a mistake from my point of view. He'll bend our ear for an hour, try to join us at dinner." Also, Ballard's appearance in Venice at this time could lead to a really big mistake. Tomorrow evening, for instance, and Sandra, and that damned letter. She had suggested Ballard as one of her possible contacts, hadn't she? What if Ballard wandered into the Piazza San Marco tomorrow evening, sat at Florian's just as Sandra came strolling by? Fenner's pulse missed a beat.

"Yes?" asked Claire, sensing his worry. Her interest quickened.

"I'm just thinking of some way to keep Ballard out of the Piazza tomorrow evening."

"That's twenty-four hours away," she reassured him. "Mike may not even be in Venice tomorrow. And if he is, he may not be anywhere near Florian's at half past six on a Monday evening."

"I'd like to make sure of that." My nerves are raw, he thought, if I start worrying about something that could possibly, perhaps, take place if only.

"Then we'll send Chris another little note. And he can send Mike for a motorboat ride all around the lagoon. Or something." She slipped her hand into his, encouragingly. And he relaxed. He could even analyze that attack of excess worry. Tension had caused it, of course—tension over Neill Carlson and Claire. He looked at her and took a firmer grip of her hand. "I wonder," she was saying, "why Mike did come to Venice? What's troubling him, do you think?"

He gave her one of the answers only. "He has the idea that I'm out to get his job."

"He's an idiot!"

"Thank you."

"But, Bill—you wouldn't." She was quite decided about that.

"How do you know?" he asked teasingly.

"I know," she told him. He was surprised by the warmth in her eyes as she glanced at him. And that small smile was all for him, too. He entered the Piazza San Marco in the best possible tradition, a general state of mounting euphoria.

The vast rectangle of the Piazza stretched eastward before them, its two long sides edged with unbroken rows of gray Renaissance palaces rising above their arcades, and ended in a sunlit blaze of light and color, of domes and steeples and turrets resting on a mass of arches and pillars, mosaic and marble and carved stone. Four Greek horses were stepping high above the bronze doorway, giant even from this distance. Angels mounted with golden trumpets, gold banners curled from every point and pinnacle, gold crosses gleamed on every cupola; and Saint Mark himself rose into the sky over the golden lion with outstretched wings. It was more than a cathedral, Fenner thought; it was a shout of joy.

They had both halted involuntarily, before they stepped out of the arched colonnade at this western end of the Piazza and walked, as a thousand or more walked, slowly across the vast stretch of worn marble pavement. Close to the pillared arcades, there was a thick fringe of café tables and chairs, crowded with another thousand people. And another thousand or so were gathered thickly in the center of the Piazza, where the municipal band was giving a Sunday-evening concert and had silenced, temporarily, the sweet and swing music from the newer cafés. Florian's provided no music, having survived very nicely for more than two hundred years on the devotion of its clients and their ability to be amused by others. Its tables, spreading out into the Piazza in neat rows, were densely populated, mostly with well-dressed foreigners, but here and there was a small advance guard of real Venetians, venturing out to recapture their Piazza now that September had arrived.

Claire turned her head away from the mass of tables to look at the band. Very softly, she said, "I see Chris. And not far away is Rosie."

Fenner nodded. So Rosie, looking like a totally unperturbed and harmless tourist—tweed jacket, sports shirt, camera, Blue Guide, and all—had come to see how his two staked lambs were faring. Carlson's death was not only a personal loss; it had been a warning. Rosie, sitting over a drink at a small table, listening to the shimmering crescendos of *Swan Lake,* watching the pigeons soaring as drums ruffled and cymbals clashed, could only mean one thing: urgency.

"We're going to have trouble finding a table," he said, steering her casually past Sir Felix Tarns, who sat with two admiring friends in Florian's front row. Tomorrow night, Fenner thought, we must come here early and be prepared to sit and wait for Sandra. It might be a comic touch to arrive for an assignation and find no table vacant, but it was one that wouldn't appeal much to Rosie's sense of humor. Nor mine, nowadays: I wish to God that Claire was back in Paris.

"We're in luck! Someone is just leaving," she said delightedly.

Luck? Two men were rising from a front-row table just beside them. One was Pietro, starting his way as expertly into the crowd on the Piazza as he had steered his motorboat from the Lido back to Venice. He no longer wore his rakish Captain's hat, or his English tweed coat. His short, dark jacket, with sloping shoulders, was primly buttoned; his legs, thin in narrowly cut trousers, looked like a fencing master's. He and his friend merged perfectly with the hundreds of other dark-haired young men who wandered purposely, pleasantly, around the outcrops of pretty girls. We can use this kind of luck, thought Fenner, and captured the table just ahead of two elegant Frenchwomen, who looked at him with annoyance, waited to see if he would weaken, and at last retreated in an indignation of click-clacking high heels and jangling bracelets. He glanced after one of them briefly, kept surprise out of his face. Yes, that had been Miss Bikini, all right. Their luck in finding a table had been openly established, and very neatly. He saluted Rosie, mentally.

"Difficult to recognize with her clothes on," Claire murmured in agreement, as he helped her slip her coat from her shoulders. She pulled off her white gloves, laid them neatly on her dark-blue purse. Her hand rested briefly on its small, well-filled bulk. He had noticed, but he made no remark at all. "You've changed," she said. "You no longer joke about—" She looked at the purse, resting so innocently beside a mock-silver tray with its used glasses and the lire Pietro had left to cover the waiter's chit.

A joke was a good way to mock reality, to dodge an issue, to escape involvement, to twist an argument, to rout an opponent. Except that his opponents weren't men to be defeated by laughter; the argument ran too straight and deadly for any twisting; he was involved up to his eyebrows, perhaps even over his head; the issue was one that couldn't be dodged; and reality, the lurking face behind the mask of safety, was grim and unrelenting. "Tomorrow night," he told her, "I can start making jokes again." Tomorrow night, he thought, the mask goes back over the face of reality: I'll return to my normal world. "If you'll listen to them," he added.

She almost smiled, and looked away, watching the children playing silent hide-and-seek among the forest of grown-up legs. Fenner could study her unobserved for one long and perfect minute. The glow from the sunset sky fell gently over the Piazza, bathing stone and flesh in its golden shower. But the music ended, a waiter came for their order, voices around them were released from the occasional low murmur into a surge of talk, the children laughed out loud, the massed groups broke loose into whirls and eddies, and high on the clock tower, in one corner of the Piazza, two giant Moors began to strike the hour.

"Seven o'clock. Mike's late," Fenner said, as their booming sledge blows stopped, and the pigeons settled again.

Claire had been watching a round-bottomed two-year-old, well padded under his short white trousers, ankles stoutly held by short white boots, ending his dash for independence in a trip and plump, right at the feet of two tall Municipal Guards, with sashes and epaulettes, cocked hats, swords, and white-gloved hands clasped over the tails of their dark-blue coats. The child yelled as his buttocks and pride were jolted, fell into open-mouthed silence as his eyes traveled all the way up to the cockades on the hats. His father rushed in, to bend and pick up and solve a problem for uniformed dignity. There were smiles and bows all around. Claire's own smile widened, and she laughed. And like the child, she fell silent, staring at Fenner. "I laughed," she said in amazement, "I actually—" She halted, her eyes observing a distant table. "What was that you said about Mike Ballard?"

"He's late, blast him."

Her eyes veered slowly away from what she had noticed. She said softly, "He's here. He was early, I think. And someone joined him. No, don't turn around, Bill." Her hand had touched his arm before her warning ended, stopping the involuntary movement. "His table is at the back, near the arcade, just two rows behind Chris."

Laughter might be a limited weapon, Fenner was thinking, but it was good medicine. Claire was no longer remote, withdrawn: some of her vivacity had returned, and all her quick intelligence. "Who is with him?" he asked.

"A man with very broad shoulders."

"What?"

"Yes. Give me a cigarette, Bill."

"And Chris hasn't recognized him?"

"I wouldn't have," she reminded him, "if you hadn't pointed him out today."

He sat quite silent. At last he said, "We've got to make Chris notice. He's a bright boy. He won't need much of a hint." He lit her cigarette carefully, and his own.

"But how?"

"I think I've got it."

"Bill—" she pleaded.

"Nothing to it," he reassured her. "All I need is a chance to turn around and see Ballard quite naturally."

She looked at him. "All right," she said, and let the cigarette slip from her fingers onto her lap. "Oh!" She half rose, abruptly, brushing the burning ash from her dress. He had risen, too, his chair toppling back with his speed. "It's all right," she assured him, her voice at its natural level. "I jumped just in time." So they could laugh, and she sat down again, saying, "How silly of me!" He turned to pick up his chair and put it back in

644

position. He looked at the curious and amused faces which glanced in their direction. And at the back of the rows of tables, just behind Chris, as she had warned him, he saw Ballard and Jan Aarvan.

"Why, there's Ballard!" he said clearly. "I think I'll let him know we're here. Won't be a minute, Claire." And there wasn't even a minute to waste: the band was tuning up again. Soon, voices wouldn't carry two rows of tables. He made his way quickly toward the arcade. He passed Chris Holland, didn't even glance at him. Aarvan was talking quietly, his back turned to the Piazza. Ballard, lost in his own world of trouble, could only stare blankly at Fenner as he approached them.

"Hello, Mike!" Fenner said. "We found a table at the front, just over there." He gestured toward Claire. "Thought I'd let you know in case you didn't see us arrive."

Aarvan had turned. It was a quick aggressive movement, from a man who thought in terms of danger. Rosie, playing with the view finder on his camera, had noted it. Chris, two rows to the front, could not look around. But he could hear.

"Say, haven't I seen you before?" Fenner asked Aarvan. "On a raft?"

Aarvan's brief show of interest had reverted to a cold stare.

"Yes," Fenner continued cheerfully, "that was it—out at the Lido today. Well—" he looked at the unhappy Ballard who had made no offer of an introduction—"see you later, Mike." He walked briskly away. Chris was examining his check and counting out some lire. Rosie had shut his camera and was waiting for the music to start.

Fenner dropped quietly into his seat as the first bars of *Sicilian Vespers* sounded over a silenced Piazza, noted with thankfulness that the waiter had brought their drinks, and gave Claire a reassuring smile. Why, he thought, in amazement, she was actually worrying about me. About me. Not about the job. About me. And he could calm down, forgetting the nervous tension that had tightened his stomach as he had faced Aarvan. That hadn't been as easy as he had pretended it to be. Now, he could admit that. It was one thing to be an actor, he decided; quite another to make up your lines as you went along. He had to wonder, of course, whether his action had been necessary. Or had he been foolish, had he made a mistake? Some men, judging from their assertions in newspapers and on television, always seemed to believe they were right, knew everything, and had chosen the only intelligent approach to any situation. Fenner could only hope that, out of the several approaches he could have made to this particular situation, he hadn't taken the worst one. It had been an instinctive action, arriving out of nowhere, startling him now as he had time to think about it.

"How was Mike?" asked Claire softly.

"Hopeless."

"If only he would stand up and fight—" She shook her head sadly. "There's no disgrace so great as the one he is heading into. Can't he see that?"

So she knew about Mike Ballard's particular mess of pottage. No need to avoid the topic any longer. "If we could make him see—" He paused, thinking over that, wondering if it could be possible and how.

"If he comes," she suggested.

"Sh!" said a music lover near them, ending their murmuring.

If he comes, Fenner thought morosely, Ballard will be one step farther into the net that Fernand Lenoir has spread for him. He began wondering how Jan Aarvan had entered this picture. Aarvan was Kalganov's man. Was Kalganov in Venice, taking full control?

The band was packing up, dusk was beginning, the balls of light suspended from each arch in the long arcades were being switched on, the crowds were having another stroll before they went home to supper; and Mike Ballard arrived. He had had one drink more than necessary. His manner was too jocular, too determinedly confident. "Well, well, well—" he began, pumped Fenner's hand, kissed Claire on the cheek and patted her arm. "Good to see you. Pretty picture you make, sitting there with Bill. Been admiring you from a distance."

"We thought you had forgotten about us," Claire said. She looked at him anxiously. He wasn't drunk. He could be, though, if he ordered anything more.

"Forgotten you? Never, my love." He pulled a chair over, and sat down. He glanced around him: the tables had become less crowded. Nearby, there were only two smartly dressed girls, with heavy bracelets that jangled as they talked with precise gestures. "French," Ballard noted. "You can always tell. Nothing like the French for that extra *je-ne-sais-quoi* touch of what-you-call-it."

Fenner looked at Miss Bikini and back at Mike Ballard. Let's get down to business, he thought. "What's the trouble, Mike?"

Ballard's eyes flickered away. "Trouble?" he asked vaguely. "Who hasn't got troubles?" His voice became louder. "Where's a waiter—what are you drinking?" He snapped his fingers furiously.

"We're all right," Fenner said. "You order some coffee, and we'll listen."

"Coffee? You sound like Eva."

"How is she?"

"And the children?" Claire asked, pressing Fenner's point still farther.

"Fine," Ballard said, avoiding her eyes, "just fine." The bluster left him. He stared down at the table. "They are good kids," he said dejectedly. He let Fenner order coffee without any further resistance. "Well," he said, trying to get back his first burst of enthusiasm, "and how is Venice treating you? Having fun?"

"Everyone has lots of fun in Venice," Fenner said. "Except you, seemingly. What's wrong?"

"Wrong?" Ballard tried a smile. "Nothing's wrong."

"Just over an hour ago, I had a telephone call. Remember? The man who made it sounded pretty worried, worried enough to make me invite him to join us here. But when he arrives, he hasn't a care in the world. He's here on false pretenses." Ballard looked at Fenner quickly. "Scram," Fenner told him with a smile. "Blow, disappear, vanish. Two's company, didn't you know?"

Ballard stared at him, completely off balance. For the last twenty minutes, since the stranger had left, Ballard had sat swallowing three double Scotches, working up his courage, his story, and his bile. He had been tempted to walk right past this table and keep Claire and Fenner out of this mess, or—if he did sit down—to forget the warning that had been sent to him through that cold-eyed stranger, and tell Fenner his troubles. As he had meant to do when he first walked into this Piazza. But that impulse must be choked back. He could sense the stranger's eyes still watching him from some safe distance. Who was he, who were the people who had sent him here? Friends of that beggar Spitzer, certainly. How else could a stranger threaten him so completely? Blackmail. It was blackmail, a quicksand with slobbering lips already sucking at his ankles. He had a return of the impulse to rise and walk away, saying the hell with all their threats. And then he thought of the kids, his job, Eva—and he sat still, trapped and helpless.

"Hold it, Bill," he said, feeling the sickliness of his forced grin after his long silence, "you don't chop off an old friend like that. Do you?" He turned to Claire. "By the way, you seem to have done well with those fashion drawings."

"Thank you," Claire said.

"Not at all. Glad to get you the job. Any time." His coffee arrived, and he gulped it down, scalding as it must have been. He drew out his cigarette case. His lighter matched it. Cuff links for his white silk shirt were of gold, too. Shot-silk tie from Florence. Silk tweed suit from Rome. Shoes, carefully displayed with a crossed leg, from London. Lenoir had supplied Ballard with more than a pretty mistress. Fenner and Claire exchanged a brief glance. He misinterpreted it. "So you are wondering why I'm in Venice? That's easy. There's a story to be dug out. I'm here to dig."

"And who is minding the store meanwhile?" Fenner asked. "Surely not that fellow Spitzer?"

"Oh, I'll be back in Paris tomorrow."

"You left Spitzer in charge?"

"Why not?"

Fenner just shook his head. Perhaps Ballard really did want to commit suicide.

"He's a bit too eager, that's all."

"Yes, eager for your job."

Ballard finished a second cup of coffee.

"Hadn't you thought of that?"

"No," Ballard said shortly. Spitzer and his friends weren't going to take away his job as long as he listened to them. That had been made quite clear. He added, "If so, he isn't the only one." He looked at Fenner.

Claire said, "Nonsense, Mike. You're an awful fool."

There was a pause. "I hope that was a joke," he said. So that's all the thanks I get, he thought bitterly.

"At present, you don't amuse me one bit," she said coldly. "You aren't the Mike Ballard I used to know."

He almost rose, hesitated, tried to laugh it off. "She's spoiling for a fight," he said to Fenner. "Have you been telling her tales about me?" Women always closed ranks against men. Claire was taking Eva's side. As if he hadn't been a good husband, a good provider, when he was in the money. Was all that to be forgotten because of one mistake?

"No need," Fenner said, glancing at the gold cigarette case. We're wasting our time and sympathy on this soft slob who'll persuade himself into believing anything just to hang on to his comforts. "Let's take a walk," he told Claire quietly. She didn't move. Her eyes seemed to say, "Wait, Bill, wait a little. . . ."

"Say, what's come over you two?" Ballard was really worried. Three questions, he remembered in immediate panic, and he hadn't even asked the first one.

"What has come over *you?*" Fenner asked bluntly.

"But—nothing."

"Why did you call me?"

Ballard saw an opening and plunged. "I'm worried. And I think I've good reason to worry. Bill, tell me—why did you come to Venice?" And I'm not just asking this for the stranger, he thought. I want to know the answer to this, too.

"You know why." Fenner was looking at him curiously.

"Those interviews? Bull— Sorry, Claire." He patted her arm and turned to Fenner again. "Does it matter a plugged nickel what a couple of neutralists think? You could write those interviews sitting here, or in Paris."

"I'd rather let them speak their little piece. Much more telling."

"You could have refused this assignment. You're not under any contract to write—"

Fenner cut in. "Who would refuse a week in Venice?"

"You're staying a week?"

"Wouldn't you?"

Ballard looked at Claire. "She'd fight with me," he said with a sudden grin.

Fenner picked up the tab that had been left tactfully under a saucer.

"Hey! What's the rush?"

Fenner said, "Your problems are over, aren't they? I've solved your worry. I'm not in Venice to take any story away from you. It's all yours, Mike. We're off to dinner."

Ballard's grin had faded. "So my problems are over." He looked at the lighted Piazza, at the men and women who walked and talked together, at the laughing children, at the crowds now gathering at one of the cafés opposite where a jazz band was stomping out a new version of *Tiger Rag*. "You two don't need to look so god-damned happy," he said bitterly. "It might do you more good to start looking for that story, Bill. Because you're in it. Somewhere, you're in it."

"In what?"

"You haven't an idea?" Ballard was incredulous.

"Not one."

"Why did Spitzer telephone a report on your plans? Yes . . . just after you left the office yesterday, he picked up the telephone and called Venice."

"He did that, in front of you?"

"Of course not."

"You caught him at it?"

"I'm not such a fool as some people think." Ballard glanced at Claire.

"And you let him get away with it?"

Ballard said testily, "Let me handle Spitzer my way."

"What way is that?" asked Fenner sharply. Ballard fell silent, his false confidence slipping. He looked the unhappiest man in the whole Piazza di San Marco. Which might be true, Fenner thought, and relented. Sympathetically, he added, "Who's behind Spitzer, Mike? Who got him into the office?"

"I hired him. He was highly recommended. Good qualifications, languages, all that. He's thoroughly capable, no doubt about it."

"Recommended by whom?"

"A friend of mine. You can take that look off your face, Bill. My friend had no personal interest in Spitzer, just heard about him. He will be as shocked as I am—"

"Who is this friend?"

"An important guy. Carries a lot of weight, has contacts. Will you listen to me? He's reliable. He has too big a career ahead of him to get mixed up with men like Spitzer. He has got brains, he has got standing."

"Hasn't he got a name? All right, all right. Your friend is an honorable man. He isn't trying to crucify you, in order to keep Spitzer planted in the *Chronicle* office."

Ballard's eyes widened. His lips closed tight. He said angrily, "My God, Bill, if we can't trust our friends, where are we? Look—this man has done a lot for me. He has done a lot for other people, too. You don't believe me? How do you think your wife stayed alive for those last three years? She was a refugee, no money, no friends—"

"Sandra Fane is not my wife."

"That's right." Ballard's eloquence went into high gear. "You and all other Americans were too good for her. When she needed help, did any of us give it? No, it was Lenoir who had the guts to help her start a new life. Would a Communist have done that?"

Claire asked, "Where do Communists come into this, Mike?"

He knitted his brows, tried to pour another cup and found the pot empty. "Perhaps Spitzer—" he began slowly, hesitated. "I don't know. But I'll find out." He looked at Fenner bitterly. "You don't have to go running to old Penneyman with reports that I'm doing nothing. I'll handle this—" He stopped, seeing the anger in Fenner's eyes. His voice eased. "I'll handle this, my way. The *Chronicle* won't suffer."

"Mike!" Claire said. "Of all the spiteful, unfair things to say!" Her eyes still told Fenner: "Wait, Bill, wait a little. . . ."

For Ballard was sorry, and didn't know how to express it. Fenner had his faults, but talebearing wasn't one of them. "I guess I spoke too quickly there," Ballard said at last, flicking his lighter off and on, off and on. He tried to laugh. "I really get her riled when I criticize you, don't I?" He saw the opening for that second question. "Say, how long have you known each other?"

"I know Bill better than you know him," Claire said. "That's obvious."

"But you never mentioned him to me. Funny, isn't it—you knew Bill, I knew him, and—"

"What's funny about that?" Claire asked. "Why should I tell you about my—" She paused delicately, looked embarrassed and amused. "Really, Mike!"

Fenner had dropped enough money on the table to take care of drinks and tip. He pulled the coat around Claire's shoulders. He hadn't looked at Ballard for the last minute. He didn't look at him even as Claire slowly gathered her bag and gloves.

"What have I got, leprosy or something?" Ballard asked angrily. "Why the hell did I bother to telephone you?"

"I keep wondering about that," Fenner said.

"Well—I warned you, didn't I?"

"About what?"

"You know damned well."

"I don't. I don't even believe there is any story—"

"Isn't there? If not, why was Neill Carlson coming to Venice?"

"He likes Venice, I guess," Fenner said. "And who is Neill Carlson?"

"He's some kind of *pro tem* press attaché at the Embassy in Paris. You never met him?"

Fenner looked puzzled. He searched his memory obligingly. Claire said, slipping in quickly to the rescue, "Oh, I remember. I met him at one of your parties, Mike. So Neill Carlson is in Venice?" Her voice was even.

Ballard shook his head, his eyes watching them. "He was killed last night. Fell from a train." So there, Ballard thought, is the answer to that third blasted bloody question. He felt a great relief: they knew nothing about Carlson's movements. And with the relief came a hot flush of embarrassment, a touch of shame as their quiet faces looked at him. He had a compulsion to talk, to explain, to make amends. "A lousy deal," he said. "I don't know what happened. But if it was murder, we'll get the son of a bitch who did it. That's one story I'm going to spread all over the headlines."

"Murder?" Claire asked faintly. That was what she would be expected to ask. But this attack of cold nausea and hot anger was real. Blindly, she stared at Ballard's smooth, well-shaven face and wanted to scream.

Fenner said quickly, "Perhaps you are onto something, Mike, after all."

"You bet I am." It was pleasant to be accepted again. Fenner was no longer disbelieving. "Lenoir himself gave me the first steer. Telephoned me this morning. I caught the next plane to Venice." Fenner looked impressed. "You don't know Lenoir, but he is a man with plenty of contacts. When he passes on a tip, it's worth considering."

"Did you go over and talk with him before you left Paris? Or could he give you enough information over the phone?"

"He isn't in Paris. He's here. I'll see him tonight and get more details. This isn't the kind of stuff you talk about on a telephone. Of course," Ballard added quickly, "I'll have to do the work on this story."

"Of course."

"And there will be plenty."

"Want any help?"

Ballard retreated in alarm. "It's my story, Bill."

"Sure. But you can't expect to keep it all to yourself."

Ballard grinned. This was the kind of fencing he understood. "You just stick to your neutralists, and write some of that immortal prose of yours."

"By the way, who was that character who was talking to you before we arrived?"

Ballard's amusement sloughed off. "Just some two-bit journalist."

"Did Lenoir tip him off, too?"

"No connection. He has nothing to do with Lenoir." And Ballard believed that, quite obviously. "Never saw him in my life—until he sat down at my table."

Fenner said nothing. The pattern around Mike Ballard was emerging. And there was nothing Fenner could tell him that wouldn't break security, endanger everyone. Someone else would have to find out why Ballard came in such a rush to Venice: the story Lenoir had promised him wasn't supposed to break for at least four or five days. Yes, thought Fenner, someone else will have to talk with Ballard. And soon. He looked casually around the other tables—neither Rosie nor Chris was there. Out on the Piazza, there was still a dense crowd of people. He saw Pietro and his friend, walking with two smiling Italian girls. He thought he saw Chris Holland, too, feeding some pigeons. And then, strolling slowly back toward the half-emptied tables at Florian's, he saw Jan Aarvan, completely nonchalant, just drifting along on a fine Sunday evening. Aarvan was confident. Aarvan felt secure. He's had too many triumphs recently, Fenner thought: he is swollen with success. But unexpectedly, Aarvan disappeared into a crowd of tourists. Aarvan might be confident but he was still watchful, a clever and cagey operator. "Time to go," Fenner said, rising definitely, glancing over at the big clock across the Piazza. "Quadri's won't keep that window table much past eight o'clock." He pulled back Claire's chair for her.

Ballard looked up at them. "What about dinner tomorrow night, before I leave? And I can tell you about that story—I'll have it filed by then." He studied Claire's face. She hadn't spoken for a long time. "Don't be mad at me, sweetie. I said I was sorry, didn't I? And I still think you're the prettiest girl I've seen in Venice."

He watched them walk away. He thought of ordering a drink. He needed one. High on the clock tower, the big Moors were raising their bronze arms to strike. Tourist stuff, Ballard thought, and eyed the waiting crowds gloomily.

Fenner said quietly as they walked across the Piazza toward the brightly lit arcades on its other side, "How do we get a message to Chris?"

"By way of Pietro, I'd think. It's a risk, Bill."

"Got to be taken." Fenner calculated their course to pass as near Pietro as possible. He and his friend seemed only intent on an animated conversation with their girls.

"I'm dropping a glove," Claire said. "Don't notice."

Indeed he hadn't. It was a most natural accident. "Signorina!" they heard behind them, and stopped. Pietro was brushing off the dust, presenting the glove with a bow. Claire was appropriately startled by her carelessness, thanked him for his kindness. But it was Fenner's quick sentence that Pietro listened to. "He is seeing Lenoir this evening. Deadline tomorrow night."

They walked on, at the same leisurely pace. And paused, like everyone else, to look up at the clock tower when the two Moors bludgeoned the hours. A sea of sound washed over the darkening Piazza into the lighted arcades, drowning the voices and the café music, breaking high into the cool night sky above. A silver cloud of pigeons swirled and settled. "Eight o'clock and all's well," Fenner said wryly. People were moving once more; thinking of dinner, too. Among them were Pietro and his friends, as merry as a Christmas card. What if he doesn't understand English? Fenner thought, and began to worry again. "I think I botched it," he told Claire.

Ballard watched the swirl of pigeons, the people beginning once more to move around. Across the Piazza, he saw Claire's blonde head gleam under an arcade's high lamp, as Fenner led her through the curved arch into Quadri's. But the crowds closed again, and they were hidden from view. The restaurant's second-floor windows were wide open and softly pink, each table glowing warmly with its small shaded lamp. Fenner had all the luck, Ballard thought, staring at the pink lights, and he felt a hideous sense of loneliness. And then, from a group of people strolling past in the darkness, the inquisitor came forward and sat down beside him.

"Well?" the man asked.

"You're damned impatient. What's all the hurry?" He glanced nervously across at Quadri's windows. Could he be seen from up there?

"What did you learn?"

"Nothing." And thank God for that, Ballard thought. His sense of shame lessened: in a way he had helped clear Fenner of any suspicion. Certainly no harm was done.

"Nothing?" The stranger's cold blue eyes were fixed on Ballard's face as if they could bore their way into the truth.

"Nothing." Ballard's confidence was returning. "Now beat it. You leave me alone."

"And what did you tell them?"

"Nothing."

"You talked a lot. Three small questions did not take so much time." His voice was harsh, skeptical. His words held a new threat.

Ballard's confidence ebbed. There would always be a new threat: no release, no end to the demands. "Damn you to hell, will you leave me alone?"

The man smiled contemptuously and rose. He turned and made one step away. No more. Two quiet men in dark suits blocked his path, and signaled. Two policemen closed in from either side, took a businesslike grip on his arms. There was a spasm of struggle, a brief scuffle, and then the small tight group moved away. Two men exchanging a quick French phrase rose from a table and brought up the rear of the solid little phalanx. The arrest, like the surprise, was complete.

It was so quickly, quietly, expertly done that Ballard wondered if he had dreamed it all. Only a nearby waiter had noticed, only a few people passing closely. There were some shrugs, some remarks about pickpockets, and the incident was over. Except for Ballard. Four men were standing at his table. He stopped staring after the man who had been arrested, looked stupidly up at them. Two policemen in dark-green khaki; a young man, also Italian, judging from his suit, and a man in conservative gray flannels, speaking in an English voice. "You are Ballard of the New York *Chronicle's* Paris Bureau?"

My God, thought Ballard, am I being arrested, too?

TWENTY-ONE

Yes, decided Christopher Holland as he saw the complete consternation on Ballard's face, this was the right moment. He nodded to the two policemen, who saluted and strolled on. "Lieutenant Rusconi," he said to the man who accompanied him, as he sat down opposite Ballard, "do you mind?"

"*Niente.*" Lieutenant Rusconi took a chair at the next table, and adopted a severe and thoughtful expression.

Ballard came out of shock. "What happened?" He gestured toward the tight group of men already vanishing into the dark shadows around the base of the Campanile, the bell tower that rose abruptly from the Piazza, well separated from the cathedral. He watched the group disappear around its corner. "Where—where are they taking him?"

"To a motor launch, which in turn will take him to the Prefecture. Your friend has just been arrested—for extradition to France." Holland's voice was businesslike, but not unfriendly. "Why did he come over to your table?"

"He's no friend of mine—never saw him before—" Ballard was starting to rise. "And what business is it of yours?"

"Please sit down, Mr. Ballard. Or else Lieutenant Rusconi, who is now waiting most patiently, will make it *his* business to accompany you to the police station. Perhaps you would rather answer our questions there?"

Ballard glanced at the detective, one of those young eager beavers with a quick eye for promotion, who was watching him with a disapproving frown, and sat back in his chair. Also, the two policemen were still patrolling this side of the Piazza.

"I thought," Holland said, "that you'd find it simpler to talk here. Less formal. And much quicker."

"Why pull me into all this?" Ballard asked angrily. "That man who was arrested—I don't even know his name."

"Who sent him?"

"I don't know. He just stopped to talk to me."

"Twice. He talked to you twice."

"So what?"

"So there is some explanation needed. Especially since the man is being extradited for murder."

"What?" Ballard's aggressiveness vanished.

"His name is Jan Aarvan. Have you ever heard of it?"

"Never." Ballard was worried enough to be honest. "What did he want?"

Ballard hesitated. He was conscious of the Italian detective's cold watchfulness, of that possible visit to the police station, which would only waste his time, keep him late for his appointment with Lenoir. "He was trying to blackmail me." Ballard noticed that the quiet Englishman wasn't amazed. He had an uncomfortable feeling that more was known about him than just his name.

"I'm glad that you told the truth, Mr. Ballard. It saves so much time all around, doesn't it? Did he ask for money?"

"No."

"A favor?"

"That's about it," Ballard said awkwardly.

"You refused him, of course?"

"I told him to clear out."

"Most courageous of you."

Ballard looked uncomfortable. He glanced sharply at the pleasant face watching him so quietly. Ironical? No, the Englishman was being encouraging, sympathetic. Any minute, he'll offer me a cigarette and establish complete confidence, and have me blabbing out my life story, Ballard thought: I know this type. Well, I'll find out more from him than he'll find out from me. That's for sure. He'd make a good story himself, this guy.

"Are you on holiday, Mr. Ballard?"

"No. Just got here. I'm checking up on a story."

"And you came all the way from Paris? How long will you be in Venice?"

"Until tomorrow night."

So Fenner hadn't made any mistake about that. Tomorrow night. Chris Holland smiled gently and said, "It must be a very short story for such a short stay."

"Interested in it?" Ballard was amused. "You know, you begin to sound like a newspaperman."

"Haven't the brains."

"What are you, anyway? Intelligence?"

"Haven't the stamina."

Ballard's grin broadened. "What's your angle? You aren't French, or Italian. So what's your interest in this fellow Aarvan?"

"He is wanted by the British, too, you know," Holland said smoothly. By this one Briton, certainly.

"Quite an international character?"

"A political criminal. He is employed by Communists. Did you know that?"

Ballard only stared.

"Just what kind of favor did he want from you?"

"Does that matter now?" Aarvan's off my back, Ballard thought. And who sent him, I wonder. Spitzer?

"Mr. Ballard," Holland said very quietly, "I shall ask the questions, and you will give the answers." He paused, and added, "Or else this little interview can drag on for hours. I have no objection. But you?"

"I—I haven't much time to spare. I've an appointment."

So Fenner's message about this evening could have been right. "Well, in that case—the quicker, the sooner. Why are you in Venice?"

"I've just told you."

Holland shook his head sadly. "You disappoint me, Mr. Ballard. You really can't expect us to believe that you yourself would come here for some story or other when you could have sent one of your staff."

"It would have been no use sending any reporter. This story is to be delivered only to me."

"That's the deal, is it?"

Ballard was amused in spite of himself. The Americanism in an English accent was comic. But friendly. He relaxed a little. "Yes, that's why I'm here. Also, the story *is* big. The biggest of the year—that's the tip I got. So I came."

"And you expect to find some scandal in Venice? Dope smuggling among the tourists, adultery by the Adriatic?"

"Nothing like that." Ballard's smile was broadening. "My source of information happens to be in Venice. That's all."

"You must trust him a great deal," Holland murmured. He lit a cigarette, carefully. And how can I warn him about Lenoir? he was thinking. Later. First things first.

"I do." And you aren't going to pry his name and address out of me, either, Ballard thought. That's none of your business, bub. Do you think I want a lot of Italian reporters pestering Lenoir? What story would I get then? Or ever get in the future? Ballard glanced at his watch. There was just time for a quick dinner before he kept his appointment at half past nine. Lenoir's directions to this Ca' Grande had been simple enough: it shouldn't be too hard to find. The story must be really big or Lenoir wouldn't have been so cagey in the way he gave his address: the house name and street number when he telephoned Paris; the route itself, but no Ca' Grande mentioned, in his call to the Danieli. Yes, this story must be really big, all right. Ballard looked at the Englishman's cigarette, lit one of his own. "Well," he said, "if the Lieutenant has no objections?" He pocketed his cigarette case and lighter, preparing to leave.

"I'm afraid he may have," Holland said very gently. "You haven't been quite frank with us, have you?"

"Look—" began Ballard angrily.

"We are worried about your safety. Can't you understand that? So please be patient. We still have a few necessary questions to ask. Just what is this remarkable story?"

"Safety?" Ballard's anger subsided into worry. "I don't know yet."

"You don't *know* what it is? Good heavens, man, how can you put together an important story like this in one day?"

"I'll have to," admitted Ballard. "Or else the headlines I never wrote will be screaming at me by tomorrow night. In this game, you get in ahead of the others, even only by a couple of hours." He noticed the Englishman was looking at him, incredulous. "Oh, it's not so difficult—some concentrated work, a little know-how, and the right contacts."

Screaming headlines . . . Holland studied his cigarette. "So you must expect to get all the details very easily, all nicely packaged and wrapped up for you? How very pleasant."

"I have to write the story," Ballard reminded him sharply.

"And have it ready when the news breaks? But how can your inform-ant predict some event—"

"Who is talking about any event? He has collected information—international implications—big stuff. Too big for him to keep. He's re-leasing it to the press tomorrow evening. The Paris papers will have the flash reports, but I'll have the full details. What's wrong with that?"

"You have it made." Holland's smile was gentle. "But why should this informant give you such an advantage—such a break?"

"He happens to be an old friend. That's all."

"And he expects nothing in return? He has no ax to grind?"

Ballard shook his head. He was amused. "And don't ask me his name," he said. "I never give away my sources."

"I didn't ask his name, did I? I just wondered about his politics. Aarvan, after all, must have been told that you had arrived in Venice. Who could have told him?"

Spitzer, thought Ballard, André Spitzer did that. "I think I know," he said grimly. And caught his breath. Spitzer? I didn't tell Spitzer anything about this trip. He might have found out, though. Must have found out. Who else could tip off Aarvan?

"For *your* safety," Holland was saying, very mildly, "I hope you do. You see, Aarvan's attempt at blackmail—" He paused. "Does this interest you?" He didn't have to wait for a reply. Ballard, who was a restless type—his hands had played with cigarette case and lighter, his legs had been crossed and dandled and uncrossed, all through this meeting—was absolutely still. "Aarvan's purpose was to find out if you could be pressured into doing something repugnant to you. That was more important than any information you could have given them. Because his friends would learn, from your reactions, how to manipulate you in future. And you may be sure they are going to apply more pressure. You won't, of course, listen to them. Will you?"

Ballard sat quite silent, not altogether believing, yet wanting to know; like a patient listening to a doctor's diagnosis which he resists but can't ignore either.

Holland's eyes were looking beyond Ballard to another table. "Over there is a good example of what I've been talking about."

Ballard came out of the fog, and glanced around. A group of three men had risen and were making their good-bys. One of them, tall and thin, was wearing a suit whose excellence caught Ballard's attention even at this distance.

"Do you know him? Tarns is his name."

"Sir Felix Tarns? Sure, I remember him. He used to hang around the United Nations. He still goes to the same tailor, I see." Ballard remembered Holland's phrase and repeated it, astounded. "A good example?"

Holland nodded. "In 1944, he was a quiet civil servant, with his father's title and his grandfather's money to help make life agreeable in the Establishment. He liked the ladies—his one human trait, as far as I know. There was a messy adultery, hushed up before it reached the *News of the World*. The Communists discovered it, and applied pressure. He caved in. Then in 1949, one of our traitors skipped to Russia. Sir Felix had carefully nurtured the young man's career, helped place him in a sensitive job. So just before a quiet investigation was started—very quiet; we like to keep those things within the family, you know—Sir Felix resigned. No fuss. No scandal. No headlines. The family congratulated itself, rather blindly. For Sir Felix started another career, as political observer and free-lance journalist. And that has been a most expert snow job." Holland thought, there goes another of Neill Carlson's phrases; and he paused, staring at nothing. He went on. "One small group kept pushing his name into adulatory articles, reviewed his collected essays most favorably, arranged lectures, sponsored important little luncheons. And now honest people are following the same pattern: everyone loves to get into the act, when it comes to celebrities. Yes, it has been one of the best public-relations jobs that the Communists ever put over. Beats your Madison Avenue, any day."

Ballard was absorbed in Sir Felix as he strolled past their table. His attention seemed more on the cut of Tarns's jacket than on Holland's words.

"You don't believe me?" Holland asked, shaking his head. It was always like this. Why had he bothered to waste valuable time? Those whom the gods would destroy, they first make mad, alas. . . .

"Why blame the Communists for everything? Sure, they are a bunch of twisters, but they aren't that smart."

"I didn't blame them for *everything*," Holland said coldly. "I'm blaming them for setting up a man who is a walking, talking lie."

"He has his own point of view." Ballard looked with indulgence at the Englishman sitting beside him. Narrow-minded little squirt, he thought. "I may not agree with it, but that doesn't mean he's a Commie mouthpiece."

"He hasn't any point of view," Holland said. "He only repeats what Fernand Lenoir tells him. Why else do you think he is in Venice, all expenses paid? . . . Dear me, are you leaving? So soon?" He watched Ballard walk away.

To Lieutenant Rusconi, who had moved over to Ballard's vacated chair, he said, "Well, Pietro—what's your guess?"

"You made him sweat a little," Pietro said in genuine American. "I'd have got nowhere with him." He grinned and added, "Haven't the stamina."

"Did he listen?" Holland was still watching Ballard's retreating back. He was suddenly depressed.

"Well," said Pietro encouragingly, "we got Aarvan, anyway. I just hope the French make that murder rap stick."

"They will. There's a bullet in a man's back that will fit Aarvan's pet revolver." Yes, we got Aarvan, thought Holland. His eyes flickered to the pink lights of the restaurant across the Piazza. "You never can tell, can you?" he asked incredulously. Amateurs rushed in where most professionals feared to tread. It pleased him, somehow, that amateurs could sometimes get away with it, too. His eyes followed the retreating Ballard: no need to make him any angrier. Stir a man up a little, and he could be made to think; but add anger to anger, and a man's mind was sealed tight with blazing emotion. As Ballard, far off, a small dark dwarfed figure walking up a couple of steps into the brightly lit colonnade at the western end of the Piazza, abruptly halted and looked back, Holland shook his head. "No," he told Ballard as he moved between the giant pillars toward the narrow streets of Venice, "we didn't follow you. We're sitting right here where you left us." He said to Pietro, "Time for you to stride off. You are checking with Rosie?"

"I'll call him to report—"

"No. See him. I've got a message for him." Although they had been talking in low voices, Holland dropped his still more. "Can you hear? Good. Tell him that the big blow-up could be tomorrow evening, Monday. Got that?"

Pietro nodded.

"I think it *will* be. That's my own opinion." Holland took a deep breath. He had stuck his neck out, there. His job was to report, not to form any opinion. "Tomorrow evening," he repeated tensely. "All right. Get cracking. But carefully!"

Pietro looked thoughtfully at Holland. "So you got something besides making him sweat?" He rose and left.

"Watch it," Holland told Pietro under his breath, as a middle-aged, sensibly dressed woman stopped mothering the pigeons and stumped after Rusconi. But Pietro was taking no chances. He melted into a large group of sight-seers, the first batch of after-supper visitors drifting back into the Piazza to view the floodlighted cathedral. Even Holland's practiced eye could not be quite sure where he had left them, or in what direction. My turn, Holland thought, rising, and dropped five hundred lire on Ballard's coffee tray as an extra bonus for the tactful waiter who had followed instructions not to disturb this table. He set out at a gentle pace toward the eastern end of the Piazza.

He would be followed. He had asked for that, sitting down quite openly with Ballard. But ever since Fenner's unexpected move at Florian's, a lot of quick decisions and immediate action had developed. And if ever he had been justified in following up Fenner's second surprise, the message that seemed so impossible, he certainly was now: old Rosie would light up like this cathedral, and the austere little Inspector Bernard, all the way back in Paris, would be fizzing off in every direction like a Guy Fawkes rocket, when they got his message.

His problem, at this moment, was not that he was being tailed. (Hello, Neill, still talking over my shoulder? How do you like the way we sewed up Jan Aarvan?) Rather, how was he to make contact with the French agent, André, who had been waiting somewhere in front of the cathedral in case of any emergency? For the message he had given Pietro might not get through: it was crucial enough to be worth sending twice, once to the English and Americans, once to the French themselves. Where, oh where was Bernard's man? Over there, looking very much like a retired Swiss schoolmaster standing among the insomniac pigeons. André had seen Holland, too, for he had begun to move, leisurely and nonchalantly. Which would he choose: the cathedral itself, the clock tower to its left, or the Campanile on its right? The Campanile it was, rising high above all Venice from its own small island at this southeast corner of the Piazza. André vanished inside its doorway along with a thin straggle of tourists.

Holland didn't change his slow pace. He let a group of Austrian students (short leather trousers, and open-necked shirts, even a couple of rucksacks) cluster into the Campanile ahead of him, before he veered up the few steps into a square, stone-floored hall. Speed was essential now. He had a few lire ready, to buy his ride up into the sky.

The students were checking the cost, counting out the small coins worriedly, so Holland could slip ahead of them and enter the big elevator, fairly full, but still waiting for more customers. He had a brief attack of anxiety as a newcomer entered the hall quickly and made straight for the elevator. "Tickets over there!" its attendant said severely, and pointed. The newcomer protested. The attendant's finger still pointed, and the man had to obey, but with ill grace. The attendant noticed it, waited for the first six students, said "That's all!" and closed the door. Down in the hall, the impatient man was left with the remaining students, who were keeping him firmly at the tail of their line.

Around Holland, the students were joking about their friends who were left behind, drawing him good-naturedly into this small triumph of one-upmanship. He smiled and relaxed. But once he reached the small observation terrace, which ran around the four sides of the bell tower, he would have to move quickly, before the next elevator load came up. André would be startled, probably disapproving. But this was a night for rules to be broken. This was a night for urgency. If I can't make contact in two minutes, Holland thought, I can't make it at all.

The night breeze from the lagoon to the south welcomed them as they crowded onto the narrow terrace to join those visitors who were already there. It was dimly lighted, so that the brilliance of the scene far below them would not be dulled. There was a jostling for the best view, an exclamation of voices. André was moving slowly toward the west side of the Campanile, reconnoitering quietly, expecting, no doubt, to meet Holland coming around from the other direction. He froze in complete disbelief as Holland seemingly stumbled against him in the darkness. "The attempt is tomorrow, Monday night. Get going." That was all. Holland crossed over to the parapet, near one of its few lights, looking for a view.

He found it, as some visitors decided to take this elevator down. He heard its door clang shut. He could glance around. André had gone. So all I have to do now is wait, Holland thought: I'll wait for fifteen minutes, until almost nine o'clock, and prove that whoever I was going to meet hasn't shown up.

The view of Saint Mark's Basin was magnificent, at least. He waited, hair and tie ruffled by the wind, watching the contrast, far below, of dark waters and sparkling lights. The elevator made its staid and leisurely return to the terrace. He looked around at the new arrivals. The delayed Austrians were joining their friends, with laughter and excited talk. The man following him was there, too. Not alone, either. During his wait downstairs he had been joined by a reinforcement. This may be unpleasant, Holland thought as he let his eyes travel over all the new arrivals with equal disinterest, and glanced at his watch, but in another way it is good: the more concentration on me, the safer is that gentle, self-effacing Swiss schoolmaster.

Holland stayed on the lagoon side of the terrace, observing each batch of visitors that the elevator unloaded, and the two men kept observing him. Twice he glanced at his watch. After fifteen minutes of this, he apparently decided to walk around and check the other sides of the terrace before he gave up waiting. He moved to the eastern balustrade, overlooking the flood-lit domes and pinnacles of the cathedral and the pink-and-white palace of the Doges. The Austrian students were gathered here. And suddenly, one of them began to sing. The others joined in. The young, Holland thought, had a genius for the spontaneous gesture. He listened to the gathering strength of their voices: what was that they were singing? Simple, yet complicated. One of those Bach hymns? Or perhaps one of Vivaldi's pieces written for his choir of disfigured orphans who had sung his music down there, in the cathedral, their pitiful faces and crippled limbs forgotten, their clear voices soaring? Holland was thinking of Vienna as he turned the corner to reach the north side of the Campanile, of Vienna in 1947, when he had just met Neill Carlson, of Neill's small room, where his prize Bach records were played almost to death, of death itself among the ruins outside, where peace had brought occupation and cold war, of nine bodies fished out of the gray Danube in one week—some Soviet, some Allied agents, others unrecognizable. Cold war . . . He felt a shiver of warning touch his spine lightly. The solitary man standing on this side of the terrace, watching the clock tower across the wide gulf of the Piazza, had turned as he heard Holland's slow footsteps coming over to share the parapet. It was Robert Wahl.

The two men faced each other for a split second before Holland rested his elbows on the parapet and studied the clusters of antlike people far below. Wahl was watching him. He has never seen me before, Holland reminded himself: I am only a name in one of his files. But he will know me again, that's certain. A suspicious type, this Wahl. Or is it Kalganov? Stop speculating, just watch. There he is, and here I am, both leaning elbows on the same wall, not six feet apart. One good shove might save us a lot of bloody history.

Who was Robert Wahl expecting to meet? Perhaps Jan Aarvan? Or was he just reviewing all his plans, taking a Napoleonic view of far horizons? The irony of the situation struck Holland—Wahl must have been here even as he was meeting the Swiss schoolmaster on the other side of the bell tower. Good God, he thought, if I had played the game correctly, we'd have both walked around and met right beside Wahl. He wanted to laugh—the best laughs always occurred when you couldn't enjoy them—as he left the balustrade and walked on. (Suppressed laughter was hardly the mood for one good shove. The wall was too high, in any case: it would take two men to heave a body over. Besides, someone below was liable to be hurt or killed. And I'm no Jan Aarvan, Holland thought.)

His pace quickened as he was about to turn the corner onto the western side of the terrace, wondering if he could reach the Piazza in time to find one of the Allied agents there and pass on the word that Robert Wahl was aloft and must descend sometime. He halted abruptly. The two men were blocking his path. They walked down on him, ready to jump him. They were Aarvan's friends, all right. He backed, slowly, watching their hands. They moved forward, stopped as they saw Wahl over by the parapet. They hesitated for the fraction of a second that Holland needed. He sprinted back the way he had come, right into the cluster of students. They were too intent on their last harmony to pay attention to the white-faced intruder among them.

He stayed with them, and regained a steady pulse. The two men didn't follow. They might be waiting, but he wouldn't give them another chance to find him alone on a narrow dark terrace, three hundred and twenty-five feet above marble pavement. As for Robert Wahl, he wouldn't wait to be tagged and trailed by Holland's friends—he was probably reaching the Piazza at this very minute. Aarvan's two men had not known who Wahl was, far less Kalganov. In any supersecret organization like theirs, working in enemy territory, the chain of command was carefully concealed. Kalganov's talent for elaborate precaution had saved his own life a hundred times and more. Tonight, thought Holland, with a grim smile, it saved mine.

The students moved off. He kept with them, talking about Vienna, all the way down, all the way across the Piazza San Marco to the labyrinth of narrow streets that spread out behind the clock tower. As they echoed his *"Auf Wiedersehen!"* he had already stepped into a side alley, and was lost in the shadows.

TWENTY-TWO

Sandra Fane was ready. She carried her handbag, a scarf to cover her head, her darkest coat. And that was all. She combed her hair, made up her face quickly, distributed some of the pieces of jewelry from the bulging bag to her coat's pocket. As for the map—she'd need that to get out of this rabbit warren of a city. A bus or a train? Padua or Milan? And the letter, still secure within the map—she'd throw that into the nearest canal once she was well away from this house. It would take minutes to destroy it here, and there could be scraps of evidence left. Nothing must connect her with that letter. And every second was precious. Every second . . .

At her door, she paused only long enough to make sure that none of the servants were wandering around. (There were three of them, two men and a woman, whom Lenoir had installed, bringing them mysteriously from nowhere: they seemed dull and stupid, but they were no doubt extremely dependable.) But there was no sound. She locked the bedroom door behind her, slipped the key into her pocket, and took off her shoes. Quickly, with sure footsteps and a fluttering heart, she started her silent journey down the curving staircase. Lenoir's door was shut. Thick walls, dim lights, deep shadows . . . The hall below was as empty as a tomb. Her pace increased to a silent run.

She reached the foot of the staircase, and started around the side of the circular hall, using the pillars that supported its dark vaulted ceiling as shelter. She flitted from one to another, passing several ornate doors, all deeply shadowed, all firmly shut—there were several rooms on this floor, but apart from the dining room, the kitchen, and service quarters, no one used them any more. They were too close to the canal level for any comfort. Down here, she could feel the chill of the cool waters outside, even within these thick walls. The flagstone floor turned her feet to ice.

She had half circled the hall. The heavy wooden door that led to the little street was only a few yards away. From the comforting darkness of the last pillar, she glanced back up the staircase. She could see Lenoir's sitting room, closed and quiet. Now! she told herself. She stepped out of the pillar's shadow, her eyes on the street door, studying its massive iron decorations. Which bars locked it, what ones were only part of the elaborate design?

Sharply, the hall's deep silence shivered into fragments. A bell's clanging tongue railed at the house. She jumped. Almost cried out. She retreated behind the pillar, sagged against it for a long moment. Slow, heavy footsteps had come out of a room near the street door as the angry echo died away. That was the servant called Martin, the stupidest of the lot, thank her luck. But she had been stupid herself: she ought to have known that the door to this house would be guarded.

"I have an appointment with Monsieur Lenoir," a man's voice said. "I am early, but I—"

(Whose voice? She knew it. Her thoughts were as jangled as her heartbeats. Whose?)

"—hope he can see me now. Tell him that—"

Lenoir's voice interrupted, from the top of the first flight of stairs. "Who is that? Who is it?"

She did not move. It's Mike Ballard, she thought in amazement. Ballard—here, in Venice?

Footsteps entered farther into the hall. "It's Ballard. I am a little early, I know—"

"A little?" Lenoir was furious. "Forty minutes, to be exact."

"I'm sorry. It's just that I—I had to see you as soon as possible."

"I am busy."

"I'll wait. I have some questions to ask you."

Lenoir's voice changed. "If you don't mind waiting downstairs for half an hour, I'll be able to talk with you. I am engaged at present. You see my difficulty?"

"I'll wait."

"Martin! Make Mr. Ballard comfortable. Take him into the dining room. Give him a Scotch and soda." And stay with him, the words implied. Lenoir's door closed angrily.

Martin's heavy footsteps led Ballard toward the arch at whose side Sandra Fane was standing so still. She slipped on her shoes and off her coat, dropping it out of sight at the base of the pillar, and stepped out to meet them. "Hello, Mike," she said, "how nice that you could come! That's all right, Martin—I'll entertain Mr. Ballard until Monsieur Lenoir is free. Go and have your supper."

The idea attracted Martin. "But—" he began, reluctantly thinking of his orders.

"I am here with Mr. Ballard," Sandra said sharply. She calculated a neatly placed indiscretion. "There is no need for two of us to stay with him."

Martin nodded, and left. She noted that he entered the door leading to the kitchen quarters. That's that, she thought; there remains only Ballard to deal with. Where does he stand, I wonder. Why should he have been invited to Ca' Longhi if he wasn't another Sir Felix Tarns? Yet, as she took him quickly into the dining room and closed the door, his face was a study in amazement.

"Stay with me?" he repeated. "Was that fellow supposed to *watch* me?"

"Fernand trusts no one. Not even me. Why are you here?"

"He didn't tell you?"

"No."

"Then I'd better not," he said, with a touch of humor. He looked in the direction of a chair, but she made no move, simply stood staring at him. She seemed tense; her face was pale, almost haggard. "Are you all right, Sandra?"

"No."

"What's wrong?"

"Are you one of—of us?" Keep the words safe, she told herself: use nothing that he could repeat against you, if he is a secret Communist. And if he is, she thought, he certainly took me in.

"What do you mean?"

"I never guessed you were a sleeper. You really are skillful, Mike."

He repeated, very slowly, "What do you mean?"

"You don't have to keep up the pretense with me."

"I'm not pretending anything," he said angrily, and made a move toward the door.

She had her back against it. Her voice dropped. "Sorry if I've hurt your feelings. You see, there has been such a parade of secret visitors all day." She watched him carefully. "An Italian Communist from Milan, some Cuban on his way back from Moscow—all so important, so secret. And there was Sir Felix Tarns here for luncheon." There was no doubt that she had shocked him. "Robert Wahl, and Jan Aarvan, and—"

She didn't have to go on. He was a man stupefied. He shook his head. Disbelief gave way to anger. "And you have been a Communist all along," he said slowly. "You were the pretender. My God—" He gripped her arm, tried to pull her aside from the door.

"Where do you think you are going?" she asked.

"To see Lenoir—"

"That isn't very smart. You'll blurt out what I've told you, demand an explanation. Either he will have you silenced or—if he can persuade you to do what he wants—he will let you stay alive. Why did you come here, anyway?"

"There was some information, an inside story—"

"So that was the bait to get you hooked. But what brought you here ahead of your appointment?"

"I—I had some questions. Some thoughts I had this evening—" He paused, remembering Fenner and that quiet Englishman. "They kept bothering me. I—I just wanted to see Lenoir, ask him—" He looked at her, his eyes suddenly desperate. "What do I do, Sandra? They'll blast my career to pieces."

"Blackmail?" she asked, her voice sad, sympathetic. The stupid, bumbling oaf, she thought. "There is one way to deal with blackmail of that kind, and that is to know more about them than they know about you. I'll give you an inside story that would blast more than their careers."

He stared at her.

"If," she added, "you will help me."

"How?"

"Come," she said quickly, "come!" She tugged at his sleeve.

He wasn't moving. "How do I help you?"

"I'll tell you when we get outside. If Martin stops us, say we are taking a short stroll—that we're freezing to death in here." We could get away with that, she thought. Martin was a servant, after all, and a dumb one, too.

But Mike Ballard was still wary.

"Please help me, Mike! They are sending me back to Russia. There's a freighter sailing early tomorrow, and I have to be on board at midnight. All I want you to do is to get me out of here. Hide me. Find Bill Fenner and tell him where I am. He knows where to get help. You won't have to do anything more—except write your story. Look—" Her voice and face had become tense as he stood there, silent. She opened her handbag and pulled out a folded map and thrust it deep into his jacket pocket. "Half of your story is in there—the other half is in what I can tell you. You see I mean what I promise." She took a deep sigh of relief. She felt better, somehow, that she no longer carried that damned letter.

669

"What is this map?" he wanted to know. He tried to take it out and look at it, but she pushed his hand back into his pocket.

"Oh—of Venice," she said impatiently. "It's only cover for a letter. Keep that safe, Mike. And help me escape. I'll tell you enough to out-blackmail any blackmailer."

"What letter?" he asked.

"I'll explain it. I'll tell you its whole background. Come! Hurry!" She was opening the massive door, slowly, just one careful inch.

Ballard stayed where he was. He watched the concentration on her face. I believed her once, he thought; I liked her. I was sorry for her. And all the time she was playing a part, making fools out of all of us. I never would have trusted Lenoir if I hadn't trusted her. And now—she may be telling the truth, but I don't give a damn. They can ship her off to Russia, and good riddance, I'd say. Good riddance if the whole pack got shipped off to Russia, the lying and cunning sons of bitches, all of them, blackmailers and cheats.

"Please, Mike!" she begged quietly, from the door. Her voice trembled, her blue eyes were large and pleading. "This means so much—"

Lenoir's voice asked, "What means so much?" With one arm he thrust the door wide open. In his other hand, he held a dark coat. Behind him was Martin, and the other man servant. He looked at Mike Ballard, who was standing well back from the door, and then at Sandra. She couldn't speak. She only kept staring at her coat.

She told me the truth this time, Ballard thought, she actually told me the truth. The way she stood there, white-faced and hopeless, was too much for him. He said, "Why—Sandra was only trying to get me to take her out to dinner."

"Was she?"

Sandra clutched at Ballard's excuse, even if he had got it wrong. There was some of the old sharpness in her words, but her voice was faint. "I wanted to walk in the fresh air. I wanted to get out of this horrible, hideous house."

"And after dinner? What then?" Lenoir's controlled fury began to slip its leash. He pulled a handful of jewelry from her coat pocket, almost threw it in her face. He looked at Ballard. "Where were you taking her?"

Ballard didn't have to pretend amazement. He stared unbelievingly at the glitter of diamonds and emeralds. "What the—" he began. "Have you two gone crazy or something?"

Lenoir accepted his astonishment. He dropped the coat and the jewels at his feet. He nodded to the two men behind him. "Take over here," he told them. To Ballard, he said, "Come."

Ballard stopped to speak to Sandra. "We'll have dinner another time," he said gently. "I wasn't being ungallant—I just couldn't make it tonight. I've got to take a telephone call at nine-thirty. From New York. Can't miss it."

Lenoir said coldly, "You had an appointment with me at half past nine."

"This one is with my boss."

There was a slight flutter of Lenoir's eyelids.

"That's why I dropped in early. Just took a chance—"

"Well, come upstairs."

"There's scarcely time." Ballard was beginning to enjoy himself. He glanced at his watch. "It's five after nine."

"I ended my other appointment quickly—" began Lenoir angrily.

"Sorry, Fernand. These things happen. Can't stand up old Walter Penneyman. I'll come back after his call. Good night, Sandra." He took her hands, and they were ice-cold. "Have lunch with me tomorrow?" Perhaps she got his message, perhaps she grasped that he was going to get out of this house and find help, and let her be free to walk away, have lunch with him or anyone, as she pleased. Or perhaps not. Her eyes were looking past him at the two men who had entered the room.

"Come," Lenoir said, and gestured to Ballard impatiently. He closed the door behind them. As they walked into the cavern of a hall he was saying unhappily, "Sandra hasn't been at all well. I am sorry you had to witness that little scene." He sighed. "I don't know what to do, frankly. She—she keeps stealing things. You saw the jewels—they are mine, you know, belonged to my mother. Do you know what she was going to do with them? Sell them to anyone she could find. Believe me, my dear fellow, she has done this before. I've had the most enormous trouble getting them back again. Last month, in Paris—oh, well, why bother you with my worries?"

They had almost reached the street door.

Lenoir, still speaking in the same friendly voice, said, "What happened in the Piazza San Marco this evening? I heard there was a small sensation at Florian's."

"A man was arrested." But he knows all that, Ballard thought. Whoever telephoned him the news in the last fifteen minutes gave him all the details. Perhaps that telephone call was the real reason why he had cut short that interview upstairs: suddenly, I was important.

"Who was he?"

"He never told me his name. He came and sat at my table. He was trying to blackmail me." Ballard smiled. "I told him to go to hell."

Lenoir's surprise was real.

"After that, the police arrived. They asked me some questions about him, naturally enough. But I knew nothing."

"Why was he arrested?"

"Blackmailers often get arrested," Ballard said cheerfully. "Good night, Fernand. See you later?"

"Not tonight. Tomorrow."

"I'll be here early. Around nine?"

Lenoir nodded. He was preoccupied. He didn't even pay attention to the scream of pain, distant and faint, that froze Ballard as the heavy door closed behind him and shut him out into the dark, narrow street. A light mist was condensing; the pavement was damp in patches, and the chill from the canal at one end of the short *calle* sent a shiver up his spine. Or maybe it was the memory of that pitiful scream. He set out quickly, walking away from the canal, choosing to plunge back into the labyrinth of Venice by way of the little square. He wasn't being followed; there were no footsteps except the echoes of his. Yet he still had that odd feeling of being watched.

Even as he crossed the sagging pavement of the small square, with its leaning church tower, its closely shuttered houses, its dimly lit café filled with men, the feeling persisted. He resisted breaking into a run, but his pace quickened, and—as the bright shop windows of the next *calle* helped light his way into more crowded streets—he took his first real breath of relief. His brain began to function again.

He chose the lighted doorway of a shoeshop, and stepped out of the stream of people flowing toward the Piazza San Marco. He pulled the map out of his pocket as if to study his direction. There was a letter inside—so she hadn't been lying about that, either—addressed to a Major Christopher Holland from someone called P. Trouin. He read on, quickly, then folded the letter away in his map and put it carefully back into his pocket. He stared at a row of women's velvet slippers, red, blue, yellow, pink, beaded and bejeweled, for twelve hundred lire. The letter was like an acid burning its way into his mind. That was one story, he sensed, that he never could use: whatever the truth, or the lie, in that letter, it was far outside his province. Could it be true? If so, the whole damned world was on the skids, and his own country was to blame. It couldn't be true—surely? Or supposing it was a fake, meant to be taken as true? It would work; it was working on him: he kept saying it couldn't be true, it couldn't, surely? He knew one thing definitely: he had been given the hottest package in Venice to hold. If Lenoir had ordered Martin to search him, he wouldn't be alive at this minute. Clever little Sandra, and sucker Mike . . . The sooner he got rid of this, the better. The easy way was to throw it into the next canal he crossed. The easy way . . . Had he become such a yellowbelly as that?

Someone brushed his arm, and he jerked around, ready to hit back.

"Such darling slippers," the girl was saying, "and only two dollars! Andy, you must bring me here tomorrow morning when the shop opens. Just look!"

"I'm looking." Her husband glanced after Ballard. "Say, we startled that fellow. Who did he think we were, d'you suppose?"

The girl laughed happily. "Really, Venice is the most *wonderful* place. I think I'll have the pink ones."

TWENTY-THREE

Upstairs at Quadri's, in one of its small softly lighted rooms, with a window wide open beside their table to let them look out over the Piazza, Claire and Bill Fenner dined on red mullet, drank properly chilled Montrachet, and talked. This, he thought as he watched her, had turned out to be a good idea although it had started badly enough.

At first, Claire had been so depressed by Mike Ballard's performance that she had scarcely touched her *apéritif*, seemed to have no interest in the tantalizing menu. Even this little table, with its splendid view of the lighted colonnade stretching down the other side of the Piazza, had seemed a mistake, for it had let her see Ballard still sitting over there, talking to Jan Aarvan again.

"I can't bear it," she said quietly. "I just can't bear it. Did we make any mistakes with Ballard, give anything away? Surely he wouldn't—" She bit her lip, looked down at the white cloth and gleaming silver.

"If he does," Fenner said equally quietly, putting his hand over hers, "he won't know he is doing it."

"And that excuses him?" For talking our lives away? she thought bleakly.

"No excuses offered. It's just an explanation."

"It doesn't make me feel any better," she said, trying to smile, failing. She looked back at Florian's. Her eyes widened in disbelief. "We've got him," she said, her voice unsteady with suppressed excitement. "We've got him, Bill!"

He looked as casually as he could over his shoulder, and saw the end of Aarvan's arrest. He looked back at her. "Now," he said, releasing her hand, "will you drink that Cinzano?"

"Lemon peel and all," she agreed, beginning to laugh. She raised her glass in a toast. "One down and two to go!" she said very softly.

"I'm glad I'm on your side," he told her. He glanced over his shoulder at Florian's once more. Holland was about to sit down at that distant table. So Pietro *had* understood English. Fenner took a deep breath of relief, and finished his drink.

"All I want is justice," she said, serious again, but no longer unhappy. "Without that, the world is turned upside down, and swamped with bitterness. No thank you—not for me."

"Now I know why the figure of Justice is always shown as a woman," he teased her. "Blindfolded, naturally."

"Naturally?"

"So that in spite of a soft heart, she can play no favorites." He picked up the menu.

"Soft heart or soft head?" she wanted to know. "It's strange, though, that women will say one thing and then do another. We sort of back out, find excuses, hope. . . . In a way, we earn our own disappointments." She looked across the Piazza again.

"Did you earn Mike Ballard?"

"Yes," she said frankly. "I kept hoping he wouldn't, he couldn't. But— well, he did. And that's that." She said it sadly.

"Let's leave him to old Dr. Chris, shall we?"

She studied him thoughtfully. "Men *are* puzzling," she said. "I had the idea you didn't like—" She glanced around the room. Talking softly like this, they couldn't be overheard. Their window table was isolated from those along the walls. "That you didn't like Chris too much."

"Oh, just a natural reaction. I felt he resented me." Which would be a natural reaction, too: there was I, with Claire, happy and confident and alive; and there was Neill Carlson, dead. He said quickly, to pull her away from that direction of thought, "So men are puzzling? And women aren't?"

"You don't seem too baffled by them."

He shook his head. "If we had forty years together, you'd still keep me guessing."

She looked at him.

"Or fifty," he said smoothly, studying the menu. "What about some red mullet? But first—let's see. . . ."

She watched him as he chose and ordered. She felt a strange warmth, a new sense of relaxing, of light in frightening darkness—light that didn't flicker and vanish, light that held steady and grew. I am tired of walking alone, she thought, of searching and groping and drawing back to past memories. I need someone to lean on, to have with me, and be with; never alone and lost and afraid any more. But that was only a part of the truth, as she knew when his eyes met hers, and stayed, holding hers.

"And wine, signore?" the waiter murmured politely, bringing them back from that long moment of discovery.

"And wine," said Fenner absent-mindedly, forgetting the small pride he took in vineyard and vintage. Tonight, water would have tasted like champagne.

So they dined and talked, their small table an island unto itself, the rest of the room forgotten.

And suddenly Mike Ballard stood beside them, signaling the waiter for another chair. "Do you mind if I join you?" he asked. He was too worried to enjoy the amazement on their faces. "Hello, beautiful," he said to Claire. He was never too worried for that.

"It seems as if you have," Fenner said coldly as Ballard sat down, his back to the room, and switched off the small pink lamp. He waved away the waiter's outheld menu. "Haven't much time."

"Better order something," Claire said. It wasn't only a conditioned reflex springing to work: to make the unusual seem perfectly normal. He's ill, she was thinking. Not drunk, as she had first thought: something was very wrong with Mike Ballard.

He took the menu, placed it in front of him, rested his elbow on it. "Double Scotch and soda," he told the waiter. He looked at Fenner. "I'm taking the first plane I can get back to Paris. But there are two things I've got to do right away." He leaned forward, lowered his voice. "How do we get help to Sandra Fane?"

Fenner recovered quickly. "Why ask me?"

"Cut it out, cut it out," Ballard said irritably. "She told me to get in touch with you if she escaped. She wasn't dousing me with eyewash this time. Not tonight."

Fenner and Claire exchanged a glance. He said, "She escaped? Where is she?"

"She tried to. It didn't work. When I left that place—it's called Ca' Longhi—they had started beating her. Or something." He could still hear the scream. "They are putting her on board a freighter at midnight—it sails tomorrow morning. I guess you don't think you owe her much. Still—she delivered half a story. It could have got me dumped into a canal, it's true," he smiled grimly, "but she did make sure it got out of that house. So you owe her—"

Claire had seen the waiter arriving. "Bill was explaining to me," she cut in quickly, "why he is all in favor of a repertory theater in New York. Don't you agree that if we could alternate a popular play with a classic each week, we could make one pay for the other?" She watched the waiter leaving. "Yes, Mike?" she asked softly.

"So you owe her something," he told Fenner. "That's how I see it." He didn't touch his drink. He had slipped one hand into his pocket and brought out a map. Quietly, he inserted it between the pages of the menu, put his elbow back on top of it. "What about it, Bill?"

Fenner looked at Claire. Is this true? he seemed to be asking her. Can we really take his word?

Claire said, "Couldn't we send the police in?" But on what excuse? she wondered.

"And tell them that a Frenchman is having his mistress beaten up by two servants? They would think it just some new angle in French fun and games. Besides, Lenoir would find an excuse for anything." He stared hard at Fenner. "I've learned," Ballard said bitterly. He looked down at the menu. "Can you help?"

"We'll get word to some people who might be able to."

"That's a promise? You'll get word to them right away?"

Fenner nodded. "You said something about half a story. What is it?"

"A letter. You'll find it inside this menu. Tell me one thing: is it real or is it a fake?"

"A fake."

Ballard took a deep breath of relief. "It shook me," he admitted. He picked up his drink and swallowed a large gulp. "Sure, I read it. I thought I might as well know what I was dying for." His smile was brief. "Also, I thought I could use it, perhaps. But"—he shook his head—"half a story could be the wrong story. I'll wait for the whole of it."

"You'll get it," Fenner promised him.

"If it can be told," Ballard said gloomily. But at least, he thought, Bill Fenner can't use it at all. That's certain. He brightened, and finished his drink. "Well—see you in Paris."

"Not if you go back to your hotel," Fenner said very quietly.

"You mean—? But I talked my way out of Ca' Longhi without a slip. And I wasn't tailed. I am pretty sure of that."

"Because Lenoir knows where he can find you." Fenner let that fact sink in, and added, "Wait for us downstairs. Outside. Be careful, Mike. Follow us at a safe distance. We'll take you to our hotel. You can't walk the streets all night, or sit at a café, or try to register at another hotel." His passport would give his name away, and Lenoir's men would soon track him down. "I'll smuggle you up to my room. And I'll pass word to our friends that you may need a little help, too."

Ballard's face was pale. "Me?" He sounded almost indignant.

"Sandra is being questioned right now, isn't she?"

Ballard nodded. "You think she will break?"

Fenner said nothing. Yes, she probably will. She is being interrogated by experts. How much will she tell? Everything? Or just enough to make a deal with Lenoir? We feel we owe her something, but there is one thing certain: Sandra feels no obligation, no loyalty to us.

"I get you," Ballard said dully. "If I tried to check out of my hotel to-night—" He didn't finish. "I get you," he said again, and rose.

He hadn't bargained for that, Fenner thought, as he watched Ballard leave. But he would rally, like the rest of us, when he had got accustomed to the idea of more trouble ahead. Fenner lifted the menu, felt for the map, slid it quietly under his napkin, called for the check, added a handsome tip, and pocketed the map along with his wallet. "How do we reach Rosie?" he asked as he helped Claire slip into her coat.

"Arnaldi's."

The camera shop near the bridge. It was on the way to the Vittoria, thank heaven. "It's twenty minutes of ten," he said as they went down the narrow flight of stairs into the small ground-floor room. "I think we had better cut out that gondola ride."

She nodded. Not many people down here in this room, she noted, and no one who seemed interested in them. No one was hastily calling for his check, leaving his drink unfinished. No one followed them, either, from the brightly lit arcade, except Mike Ballard, who had waited sensibly on the shadowed side of one of the arches, and was keeping at a reasonable distance. No one was interested in them at all now. Why? Were they out of suspicion? Perhaps. It was ironic that at this point, when they had managed to free themselves of suspicion, Sandra should have been trapped. What was Bill thinking, feeling? she wondered. His face was expressionless. He hadn't spoken since they had come down Quadri's stairs. He was walking quickly, though, his arm through hers, drawing her along. Sandra, she realized, that's what is driving him like this. I'll have to start planning for both of us again, she thought unhappily: emotions, in this job, only led to mistakes.

In silence, Fenner made a cautious detour once they had left the Piazza, choosing a *calle* that seemed to lead them away from Arnaldi's shop. But in Venice there was always another *calle* to lead back. The crowds had thinned out: most Venetians were already home, thinking of tomorrow's early start to work. The visitors still window-shopped or wandered leisurely in a happy daze. No one was following them, except Mike Ballard. Of that, Claire was sure. And somehow it worried her. She remembered Bill's good reason why Mike hadn't been trailed from Ca' Longhi: they knew where he could be found. That same reason could apply to us, she thought. As they came back onto the street that would lead them over the bridge, she said, "Is our hotel safe, Bill?"

"If I see anyone hanging around watching for us, I won't leave Mike there."

"Then what?" We can't take him near Arnaldi's. That is definite. We don't even know if his story is true: there may be no letter inside that map. And yet we've got to assume the story is real; and hurry; and act, perhaps even rashly. Because of Sandra, because of what she may be suffering.

"I'll think of something," Fenner said worriedly. Perhaps I'll send him off with Zorzi, and let them drift around the lagoon for a couple of hours. "First, I'll see you safely into the shop. You know what to do?"

"Telephone Chris, and have him contact Rosie. When Rosie comes, I hand over the letter."

"If there is a letter," Fenner said quietly.

"Be careful, Bill," she said, remembering the approach to the hotel's courtyard. By night, there must be patches of pitch blackness in that narrow alley. She opened her handbag. "Take this," she said, slipping her small automatic into his jacket pocket.

"What—" Then he knew. So she had been thinking, too, of that dark approach to the hotel's back door.

"The Little Comforter," she said, half smiling. She was looking at the camera shop, no more than forty feet ahead of them. "If it's closed, there's a back entrance on an alley. We're just passing it, Bill. See it?"

It was a narrow strip of darkness, wide enough for a lean Venetian to squeeze his way through. He hoped they wouldn't have to use it. You could waste a lot of time searching for the right doorway, or courtyard, or whatever particular whimsy the ingenious architects of Venice had thought up. "We're in luck," he said thankfully. The shop ahead, about to close, was still half open. The boy, Luigi, was fastening a strong grille over its window, already darkened. Fenner's pace slowed, so that Ballard caught up with them. "Walk on," he told him, "to that shoe window over there. Keep inside its doorway. I'll be with you in one minute." He watched to make sure that Ballard didn't look back at them, before he steered Claire quickly into the camera shop. Luigi's bored face brightened as he saw them, but he went on with his job.

Inside, there was one dim light shining down on the counter where Arnaldi, in shirt sleeves, was checking the day's earnings. The rest of the shop was in deep shadow. Fenner chose a corner hidden from the street by a display of photographs. He said, "We have to make an emergency phone call to our friend. Urgent. Most urgent. Can you get him for us? The signora will talk to him. I'm leaving. But I'll be back in ten minutes."

Arnaldi nodded—perhaps in his life he had seen so much that was unexpected that he had reached the limit of surprise—and limped toward the back sitting room.

"Take this." Fenner gave her the map. "Check the letter before you talk with Chris. Tell him Ballard's story, too." He gripped her arms.

"Highest urgency." She looked at his face in the half-darkness. "I know, Bill. And they'll get Sandra out of that house, somehow." She felt his hands tighten on her arms.

"I'm worrying about you," he said quietly.

For a moment, she said nothing. "I'll be safe." Safer than you, she thought miserably.

"Take care—"

"And you take care—"

His arms went around her, holding her close, crushing her body against his. He kissed her, a long kiss, deep and strong, that took her life and gave her his, a plea and a promise, a beginning. Just as suddenly, he freed her, and was gone.

She heard the door close gently. She stood very still. Then she flung her arms wide, threw her head back, and laughed with sheer joy.

Behind her, Arnaldi cleared his throat. "Your friend is waiting."

She turned, still smiling, but in control of her emotions again, to slip quietly into Arnaldi's back room. He had got that call through quickly, she thought. She still had to check on the letter inside the map. She halted abruptly. "Chris!" she said unbelievingly.

"The bearer of joyful tidings, I see, all rosy and wreathed in smiles and properly tousled. Come in, sweetie, and share this pew, and tell Uncle Chris all about it." He was sitting on the bottom step of a narrow staircase that climbed up the back wall of the room to the bedroom overhead, dressed in wildly striped pajamas and a bright dressing gown, both too loose and long. "Vicente," he addressed Arnaldi, "you go back to your counting-house. And thank you for wakening me so effectively. A cold-water sponge," he explained to Claire. "Never fails." He was making conversation until Arnaldi closed the door.

She took his cue. "Asleep at this hour?" She opened the map and found the letter. She glanced through it quickly, raising an eyebrow as she saw the name of Major Christopher Holland. He wasn't going to like that. She shook her head.

"What else was there to do? I've been quarantined, put out of sight for twenty-four hours. Seemed safer for all of us. I'm hot, my dear; I'm a wanted man. But I scored a little bull's-eye, I think. I hope so. If I guessed wrong, I'll be rusticated permanently—back to the old Finance Division, tracking down dead Nazis' loot." He paused, watching her replace the letter carefully. "All right," he said most seriously. "What's up?"

"Get Rosie here."

"Rosie is having a very busy night, my pet. Must we—"

"Get him, Chris. We have the letter."

He stared at her. "Good God," he said slowly. Then quickly, "How?"

"Telephone, first. I'll explain, once you've tracked down Rosie."

He got up and padded over to the telephone in his bare feet. He hadn't been able to borrow slippers that would fit. As he waited for his call to go through, he eyed the map she held most firmly in her hand. "I couldn't pinch-hit for Rosie, could I?"

She smiled at the mixture of phrase and accent, and reciprocated. "That wouldn't be cricket. He is my boss."

"I can read, too, you know."

"You can't expect to hit the bull's-eye twice in one night."

"Why not?" He conceded his defeat with a grin. "It was a nice try, anyway. Where's your devoted American?" He started to talk into the receiver, something about a fishing boat having docked with a full catch; immediate delivery advisable in this warm weather.

The call was over. "Rosie is on his way," Chris told her. "He won't take long. Is Bill all right?"

"Yes, yes," she said, "he's all right." She was thinking, our job is over. Bill and I are free. The job is over. I give this letter to Rosie, and the job is over.

Chris Holland, watching the emotion on her face, said quietly, "Come along, Scheherazade. Tell me the end of this story. How did you get that letter?"

Fenner found Ballard mesmerized before a window of velvet slippers, beaded and bejeweled, red, blue, green, pink. "Can't make up your mind? Take the blue."

"Sharks," Ballard said, walking on with him. "Three dollars here. I know a place I can get them for two." He sounded more like himself now. "That was the longest minute I ever lived through," he said reproachfully. "Spooky place, Venice, when the crowds leave the streets. Chilly, too." He turned up the collar of his silk tweed jacket.

"The minute stretched a little," Fenner admitted with a grin. "You're lucky I didn't take ten."

"You sound pretty cheerful."

"I am."

Ballard relaxed still more. "You know, Bill—if you had only tipped me off when I met you at Orly, everything would have been simpler for all of us."

Fenner didn't answer. They were starting up the steps of the bridge over the canal. Three men were standing together on its other side, one of them a gondolier. They interrupted their talk as the two Americans came up and over the bridge, and in that brief look, Fenner could feel their surprise. Surprise? I'm getting too damned sensitive, he thought.

As he and Ballard came down the steps, and left the street to turn onto the quay, he saw that the gondolas which usually clustered there were all out on hire except the one that belonged to the gondolier at the bridge. No Zorzi? It was five minutes before ten. Zorzi had possibly picked up another fare. And yet Zorzi had struck him as a man who'd keep his word, just as he'd expect others to keep theirs.

"Something wrong?" Ballard asked, nervous again. On the street, there had been strolling footsteps and talking voices. Down here on this empty quay, which ran briefly along the canal and then dodged under the cover of overhanging houses to become a *sotto portico*, there was nothing but the sound of water slapping idly against stone.

"It's all right," Fenner said reassuringly. He paused beside one of the heavy squat pillars that supported the low, ill-lit arches of the *sotto portico*, to watch a gondola come gliding up from the Grand Canal, floating out of the darkness, passing them silently, the gondolier not even breaking the slow rhythm of his oar as he bent low to slip under the bridge and vanish. Not Zorzi, anyway.

"Come on," Ballard urged. "What has got into you?"

I don't know, Fenner thought, but the sooner I deposit Ballard safely in my room, the sooner I can find out. So quickly he led Ballard away from the canal and the vaulted porch, into the narrow dark alley lined with two rows of shuttered windows. People lived here, for there was music from one room, faint laughter from another, and an occasional ribbon of light where a shutter was left one inch open. But he kept his hand in his pocket.

Ballard was mumbling in a husky whisper, as if the privacy around him was closing in on his voice, too. "As I was saying, if you had only tipped me off when I met you out at Orly—"

"About what?"

"That you were with Intelligence."

"But I wasn't."

Ballard laughed shortly. "That's what they all say. But if you had told me, then we wouldn't be prowling down this godforsaken alley. Because I wouldn't have come to Venice—" He tripped and clutched Fenner for balance. "What's that?"

"A cat. Or your own big feet."

They entered the courtyard. By night, it had a look of theatrical gloom—a compact stage-set, dimly lighted, for even here the heavy walls seemed to eat up the brightness of the lamps set high on the surrounding houses. By contrast, the hotel's wide doors, opened and welcoming, showed an empty lobby ablaze with gleam and glitter. Fenner's grip on Claire's small automatic loosened, and he took his hand out of his pocket. "Walk straight ahead and use the staircase. Wait for me on the floor above. I'll get the key and take the elevator."

Ballard nodded obediently, and entered the hotel. Fenner followed watchfully. No one around except the night porter, alone at his desk, and an elevator boy. Everyone else was in the bar or the dining room, or out on the town. He could relax a little as he took the slow elevator, and ponder over Ballard's new amenability. Either Ballard felt the edge of danger on which they were all balancing so precariously or he had stopped worrying that Fenner was after his job. Was that what he meant when he said, in his own peculiar form of reasoning, that Fenner had been to blame for his arrival in Venice? Because Fenner was in Venice, and a story was in Venice. But if Fenner was working for Intelligence, he could never use the story and so Ballard could stop worrying. Was that it? Fenner shook his head in wry amusement. He was relieved, at least, that Ballard had stopped glooming around.

But he could wish, when he met Ballard upstairs and noted his rising euphoria, now that they were safe in a brightly lit, comfortable hotel, that Ballard had stayed a little more scared. The edge of danger was a slippery place.

He hurried Ballard into his room, with no one to see them enter. The bed had been turned down, the light left on to welcome him. "Stay here. Keep the door locked. If the telephone rings, wait for an identification before you speak."

"What's the password?" Ballard was highly amused.

"Florian," said Fenner on the spur of the moment. "You won't forget that."

"No," Ballard said abruptly. He chose a comfortable armchair and looked around the room. "So I wait here."

"You wait here." Fenner turned back to the door.

"I could use a drink and a sandwich."

"You'll have them. Just wait, meanwhile." Fenner was getting impatient. "That's little enough to—"

"Do you know who was in the bar? Drinking brandy with his coffee, lucky stiff. Tarns. Sir Felix Tarns."

Fenner halted. "Did he see you?"

"No." Ballard was irritated. "Would that matter?" Tarns was a stinker, but not the Jan Aarvan type. His mood was back to high amusement. "You know, I was thinking how we could shake him a little. Just enough to—"

"You keep away from that telephone!" Fenner said angrily, making a quick guess.

"Okay, okay."

"All set?"

"Any cigarettes? I'm all out." Ballard caught the pack that Fenner had tossed over on his way to the door. "Stay for a couple of minutes, Bill. Claire has given the alarm about Sandra, hasn't she? So what's the rush?"

"You are part of it," Fenner reminded him, opening the door.

"When do I get bailed out?"

"Soon."

"How soon is soon? One hour? Two? Am I just to sit—"

"You'll find a couple of books on top of the dresser," Fenner said.

"Hey!" But Fenner had closed the door firmly. Ballard heard its lock snap tight. He stared angrily at the door, lit a cigarette. Not that he wasn't grateful to Bill for getting him off the streets. But all those cloak-and-dagger boys were too damned mysterious. Part of the act, no doubt. Made them feel important. It wasn't as difficult a job as they made it seem, though. Hadn't he talked his way very neatly out of Ca' Longhi? Hadn't he brought them the letter? He, a rank amateur, had done what they couldn't do. Not bad for old Mike, not bad at all. Finesse and quick wits, a little daring, that was all you needed in this or any other sport.

He smoked two cigarettes, started walking around the room. There was nothing to drink. The books on the dresser didn't interest him. (They seemed dull compared to the excitement he had been going through. Who wanted to read about Faulkner's Mississippi or the White Nile on a night like this?) The window looked out onto a blank courtyard. Quiet, restful. He turned the door's lock cautiously, glanced into the corridor. Quiet and restful, too. Not so expensive a hotel as the Danieli, but not bad. Comfortable and respectable. He watched a well-dressed, elderly couple go into a room not far away. Near the staircase, a middle-aged maid ended her gossip with a white-haired servant in a green apron and striped waist-coat. The corridor was empty again. This was the kind of hotel where Mama could let her eighteen-year-old daughter stay without a chaperone, and only have to sigh over the bill. A dull and virtuous place, cosy and safe.

He could fix the lock so that the door would open from the outside. And he did. He was thirsty, he was hungry. The bar was a quiet place. He could have his sandwich and Scotch, and the pleasure of watching Sir Felix Tarns lose a little of that stiff-necked composure, too. It was time that someone administered a little shock treatment to that quiet-faced stinker: that could have saved his wizened little soul, before now.

Mike the missionary, he thought, as he entered the small bar, paneled, softly lighted, its velvet chairs around polished-wood tables mostly empty, and ordered a double Scotch and a couple of chicken sandwiches. Mike the avenging angel, he added grimly, thinking suddenly of Lenoir as he saw Tarns's head bent over a newspaper. Finesse, just a little finesse, could hurt Lenoir where he didn't expect it. Ballard slid off the bar stool as the solitary attendant telephoned the kitchen for the sandwiches, and walked across the room.

"Sir Felix Tarns? You are a friend of Sandra Fane, I believe?"

Sir Felix looked up at him blankly.

"Sandra told me you visited her today. Was she all right then?" Ballard dropped his voice still more, to an appropriate conspiratorial murmur.

Sir Felix said icily, "I don't believe I know you—"

"Doesn't matter. It is Sandra we have to worry about. I saw her this evening. She's ill. I don't think she is going to last until morning, in fact."

Tarns's handsome, gaunt face whitened. "I beg your pardon?"

"She wants to talk with you. She needs your help. I think you'd better get over to Ca' Longhi right away. Lenoir is having her shipped off to Russia."

There was a definite pause. Sir Felix rose to his feet. "I do not know who you are. I do not know why you should tell me this fantastic story. But I do know that I do not have to listen to it." He walked quickly out of the bar, his head up, eyes cold, nostrils pinched. He had been shaken enough, though, to leave his newspaper behind him and his brandy unfinished.

Ballard enjoyed his sandwiches and his drink. Tarns was a womanizer —that had been the start of his troubles—and any womanizer had a definite drift toward Sandra Fane. I ought to know, Ballard thought. Tarns could pretend he had never heard of Sandra or Lenoir. But he had listened, all right. Now let him go to Lenoir, let him at least stop Sandra screaming.

The trouble with the bright boys like Fenner, Ballard reflected, was that they had to plan and prepare and wait and tie themselves up in double talk and high signs. Fenner's pals would have to rack their brains to find a way into Ca' Longhi. It would take them at least a couple of hours to get organized. The place was a fortress. You just didn't climb in a window. Not in Ca' Longhi. But I've got inside: I've sent Sir Felix Tarns, no less. And when he insists on seeing Sandra, and Lenoir has to start sweet-talking—well, that could hold up Sandra's questioning for a couple of hours. It could even delay her being taken on board the freighter.

How's that for an idea, Fenner?

It wasn't altogether like that, though.

Sir Felix was definitely alarmed, but he did not go to Ca' Longhi. He compromised. He telephoned, instead.

Lenoir was, in turn, astounded—indignant—amused. Sandra couldn't be in better health. She had already retired for the night—she had an early start tomorrow. Yes, she was going to visit Moscow. The invitation had only arrived this evening, and Sandra had accepted it with great excitement. Naturally.

"Naturally," Sir Felix agreed. *Shipped off to Russia*—what hysterical phrases those Americans used. "I envy her. This is such a pleasant time of year in Moscow. I am sorry I shan't see her before she leaves."

"That's possible, if you could join us for breakfast tomorrow. At six, I'm afraid. That might be a very pleasant send-off for her."

"A little early for my own plans," Tarns excused himself quickly. "But you will give Sandra my best wishes? I hope to see her in Paris when she returns. She is returning?"

"At the end of October. By the way, whoever told you this nonsense about her illness?"

"I have no idea. Just an American in one of those appalling silk suits. He said he called on you this evening. Otherwise, I should never have telephoned."

"I'm glad you did. Otherwise, my dear Felix, you would have been worried unnecessarily. Is the American staying at your hotel?"

"I suppose so. At least, he was ordering sandwiches in the bar. He is no doubt eating them there at this minute. Peculiar habits they have, I must say."

"And a peculiar sense of humor. Until tomorrow evening, as arranged? Have a pleasant night!"

The call ended. It was really indiscreet of Fernand, Sir Felix thought in annoyance, to mention my plans in that tone of voice. Surely how I choose to spend the next eight hours is entirely my business? Bridling over Fernand's slight raising of the whip, Sir Felix prepared to leave the hotel for his pleasant night. Sandra Fane was already forgotten.

TWENTY-FOUR

Bill Fenner left the hotel casually. He crossed the courtyard briskly. He passed through the alley at a light run. But as he reached the *sotto portico,* he dropped back into a quick walk as he saw a man and woman, arm in arm, sauntering toward him. They passed him, American they were by clothes and voice, seemingly bound for the alley. He halted in the shadows of one of the squat pillars at the canal's edge that held up the low ceiling of the covered way. Ahead was the short stretch of open quay, and then the street that traversed the bridge. It was fairly quiet at this hour, with only occasional tourists drifting around. The gondolier was still there. So were the two men. They weren't talking now. Just standing together.

To his surprise, as he was about to walk on, two other men stepped out of a recessed doorway near the street and joined the group at the bridge. Had they been there all along? Perhaps, Fenner admitted worriedly: the doorway was deep and dark; he could have missed them when he and Ballard came this way—he had been too busy looking at the canal for Zorzi. As he waited, puzzled (the two newcomers had looked at their watches, said a few words, moved slowly back into the doorway), he heard the voices of the American couple retreating from the alley.

The man was saying, "But it won't lead anywhere."

"It looks romantic. You never can tell—"

"It's a dead end," the man said flatly, and won. Their footsteps came back into the *sotto portico.*

"Isn't this a funny old place?" the woman asked as she halted. "Sort of an arcade. Where does it lead, d'you think? Perhaps down to the Grand Canal. Come on, Milt. Let's see!"

"There's no exit that way."

"How do we know until we try it?" High heels clacked lightly, the man's steps followed slowly, toward the far end of the *sotto portico*, a place of deepening shadow turning into black depth. "Romantic, isn't it?" the woman's voice drifted back, a little uncertainly.

"We're nuts," her husband said, balking. "There's no street down here—just a dock where they bring in supplies. Come on, Sue, let's get to the Piazza."

His voice, raised in annoyance, had carried as far as the recessed doorway near the bridge. One of the men stepped out onto the lighted quay, and started toward the voices. The gondolier's two friends had looked quickly in their direction, also. But the American couple, retracing their steps, had passed Fenner and were reaching the open quay. The man halted, went back to his doorway. "Funny, isn't it," the woman was saying, "gondolas instead of trucks."

"Funnier if they tried to float a truck."

"I just never thought how they got supplies to the shops and restaurants. You know, Milt, it must be strange to housekeep here." Their voices faded into a murmur. At the bridge, they hesitated, and took the wrong direction for the Piazza San Marco. The men on the bridge paid no more attention. The gondolier, in fact, had decided to go down to his craft, which was moored so close to the bridge that half of it disappeared into black shadow.

Fenner was about to move on. He was puzzled. He hesitated. He looked over his shoulder, to the far end of the dark and deserted *sotto portico*. Just what had worried those men when Sue and Milt had gone exploring down there?

Carefully retreating from the shelter of one pillar to another, Fenner tried some exploring himself. Quickly, he made his way back through the shadows into the black depths of the *sotto portico* and ended, as the practical Milt had predicted, at a house wall where the ground floor of the building pushed out to reach the canal. There was, also, as his eyes became accustomed to the various depths of shadows cast by a far-off and meager lamp, a heavy doorway, closed; barred windows, unlit; a coil of rope on the paving stones; some basket-covered kegs; two barrels; a crate. And on the canal side, cradled darkly against the edge of the *sotto portico*, was a heavy gondola, neatly tarpaulined and shipshape, waiting for tomorrow's workday. Nothing, no one here.

Fenner almost turned away. Then he noticed that there were two shapes of tarpaulin deep in the well of the gondola. Amidships, one was squared off neatly, stretched over the square bulk of its cargo, roped in a businesslike way, but the smaller tarpaulin-covered shape seemed loose, ill-secured, as if the workmen had been in a hurry and had dumped the last load in a bundle. It wasn't their way, though: the neatness of the rest of the gondola, and of the miniature wharf to which it was so securely moored—Fenner stopped speculating and stepped carefully into the gondola, keeping his body bent, his head low, using the bulk of the well-stowed cargo as a shield against any watchful eyes from the distant street. He felt the lilt of the canal send the gondola swaying gently with his weight. He steadied himself, paused just long enough to let the gondola right itself. He was down in the broad deep well of the boat, and invisible from the bridge up the canal. He moved carefully, reached out to the small bundle of tarpaulin. It was tightly wrapped but unroped, pliable to his touch. It stirred with a small feeble movement, felt more than seen.

Quickly, he searched for an opening in the tarpaulin, wrenched it apart. A man's eyes stared up at him wildly. His mouth was tightly covered with a broad strip of adhesive, his hands and feet tied with wire. Cautiously, Fenner flicked on his lighter briefly, shielding it with his hand. It was Zorzi.

Fenner tried to ease the cruel bandage from Zorzi's cheeks, and the staring eyes closed. But the gondolier's pulse, though weak, was still countable. There had been no sign of any blood, so Zorzi had probably been hit on the head, or at the base of the neck. Enticed near here on some pretext, and struck from behind? Fenner worked frantically at the bandage and wrenched it loose. The wires around the wrists and ankles were not so easily removed. He could feel blood there, where Zorzi must have tried to struggle free. And the more he had struggled, the more the several strands of wire had been pulled, almost welded, together. Impossible to unravel. Fenner's penknife was useless, too. He needed pincers. He needed some light to work by. He needed help, and quickly. Police, in this case, would be the simple solution. But that was all that was simple. Normally, he would have stood up and yelled, until a passer-by in the street came running, but not with those men at the bridge. He could guess what kind of help they'd give him. No, he would have to walk past them, in his search for a policeman, and if he couldn't see any around, he would have to get to Arnaldi's shop by its rear entrance—only not by a direct approach, for the waiting men might see him branch off the street into the side alley.

He disliked the idea of leaving Zorzi, trussed up like this, to regain consciousness by himself in the darkness. But there was no choice. And just as he was about to hoist himself onto the covered wharf, he heard the sound, the soft silklike sound of a gondola speeding smoothly down the little canal. He crouched instinctively, and glimpsed the two men from the bridge sitting erect and motionless as they swept past. The gondolier standing high behind them might have seen Zorzi lying free of the tarpaulin, but if he did, his only response was to increase speed. He shouted a warning to some approaching gondola coming up from the Grand Canal, and that was all.

Fenner pulled himself onto the paving stones of the *sotto portico* and broke into a run. Ahead of him, the street was peaceful and almost empty. He glanced at the recessed doorway on the quay as he ran past. There was no one there. The men had got tired of waiting and left. Or perhaps they had seen the flicker of his lighter in the freight gondola, and decided that flight was wise. As he reached the bridge, he remembered Zorzi, this noon, standing down there in his gondola, shouting up to Claire and himself. Ten o'clock . . . Their arrangement had been no secret. Now he knew why the five men had waited, why Zorzi had been eliminated, why his gondola had been taken. Instead of cursing Mike Ballard as a general nuisance and delay, he ought to be giving him special thanks for changing their arrangements.

He halted on the crest of the bridge and looked both ways along the street. There was no policeman in sight. Near him were two Italians walking quickly home, a small group of Austrian students hiking along. He tried some Italian on both, and received only puzzled frowns in return. Thankfully, he saw the American couple retracing their sadly wandered steps. "There's a man in a gondola down there!" he yelled to them, and pointed. "He has been mugged. Will you wait with him? I'll telephone the police."

He ran on, leaving Milt staring, and the students translating his words. There was a quick clatter of metal heels as the young men surged down onto the quay. (Milt, to his credit, was dragging Sue along, too, saying gloomily, "Might as well be back in New York.") The students would find Zorzi, all right. He could hear them whooping into the *sotto portico*, as he approached Arnaldi's shop. He passed it, his eyes searching for the alley. He was relieved to see the boy, Luigi, stationed near its dark entrance as if he had been waiting for him.

"Did you—" Luigi began, but Fenner was already in the alley. Luigi didn't follow him at once. He stood looking along the *calle* toward the bridge. The students' clatter had probably made him curious, Fenner thought as he concentrated on the alley. It twisted abruptly to his right. The light, at the corner wall, was worse than meager. He counted three doors ahead of him, and then noticed a fourth in a very dark patch of shadow. Was that Arnaldi's back entrance? As he hesitated, he heard Luigi's light steps running after him. The boy brushed past him, his face worried, his eyes questioning. But he kept silent, only knocked gently on that fourth door; repeated the knock; waited; knocked again. The door opened quietly; Luigi and Fenner slipped inside. Arnaldi nodded to them and switched on the light as he locked the heavy door behind them.

They were standing in a large cluttered space, half storage, half workroom, with a small stove in one corner for bachelor cooking. There was a pleasant smell of freshly made coffee. And from the next room, through its firmly closed door, came laughter and a voice (Rosie's?) raised jokingly. The mood was merry, Fenner thought, and some of his tensions left. "Get the police," he told Luigi. "Take them to the big gondola moored at the far end of the *sotto portico*, on the other side of the bridge. They'll find a man there, badly hurt."

But Luigi wasn't listening. He was talking Italian, far too quickly for Fenner to follow. Arnaldi, his smile of welcome vanishing, burst into a vehement flow of angry words. Luigi nodded, avoided Fenner's eyes, and left. "What is it?" Fenner asked sharply. "What is it?"

The door to the other room opened. "Fenner?" Rosie called to him. "Come in, come in. D'you know the lucky guy who was to receive the letter? Old Chris, here. Come and see his face." Christopher Holland, in pajamas and dressing gown was standing at a table spread with some papers and a large map of Venice, studying a sheet of paper. "Very funny, very funny," he was saying bitingly. There were two other men in the room: a small, neat Frenchman with an upraised eyebrow and an amused smile; a larger, rounder man—Italian, by his clothes—pursing his genial lips, shaking his head in sympathy even as he restrained his laughter. "Joke is over," Rosie agreed. "Any trouble with Ballard?" he asked Fenner as he entered.

"He is in my room. I told him to wait there until you sent someone. The password is 'Florian.'"

"It is, is it?"

"There has been bad trouble near the bridge. Better call the police. Where's Claire? Upstairs?"

Four faces stared at him blankly for a second. Rosie, as if he couldn't believe Fenner's question, moved into the storage room, looked quickly around it and back at Arnaldi. "Where is—" he began.

Arnaldi burst into a stream of explanation.

"Marco—" Rosie called to the Italian Intelligence officer, "what's he saying? That she *left*?"

Marco nodded. "Not long ago—perhaps seven, eight minutes, no more. She walked to the bridge to cancel an arrangement with someone called

Zorzi. Also she hoped to meet Mr. Fenner. He was late, and she was worried. Women—" Marco shrugged his shoulders. Women worried about such small things. "Arnaldi has now sent Luigi to find her and tell her that Mr. Fenner is safely here."

Fenner was already in the storeroom, making for the back door. Holland darted after him and caught hold of his shoulder.

"Wait!" Rosie moved quickly and gripped Fenner by the wrist. As Fenner tried to pull free, Rosie twisted it behind his back. "Stop it, Bill, stop it! You'll break your arm. Listen, man—listen! You can't run out there."

"Don't be a bloody fool," Holland told him. "Rosie's right. We can't go dashing in and out of that alley."

"Zorzi is tied up, unconscious," Fenner shouted at him. "They took his gondola—I saw them leave. Claire—"

"Pipe down, Bill! Do you want everyone out there to hear?"

"Come away from the door," Rosie said. "Come on, Bill. Tell us everything. Then we'll know what is to be done." He looked at the Italian, whose face was grave. "Police?" he queried softly.

Marco asked quickly, "A gondolier was attacked? His gondola stolen?" That was indeed bad business.

Fenner said tensely, restraining his impatience, "Yes. I found him in a freight gondola, at the *sotto portico* just below the bridge."

Marco moved to the telephone.

"Come on, Bill," Rosie said, releasing his wrist, getting him back into the sitting room, closing its door. "Now tell us—"

"They've got Claire." His anger was rising again, along with the hideous feeling of complete helplessness. "Claire is—"

"We don't know that. She may walk back in here with Luigi. Could you have missed her on the street to the bridge?"

"No!"

"She may have walked on to the hotel when she didn't find Zorzi. Could you have missed her while you were in that *sotto portico?*"

Yes, that was possible. It was a slim hope, but Fenner grasped at it. His voice became more controlled. So did his mind. Quickly, he told them about the waiting men, and Zorzi. But as he talked, the slim hope vanished. He knew. He knew they had Claire.

The others listened intently, exchanged a brief glance as he ended.

"*C'est Kalganov,*" the Frenchman said. His eyes held no illusions.

Marco, whose call to the police was over, lifted the telephone receiver again. "I shall tell our men to block the Ca' Longhi canal. They could stop the gondola. Quietly, of course."

Rosie nodded. If, he added to that, Kalganov has had her taken there.

Kalganov? This had his touch, all right. He has dropped the Robert Wahl pattern of action. But why? Why take such a daring risk at this stage? Was he so sure of success that risks could be taken? If so, he could not know how close he was to failure, to complete discovery. He could not know that Claire had friends here in Venice, powerful friends, ready to act. That was certain, Rosie decided. For once, we will surprise Kalganov. "Marco—can you advance your plans?"

"To what time?" Marco asked worriedly, pausing in his telephone call.

"Eleven-thirty."

Marco did some quick mental calculations. "Yes, all the material is ready, all the preparations. Just a matter of final instruction. I shall have to leave here very quickly."

"We'll all be leaving. Very quickly."

Marco nodded, began speaking urgently into the telephone.

"Will you all wait until Luigi gets back?" Christopher Holland asked the room angrily. First they said that Claire was probably safe, and then they all started talking of Kalganov, and advancing plans for the assault on Ca' Longhi. Not that he had much hope, himself. No, the more you thought of Fenner's story, the worse everything looked. "I blame myself," Holland said, giving Fenner something else to think about. "We were having a conference in here, so I asked Claire to brew us a pot of coffee." That had been a tactful excuse to get her out of the room where subjects were being discussed that weren't for Claire to hear. Her job was over, finished. ("Fancy loose and foot free," she had told Holland, holding up the letter, laughing. "Assignment over, isn't it?") Yes, her job was over with the delivery of the letter to Rosie. And she had dropped her guard. As we all do, Holland thought, when tension ends. I ought to have remembered that, but with all the excitement—the letter, Marco's plan, the arrangements— "I'm sorry, Bill," Holland said awkwardly.

Fenner wasn't listening. He moved to the door. Luigi was here. And he came alone. In his hand, he held a small blue bag.

"Where did you find it?" Rosie asked. Chris Holland was already hurrying upstairs.

"Near the bridge. Down beside—"

"Why did you let her go there?" Fenner burst out.

"I was at my post." Luigi was hurt. "I couldn't leave it."

Fenner caught control of himself. "Sorry. Sorry, Luigi. It wasn't your fault." He looked at Rosie.

"Yes," Rosie said, "The fault is mine. It goes back a long way—to Saigon." Some new speculation formed in his quick, dark eyes. "Saigon," he repeated, as if that answered a question.

The Frenchman, who had spent the last five minutes studying the letter, looked up to say impatiently, "The fault is with Kalganov. And with Lenoir. None of us would be here in Venice tonight if it were not for those men." His cold logic was salutary. The surge of emotion was over in the tense room.

"Better get back to your posts. We start leaving soon," Rosie told Arnaldi and his son. He closed the room door behind them.

"Then what?" Fenner demanded.

"Chris will brief you," Rosie said, as Holland, some clothes on his back, the rest in his hand, came at a rattling run down the steep stairs. He turned quickly to Marco, who had just finished giving his last instructions over the telephone. "All set?"

"Completely," Marco told him, putting down the receiver with a flourish. He was a beaming picture of confidence. "Have no fear, my friend. It has been well prepared. We are ready. At half past eleven—" Marco made an expressive gesture with upflung arms—"and we call the fireboat. We will give you some excitement," he promised. He was buttoning his neat dark jacket, picking up his black Homburg, gray suède gloves, silver-headed stick. He looked like a sedately prosperous civil servant, returning from a Sunday visit to his grandchildren. He knew more about arson than the terrorists he had tracked down in the course of duty. Tonight, thought Rosie, we depend completely on Marco and the skill he has learned from the men he has caught. Thank God, too, for men like Marco, who aren't vote-catching politicians co-operating with allies only when it suits the climate of opinion. Without Marco, where would we be tonight?

He grasped Marco's hand, gave it a firm grip. "Thank you. And good luck." Marco left, with a wave for everyone. "You're next to go, Jules," Rosie told the Frenchman.

Jules had already looked at his watch. Three minutes, and he would leave. "I shall report to Paris that we have the letter. After that, I shall join you at Ca' Longhi. Just about the time when our wine merchant is being flown out of Zurich." The idea pleased Jules.

"No one knows of his arrest?" That was important. One hint of Trouin's extradition, and Kalganov would be warned.

"Not even his little Communist secretary."

"By bedtime, she may begin to wonder where he is."

"By bedtime, she will have other worries." The Frenchman looked at the letter on the table. "That could be very useful to make Trouin start talking."

Rosie shook his head. "You can have one of the copies that Fernand Lenoir must have at Ca' Longhi."

"He may destroy them when Marco's little excitement starts."

"I doubt if there will be time." Rosie was polite, but obdurate.

The Frenchman looked with regret at the letter. "A pity. It would certainly loosen Trouin's tongue."

"He will talk, in any case. He is no Jan Aarvan."

The Frenchman nodded. He glanced at his watch and moved to the door. "*A bientôt!* And please leave Monsieur Fernand Lenoir to me."

"He is all yours. At half past eleven!"

With a polite bow, the Frenchman left. Rosie said to Holland, "You're next, in four minutes." He turned back to the telephone. Once he made contact, he began speaking quickly, giving seemingly precise directions, but nothing he was saying made sense to Fenner.

"You see," Holland said, drawing Fenner's attention to him, as he knotted his tie and pulled on his jacket, "it is less than six minutes since Luigi got back, and everything is moving."

"I see." Six minutes . . . six hours, six days.

"Cut out the bitterness. It gets us nowhere," Holland said sharply.

"I can be bitter with myself, can't I?"

"No—you can't afford any emotions whatsoever. We're going into action. Keep your mind cold, your reflexes quick."

Fenner found a cigarette, lit it, took a deep long drag. "What's the action?" His voice and face were hard.

"A little fire. Nothing dangerous, mostly a nice cloud of black smoke. Marco will see that the fireboat is there at once. And, of course, the firemen will have to go through Ca' Longhi to make sure nothing is smoldering. There will be a number of volunteers who'll push in with them. Like to be one?"

Fenner said nothing. But his eyes held new interest.

"The police will enter then, too. Tricky business to arrange. If we simply sent the police knocking at the door, there would be some delay in getting it opened—a lot of talk back and forth about illegal entry and search—enough delay, at least, to allow Lenoir to get rid of any evidence and let the Grand Canal take the blame for two deaths." He had used the callous phrase purposely. He was watching Fenner. Damned, Holland was thinking, if I'll risk taking anyone along with me on any action unless he has a good grip on himself. But the American had taken his advice: he was in tight control of his emotions.

"Sandra Fane," Holland went on, in the same quiet voice, "is in a pretty bad spot. But Claire? No. I don't think so. If Kalganov had wanted her killed, she would have been found under the bridge instead of her handbag. She could be a hostage, held to blackmail you—keep you immobilized."

"But why? We gave nothing away. They had even stopped paying attention to us."

"Lenoir stopped paying attention. But Kalganov—" Holland shrugged. "He always has some reason. But this time, I rather think he has made a mistake."

Bill Fenner looked at his watch.

"We *all* make mistakes," Holland insisted, "even Kalganov."

Cold, cold comfort. Fenner stirred restlessly, his eyes on his watch. "Do we have to wait?" he asked impatiently.

"Yes," Holland said most definitely. "We wait. We can make no move against Ca' Longhi until Marco's men are ready. Surprise—that's our strongest weapon, Bill. Calm down, calm down. We'll get Kalganov. He's in Venice. A general alert has been sent out." He glanced over at Rosie, who was finishing his long call. "This is the first time we've ever been ahead of Kalganov. We'll get him."

"So you have all decided to call him Kalganov," Fenner said grimly. That might sharpen their morale, but it only plunged him into deeper depression. Kalganov. And Claire . . . What chance did she have with him?

"It's his name. We are sure of that now."

Fenner raised his eyes from his watch. "How?"

"Through Neill Carlson. He finished a report on Robert Wahl shortly before he left Paris—a study of time and place in Wahl's travels abroad, coinciding with outbreaks of violence and terror. That report was compared yesterday with our files on Kalganov's known activities. The times and places matched."

"That won't be enough evidence for a trial."

"No. And so he will be arrested and tried as Robert Wahl, conspirator in an assassination attempt. But in our minds, it will be Kalganov who is sentenced. That's one file we can close, at last."

"*If* Wahl is executed," Fenner said savagely. There was going to be a lot of sympathy stirred up for a poor unsuspecting film producer who had been used by crooked politicians. "You'd be more sure of closing that file if you could have him tried as Kalganov." The man who stated, fifteen years ago, that he had killed over two thousand men. . . .

"We may manage that," Holland said very quietly.

"But no one can identify him as Kalganov except Jan Aarvan." And he wouldn't talk. Nor would Lenoir.

"Or perhaps Sandra Fane?"

Fenner's lips tightened. Ironical, he thought, that Sandra was, at this moment, more important to Rosie and his friends than Claire. He looked at his watch again. "Time to go."

"Still a minute left." Holland had picked up the letter as Rosie left the telephone. "What do you plan to do with this little document?"

Rosie came out of his own thoughts. "Burn it."

"Couldn't agree more," Holland said. "May I?" He had his lighter ready.

"It's addressed to you, isn't it?"

Holland watched the flaming paper curl. "I'm sorry to disappoint Jules. He wanted it. But it's too good—a masterly job, one I wouldn't even trust to most-secret, triple-locked files." His foot stamped on the black gleaming ashes, pounding them into a smear of charcoal dust on the floor. "Arnaldi will give me hell," he said, smiling.

"Come on," Fenner told him from the door. He looked at a strangely silent Rosie. "Did you get any report about the gondola? Was the canal blocked in time?"

Rosie shook his head. "Two gondolas reached Ca' Longhi just before Marco's orders got through. One brought a visitor—"

"Who?" asked Holland quickly.

"Couldn't be recognized in the darkness. He was expected: he didn't have to wait at the door. Just slipped in—"

"And Claire?" Fenner asked. "She was in the other gondola?"

"Yes. At least, two men carried something—"

"Come on!" Fenner said savagely, and left.

"Keep with him," Rosie told Holland. "He's in an ugly mood." He paused and added angrily, "Why the hell wasn't I told that he and Claire—"

"They weren't. It must be one of those first-take, fast developers. That does happen."

"But why *now*, of all times?"

"Something always goes wrong," Holland said philosophically. "You ought to know that, old boy. Coming!" he called to Fenner, who had shouted back to him. "And I thought I had got him all quietened down," he told Rosie as he left. "See you at the café on the square; just before eleven-thirty?" And then the balloon goes up, he thought, as he hurried through the storeroom. Fenner was waiting, grim-faced and silent. But he did listen to Holland's quick instructions on how they'd leave separately, and where they'd meet.

Something always goes wrong, Rosie thought as he folded up the map of Venice, gathered together the sheets of paper on the table and began tearing them to shreds. Because people were people, not to be arranged like schedules. Such as this one he held in his hand. He studied it for the last time: nothing forgotten, nothing omitted. He tore it up and burned it with the rest of the scraps of paper.

Arnaldi had come back into the room. "They have both gone," he told Rosie. He was still upset. He didn't even notice the black ashes. "The young lady—I thought she left under orders. I am sorry. It was my fault."

"The fault is mine. I didn't give her orders to stay with you. Don't worry, Vicente, we'll find her. She'll return. Keep her purse until she comes. Right?"

We'll find her, he repeated to himself as he stepped out into the alley. Will we? Good God, why did this have to happen? Her mission was accomplished with the delivery of the letter. By this time, Claire and Fenner ought to have been back at the Hotel Vittoria, enjoying a nightcap in the bar. That's the way it should have been. The Hotel Vittoria . . . Ballard!

I mustn't forget him, Rosie reminded himself. He is safe enough in Fenner's room with the door locked; a damned sight safer and happier than Fenner will be this twisted night. If we have a minute to spare before the fireworks start, I'll get Marco to call the tourist police, tell them to pick up Ballard and take him to their station, keep him there until I can turn up. By that time, all going well, he will be free of Fernand Lenoir—but for good.

The end of the alley was in sight. Luigi had seen him. He gave no warning signal. All was well—so far. He passed Luigi silently, gave the boy a broad wink to make him feel better, and set out on his detour to the little piazza behind Ca' Longhi. It wasn't far away. Marco would already be there. Jules, too, perhaps. And Chris, with Fenner, should now be taking the water route.

Cautiously does it, Rosie told himself, entering a long narrow street of closed shops, quiet and peaceful. Abandoning all worries, all thoughts, his mind only responded to each second, commanded only his ears and eyes.

TWENTY-FIVE

They had left Arnaldi's shop separately, Holland walking ahead, Fenner following at a little distance. Holland was leading him away from the direction of Ca' Longhi, Fenner realized, but there was nothing he could do about it except hope that there was safety in this madness. They were almost back at the Piazza San Marco before Holland cut down toward the Grand Canal and reached a considerable cluster of gondolas. To Fenner's further doubts and dismay, Holland stepped into the first gondola he reached. Once Fenner joined him, they were quickly away. Even so, it was a leisurely method to travel up the broad curve of water. Fenner looked at the *vaporetti* still bustling up and down the Grand Canal, cutting through its dark ripples with a steady, soft-sounding swish. He said nothing, just set his mouth more grimly. Holland was the expert, but damn his eyes all the same.

Holland guessed his thought. "*Festina lente,*" he said quietly. "We can talk here without being noticed." He looked at one of the water-buses, all lit up like a Christmas tree, passengers clearly visible inside its glass windows. "I thought you ought, first of all, to look at Ca' Longhi from its canal side. Here is the setup briefly." He began a clear, concise description of its immediate surroundings and entrances. And then he gave an exact account of its interior.

"How did you get a man inside?" Fenner asked quickly. If one man had got in, he could.

"We didn't. The place is a citadel. Marco got the information."

"But how?" Fenner insisted.

"Through the servants who were discharged. Lenoir brought his own." Holland was scanning the right bank of the canal, studying the façades of the houses which formed a continuous row with occasionally a walled garden, a small indented piazza, the mouth of a *rio,* or a landing stage to break the line of buildings. The sparkling edge of hotels had been left behind. The houses were more somberly lit, some almost in darkness except for the steady glow of lanterns at their water-washed front steps. "They are all so different, and yet so—" Not alike, certainly. A mixture of centuries, Holland thought. Perhaps it was their variety of detail that made it so easy to pass over one that was less distinguished, to travel beyond it. Suddenly, he nodded. "There it is!" He signaled to their gondolier to draw toward the left bank of the canal, opposite Ca' Longhi.

"Which?" Fenner asked. Over there, he could see a narrow waterway joining the Grand Canal, with large houses rising on both corners. Gothic, or Renaissance with nineteenth-century restoration? His eyes, accustomed to the dark half-lights of the canal, picked out the house that seemed more closed than the others. Not a light from any window, no lamp on its solid wall. "That one," he said softly. "Three floors above the water line, four attic windows jutting up from its roof. No front entrance."

Holland nodded. So he did listen to me, he thought in relief. He called back to the gondolier, "Slowly, slowly! We want to admire the architecture."

"Venice is the place for architects," the man shouted back. "They have not lived until they see Venice."

"How true. Perhaps we could stop for two minutes? Let us see the view?"

The gondolier swung them expertly out of the way of traffic, brought them close to the left bank and rested in the dark shadow of a large palace-museum.

"Keep looking at the whole sweep of the canal," Holland advised Fenner, "not just at one house. That's the idea. And let's go over the interior of Ca' Longhi again. First the cellar—" He paused, waiting.

"Partially submerged, not in use any more. Above that, the first floor, with three entrances: one, at the side, on that small canal over there; one at the back, on a narrow street; one a service entrance, near a small piazza linked to the canal by the narrow street. The hall is circular, with pillars . . ." His voice went on with the quiet recitation, floor by floor, particular by particular, and ended with "—Then the attic. Four small rooms, once occupied by servants, now used as storerooms."

Yes, he had listened, thought Holland. He is ready and fit to go along with us: his mind is working, his emotions are in control.

"How many men have they got?" Fenner asked. He was studying the façade of Ca' Longhi, its second-floor balconies, its upper-floor decorations. If I could get in—by one of those windows—

"Two men servants—one is now a colonel in Intelligence," and, remembered Holland, well trained by the old MVD. But he didn't mention that. "Kalganov slipped him in."

"He doesn't even trust Lenoir?"

"He trusts nobody. Then there is the cook—a woman, but she could be counted as a man—a Kalganov agent, just to keep an eye on the colonel, no doubt. And there are the two men who abducted Claire. And there is Lenoir's visitor, unless he has left. And Lenoir himself. That makes possibly seven, certainly six, inside the house. Outside, they have two on patrol—one near the side canal, one on the small square. We've spotted them. We'll deal with them before we make our first move. Seen enough?"

"Almost." Fenner's eyes were studying the roof of the adjacent house. "The next house—its back overlooks the little piazza? And do some of the houses on that square run up to it? The roofs are continuous?"

"Yes"—Holland was watching him curiously—"with some ups and downs, of course."

"But no gaps? That house, adjoining Ca' Longhi, really forms one side of the little square?"

"Bill," Holland said worriedly, "this isn't in our plans. Better stick to—"

"It could be done," Fenner said softly. From some house top on that small piazza, he could reach Ca' Longhi's neighbor. It could be done. The roofs had varied pitches, but all of them were sloped gently. The tiles would be fluted. There were wide chimneys, decorated gutters to help block any fall. "There is some kind of a balcony in front of the attic windows, isn't there?"

"Only a ledge—"

"But with a fairly high balustrade. It's safe enough, Chris."

"Not so easy. It looks simpler from here—"

"The moon's just right." A quarter-moon, its light not too strong, but sufficient. Clouds were small, dimming the moon only briefly. Above the vagrant clouds, the sky was dark and clear with bright stars.

"Have you a head for heights?"

"I'll manage. I've done some rock-climbing."

Damn, thought Holland, and searched for another reason to dissuade Fenner. "We can't really have anyone clambering around the front of that roof, being seen from the Grand Canal. Can we? And we certainly are not going to have anyone skittering over the roof, raising any alarm in that house to give them warning of trouble to come. The only alarm is the big one. Throw them completely off balance. Without that—"

"Calm down. I won't raise any alarm. I'll get up there and wait. Until half past eleven. That's zero hour, isn't it? Then I'll go in. Okay?"

"You'll have to clear it with Marco. He's in charge of this operation." Holland was both annoyed and sympathetic. And in a way, he even liked the idea. If it didn't raise any bloody alarm, he thought. He tried again. "Why aim for the attic? There are plenty of closed rooms in that house. The ones on the ground floor—" He caught himself in time. If Lenoir had time to eliminate evidence, a body could be dropped very simply into the dark waters of the canal, only six feet below those ground-floor windows. "They may be holding Claire down there. It's logical."

"If they expected attack, which they don't," Fenner said. His eyes were still studying the roofs, as if he were already choosing his route across them.

Holland called softly to the gondolier, who had been back-oaring gently to keep the gondola close to the museum's wall without scraping against it, "Take us across to the other side. No, not that *rio* opposite! Take us to the one just above it." And we can walk from there in one minute to that small piazza, Holland thought as he glanced at his watch. They were in good time: not too early, not late. To Fenner, he said gloomily, "You'll end up in the canal, old boy. One glissade, and I'll have to fish you out. Miss all the fun."

Fenner didn't answer. He was staring up at the attic windows. "Thought I saw a light. Just a thin sliver—a crack in the shutters."

Holland looked quickly. There was nothing to see.

Their gondola was slowing up to avoid the rush of water from a *vaporetto* on its quick way up the canal. Sharply, there sounded a warning hoot from its siren. Floating down toward the water-bus, in the middle of the canal, was an island of gay lights and music. The water-bus altered course slightly, with a last pay-attention blast on its siren, and passed the two decorated gondolas, roped together, crowded, their three-piece orchestra throbbing into O *sole mio* under a canopy of colored lights and flowers. See Venice by night. Indeed, yes. Fenner watched the shimmering drift of the linked gondolas, listened to the music as it floated along, looked back at the attic window. I'm going in that way, he decided. How strong are the shutters?

"*Bellissimo!*" their gondolier shouted to encourage everyone's enjoyment, and began his rhythmical sway once more on the flat-topped stern, judging the backwash of the *vaporetto* skillfully, rowing his way in earnest now across the canal.

"*Bellissimo!*" Holland agreed, tactfully. He started as Fenner's arm grasped his. Fenner was staring up at the roof of Ca' Longhi.

Holland looked, too. He saw a thin edge of light from the second attic window. Then it vanished.

703

"Watch!" Fenner told him.

The light came on again. It went off. On again. Off. On.

Their gondola was drawing closer to the bank, up canal. They could no longer see the attic window.

That might not be Claire, Holland thought. It could be Sandra Fane. But all he said was, "That's what I like about women. They never give up, do they?" He added, "You'll have company on the roof. Two of Marco's specialists."

Fenner looked at him swiftly.

"Did you notice those nice big Renaissance chimneys, filled with soot? No, don't ask how they'll do it. Just guess. You'll come near enough the truth."

They both half smiled, fell silent.

Had that been Claire, Holland wondered again, or Sandra? He was too old a hand at this kind of work to hope for anything: you did your best, made the most of every small advantage, and that was that.

It was Claire, thought Bill Fenner, it was Claire.

Claire drifted out of the black sleep of unconsciousness into blind suffocation. She couldn't see, couldn't hear, couldn't breathe. Her hands went up to her face, pushing, pulling, and she came free of the long dark cloak that had been twisted around her.

She was lying on a narrow bed in a square-shaped room with a light, one naked bulb dangling from the ceiling, setting her head throbbing as she looked up at its knife-sharp gleam. She looked away, to the other side of the room. It was filled with a mass of old furniture, trunks, crates. She pulled the cloak's cocoon-like wrapping away from her thighs, freed her legs, and sat up slowly. The thin straw mattress crackled; the rickety bed creaked and trembled. From the cluttered side of this boxlike room came the scrabble and skitter of mice back into the wainscoting. If I frightened you, you frightened me, she told them silently; and rose unsteadily. Wooden floor, dusty. One door, very closed, in the center of the wall that faced the window. A single window, stoutly shuttered on the outside. And silence. Silence complete. Where was she? At Ca' Longhi? It was only a guess: she had no way of knowing. She had seen nothing, heard nothing, since she had come down the bridge onto the quay to talk to Zorzi, waiting half asleep in his gondola.

The gondola had certainly been Zorzi's. From the bridge above, she had seen about two thirds of it clearly and recognized the brightly polished dolphins that held up its black side cords, the black leather cushions with their bobbed red fringes, the red rug at the feet of the two upright armchairs. She ran down the steps and saw Zorzi stretched along the stern under the shadow of the bridge, resting gondolier-style on his back, knees raised, one leg dangling over the other, hands behind his head, hat tilted over his brow. But it wasn't Zorzi.

The man had a ready explanation as he rose and came forward to where she stood by the side of the gondola. Zorzi's little boy was ill: Zorzi had asked him to take his place tonight. As she quickly searched in her purse to give the man some lire and ease the broken appointment, she heard quiet footsteps behind her. And sensed danger. She had snapped her bag shut, turned to see who this was—two men, pleasant-faced, smiling. But across the quay, in a dark doorway, were standing two other men, one looking along the lighted street, raising his hand. As a signal? Before she could scream, the gondolier behind her had struck a sharp blow against the back of her neck. She had dropped her bag as she felt the pain, the paralysis that turned the scream into a moan. And then blackness complete. And nothing more.

Where was she?

She walked over to the casement window. It opened inward, showing a deep recess between it and the shutters. No problem there. But the board shutters were another matter. They were sturdy, unpainted, weathered by age. They met together tightly, as if sealed by sun and rain. And they were most definitely secured: a combination of hasp over staple was clinched by a padlock. The hasp and staple were of black iron, antique in design, massive. The padlock was new, small, made of steel. She looked at it in dismay. Then she noticed the contrast between the large staple, made for some heavy ancient lock, and the padlock's slender link. There was a lot of room to spare there, enough to give the hasp some free play.

She reached up, across the deep stone sill, and pulled the hasp toward her as far as the padlock would allow. This would permit the shutters— if she could force them apart—to open for at least one inch. One good inch of view. That was all she needed. She would know where this window faced—a courtyard, a canal, a street. She could scream for help. Her throbbing head might split open, but she would like to scream right now. Useless, though; unless she knew there were other houses, other people near enough to hear her cries, she would only give warning to her captors that she had to be gagged and bound.

But she couldn't force the shutters apart. She pulled and tugged. They should open inward, obviously, judging by the depth of the stone sill. But they didn't move. She could get no grip, no fingerhold on their closely met edge. They were jammed. Warped? Too long unopened? She stepped back, letting her tired arms rest, easing the hard pressure of the sill against her waist. She stared at the shutters helplessly. And in that moment, she felt her complete loneliness.

Where was Bill? Was he safe? The two men in that dark doorway had made no move toward her—only signaled that the lighted street near them was clear, that no one was about to reach the bridge. Had they been sent to deal with Bill? Would they have taken him, too? Or left him there in some dark corner? Was he lying somewhere near that alley?

Rosie, Chris, Marco, the Frenchman they called Jules—where were they? Had her handbag been found? She didn't even know if it had fallen on the quay or been kicked into the canal in the quick scuffle. If it had been discovered, and she *must* believe it would be or else she'd be paralyzed by helplessness, the search was on. Her optimism was qualified, though: the first search must be for Sandra Fane. Her escape was vital if Kalganov was ever to be tracked down. When Ca' Longhi was raided (and Marco had plans all made and ready, hadn't he? That was when she had been asked to leave them in peace while they talked, to make coffee—tactful Chris . . .), Lenoir would certainly be caught. But Kalganov, where was he to be found? So Rosie and Chris—they had to concentrate on Sandra, free her, protect her, get her tongue unlocked, find Kalganov before he could change his plans again, perhaps even pull a victory out of threatened defeat.

Strange that Sandra was the one who would escape. Where was justice now? Very much there, she realized sadly: Justice, blindfolded, so that she would play no favorites, and Kalganov could be caught. You'll have to settle for that, she told herself: what is unfair to you is fair to others. How else would people be able to go on spending pleasant Sundays in their free-walking, free-talking, free-thinking world? Kalganov, uncaught, would end all that: if not this time, the next time, some time. He had the will, and he had the cunning, and he was gathering the power. Strange, she thought, the Russians may yet be thankful to us— although they'll never admit it—if we can stop Kalganov. Unless, of course, they want a return to Stalin the Awful . . . Ivan the Terrible . . . Kalganov the Frightful.

All right, she told herself, you've talked yourself into accepting Sandra's importance. She comes first. You're a poor second. As far as the Kalganov problem goes.

Strange, though, so many things are strange. . . . For eight years, you've had no personal need to survive. Since Jim's death, no real meaning in your own life. All you wanted was the cause of Jim's death removed, the cause of those other murders exposed, the blackmail of terrorism and the threat of violence gutted out—the way cancer is destroyed before it runs through the whole body. And you had fine words to speak: you said you'd die happy if, in one small way, you could help. You told Rosie that. You meant it, too. You still mean it. Only now, today, you would like to have helped and stayed alive, too. Strange . . . on the day you found life anew, you may lose it.

She closed her eyes. She allowed herself one long, unhappy sigh. The mice rustled. She came back to the room again. She stared at the shutters. How long shall I be kept here? How long have I been here?

She couldn't even tell that. Her watch had been taken off her wrist. Regrets and sad thoughts vanished. She was suddenly angered by the very meanness, the calculation of that theft: she was to know neither place nor time. She stopped staring hopelessly at the shutters and looked around for something to use on them.

Spindle-leg chairs, a broken marble table, cracked or spotted mirrors in gilded frames, antiquated footstools, a carved chest, chipped golden cupids, a high old-fashioned trunk with curved lid, smaller trunks of battered tin, an elaborately carved candlestick with broken feet and a chunk of wax still in its holder, uncovered boxes exposing a clutter of yellow-paged books half fallen from crumbling bindings, a music stand tra-la, a do-re-me recorder, two repellent busts of Roman matrons, inlaid trays, broken chessmen . . .

Her eyes traveled again over the most likely objects. Quietly, she moved through the crush of junk. She was searching for something strong enough to act as a lever, force the shutters apart; something sharp enough to try to turn the padlock. Everything was made of wood, or marble, or plaster, or glass, or tin. Inside the large trunk, she found faded brocades and silks. She picked up the tall candlestick—wood, too, but a solid piece of carving —and studied the remains of its broad candle. The wax was so hardened by age that even a mountaineering mouse had only fretted its edge with gnawings. Possible?

She hit the squat chunk of wax against the edge of the marble table. It split after three quick, hard blows, and the candle could be gouged away from its holder. She found what she had hoped for: a metal point almost two inches long onto which the original candle, tall and heavy, had been jammed for safe anchorage. She found, too, something she didn't want: after the sound of the blows, someone outside the door had walked a few heavy paces, and stood listening. She waited. The footsteps receded again, and silence returned. The guard must have sat down on a chair; the guard, by the footsteps, must be a man. So she knew what was outside in that direction. She would have to work cautiously.

She carried the largest footstool over to the window to give her ten more inches of height. She examined the padlock more closely. Its keyhole was too small for the thick point of the candle holder. That was a bad disappointment. She would have to concentrate on the shutters. It should have been a simple job, but it wasn't. The candlestick wasn't too heavy, but it was cumbersome to handle. Its spike, once she had managed to insert it between the two shutters, refused to catch on either wooden edge to give her enough leverage. It slipped, held, slipped, almost caught again, slipped. If she could have risked noise, it would have been easier. She was almost weeping in frustration when she felt the point hold as if, this time, it meant to keep its grip. She pressed, pressed. One shutter trembled for an instant, sighed, and moved free.

She pulled it inward, as far as it would come. She had her full inch of view. Of black nothing. Idiot, she told herself, kicking off her shoes and running over to the light switch near the door. She remembered the guard outside, looked down at the gap of door above the threshold. Not always an idiot, she thought, as she dropped her coat along the edge of the door, and switched off the light. She could see what lay outside.

It was a view of night sky, black suffused with red. So she was in Venice —that was a city's glow—and not in some remote house far out on the shores of the lagoon. Stars, bright when the light clouds drifted away from them. A small piece of moon. Some distance away, directly opposite her, there were roofs, a row of them, broken in silhouette, possibly belonging to large and handsome buildings. But she could only see their unlighted upper floors—her downward view of them was blocked by some kind of balcony outside this window. Did they rest on water, or on some broad piazza near water? (She had been brought here by gondola, hadn't she?) To see the ground floor of that row of houses, she would have to stand higher, be able to look down over the high balustrade that cut the view in half. She would have to drag apart some of the clutter behind her, pull that marble-topped table to the window.

The idea, when she had switched on the light again and could study the table, defeated her. She couldn't move it six inches. She stood there, dispirited, looking down at the silks and satins in the opened trunk. It was made of light wood, covered with leather. The lid felt thin to her touch. Perhaps she could empty the trunk, drag it gently over to the window. But even as she pulled at a piece of heavy brocade, white turned yellow, she knew she was too tired, too weak. She sat down on a low chest beside the trunk, her hand fallen on the silks. She'd rest for a little. Opening those shutters had been harder work than she had thought at the time. Or else she had hoped then; and now it was slipping away.

Bill—what had happened to him? Where was he? Her thoughts kept being forced back to him, as if they were being drawn. . . .

She raised her head. From the silent darkness outside there had come a ship's warning traveling over water—not the heavy blast from a liner or freighter, but the peremptory little siren she had heard today on a water-bus traveling to the Lido. Could that be a *vaporetto* plying its way up the Grand Canal? She rose, moved quickly to the door, switched off the light, returned to the window. The shutters had swung closed again. She forced the inch of space open. As if to answer her question, she heard music floating toward her, at first faint, louder, very loud; less loud, decreasing, passing. *O sole mio.* So it was the Grand Canal down there, far below her. And there were gondolas, with their people looking up to admire the view on either side. And even if the dark houses far opposite were museums or offices, closed for the night, there were other houses near them where people lived and stepped out onto their balconies to look at the night. People . . .

She picked up a shoe and wedged its toe into the little opening between the shutters. That would hold them. She ran to the light switch, her exhaustion forgotten.

She flicked the switch on. And waited. She flicked it off. Count a slow five, switch on. Count a slow five, switch off. Count; on. Count; off . . .

That was all she could do. That, and hope.

TWENTY-SIX

Hurrying, but not too alarmed, Robert Wahl had made his quiet return to Ca' Longhi. A black gondola in a small dark canal, an unlighted door waiting to open for him, and he was safely inside the heavy walls. He was more annoyed than worried. Lenoir's guarded telephone call only told him that there was trouble with Sandra, that he was needed. He arrived, expecting to stay for ten minutes, blaming Lenoir for any difficulty that had arisen: Sandra Fane had been obedient enough when he had left her.

Then he heard the details. The problem had developed a different dimension. The quiet, understanding, wisely tolerant smile of film producer Wahl was wiped out; the handsome face became Kalganov's mask, eyes narrowed and calculating, mouth grim and unrelenting. The voice changed, too, from ironical innuendo to savage contempt, goading Lenoir into a flood of self-justification.

The situation was not out of hand, Lenoir insisted at the end of his detailed report. Sandra had realized her situation was hopeless. She had confessed. She was in the library, next door—writing out a statement of her guilt. Martin was guarding her.

Kalganov listened impatiently. "And what have you done about Ballard?"

"Tarns reported he was in the Vittoria bar. I took immediate action, of course."

"Such as?"

"I had a man pick him up at the hotel."

"How?"

"He met Ballard coming out of the bar. He persuaded him to walk to the front door."

"With what?"

"A gun concealed under a raincoat over his arm. It was discreetly done. Ballard made no trouble. He was taken completely by surprise." Lenoir's temper was shortening, his voice became more clipped.

"And at the front door?"

"I had a motorboat waiting." Lenoir paused. "Naturally."

"And the letter? Did Ballard have the letter?"

"I am waiting for a telephone call about that."

Kalganov's silence lasted a long minute. At last, he said, "They will not find it. He will swear he never saw it. That is why he walked out so quietly from the hotel. Nothing could be proved against him, and so he felt safe."

"He also felt the gun hard at his ribs." Lenoir eased his voice. "I think he still has the letter. That could be the only reason why he was in the Vittoria bar—to meet Fenner and give him the letter."

"Fenner," Kalganov said very softly, and frightened even Lenoir. Nervously he glanced at the telephone. "We'll soon know whether Ballard has the letter or not. Meanwhile, we have to deal with Sandra's written confession. It is important to us."

"To you, particularly. The first question that Moscow will ask when they hear of her treason will be, 'How did Comrade Lenoir live with this woman for three years and not notice anything wrong?' You are in trouble, Comrade, if she does not confess correctly."

And so are you, Lenoir thought. "I am aware of that," he said coldly.

"I hope you have instructed her adequately."

Lenoir almost smiled. "Certainly, I persuaded her to leave out the reason for her defection. She blames you for that, Comrade Wahl."

"She has put the party in jeopardy, and you make jokes?"

Lenoir's amusement died away. "It was no joke." His voice was bitter.

Kalganov stared at him. "I shall see her. I am taking charge here. Your part of the operation is over. Without the letter—" He snapped his fingers.

"There can still be a campaign of rumors and newspaper speculation. It worked last April."

"And failed, because we had no evidence. This time we had evidence. And we let it slip."

"Along with the ten-thousand-dollar bills," Lenoir reminded him. That had been Kalganov's project. Its failure had not been emphasized, Lenoir couldn't help remembering.

Kalganov changed the subject, and his manner, abruptly. In a more normal tone, he said, "Fortunately, the main operation goes through. That is what counts, anyway. The essential action—that is the heart of the matter."

"Fortunately, too," Lenoir suggested, "I did not mention De Gaulle's name in the letter, nor the actual time and date of the assassination." He paused, waiting for some recognition of his skill in the letter's wording: it would make clear sense once the event had taken place. Its careful phrases only implicated, meanwhile, the Americans and the British go-betweens in some cynical and devious plot holding an enormous threat against France. "I shall concentrate instead on the co-operation of progressive newspapers. You still need their headlines in order to give some reasonable cause for Trouin's panic and suicide." My part in this operation is not over, he thought: Kalganov needs me. He relaxed. "You agree?"

Kalganov was scarcely listening.

"You agree?" Lenoir insisted.

Kalganov said slowly, "Are you sure she did not tell Ballard about the assassination?"

"Martin examined her thoroughly on that point. She insisted she had told Ballard nothing. She had simply given him the letter to pass on to Fenner."

"Did she tell Fenner about the assassination?"

"How could she? She hasn't seen him yet. She was to meet him to-morrow night."

"Who made this arrangement with Fenner?"

"Ballard. She asked Ballard to make contact with Fenner in Paris—and he did, as we know from André Spitzer's report."

"She asked Ballard? Why?"

Lenoir hesitated. "She had discovered you were having her recalled."

"You told her?"

"Not I." Lenoir returned Kalganov's cold stare and hoped he was believed. If she learned from me by subterfuge, he thought, that was not a calculated error on my part: it was a personal betrayal on hers. "She was afraid, because she did not know the reason for her recall," he went on quickly. "She says she was driven into an attempt to escape. She thought Fenner would help her. She used the letter only to bargain for help."

"You believe her?" Kalganov did not.

"Who can believe a traitor?" Lenoir asked diplomatically.

"We have other ways of learning how much Fenner knows. Where is the woman, this Mrs. James Langley?"

Why should he speak so bitterly of that name? Lenoir wondered. He said, "She is upstairs. A pity—" He paused delicately.

"What is?"

"That you did not have Fenner brought here, too," he said innocently. And that is one mistake for which I cannot be blamed.

Kalganov moved to the library door. "We are wasting time. I have business of my own tonight," he reminded Lenoir. Aarvan's arrest had to be investigated, thoroughly, and this fool had brought him here. "I'll deal with the confession and with Langley. After that, I go." This house smelled of stupidity and bungling, of evasions and excuses. . . . Kalganov's instincts urged him to finish what had to be done and leave. Quickly. Too many unanswered questions, too many imponderables. More might lie behind Aarvan's arrest than just some mistake Aarvan had made on the Simplon Express. The mistake could have been Fenner, Fenner the seemingly negligible. . . . Kalganov looked at Lenoir bitterly as he paused at the door. These intellectuals were all the same: elaborate little plans, fussy attention to small perfections, and then, when something went wrong because of their inborn blindness, they screamed frantically for help, for someone else to act. To do. To complete. "We shall see how well you have instructed Fane," he said bluntly, and entered the library.

Lenoir had been right about one thing though. Sandra Fane was without any hope at all. It was possible, Kalganov thought as he looked at her, that she would confess everything sooner than he had expected. Despair was the necessary catalyst to produce satisfactory obedience.

She was sitting at the table, staring down at what she had written on a piece of paper. She had cried. Tears were still half dried on her cheeks. Crying from pain? Or crying because she was defeated? He congratulated Martin on leaving so little evidence of his work. She looked almost normal except for the fear in her cringing body.

He picked up the confession and read it. "Totally inadequate," he said, letting it drop.

She looked at him, put a hand over her aching mouth. She took a deep breath. "What do you want me to write?" she asked faintly.

"The truth."

She picked up the pen, waiting for him to dictate. "Yes?" she asked. He eyed her coldly. Was she still capable of insulting him?

"You forgot to mention that your ex-husband, William Fenner, has been an agent of American Intelligence since Korea; that you kept this secret, deceiving your comrades in New York, Mexico, Prague, even in Moscow itself. Because you knew that this fact would damage your career."

So, she thought slowly, I not only deceived Kalganov, I deceived everyone. Everyone must share the blame. The more blame shared, the less for him. Cunning, clever Kalganov, so generous in sharing.

"Why," he was demanding, "didn't you mention the fact that Fenner made secret contact with you as soon as you came to Paris?"

"Three years ago?" Her eyes, half closed with the knifelike pain that jabbed inside her left shoulder, opened in wonder.

"Three years ago. He pretended he was still in love with you, didn't he? Poor Sandra—you believed him. Because you are still in love with him. Aren't you?"

His voice was gentle, suddenly, like the first touch of a wire noose against her throat. His eyes narrowed, watching her face. The wire noose seemed to tighten.

"Complete the confession," he said. "Add one more page to what you have written. Give the facts. All the facts. The blame for your treason lies with Fenner. And with you, for your weakness." His eyes were satisfied now. He laid a fresh sheet of paper in front of her, and turned away. "I shall see you in fifteen minutes. If it is not correct—" He looked across the room at Martin. The wire noose, which had slackened, tightened again. "But if you write the truth, Moscow will take your honest remorse into consideration. You might even stay alive."

He left, stopping to tell Martin something she couldn't hear. Martin nodded and looked at her. Her hand fell away from her painful mouth, and the pen began to write. Martin, big and slow and thorough, studied her with amusement, as if he were admiring the artistry of his persuasive powers.

The door closed behind Kalganov.

He found a frowning Lenoir standing beside the telephone. "She will confess the truth," Kalganov said, "the whole truth, this time. I'm going upstairs. You would like to be present, of course, when I question Claire Langley?" His heavy sarcasm ended. "What's wrong?" he asked testily as Lenoir's frown deepened.

Lenoir gestured toward the telephone. "Ballard—he hasn't got the letter."

"So he has already passed it to Fenner!"

"He would not tell us."

"He did not talk?" Kalganov was scandalized.

"No," Lenoir said quietly, "he didn't talk this time. Odd, isn't it? He was the biggest talker I ever met."

Kalganov was outraged. "They did not keep him alive to talk?" he asked unbelievingly.

"There was an emergency. He tried to escape." Lenoir waited for Kalganov's outburst, but it didn't come.

"I know one who will talk," Kalganov said very quietly, and moved to the door. He waited there for Lenoir.

"I am going to call Zurich, to find out if Trouin has been arrested," Lenoir said quickly. Kalganov's methods are his; mine are mine, he thought. I will not go upstairs. I will not go into that library next door.

"I did not forget Trouin. But there is a quicker way of finding out if the assassination plan has been discovered by Fenner. The answer to that question lies no farther away than your attic room. Are you coming?"

"First," Lenoir said evasively, "I must send out a general alert for Fenner. He may still have the letter."

"Scrap that letter! Forget it! It's lost to us—for good!"

"I want Fenner," Lenoir said grimly.

"And so do I." But, thought Kalganov, I do not use that as a subterfuge to evade what has to be done. These intellectuals are always the same: they talk of sending in the tanks to shoot down rebellion, of using firing squads and bulldozers to plow traitors into massed graves, of forcing prisoners into screaming insanity for the sake of information, but they do it from the end of a telephone, from the committee table, from the anonymous distance. There he is, Comrade Lenoir, about to order torture if need be, death eventually, for the American called Fenner. But he will command it from this quiet room, among his books and records. And he is looking at me as if I were the monster. "Are you coming?" Kalganov demanded, opening the door onto the landing.

"Shortly," Lenoir said. "I have to—"

"Indeed you have," Kalganov said contemptuously. He walked out. Lenoir was picking up the telephone receiver with a great flourish of urgency.

Kalganov passed the library door, halted—that was Martin's voice, raised in anger—and retraced his steps. More trouble, was it? He entered quickly. Yes, more trouble. Martin was standing over the desk, threatening. Sandra Fane was cowering back, yet strangely determined.

Kalganov picked up the confession. One paragraph was all she had added, a very bald statement, but adequate enough. The names were there. That was what mattered. Fenner would never escape from that indictment. Even if, tonight, he slipped out of reach, his name would stand on file. Fenner's end was only a matter of time and convenience. His death was written on this sheet of paper. But there was no signature. "You have forgotten something," he said, too gently.

"I'll sign it when I reach Moscow." Her voice was still faint, but her eyes were sullen, steady. He won't kill me until it is signed, she thought again. And when I reach Moscow, I'll write a new confession. I'll denounce him as a Stalinist, a Leftist deviationist, terroristic opportunist, dogmatist. There are plenty of phrases to pin on Kalganov. I'll pin them all.

Still planning to escape, Kalganov thought as he watched her. He glanced pointedly at the clock. Twenty-three minutes past eleven o'clock. "Sign it," he said, smiling. He drew a revolver from inside his jacket. "If you wish to sail from Venice, Sandra, you must sign." His voice was most reasonable.

She looked at the revolver. She saw its strong barrel. She remembered Lenoir telling her in amusement about it: specially made, custom built like Robert Wahl's suits, to shoot the terrible bullet with the grim name: Jugular —a Harvey Jugular bullet. And Lenoir and she had laughed: Kalganov and his fads; Kalganov, the great producer of real-life dramas, action guaranteed.

"After all," he was saying, "a signature is a mere formality. The confession is in your handwriting, isn't it?" He glanced over at Martin. "I won't shoot you if you sign. I shan't touch you. You will rise from that desk and walk away. I promise you. I keep my promises. And my threats. You know that."

Yes, he kept his threats. She looked at the revolver, so casually held, so deadly. And he had kept promises, too. Something about this promise seemed—seemed—what? She was too tired, too cold, too sick, to hold on to the small warning. It faded; she couldn't even remember what had troubled her. He had promised: he wouldn't shoot her; she could rise and walk away. She picked up the pen, fumbling, and signed her name.

Kalganov nodded, slipped the revolver back into its hiding place, lifted the two sheets of paper, folded them neatly, placed them in an inside pocket. "Thank you, Sandra. You can go to your room. Martin will put you on board the ship at midnight."

The blue eyes, once so beautiful, so confident, looked up at him thankfully. She rose, began her slow painful walk toward the door. Martin was waiting for her. He held out his arm as if to help her. She saw something like a black fountain pen in his hand, pointed at her face; and suddenly, a little cloud of vapor, of—

That was all she ever knew. She dropped where she stood.

There was a slight, bitter odor in the room. Martin opened the window quickly, flung back the outside shutters. "It soon dissipates," he said reassuringly. He smiled. "I'll put her on board the motorboat at midnight."

Kalganov had clamped a handkerchief over his mouth and nose. He knelt to feel Sandra Fane's pulse, to make sure.

"Fatal heart attack," Martin said, "you can depend on it. And you don't need that handkerchief. It is only the first impact that is deadly."

Kalganov rose. "Quick and efficient." He glanced for the last time at Sandra Fane. "Too quick," he said, "for a traitor." He avoided the door near which she lay. He didn't have Martin's trust in the rapid dissipation of that gas. "You did a good job, Comrade Colonel," he told him as he left by way of the sitting room.

Lenoir was still at the telephone. He seemed to be waiting for his call to be answered.

As Kalganov passed through the room, he said, "I'm expecting you upstairs. Don't forget that!" He paused at the door. "Come up in ten minutes. And bring the news that Fenner has admitted everything."

Lenoir stared at him.

"We've caught Fenner, didn't you know?" Kalganov smiled widely. "I'll tell her that. She'll try not to believe me. But your news will add just the right pressure. Psychologically—"

"Yes, yes," Lenoir said irritably. He looked at the receiver. "It's this damned connection to Milan. I seem to have been cut off. I'll have to try again. I am extending the alert on Fenner. I think he has left Venice. But he can't have got very far."

"You are wasting time," Kalganov said sharply. "The answer is upstairs. Ten minutes?"

Lenoir was complaining into the telephone. He nodded to Kalganov, and glanced at his watch to check the hour. It was almost half past eleven. No, Fenner could not have run very far, as yet.

TWENTY-SEVEN

Fenner said softly, "One minute to go." He edged his way carefully over the crest of Ca' Longhi's roof toward the concealing shadow of a large and ornate chimney on the Grand Canal side of the house.

"Keep off the sky line," Holland whispered warningly. He gave a brief wave to the men, Marco's experts, who were waiting farther back, by the kitchen chimney. They were too busy to acknowledge. They had been warned by their miniature radio, anyway, to expect two more on the roof. The blessings of scientific invention, thought Holland; a pity that there were no similar aids to crossing three roofs, climbing a parapet, dropping down a short gable end. He shook his head, remembering how he had slipped in spite of his rubber-soled shoes. Dirt-colored sand shoes they were, compliments of Marco, along with the old dungarees he had provided—Fenner called them sneakers and overalls. Logical enough: the shoes sneaked along, the one-piece outfit went over all. But words aside, Fenner's actions were quick, instinctive. Holland had not ended in a bottom-down slide into the canal. And I came to keep an eye on him, Holland thought, and grinned. Also, Marco wasn't going to let Fenner climb up alone. Also, I still like Fenner's idea. So here we are, up on the roof of Ca' Longhi, slightly bruised and bleeding at the knuckles, and two minutes to go.

Either Fenner's watch was fast or he was just forcing the time as he had forced the pace. He was still forcing it. He left the chimney and started along the red fluted tiles, silvered into faint pink by the moonlight. Dammit, he should have waited for that large batch of light clouds to start sailing over the quarter-moon, Holland thought. That might take too long, though. And Fenner was moving slowly, being careful (as Marco had warned them) not to scrabble above the attic corridor, where there might be someone on guard outside the room.

The attic windows had their own small roofs emerging out of the gently sloping tiles. Fenner's plan was good. He had approached the second room at the point where it met the pitch of the main roof. He was sliding onto it, taking shelter behind the decorated arch that jutted up over the window beneath him. From the canal, he would not be noticed.

Not bad, thought Holland approvingly, not bad at all; the only bad thing is getting there. He set out, following Fenner's route. And the part that had looked the easiest, that small slide onto the attic's roof was, astonishingly, the worst. But Fenner may have had the same experience, for although there was a welcoming grin on his face, there were beads of sweat on his brow as he blocked Holland's unexpected momentum.

"The immediate problem," Holland whispered, regaining control, feeling a sharp edge of tile bite into one knee as he braced his hands gingerly against the back of the window arch, "is whether this holds." It felt solid enough. It was only the elaborate curlicues and cutouts of stone that had given this piece of Venetian Gothic its fragile look. He sucked his skinned knuckles and studied Fenner's next move with sympathy. "We must look like a couple of gargoyles," he added as they raised their shoulders cautiously to look over and down.

Fenner was noting the two pillars that decorated each side of the window beneath him and pretended to hold up its arch. They were slender, and fluted twistingly. They would give him enough grip as he pulled himself onto the narrow balcony from the slope of the main roof. He couldn't drop directly onto the balcony from where he knelt. There wasn't enough breadth on that glorified ledge to allow for any lost balance. It had a balustrade, but that could have developed a weak patch or two in the last four hundred years; and below it there was only a short stretch of sloping tiles to the roof's edge. No, he would have to back up to the main roof —thank God its slope was gentle—and come down it by the side of this outcrop of attic, and then swing around its front corner, holding that pillar, onto the balcony's balustrade. After that, it was simple. The balcony was narrow, but there was room to maneuver.

He sign-languaged his plan quickly to Holland. "It's only a dormer window with some fancy trappings," he added to encourage himself.

"That's all. Nothing to it," Holland agreed with a small smile. His whisper strengthened in alarm. "Hey, wait! Still seventy seconds to go."

"It's time." Fenner was already backing onto the main roof.

"Take this—" Holland unbuttoned a pocket.

"I've got one," Fenner whispered up, as he started down the side of the attic roof.

"What caliber?" Holland leaned over and gripped his arm.

"A .25. It's Claire's."

"You may need more than that peashooter." Holland passed down a .38/32 Smith and Wesson. "Straight and true," he murmured. "You may need this to shoot out the lock on the shutters. You'll only have time for one shot if there is any guard around to hear it." He watched Fenner stick the short-barreled revolver deep into a pocket, button it. "Slowly does it," he whispered as Fenner moved on. He spread-eagled his body, face down, on the slope of attic roof, dug in his toes, leaned over near its front corner, held on with one hand, held out the other for an emergency grip as Fenner worked his way toward the pillar. He tried to keep his eyes fixed on the top of Fenner's head, descending step by step down the main roof, his hands flat against the rising attic wall. Fenner was reaching up for Holland's hand. He grasped it, and their two arms, fully extended, let him swing around the corner to catch hold of the pillar.

My God, how I hate heights, Holland thought as his body strained against the pulling arm and he felt his eyes drawn down to the canal far below. He closed them quickly; Fenner released his grip, whispering, "Okay, okay," and Holland could have both his hands to clamp on those comforting curlicues of carved stone. From away behind him, on the other side of the roof, came a long, clear whistle. He called softly down to Fenner, "Thar she blows!" Eleven-thirty it was. He settled back contentedly on the tiles. He was imagining, with considerable enjoyment, the little scene from hell that was now bursting into Ca' Longhi's kitchen.

Fenner caught his breath and balance. This was a devil of a time, he thought, as he held onto the pillar, to discover he had lost his head for heights. But if he had got this far, the return could be managed: climbing up was always easier than coming down, and Holland would be there to grip Claire's hand. He moved carefully along the narrow balcony—it shook a little under his weight, but held. There was no light from the small opening in the shutters. The fear he felt now was for Claire. Had they taken her away? Was she no longer— At that instant, the room light flashed on. And it was Claire he saw. Claire. Thank God.

She was standing opposite the window, her hand on a light switch. Her coat, thrown on the floor at the door beside her, covered the threshold. So there was a guard, outside in the corridor.

Gently, he rattled the shutters, called, "Claire!" softly. She seemed to freeze against the wall. Her eyes stared at the window with disbelief, her face tense and white, so tense and white and exhausted. Then she was

720

running toward him. She slipped her fingers between the shutters. "Bill?"

He touched them. "It's Bill." That was all he could say.

From somewhere, not too far distant in the house, there came a roaring shout.

"They've found out!" she whispered in anguish. She glanced back at the door, expecting to hear the key turn in the lock, the guard burst in. There was a movement in the corridor, but the footsteps weren't coming here. They were running away from the room. Another shout, fainter . . .

"No. It's a fire," Fenner said quickly. "What's holding these shutters?" A large black iron band was all he could see. "Is there a padlock behind this thing?" He tried to grope for it.

"It is tight up against the hasp to let the shutters open."

"Take this and shoot its lock out." He pushed Holland's revolver between the shutters. It stuck. It wouldn't go all the way through. It needed another half-inch for clearance. He tried to force the shutters farther apart. They wouldn't move. "Take your automatic, Claire. Shoot twice, quickly." Would twice be enough?

She whispered, "The guard is coming back. I hear his footsteps."

"I'll keep the door covered with the thirty-eight. Shoot quickly."

"Stand away from the shutter," she told him anxiously. "It's dangerous—"

"Shut up. And I love you, too."

She gave a smothered laugh, and looked at the automatic as she raised it. It was so small, so light, not even comforting any more. The padlock was small, strong. Would two bullets be enough? Perhaps three? She wished her hand would stop this nervous trembling.

It is always the same, thought Fenner grimly; if anything can go wrong, it will. Always? No. There was another side to that coin: if something could go right, it might. It just might. "Quick," he whispered as he heard the piercing shriek of a fireboat's siren, far below in the Grand Canal. "Hurry, Claire!"

It was Kalganov who had shouted.

He had reached the third floor of Ca' Longhi on his climb to the attic. He was still thinking contemptuously about Lenoir. The Frenchman ought to have handled that confession himself. He should have dealt with Sandra Fane. Instead, he hadn't even asked what had happened to her. He knew, all right, but he wanted no share of the responsibility; so he hadn't asked. Lenoir would never—

What was that? Some disturbance. Far downstairs.

He looked over the yellow marble balustrade. He heard the cries more clearly: "Fire!" Down in the hall, a billow of black smoke gushed from the kitchen quarters; it spread and thickened, pouring over the flagstone floor far below him. As he stared at the forming cloud, the cook came running out from the kitchen corridor still screaming, "Fire, fire!" The cloud enveloped her, and turned her scream to a choking cough.

Kalganov shouted.

The guard, posted outside the girl's door, started to his feet and came running along the attic's corridor. Kalganov, turning to race downstairs, signaled to him to stay where he was. He shouted again, bringing Lenoir away from his precious telephone and Martin out of the library. Lenoir stared over the balustrade. "Fire!" he cried, as if he had discovered it. "Look! Fire!" He pointed down to the hall.

"You amaze me," Kalganov said bitingly as he passed Lenoir at a run. Then he halted, really amazed, when Lenoir didn't follow: just stood, hands on the balustrade, looking over into the hall. There were three figures down there now, running around in the cloud of smoke like chickens with their heads chopped off. "Get them organized," he told Lenoir sharply. "Come on, get moving! It's only a kitchen fire. We can deal with it."

"It's spreading!" Lenoir cried, pointing down to another room where a thick ooze of smoke soaked its way into the hall from under the closed door. "That whole wing—"

"Don't open it!" Kalganov yelled down to the hall, "don't open that door!" But one of the men had already thrown the room door open, and was entering. "Don't open any windows, you fool!" Kalganov was screaming after him. "Do you want people outside to give an alarm?" He was clattering down the last flight of stairs, a handkerchief covering his mouth and nose. Martin was at his heels.

Who was the fool? Lenoir wondered, following more slowly. Windows had to be opened to get rid of that smoke. No one could breathe. The shouts had become gasping coughs. He choked into his handkerchief— burning grease, obnoxious, sickening—and retreated a step.

"Fire extinguishers—" Kalganov was yelling. "Where are they?" he shouted up to Lenoir.

"I—I don't know. How could I?" Lenoir kept his voice as normal as possible. This screaming was grotesque. This speed of action was close to panic.

"Water!" Kalganov shouted, now. "Buckets—"

"Water makes the smoke worse," the cook called to him, groping her way to the staircase, her eyes white in a blackened face, hair soot-heavy. "Whose carelessness?"

She shook her head helplessly. "The fireplace was filled with flames. They just—"

"How far have they spread?" Kalganov stared at her. "The fireplace? That's all?" He turned to Martin. "Take charge. It's nothing serious. A chimney fire. Use salt—" He broke off, listening. Far distant came the high wail of a fireboat's siren. Loud, louder, nearer and nearer.

But it's less than a minute since Kalganov's first shout, Lenoir thought in complete amazement, much less. How quick they are!

Too quick, Kalganov thought grimly, and started back up the staircase, pausing only to yell down to the startled faces in the hall, "Keep the doors barred! Tell them the fire is under control!" But his voice was lost in the siren's hideous scream, blaring into the small canal. As it sobbed into silence, heavy pounding began on the street door.

Lenoir caught Kalganov's arm. "We must let them in—it's the law! They've seen the smoke." Someone has to use his intelligence, he thought, but he wondered why Kalganov was looking at him with such a strange small smile. "I'll keep them downstairs—"

There was a shot, light, muffled by distance. Another. And another. They came from the attic.

Kalganov pushed Lenoir aside, and was racing along the first landing to the next sweep of stairs.

"Open the doors!" Lenoir called out. "Open the doors, at once!" If the firemen had to use axes to get in, there would be questions, suspicions, a search. Show no panic, Lenoir told himself as he started downstairs. This is a matter of tact and reason.

Again there was a shot. Only one, this time, sounding loud and clear from overhead.

Lenoir halted in surprise. Kalganov hadn't yet reached the attic stairs. He was only on the second landing, racing past the bedroom doors. That must have been the guard who had fired, Lenoir thought worriedly. But those three lighter shots? The girl had carried no gun, no weapon of any kind. So the men who brought her here had reported. Or had they blundered? Let Kalganov puzzle that out. Upstairs is his problem. Mine is here.

Lenoir looked down at the shadowy figures who were moving into the swirling cloud in the hall. The cool air from the wide-open door cut through the black smoke, dissolving it into thin gray wisps. The number of men alarmed him. He raised his voice, "The fire was only in the kitchen. It has been confined. No need—" He broke off as four men came running up the staircase. "Gentlemen!" he insisted. "There is no need whatsoever—" He stared at them. These men were not firemen. And behind them were

723

policemen. Suddenly he remembered Kalganov's small smile. Kalganov had guessed, Kalganov had escaped.

Lenoir caught his bitterness, choked it off. Kalganov would do more than escape: he would eliminate all evidence. Lenoir blocked the path of the men as they reached him. "Get out! Get out, all of you! Do you hear me? The fire is over. You have no right—"

"Don't we?" asked an American, a dark-haired man with angry dark eyes. He shoved Lenoir aside. "He's all yours, Jules," he said over his shoulder, hurrying on, two others at his heels.

Jules nodded with grim satisfaction, and stepped aside politely to let the Italian policemen make the arrest.

Lenoir didn't even listen to them. He was watching the American and the two men, spreading out along the landing, opening doors, searching. "Here, Rosie!" one called urgently from the library. Lenoir almost panicked. Sandra . . .

He glanced quickly down at the hall. Martin was there, handcuffed, watching the search, too. But he had no alarm on that stolid face, upturned to the library door. There could be no sign of bullet or knife in Sandra's body. Lenoir relaxed. He stared at the handcuffs closing on his wrists. "What is this ridiculous charge?" he asked.

"Abduction," Jules said. He added, with a thin smile, "Meanwhile."

"Abduction?" repeated Lenoir unbelievingly. Three more men pushed their way past him to help with the search upstairs. The man called Rosie had come out of the library, and was signaling to the others to follow. But I have given Kalganov time, Lenoir thought rapidly; without evidence, what can be proved? I've given Kalganov at least two minutes. The strong attic door would give him more: locked and barricaded, it could stop the search for many minutes; more than enough to let Kalganov go free. He wouldn't leave the girl, either. No evidence—no proof; only guesses and suppositions. A body found floating in the Grand Canal was proof of nothing except death. "Whose abduction?" Lenoir demanded with an appropriate show of anger.

Jules did not answer. His hand tightened on Lenoir's arm. "Start moving!" he said. Then the little group on the staircase halted, looked up. One shot, distant yet clear, echoed down from far above.

One shot, definite in every way, thought Lenoir. The American with the ridiculous name had not even reached the attic staircase. He was racing now, the other men clattering wildly after him. Too late, Lenoir's mocking eyes told the backs of the running men, too late. By this time, Kalganov is out on the roof. The girl is gone. Kalganov will escape.

And so shall I, Lenoir thought. Since when has propaganda become a felony? He looked at the Frenchman beside him, coldly. "You are making a grave mistake."

"You must tell that to Trouin, the wine merchant," Jules said with his thin smile. He tightened his grip on Lenoir's elbow as another shot rang out, and Lenoir's indignant innocence crumbled into blank silence.

The siren had screamed high as the fireboat curved from the Grand Canal into the *rio*, swooped down two full octaves, and stopped.

Claire started when the shrill note blared into the attic. Then, as it ended abruptly, she took a deep breath, steadied her nerves, and took aim once more at the padlock. "Hurry, Claire!" Bill's whisper urged her from the balcony.

"Three shots," she warned him. Three to make sure. She fired rapidly. And accurately. For when she wrenched at the padlock, it broke loose. Fenner smashed the shutters open, jumped down beside her.

"Out!" he told her, regaining his balance, a revolver pointing at the door, his eyes glancing around the room. His free hand steadied her as she began to raise herself over the window sill. She heard the guard's footsteps, the heavy key turning in the lock. We'll never make it, she thought, and dropped back onto the floor, turning to face the door with Bill. He caught her, swung her to the side, sent her tumbling, sliding over toward the heavy, carved chest. She fell prone behind it as the door crashed open. There was a shot. One shot.

Cold with fear, she raised herself on her elbow, her automatic ready. But Bill was all right. He was looking at an empty doorway. She pulled herself to her knees, and saw that the guard had fallen backward across the threshold, half in, half out of the room. He was clutching a shattered right shoulder, and beginning to moan.

Bill had heard something else, for he moved quickly to the door, kicking aside the guard's pistol, switching off the light. "Keep down!" he said softly, and she obeyed him, letting herself drop back again onto the dust-coated floor.

Running footsteps, that was what Fenner had heard. And so had the guard. For he made an attempt to rise and lunge forward with his one good arm. Fenner smashed down at the upraised head with his revolver, sent the man toppling back into the corridor. He pulled the large key from its outside lock, tried to close the door, found that it jammed on the man's leg, lying stiff and straight over the threshold. From the far end of the corridor, the light was switched off.

The footsteps, careful, no longer running, were coming close. Too close. No time to clear the threshold, get the key into this side of the lock. No time to do anything at all except step behind the gaping door, and wait. He glanced over at the chest. Claire could be seen from the threshold if she didn't keep herself flat on the floor. Keep down, Claire! he told her silently, for God's sake, keep down.

Any minute, now . . .

He waited, spine pulled taut against the door in the hope that he couldn't be seen through the close-angled crack at its hinges, left hand lightly holding its knob to sense any touch on it from outside, right arm close across his ribs with the revolver's two-inch barrel pointing just where someone would step across the guard's ankle.

But the man was waiting, too. His breathing, audible at first, had been controlled. There was only silence in the blackness of the corridor. Neither breath nor footstep. A clever type, thought Fenner: not one who came bursting into a room with his gun blazing. What was he waiting for? Reinforcements? Or was he studying what he could see of the room from the gaping door? If so, he would see that the shutters had been burst open, for a stream of faint moonlight stretched obliquely toward the crowded furniture, played over it gently, set two dark mirrors gleaming, turned a golden cherub into silver, shimmered over the silks and satins lying in an opened trunk near the chest where Claire lay so still, whitened floor and walls, sharpened shadows.

Why didn't he move? He knew he had little time.

He is more than a clever type, thought Fenner tensely, eyes now fixed on the edge of the opened door. He isn't just standing somewhere in that corridor (and I wish to God I knew exactly where), waiting for someone to make a false move: he is goading us into one. Us? He doesn't know I am here. He didn't see who was trying to close the door. He can't see me standing here. That's the only good thing about this position: he can't see me. But if he throws this door wide open, he could fling me off balance for one second. And seconds can mean everything—for proof, just look at that damned foot lying wedged across the threshold. So that's one advantage he has. There is another, too: he is in a black corridor looking into a moonlit room. Or now and again moonlit. For the light, ebbing and flowing, was once more veiled by a passing cloud.

Fenner heard the first careful movement from the other side of the door. Here it comes, Fenner thought, here it comes, whatever it is. He braced himself, waiting for the darkness to end once the cloud had passed over. The pale, uncertain light began to flow back into the room. He gave one quick glance in Claire's direction, for the low chest had worried him: unless she lay absolutely still, she might be seen. Invisible, thank God. Then, as the light played briefly over the mass of furniture, he froze. That mirror tilted drunkenly forward from the wall, that mirror catching a beam of moonlight— He stared at Claire's trapped image. She had moved behind the trunk, using its upraised lid as a shield. Abruptly, the moonlight fled; Claire's reflection vanished. He was left staring at a jumble of dark shadows. But the position of her head and shoulders behind the trunk's lid as she knelt, motionless, waiting, her automatic ready, would be marked and remembered. From the corridor, he heard another careful movement, the slight scrape of metal on metal (a silencer, perhaps?), a small click of readiness. When the light strengthened again—but Fenner didn't wait for that.

He wrenched the door open, dropped to the floor. The man just beyond the threshold swerved his aim from trunk to door's edge, and fired silently into the darkness. The bullet smashed savagely into the wall behind Fenner as he shot from the floor at the black shadow emerging from the corridor. It gasped and fell, lay motionless. The moonlight was spreading across the room again, sending the mirror glancing.

"Don't move, Claire!" he called warningly. He began to rise, and stopped, watching the man's still body. A clever type, Fenner remembered. He could be faking. And his aim was good. If I had been standing as he expected, his aim would have been very good.

"Look out!" Holland shouted from the window, and fired. The man's long revolver, grotesque and grim with its silencer, lifting slowly, painfully, clattered back to the floor.

Holland jumped into the room, side-stepped out of the flow of moonlight, circled toward the door like an alert and capable terrier flushing out a rat. "He's had it," Holland said very softly. "No more strain." He took a deep breath. As Fenner rose, he switched on the light. They stood half blinded by the naked bulb's jagged glare. "It's Kalganov," Holland said unbelievingly. He looked at the doorway, where Rosie stood, revolver ready, his breath coming in sharp gasps. "Kalganov," Chris Holland told Rosie. "It's Kalganov!"

Fenner looked down at the man who had almost ended their lives. He had died badly. The handsome face was distorted with his rage to win, the clever eyes staring with savage hate, fanatical refusal; declaring a perpetual war; damning all and everyone to everlasting hell. As it might have been, Fenner thought, as it could have been if this man had won. If the moment of death was the moment of truth, then in Kalganov's truth there was nothing but menace.

He turned away, started toward Claire. She had not moved.

Holland was saying quietly, "It was a close thing, a damned close thing." He had picked up Kalganov's revolver, which he was examining

727

with interest. He shook his head over the bullet he had ejected into his palm. Silently, he showed it to Rosie. Outside in the corridor, there were many footsteps, voices. Let Rosie and Chris deal with all that, Fenner thought as he made his way toward Claire. He felt no triumph in Kalganov's death. Only a sense of warning. The Kalganovs died, the Kalganovs lived. No end? No peace? Yet this one had been defeated. This one, at least. He wasn't the first to have been defeated, either. He wouldn't be the last. They were not invincible—if you knew they existed. If you knew, and faced them.

He stepped over a footstool, pulled aside a chair. His movements were slow, exhausted, deliberate. And at last he reached Claire.

She had started to rise, and then, as all strength left her body, sank behind the trunk again, her shoulders drooping, her hand—still clutching the automatic—lying inert on her thigh. Her head rested against the lid of the trunk; disheveled hair fell over her white face. She had been crying; slow tears still escaped from the dark curve of eyelashes, down over the dust-streaked cheeks.

She heard his footsteps now. She looked up at him; tried to smile, but she couldn't. He loosened the tight clasp of her fingers from the little automatic, slipped it into his pocket. That's all over, he thought, all over. He reached down and gripped her waist, raised her slowly to her feet. She said, "Oh, Bill—I thought you were dead. For one whole minute, I thought you were—"

He caught her, drawing her close to him. Their arms encircled each other, and held.